Ten Days in the Hills

Jane Smiley

.

Ten Days in the Hills

Alfred A. Knopf

NEW YORK · 2007

This Is a Borzoi Book Published by Alfred A. Knopf

Copyright © 2007 by Jane Smiley

All rights reserved. Published in the United States by Alfred A. Knopf,
a division of Random House, Inc., New York, and in Canada
by Random House of Canada Limited, Toronto.

www.aaknopf.com

Knopf, Borzoi Books, and the colophon are registered trademarks of Random House, Inc.

Grateful acknowledgment is made to the following
for permission to reprint previously published material:
Jörg Friedrich: Excerpts from "Beyond Slaughter: Memories of '45" by Jörg Friedrich
(Los Angeles Times, March 28, 2003). Reprinted by permission of the author.
Los Angeles Times: Excerpts from "Transgender Prostitute Guilty of Manslaughter," by Tracy Wilson
(Los Angeles Times, March 28, 2003). Copyright © 2003 by the Los Angeles Times.
Reprinted by permission of the Los Angeles Times.

Library of Congress Cataloging-in-Publication Data
Smiley, Jane.
Ten Days in the hills / Jane Smiley. — 1st ed.
p.   cm.
ISBN-13: 978-1-4000-4061-2 (alk. paper)
ISBN-10: 1-4000-4061-2 (alk. paper)
1. Interpersonal relations — Fiction. 2. Hollywood
(Los Angeles, Calif.) — Fiction. I. Title.
PS3569.M39T46 2007
813'.54 — dc22   2006046579

Manufactured in the United States of America

First Edition

To Jack Canning, Mr. Inspiration

I thought that I had arrived, like the Caliph in the *Arabian Nights*, in the nick of time to rescue a man who was being beaten, and in fact it was a different tale from the *Arabian Nights* which I saw enacted before me, the one in which a woman who has been turned into a dog willingly submits to being beaten in order to recover her former shape.

—**Marcel Proust,** *Time Regained*

Gogol once boasted of *Dead Souls*: "All Russia will appear in it," but later confessed that he had made it all up.

—**Richard Pevear,** Introduction to *Anton Chekhov: The Complete Short Novels*

But a little after nones, they all went and refreshed their faces in cool water before assembling, at the queen's request, on the lawn near the fountain, where, having seated themselves in the customary manner, they began to await their turn to tell a story on the topic the queen had proposed.

—**Giovanni Boccaccio,** *The Decameron*

Ten Days in the Hills

DAY ONE · Monday, March 24, 2003

Max was still sleeping, neatly, as always, his head framed by the sunny white of his rectangular pillow, his eyelids smooth over the orbs of his eyes, his lips pale and soft, his bare shoulders square on the bed. While Elena was gazing at him, he sighed. Sometime in the night, he had turned back the white comforter; its fold crossed him diagonally between the hip and the knee. The morning sunlight burnished his hands (right on top of left), and sparkled through his silvery chest hair. His cock lay to one side, nonchalant. Elena smoothed the very tips of his chest hair with her hand so that she could just feel it tickling her palm, and then circled his testicles with her index finger. She was sleepy herself, probably from dreaming of the Oscars. What she could remember were more like recurring images of the bright stage as she had seen it from their seats, smiling figures walking around on it, turning this way and that, breasting the audience suddenly as if jumping into surf—not unhappy images, but not restful. The bright figures had stayed with her all night, sometimes actually looking frightened, or turning toward her so that she had to remind herself in her dream that they were happy, well fed, successful.

She sat up quietly, so as not to disturb him. She saw that all of their clothes—his tux and her vintage gold silk-velvet flapper dress—were draped neatly over the backs of a couple of chairs. Her silver sandals and her silver mesh evening bag lay on the windowsill where she had set them when she walked in the bedroom door. He had taken her to the Oscars and then to the Governors Ball, because she, of course, had never been, though he himself had an invitation every year—his movie *Grace* had won Best Screenplay in the 1970s (and in fact was listed on three "hundred best films of the twentieth century" lists that she had looked up on the Internet: seventy-seventh on one, eighty-third on another, and eighty-fifth best on the third). At fifty-eight, Max had a certain sort of fame in Hollywood: most people had heard of him, but lots of younger ones assumed he was dead.

Elena, who wrote self-improvement guides (she was currently working on *Here's How: To Do EVERYTHING Correctly!*, chapter four, "Eating and Drinking"), had also managed to earn herself a house, but it was a bungalow in the flats of Beverly Hills, not a mansion that cascaded down a mountainside in Pacific Palisades, looked across Will Rogers Memorial Park at the Getty Museum, and had five bedrooms, a guesthouse, and a swimming pool down the mountainside (three flights of stairs) that caught the morning sun. There were two gardens—the herb garden and flower garden, one level down from the kitchen, and the Japanese garden, twenty feet below the swimming pool, which was utterly cool and silent, as far away from Los Angeles as the island of Honshu.

Elena put her feet on the floor and thought of the war. The war had begun on Thursday. As soon as she thought directly of the war, which had been until this moment of her day a presence but not an object, her fragmented, Oscar-colored mood jelled into a general feeling of shame and fear. The fact was, the war was going forward no matter what, no matter how threatening and dangerous it was, no matter how many people were certain to die, no matter how many people protested and complained, no matter what a bad bet it looked like. Other people could understand the war and explain it—there was, indeed, something reasonable about the war that other people seemed able to comprehend—but for Elena the war was entirely counterintuitive. She supposed it came down to that very word— "war," a word she had avoided reading, saying, looking at for a number of years when she was a child during the Cold W——, when "war" meant annihilation, mutually assured destruction, better dead than red, except that as a child she had understood "dead" much better than "red"—she had understood "dead" perfectly. Elena remembered herself at eight, standing in the kitchen with the radio on and her fingers in her ears, blocking out the sound of the television in the living room that was reporting the random progress of various threats to her life. One name she remembered was "Francis Gary Powers," a man who endangered everyone by spying. After more than forty years, Elena could still remember that name and see his snowy black-and-white figure, a tall man with dark hair, being hustled from one room to another by other, more shadowy figures. She remembered him because she had known that there was a train of circumstances that could begin with Francis Gary Powers and end with her death. Even then, even at eight years old, Elena had understood that tipping over into mutually assured destruction would have been an accident. This war, though, was not an accident but an intention. People who knew people whom Elena knew planned to visit assured destruction on other people whom Elena didn't know. She sighed so deeply that Max turned toward her and opened his eyes. He said, "Did you have fun last night?"

"Yes, but I dreamt about the stage all night. What I liked best was that so many people were happy to see you."

"The troll emerges from under the bridge." He pulled up the coverlet. "It's always a pleasant surprise."

"It looked to me like they were genuinely happy to see you. Actual smiles that included their eyes. Involuntary twinkles and sparkles and body twitches."

"They're actors. Nothing is involuntary."

"Well, thank you anyway for taking me."

"The best part was them wondering who you were and where you got that dress." Now he rolled her into his embrace, right up next to his shoulders and chest. He kissed her between the eyebrows and pulled the quilt over her. "The worst part is that I think we have a house party shaping up."

"Isn't your friend Charlie Mannheim coming soon?" She had met Charlie the previous summer with Max on a trip to San Francisco. She had observed then that with men you often didn't quite understand why two people who became friends when they were ten years old remained in contact almost into their sixties.

"That, plus Stoney has to vacate his place while the floors are being redone. And Isabel wants to visit all of a sudden. I guess she broke up with Leo and he won't leave their apartment."

Stoney Whipple was Max's agent, a position he had taken over from his father, Jerry. Elena hadn't known Jerry. She'd met Max in the cheese section at Gelson's last Easter, when Max was buying a Piave and Elena was buying a Gruyère de Comté and their hands touched as they both reached for the Epoisses. Jerry had died by that time. She had come to understand that Jerry Whipple was, by all accounts, a legend. Stoney Whipple was sweet, Elena thought. He was in and out of Max's house in a way that reminded her of her Midwestern roots, and so she felt friendly toward him for that and also because his career didn't seem to be shaping up into a legendary one.

But Isabel! Isabel was Max's daughter, whom Elena had not met. She said, calmly, she thought, "That's three. That isn't so bad. It isn't bad at all."

"Stoney can sleep in the study. He's going to be in and out."

Without wishing to, she felt a surge of nervousness. The spacious peace of this luxuriously sprawling house to be broken! Although Elena loved to contemplate pork roasts and thread-counts and bottles of spring water on bedside tables, having to provide them made her anxious. She said, "At least we got rid of Simon." Simon was Elena's own son, a senior at UC Davis, who, Elena thought, was spending too much time in L.A. and too little time in Davis. He had left only a week ago, after twelve lazy days of vacation during which he did not look for post-graduation employment.

Max said, "What do you want to do today?"

"Hide out from the war."

"Oh, that." He frowned and flopped over on his back. Max's feelings about the war, she knew, were compounded less of shame than of anger. When Elena said that the war was stupid and then Max replied that, yes, it was stupid, she then went on to point out that those prosecuting the war didn't comprehend the chaotic and agonizing nature of war, and he went on to exclaim, "What's the plan? It's evident they have no plan!" As a movie director, he had directed *Bull Run* in the late 1980s, an epic Civil War movie that ran three hours and five minutes, had taken eight months to make, employed hundreds of extras and horses, and had, perhaps, killed the studio that made it. When he talked about planning, she was sure he was thinking about projects he had planned and executed over the years. And he was thinking of the army, since he had been in Vietnam.

She lifted the quilt, then let it drop. She said, "The war is too much for your cock."

"I admit that."

"Say, did you notice that when I spoke to Michael Moore after the cere-mony, about his speech, he seemed a little shocked by the booing? You don't expect Michael Moore to be shocked by anything. I was disappointed. I mean, if Michael Moore is intimidated by a little booing, what's going to happen to the rest of us?"

"But who was booing him? Studio executives. You don't want to be booed by studio executives, even if you are filled with contempt for them. Anyway, I bet by this time you're the only person in the world who knows he was shocked. I bet even he doesn't know he was shocked anymore. And who's to say that they were booing his remarks about Bush? Maybe they were booing his remark about having Canadian financing."

Elena smiled, then Max smiled. He said, "I want Canadian financ-ing, too."

"What for?"

"A movie I am going to make about you."

"Oh, yes, about posture. I'm going to be sitting in my chair with both feet flat on the floor and my spine perfectly aligned, and then I'm going to rise from my chair and walk across the room without turning my toes out, pronating my ankles, or, God forbid, turning my toes in. We'll put small white circles all up my spine and across my shoulders and down the backs of my legs, so that my physiologically correct and evolutionarily correct posture will be evident to anyone."

"No."

"Then maybe I'm going to get stains out of some delicate items? Not just red-wine stains and bloodstains, but rust stains and grass stains and oils of various kinds? Using lemons and other citrus fruits?"

"No. You are not going to be useful in my film about you." He was propped up on his left elbow now, looking down at her. His right hand slipped behind her back and turned her toward him. She let her head loll backward, lengthening and exposing her neck, and he kissed her along her jawline. When she turned her head toward him, he kissed her on the lips. He had a certain way of kissing that Elena liked very much, not active but quiet, springy, and full of suction. During the kiss, she contemplated their connection—tight, warm, and comfortable. Everything promised was delivered, adjustments were made in which he claimed more and more of her lips, and then, in a moment of common agreement that she suspected was visceral or even biological, they broke apart, in order to kiss again. Each long kiss built on the previous one as more and more nerve endings came into play. Each kiss was a surprise to her lips. Her brain remembered that they had kissed and that the kisses were always seductive and good, but her lips were won over anew every time. Each kiss, also, she felt as a material and particular assertion of his masculinity—steady, strong, orderly, desirous, and, above all, intentional, as if kissing her were something that he paid attention to each time. Elena, of course, had been kissed thousands of times over the years—she was fifty, after all—and she had been married once, and of course there had been high school and college and graduate school, and if marriage was like a thousand-dollar bill, rare but tangible and possessable, and going steady was like a hundred-dollar bill—more common than you thought when you didn't have one—then kisses were like pennies, easily disregarded, hard to remember, or even inconvenient and annoying. And yet she could say with perfect honesty (and she was far too meticulous to allow any other kind of honesty) that Max's kisses were always to be noticed, valued, and cherished, since they could not be preserved, which was, by the way, too bad.

They stopped kissing. He put his leg over hers and pulled her more tightly against him. Now that the kiss was over, she thought maybe it was this she liked best, the skin-to-skin contiguity of solid flesh, which, of course, was not solid flesh at all, but layers of various tissues, and, from the point of view of physics, lots of empty internal space. Perhaps as a young girl in biology class, when the elderly biology teacher set the orange on the lab table and said, "This is the nucleus," and then walked to the far corner of the room and held up a pea and said, "This is the electron," and then demonstrated, as best he could given all the junk in the room which they were to imagine as emptiness, the passage of the pea around the orange, she had hardly paid attention to him, because what she could not stop noticing was that her best friend, Linda, was whispering to her other best friend, Margie. The way that teacher lifted his arm, clad in brown tweed, and the way she could not really see the pea between his thumb and forefinger, and the way that the orange was bright against the smooth blackness of the lab table, was as vivid to her at fifty as it had been at thirteen, though, and of course that was why he demonstrated that space in just that way, so that indifferent twelve-year-olds would notice and remember. As a result of such idle biological experiences: here was the arm, here was the leg, here was the hip and the curvature of the chest. As they squeezed her and pulled her even more tightly against his vibrant warmth, she had in her mind an idea of the long limestone-white bones with their striated brick-red bulging attachments, and over those the bright azure-and-magenta network of blood vessels, and encasing them the squamous cells and the dermis and the epidermis, with its tear-shaped hair follicles out of which sprang those single dark hairs—each hair having a follicle of its own. When he held her and squeezed her and pressed up against her and warmed her and comforted her, she was aware of the variety of his anatomy. He was a mesomorph. As he moved, the layers slid smoothly and noiselessly across one another. As she pushed against him, the springing hairs flattened; she felt the different texture of his skin against hers. When children were raised without biology teachers and encyclopedias, how did they perceive the bodies of their lovers? It was impossible to know, Elena thought.

"I want to make a movie about this very thing," he said. "I was thinking about it last night at the Oscars. *My Dinner with Andre,* but in bed naked. *My Lovemaking with Elena.* This is how her body looked. This is how my body looked. This is how the light in the room changed as the sun rose and the clouds came in off the ocean. This is what we said. This is what we did. This is what we felt. Ninety minutes. Doesn't that sound great? We've made love for ninety minutes any number of times, and every time was interesting and most of them were worthy of film. But, and here's the great part, it would be a real filming challenge. How would you get in close? How would you set up the camera? What sort of film stock would you use? I mean, look at the skin of your arm here." He lifted her arm. It looked brownish and mottled to her, like a fauxed wall, though not shiny. "With the right lighting, we could make that skin look any way we wanted to. Rich, deep peachy pink. Parched, bleached-out sand color. But how would we make it look like you, just like you? That's what I would want, except, of course, the actress wouldn't be you. Frances McDormand, maybe. I thought of her. Anyway—"

He turned her palm and kissed it. "This is a fabulous idea. Never been done before. But you can do almost anything as an indie feature now. Not like fifteen years ago, when you were stuck with what they gave you." He grinned. "Let's look at your arm again. Put it here, next to your stomach. Now, see that contrast? That's a beautiful thing, only seen in fifty-year-olds."

His hand was the beautiful thing, she thought. It cradled her wrist, made a contrast with her own hand, about which she had no opinions—it was hers, she made do with it. But he said, "I mean, this film would have things that *My Dinner with Andre* didn't have, like penetration and a variety of camera angles and lots of point-of-view shots. Voice-over. I don't think *My Dinner with Andre* had very much voice-over at all—I need to watch it again. The actor who plays me is talking, and the camera reveals things that he's looking at, sometimes things that he is staring at—for example, the skin on your arm. What if the camera focused on the skin of your arm for five minutes, or even for a minute? Probably I haven't stared at the skin on your arm, or, say, your belly, for five minutes, but I bet I've stared at it for a minute more than once. What did I see? I can barely remember. But I know I stared at it with fascination. After all, it was your arm! Love you, love your arm! I mean, just as an example, let's turn your arm over and look at the inside of your wrist. Here's the base of your hand, kind of rounded and mounded up, and then here are your tendons. If we move your hand backward and forward, we see that the right tendon, as we are looking at it, pops in and out—when your hand is flexed forward and backward—but the left one barely moves. That's interesting. Don't you wonder why that is? And then the veins are so visible—down here, where they begin to emerge from the forearm and then branch around the right tendon—and then up here, right where the lines you've made in the skin by bending your wrist cross laterally, the veins branch again, but very faintly, and disappear into the fatty tissue of the palm. Isn't that beautiful?"

Elena made a waving gesture with her hand, mimicking a sea anemone.

"How much of that sort of thing is too much in a film?" he went on. "I don't think our models are really Hollywood movies at all, more like National Geographic specials. But even so, if I can look at your hand for a minute, in fascination, then why couldn't an audience look at it for a minute, too? Maybe they could. And, of course, there would be just the tiniest difference between how he sees the room and how she sees the room. Her arm would look different to her from the way it looks to him, so let's say for part of the movie—and not exactly half, that's too obvious—the room is slightly brighter or more vividly colored, or more full of depth than it is in the other section of the movie. His film stock, her film stock. Anyway, think of it this way. Frank kept that show to three hours. Everyone said he was draconian about it. You open your mouth for one more second than your allotted time, and you get the hook. Hallelujah, they held the Oscars to three hours! But, my God, it was three hours long! No camera work! No story! I mean, yes, there was better material than maybe they've ever had at the Oscars, what with Brody kissing the girl like that, what's her name?"

"Halle Berry."

"Of course he couldn't resist the chance, everyone saw that immediately. And all the stuff with Michael Moore, and then, when they got everyone onstage for the portrait, even Luise Rainer, that was significant drama right there. Just the sight of Luise Rainer all dressed up in that gown and made up and helped out onto the stage. Shocking! We thought she was dead! This one was surely dead, but no! So Frank had a lot to work with, and he did a wonderful job moving it along, and millions of people watched it, so why wouldn't they watch a minute of your arm, or, you know, Frances McDormand's arm, while the voice-over makes remarks about things?"

Elena said, "You want to have penetration?"

"Well, that would be the promise. I don't see, if it's *My Lovemaking with Elena*, how you could avoid penetration."

"You would never get it on the screen. It would be pornography."

"Just because of a little penetration? A little penetration embedded in a long conversation? I don't know about that. Anyway, if the conversation were interesting enough, and the audience got inured to seeing them, us, on the screen, fifty and fifty-eight, who cares? If penetration has a context, then it isn't pornography, it's a story. The mere sight of penetration doesn't arouse, isn't meant to arouse. It's *their* penetration, not an abstract penetration taken out of context. It would be much easier to simply observe and consider a penetration if it were surrounded by other things, especially voice-over. In some sense, the movie would sort of bore the viewer until he was beyond caring about the penetration as penetration. And anyway, in porn movies, they don't do much with the penetration, because they always want the ejaculation to be on the screen. Our ejaculation would be normal—entirely invisible."

"I don't know that people would see it like that. Don't you think the penetration would be the news, and that everyone would go to the movie to see the penetration and more or less ignore the other stuff?" Max rolled onto his back and put his hands behind his head. Now the sunlight was stronger. She said, "Are you ready for a cup of coffee?"

"But having no penetration would be just avoiding the issue. Everyone knows that when you make love you have a penetration and all the various sensations that go with it. How would this movie be different from *My Dinner with Andre* if there were no penetration?"

"But here's another thing. Who would be seeing the penetration? We don't see the penetration, except from various odd angles."

"I see it. I see it in the mirror, and you don't because you aren't looking. I also see it from better angles than you do, just because of anatomy."

"So would the actor playing you wear one of those little cameras around his head like they do in sports events?"

"That's an idea. I'll have to think about that idea. I actually haven't seen one of those, so I don't know how you would fit it onto a regular head, you know, without a helmet or something like that. Also, I would have the penetration in the first act of the movie, not the third. The penetration is not the climax."

"What is the climax, then?"

"Well, think about every Hollywood movie you've ever seen. What's the climax?"

"A warehouse explosion?"

"No. The kiss."

"They, we, would be making love but not kissing for ninety minutes?"

"Well, eighty-five. The kiss itself would be quite lengthy, but it would take a while to get to it."

"How could they make love for eighty-five minutes without kissing? I don't think that's very realistic, especially for us. We kiss all the time."

He kissed her. Elena closed her eyes, which shut out the brightness of the room and relocated her back inside her sense of touch. The sensation of his lips on hers flowered along her cranial nerves, which she imagined fanning outward from her lips over and around her head like a spiderweb, and within that web was a darkness whose life she could better sense when her eyes were closed. When her eyes were open, she was all surface, facing the world. When her eyes were closed, she was all hollow, facing inward. And what shape was she? Not precisely human, not precisely bipedal, but more amorphous. She opened her eyes. His face was right there—she could see the bridge of his nose, the orbit of his right eye, and the lid slightly wrinkled across it. Three creases in the corner. The plane of his cheek. She said, "But in some ways, watching people kiss is the most pornographic of all, because, from their point of view, the kiss is in darkness. It's felt in the body, and there's no way to get that on film, or even to get that weird view you have of the other person while you're kissing, just his eye and his hair and the far wall. As soon as they start kissing, no matter what point-of-view shots you've had before, you're out of their consciousness, and you couldn't have voice-over, either, because they're kissing. So you're stuck with watching the two people kiss. I don't think you—"

He kissed her again. This time her sense of herself was located between her lips and her hands and arms, because between kisses, more or less as an involuntary response to kissing, they had repositioned themselves in order to address the kiss more fully. Now their heads were tilted at more of an angle, their arms were fully around one another, and they were pressed together all down her breastbone, and belly. It was a satisfying kiss, a whole-body kiss, definitely a kiss of the nerves and the epidermis, not a kiss of the mind. They parted, kissed again for a second. He said, "Of course you could have some cut-away shots that represent the kissing. That's a technique. It can be kind of cheesy, of course, if you cut away to trees blowing in the wind or surf crashing on the shore. But what if you cut away to something simple and abstract, like mere blackness with some indefinable shadows or light patterns? Just for a second. I mean, at this point, artists have been visually representing the inner life by means of abstract color and shape for more than a hundred years. Why hasn't this made it into film? That's a question in itself. It's a challenge. That's why this whole thing is a good idea."

Elena said, "What if you cut away as soon as their lips touched to that *Scream* painting? I would like to see that. It would make the whole movie not quite so domestic."

But even after two quite superior kisses, he didn't have an erection. And she was stiff from lying in bed. She was fifty, after all. If she remained too long in one position, muscles contracted, that was just the way it was. She rolled away from him, got up, walked across the room, and picked up the velvet dress. He lay there with his hands clasped behind his head, happy with his idea.

She picked up the velvet dress and smoothed it. The velvet dress added up to, in every sense, a private triumph for her. As far as she knew, no one at the Oscars or at the Governors Ball had noticed the velvet dress. She had not detected a single lingering glance or turn of the head. Whether this was owing to her own obscurity or to the apparent unimportance of the velvet dress she did not know, but the velvet dress was true silk velvet, of a rich, deep gold color, and it had a lineage—it had belonged to Gene Tierney, and been worn by her, though certainly not to the Oscars. Maybe she had worn it as a young woman. When the dress was new, in 1927, Gene Tierney was only seven years old, so perhaps she had inherited it from her own mother. At any rate, the dress had gotten from Gene Tierney to her niece, and when Elena had told the niece, whom she knew from a cooking class, that she was going to the Oscars, the niece had handed her the dress in a brown paper bag and said, "It's in terrible shape, practically unwearable." The niece, whom Elena did not know well, seemed to be the sort of woman who had transcended material considerations, and so no longer valued the dress except as a mildly arresting artifact. Elena, having nothing else to wear and not wanting to spend actual money, had taken the dress to a shop full of Iranian seamstresses. Together, she and two seamstresses had inspected all the frays and tears and holes in the dress. Gestures by all three of them had expressed amazement, hope, despair, willingness to try, willingness to acknowledge that with such an old fabric there were no guarantees, willingness to keep the shop open an extra hour on Saturday for pickup, willingness to pay extra for extra effort. It was an exchange of perfect mutual satisfaction in the end—the repairs were invisible, they cost $144.89, the seamstresses were happy with their work, and the dress fit perfectly, shimmering from her shoulders to her mid-calf in a gold that contained shades of red and silver and brown as well as yellow. Now its nap picked up the slanting sunlight and the velvet seemed to smolder around the sparkling beads. And it had been a practical dress for the Oscars, having no train. Her worst moment, the night before, was when she and Max were standing at the bar, waiting to get a drink, and she and the woman beside her realized simultaneously that she was standing on the woman's ruffled pink train with both feet. After that, Elena had more or less stayed close to the walls of the room or occupied her seat in the Kodak Theatre.

She took the dress to the closet, where she opened the closet door and took out a hanger. Max said, "This is a shot I would put in, just a shot of you, perfectly naked, walking across the room and hanging up a dress. No bending down, no shimmy, just your hair falling across your shoulder, the muscles of your back, your waist, the backs of your thighs, your calves and Achilles tendons and heels, moving casually across the room."

"Maybe Nicole Kidman would play me."

"Wrong type. Too young. I mean, apart from the fact that, after last night, there's all the added factors. If she got out of bed and walked naked across the room and hung up a dress, she would be hauling her whole career with her, if not in her own mind, then in the mind of everyone in the audience, and in my mind as the director. Frances McDormand is perfect for you."

Elena folded up the silver shawl and set it on the table by the door—that was borrowed, too, from her friend Leslie, who had an antique-clothing collection. "Frances McDormand is not my type at all." She knew she sounded a little waspish.

"Who is your type?"

She turned and looked at him. He looked jolly and irreverent. She said,

"That's a dangerous question to answer. Lots of potential for vanity on the one hand and false modesty on the other. What if I said 'Audrey Hepburn'? What if I said 'Marjorie Main'?"

"What if you said 'Liv Ullmann'? She's Scandinavian, like you. Or 'Constance Bennett'?"

"Constance Bennett was a lifelong blonde and at least four inches shorter than I am. Not to mention that she's the same age as my grandmother."

"But she's your type. Every move she makes is organized and precise. Every moment she's onscreen, she's taking measure, observing. She would never get herself into that situation that, say, Joan Fontaine got into in *The Women*, where she leaves the husband in a fit of petulance and talks in a baby voice. It's not in her. The thing you just did, walking across the room naked, hanging up the dress, turning to face me down though I lie at your mercy in my bed, Constance Bennett would have done that effortlessly. Joan Fontaine would have made a fuss about it. It's one take versus twenty takes."

"Thank you, you're forgiven, she's dead, so who else?"

"Frances McDormand." But he was teasing her.

"Say who for you."

"I don't know."

"We're not actually casting the movie. Just say someone who's dead. Say someone who's too attractive, too unattractive."

"Let's see. Gregory Peck in *To Kill a Mockingbird*. Too thoughtful and wise and forbearing. So full of virtues that the good looks slip into the background. That's not me. Walter Huston in *Treasure of the Sierra Madre*. Too garrulous and hairy. I can't jump up and down like he does. I'm too nervous for that."

"What if I say Dana Andrews is your type?"

"I like that."

"Whatever he's doing, you want to watch him. You don't have to watch him, the way you do Humphrey Bogart. The whole time you're watching Humphrey Bogart, you're thinking of reasons to stop watching him, but you keep watching him anyway, even when he makes that little move with his upper lip and you go, Ughh, don't do that! With Dana Andrews, you just sit there and when he's onscreen you're happy and when he's not onscreen you're less happy."

"That's a very female perspective."

"I'll tell you what. It's going to be harder to cast you, because it's harder to cast a man as a regular man, a man with a brain and a point of view. As soon as you have a man on the screen, everything about him is exaggerated.

When he's lying around in bed, he's got a manliness problem. When he's sitting at the kitchen table, he's got a manliness problem. He's got to get out of bed and stand up and prove he's a man and then do that all day and all night, and every time he does something or fails to do something, either he's more of a man or less of a man. I don't think that's going to work in a simple tale of *My Lovemaking with Elena*."

"I didn't realize you were such a theorist of the cinema."

"Adrien Brody could do *My Lovemaking with Elena*, but not with Frances McDormand."

"I think he solved his manliness problem last night, for sure. He took her in his arms, he pulled her to him, he bent her back, he gave her the kiss of a lifetime and took her completely by surprise. His rhythm was perfect."

"He did, but men in European movies don't have a manliness problem. They can do whatever they want."

"Brits, too?"

"They're transitional. For example, Hugh Grant never has a manliness problem. He has abdicated all considerations of his manliness, and if a question of manliness comes up, he ignores it, so he's fallen back to the default option—he's a man. That makes all movies with him much more simple and relaxed. Colin Firth, on the other hand, always has a manliness problem, because his willingness to keep working on the issue is evident in his face every time he's onscreen. He has to win something or get something or understand something. Hugh Grant only has to allow things to be thrust upon him. So English actors have a choice. American actors have no choice, and European actors are outside the manliness problem altogether."

Max laughed.

By now she had put away everything, closed the closet doors, raised the shades, looked across the canyon at the Getty shining through the smog, straightened the pillows on the settee, and flipped a corner of the area rug, a rose-colored Oriental, so that it lay flat again. The room looked neat and quiet. For her, disorder was what noise was for most people, distracting and irritating, but, oddly, she didn't mind noise. If the room she was in was straight and the windows were clean, no amount of noise disturbed her.

He threw the quilt to one side and said, "Here's a manliness problem right here."

She sat down cross-legged on the bed and regarded his member. Once, in the Hustler Store on Sunset, they had gone through all the dildos on the shelf to find the one that most resembled him. In the end, they had settled on the "Big Classic." Now, though, the Big Classic had subsided into cushy somnolence, though as far as Elena was concerned it was still appealing. It lay over to the side, not a straight, evenly shaped sausage, but more of a baguette, bulging comfortably in the middle and then narrowing just below the cap. Blood vessels of various shapes and sizes ran all over its length. The major artery ran up the left side and branched at about the middle. The cap itself was large. It swept back in a fire-helmet sort of shape and bore a faint triangular discoloration, a birthmark, that was only visible in bright daylight. The most interesting thing about the Big Classic was that, even though it was fifty-eight years old, the fineness of the skin, its smoothness and softness and resiliency, seemed not to have diminished over the years. Was this from lack of exposure to the sun, or simply a feature of this special sort of skin? It differed in this from all the other skin on his body, even the skin in the creases of his hips and the tops of his thighs. And his scrotum showed considerable wear and tear, even though one couldn't actually say what the wear and tear on a scrotum would be. She said, "I told you I consider this a geopolitical problem."

It was true that the war felt like it was just outside the room, not visible through the windows looking out upon the Getty, but still there, like two gunmen hiding in the bushes, waiting to mow them down. You could film it that way—cutting from herself and Max, idly considering his dick, to the brutal-looking hit men, glancing at one another as they took up their positions, then back to her running her index finger up the artery on the Big Classic, then encircling the shaft with her hand, and the two of them smiling at each other, then back to hit man number 1, taking off his jacket as the sun struck the house and laying it neatly under a bush, then back to her rolling the shaft gently against his belly, then back to hit man number 2, setting down his weapon and surreptitiously wiping his nose with a used tissue, then tossing aside the tissue and picking up his weapon again.

Or you could film the Iraq war as a fog, a thick toxic pall, approaching the house from the other side. While they unknowingly laugh and chat, the suffocating miasma engulfs the house board by board, roof tile by roof tile.

He said, "Don't you think it would be able to transcend the geopolitical problem?"

"I don't know, because I think this particular geopolitical problem is unprecedented. I think your cock is saying what now, why bother, he's distracted, she's distracted. At this point, I think it's just reacting. I think it will naturally either reject or assimilate the geopolitical situation."

He flipped his cock back and forth in a way that she always found a bit disrespectful, or at least overly familiar, but of course perfectly understandable since it was his cock. He said, "Why don't you turn over, and I'll just massage your ass?"

She stretched out on the bed and then turned over, facing away from him. The sheet against her skin was cool and clean. She said, "Don't you always wonder what you would do in your last hour or so, as the bombs were falling all over Los Angeles? Would you really have the fortitude to sample one last pleasure? Would you really have the strength and fatalism to maintain your privacy, to not show off your end in any way? And say we were together. What would be the most comfortable connection? Just lying in one another's arms? I guess it would take a lot of savoir faire to do anything else." Of course she had images in her mind of *Mrs. Miniver* and of Margaret O'Brien, but she had no images of real deaths, real escapes, real panic, or real fortitude, because the closest she had ever come to such a thing was crouching in a corner of the basement with her babysitter during a tornado as a child. Elena would have been nine and Eric maybe four. They were sitting at the kitchen table after school when the sirens went off, and they stared at one another for a moment, then the girl herded the two of them to the top of the cellar steps. As she opened the cellar door, they looked out. The spot they were standing in was quiet, but ten feet away, the curtains to the windows of the screened porch stood out horizontal in the wind. The two of them went down the steps while the sitter went for Andrew, who must have been about a year old. A minute or two later, here she came down the steps, lightning flashing behind her, with Andrew clinging to her shirt. Yes, trees fell like bombs as the winds broke them over the house, and, yes, the noise was too loud for any kind of communication. Andrew clung to the babysitter, and the babysitter held Elena and Eric in place beside her, their backs pressed against the bricks, until the door opened at the top of the steps and Elena's mother's face appeared and they realized everything had been quiet for some period of time. Now she turned toward him and said, "I was in a tornado once. A house two streets over was knocked off its foundation, and all the windows on the west side of the school were blown out. But you were in Vietnam."

"I guess the scariest thing that happened directly to me over there was when this crazy guy in our company turned the rocket launcher toward the officers' tent, which was up the hill. I was actually stepping into the latrine. I'd just closed the door when the force of the explosion knocked it over onto the door and it slid down the hill maybe ten feet. It took them at least a half an hour to roll it over and let me out of there. I wouldn't say I panicked, but my attitude was far from resigned and accepting. I was the company clerk, so I wasn't out in the firebases, taking incoming rounds all night. I knew some of those guys, though. Lots of the time they were drunk, of course. Or stoned to the eyeballs, though the real marijuana period was more after my time. I think if you'd asked those guys what they wanted to be doing all night, they would have said fucking, of course, but who knows? They didn't have that option." He leaned forward and kissed her breasts, first the left one, then the right one. She put her fingers in his hair and felt the shape of his head. Her nipples lifted. The left one seemed to spark, as if the nerves within were switched on by the unexpectedness of the kiss. Both breasts seemed suddenly lighter and less dense. His skull was hard under her fingertips, and he breathed out a little groan. But the Big Classic was nonresponsive. She pulled him on top of her. The Big Classic fell between her thighs.

"We were in that tornado with a babysitter. She was fourteen or something, maybe only thirteen. She sent Eric and me down the cellar and went for Andrew. When she appeared in the doorway, her hair was puffed out from her head because of static electricity, like a helmet. Andrew's hair was standing straight out, too. He didn't cry until he saw my mother when she got home and found us. The babysitter charged fifty cents an hour, and my mom gave her a ten-dollar tip for saving our lives. She said, 'Oh, you don't have to do that, Mrs. Sigmund.' Then my dad came home and we ate dinner and he told us how the tornado went right down our street just when he would have been coming home, except that he had to stop at my uncle George's house to give his car a jump." Now she could feel the muscles in his back and buttocks as she stroked him up and down. He pressed her comfortably into the mattress, and she felt completely safe. She said, "I would do this if the bombs were falling. I would pull you on top of me and be crushed by falling debris."

He lifted his head and put his hand behind her. "My friend Charlie who's coming today and I were in a thunderstorm in high school. We were watching TV with our girlfriends in his living room. Marnie Cushman and Patty Danacre. Lightning came down the cord and blew the thing up right in front of us."

"Oh my God!" exclaimed Elena.

"Charlie threw himself over Marnie so he would get some credit for saving her. They made out for the first time right then and there, with the TV smoking against the far wall. I tried to get that scene into a movie once, but I had to leave it out." His weight along her body was reassuring. She gently pulled his cheeks apart and pushed them back together; pulled them apart, pushed them back together; then she made deep circular strokes, her right hand clockwise and her left hand counterclockwise. She said, "What would you have to leave out of *My Lovemaking with Elena*?"

"I wouldn't have to leave anything out. That's the challenge. Say, for example, there is no lovemaking with Elena, or at least no penetration, because part of the team isn't cooperating. You might be tempted to leave that out, or to film another day, or to use a body double or some sort of special effect. Even as I say it, I can imagine how I would do it. But the nonco-operating member does have a contribution to make. What is it? This here seems to be intimately related to the manliness problem." He was smiling.

"I'm not sure that it is, actually. The manliness problem is more of a social problem. The noncontributing-member problem could have a more idiosyncratic context, and anyway would be a problem that lots of people could relate to. Really, how many guys are going to boo or jeer? People might get up and walk out, but not just because the protagonist can't get an erection. What is it that lawyers say? His manliness problem is mooted. It's personal. Members of the audience don't judge. It's bad luck to judge something like that, and they know it." She was smiling, but again the war was imminent. It was fun to lie here beneath him in the bed in the tidy room in the well-cared-for wing of the charming house nestled at the top of the canyon on the west side of L.A., overlooking the shining Getty in south-ern California, far from Washington and even farther from Iraq. It was a relief not to know personally any of the government officials who were set-ting up the deaths and dismemberments and talking about them reason-ably. But now that she had remembered that old tornado and had in her mind simultaneously the dim memory of the babysitter's hand on her arm, holding her against the wall, the earthen smell of the basement of that house, and the soundless roar of the wind, but also an image of them as if from her mother's point of view as she would have opened the cellar door and looked down, four children pressed into a dirty dark corner, only the pale colors of their clothes and skin visible at first, that was the image she now had of the waiting-to-be-bombed ones in Iraq. What if the mother never came home, what if the bombs, unlike most tornadoes, came right through the house into the basement, what if the babysitter was killed, leav-ing three, two, or one child to linger in shock and pain, what if the bombing went on for days instead of an hour or so, what if the basement was flooded, what if rats came around and ate the children, what if the mother showed up but way too late? It might be that these what-ifs didn't cross the minds of those prosecuting the war, and it might be that if they did cross those minds, those people said to themselves, So what? Elena could imagine that, too. She could imagine how it was when you wanted to do a certain thing—you thought, that's the way life is sometimes, or they'll get over it, or that's not my problem. There was a little frisson to that, a frisson of selfishness com-bined with willfulness. Who had not felt it? Of course the architects of the war felt that. And then there would be the afterthought, after the war was done and countless agonies had gone unwitnessed or unexpressed. The afterthought would be, we did our best. Mistakes were made; some things are always unforeseeable. But actually, from beginning to end, indifference would be permanently on display, the indifference of those who made the war to the war's resulting deaths and dismemberments. The war-makers knew they should care—everyone agreed they should care—but in fact they didn't, and you couldn't get around it. They themselves would say that they cared about something else more than the deaths and dismemberments, that one had to have priorities, but that was a rationalization of the fact that, no, they didn't care.

At any rate, now that those tornado-generated images were in her mind, she didn't really want to kiss, or to have him lie on top of her. She pecked him on the lips and eased him off. She said, "You know, I can't get this war out of my mind. I hate it."

"It's a dilemma." He looked regretful.

"What's a dilemma?"

"What to do about the weapons of mass destruction. What to do about Saddam."

"You know I don't believe in the weapons of mass destruction."

"I know that. But he didn't prove they aren't there."

"You can't prove a negative."

"You can be open and aboveboard. You can let in the—"

"Or bend over and take it in the ass. You can do that. If you'd been to enough movies, though, you would hesitate to do that because of the manliness problem."

"I'm sure Saddam is beyond the manliness problem. I mean, the manliness problem doesn't seem really to apply to him."

"Why not? Don't you think he watches movies?"

"You sound a little aggressive."

"You sound a little condescending."

"Do I?"

She sat up and looked around the room. The angle of the slanting sun had risen, and it crossed the feet of the woman in a photograph she liked. The sight of it relieved her a degree, and she said, "No. You just sound like you disagree with me. Supposedly, in some abstract way that I can't quite comprehend right now, that's not only okay but inevitable and even desirable."

"I do agree with you. I just can't quite gauge what will satisfy you."

She thought for a moment. "Okay. Here it is. I don't want arguments to be made. I don't want logic to pertain or issues to be carefully weighed. I want the whole idea of the war to simply be disgorged from the body politic like the poison it is, and I want those who thought it up to feel sick with overwhelming nausea and horror that they somehow ingested the poison to begin with. I want them to sincerely and abjectly plead for forgiveness.

Then I want them to spend a lot of time thinking about what happened. And I want them to make a solemn vow to change their ways and do better in the future. I don't think it's too much to ask."

"But you know it's too much to expect, right?"

"A remote part of me knows that," she acknowledged.

"You know that there are people whose job it is to know more about this than you do and that they think this is a regrettable necessity, right?"

"I've heard that rumor, but I question their motives. If their motives are humane, I question their logic. If their logic is reasonable, I question their worldview and their right to impose their worldview on the lives and bodies of others."

"Then, honey, you question the nature of civilization."

"And you don't?"

He sat up, put his arm around her, and brought her down again, but now they were lying face to face in the sunlight. His face had that clear, open shape she liked so much, prominent nose, smooth brow, well-defined chin, blue eyes. He was smiling. He said, "Do you know how long I've been in Hollywood?"

"Thirty-five years."

"Do you think I have any faith in human civilization after that?"

"No."

"Let me tell you how I see it."

She rolled over onto her back and said, rather petulantly, she was willing to admit, "Okay."

He rolled her onto her side again. He said, "Look at me."

"Okay."

"The people who are running this thing have spent their whole lives as corporate executives, more or less, and not only that, corporate executives with in-house philosophers of the free market. Not only are they rich and powerful, they feel that they deserve to be rich and powerful, because the free market is the highest good and they have worked the free market and benefited from it, and so has everyone they know. There are two things about them that you have to remember—that deep down they feel guilty and undeserving and that they live very circumscribed lives. Inside the office, inside the house, inside the health club, inside the corporate jet. Iraq is the size of California, right? But none of these guys has driven from L.A. to, say, Redding, in living memory. They have no idea what the size of California is, much less what it means in terms of moving armies and machinery, or having battles or conquering territory. They are used to telling people to get things done and then having them done—or partially done, or done in a good enough way, or done in a half-assed way that someone has

convinced them is good enough. The real problem is that they don't understand logistics and that they've been downsizing for decades. Even though
Iraq is the size of California, they think it is the size of United Airlines.
United Airlines could possibly be reorganized and made to sustain itself in
a couple of years with the right sort of ruthless leadership, but California
doesn't work like that. That's how I see it."

"As an administrative problem that can't be solved."

"In a way, but more as a testament to inexperience and lack of imagination. If one of them had been in the army, or even just drove around in the
Central Valley for a week and saw the scale of things, that might help everyone emerge from the fantasy. Or if everyone all the way up and down a
single chain of command—let's say forty levels of authority, down to the
guy fixing the carburetor on the Hummer—just came into the office and
told one of them what he had actually done for the last twenty-four hours,
the inevitability of fuckups and waste would be so evident that even the idea
of ordering up a successful invasion would seem laughable. Situation Normal All Fucked Up, as we used to say. But I know it isn't going to happen. I
know the machine is going to keep running and lots of people are going to
be crushed beneath the wheels and mangled in the gears. I can't not know
that. I can't even have hope that it won't be so."

Now she rolled on her back again, and he let her, though he kept his arm
comfortingly under her head. Though no theory worked, she couldn't help
toiling at her theorizing. Her fellow citizens had become unaccountable.
She had lost even the most rudimentary ability to understand their points of
view, but she could not stop theorizing. Each new theory was accompanied
by a momentary sense of uplift—oh, *that* was it—fear, native aggression,
ignorance, disinformation and propaganda, a religious temperament of
rules and punishments. But in the end, it was that they didn't mind killing;
they didn't think killing had anything to do with them or their loved ones. It
was unbelievably strange, a renewed shock every time she thought about it.

She said, "I think I'm becoming deracinated."

"Then it's time to get up."

"Is there a word beyond deracinated?"

"Only in the realms of mental illness."

"Well, mental illness is not the problem. Moral illness is the problem."

He put a hand to each side of her face and turned it toward his face. He
spoke slowly and clearly. He said, "I agree with you even when I don't feel
exactly as you do. That's the best we can do." He took his hands off her face.
She nodded, feeling at first a bit chastened and after that comforted. Now
he rolled her up against himself, her head in the crook of his neck, her
breasts against his chest, his belly pushed into hers, his leg crooked over her

leg and pulling her legs toward him. She could feel his warm solid body all the way down hers, no gaps. His wide hand was on the small of her back, pulling her tightly against him. Then he shifted toward her a bit, not on top of her but pinning her nonetheless between his weight and the resilience of the bed. She felt him breathing, then felt her own breath synchronize with his. She let this happen. It was slow, but they had done this many times, this exercise of physical agreement, usually as a way of getting back to sleep in the middle of the night. Even now, after only a minute or two, it made her feel relaxed and then sleepy. Should the occasion arise, she thought, this was a good way to be buried, and she should remember to put it in her will.

She said, "What time is it, do you think?"

"It is eight-oh-six. Time for a cup of coffee."

When he walked across the room, she thought, This is the thing you never get to see in the movies—a naked hairy middle-aged man walking past the window in a graceful, casual way, pushing his hair back, adjusting his testicles, looking for his glasses, rubbing his nose, coughing—and yet it is a beautiful sight, no manliness problem at all. He went into the bathroom. She heard him blow his nose, urinate resoundingly into the toilet, and flush. She heard him go out the other door of the bathroom. After that there was silence for about a minute, and then he was back.

She said, "What's the matter?"

"The house is full of people."

"How many people? Do we know them?"

"Stoney, Charlie, Delphine, Cassie, Isabel, and Simon."

"Simon! What's he doing here?" She sat up.

"I don't know what anyone is doing here. I got out there in the altogether, realized the place was teeming, and came right back for my bathrobe. Do you think we invited all these people for today? I thought they were going to be dribbling in one at a time over the next couple of weeks."

It was, indeed, unusual that they all showed up at once. Normally, Max lived alone in the house itself, but his former mother-in-law, Delphine Cunningham, lived in the guesthouse. Even when his ex, Zoe (Isabel's mother, the pop icon and sex goddess Zoe Cunningham), left, there had, apparently, been no question of Delphine going with her. As Delphine was Jamaican, Zoe said, it was wiser not to move her. But really, of course, the arrangements were more about Isabel than anything else. Delphine was tall, thin, and imposing, but Elena had found a small, perhaps pinpoint-sized, area of common ground with her on the subject of correctly roasting pork. Delphine and Elena agreed that brown sugar in the marinade, soy sauce, and slivered ginger and garlic (always sliced lengthwise) thrust into cuts stabbed into the meat with the tip of a good sharp knife were key, along with, of course, laying the roast in the pan fat side up, and setting the oven temperature low—325. Thirty-five to forty minutes per pound was not too much, either, if you wanted juicy. And they had come to these conclusions independently, only happening to compare notes one afternoon in Max's kitchen.

Delphine's best friend, Cassie Marshall, also in her seventies, lived next door. Whereas Delphine was tall, Cassie was short. Whereas Delphine was laconic, Cassie was voluble. Whereas Delphine did not drive and almost never made any noise, Cassie drove, ran an art gallery down in the Palisades, and was notoriously well connected. Delphine was reserved and Cassie was busy (and Max didn't like to be disturbed), so Elena could not say that she had become actual friends with them.

Max said, "Simon shaved his head."

"He did what?"

"I guess he did it yesterday."

"Oh, for God's sake!" But this exclamation was mostly for show. She was a veteran of worse surprises than head-shaving. She said, "What about Isabel? I thought she wasn't coming for a few days."

"She looks good. Get up. They're making pancakes. I had no idea Charlie would be here. I thought his plane was due this afternoon."

She got up.

The kitchen was the only other room on the same level as the master bedroom, but whereas the bedroom seemed to stand out over the hillside, anchored to the rock but jutting into the air, the kitchen was set back under the trees, on what had been the original tableland. It was shaded most of the day by overhanging purple bougainvillea that grew up through a spacious deck. It was not terribly modern—no restaurant range with grill, for example, and the work space was limited—but you could cook there happily day after day, as Elena sometimes did, making bread or cookies or authentic Bolognese sauce with milk and white wine, just to prolong the pleasure of puttering around in the wood-paneled quiet. Her own kitchen, which she had installed after much thought, research, and consultation with experts, was more up-to-date, but she found herself cooking there less than here, in what had become, more or less, her territory.

Not, she supposed, in the minds of Delphine and Cassie, who were busy flipping pancakes, or the tall girl, who would be Isabel, whose head turned in her direction as she came into the room. She was opening a jar of jam. She gave Elena a friendly smile, set down the jar, and stepped forward. Though she didn't have the same attention-riveting incandescence that Zoe had, she did have a bright, intent look to her, and Max's natural grace. She said, "Hi. I'm Isabel. You must be Elena." And then she put a hand on each of Elena's shoulders and kissed her. Simon said, "Hey, Mom."

She turned from Isabel with what she hoped was a smile that matched Isabel's in warmth. "Hey, Simon. What are you doing here?"

"Something not bad. Something fun."

"That's not a good start, Simon. I see you had your hair done."

He put his hand on the top of his shining head and rubbed. "What do you think?"

She was more suspicious about his purpose for being here, but she knew not to openly pry. She said, "Honey, your head has a nice shape." She kissed him on the cheek. "You're lucky. Some people are entirely flat behind." She decided to leave it at that. Cowardly. "How's your car running?"

"It's fine."

"So have you two young persons been formally introduced?"

Simon said, "A long time ago. Do you remember that guy Decker, Roman Decker, that I used to hang with?"

"Not really."

"Isabel goes with his cousin Leo."

"Well," said Isabel, rolling her eyes and spreading her hands, "I think Leo and I would have different views on that. I thought I was so relaxed about it, and I was going to take my vacation-time buildup and come next weekend, but then I just couldn't stand the sight of him for one more minute, so I flew standby last night. The plane was four hours late, so I sneaked in after you guys were asleep. Little did I know that the bed and breakfast here was full."

"I'm just staying for a couple of days," said Simon, with a glance at Elena.

But Elena didn't ask. She would ask later, she hoped.

Isabel turned suddenly toward her and said, "Do you mind that I called my mom? I mean, of course you don't mind that I called her, but do you mind that she's coming over? If she comes over she can see me and Delphine at the same time, whereas if she doesn't come over who knows how she'll fit us in."

"I don't mind. I like your mother."

"Do you? You're one of the few, then. Have you met Paul? Here are his credentials: He's a terrific healer and he got back from China less than a year ago, where he climbed the seven holiest mountains. And, let's see, as Mom would say, he has a boat."

"What kind of a boat?" asked Simon.

"Well. He doesn't have a boat. I am making fun of my mom. That's what she said about her last boyfriend all the time—'and . . . he has a boat.'"

"I have met Paul, actually," said Elena. "I didn't really form an impression of him, though."

Isabel opened the refrigerator door and took out the package of butter. She said, "You *are* smart. I like you. I'll have to consult you on what to do about Leo." She unwrapped a stick of butter and set it on a plate, then she wadded up the paper and tossed it over her shoulder into the wastebasket without looking. Elena and Simon shared a glance.

Simon put his arm around her and gave her a squeeze. She said, "Just tell me one thing. Are you going to get a big tattoo on the back of your head?"

"Isn't that the best place?" But he slipped away from her without committing himself. He had only two tattoos so far, one on his calf, of a skull, that he had gotten in high school ("When I have to get a job, I'll just wear pants"), and one on his upper arm, of a tree, that she rather liked. By the time he got that one, it seemed as though his future in corporate America was improbable, anyway.

Across the room, the pancakes, cooked and served without her help, were now being eaten. Cassie, Max, Delphine, Charlie, and Stoney were sitting around the island, hunched over their plates and laughing. Behind them, framing them, the lemon and quince trees she had installed in tubs on the deck looked simultaneously bright and dark, yellow and green, promising and calm, just as she planned they would. The pancakes were small, maybe three inches across, and delicate, with crispy edges, cooked in butter. She slipped under Max's arm, gave him a squeeze around his middle, and reached for one, then said, "Hi, Charlie." Charlie opened his mouth to speak, but Cassie said, "So how did you enjoy the Oscars? We watched for a while, then we turned it off and missed all the good parts."

"They hid the red carpet around behind the building this year, for fear of snipers," said Max, "so it wasn't terribly festive."

"It was all new to me," said Elena. "I liked it. And at one point, they got every actor who'd ever won up on stage for a group picture. I thought that was fascinating. I understood that they did that during a commercial break, so no one at home saw it."

"Frank still looks good," said Max.

"Who?" said Cassie.

"Frank Pierson, the president of the Academy. You know him."

"I do," said Cassie. "He's older than I am."

"I don't think so," said Delphine. Elena didn't know how to react to this. In fact, she didn't know how to react to a lot of things Delphine Cunningham said.

Stoney smiled. His plate was swimming with syrup. He lived by himself three streets down the hillside and hated to cook.

Max said, "Frank told me a funny story at the Governors Ball."

"What was that?" said Stoney.

"You know he worked on *Gunsmoke* for a while. And he said that, once, they were sitting around, waiting while the scene was being set up, and one of the old cowboys was sitting sideways on his horse, having a smoke. Well, the horse reached forward with his hind leg, I suppose intending to scratch some itch, and it got its foot in the stirrup of the saddle. Frank was standing right there, and he said the old cowboy just drawled, easy as you please, 'Weelll, if yer gittin' on, I guess I'm gittin' off.'"

Everyone laughed.

"Frank has been around this town as long as I have and he's still alive," said Cassie. "Most of them aren't."

Stoney said, "Cassie won't tell me how she came to Hollywood, but she says it's mythic. So, Elena, you tell me how you got to Hollywood."

"I never got to Hollywood. I only got as far as L.A."

"We want to know," said Cassie. "Then I'll tell how I got to Hollywood."

"You will?" said Stoney. Isabel leaned over his shoulder and took a strawberry off the plate in the middle of the counter. "You will?" she said.

"You tell first," said Cassie to Elena.

She glanced over at Simon's bald head. He was going down the stairs. "Well, my first literary work was a pamphlet called *You and Infertility.* What was this? Oh, twenty-five years ago now. I mean, I was married to my husband, and I could never get pregnant, so I did my usual thing, which was to find out all about it. Every time I made an appointment with an expert to find out more, he would ask me if I were writing a book, so eventually I started saying yes. Then that marriage broke up, which actually happens with infertility more than most people realize. Anyway, I wrote that book, and it made a fair amount of money. Then I got pregnant and had Simon, and I got interested in babyfood, though of course Simon was on the breast for"—she leaned forward, more as a joke than anything else, because Simon knew this about himself—"thirty-one months. I wrote the next book, with recipes and little pen drawings, called *Don't Feed Your Baby What You Wouldn't Eat Yourself!* That was put out by a press that published baby and child-care magazines with a natural slant, you know, homemade diapers, and how you could put a four-year-old child in a warm bath and ask him to remember his birth. When those magazines went out of business, another press bought it. They were more of a media conglomerate, so they brought me to L.A. to do a little demo tape—an infomercial, really. I made little messes and showed how to freeze them in ice-cube trays. That sort of thing. Once we were installed in our rental in South Pasadena, it wasn't really in the cards to go back to Chicago. And Simon, of course, has never had a trans-fatty acid in his life. You can tell by his head of hair, can't you?"

Max laughed and the others smiled.

"Very dull," she said. "Now you." She pointed her fork at Cassie.

"We're ready," said Stoney.

"Well," said Cassie, "when I was a small child, in the thirties, I didn't really know who my father was."

"Don't believe her," said Delphine.

Cassie tossed her head. "I lived with my mother and my sister on the Upper East Side in Manhattan, and there were these two men who came around. One was a guy in a suit—he was in advertising, and he later got to be famous for the slogan 'I'd walk a mile for a Camel.' His name was Ewan Marshall, like mine. The other one was named Morton Hare. He was an impoverished artist. I preferred him. He would get me up early on Sunday mornings and take me out into Central Park with a gun and he would shoot ducks for food. They both had volatile relations with my mother, who also worked in an ad agency."

Cassie took another pancake. Stoney said, "New York always leads to Hollywood."

"So, when the war started, both of them went into the army, and my mother wrote a best-seller called *Since You Went Away*. David O. Selznick, who made some big movies—"

"Like *Gone with the Wind*," said Stoney.

"Bought the book and brought my mother out here to write the screen-play, and us with her, of course. We started at the Westlake School. I was in the sixth grade and my sister was in the ninth grade."

"A big movie," said Max.

"Claudette Colbert played my mother, Jennifer Jones played my sister, and Shirley Temple played me. She had to follow me around and learn how I did things and my facial expressions. In the movie, she's incredibly spoiled and bratty."

"That was you," said Delphine.

"Well, she followed me around a fair amount, but she was slightly older than I was and way more mature—when we went to gym class, I saw that they were wrapping her chest to make her look flat, because she was always having to go on good-will trips. She was nice to me, but even I knew she was having a difficult transition to more mature roles, and I think maybe they bought the book not because of how great it was and how noble and long-suffering and brave my mother was, but because Shirley's career needed a boost. Anyway, Jennifer Jones followed my sister around. She was in her twenties, I think, and married to Robert Walker, who was in the movie as her boyfriend, but actually she was having an affair with David Selznick. Robert Walker was fairly crazy. You remember him, right? He was in *Strangers on a Train* as the guy who proposes that Farley Granger kill his father and he will kill Granger's wife. It was all a very big deal, because Jennifer Jones had won the Oscar for *Song of Bernadette*. Delphine and I watched *Since You Went Away* a couple of years ago. Joseph Cotten played Morton Hare, and he was all over the picture, even though the 'you' in the title was supposedly my father, who was overseas. Anyway, at one point, Joseph Cotten gives Claudette Colbert a bigger-than-life-size picture of her-self as a naval recruiting poster. She's in a short-short skirt and high heels, no stockings, and she's leaning forward. Her derriere is out to here, and a little skirt is fluttering around it, and she has a mysterious smile on her face, luring young men into the navy. Claudette Colbert is, of course, a little scandalized when Joseph Cotten gives her this picture, and they hang the picture somewhere out of the way, but not before the camera gets a good full-frontal look at it." Max and Stoney chuckled.

"Except that we had that picture in my mother's room for years, the very same picture that Morton Hare painted. Only it was a nude."

Everyone laughed except Isabel, who produced an authentically shocked look. She was a handsome girl, Elena thought, so similar to Max.

"Of course, in the movie, they are very careful to establish that Claudette Colbert only has eyes for my father. I had realized which one was my father by that time, of course." She jutted her jaw saucily at Delphine. "But Joseph Cotten only has eyes for my mother. He keeps turning up and giving us things."

"He was sinister onscreen," said Max. "Effortlessly sinister."

"What made me cry was the dog. It was my dog! He was an English bull-dog, and I suddenly remembered that at some point they took him away, and then at some point they brought him back. In the movie he does exactly the same thing as he did around the house — nothing. But there are lots of shots of him doing it. It's a very slow movie. Delphine and I had to stop watching at the intermission."

"Well," said Max, "it was basically propaganda. People were in the mood for it at the time. It was nominated for a lot of Oscars. I don't remember how many it won."

"I think I ended Shirley Temple's career. The better job she did acting, the more accurate and convincing her portrayal of me, the more unappealing she was onscreen. But it was fun for us. My mother wrote a few more movies about the war, I rode ponies and horses, my sister became a specialist in international law and later met Shirley Temple at diplomatic functions, Selznick married Jennifer Jones, Jennifer Jones got rid of that strange young man, Morton Hare got a wife of his own in Europe, and the Allies won the war in part thanks to all the good-will trips Shirley Temple had to do."

"More pancakes?" said Delphine.

Isabel gave her grandmother a kiss on the cheek. Delphine said, "Did you eat, Isabel?"

"I ate some of the cantaloupe, an orange, two slices of whole-wheat toast, and a piece of pineapple."

Delphine said, "Isabel is a vegetarian."

"Vegan."

Everyone looked her up and down.

Delphine said — fondly, Elena thought — "When Isabel was five years old, she came through the kitchen while I was fixing a chicken and she said, '*God*, what's *that?*,' and I said, 'It's a chicken,' thinking that she had eaten plenty of chicken, but she looked at that chicken, and that was that. No chicken ever again."

"I am an overtly self-righteous vegan," said Isabel. "My position is the moral-high-ground position."

"Except around me," said Delphine, "because I know that all this started not because you knew anything about agribusiness, but because you couldn't stand the sight of an undressed chicken."

"It had feet on it. And a neck."

"It was a good chicken. And it tasted good, too."

"I'm sure of that," said Max.

"Anyway," said Isabel, lifting her chin, "Mom left me a message that she and Paul have decided to go wait out the war at some Buddhist monastery up north, and they are leaving today, and so they are stopping by on their way out of town."

"Do you think they've eaten?" said Elena.

"I'm sure they have," said Isabel. "They're on a diet where they have to get certain foods eaten by certain times in the day, and the first time is six a.m."

Delphine rolled her eyes and got up from her chair. Isabel continued, "He makes her get up at four-thirty so they can get whatever it is cooked and digested. I think it's organ meats."

"You're kidding," said Charlie, who hadn't said much yet.

"Kidneys, hearts, sweetbreads, brains. I don't think I could even open their refrigerator. When I was here last, she was low-carb, but now she's gone beyond that."

"Not very Buddhist," said Cassie.

"I know," continued Isabel, "but Paul has his own system. He's got all these students he counsels over the phone. They call him at all hours, too, because some of them are in Australia and France and one is in Croatia. It's been very taxing for Mom, I have to say, having him get out of bed in the middle of the night and talk some Frenchwoman through an anxiety attack." Isabel grinned merrily. Elena couldn't help smiling, though she did like Zoe, as she had told Isabel—who didn't? Zoe was a mostly good-natured and generous woman, and she was also agelessly and effortlessly beautiful, with a singing gift that no harebrained script or crazy producer had ever been able to dim. Zoe Cunningham could sing any song from "Stormy Weather" to "Happy Birthday" and break your heart every time. Once before this Paul, who had been in the picture now for about three or four months, she had come by to look in Max's storage room for an old port-folio of photographs that she couldn't find anywhere else, and Elena had listened to her singing in the bathroom—flushing the toilet, washing her hands, no doubt fixing her hair, and at the same time offering a rendition of "It Had to Be You" that segued neatly into "Bob Dylan's Dream." Elena had positioned herself cautiously so that she could listen. When Zoe suddenly opened the bathroom door and there she was, Zoe had said, "Doesn't that bathroom have great acoustics? I always loved them," and went past her up the stairs.

In spite of her good nature, though, Zoe Cunningham was irritating, or perhaps "maddening" was the word. Every so often there would be "a crisis," and when "the crisis" hit, she sought advice and support from everyone around her. Everyone around her gathered and helped her weather "the crisis," always dishing out much advice, for which Zoe expressed profound gratitude. And then the next crisis would come along, and its terms would be exactly the same as those of the previous crisis, and not only had Zoe not learned anything about how to weather this crisis, she didn't seem to realize that the two crises were similar. In the year since Elena herself had come into the picture, there had been more than five but fewer than ten (well, six—Elena was a counting sort of person) crises. When Paul turned up, Max had said, "Well, finally she's got her own in-house healer and guru," but Zoe had called within a couple of weeks, and "the crisis," as far as Elena could tell, was no different from the others.

None of her crises were career crises. She was a working machine, which Elena had to admire. If she put out an unsuccessful CD or acted in a stinker of a movie, she laughed it off and did something else, like a concert of standards in New York or a mini-tour of Europe singing cowboy songs (she sang "Red River Valley" like you wouldn't believe). It was only men that made her crazy. Delphine was reserved in these crises; Elena had no idea how Delphine felt about her daughter or anything else.

Isabel said, "I don't think Paul considers serving Mom his number-one priority. In fact, I think he sees Mom as just another unit in his array of female admirers."

Elena looked at Max, and Max looked at her.

Charlie said, "I can't believe Zoe Cunningham is just going to walk through that door in a half an hour."

Max turned toward Charlie in exaggerated amazement. He said, "Zoe Cunningham has walked through that door thousands of times, and you were here for some of them, so what does that mean?"

"I don't know. I mean, yes, Max, Zoe was your wife and my friend, but that was twenty years ago. Now—"

"Now you're separated."

"I don't think that's a factor. I mean—"

"Face it, Chaz. Here you are almost sixty and you have to make up for lost time." He turned to the group. "You should see Charlie's suitcase."

"It's a sample case."

Max said, "Charlie decided to live his life backward. He got married at twenty and had five kids. Now the kids are all married and he has twelve grandkids, and he's decided to live a little."

"You laugh, but taking advantage of your best reproductive potential and highest fertility is the responsible thing to do. You pass on the optimum genetic material, for one thing. Pregnancies tend to be more trouble-free, and the likelihood of producing a child with problems is less—"

"Yes, ladies and gentlemen, Charlie Mannheim has been boning up on the latest research by the Cato Institute, or is it that Richard Mellon Scaife thing, what's it called?"

"Fertility decline in women of European descent is—" He coughed and glanced around, then smiled. "Anyway, I'll be happy to see Zoe. I hope she remembers me positively. I was a little self-centered in those days, I admit. The separation has been a real growth experience for me."

"What about your wife?" said Cassie.

"Well, in the end she's glad to get rid of me, she says now."

"And he is giving her everything," said Max. "That softened the blow. She gets the house and the money, and he gets the nutritional supplements."

"Who gets the kids?" said Cassie.

"I know just what you mean!" exclaimed Charlie. "Everyone is in their thirties and married and has kids of their own and all, but every single one of them has an opinion, including my two sons-in-law."

"Charlie is an outcast," said Max.

"Well, I wouldn't go that far. But there hasn't been a lot of sympathy for my point of view."

"You vacated your fancy job at PepsiCo just when you hit your earning peak, so I'm sure part of it is that they see their inheritance flying out the window."

"That wasn't completely part of the separation. That was more of a health issue. But I'm telling you, these supplements are a growth industry. Junk food is going to level off. Anything geriatric? Hunh! Out of this world. I mean, look at it this way. My grandkids aren't allowed to drink soda, much less energy drinks. My kids drank free soda all their lives, and now they put soda down in the basement like it's booze or something. All investments are ultimately driven by demographics. The soft-drink market seems permanent to outsiders, but it isn't. There's no telling what the Chinese market is going to do. The days when you put up a Pepsi sign and they all came running are gone. The market is too splintered. I mean, I told them—" Everyone was picking up plates and evidently beginning to think about other things. Charlie looked around the room for the rest of his audience, Elena thought. "Anyway," he said, "I'm here. I'll be glad to see Zoe again." He glanced at Elena. "Of course, it's wonderful to see you again, Elena."

"Thank you, Charlie," said Elena, picking up her own plate. That was the correct reply. She didn't say that Simon had only had access to fresh, filtered water and organic low-fat milk. She had met Charlie once, the previous summer, when he and Max had happened to be in San Francisco at the same time. They had all gone to Postrio, and Charlie had talked about his separation for three and a half hours. She said, "You seem happier."

"You know, I'm glad you said that, because I am—"

She smiled warmly and turned away from the island before he could continue. As she did, Max gave her a friendly pinch on the ass.

Simon emerged from the stairwell. He was wearing a different shirt and pants. It looked like he had shaved everything all over again. He said to her, "May I turn on the TV?"

Everyone looked at him, and there was a long silence.

Elena's first thought was that this was an odd question for an American boy to ask, especially one like Simon, for whom the TV had often been his only friend. Simon had been a loner for years before he, rather unaccountably, blossomed. That pattern of middle-school life, where betrayal was routine and hurt feelings were intentional and you didn't know what was going on most of the time, was simpler on television. Simon had always watched television because television was safe and predictable; even when he himself got handsome and graceful and attractive to women (he still didn't have many male friends), he watched television automatically. But not now, not here.

Because there was the war. The prospect of opening the communications tap and letting the war flow over them made Elena feel tense and ill. She said, "I think we're all talking, Simon, and the TV would interfere."

Everyone else was silent, too. Simon said, "So okay. I won't turn on the television."

After a pause, Charlie said to Isabel, brightly, as if eager to be part of the conversation, "So—did you see *The Hours*? I was wondering why what's-her-name got the Oscar. I didn't see it myself."

Isabel said, "Oh, I saw it." She glanced at Elena in a friendly way. "The weirdest thing happened. Explain this to me. We got there kind of early, because they were showing it in a smallish theater in Cambridge, where my friend was living. We had to sit toward the back and off to the side. I was sitting next to Tara, and there was one seat between me and the wall. Behind Tara, all the seats were full except one seat over toward the aisle. About a minute or so before the lights went down, this couple walks in. They must be in their forties or early fifties. Perfectly normal couple, nice-looking and tall. She's carrying the popcorn. No seats anywhere by this time, so he squeezes in past me and sits in the seat by the wall, and the wife sits up behind Tara. For some reason, everyone in this section is friendly, and these two are perfectly pleasant, just like everyone else. The movie starts, and we're watching. About fifteen minutes into the movie, I realize that the guy next to me is making noise, so I shift over toward Tara an inch or so. The movie goes on, and he's really bothering me. I mean, he's not touching me or anything, but I can't stop being distracted, so I turn and look at him. It must have been in one of the California scenes, because this man is all lit up from the reflection of the screen back into the audience, and he is leaning up against the wall on the other side of his seat and crying his eyes out. His eyes are open and I can see glints of light in them, and also in the tears running down his cheeks, and he's resting his head against the wall like he can't hold himself upright. So I poke Tara and she looks at him, and then we turn and glance at the wife. She's just sitting there, eating popcorn and watching the movie with that movie-watching face you get. We look at the husband again. Floods of tears. We look at the wife again. She never looks over at him or seems to notice or have any sixth sense that there's something wrong. I thought we should report him to the wife, but she was too far from Tara for her to poke her on the leg."

"I would put that shot in a picture. Especially with the light from the screen glinting off the tears," said Max.

"Are you sure they were married?" said Cassie.

"We couldn't figure out if she even realized what was going on. Tara said, 'Aren't you so glad those aren't your parents?'"

Cassie said, "Maybe they'd been fighting on the way to the movie."

Simon said, "Maybe he had a friend with AIDS or something. I mean, maybe they weren't married at all, and he was gay, and the movie made him relive the death of his lover."

"They had that married look. Used to each other. I think women and gay men who hang out together look like they feel lucky."

"Or maybe his mom had been schizophrenic and he was reacting to that part of the movie, where the little kid realizes something is really wrong and he's the one who has to deal with it. I thought that was the most affecting part of the movie myself," suggested Stoney.

"Maybe," said Elena, "he sympathized with Virginia Woolf's decision to kill herself because of the onset of the Second World War."

"But he didn't try to stop or wipe his eyes or hide his face. He just leaned up against the wall and bawled. What if he hadn't gotten that seat against the wall and had been out in the middle somewhere, or sitting next to the wife? It was just the sort of seat in a movie that nobody ever wants, but it was perfect for just this guy in just this movie even though he was the last person to get to the theater. So, yes, I saw *The Hours*."

Simon said, "I couldn't get over the nose thing. I guess I didn't understand the movie, really. I liked that guy Ed who played the gay man."

"Ed Harris," said Max. "No manliness problem there. That would be why they cast him as a gay man dying of AIDS. I've tried to put him in at least three movies, but he's always had scheduling conflicts. I saw him do a movie about twenty years ago, *Under Fire*. He played a mercenary. He was funny and happy and entirely without a conscience."

"What's a manliness problem?" said Charlie, leaning forward.

"Ask Elena. It's her theory of American film."

"Oh." Charlie slightly deflated.

"It has nothing to do with your sample case."

"So, Max," said Simon, "what's your favorite movie? What movie do you wish you had directed?"

"Well, those aren't really the same thing. I have a lot of favorites. There's the one I wish I had directed, which was *One Flew over the Cuckoo's Nest*. There are all the ones I love but couldn't have possibly directed, like *Pennies from Heaven* and *Ashes and Diamonds* and the Judy Garland version of *A Star Is Born*. There are my Hollywood favorites and my non-Hollywood favorites."

"Hunh," said Simon. Then he added, "So what was it like to win the Oscar?"

"You know what?" said Max. He leaned forward, a playful look on his face.

Elena thought how much she enjoyed watching them interact. She did not think that Max was going to be the father Simon had never had, but she did think that it was positive for Simon to know Max. She would go that far.

"About two weeks before the Oscars that year, I was driving out in the Valley, by Middle Canyon, you know that area? A dog bolted out of a driveway to my left and ran across the road. I just saw him out of the corner of my eye. I swerved right, and my tire went down over the rim of the pavement. When I turned the wheel to come back up onto the blacktop, the wheel jammed, and the car went end over end."

Elena gasped.

He glanced at her. "I didn't have a seat belt on, and I was thrown under the glove box. Both the roof and the left side of the car were crushed, and I was disoriented. I kept trying to get the window open by pushing the button, but because I was upside down, I was pushing the wrong direction. A guy showed up who told me to push the button the other way. That's all I remember about him. The window opened, and another guy pulled me out. I had to go to the hospital for the night but that wasn't the weird thing, the omen."

"What was the omen?" said Isabel.

"The omen was that when the car flipped over it landed on the dog."

Simon laughed.

Isabel looked a little shocked. Max said, "So I was convinced that, because I survived, I was going to win. When I won, I wasn't very surprised."

"I don't—" Elena was saying, but then the front door opened and there was Zoe Cunningham, and everyone turned to look. Behind her, Paul, who had a bushy beard and was thin and catlike from years of doing yoga, smiled. Zoe seemed to spring into the foyer in a way that reminded Elena that once, in her stage act, she had entered by leaping from the wings almost halfway across the stage (she had used a trampoline to launch herself). Paul closed the door behind them. Zoe dropped her handbag on a table and swept toward them, Elena thought. She was only wearing jeans and a white shirt, with black-and-white zebra-print flats, but she wore it all with such flair that, had she worn it the night before, she would still have appeared on the best-dressed list. What you could not get used to, Elena thought every time, was that face appearing suddenly near you, and her hair, swept up in a luxuriant bundle and pinned with careless expertise at the back of her head.

"We're here!" exclaimed Zoe. "You wouldn't believe the traffic. We should have come over Mulholland, I guess, but we came by the 101. Hi, Max. Hi, Ma. Isabel! Oh, you look great, sweetie! Elena, are they driving you crazy? Who's this?" She put her hands on Simon's shoulders and looked into his face.

"I'm Simon."

"You're so cute! Are you Isabel's boyfriend?"

"Not yet. I'm Elena's son."

"Are you? Stoney! How are you, you should just move in. We should all just move in. Can we move in, Max? Hi, Charlie. I heard about the divorce, but I didn't hear how to feel about it."

"It's a separation," said Charlie.

Cassie said, "Charlie says his wife is relieved, so I guess we can be relieved for her, too."

"Hi, Cass. Is my mother behaving herself? This is Paul Schmidt, did you meet Paul? Paul, this is Cassie Marshall. Cassie knows everyone and has seen everything, and that's why she hides out up here in the hills with these people."

"I do not! I open the gallery six days a week, and I have to deal with artists on a regular basis, and I met Paul a month ago. Nice to see you again, Paul."

"Charlie, Paul Schmidt. Stoney Whipple, Paul Schmidt. I am so hungry! We haven't had a thing all morning. Did you have pancakes?"

Isabel said, "I thought you were eating organ meats."

"Paul does, but I stopped. It's harder than you think."

"How could it be harder than you think?" said Cassie.

"Brains was the hardest," said Zoe. "In the end, I couldn't actually incorporate the brains into my body. I talked Paul into substituting tofu that's been made to taste like organ meats. You can get it in Chinatown. Oh my God!" Zoe strode into the living room and dropped into a chair.

Isabel said, "You want some fruit, Mom? I cut up some pineapple."

"Oh, I don't know," said Zoe.

Paul said, "I'd like some fruit, if you don't mind, Isabel. May I help you get it?"

"Sure. If we bring it out, Mom will see it and start picking at it and pretty soon eat all the best pieces." But she smiled.

Paul was wearing khakis, a cream-colored polo shirt, and bone-colored Timberland boat shoes trimmed in tan. The way you could tell he was a healer, Elena decided, was the full beard, so thick that for any normal person it would clearly present a style problem—how was such a beard to be groomed? Shampooed like a thick head of hair, but then what—combed? trimmed? roughed up with fingers? shaped with hair gel? Clearly not. He was a walking paradox—slender and elegant and clean and even careful, the way dapper men were often careful of what they chose to wear and how they wore it, but with all this grizzled hair around his mouth and down to his collar, like a rabbi. Probably, Elena thought, he should not be handling food. Isabel and Paul opened the refrigerator, chatted, took things out. They were the same height and build, taller than she was by five or six inches, and taller than Zoe, who was more or less what you would call "petite." Max, who had disappeared for a bit, now came out of the bedroom with his clothes on. In the meantime, Zoe continued what she had been saying while Elena had not been listening to her.

"It's a place of miracles, actually. Miracles are absolutely routine there. It isn't just that some fire they had up there a few years ago literally stopped at the property line and went *back* the other direction. Isn't that interesting? I guess there was a big fire in that whole forest that was set by a lightning storm that came in September. No rain, just lightning. Talk about an act of

God. Thunderbolts being cast here, there, and everywhere. And the country was so rough that all there was back in this part of the forest was a Franciscan monastery and a Buddhist monastery, and of course some marijuana farms. The firefighters came after about four days, and they told the monks they had to clear out, even though the monks were doing everything to remove the brush and save the place. So the monks were resisting, of course, though politely. The way they do it is to just not respond to what you're saying. People think they keep smiling, but they don't. If you are a true Buddhist, smiling has nothing really to do with it, though you might have been smiling, and the smile could linger, but you are not trying to smile. Anyway, the monks did not want to move, so they just kept clearing the brush and giving the firefighters water, and here came the fire up the side of the mountain, and as it got to the property line, which was visible from the buildings, the wind shifted and the fire stopped, because of course it couldn't go back down the hill. It just burned out, and the firefighters and the monks dug a trench. The firefighters were really impressed, but the monks considered it fairly routine, all things considered. Buddhists don't really get excited about things, I've noticed. I don't think the Franciscans had the same sort of miracle, but I don't remember. Do you remember, dear one?"

Paul sat down across from her and put the plate of fruit on the table between them. Pineapple, strawberries, a couple of slices of kiwi, and some wedges of orange.

"Do I remember what, Zoe?"

"About that fire up at the monastery. What happened to the Franciscans?"

"They ended up rebuilding the residence, I believe."

"There you go," said Zoe. "I gather that the Franciscans pray for miracles, but the Buddhists expect nothing."

Paul might have been smiling, but, Elena thought, it was hard to tell. She said, "Are you going up there today?"

"We were," said Paul.

"But what time is it? Oh, about eleven. To us that's like three or four in the afternoon, because we get up at four, so my own opinion is that it's too late to go all the way up there. It's six hours just on the highway, then another couple of hours on very treacherous roads with no guardrails, and at this point that would be in the dark, which I don't like, so maybe tomorrow, don't you think, dear one?"

"We'll see." He ate another piece of pineapple.

Elena glanced at Max. He looked amused and benevolent. She glanced at Isabel. She looked amused and irritated, the way Elena herself could remember feeling so well, that overwhelming weariness that came from being too familiar with your parents, more familiar than anyone should be with any other person. She glanced at Delphine. Delphine was smiling in Isabel's direction, not as if she expected Isabel to return her gaze, but as if she didn't and was simply enjoying the chance to look at her granddaughter. It was sort of like watching Delphine reveal a secret, something that Elena, at any rate, had never seen Delphine do before. In fact, secrets abounded in this house. The biggest one, as far as Elena was concerned, was how long it had taken Max to get over Zoe, if he was over her yet. As Max beamed (a low beam, for sure, but nonetheless a beam) at Zoe reaching for a strawberry, Elena suspected that he was surveying Paul for clues, using this new guy to ask, What does she want, what did she want? And Elena herself was staring at Zoe, as she always did, thinking, What does she have, is there something beyond the beauty and talent, or is it just that surface thing?

Officially, of course, Max didn't love Zoe—she had devolved into just another person who was around from time to time, important as Isabel's mother but otherwise more tedious than attractive. Officially, Max's adult life, at least with regard to women, had flowed like a river, through several sets of locks and dams, and no reach of the river was that much different from any other, except in regard to landscape. When he was first in the business, he told her (he told her all of this in an easy, good-natured voice), he was married to a girl named Ina that he had met at the Actors Studio in New York. They had come to Hollywood, but she had been artistically offended by the parts she landed, and so she'd gone back to New York. After Ina, who lasted only two years, he dated Dorothy, who was the daughter of Bo Levin, the famous agent. When the time came to break up, Dorothy and Bo had sat Max down in Bo's office and told him he was too antisocial ever to make it in this town, and so Dorothy was leaving him, no hard feelings. Later, she married Jerry Whipple, who worked in Bo's agency and was Max's agent. Jerry had Stoney from his previous marriage to Diana Carstairs, a starlet who died in a car accident under mysterious circumstances when Stoney was not more than a year old. Jerry went on to make the sort of money that Dorothy and Bo were comfortable with, and to have three more children, while Max dated beautiful women. In 1979, Max met Zoe at a party, where she was singing with the band. In 1980, as a result of winning his Oscar for writing *Grace*, which had been about a classic British actress that Elena couldn't now remember the name of and a child actor named Josh Lane escaping the Russian Revolution and ending up in Japan, but was really about Max's great-grandmother and his grandfather, Max got Zoe a part in a comedy about college students in San Francisco, and she was so sexy and gorgeous, even before she sang, that for her next movie she had to hide the fact that she was pregnant with Isabel through almost the whole shooting. After Isabel was born, Zoe made one movie after another, with no one realizing that the woman on the set taking care of the baby was Zoe's actual mother (because Delphine insisted on wearing what seemed to be a uniform, but was, according to Max, just the sort of cool, natural cotton trousers and shirts from India that Delphine liked to wear). Max didn't make movie after movie, but he wrote two more and then directed his first, which was a success, and then directed his second, a blockbuster called *A Very Bad Day*, in which the Beverly Center was destroyed by a flotilla of tornadoes and the La Brea Tar Pits gaped open and swallowed up UCLA. After that movie, Max and Zoe bought this house. In 1990, Zoe suddenly bought a house in Malibu, and they broke up. In the late nineties Zoe had fallen in love with the costar on her most ambitious film, which was a remake of *Green Mansions*, set in the Amazon, written expressly for Zoe, though they actually filmed somewhere in British Honduras, and Zoe got malaria, which stopped filming for a while, and by the time the movie was in the can, Zoe didn't want to see that director ever again.

To Max (Elena was sure), Zoe felt like the main event of his life, but to Zoe (for some reason), Max felt like the opening act. Elena understood that this was a common pattern in Hollywood, where the calibrations of success, especially for "talent," were highly refined, and every marriage was simultaneously an assertion of who and how important you thought you were at a particular moment in your career and a sign of how you were to be treated by others. But Max's feelings (Elena was sure) about Zoe went beyond those prescribed by the system, even, as far as Elena could tell, beyond his history or psychology. He found her at a party, he was married to her for ten years, fixated on her for another ten, and never for a moment did he cease—what? Maybe it was something Elena could not imagine, but it was very romantic, larger than life. Desiring her, of course; contemplating her, of course; longing for her, wondering about her, molding her, wishing to touch her, be next to her, look at her, fuck her, make love to her, give her things, serve her, make an impact on her even when she was thinking about something else. Once he had said to Elena (and she thought about it for days), "What I wanted was to be fused with her, for our molecules, atoms, and subatomic particles to be intermingled, and then, when Isabel was about two and we were watching her and talking about how she looked like each of us, I realized that I had had my wish—in the fusing of sperm and egg, there it was, we were intermingled at the minutest possible physical level, but it didn't satisfy me. The result was Isabel, an entirely separate human being, a child that I loved, but not what I wanted in terms of the potential outcome of my feelings, which felt like it should be an explosion or a melding, not another person. I considered this a tragic revelation about the impossibility of true love." When he told her that, he laughed at his folly, but what he said was so like what she felt about him that at first she felt like she wasn't going to get over hearing him say it about Zoe (though jealousy was the ultimate incorrect thing).

In the end, Elena saw what Max had felt for Zoe (she saw this privately—she had never confided this idea to Max himself) as a gift, an example of unprecedented inspiration on Max's part in which he recognized the inherent possibilities of romantic love, not only for himself and Zoe, but for everyone. He had been in the grips the way everyone wanted to be in the grips but couldn't manage, or was afraid to permit. And furthermore, it was *his* inspiration, not *theirs*—that much was evident in Zoe's attitude. She treated Max as if he were her father or uncle, whose affection she could rely on but whose wrath she preferred not to incur, not because she was afraid of it, but because it would inconvenience her. Look at how she had apparently consigned Delphine to him, and he and Delphine continued to live together the way estranged couples were said to do in Japan—separate living quarters, separate entrances, separate recognitions that the arranged marriage didn't work as a form of intimacy, but did work as a way of life. He did say, "It's okay for me that Zoe and I aren't married anymore. I never actually wanted to be a family with her. It was just that that was the only form available to embody what I felt about her." Elena contemplated this as she gazed at Zoe.

The new Max, the Max that loved her, Elena, had chosen not to engage in that Zoe sort of love anymore, or ever again. He was kind, attentive, faithful, thoughtful, conversational, and sexy, just exactly what Elena had always looked for. Every day she marveled that she had found him, attracted him, and had many minutes and hours to enjoy him. It was love of a very correct sort, much like finding your notions, plans, and presuppositions satisfactorily confirmed—you thought that you wanted a certain thing, you got it, and it turned out to be everything you had hoped for and more, because your capacity for enjoyment turned out to be larger than you had realized. So—nothing wrong there. But how was she to think of Max's progress? Had he been sick before and now he was well? Had he transcended before and now he had come back to earth? Had he painted his masterpiece and now he was idling out his later life? Had he embraced an illusion and now he was back to reality? Had he been an older man falling in love for the first time with a younger woman and gone a little crazy? Or was it just pure Hollywood? She could have asked him about that when he was talking about his joke film, *My Lovemaking with Elena*, but she had forgotten to. Or not dared.

Paul and Isabel offered the last strawberry to Zoe, who took it and said, "I could eat a piece of toast. What kind of bread do you have around, Max? Dear one, do you want a piece of toast?"

Elena said, "I bought some of that nine-grain loaf that they have at Gelson's Friday. That's good toasted."

"Do you have any hummus?" said Zoe. "We've been eating that instead of dairy products."

"Oh, for God's sake, Mom," said Isabel.

"I thought you were a morally superior vegan," said Cassie.

"I am, but not being greedy is a moral category that trumps vegan. Sometimes, when the virtues you want to promote contradict one another, you have to choose one over the other. In this case, I notice that Mom came into the house, made herself the center of attention, asked for food, didn't like what was offered, and then asked for what else we might have as if this were a restaurant."

"No one minds," said Elena.

"We're used to it," said Delphine.

"Are you joking, Isabel?" asked Zoe.

"What do you think, Mom?" said Isabel.

"I don't know," said Zoe. After a short, meaningful pause, she went on, "Honey, why don't you show Paul where the bread is."

"I'll do it," said Elena.

"Do you know how irritating you are, Mom?" said Isabel.

"I irritate you because you can't give me a break, Isabel," said Zoe, and as Elena passed her to go into the kitchen, she thought that that was probably true. She herself would have never gotten along with a daughter. However, had she been Zoe's daughter, she would have found her irritating also.

The nine-grain bread was in the freezer. She took out the loaf and broke off four of the frozen slices. While she was putting them in the toaster, Paul came up behind her. He said, "Let me do that. We meant to pack some food, but we forgot, and then we meant to stop for something to eat on the way over, but the traffic was terrible and there wasn't anywhere I was willing to eat. Probably Zoe's a little annoyed about that."

Elena considered how not to offend by showing that she knew more about him than she had learned from actually talking to him. Finally, she said, "Are you on a special diet? I mean, other than the organ meats?"

"Well, the organ meats are temporary. I only do that once a year, for about four weeks, for the iron mostly. Zoe never did it before, so it's a big deal to her, but I'm so used to it I just think, 'March—organ meats.'"

"Why March?" The toast popped up. Elena picked out the slices, turned them over, and put them back in so they would toast evenly.

"By now, it means spring, I guess. I used to live in Ohio, where spring actually came in March, but if I remember correctly, I just happened to do it the first time in March, and so I did it a year later, and so on."

Elena opened the refrigerator and took out a container of roasted-garlic hummus. The toast popped. She opened a drawer and took out a knife. He took it from her in a smooth, courteous way, and began to spread hummus on the toast. It was awkward to stand there not knowing anything significant about him and to make assumptions based on someone's saying that he was a "healer" and that he ate organ meats before six in the morning. He was too vivid in her mind to be a stranger, and yet he was a stranger. So she said the wrong thing. She said, "If it's too late to leave for the monastery, you ought to spend the night here. I mean, if you go back to Zoe's house, that's going to add an hour to your trip starting out again tomorrow."

"We could stop somewhere along the way, though my idea of a good place to stop isn't going to be the same as Zoe's. I like a nice dive myself. There's a motel in San Miguel. It's right out of *The Postman Always Rings Twice*. You know, two hard beds and a lightbulb hanging from the ceiling."

"You like that?"

"I like paying $44.95."

"It's probably better that you get all the way to the monastery in one day, then."

"The first time I ever stayed there, I couldn't figure out why the doors were slamming all night long. Every time I would drift off, bam, the door next to mine or down the line would go off like a shot. And the semis were idling in the parking lot. At about five, I finally woke up for the day when someone came pounding on the door next to my room and shouting, 'Let me in!' and the girl inside called out, bright as you please, 'Who is it?,' and the guy shouts, 'It's me! Let me in!,' and the girl calls out again, 'Who is it?,' and the guy says, "Come on! Let me in! You know who it is!' They go on like this for about ten minutes, and she never lets on that she knows who it is or that she's intimidated in any way, always just calling out 'Who is it?,' and he refuses to say his name. So the guy heads off to the office, I guess to wake up the manager and get another key, and there's quiet for, oh, say two minutes, and then, all of a sudden, the girl runs out of the room, jumps into the car, and races away. When the guy comes back with the key five minutes later, she's miles down the road. I always thought that was brilliant, the way she did that."

Elena laughed. As he told this story, he carefully cut the crusts off the toast, cut the four slices into eight triangles, picked a sprig of parsley off the plant in the window, and set it on the plate. Elena said, "What about water? I have some Pellegrino."

"We drink Pellegrino."

She opened the refrigerator again and took out a big green glass bottle. There were two glasses in the dish drainer. He said, "Do you have room for us?"

"Oh my goodness," said Elena, "I think it's a crime the way the rooms in this house sit empty. And Delphine lives in the guesthouse, so that's four bedrooms that hardly ever even get aired."

"It's a thought," said Paul as they carried the food into the sitting room.

"Dear one!" said Zoe. "Guess what. We're staying here for the night! Isn't that a good idea? We're right above the 405, and we don't have to go all the way back to my place and start all over again tomorrow morning. Max said we could stay in the garden room. It's a cave! You'll love it. The previous owners actually dug it out of the hillside for their wine cellar. You could never do that nowadays. And then they got divorced, and all the wine went to some bank or something. Anyway, it's totally quiet, it looks onto the Japanese garden, and when you get up, you can go out and pull weeds. It'll be just like spending the night in the monastery. It even has a tiny little kitchen, if we want to cook. It is just my favorite room, even though it's forty-eight steps down and forty-eight steps up."

"It sounds perfect," said Paul.

"We'll stay, then," said Zoe.

Isabel made a little noise, as if she couldn't believe that Zoe had gotten away with something yet again.

DAY TWO · Tuesday, March 25, 2003

The nice thing about Isabel's bedroom, which Stoney had discovered years ago, was that it had windows on all sides but it was entirely private, like a fire lookout. The Getty on one side, mountainsides full of houses on another, the cul-de-sac and another street beyond that. It was a California view for sure, one of the best Stoney had ever seen in Los Angeles. Isabel had been living in this room since she insisted upon moving up here when she was ten, and the room had remained more or less the same over the years, since it had too many windows to be decorated in any style. The bed sat in the middle of the floor; cream-colored Japanese shades hung in each of the windows, and a few inexpensive bright area-rugs were thrown around that sort of matched the bedspread. The only thing Isabel had collected over the years was pillows, and there were pillows everywhere—in the corners, stacked against the walls, on the bed. There were also a few small palms and rubber plants, because of the light, but no pictures or paintings. L.A. was the panoramic picture, out of every window. Stoney felt that it was this view that had formed Isabel's perspective, literally. She was entirely self-confident, a tad remote, unimpressed by luxury or comfort, and tall. It was when she had gotten tall—at fourteen—that Stoney, who had known her all her life, really noticed her. It was when she had gotten self-confident, at sixteen, that he had started coming to this room and smoking dope with her, and talking to her. He had been nervous from the beginning, but there was a separate entrance, which, most important, was not visible from Delphine's place or Cassie's place (just around the cul-de-sac, but hidden by thick olive trees).

Of course, Stoney knew that the sense of remoteness and security he felt here was an illusion—for years he had parked his car a hundred yards down the street and walked up the hill, his heart pounding in case Delphine or

Cassie or Max should emerge suddenly and ask him what he was doing—but it was something he could not shake and was always reassured by. It was the reason he had recently bought himself a lesser house in the same neighborhood, even though he could afford something bigger, better, and more convenient to his office across the 405. His house was much less interesting than this one—just a 1970s rambler with lots of rough wood paneling and the remnants of psychedelic wallpaper here and there and beaten-copper fixtures. He had not quite started to update it—his floors weren't really being refinished for another month, but when Isabel called him and said she was coming, floor refinishing was the first excuse he could think of to get himself inside Max's house for a week. There were so many ways that his relationship with Isabel was unacceptable to almost everyone he knew that when he was in this room he was grateful for everything that permitted it, but when he was out of this room he thought he probably wouldn't come back again. Nevertheless, he always did.

The bathroom door opened, and Isabel came out. She was wearing pajama bottoms—black and white, patterned like the hide of a cow—Uggs, and a yellow sweatshirt from UC Santa Cruz. She looked willowy and tired. She said, "It's five a.m. to me. I am so baked. Where did you get that stuff?"

"Some guy. I hardly smoke it anymore, because it's so much worse than cigarettes, and I quit those last summer. I read that book, *The Tipping Point*? Have you read that? He said there were something like five different degrees of being a smoker, and you could tell what degree of commitment you had to it by whether you had a buzz the first time you ever smoked. So I remembered I hated smoking and it took me real effort to start. I thought I could probably quit pretty easily, and—boom—I quit."

Isabel paid attention to him for about the first five seconds of this dissertation, and then began looking around the room. Long after he stopped talking, she said, "I think my grandmother was in here and threw away my bong, because I was looking for it before dinner and it's nowhere to be found. She used to do that in high school. She never forbade anything, but she would make it hard to do whatever it was, so, if you got an impulse, four or five times out of ten you couldn't give in to it, because it was too much trouble."

"He also said that real smokers tend to have a certain type of cool personality. You know, rebellious and funny, kind of the high-school version of a Lenny Bruce personality. I realized that I don't actually have that personality, I just used to aspire to it. You look good."

She looked down at herself in a speculative way, then said, "You don't."

"I don't? I've been going to the gym. I was going to put a workout room in my house—"

"That's what I mean. You look like you don't have anything better to do than polish your presentation."

"Oh, thank you."

"Well, it's true." She scratched her cheek and pushed her hair out of her face. She did look good—a perfect meshing of Zoe and Max, or maybe she just looked like Max as a woman with Zoe's hair. She had a rectangular face and a wide mouth and a narrow nose with a bit of beakiness to it, a long neck, and broad shoulders. Under her sweatshirt, he knew, her back was long and her waist distinct. She had prominent hip bones and a flat ass. She was not his type, but he had been sleeping with her at this point longer than with anyone who was his type, including his former wife, Nina—petite and ballerinalike, with wiry muscles and a lot of surface tension. Nina was Italian; her family had moved to New York when she was ten and had a shop full of luxury goods there. Luxury goods had turned out to be more of a feature of her personality than he'd realized when they got together in the early days of her career in wholesome Disney movies. He said, "So what do you think of Elena?"

She came over and lay down on the bed. She looked around the room for a moment, staring toward the west bank of windows. Finally, she said, "She's cute. She's not like anyone my father ever was interested in before. She's kind of dry and neat. She makes my mom, the legendary Zoe Cunningham, seem quite out of bounds. I like that part. I guess she's okay with my grandmother."

"What makes you say that?"

"No emanations."

"Excuse me?"

"Delphine is so vibratory. It comes off her in waves. If she doesn't like something, she just zings."

"I never noticed that."

"Oh, Stoney, you never notice anything. You are like the least intuitive person I ever met." She yawned. "Do you think it freaks Elena out to have us all descend on her like this? The *daughter*! The *ex-wife*! The *best friend*! The *neighbor*! It's right out of a horror movie. '*And they weren't leaving!*'" She laughed.

"Not to mention the strange guru from nowhere, the sinister Jamaican grandmother, and *her own son*, grotesquely changed!"

"What about you yourself, the mysterious stranger?" Now they laughed together, maybe longer than this joke warranted; then she said, "But of course this family reunion is weird to all the rest of us, too. We never had one before." She shrugged.

"It's been a whole year since I've seen you. When are you moving back?"

"To L.A.?"

"Well, yeah."

"You don't mean to be with you or something?" She sat up and looked at him in a critical way, then pursed her lips. Suddenly she opened her mouth as wide as she could, then closed it as tight as she could, then opened it again. Then she looked at him. He said, "What does that mean?"

"What?"

"You just made a face at me."

"I didn't make a face. I exercised my facial muscles."

"Your mouth is the biggest mouth I've ever seen."

"Look at this." She opened her mouth and introduced her clenched fist almost entirely into the space between her teeth, then took it out, looked at it with satisfaction, and said, "You try it."

"Put my fist in your mouth?"

"No, put your fist in *your* mouth. Try it."

He opened his mouth as wide as he could, wide enough so he could hear the tiny sound of his mandibular joint creaking. He got his fist in up to the dip between his second and third knuckles.

"See?" she said. She smiled, then stared at him again.

"See what?"

But she was stoned. She said, "You know I wouldn't come back to L.A. and live in this room."

"Why not?"

"Because, you loser, I am not going to live with my family. I am twenty-three years old. So any fantasies you have of this life where you sneak up the hill and we cultivate eternal youth behind the backs of my grandmother and my father, it ain't gonna happen. This right here is, as they say, your last hurrah."

"This is the best bedroom in L.A."

"Well, of course it is. It is the best room, and I have had the best adolescence in it, so what now? I quit my job."

"What job was that?"

"My job at the Wildlife Conservation Society. At the Bronx Zoo."

Stoney knew that he looked blank, that once again he had forgotten the terms of a woman's personal drama even though, evidently, he had been informed of them in some detail. But last year, when she came back for Jerry's funeral, he had been in no shape to take in anything about her job.

Stoney now did what Dorothy had always taught him to do. He looked Isabel right in the face and said, "I'm sorry, Isabel. I didn't remember where your job was, which I should have done, or maybe would have done if I had been paying attention, which probably I wasn't, but I am really sorry, so tell me about it."

"I'm too fucked-up to talk about it right now."

"Okay."

"Did you smoke any of this shit at all?"

"I had a hit."

She slid down in the bed and moved over toward him. A moment later, she turned off the light and then said, "Take off your jeans."

He sat up and took off his jeans.

The room was, in some sense, no less light than it had been when the light was on, but the light in it was blue and white rather than yellow and red. As she snuggled against him and he put his arm around her, he could see her profile, moon-colored against the bright windows. It was funny that, in spite of the fact that he knew Delphine and he knew Zoe, he almost never thought of Isabel as being of "mixed race." In California, she looked vaguely Hispanic, or unidentifiable, or simply herself, Isabel. He must have been stoned, because he had one of those stoned thoughts about how her lips were beautiful because they had to open that wide in order to accommodate the size of her jaw, or maybe it was the other way around—her jaw could open that wide because her lips were so elastic. And then, when she closed her lips, they had to do something to fit into a much smaller space, so they bunched up and curved in an attractive way. Then she put her hand up his shorts and began tickling his scrotum. He let his legs relax and fall apart. Her fingertips tickled down one side and up the other, then underneath and behind, then made little circles. His cock began to press against the seam of his boxers and pretty soon showed its tip above the waistband, and it, too, was pale and moonlike in the air of the room. He closed his eyes and pulled her a little closer. She continued to tickle him, sometimes only brushing the tips of his pubic hair, sometimes stroking the skin. He shifted position and pushed his boxers down. She stroked his cock lightly upward once, and then made a ring of her thumb and forefinger and ran it downward from the tip. This was something he had taught her to do, and it was very exciting. He gave out a little bark of pleasure. She said, "Remember the first time we slept together? You were twice my age."

"I was not twice your age. I was twice your age when you were fifteen, but when we slept together, you were sixteen, so I was only about 187 percent of your age. I worked it out at the time."

"How about now?" She gave a big sigh.

"Now . . ." Her hand wandered up his chest and pinched his nipple. He said, "Let's see, I'm about 162 percent of your age."

"You took off my clothes very slowly. I was wearing a shirt with some-thing like sixteen buttons, and you unbuttoned every button from top to bottom, and then you unbuttoned the two buttons on each sleeve, and then you unbuttoned the two collar buttons. I thought that was so romantic, the way you undid the collar buttons before you opened my shirt and unbut-toned my jeans."

"Your bra had hooks in the front, too."

"One hook. It was my first bra from Victoria's Secret. My friend Daria got one, too. We thought we were so hot." She laughed and then rolled over against his chest and kissed him between the eyebrows. He could feel her breasts sway beneath her sweatshirt and then press against his chest. "And we got thongs. Mine was black stretchy lace. Daria read in some magazine that if you got the stretchy lace ones they would be pretty comfortable, but they weren't. It was better just to not wear any underwear at all."

"No panties."

"No panties. But girls don't call them panties."

"I remember that you didn't wear panties for a while. It was nice."

"You were so hot for me. Remember we had the bed kind of turned around, closer to that set of windows, and you would look at my reflection in the glass?"

"It was ghostly and really erotic." Now she lifted her sweatshirt and arranged her breasts against his chest, rubbing the nipples up and down lightly in his chest hair. He said, "I loved trying to make out what I was see-ing, and I would think, Oh, that's her ass, or Oh, that's her tit."

"So you know that when you took my shirt off, and took my jeans down and began to stroke my ass, I was thinking how no one had ever stroked my ass in my entire life up to that point, and I thought it felt so good, the best thing I had ever felt. I think you should do that now." She swung her leg over, sat up, and took off her cow pants, letting them drop over the side of the bed. She was not wearing any panties. When she sat down on him again, she made sure to position her labia right on his cock. That was excit-ing, too. He slapped her ass a little bit, first right, then left. She muttered, "Oh, I just love that. Why isn't it the same when you try it yourself?" She moved back and forth on his cock, and his erection felt like it swelled a bit, if that was possible. He knew there would be a moment when she hitched her hips upward and he slipped into her, but it wasn't just yet. She said, "That's good. Oh, just like that. Right there. Now run your hands down a little bit and pull apart the inner thighs, right there at the top. Oh, yeah. Just stroke there. That's nice, too. Remember how surprised I was at what your erection looked like?"

"No, I don't remember that."

"Oh, shit. I was sort of dumbfounded."

"I thought you had seen some erections before."

"I must have said I did. I guess I'd seen a picture and maybe some porn movie. Did they have erections in *Boogie Nights*?"

"I don't think so. Anyway, *Boogie Nights* wasn't out by then."

"Daria had access to her dad's stash of porn movies, so we watched one together. She watched them all the time."

"Daria did? Little Daria?"

"Little Daria tried to seduce both her stepbrother and her cousin. She was very curious. She was the one who talked me into doing you. She said it was perfect, because I'd known you all my life, and you were into it, and we weren't related in any way, not even as steps, and you were married. She said you would be nice. Oh, it was funny, she also said, 'There are bonus points if he's married.'"

"I had no idea." He slid his hands slightly upward and positioned her on his cock again. She rocked slowly back and forth, and he moved with her. It was gentle, like the motion of a boat on a calm sea.

"We talked about it every night for a month. We aren't friends at all anymore, but Daria pretty much made me who I am today, since our first project together was caring for that baby mole. Remember the baby mole?"

"No."

"Oh, God. We were about ten, and her dog was out in her yard playing with something, and when we looked at it, it was a baby mole. It wasn't hurt, but I guess the dog had killed its mother or something. So Daria got a box and an old doll bottle, and we took care of that baby mole for weeks. I guess she went to the library and asked the science teacher, and in the end, we managed to save the mole, and she wrote it up as a science project for school, and then, when summer came, she gave the mole to her teacher. Daria was just so serious about everything, even sex, really. And she got worse. Eventually nothing was funny for her at all. She came for a visit to Santa Cruz sophomore year, and we pulled into a convenience store on Mission Street. There was some junker on her side of the car, all decorated with stickers about Wiccans, you know, like 'Wiccans do it in a circle.' I saw her looking, and I saw the couple and their kids. He was wearing a suit and she was wearing a *Little House on the Prairie* sort of dress. The car was full of stuff—two kids in car seats, coolers, clothes, little objects glued to the dash. So, as we pulled out of the parking lot, I said, 'I bet they live in that car,' and she said, 'The guy in the suit was a woman.' I said, 'Probably. This is Santa Cruz.' And she said, 'That's too freaky for me.' And I said, 'They're just lesbians, what's the difference,' and she said, 'They're homeless Wiccan lesbians living in their car with two kids. Is that a choice or a misfortune?'

After that, we sort of lost touch. She works in her father's law firm during all her vacations now. I guess she's already in her second year at Boalt Hall."

"Who's her father?"

"Robert Shengold, but he's not an entertainment lawyer. He's a patent attorney. They argue all the time. I would hate that."

"I can't believe she would get along in Berkeley if she can't accommodate a couple of homeless lesbians."

"I don't know. But the butch one really was carefully turned out. She had on a striped button-down shirt and a bow tie and everything. Her hair was slicked back. Usually in Santa Cruz, lesbians make an effort to look like lesbians, not like a straight couple from the 1930s."

Stoney said, "We're losing momentum here."

"Did we have momentum?"

"I had momentum."

"Thanks to that shit you brought, I have no momentum at all. What time do you think it is?"

"It's about two-thirty."

"Oh, God."

Now she rolled over on her side and pressed up against him with her face in the crook of his neck. She was relaxed and heavy, but it wasn't uncomfortable. He imagined himself at thirty-one, three years into his marriage to Nina, the subject of conversations between Isabel and Daria. Daria was short, flat-chested, and squarely built, with ungovernable curly hair that she had kept neatly trimmed. He had thought Daria was a tomboy. He had thought seducing Isabel was entirely his own bad idea and all the more exciting for that. He slipped his hand under his cock and wiggled it back and forth. He was not tired at all and had planned on making love to Isabel as a way of getting to sleep, since he knew that even if he fell asleep in her bed, he would be awake by dawn and ready to exit without anyone's being the wiser. And if he managed to fall asleep now, he could get four hours, which would be a good night for him. But they had lost the momentum. She said something that he couldn't hear.

He said, "What was that?"

"Did you like that movie we watched with them?"

"Did I like *Sunset Boulevard*?"

"Was that what it was called?"

He lifted her up and looked into her face. He said, "You've never seen *Sunset Boulevard* before? Or heard of it?"

"I never saw it. If I heard of it, maybe I just thought they were talking about Sunset Boulevard. Didn't you think she was weird?"

"Gloria Swanson is supposed to be weird."

Isabel sat up on her haunches and stared at him. She said, "Do you think he was actually fucking her?"

"You mean Joe? I guess so. That's the implication. After the New Year's Eve thing. He moves in, she buys him all those clothes. He's her gigolo."

"But maybe he's only her escort and friend. Maybe he's not actually fucking her."

"I'm sure they want you to think he is."

"But how does it work? He isn't into her. She's old. She has all these weird mannerisms. I can just imagine what she would be like in bed, like with all the lights low and the room full of candles, and she's wearing a headdress of some sort. And a kind of filmy garment to hide her body." She laughed. "What's he? Like forty? How does he get it up?"

"Forty-year-olds get it up."

"Well, yes, they do, but I saw this chart in a men's magazine that showed that as time passes they don't get it up as high or as easily. I think the line for the forty-year-olds was at a thirty-degree angle or something like that. The line for the sixty-year-olds wasn't even above the horizon. It was minus thirty degrees."

"Something to look forward to."

"Well, it's a good thing you stopped smoking, according to the article, because that's the biggest single factor. Anyway, everyone was sitting around saying what a great movie that was, and how they don't make them like that anymore, but I thought there was such a basic unanswered question that I couldn't get into it."

"I think he's meant to be in his late twenties."

"You're kidding me. His face looked so wrecked and old."

"Well, in real life I think William Holden was thirty or so. Gloria Swanson was just over fifty."

"So they were implying that he could just get it up no matter what? I mean, yeah, I knew this guy in college who would get an erection on the bus, just from the vibration, but what is the implication here about this guy—"

"Joe Gillis."

"About Joe? He's made out to be humiliated by the whole situation and not into her, and yet he's supposed to be getting it up and fucking her on a regular basis. I don't understand it."

"Well, it's Hollywood. Maybe he's thinking about her money. Or maybe he's closing his eyes and thinking about that other girl, Betty. Or maybe you're right and he's just her escort. I mean, there was a lot of censorship in those days, precisely so that the audiences out in Iowa wouldn't start thinking about those very things you're thinking about. If the censors let the movie through, then maybe they saw it as an unsavory situation, but not a sex situation. We could ask your dad."

"I would. But everyone just accepted it."

"It's a classic movie. We've all seen it a dozen times. It just is what it is."

"We're going to have to watch that sort of thing for days now."

"Your dad likes European movies."

"Those are worse. I mean, yes, American movies are slow because everyone says everything. You know. A guy walks into a room. He says hi. She's sitting there. She looks up. She says hi. He says, How are you? She says—after a pause, of course—I'm okay, how are you? He says, How've you been? She says, How've *you* been? They aren't questions, either, so they aren't even that lively. But European movies, they sit there and sit there without saying anything or doing anything. If you're lucky, at least they aren't sitting in a car stuck in traffic."

"That's *Weekend*. That's only one movie. And it's French. French movies are a special taste. What would you watch?"

She flopped back on the bed. "Nothing. I would read a book. Books move a lot faster."

"There's a revolutionary idea."

"Well, they do. You never have a shot in a book of two people walking down the street in real time, step step step. That drives me crazy. And then their mouths open and then words come out of one and then words come out of the other. You might as well be watching two real people walk down a real street, but why would you? And you can't speed it up. You can cut in and out of it, or you can cut to another scene, but otherwise you're just stuck, because if it moved faster they would be running and that would look weird. If I'm reading a book, it takes a few seconds for my eye to pick up the lines of dialogue that in a movie take much longer to say, and once my eye has picked it up, I can go on to the stuff I'm really interested in, which is what the characters are thinking or whatever. I think books move a lot faster even than a movie everyone thinks is fast, like *The Matrix*. I hated in *The Matrix* how you were always having to stop with the story and watch them fight. I would rather the story would go on and on, and then the fight would start, and then, right away, they would cut to the end of the fight and you would know who won, and then the story would pick up again."

"Spoken like a girl."

"Well, so what? I don't like chick-flicks, either. I don't mind documentaries. I saw this one about an art class for schizophrenics at a mental institution in New York State that I thought was wonderful. So I'm not cinematically impaired."

"I thought you were stoned."

"I'm not anymore. It wore off."

"Want another hit?"

"No. I still like *The Lion King*. I made Leo watch it just the other day. If they ask for suggestions, that's going to be mine. What's going to be yours?"

"I don't know yet. I have to think about it. I don't want it to be anything symptomatic." He said this seriously, thinking how much people could tell about you when you suggested a movie for everyone to watch, but she barked out a laugh, which made him smile. Then she said, "Sweetie, I don't think anyone but me cares enough about you to want to diagnose you."

The effect of this remark on his body was instantaneous, like an electrocution. He felt the nerves in his chest and arms light up and blood rush to his face, which, in the dark, thank God, she didn't notice. He cleared his throat. She was moving around, making herself comfortable, totally unaware, as far as he could tell, that she had more or less done him in. Of course it was true. He knew that because nothing, no name, no face, popped into his head at the moment she said it. He cleared his throat again, and said, coolly, he thought, "But you do?"

She turned her head in the blue light and was still smiling. She said, "Well, I do, yes. You were nice to me. You are nice to me. I don't care about diagnosing you the way I did Leo, so we could fix it because it was interfering with my plans. I don't have any plans with you. So I care about diagnosing you for you, so that something better could happen to you."

He said, jokingly, he hoped, "I hate that thing where you suddenly see yourself as others see you."

"That is a bitch, honey." She reached up and stroked his forehead, and just then, as if his electrocution had turned something on, no more voluntary than that, he felt tears run down his cheeks. She said, "You're crying."

"Well, I'm not actually crying. I'm just reacting."

She said, "Stoney. Stoney Whipple. I hurt your feelings." She sounded genuinely surprised.

"Talk about a diagnostic."

"Oh, honey. Gosh." She pushed the hair out of his face and continued to look at him; then she picked up a pillow and wiped his tears away with the corner of the pillowcase, first the left cheek, then the right cheek. Then she put the pillow down, got off the bed, and stepped across the floor toward the bathroom. When the bathroom door opened, a big square of yellow light yawned into the darkness of the bedroom, blacking out all the blue windows. She came out, closed the door, came back to the bed. She handed him some tissues and said, "So blow your nose."

He blew his nose and wiped his face more thoroughly. The tears had stopped, and now he felt that washed-through feeling of involuntary relaxation that could have been pleasant if it didn't remind you of the agony you had felt and didn't also suggest that this could happen again. As a rule, Stoney preferred sensations to be spaced widely apart and to be mild. He liked the hours to become days and the days to become weeks and his life to seem as endless as possible.

Isabel said, "You know, I think it is really time for us to go to sleep." She was standing beside the bed with her hands on her hips. When he nodded, she began straightening the bedcovers and the pillows around him and over him. He said, "I guess I should go back to my room."

"I guess not. You should stay here. I'm twenty-three. Even if they find out we've been together, we don't have to give them the whole history, at least right away. You're not married anymore. I'm a consenting adult. Blah blah blah." Her voice was soft. When she had straightened the covers and patted the pillows, she folded back the quilt, took off all her clothes, and got into bed. She said, "Go to sleep. I'm sorry I said that. It was just something to say." She cuddled up against him, and he could feel how cool her skin was all the way down, shoulders, back, waist, arms, belly, thighs, cool and silky and warming bit by bit against him. Her hair was in his face, but then she turned her head and pushed it out of his face with her hand. She seemed to fall asleep. The blue light seemed to pervade him, and the main thing he sensed was all the windows around the bed, was it eight on a side, that would be thirty-two windows, or was it sixteen on a side, that would be sixty-four windows, except you had to subtract for the bathroom, was that half a side? So that would be four windows you would subtract, except the bathroom had windows, too, so would you subtract four or add two, or subtract four and then add six? He knew he could open his eyes and count all the windows in the room, but he could not get his eyes open actually, and then the door to the bathroom disappeared and there was a bright light and his father was standing by the bed in a brown suit with cordovan oxfords and a maroon tie, and Stoney knew that this was the outfit his father had worn to the Oscars for some reason. Maybe it was what he had been wearing for the last year, while he was away, and since he had come back through the Oscars, he hadn't had time to go home for his tux, it was a mystery, because his father wasn't saying anything. Stoney felt himself twist and contract a little bit, and then he woke up and turned over and Jerry was gone. He said to himself, though not out loud, Well, you are on the downward slide now, and what he meant was that sleep was like a big pool he was heading into, feet-first, and he didn't have to worry about it and here it came, and then he woke up because Isabel was somehow under the covers and was giving him head, and he had a huge erection, which she was anchoring with her hand. He opened his eyes.

It was true that she was under the covers giving him head. Not only could he feel her lips and tongue on the end of his cock, making some kind of flower motion, but if and when he could keep his eyes open, he could see the hump of her hips and one foot, sticking out of the covers at the bottom of the bed. He groaned, which woke him up more thoroughly, and then his back arched a bit because she was doing something with her fingers on his balls that sent a charge directly into his spine. He placed both of his hands, which were on his chest, onto her head and he scratched her scalp a little bit through her hair and it was the least he could do until all of a sudden she rose out of the covers, lifting them high and throwing them off, exclaiming, "Oh, it's so hot under there!" and she was brightly naked for a moment against the dark underside of the quilt, smiling, only the circles of her eye sockets and her areolae and the triangle of her pubic hair were dark, making a triumphant pattern against her skin, and then she swung her leg over him and sat down ever so slowly right on his cock, introducing it millimeter by millimeter into herself. She said, "I'm always amazed at how much bigger my cunt is than my mouth, when my mouth seems so big," and he gave a loud sudden laugh and finally he was wide awake and fucking her, arching his back and looking at her face, which was, since her hands were on his shoulders, an arm's length from his. As she gazed at him, she puckered her very fine curvaceous lips and then opened them and let her tongue float out between them, which he could not stop staring at, until he decided to stare at her breasts, which were small but round and good to look at the way they moved slightly as she leaned over him. "Oh, yes," she said, and lifted herself and then she put her hand between them—her fingers were still cold, which was exciting—and somehow the coolness of her fingers and also sensing that at the end of his cock inside her he was touching something, what would that be, something deep inside her, that must be her cervix, made him come, so he arched up into her and it felt like all sorts of things were happening—his come was spraying out of him in a shower that was flowing back over him and warming him and her and running out of her onto his scrotum in a honeylike way, or not that, but something. "Ah," she said. "Hmmm." And she slumped forward over his chest, warm and comforting. After a moment, he said, "What happened to me?"

"Well, let's see. I was drifting off and you were pushed up against my back, and I felt you getting an erection, so I thought I would kind of slide down there and give you a happy surprise."

"It was a very happy surprise."

"Were you having a dream?"

"Yes. My father was standing beside the bed, but I think he was you, because he was standing where you were when you came out of the bathroom and handed me the tissues. That sounds better, anyway."

"Well, dreams don't mean anything."

"They don't?"

"Just random images firing in your brain, and you make a story out of them. That's what they said in my psych class."

"That's very boring."

"I know. We were all a little disappointed." She sat up and looked at him seriously, as if, after all this time, she was finally saying what she had been wanting to say. "Stoney?"

"Yes?" He arranged himself a little bit in order to answer this question, whatever it was.

"Does my father have a career left?"

He knew instantly what she meant, which was a bad sign, and then he didn't say anything even though he had intended to, which communicated to her the fact that it was a bad sign. She added, "Does he think he has a career left?"

"Well, Max has been in Hollywood for a long time. And he doesn't fool himself about anything, so my guess is he's got a pretty good idea of, you know. Anyway, he has a career left, but it's harder, and I don't know that he's made up his mind to do the hard stuff. I've only officially been his agent for a couple of years, and we've hardly worked together, because he hasn't shown much interest." He didn't say that, once or twice when he was still lucid, even Jerry had expressed worry about Max.

"What's the hard stuff?"

"Keeping on writing and pitching and sucking up. I think it's a toss-up between the three of those which is the hardest. I've suggested him for a few things and I've suggested a few things to him, but nothing's connected in a little while. I thought he was going to make this mountain-climbing thing in British Columbia, but then he had that angioplasty when they were in pre-production, remember that? And they'd already rented the helicopters and everything, so they couldn't wait. But after I saw the rough cut, I was glad he didn't do it. Talk about slow. Step step step is nothing compared to handhold, grunt, foothold, heave, handhold, deep intake of icy breath, foothold, groan. And then it didn't even look very good. It reminded me of that old Monty Python routine where you're watching one of the Pythons hoist himself in agony up the sheer side of the icy cliff, and then the camera pulls back, and there's Eric Idle standing there on the sidewalk with a microphone, and he says, 'Will he make it? Yes, here we are, watching the famous mountaineer Marvin Parvin climb the Edgware Road! Marvin, can we have a word with you?' And then he bends down and holds the microphone to the other guy's lips."

"That's so funny."

"Believe me, that was an angioplasty sent from God."

"Maybe my dad could have made it better."

"Well, he would have been more organized, I'm sure, but I don't think he would have been able to screw more money out of what they laughingly called the production company. They were very cheap, which is not to say that the insurance people weren't making them pay through the nose, too. But he has to write something. Something with two characters about your age that takes place in three small rooms and an old car."

"Something really cheap, in other words."

"Really cheap would be the key, and with the right angle, probably about stepparents and the eternal screwups of the baby-boom generation, something that would be independently financed and that we could take to Sundance." He looked at her in the blue light. "Actually," he said, "Max should do a documentary. I showed him a book a few months ago, about salt. It was a great book, and I thought it would make a great documentary. He said, 'I would rather make a movie about asphalt.' I didn't know whether he was joking, or whether there was something really interesting about asphalt. And then it turned out that there's a famous old movie named *Asphalt*." He shrugged. "So I haven't mentioned the documentary thing, but people love documentaries now."

"Everyone in Cowell College at the University of California at Santa Cruz is intending to be a documentary filmmaker."

"There you go."

"I like documentaries. Didn't I tell you that?"

"Yes, but you were stoned."

"Should I worry about him?"

"No."

"Why not?"

"Because, as my father, Jerry Whipple, always said to me, 'It's not the job of the kids to worry about the parents, because the parents' problems are way beyond anything the kids can fix. So go worry about yourself, and then I will stop worrying about you, and then I will have the time I need to worry about myself.'"

"That's just a general principle."

"Let Elena worry about him. That's her job."

"Maybe she doesn't know enough about Hollywood to worry about him."

"All the better."

"They did screw up."

"Who?"

"The baby-boom generation."

"Well—"

"You should live in Santa Cruz, the town that time forgot. You can get to know two generations of hippies there. I had this roommate freshman year. Her name is Gloria. She's from up near Redding somewhere. She was raised in a tepee. She was always setting off the smoke alarm in our room, smoking dope. She would smoke in the closet in the middle of the night, even though I pointed out to her that that was a definite fire hazard. One time, we were having a party, and somebody else set off the smoke alarm with a cigarette, so the dorm manager came down with a couple of security guys, and they opened the closet door and there she was, smoking a joint. So that was her last chance, and they told her to come out of the closet, but all she did was curl up in a fetal position and go limp. They had to drag her out and down the hall. She said it was 'nonviolent resistance,' but, really, she was just too baked to move."

Stoney laughed.

"Another time, everyone was talking about what their parents liked to do, and Gloria said that her mom's favorite thing was to go to one of these competitions where she would catch a sheep, shear it, card the wool, spin it, and make something before the end of the day."

"What's wrong with that?"

"It does not prepare you for this world! And then we would have this constant discussion about a certain ethical question—should parents sell dope in front of their children? Whenever I said no, they all said, Well, she's from *Hollywood*. Then they would talk about 'white-skin privilege,' and I always thought"—she turned her face toward him in the blue light and spread her hands under her chin—"'Hello! Look at me, you blondes!' but I didn't say anything, because of course I knew what they were getting at, so I was just as bad as they were, and cowardly, too."

Stoney laughed.

"I'll tell you something. You're fifteen years older than I am. People normally think that's good, to be the younger one, but I think the fifteen years that I have more than you, say, I think it's going to be a nightmare. I mean, I'm *scared* of global warming. I'm *scared* of estrogen imitators in the water. I'm *scared* of the death of the rain forests. I'm *scared* of fish with no eyes. At my job, we talked about that stuff all the time, and you know what, there are people at my job who've been there for a whole generation, as long as I've been alive, just about, and they're still going at it, and it's gotten worse, not better. I mean, there's this group of gorillas saved here, and that group of hunters and gatherers who don't drink Coca-Cola there, but in general, it seems like they've done more harm than good, because they've just been feeding the other side and making it bigger and bigger. Here you are, you sixty-year-old woman, in your Birkenstocks and your homemade wool sweater and your gray hair, and you think globally and act locally, and they just sneer at you! And everything you say or do increases their contempt."

"The two halves of your analysis don't really seem to mesh—"

"Well, aren't you scared? Aren't you angry?"

"Oh, I don't know. Angry? Of course I'm angry, I guess, but I'm angry that here *I* am, doing the same thing as my father and my grandfather, but I'm not doing it very well, not as well as they did, and I'm angry at Dorothy for being angry at me that the power in the agency is shifting to people that Dorothy doesn't like and never had any respect for, and I can't stop it, even though that's my job. We all know that I am the interregnum while Monty and Clark get it together, and believe me, they have a perfect right to be named Monty and Clark, because Monty and Clark were tremendous friends of Dorothy and her father, Dorothy is Hollywood *royalty*, and her father's father came over with the original Hungarians, and before they came, they were very important in Hungary, which means that Dorothy was born to be important, or maybe not, depending on what day it is, maybe they were extra unimportant and that's why it is so amazing that Dorothy is who she is today. So—someday Monty and Clark are going to take over the agency, except that Monty plays the guitar and the piano and the saxophone and wants to write music for video games—that's his consuming ambition—and Clark wants to ride reining horses out in the Valley and live with that girl who trains dolphins at SeaWorld, and Dorothy is of course happy that they have talents, but in Hollywood, if you've got talent but not genius, then you are nobody, really. So . . ." He shrugged.

"You don't sound angry. You sound like you think it's funny."

"Well, I do think it's funny. But I am angry."

"But you're not scared?"

"Honey, I'm scared your father is going to find out I've been putting it to you since you were underage, since my father was alive, since I was married. If this were a Hollywood movie, it would be *Badlands* or something like that, and probably I would have to die in a major shoot-out in the end, or at least a car wreck."

"What's *Badlands*?"

"*Badlands* is that Terrence Malick movie where Martin Sheen and Sissy Spacek go on a killing spree in South Dakota, and she is about fifteen, though I think she was about your age when she made the movie. Anyway, they have fun, but he has to die in the end."

"I can't believe you're not scared about bigger things."

They stared at each other. Stoney knew that now it was time to mention the war, which had come up for discussion at the dinner table after an entire day without television. In the afternoon, Stoney had walked down the hill to his own house and watched CNN for an hour, but he didn't say anything about it when he got back, implying that he'd gone to the gym, where, of course, CNN or Fox News would have been blasting away anyway. Whatever show he'd been watching on CNN at his house amounted to a parade of experts interspersed with footage of the soldiers crossing the desert, and Stoney found himself agreeing with all of them, even when the moderator advertised them as being in violent disagreement with one another. What swayed him, he thought, was the conviction with which each one spoke, even those speaking for the administration, of whom Stoney was inclined to be suspicious. Part of the reason he didn't say anything at the dinner table was that he hadn't learned anything from the television except maybe that if all premises were true then no conclusions could be drawn, a remark that would confirm Isabel's impression that he had arrived prematurely at some plateau of uselessness, though his own idea was that he had risen artificially and reluctantly to a higher stage of development (marriage, moderate career success, pretty good money, though not children) than he had actually been capable of, and was now falling back to his natural level, which was more or less adolescent (eating whatever was in the refrigerator, getting to work most of the time, driving around even when he didn't need to, and watching car chases on TV). He said, "I am not for the war."

"There's this woman at my job whose husband was killed in the Trade Center eleven days after I met her. She's convinced that he was one of the ones who jumped. For a long time after, she would stare at pictures of the ones who jumped, trying to figure out if she could recognize him, and then she said that she saw him, something about his face or his body or something, and so she knew that he jumped, and she began to wonder if when he jumped he was on fire, though that didn't appear in the picture. She stopped talking about it, but if you asked her she would tell you her latest ideas, because she said she had decided that the best policy for her mental health was not to offer to talk about it, but not to resist talking about it, either. I thought that was good myself, in principle. Last year, we were working on a project together, just working up a proposal about funding research into temperate rain forests, and when we began reading up on the material, we came across these guys up north who climb the sequoias to look at what's going on in the canopy. One time, she said, sort of to herself, 'Well, that's like the thirty-fifth floor,' and these images came into my mind of her husband jumping from the sixty-fifth floor, because that's where his office was. So we were reading along and working, or pretending to work, saying this and that, and all of a sudden I felt like I was in her mind and it was hell. It made me breathless to think that for over a year she'd had this constant, pounding image of her husband jumping out of the window of his office, maybe on fire. While I was reading a book or sleeping or riding the subway thinking how lucky I was to be in New York or, you know, arguing with Leo, she was seeing that repeat over and over again. The husband doesn't have that. He's dead. I feel sorrier for her than I do for him. So that's what I mean by a larger fear."

"You mean a fear of being alive."

"Yes, I do. I am afraid of being alive. And I think my job has made it worse, because we're always talking about endangered things. Do I sound suicidal?"

"Excuse me?" At this word, Stoney felt truly startled.

"Do you think being afraid of being alive is the same as being suicidal?" As she said this, she had her most typical Isabel look on—inquisitive and intent, vaguely threatening (which surely she inherited from Zoe, whose displeasure was a sight to see), not at all suicidal as Stoney had seen it— strung out on drugs or depressed. He said, "I have no idea." And then, "I hope not." Then he said, "You watched television today, didn't you?"

She nodded.

"Me, too. But I didn't get anything out of it."

She nodded. She looked less intent, and younger, too. Since she was as tall as he was and broad-shouldered, like Max, and strong, he was not in the habit of worrying about her—more in the habit of trying not to offend her. This went back to when she was sixteen, too, and full of teenaged-girl bravado. Now, though, he saw it was time to do what his dad meant when he said, "Be a man." He put his arms tightly around her and pulled her into him. He even put his chin on her head, as a way of enclosing her protec- tively. Then he said what Jerry might have said: "But, Isabel, you don't have to think about the whole world. In fact, I think you should try *not* to think about the whole world. That's what crazy people do. That's why they end up thinking they are Jesus Christ or Genghis Khan or someone like that. Did you ever see that Albert Brooks movie *Defending Your Life*? There's a place where he talks about how everyone thinks he is a reincarnation of Napoleon or Alexander the Great, when actually he's just a reincarnation of someone who got chased by a bear, or hit by a car."

"I don't see what you're getting at."

"Well, of course you're afraid to be alive, if you think being alive is recti-
fying or even sorting out all the causes and effects that produce the war, or
the fish with no eyes, or the women whose husbands have been killed. You
should be afraid if it's that. But maybe it isn't that."

"What is it?"

"What is life?"

"Yeah."

Sitting like this, with his arms around her and her warmth and fragrance
engulfing him, he thought that it would be romantic to say, This, this is life,
just like that, the way you would say it in a movie, but in fact he could not
say that, because for such a long time he had been careful to define this as
not life. Life was everything outside of this room-in-the-sky. So he said,
"Okay, let's say that life is a much smaller thing, the thing of doing what
needs to be done when it needs to be done. Accomplishing the tasks or
making the decisions that present themselves to you as they present themselves to you."

"How would you come up with a plan, Stoney, if you just did that?"

"I don't know."

"It would just be chaos."

"No, it wouldn't. I mean, look at what happens when people die. It
doesn't matter what they planned, really. Their lives are consistent. In fact,
they did the same things over and over. Even if they have the luxury of years
of psychoanalysis, like my father had, in an effort to break old patterns and
destroy the hold of the past on the present, blah blah blah, he talked about
it for years, it was all of a piece when he died. Even though he died of a
brain tumor, and everyone thought, 'Well, where did that come from?,' I
remember thinking as soon as he told me the diagnosis, 'Well, what do you
expect, Dad? You think too much, and now you broke it.'"

"Oh, Stoney!"

"Well, I was sympathetic and really devastated, actually, and the whole
year of his decline was the worst year of my life, but my dad aways had a theory, and his brain tumor was a perfect example of theory buildup. The neu-
rons were crusted over or worn out or something like that. At one point, I
read that book by Oliver Sacks, *The Man Who Mistook His Wife for a Hat*,
and I thought that I had located my father's tumor right in the spot where
all the psychoanalysis had taken place. Five times a week for decades. But I
don't know. It would be nice to blame Dr. Epstein. But anyway, whose life
have you ever heard of that turned out random? No one. Everybody turned
out to have made a life that looked like a package, no matter what they
thought about it as it was going on. If you ask me what life is, well, that's

what I say. It's what you were going to do anyway, before you started worrying about it."

"Oh, Stoney, you are such a slacker." But she was smiling and light again. He looked at her and pinched her cheek, then stroked her arm. No suicide there, he thought. Her skin was resilient and hydrated, her eyes were clear, her whole body was well oxygenated and vibrant. When people used the word "suicidal," Stoney thought, they didn't know how hard it was to kill the animal. That's what he'd discovered when his father was dying. For a year after the diagnosis, which was now just about exactly two years ago, all they had done really was try to enable his mind to last as long as his body, and they had failed. In the last two months, when Jerry really hadn't known what he was doing at all, he had gotten out of bed and wandered around, fortunately setting off all sorts of alarms, night after night, shouting and disoriented, stumbling over furniture, evidently in terror and pain (which was worse?), until Stoney thought it would be easier to shoot him or let him fall in the pool, except that if he had fallen in the pool he would have surely kept swimming, in the same way that he kept eating and walking and yelling and pissing and shitting, a big man, a big animal, but not, of course, Jerry Whipple, husband, father, mentor, boss. The tumor did finally kill him, but only by shutting down the brainstem somehow. By that time, Stoney didn't care about the details. Thinking about it now, he stroked Isabel's arm again. Then he said, "Personally, I try to think the smallest thought I can at any given moment."

"So what thought are you thinking now?"

"I'm thinking that your arm is very nice and that I enjoy stroking it."

"I am so wide awake. We have to get to sleep before the sun comes up, or we won't get to sleep at all. If you go to sleep, I will, too. So this is what I'm going to do. Lie back." She arranged his pillow and he lay back. "Close your eyes." He closed his eyes. "Now look right at your eyelids. You feel that sensation of being blocked inside your skull? That's good. Leo taught me this. He can sleep anywhere. Keep looking at your eyelids. Now take a deep breath and imagine yourself humming. Just a low hum." As he was doing this, she began stroking his forehead very lightly, up by his hairline. One more time, she said, "Look at your eyelids, and don't forget to hum." Here was his dream. He was driving up the 405, and the air was a little smoggy, and he saw a glacier inching down a mountain off to his left, right beside the highway, brilliantly white in the Southern California sunlight, and he thought he knew what that was, but he couldn't remember.

•

As Stoney stepped out onto the deck surrounding the swimming pool, carrying the scripts he had intended to read the day before and really had to read right now, before he went to the office, he heard Cassie say to Zoe, "Did you ever meet this guy Aaron Tolchin?"

"I met Michael Tolkin. He and his brother talked to me once about a movie they wrote that they thought had a part for me."

"No, not him. This other guy, who was in the paper for the fund-raising scam. What was his name?"

"Tonken," said Stoney. "Aaron Tonken." He set the scripts down on a table. There were five of them. Five scripts had been nothing for Jerry—he read five scripts every night before going to bed. Stoney had been lugging these around for three days now.

"I don't know," said Zoe. "What does he look like?"

"Odd," said Cassie. "Not pretty. His head and neck look like they have the same circumference. He came into the gallery once and asked if he could do a fund-raiser there, but then he never came back, so I didn't follow it up, but then I saw that article in the paper yesterday."

"Paul and I don't read the paper. Maybe he did that fund-raiser for the West Hollywood Book Fair."

"The West Hollywood Book Fair *is* a fund-raiser."

"Remember I cooked something there? I cooked orange tarts with raspberry sauce and sang songs about desserts, like 'The Good Ship Lollipop' and 'Big Rock Candy Mountain.' I had to appear at ten a.m., and there were about twenty-five kids there, and the accompanist didn't show up, but it was fun. All the kids came up and ate the tarts afterward."

"You're lucky you didn't get sued," said Cassie.

"Well, the parents had to sign a release," said Zoe. "This is California, after all."

Stoney moved one of the lounge chairs into the sunshine and sat down on it. Max's pool, which was on a deck about fifteen feet below the kitchen, got sun for only about four hours on the best days, but it was quiet and you could look down the hillside and get a bird's-eye view of the Japanese garden, which was in a cleft in the hillside another thirty or forty feet down. And there were potted flowers and bonsai on many of the steps. The garden was Max's indulgence, and Stoney knew that it cost him a lot of money that other people would have put into refurbing the house, but Max was content that the house not be grand, and, in particular, not look grand from the street. Stoney thought he would wait for Max here, and then he would lure Max down the steps to the Japanese garden, and then he would make his proposal. He said, "I talked to Tonken about doing a fund-raiser once for Dorothy, for the L.A. Philharmonic. He said he could get Jack Nicholson."

"For the L.A. Philharmonic?"

"Oh, Dorothy had some idea. I think the only movie Jack ever made that Dorothy saw was *Five Easy Pieces*, and that stuck in her mind, and of course Dorothy is she who must be obeyed, so I sent out a few feelers, and Tonken called me, but he was such a gossip, and nothing he said about anyone was nice, so I got a weird feeling about him and didn't pursue it. In the paper it said he was paying a lot of celebrities to show up at the fund-raisers, and the paper was treating this as if it were a big deal."

"Hunh," said Cassie. Stoney eyed Zoe, to see if this last remark would get a rise out of her, but she didn't react, and he couldn't tell if it was because she hadn't heard him or she didn't care. Zoe interested him. She was a terrible actress, the sort of actress who moved twenty facial muscles in preference to two, and so he couldn't watch any of her movies—she always seemed to him to be bursting off the screen, like the monsters in *Alien*—her mouth opened, and then another mouth seemed to open, and in some cases it was a song pouring forth, and in other cases it was some sort of emotion manufactured for the occasion. But Stoney kept his opinions about her acting ability to himself, and he liked Zoe. She had been nominated for a Best Supporting Oscar once but hadn't won. She was very beautiful, though not as beautiful as she had been ten years ago, and Stoney felt he was entitled to this opinion because he and Zoe were only about five years apart in age. If this guy Paul was a healer, well, once again Zoe had done just the right thing, because now she was forty-three, and every actress in Hollywood who was forty-three needed a healer to help her accommodate herself to the decline of her looks, her career, and her prestige.

And she didn't act like any beautiful woman he had ever met, young or old. Deep in her heart, Stoney thought, either she didn't care about men and her effect on them, or else she didn't care about her effect on anyone, men or women. In Hollywood, where talent and looks were always seeking financing, and financing was always surrounding itself with talent and looks, Zoe's bone-deep indifference was very unusual. Yesterday, when she came in, Stoney had watched her, trying to gauge who her eyes sought out—Delphine? Isabel? Max? Paul? even Charlie or Elena or himself? To whom did she look for reassurance? But she didn't look at anyone—that is, her look didn't pause on anyone. It paused on the windows to the deck, on a painting Max had that Stoney, too, liked, of a woman lying on a beach under a thundery sky. So, even while Zoe was talking vivaciously, being friendly and affectionate and entertaining, and even seductive, Stoney saw that it meant nothing—there was nothing she wanted, even from Isabel (who on principle wasn't giving her anything), even from Paul (who seemed to think Zoe wanted something from him, though perhaps she was only performing some sort of ritual supplication toward him). There was nothing she wanted even from her mother. This Stoney found the most interesting of all. Supposedly, everyone in the world wanted things from his or her mother. Supposedly, every mother in the world was a power in the life of her child. He would have expected a woman like Zoe, with a Hollywood career, to at least cultivate her relationship with Delphine as an emblem of her humanity and her connection with average people, but she didn't.

Now Paul came up the stairs, head, neck, shoulders, torso, legs, feet. He was wearing swimming trunks and flip-flops and carrying a towel. His beard, of course, was heavy and thick, but he had no hair on his chest, which looked to Stoney to be older than the rest of him—the skin over his pectorals was shiny and wrinkled. Zoe said, "Did you do your yoga, dear one?"

"I did. I rolled out my mat in the garden. It was very pleasant."

"I love that garden," said Zoe.

"Good morning, good morning." Paul nodded congenially to Cassie and then to Stoney. Cassie said, "Do you do yoga every day?"

"I do," said Paul, and as he opened his mat on the deck and sat down on it, Stoney saw that this must be true, because he was very supple—not showing-off supple, but simply catlike in the smooth efficiency of his movements. He leaned down and kissed Zoe on the lips, while she turned upward to meet him in a natural way, then he sat on the mat with his legs crossed and looked around. He said, "This is a nice spot. What an interesting house to find in L.A." His back was perfectly straight, right out of a yoga manual. Stoney said, "So—how long have you been doing yoga?"

Paul turned to looked at him. "Thirty-some years at this point."

"Every day?"

"I think I can say every day, yes. I can't remember missing a day."

"Paul is very disciplined," said Zoe.

"I don't call it discipline anymore," said Paul. "Or even habit. I don't call it anything, actually."

There was a long pause, during which Stoney expected Paul to continue talking, but he didn't. Out of the corner of his eye, Stoney saw Cassie throw him a glance, but Stoney didn't acknowledge it. Zoe offered, "Paul doesn't narrate his life. He simply lives, don't you, dear one?"

"I've become less attached to certain uses of words, yes," said Paul. Then he was silent again. His silence did have an authentic quality about it, Stoney thought, and even though he was sure that Paul had done yoga for thirty-some years and that the testament of the healer's straight spine and the weight evenly balanced on his two buttocks was true, Stoney felt tendrils of skepticism growing out of him toward the other man, originating, perhaps, only in some sort of who-do-you-think-you-are response toward the formal diction and upright manner. He said, "Have you been in L.A. for a long time?"

"I have an apartment in L.A., but it's been more or less just for stowing things for some years." Silence again.

Cassie said, "Where is it?"

"In an old apartment complex in Westwood. It's a one-bedroom that I started renting in the eighties."

"There's no bed," said Zoe.

"I have a futon rolled up in the closet. I sleep there from time to time."

"Paul isn't attached to *things*," said Zoe.

"Well, I try not to be," said Paul. His tone was inhumanly even, Stoney thought. And his next thought was, Well, if he's so enlightened, why isn't he famous? He could see that Cassie was thinking the same thought. It was a very Hollywood thought.

Cassie said, "Are you from L.A.?"

"I grew up mostly in Michigan and Ohio."

"You don't see that very often," said Cassie.

Stoney gave a bark of laughter, and Cassie glanced at him. She said, "Well, you don't. I don't know why that is, but people from Michigan and Ohio don't seem to turn up in L.A. as much as people from Iowa and Wisconsin, for example, even though there are more people in Michigan and Ohio than there are in Iowa and Wisconsin. So how did you end up in L.A.?"

"I had a football scholarship to UCLA."

At last, Stoney was impressed. If Paul had been doing yoga for thirty-some years and his hair was white and his beard was gray, then no doubt he was in his fifties, anyway, so he would have maybe played football in the sixties. Of course, Stoney didn't know anything about UCLA in the sixties, but he said, "You got a scholarship all the way from Michigan and Ohio?"

"I did, yes. We all had crewcuts, and when we sat down to training table, you couldn't tell us apart." He smiled. When he smiled, Stoney realized that he hadn't seen Paul smile before. He said, "Did you start or anything?"

"I broke my foot freshman year, jumpng out of a second-story window in the dorm, and after that I really wasn't fast enough anymore. I was an end. My only claim to fame was speed. But they let me stay at UCLA."

"Dear one, why were you jumping out of a second-story window?" said Zoe.

"I was drunk, and my roommate dared me. It was the second time that night. The first time, I made it."

Once again, Stoney waited for Paul to make this into a story, but he didn't. They sat in silence, watching the sun expand its range around the swimming pool, until Zoe said, "You can't believe all the exciting things Paul has done."

Paul didn't respond to this. Cassie said, "Name one."

Paul didn't respond to this, either, until Zoe said, interrogatively, "Dear one?"

"Excuse me," said Paul. "I thought that remark was addressed to you."

Silence again. Dorothy and Jerry, Stoney thought, would have dismissed Paul by this time as passive-aggressive, as they dismissed everyone who failed to rise to their requirements for sociability and congeniality—they had accused Stoney of being passive-aggressive when he refused to sing a song at a family party when he was thirteen years old—but Stoney found Paul's manner fascinating. He was not at all able to divine the healer's motives or level of self-consciousness. It was entirely possible that he was so self-conscious that he was no longer self-conscious at all—wasn't that what yoga was for?

Zoe said, "Last year, Paul climbed the seven holiest mountains in western China. He's been to China three times."

"Is that one exciting thing?" said Cassie. "Or seven?"

"I did take some photographs," said Paul.

"We should have a slide show," said Zoe. "I'd like to see them."

"I don't mind that," said Paul. "But I don't have them with me." Then he stood up suddenly, walked over to the edge of the pool, and dove in. Just then, Max and Isabel came down the stairs from the kitchen. Stoney eyed Max. He looked normal. Then he looked at Isabel. She looked sleepy, but not tired or depressed. She glanced toward him and smiled. It was the same collusive smile she had been giving him for years now, impish and pleased with herself, and therefore pleased with him. He said, "Hey, Max," and cocked his head toward the steps down to the Japanese garden. Max said, "You been to your office this morning?"

"Not yet. I've talked to them several times, though."

"Are you getting reception down here?"

Stoney looked at the cell phone in his hand. There were no towers. "Nah. I went out the front door and stood in the middle of the cul-de-sac. I can get about two towers there. I get three at my house. I guess the hillside is pointing in the right direction there, because that's lower than your house."

"That reminds me," said Zoe. "We'd like to stay rather than go to the monastery. Paul is thrilled with the room, and I'm not looking forward to the drive at all. We've put it off three times already, and by the time we get there, my guess is the war will be over, and we'll just have to come right back."

Stoney looked at Isabel, but Isabel forbore to say anything. Only when Max said, "Sure, Zoe," did Isabel poke him in the ribs. Zoe evidently noticed this, but she didn't comment, just turned her head elaborately away, toward the pool, while saying, "Thank you, Max. I appreciate it," rather stiffly. Max, who was carrying the morning paper, sat down on the end of a deck chair and opened it up, taking his reading glasses out of the pocket of his shirt and balancing them on the end of his nose. Paul hoisted himself out of the pool, and Zoe told him they were staying. Paul went over to Max, who looked up from his paper. Paul said, "You're kind to let us stay. Thank you."

"Sure. No problem," said Max, and he went back to his paper. Stoney knew that it was no problem, but the exchange Jerry and Dorothy would have been having about this whole setup ran through his mind:

Jerry: He put them in that room off the garden for ten days, so what?

Dorothy: She's got a perfectly good place of her own, though how she got stuck with that Tudor monstrosity I'll never know. If she'd come to me when she was moving from Malibu, I would have set her up with Delilah Mossadeh. She's Iranian, she knows every house on the market.

And then Jerry would have come prowling in the front door. He would have felt the soil in the potted plants and looked into the refrigerator and straightened a picture and peeked into Max's room, and maybe into his closet (to see where he was buying his suits and how old they were). He would have knocked on Delphine's door and gotten her out on her front porch and said, "Hey, how ya doing? You look good for an old lady. How about me? You need anything? How's Isabel?" Then he would have stood on the deck for five minutes with his hands in his pockets, staring at the Getty, and finally he would have gone down the forty-eight steps, plucking leaves off the plants as he went down, rolling them between his thumb and forefinger and smelling them, putting a gardenia in the lapel of his jacket. Then he would have walked right into the garden room, and Stoney imagined Paul and Zoe engaged in some sort of sexual congress, let's say she is up against the wall with her legs wrapped around his waist and he's kissing the base of her neck and her head is thrown back, and just then Jerry says, "Hey, how ya doing? Everything okay in here? I just had a thought. What d'ya say? Seems a little damp to me. Maybe I could have them send over a dehumidifier. Nothing loud." And then he would stroll through the Japanese garden and climb the steps and walk around the house on the deck instead of going through, and he would look at the exterior walls in a critical way, as if he could tell whether the house was going to fall down the hillside, and he would get into his Jaguar, and as soon as he had decent reception, he would tell his secretary to order Max a dehumidifier, "But tell Delivery that they have to carry it down a lot of steps, got that? Great." Stoney laughed to himself, and Max looked at him over the paper. Stoney said, "I miss my dad."

And Max said, because he knew why a laugh would mean that Stoney missed Jerry, "Me, too. I miss your dad every single day." He folded up the paper, then he said, "I would have liked to hear what your dad would have said about this war."

"I don't know what he would have said. He never forgave Saddam for lobbing missiles at Israel during the Gulf War. But he hated Cheney, too. One of the last political conversations we ever had was about the energy crisis a couple of years ago. He said to me, 'You mark my words, there's some kind of shit happening at Enron, and they're trying to cover their asses by fleecing California, their biggest and richest customer, and Cheney knows all about it.' So I think this would have been a tough one for him."

Max sighed.

"Say—" said Stoney. But then Simon and Elena came down the steps, and just by looking at them, Stoney could tell they had been having it out. He picked up his script again and pretended to read it. She came over and sat behind Max on the chaise. She had her sunglasses on, and after smiling politely at Stoney, she turned her head the other direction and laid her cheek on Max's back. He said, "You okay?" but she didn't answer. In the meantime, Simon went and sat down on the most distant deck chair, not even in the sun, and acted casual. If Zoe was the most beautiful woman here, and possibly the most beautiful woman now within the limits of Pacific Palisades, then Simon was the most beautiful man, or boy, or combination of the two. Stoney didn't think the older folks would be able to see it—after all, Simon had no hair, he had two large tattoos, his eyebrow was pierced, and his pants were being held up by friction with his shorts. Stoney himself remembered being twenty perfectly. This is what he wore: 501 jeans with a Members Only jacket and Doc Martens. This is what he listened to: U2. This is what he watched on TV: *Moonlighting*. This was his favorite movie: *F/X*. This was his favorite activity: snorting cocaine. This was the book he was reading: *Less Than Zero* (he was snorting so much cocaine that it took him almost a year to read it). This was how he was wearing his hair: shaggy and clean. This was his college major: oceanography. This was the name of his girlfriend: Amber Kimberley Marzetta, aged fifteen. This is what they did together: drive around. This was her greatest pleasure: being allowed to take the wheel of his Blazer and push it up to eighty-five or so up Highway 1. This was what his father felt about him: disappointment. This was what his father should have felt about him: despair. Probably, Stoney thought, looking at Simon, who now leaned carefully back in his chair and let his facial expression fade out of defiant good nature to resignation, who he had been at twenty was the reason he had no kids now. He heard Max say to Elena, "You want to talk about something?" Then he heard Elena say something that he couldn't make out, and then Max said, "Okay, it's up to you."

Stoney said, "Say, Max, can we do a bit of business?"

Max looked over at him and took off his reading glasses. He folded up the paper and set it on the little table between them, and then he said, "Let's do. A short bit of business that acknowledges that life goes on." Elena sat up, then leaned back against the chaise and closed her eyes. Max stood up. First he kissed her on the forehead, and then he propelled Stoney past Zoe and the others and down the steps. He said, "It feels a little crowded."

Stoney offered, almost reflexively, "I can go back down to my house—"

"Elena likes it."

"Does she?"

"Let me put it this way. If one young person would go back up north and resume his classes in graphic design, she would like it fine."

"Why is he here?"

Max gave him a speculative look, then shrugged and said, "I don't know for certain, but probably because he has a stupid idea. You were twenty once. What was the stupidest thing you did?"

"Overall, I would say teaching my fifteen-year-old girlfriend to drive. How about you?"

"Well, I was actually twenty, but almost twenty-one. My buddy and I took the company jeep and went to Saigon to do an errand. The stupid thing we did was decide we were going to explore the city because we had a couple of hours to kill. We didn't have our weapons with us. Anyway, we were driving around and we got into some kind of crowded dead-end street and the jeep ran out of gas. We were sitting there trying to decide what to do, and a crowd started to gather. They weren't smiling and they didn't look friendly, and we had no idea where we were. There were certainly no other GIs anywhere around. My buddy kept trying to start the thing, though we knew it was out of gas, and I was looking up and down the street, wondering if we could walk away or run away, when this kid came up to the car on my buddy's side, and started pulling on his jacket. He didn't speak English, other than 'Come on, Joe, come on, Joe,' but he looked okay, and the guy's name really was Joe, so we climbed out of the jeep and followed him. We walked for a while, and we turned a couple of corners. At that point, the kid started running, still calling, 'Come on, Joe, come on, Joe,' and all of a sudden he ducked into a tiny little house, and gestured us to follow. I held back, but Joe went in. The door closed, and I thought, Well, I am really fucked now, but the door opened, and Joe pulled me inside just as some of the people in the crowd showed up at the corner. Inside was a typical Vietnamese house, and the kid was standing there with his grandmother and a couple of younger kids. They were all smiling, and so was Joe. After a moment, the kid took me over to the family altar, and pointed something out. When I focused on it I saw the strangest thing I'd ever seen in my life up to that point, which was a picture of Joe in a blue tux with a white-and-blue ruffled shirt at his senior prom, and on his arm was a Vietnamese girl. Well, it turned out that Joe was a family saint or god or something, because when the oldest daughter of the family was an exchange student in the U.S., she went to Joe's high school, somewhere in Texas, and Joe took her to the prom because his steady girlfriend was already away at college. This girl was out in the countryside teaching, so we didn't see her, but the grandmother kept patting him and the kids were grinning. We stayed there for a little while and had tea, and then, when an uncle came home, he got gas for the jeep and showed us the way out. We finished our errand and went back to the base with no one the wiser."

"Well, the most I can say for teaching Amber to drive was that we never actually got into an accident."

By now they were in the garden, which was just beginning to get sun. What Stoney liked best in this garden was the bamboo, but water lilies in the pond were nice, too, the way they led your eye to the willows, and behind them the cypresses. Max stopped walking, and put his hands in his pockets and rocked back on his heels. He said, "I want to make a movie. I can put a shooting script together in a week. I've got it completely in my head. If I had the equipment, I could start shooting right now. It's a cheap movie. Indie type."

"Oh," said Stoney. He felt a little disoriented, because for a moment he'd thought Max was reading his mind. Only when he heard that word "cheap" did he realize that they were thinking not at all the same thing. He said, "How about making a big-budget movie? You want to do that?"

"Who for?"

Stoney knew that Max was especially suspicious of several producers. He said, "Nobody you know."

"Then how did they get the money?"

"It's not Hollywood money. It's not even a Hollywood movie, really, but they want it to look and feel like a Hollywood movie."

"European?" That notion livened him up.

"In a way. Partially. It's a lot of money, and you have the final cut. It's a good deal, Max."

"I don't like the sound of that."

"Why not?"

"Because it sounds like someone is giving something away."

"Well, they want to film on location, and the location is far, far away."

"Where?"

"You aren't going to like it, but they have so much money, you can essentially do anything you want. You could make a masterpiece, you really could. I read the source material over the weekend. It's fabulous."

"Where's the location?"

"They thought of you because of *Grace*. They all saw *Grace*. And *Bull Run*, too. You could see this movie as a kind of combination of *Grace* and *Bull Run*, set in the sixteenth century."

"Where's the location? You know I don't even like to leave my bedroom and go across the 405."

"I know that, but I said I would approach you."

"Where's the location, Stoney?"

"Ukraine."

"Ukraine! What is this movie?"

"A remake of *Taras Bulba*."

"A remake of *Taras Bulba*! That old Yul Brynner movie? No one wants to see that movie, Stoney."

"These guys do."

"Have you ever seen it?"

"I screened the DVD last week. It wasn't bad. But it isn't like the book. They want it to be more faithful to the book—no romance. I mean, yes, romance, but I guess in the book when the son takes up with the Polish princess the father kills him for being an unworthy Cossack. And then the other son is captured and tortured to death while the father watches. They want all of that stuff to stay in. They want you to be true to your sources. I thought you might like that. My guess is that they think this is going to fly more with the world market than with the American market."

Max was looking at him in disbelief.

Stoney said, "It really is a lot of money. I guess you would have a free hand. They have someone in mind for the music, but they aren't firm on that. Actually, that sounded like a good idea to me. Apparently this person knows all about Cossack music and church music from that period, and has found a few haunting melodies—"

"How much have you talked to them? How did they find you?"

"Did you ever meet Avram Cohen Ben Avram?"

"That Israeli guy who was a friend of your father? The one who owns that house on the top of the hill above Bel-Air that they've been building for twenty years?"

"Yeah."

"Well, I met him, of course. But I never figured him out. Isn't he a big deal in Mossad or something like that?"

"I wish I knew. But anyway, he knows these guys, and through him they got to me. Your name came up right away. I mean, I said that it was unlikely that you would ever do this, but they got me to look at the movie and read the book—the book is really short. I liked it. It's good material. I said I would ask you."

By this time, they had gotten to the far end of the garden and walked around the cypresses. From there you could see up the 405 through a cleft in the mountains. The highway was bright and busy. You could hear the sound of the breeze rustling the cypresses, and the trickle of the water in the Japanese pond. They sat down on the bench. Max stretched out his legs. He said, "Well, I never saw that movie, but I saw ads for it when it came out, because Brynner was such a big star, and someone else was in it, too, who was that—"

"Tony Curtis played the misguided son."

"Yeah, they were pushing him as a heart-throb in those days. Anyway, in the ads, as I remember, lots of horseback battles and raids in native costume and that sort of thing."

"From that point of view, Max, it could be an important movie. I mean, here it is in the Middle East, Ukraine and Russia on one side, Muslims on the other, lots of religion, but, you know, removed by five centuries. Jews in traditional costume. Everyone in traditional costume. The time is ripe for something authentic like this that kind of comments on what is going on nowadays but doesn't actually make a statement. This could be big for you. And the Cossacks had certain fighting techniques. I don't know what they were, but I was thinking of *Crouching Tiger* when I was reading the book. *Crouching Tiger* on horseback. I guess they were great horsemen."

"That's another thing. Who's going to wrangle the horses? When they made that movie before, there were guys all over Hollywood who did horses for a living because of all the cowboy movies and TV shows, but those guys are gone now. I don't know who can train a horse to go over the tripwire anymore. Did you hear that they're making a movie about Alexander the Great? Oliver Stone is directing. Anyway, someone was talking about the pre-production—who was that?—oh, Norman Ballantine. He's advising them about horses. I guess they went with some kind of black horse called a Friesian that has a big head and lots of hair on its legs and a thick mane and tail. An unusual-looking horse, but too unusual-looking, if you ask me, because it's going to pop off the screen and look not like a regular horse. And it wouldn't even matter if that horse were the spit and image of the original Bucephalus. If the audience is gawking at that horse, then there goes every other authentic detail that you were working toward weaving into a seamless film. I hate making movies with horses in them. Even when they behave, they don't work. The more horses, the more problems. So we've got Cossacks, and therefore we've got horses."

Stoney gave Max a moment to recover from his rant, then said, "Will you meet with them?"

"Will I meet with whom?"

"The guys who have this money and this idea. They're afraid someone is going to steal the idea, because the book is in the public domain, so they would like to get a script written."

"They're afraid that more than one person is going to want to remake *Taras Bulba*?"

"Look at *Dangerous Liaisons*. Who ever heard of that? And then there were two movies in production."

Max was not laughing, but he was definitely grinning, as if he hadn't heard such a preposterous idea in a long time and he was really enjoying this one.

Stoney had to admit that he was a little disappointed in Max's reaction— surprisingly so, since he had been telling Ben Avram for at least a week now that it was never going to fly. As usual, talking about a project made it live, at least a little. He tried one last thing. "Max. Think about being the boss. Think about doing it your way and not having some twenty-five-year-old studio guy on the phone to you every day, second-guessing everything you do and worrying about money. Wouldn't that be fun for a change? You should just read the book, anyway. You like to read."

Max turned suddenly and leaned toward him. He said, "I'd rather do my movie."

"What's that one?"

"*My Lovemaking with Elena.*"

"Excuse me?"

"Did you ever see *My Dinner with Andre?*"

"Set in a restaurant in New York or something like that?"

"Yeah."

"I saw a bit of the beginning. I think I fell asleep after that. This is a joke, right? You're getting back at me for *Taras Bulba*, but you should read—"

"No. I think I could do it. It's interesting. A man and a woman are alone in their room for ninety minutes, and they make love and have a conversation."

Stoney said, "Max, that's called pornography."

"Not if they have a conversation."

"What would they talk about?"

"That would depend on what day it was. If the movie were made today, they would talk a lot about the Iraq war. Obviously they would talk about their children. They could talk about anything. That's what conversation is, associating ideas."

"Are these two married?"

"I don't think so."

"How old are they?"

"Early- to mid-fifties."

"You want to make a Hollywood movie about an unmarried couple with grown children talking about the Iraq war and making love, with graphic sex? You know better, so this must be a joke. It has every single thing that Hollywood producers hate and despise, and that American audiences hate and despise—fornication, old people, current events, and conversation. You might be able to do it with Clint Eastwood, but unless the girl was forty years younger than he is—" But Stoney couldn't go on with that. Even thinking about Eastwood made him too nervous. He shook his head and said, "How did you get this idea?"

"Oh, I've had it for years in a general way. I think I first got it when I was watching an old Anthony Hopkins movie, what was it? Brad Pitt was in it."

"*Meet Joe Black?*"

"That was it. I don't remember a single thing about it except that when
the two kids started making love the camera angles were very tight. Just his
head and torso and her head and torso, and a lot of moaning and eye closing, and I thought, first of all, how boring that was, and, second of all, how
trapped I felt by those camera angles. They made me want to get up and
leave the theater and get a breath of air. And the lovemaking was not actually a relationship. I mean, that isn't the only example. That's just the one
that started me thinking. I like *My Dinner with Andre.* It was about a real
connection that these two guys had. Why not make a film about a real connection that a man and a woman have?"

Stoney eyed Max, who was gazing out over the 405. On the one hand, it
was unimaginable that a man who had been in Hollywood for such a long
time and knew how the town worked would have seriously come up with
this idea. On the other hand, at a certain point in everyone's career, especially if that career had been successful and critically acclaimed, as Max's
had been, everyone in Hollywood came up with a pet project that was so off
the wall that no one they knew could believe what they were saying. It was a
pattern, especially for directors. He said, "You know, Max, I guess I can see
it, but it's a French-type movie, not a Hollywood-type movie. I don't
think—"

"Yes! Good idea! Did you ever see *The Magnificent Seven?*"

"Yes."

"That was a Japanese movie made in the Old West. Did you ever see
Ran? That was an English play made in Japan. Did you ever see *The Birdcage?* That was a French movie made in Hollywood. We can do this. We
just have to find some property, some old French movie, to show them.
Like *A Man and a Woman,* something like that. Then we rewrite it and do
what we want."

"I think you're serious. I think you want me to actually take this project
around."

Max leaned back and looked at him. "I see exactly how it could be.
Exactly. It's running in my head. I can hear the music and the conversation.
I can see them making love. It's like when I was writing *Grace.* The images
in my mind were so thick and alive I never had to think once. Writing the
screenplay was like dealing cards off a deck. Each scene, each bit of dialogue was just there. All I had to do was place it on the page. And then,
when they did the filming, every time I was on the set it was like looking at
something I remembered, even though of course all I ever knew about what
really happened with my grandfather and his mother was how the stories
were told. Why do you think that movie was so good? Why do you think the
screenplay got the Oscar? I'll tell you. It was because it pre-existed me. It

pre-existed Apted. It was a room we walked into. Even when it felt like work, it was the work of reconstruction, not construction."

"My dad said that did go pretty smoothly."

Max smiled. He said, "That was very grudging. But I take it as a yes. Here's our deal. I'll write something up. You get me that book. You read what I write and I'll read the book, and then we'll talk again."

Stoney said okay, and felt some tension that he hadn't recognized before flow out of his chest. The thought in his mind as the tension dissipated was of Isabel, not Max. They stood up at the same time. Max was taller than Stoney. He led the way around the cypresses and back through the garden. Stoney thought he should probably go to his office now, or at least down to his house. It was nearly eleven.

Around the pool, every seat was taken, and on the big table sat a plate of fruit and another plate of toast. Zoe was saying, "That's what he told me." She shrugged. Isabel gave a snort. It was such a loud, indignant snort that Stoney and Max both glanced at her just as she said, "Oh, I can't believe you would repeat something like that, Mom! Don't you have any sense at all?"

"I think it's interesting," said Cassie, "and I'm not surprised." She looked at Delphine, and Delphine nodded.

"What's interesting?" said Max. Now all the eyes turned toward him and Stoney. Stoney noticed that Simon was smiling and that he had pulled his chair closer to the group. Elena was still sitting where Max had left her. Zoe said, "Remember when I did that movie about the French Revolution, when was that, '88 or '89? I played Sophie, who had lost her parents and was on her own. I was supposed to be about seventeen, I think. Anyway, in the course of three hours—God it was a very long movie, truly endless, which is probably why it died, it even had an intermission—Sophie goes all around the countryside and meets everyone and sees everything, and eventually she gets thrown into the revolutionary prison—"

"The Conciergerie," said Isabel, schoolmarmishly, but Zoe ignored her.

"—and she gets tried and she meets all the aristocrats and then all the first wave of revolutionaries that are killed, and Danton and Marat and de Sade. She rides in the tumbrel to the guillotine but is saved at the last moment, and she and her lover escape and they go to America, where she meets Thomas Jefferson and writes a book."

"I remember that one," said Max. "I wonder if it's out on DVD? I wouldn't mind seeing it again."

"Well, when we were just starting that one, maybe on the fourth or fifth day of shooting, I had to do a scene where Sophie realizes that the little band of people she had fallen in with are thieves. They take something they find on her—maybe it was her jewels that were strapped to her leg under her gown, or something like that. So they rob her and beat her up and leave her for dead in a bush, and when she revives she is watching two men hidden in a grove behind the bush, and they are obviously having sex, though of course the director did something so that you only had to know they were having sex if you already knew about that sort of thing. You could barely see them, for one thing. So, when Sophie comes to and sits up, they hear her and they stop buggering one another and run over and grab her and pull her out of the bush, and they are going to kill her—the younger one pulls out a pistol and puts it to her head—but the older one sees she is beautiful and saves her, not because he's attracted to her, but because he thinks he can sell her. So they give her a shot of cognac and sit her on a rock, and she asks them who they are and all, and it turns out the old guy is the local bigwig aristocrat and the young guy is his servant, and as they are talking, the old guy says that all girls are for sale, the more beautiful the better, but no one really actually wants to fuck them. What all men really want is to be buggered by their servants—girls are just bargaining chips. I mean, this movie was really supposed to be a hard-hitting analysis of the French Revolution, and this scene was meant to be a shocking revelation of political reality. I think we did about four takes, and after the fourth one, the old guy—was that Peter O'Toole or someone else? That movie was full of great English actors. Anyway—he laughed and said, 'Well, *plus ça change, plus c'est la même chose!*' and I said, 'What does that mean?' and he said, 'What was good enough for the Ancien Régime is good enough for Hollywood, isn't it?' I guess I must have looked shocked, and he just laughed and said, 'Oh, darling! Where have you been keeping yourself?' So, anyway, we were talking about that, and I was saying that once I came to realize that Hollywood does work like that, everything got a lot easier, and all of a sudden Isabel got upset. You know, I think if I were to recite 'Mary Had a Little Lamb' Isabel would get upset, and I am getting tired of it."

"Well," said Max, "apart from the fact that O'Toole, like all Brits, would say anything just to get a laugh out of someone, or, preferably, just to get up the nose of some Yank, why is this shocking, Isabel?"

Isabel exclaimed, "It's tremendously homophobic and sexist at the same time. It, like, encapsulates everything about how women and gays are destroyed by conventional social arrangements. And she just started talking about it as if that's the way things are and it doesn't really matter and there's no reason to do anything about it. *And* she went along with it, and made use of it for her own purposes. And she was trying to get a laugh, too." Isabel was pressing her lips together angrily, and Stoney thought that he was the only one who knew the roots of her overreaction. He went over to get a piece of toast, and while he was putting some pineapple on a plate with one hand he touched her on the shoulder with the other. She stepped away from him. Of course, this was the downside of their secret intimacy—he couldn't actually comfort her, or rein her in. The best he could hope for was some later conversation about it, but that rarely happened. He took some toast and watched her stalk round the pool and sit down on the corner farthest from her mother, where she said, "If things work like that, then you should make an effort to change them." Stoney was looking down at his toast, but he felt his eyebrows lift at this sentiment.

"But what if it's true?" said Cassie. "I think it is."

"Oh, you do not," said Delphine. "I'm the one who thinks it's true."

"I do, too."

"We were talking about a year ago," said Delphine, "and if you'll remember, it was my idea."

"You are teasing me," exclaimed Isabel.

"How did this come up, anyway?" said Max.

In the ensuing silence, Elena sniffed. Simon, who Stoney saw was much livelier now than he had been, said, "I started it."

"Simon has a part in an alternative movie," said Cassie. "That's what he called it."

"I heard about that," said Max.

"It's just for fun," said Simon. "And it's good money for, like, two days' work. Everyone is my age. They're all at USC film school. It's funny."

"What's an alternative movie?" said Paul, who was relaxing in lotus position, with his head tilted back and his eyes closed.

"Porn," said Elena.

Paul opened his eyes, but his facial expression didn't change.

Simon said, "They're in film school, Mom. It's a project."

"It's a project they're going to turn in to their teachers?"

"Well, I think so. That's what they said. I mean, why not? It's got some very funny bits. There's a naked male chorus line tap-dancing. It'll be funny. It *makes fun* of porn in a way. I mean, most porn movies are all about dicks, if you excuse me saying so, and here are sixteen dicks flopping around. It should be interesting. We're all going to have umbrellas that we twirl. I laughed for days after they told me that."

"What's your part?" said Zoe.

"Well, in addition to the tap dance, I'm in the fantasy sequence where there are two dicks and two pussies out on a date. I mean, there's a whole bar-full of dicks and pussies, so they needed lots of bald guys to play pool and sit around and do the things you do in a bar."

"How are the girls dressed?" said Cassie.

"Well, they're naked, but they have secondhand fur coats on, and whiskers and cat ears. Every bald guy is wearing just a stick-on name tag, stuck to his chest, with 'My Name Is Dick' written on it."

"I think it's cute," said Zoe.

"It's about the college dating scene," said Simon. "It's a satire! I don't understand why my mom is so upset."

Everyone looked at Elena. She said, "Well, you make it sound very innocent, but there's explicit fellatio and masturbation, you said. I just don't think—"

"Yes, but in my scene the masturbation is mental. When the pussies walk by, we're supposed to take both of our hands and rub our heads and close our eyes and moan."

Everyone laughed. Even Isabel smiled, though she was studiously pretending not to be part of the conversation. It occurred to Stoney that he should take Simon aside and find out who these kids were and see if they had representation. Elena sat up. She was smiling, too, in spite of herself. She said, "Well, it seems like fun now, but these sorts of things come back and haunt you in your later life. What if it gets popular? That defines you! For the rest of your life, people say, 'Oh, were you in some movie I saw?' Especially now, when everything is in some Internet database."

"So I'll grow hair. I don't think I'll be that recognizable. Anyway, we have to shave our eyebrows the night before the filming of our scene."

Elena frowned. Stoney could see that she felt a little defeated, but he could also see her point of view, and he didn't think it was about the kid's being haunted in the future by this particular youthful indiscretion, more about what were probably a train of youthful indiscretions one by one taking their toll. Simon had that look—the bald head, the tattoos, the piercing—but more than that a certain look, the look of a smoker, right out of that book he had been talking to Isabel about. According to that book, smokers had a natural nervous daring that they realized very early on, primarily through the process of learning to smoke cigarettes. Stoney was willing to bet that Simon was one of those who had been in and out of trouble since high school, and that Elena was mostly reacting to this episode as yet another item on a long list.

"What about classes you're missing in order to come down here?"

"We're just working on our final projects this quarter."

"I'm not even going to ask what that is," said Elena.

"Well, I'm not quite sure yet, but I have some ideas and some photographs, if that's what I choose to do."

"That's why I'm not asking."

"Oh, Mom," said Simon, but he knew he'd won.

The sunlight had now spread everywhere around the pool and spilled down the hill into the Japanese garden. Conversation subsided, and everyone stretched out and did something in the sunshine. Sure enough, Simon reached into the pocket of his shirt and came out with a cigarette, which he quietly lit. Here's why I need a wife, Stoney thought: with a wife you could say, "This is what I think," and then, after a while, after something had happened, she would say, "It was just the way you said it was going to be." And then all of your passing good ideas didn't simply vanish into thin air. For a while his former wife, Nina, had been good at reinforcing this feeling of having a life and building toward something—not a fortune, exactly, or a family, or a legacy, or the things that Jerry and Dorothy cared about, but something more like the idea that one thought was adding to another and eventually there would be a state of understanding. He looked at the scripts on the table. There would also be a reason to not just let his career slide into the maw of his natural temperament.

After a few minutes of quiet, Cassie said, "Well, I need to get to the gallery, and I wondered what about dinner, because Delphine and I can go get something. Let's see." She reached for her handbag and took out a small pad. "Okay, how many regular vegetarians?"

Zoe's hand went up, then Paul shrugged and put his hand up.

"Vegans?"

Only Isabel.

"Anyone lactose-intolerant?"

Delphine nodded.

"Low-fat?"

Max's hand went up. Cassie said, "What about Charlie?" and Stoney realized he wasn't present. Max said, "If he isn't, he should be."

"Okay. Let's see. How about hot-pepper-intolerant?"

No hands went up.

She said, "Do you care, Elena?"

"No okra."

Cassie wrote that down, then said, "I don't like lamb. Hmm." She showed the list to Delphine. "Simon likes everything?"

Simon nodded.

"I know Stoney likes everything."

Stoney nodded.

Cassie and Delphine stared at the list for a moment. Then Delphine said, "I think baked tofu in a spicy orange sauce with pea pods and pea tendrils, Szechuan green beans, some with shrimp and some without, and some baby greens with champagne vinaigrette—"

"How about Black Japonica fried rice?" said Elena. "It comes out the most beautiful rich purple color. I can sliver up some bamboo shoots and baby carrots and chanterelle mushrooms to go in it."

"Tell us what to buy," said Cassie.

"Get a *New York Times*," said Max. And everyone who had been smiling sobered up. Stoney saw Isabel survey everyone with a belligerent air, then get up and go into the house. Moments later, she called from the doorway, "I'm going now! Here's Charlie!" And then Max's friend walked out onto the deck. He said, "Hey! Wake up, you sluggards! Some of us have been running on the beach!"

"Where'd you go?" said Elena.

"Well, Santa Monica, where else? Look at this!" He held up a small capsule. "It's a grain of rice with a yin/yang symbol etched on it. Isn't that great? I love it." It was strung on a thin chain, which he hung around his neck. He sat down on a chaise and stretched out his legs. He said, "And here's some papers. I got *The Wall Street Journal* if anyone wants that, and a *USA Today*."

There was something about Charlie's enthusiasm that was mildly disturbing, but still no one stood up. The sunshine was so pleasantly comforting that Stoney nearly fell asleep. Then, at some point when he was thinking something about cars on the 405, he heard Paul's voice say, "So, Max, how did you get to Hollywood?"

At this point there was a creak, the creak of Max's chair as he shifted position, and Stoney opened his eyes. He was slightly surprised to find that he was still here. He sat up. Max said, "Oh Lord. Well, I have to blame Bette Davis."

"How did you know Bette Davis?" said Charlie.

"I did not know Bette Davis. Remember Laurie Lehman, though?"

"Oh, yeah," said Charlie.

Max turned toward Paul. "I had a girlfriend in high school named Laurie Lehman. She was very smart and went off to Radcliffe, at which point she broke up with me. Well, her mother wasn't old, less than forty at that point, and she and Laurie's old man were divorced. He was a dentist. So Mrs. Lehman modeled herself on Bette Davis. Women did that in her generation. A girl had a type—the Barbara Stanwyck type or the Ingrid Bergman type. Anyway, after Laurie went off to college, Mrs. Lehman started inviting me over. She would carry a drink in one hand and a cigarette in a holder in the other and stalk around the house trying to cook dinner and saying all sorts of Bette Davis lines, like 'Fasten your seat belts, it's going to be a bumpy night.' She had a way of opening her eyes very wide and enunciating her words, and she always cultivated the idea that she was hard to handle. Bette Davis wasn't a tremendously big star anymore at that point, so I hadn't seen any of her movies until one night when I stayed up to watch *Dark Victory* on TV, and I was amazed. It was exactly like watching Mrs. Lehman walk across the kitchen."

"Did you sleep with her?" said Cassie.

"I did," said Max. "For about two weeks, then I went off to college myself, and then I got drafted. She wrote me when I was in the army, and her letters were always newsy and happy, full of funny gossip, and not at all concerned about what might happen to me. She acted as if nothing bad could possibly happen to me, and my sojourn in Vietnam was just a little break in the general life of good times that I had been and would be leading, so I liked getting them. Letters from my parents were much more anxious and full of advice. She was talented. She always put in little drawings of people we knew that she had seen at the grocery store or the hairdresser's. One time she drew a whole line of women sitting under hair dryers, and I could recognize every one of them. By the end of my tour, I felt like she was about my best friend, so, when I got back Stateside, I went to her house for a few days before I went home to my folks.

"Laurie was married and living in England by that time, and her mom's place was a mess. As soon as I got there, I realized that she was drinking very heavily and that she and her house and her alcoholism were way more than I could handle, so I only stayed two days. In those two days, though, she pulled some string, some very, very old string she had from her days in New York, and who should show up the second night but Lee Strasberg. And he must have known her pretty well, because he came for dinner and he brought the food with him—Chinese food. So he sat down and ate dinner with us in the middle of the mess, and he didn't talk to me much. He just was nice to Mrs. Lehman, and she was Bette Davis all night long. I have to give it to him, because he never even gave me a complicit glance. Her role was that she was Bette Davis, and his role was that he was happy to be there and interested in her, and my role was more or less to clear the table and wash some dishes so we could eat, and pick up magazines so we could sit down. The next day, I made her realize that I had to go home to my parents' house, which was about twenty-five miles away, and I managed to escape, but then, a couple of days after that, she called me and said that Strasberg thought I had potential and would I come to New York and talk to him, and my parents thought I might as well do that while I was getting ready to go to chiropractor's school, which was going to be my real vocation. So I did, and he let me in, and I met Ina the first day, and Ina was a Natalie Wood type."

"Yes, she was," said Charlie. "She was Natalie Wood all over."

"And Ina couldn't sit still till she got us to Hollywood, and I just came along with her. We rented a place not far from here, where you get off the

405 onto Sunset, but then you make two lefts and you end up in a dead-end street right up against the highway. Anyway, she was acting, and I was acting and writing, and here we were." He shrugged and looked at Stoney. He said, "It wasn't until I fell in with Dorothy and Bo and Jerry that I really got to Hollywood Hollywood."

"You were a very nice boy," said Cassie.

Max smiled at her, and somehow that was what made Stoney actually want to go to the office. What was really his secret treasure, though, was that he would be back for dinner, tofu and all. And then Isabel walked by as if by mere coincidence, and her hand brushed his lips, and he kissed it on the palm, and no one noticed.

The phone rang exactly at midnight, which would be 9 a.m. in Paris, where Paul's client Marcelle Vivier lived. Zoe, of course, had been very proactive in setting up this appointment. She had pointed out to Paul that his cell phone was not going to work in the garden room, or even in the garden, and she had gotten Max to give her an extension from some other room, and she had found the jack in the wall and written down the number for Paul so that he could send it to Marcelle. Even so, when the phone rang, it startled her because she had drifted off, and as she woke up and reminded herself of what was going on, she felt several involuntary jolts of annoyance, as she always did when Madame Vivier called for her session.

Paul answered the phone — "*Bonjour, Marcelle, bonsoir! Ça va? Ah, mais oui. Oui, oui. On marche bien*" — and as he was talking, he got up, kissed Zoe discreetly on the forehead, and carried the phone and its cradle over to the yellow armchair, which sat in the alcove. There he folded himself into the chair with his back to Zoe. She could hear him mumble in French, but she really couldn't make out his words, and anyway, her French wasn't the best, so when he really got into the session she wouldn't be able to understand him at all. Paul's French seemed to be quite fluent, though Zoe had no idea what Madame Vivier thought of it. She called him precisely once a week at this time, and had been doing so for seven and a half years, ever since Paul did a healing weekend in Biarritz in 1995. Paul made sure that every Tuesday night, wherever he was except when he was on his yearly three-week vacation, Madame Vivier had his phone number. When he was at Zoe's, he used his cell phone (free minutes after 9 p.m.) and went into Zoe's glassed-in breakfast room overlooking the pool, all the way on the other side of the house, in order not to disturb her. Sometimes she watched him from her bedroom window as he moved around in there, talking to

Marcelle for exactly fifty minutes, for which she sent him a check for ninety dollars, drawn on the Bank of America, where she had an account specifically for this purpose. The other overseas clients called during the day, when Paul kept hours in his home office.

Paul was a precise person, and he had precisely twenty-one clients, for whom he did thirty sessions in a week (one client did three sessions, seven clients did two sessions, and thirteen clients did one session), and so his gross income for the week was $2,700, which came out to $129,600 per year, since he took three weeks off to travel every year and one week off to go to the monastery. Paul had no tax deductions of any kind, not even his telephone expenses, since the clients always called him, so he paid $53,400 in taxes, and so had a disposable income of $76,200 every year. And he expected to keep giving sessions for the rest of his life, so he didn't have an IRA. On the one hand, Zoe was impressed—that he could make the numbers add up so precisely, that he could pay such a large percentage in taxes without caring, that he could go through life without a single deduction, that he never worried about it—and on the other hand, she was not impressed. Fifty-five years old, and his disposable income was not into six figures. And of course she was impressed with herself for coming up with such an unusual man, not like anyone she had ever dated before. She thought of him not as a therapist—of course there were plenty of those—or even as a religious person or teacher—there were plenty of those, too—but as a solo sailor or flyer, the sort of person who leaves L.A. one day and turns up in Honolulu months later, having sailed across the Pacific on a diet of nuts and dried fruit. Her idea of him was of course metaphorical, but it encapsulated a certain excitement she felt in his presence.

As a part of the perfect package, he was too enlightened to be compliant. She occasionally, as, for example, now, found this grating.

He guided her in her sessions to understand that this was simply a habit with her. She was used to having her own way with men, because she was beautiful and talented, but, of course, having her own way was the worst thing for her, since as soon as she had her own way she lost interest and began finding fault. It was the oldest story in the book, the Cleopatra story, the Salome story, the Medea story. Zoe, who never liked school, had only the vaguest notion of what really happened to Cleopatra, Salome, and Medea, but she knew it was all bad, and that they got blamed for it, whatever it was. Of course, of course, of course. One especially appealing thing about Paul was that he spoke as if he considered all his opinions self-evident.

Zoe herself was the three-session-a-week client, and Paul didn't give her a break on fees. "No sliding scale for you," he had said at the beginning, but, of course, there was no sliding scale for anyone. In these sessions, they did not explore her childhood; Paul considered that banal. "Self-knowledge," he said, "can be fun in a way, but it convinces you that you are special, when in fact you aren't. You are only unique, and uniqueness doesn't have to be a problem. What you really want is training, and it doesn't matter what kind of training you already got or why you didn't get what you might call the proper training. No one did. You're forty-three years old, and now you need some more training, and you can afford it, so get as much as you want."

When she said, "Discipline will be good for me, I guess," he replied, "Not discipline. You are not being disciplined, and we are not engaged in a discipline. Your child is grown, your career is established, and you are training for the third quarter of your life, that's all."

Paul had several theories, and one of them was that, although at one time biology had constituted destiny, it no longer did so. The great enigma of existence was the wholesale longevity of twentieth-century humans. The mystery of life was what you were supposed to do after surviving and reproducing, and obviously the clue to this question was the extra brainpower humans had. It was there for something, and almost everything it was usually used for was a waste of time and resources. It was only "getting ready for translation to a higher sphere" that was not a waste of time. Paul liked and approved of gardening, and so his theory of this preparation was a gardening theory: pruning. First you pruned your faults, then you pruned your habits, then you pruned your idiosyncrasies, and eventually you disappeared. You didn't die—that was too dramatic a way of looking at it. Paul liked to think of it as drying up and blowing away—saying less and doing less and being less noticeable until, with only a blink of an eye or a movement of a finger, you slipped out of this world. His conversation was full of comforting vegetable images of this sort.

Zoe sat up and straightened the quilts on the bed and arranged the pillows. The room, which had been yellow when she lived with Max, was green now, and the sheets and duvet cover were a mossy sateen stripe with a very subtle peach accent. There were two rugs on the floor from Kashmir, different sizes and slightly different patterns, but both picking up the subtle green of the walls. It looked good. It looked like her mother had had a hand in it, because Delphine liked uniformity (her own place was uniformly oatmeal-colored, with a Japanese ambience; she slept on a futon on a low platform, and the only decoration in her living room was a beige kimono with a scene on the back of a path going up a mountain).

Now that Zoe and Paul had been here for a couple of days, how well she remembered sitting in that kitchen for four years, watching Max talk on the phone, watching her mother cook something for Isabel, watching the assistant they had then, Gabrielle, talk on the other telephone—about what? About her, of course, about which project she should say yes to, where the tour should take her, what the album cover should look like, what she should wear, which fund-raiser she should attend. And as they talked, she would herself swell up with unexpressed, and no doubt adolescent, ire (she was about the same age then as Isabel was now). The most annoying thing was very specific—over and over, each one of them would say, "What do you want to do?" and each time she would answer, because she always knew what she wanted to do, and each time her answer would be the occasion for an argument or at least a discussion about what it would be better to do than the very thing that she wanted to do. And the argument would continue until she gave in, and they did with her what they had wanted to do in the first place. Then she would get worked up—she admitted that—and demand to know why they had asked her in the first place if they didn't intend to do—for her to do—what she wanted? And they would act a bit astonished, as if this were a tantrum on her part, a mere expression of temperament, rather than an actual grievance. Had they talked about Max's career, too? She didn't remember.

One day at the end of those four years, she was looking at her financial situation—like Delphine, she always knew what money was where, how much she was worth, what taxes she owed, and how much things cost—and she saw that it was time to make some sort of investment. She had a big wad of cash, and no one had asked her what she wanted to do with it yet (preparatory to overriding her decision), and so she drove out to Malibu and bought the second house she saw. The place had one bedroom for her and one for Isabel, and none for Max or Delphine, and since Max was away for five weeks on a shoot, she moved her things over there in her car, trunkload by trunkload. It was a beach house, so it came furnished, and for a long time it was most ravishingly like living in a hotel, and she was never lonely or nervous there, even with glass windows in big storms. No one liked it there. Isabel hated the roar of the ocean and the damp smell of the run-down furniture, nor did she like the beach, which Zoe had thought all children liked. Delphine complained about the drive; Max thought there was too much sand everywhere. And so all she had to do was squat there, and pretty soon, like a tide running out, they flowed away, and she got to visit them when she felt like it, and to not visit them when she didn't feel like it. In a way this pleasure was her greatest secret sin—"Come out here," she would say, but they rarely did. The Malibu place was quiet—no one asked her a single question—and she didn't even care whether she was actually in residence there or not; she could be on location or on tour, and all she had to do was think about 87549 Rokeby Road in Malibu, and she would feel calm and adult.

And then, in the winter of '97, the house fell down. She was away for four days in San Francisco, doing some looping, though why up there she couldn't remember, and while she was gone there was a big storm, though not so big that it got into the San Francisco papers. When she got back, part of the foundation had slipped, and the right front corner of the house was listing to one side, and some of the floor and the roof had broken away, and rain had gotten in. Of course it turned out that the whole place was rotten and would have to be completely rebuilt, which defeated its original purpose, so she sold it as a teardown for more than she had paid and bought a place in the hills not far from the Hollywood Bowl, where she now lived, still gloriously alone except for when Paul stayed over.

Paul never asked her what she wanted. If a question came up, he stated what he wanted, and expected the same of her, and quite often, since she wasn't asked, she didn't really care. In the end, that was what had bothered her—the effort of having to come up with a response in the first place. Once, she had done a personality test, and on it was a telling question: "At the end of a party, do you prefer to go home and be by yourself, or to go on to another party?" Alone, perhaps, in all of Hollywood, she would have said, Go home and be by myself. And not at the end of the party, either, but in the middle, or at the beginning. That was the sign, the quiz said, that she was an introvert. People thought that if you were a singer and could stand up in front of thousands of people and sing for an hour or two, then you must be an extrovert, but no. In the first place, the stage lights were so bright, how would you even see anyone out there? And in the second place, you weren't relating to the people, you were relating to the song. You were singing; they were eavesdropping.

The best thing about living in Malibu had been the drive. She could find her way around Los Angeles better than most limo drivers, and none of it came naturally—all of it came because of how much she loved to drive by herself from Malibu, in the car as in the house—alone. Cars were wonderful philosophical things, zones of privacy and occasions for cooperation. There was something especially fine, she thought, in world-historical terms, about a car belonging to a stranger whom you had never seen before moving into the left lane in order to allow you onto the freeway. There was something politically beautiful about four cars at a four-way intersection smoothly taking their turns. Good traffic made you a benevolent person and a believer in basic human goodness. A nice drive from Malibu to Universal, quiet, comfortable, expeditious, and deliberate, was a form of meditation, the truest experience of being yourself, and the closest you could come to passively sensing the unity of time and space, which always put her in a good mood. Paul had liked this idea, too, when she told him about it, but, unfortunately, it was something they couldn't experience together, because the whole thing vanished if there were two people in the car, even if the other person was enlightened, as Paul was.

Across the room, in the arc of yellow light that shone on the pea-green armchair, Paul laughed out loud. Zoe looked at her watch. It was twelve thirty-one. Zoe imagined Marcelle Vivier, whom she had never seen. She would be dark-haired and pale-skinned and thin. Normally, French people did not interest Zoe in the slightest, though she was popular in France because she was a woman of color and she sang songs they liked, but this Marcelle woman was slightly different from Paul's regular set of lugubrious complainers such as herself, and she knew that he enjoyed doing the weekly session with her. It didn't help, of course, that the session was at midnight and that they talked about sex. Obviously, all of Paul's clients talked about sex. Zoe talked about sex, too—Paul considered sex and enlightenment to be intimately connected, and part of his theory was that once you had talked about sex to your absolute heart's content, you could then go on to other things wholly and sincerely. You could talk about sex in any way you pleased with Paul. Neither he nor his theory made any promise that your sex life would improve or that you would have better relationships. There was only the promise that you would eventually get bored with talking about sex and discover that life had more to offer than sex and relationships, at which point it might be that your sex life and your relationships would improve, or it might be that you would forget about sex and relationships altogether—both things had happened with Paul's clients. He didn't have a theory about which was better, or even about what constituted improvement—more, less, more orgasmic, less orgasmic, fewer partners, one partner. The only goal was to have your say about it and see what might happen. Marcelle Vivier had been talking about sex once a week for seven and a half years—that was 360 conversations about sex, give or take a few— which struck Zoe as a lifestyle rather than a therapy. In her own sessions with Paul, her sense was that she was doing an extra-large housecleaning. Obviously, some tasks get performed every day, others once a week, and some only once, but eventually, in much less than seven and a half years, the house is clean. However, Paul said that Marcelle was really benefiting from the therapy, and that in his experience of French people, the act of doing something is in itself sufficiently healing. He said, "French people aren't obsessed with finishing one thing and going on to the next. They are obsessed with doing each thing properly. It's not necessarily better, but it does pass the time and offer a feeling of satisfaction."

Zoe felt that it was time for Marcelle Vivier to move on.

He laughed again. Zoe had not thought that French people were witty enough to provoke a guffaw, or that therapy was the appropriate occasion for laughter. She wiggled down under the covers and closed her eyes. Marcelle was really the only client she was jealous of, though seven of the other nineteen besides herself and Marcelle were women. The men she didn't mind at all. They could talk about sex for the rest of their lives and she would feel nothing but indifference toward them.

Paul's days were exceptionally peaceful. She had seen it with her own eyes. He slept, he ate, he defecated, he urinated, he groomed himself and his home. He traveled near and far. His hair and beard were shiny, his breath was pleasant, and his sweat smelled good. He could walk for hours and stand on his head and do yoga postures that defied belief. He could sink ten baskets in a row and make a penny travel back and forth along the tops of his knuckles. He could go without speaking for half a day. He had no children, and his parents were dead. He never had crises in his life that he spoke about, and he progressed by means of minute adjustments—no lurching from one thing to another. She recognized that he would and did have no appeal for many people. His appeal for her was that in part his way of being constituted a rebuke to her own way of being, but also in part that she was enough like him that she could see how well he lived, a still point inside the frantic chaos of a world that neither acknowledged nor affected him.

And he loved sex. They had met during her last film shoot. The mother of the kid whose mother she played brought Paul onto the set one day, and they got to talking over lunch. The picture had a vaguely Buddhist theme, since it was about a man who has been living in a Buddhist monastery for ten years. The backstory in the movie was that the man, who had been a cop and was played by Denzel Washington, had quit being a cop after investigating an especially brutal murder, and gone to live in a monastery. At the beginning of the picture, someone comes and tells him that his younger brother has been killed by street kids. Denzel leaves the monastery to go to his brother's funeral, and when he's there, he becomes suspicious and gets the urge to investigate the crime, though he's conflicted, of course, partly because he's hardly said a word in ten years. What finally draws him into the case is the fact that Zoe's son, who was played by a first-time actor named Ty Griffin Abbas (who was truly, truly gorgeous, a real mix, not only black and white, but Vietnamese, too, small but quick and graceful, and brilliant on the screen, much too good, in a way, for this movie, Zoe thought), had witnessed the murder and didn't recognize any of the alleged street kids who did the killing. So Denzel is moved by the vulnerability of

Ty and Zoe and decides to watch over them and investigate his brother's murder, even though his brother had made much different and more dangerous choices than Denzel has made over the years. Of course it turns out that something much bigger is going on, something that goes right up to City Hall, though now, four months later, and not having seen the final cut of the movie yet, Zoe was a little vague on what exactly that was. Her character and Denzel's character do have a bit of a flirtation—he's a good man, after all, and her savior—but he goes back to the monastery, fade out. The movie was called *Zone of Light*, and she only sang one song, a lullaby to the kid, which Denzel overhears when he is sitting in the living room of her house, staring out at the street, waiting for the bad guys to come and try to smoke them out. The sequence went: lullaby, quiet glances between Zoe and Denzel, explosion of gunfire, with Zoe and Ty diving under the bed, then the shoot-out, then quiet again as Zoe and Ty crawl out from under the bed, and Zoe and Denzel exchange another series of quiet glances, then the cops show up to clean up the mess.

Ty's mom, Milena, brought Paul to the set because he was interested in how they were doing the Buddhist aspect. He had been her yoga coach at some point. In September, before coming to the set in November, he had gotten back from this trip to China, climbing the seven holiest mountains, and he was in great physical condition, even better than Denzel, who was himself in excellent shape. Paul sat quietly, watched, dug his fingers into his beard, laughed from time to time. When he was sitting across from Zoe at the lunch table, he asked her what her name was. It turned out that he had never seen any of her movies and had only heard her rendition of "I'll Fly Away" on a Chevy commercial. He was so simultaneously straightforward and relaxed about his total ignorance of her career that it tickled her, and then he said, "Don't be insulted. I think I was actually the last person in the Western Hemisphere to learn who Monica Lewinsky was." Zoe took his number and called him a few days later. They went out to dinner at a vegetarian Indian restaurant in Culver City, then went for a walk at Venice Beach, then went to her house and made love six times in four hours, before she had to get up and go to the set and film the last scene, where she drops Denzel at the bus station and he takes the bus back to his monastery. She was great in that scene, because she was exhausted. In the dailies, she looked quietly distraught and self-sacrificing, some of the best work, she thought, that she had ever done. Now it looked like they were going to release the movie in the late fall, when all the serious-contender sorts of movies were released, so she had some hopes for it. In the meantime, here was Paul.

It was only after maybe a month of dating and great sex that Zoe asked

Paul whether she might start having sessions with him, and as he was not a member of any professional organizations or certified by any board, he said of course she could. It turned out that he said of course because it was his policy and his theory never to say no, though sometimes he waited three seconds for you to make a different request, one that was better for you. It was impossible to say whether these sessions were productive, but they were always interesting and sometimes fun. Usually they were in person, but she had had some phone sessions, too. What happened was, she lay down on a yoga mat. He sat in a chair with a clipboard on his lap, and she issued her complaint. Often her complaints were about Isabel. Once, she remembered, she had called Isabel in New York because Delphine had told her Isabel had the flu. She called Isabel to find out how she was feeling and got her voice mail. She left an affectionate and interested message. As soon as she hung up, her cell phone rang, and it was her hairdresser—they had to discuss whether her hair was to be redone for a reshoot of the scene where she came out from under the bed (there were a couple of shots of her with Ty under the bed, too). What could they get away with when she came out from under the bed? What would cobwebs say, for example? The director now wanted cobwebs, but both Zoe and Eileen were against cobwebs in her hair, especially as they had to stay in her hair for the whole next scene, when she and Denzel were to look at each other and understand exactly what there was between them and what it meant, and if they reshot with cobwebs for one scene, they might have to reshoot the next scene, too. So they discussed the cobwebs for about five minutes, and in the meantime Isabel called on the landline and Zoe said, "Call me back in five minutes." Ten minutes later, just as she was wondering when Isabel was going to call her back, the phone rang, and as soon as she picked it up, Isabel said, "I thought you were going to call me back in five minutes."

"I thought you were calling me back."

"I hate playing phone tag with you. You're impossible to get a hold of."

"I called you, and as soon as I hung up, someone called me. That's not so unusual. It's pretty normal, in fact."

"Maybe, but all I know is you are the hardest person I know for me to get in touch with, so there's a certain level of frustration already built in."

"How are you?"

"I'm fine."

"I thought you had the flu."

"That was days ago."

"When?"

"Tuesday."

"Tuesday was yesterday."

"Well, it seems like days ago. I've nearly forgotten about it. I can't talk, anyway." And so they hung up, with Zoe trying to make one last agreeable remark. Lying on her mat, Zoe related this conversation to Paul, and then she came up with a theory about why it bothered her. It bothered her because Isabel's tone was unforgiving and full of grievance, as usual, and she was tired of failing to please Isabel in even the most mundane sorts of ways, and yet having to keep trying. She felt that their relationship was based on Isabel's resentment combined with her sense of guilt, but Isabel wasn't resentful enough to break off the relationship, and she, Zoe, didn't feel guilty enough to submit to whatever punishments Isabel might like to impose. So they were at an impasse. That was her theory.

Paul then thought for a while, and declared that her theory was wrong. What was going on had nothing to do with Isabel herself or Zoe herself as they appeared to exist in this life. What was really going on was that in a previous life Zoe had been Isabel's husband, and Zoe had taken a mistress. Since the society they lived in allowed and even encouraged wealthy men to take mistresses, Isabel had no recourse against either Zoe or his mistress, and so she had begun behaving in a classic passive-aggressive manner. This issue had been unresolved at Zoe's death, especially since the mistress showed up at the funeral with Zoe's two children by her, and Isabel, of course, was there with Zoe's three children by her. It was apparent from the ages of the children that Zoe had been carrying on with both women simultaneously for many years, and Isabel had felt publicly as well as privately humiliated. She retained this grievance into her next life as Zoe's daughter (though the lives didn't have to be precisely sequential—Paul had the impression that their wedding had taken place in the nineteenth century), and she was still trying to exact remorse from Zoe. In fact, according to Paul, Zoe did owe Isabel a karmic debt.

Zoe, who had been expecting to discuss Delphine and Max and Isabel's childhood and how young she was when Isabel was born so early and the pressures of her career, was thrilled by this story, and the possibility that it revealed Paul as a charlatan made it all the more thrilling. She had been expecting to work through guilt and remorse, and here all she had to do was embroider upon this narrative of her past life. Where was it? In Italy! What kind of man was she? A small-time landowner who married rather late, and managed to increase his holdings. Flushed with success, he took first a wife and then a mistress. He also bought a car, one of the first cars in his region. What region was this? Emilia-Romagna! Where was that? Bologna, Ravenna, Parma! And Zoe had been to both Bologna and Ravenna. Had she felt any sense of familiarity there? Any sense of déjà-vu? She had to admit not, but even so, it was the only place in Italy she had been, so possibly that meant something! They talked about the wife, Isabel, and the mistress, and the children of both relationships, until Zoe could just see the movie, and then, after they had filled everything in, Paul had guided her through a meditation in which she recognized that this Italian life not only was over, but had been an illusion in the first place, a conceit, a fiction, as all lives are, as this current life as a movie star was also, and for that reason she and Isabel were not required to act out all the emotions of every life they lived together over and over. They could, if they chose, let all of that go. He had her imagine that former Italian life as the membrane of a balloon, filled with bad thoughts and bad feelings as with air, getting larger and larger, the resentments and jealousies and murderous impulses, the pall of disappointment, the anger and the fear and the threats, and then he had her pop the balloon and allow all of those feelings to dissipate in the fresh air and blue sky of Emilia-Romagna. After that, she said, "What do I do now?" and he said, "What do you want to do?" and she said, "Well, I could call Isabel and apologize for not calling her while she had the flu," and he said try it, and she did, and they had a nice talk about Enron. It did not escape Zoe's attention that Paul's "technique" had eased her relationship with Isabel at least for a moment, if only because it was more interesting to think about this past life than it was to think about their relationship as mother and daughter.

Across the room, Paul had hung up, and he stood up from his chair in the light, then turned the light off. Zoe looked at her watch—twelve fifty—stretched out in the bed, let her eyes drift closed, and sighed a few deep sighs. She even let out a pleasantly satisfied groan of the sort that you make when you are happily transitioning into or out of sleep. In fact, the very sight of him dismissing Marcelle Vivier and turning his attentions to her woke her up all over. She stretched seductively.

He said, "Marcelle is very agitated about the war."

"I'm sure she is," said Zoe. "It must feel very close to them. Closer than it does to us. Personally, I worry more about the North Koreans. I heard they could get a bomb here to California if they wanted to."

"I don't know that proximity is the problem. She didn't mention that. She just feels that Bush is a monster. She feels very personally imposed upon by him. I thought that was interesting."

"Why?"

"The size disparity. The sense that she is a small child and he is an inhuman, insensate, mysterious creature that can't be understood in human terms. He's quite present to her, as if he were in her closet or under her bed.

Of course we talked about that, and she went straight to the difference in size between the U.S. and France. Apparently everyone she knows in France has the same view of Bush and the U.S." He stripped off the light-weight cotton pants he had been wearing and got into bed. He took her in his arms easily and comfortably, without any preliminaries or awkwardness, in a way that told her exactly how he felt about Marcelle Vivier, indifferent, and her, welcoming. Zoe felt herself smile as she cuddled into him. One of the abiding concepts in Hollywood, and one she had wondered about over the years, was the concept of "chemistry." The odd thing, really, was that you couldn't tell during the shoot what sort of chemistry you were going to have onscreen, and it wasn't predictable. She'd had no chemistry with men she liked and respected, and plenty of chemistry with men who put her off, but also vice versa. One famous actor she had found repellent in every way, including his physical type (fleshy), had looked onscreen like her born soul mate. But it wasn't until Paul came along that she knew what "chemistry" really was—it was the way one body conformed to another one, no matter what the brain felt about it. Take Max, for example. For a few years she had loved Max in the most innocent and classic way, happy that he had found her, grateful for his love, buoyed up by his company day and night, well married. But their bodies couldn't get along. Where his eye was, there was her elbow. When he was awake, she was asleep. When she was awake, he was snoring. When he hugged her, she got uncomfortably hot. When she kissed him, she often missed his lips entirely and felt the grit of his beard grating across her own lips. They could not walk in step, and often didn't hear what each other said, even though they both had resonant voices. It was nothing like this with Paul, his body, her body acting like the same body but always pleased with the other body. He said, "I don't feel I helped her much. But she and Jean-Pierre do agree on the war, so that will please her for a while. She said, 'We have angry agreements about these Americans, and then we feel very good in a martyred sort of way, and so we make love. He is nice to me for the sake of the Iraqis.'"

Zoe didn't know quite what to make of this remark, so she said, "Does she realize how you feel about the war?"

"She didn't ask. And I told you, dear one, that I don't have a feeling about the war, at least a for or against feeling. What she says is interesting, what you say is interesting, what Saddam Hussein says is interesting, what George W. Bush says is interesting. The more dramatic any situation is, the more people reveal themselves. I don't think that's a 'cold' point of view, as you say. But, whatever, it's my point of view."

"I know that. I was just asking a question." She knew she sounded defensive, but still they pressed close, and she felt her whole body relax and open up in a tingly sort of way. He began kissing her, which was very nice, too, beard and all. She had not thought his beard very appealing at first, but now it was delightful, a part of him and therefore sexy and alluring. She felt his body charge up slightly with intention, and then hers did the same. They kept kissing, tongues, lips. He sucked her tongue into his mouth and she felt as though she were fucking him, in-out, in-out. She pressed him onto his back, and crawled over him, not in any way mitigating the kissing, but intensifying the kissing. She could feel against her stomach that his prick was hard, and she thought the word "throbbing," which was a common and lovely word having to do with erections. She had never actually felt one throb, but she thought the word "throbbing" anyway, and then felt a certain throbbing, but it was their hearts—her heart in her chest against his heart in his chest. Then he introduced his hand between them, and reached for her pubic area. She felt his fingers in her pubic hair.

She pulled away from the kiss for just a moment and said, "You're stroking it the wrong way."

"I'm sorry, what way would you like me to stroke it?"

"I mean, the wrong direction. You need to go down rather than up." She kissed him, but it was a compensatory kiss, not a passion kiss. She said, "You need to stroke with the growth pattern. Otherwise it's irritating."

"Pubic hair doesn't have a growth pattern, dear one."

"Mine does."

"Why is this the first I've heard of it?"

"I don't know. It came up before, but I didn't mention it."

He sat up and pushed back the covers. They both looked at his crotch, but it was too dark to see anything other than his half-detumescent prick listing toward her. He said, "Turn on the light."

She said, "Why are we doing this?"

"Doing what?"

"Looking at our pubic hair. We were making love."

"I want to see."

"I want to fuck!"

Three seconds went by. She said, "Okay," and turned on the light. Since the light was on her side, he squirmed over toward her so that it could shine equally on his pubic hair and hers. His rose like foam around his member, blondish-gray and curly. Then they looked at hers. Hers lay flat, and, compared with his, most of the individual hairs were oddly straight. They turned this way and that. He said, "Hmm. They look more like eyebrow hair than chest hair. It's funny how pubic hair never looks like the hair on your head.

Hmm." He touched her pubis with an index finger. She said, "See? There's a growth pattern. There's almost a cowlick." She tried to sound mildly interested, but really she was getting quite annoyed. If she had known what a simple statement of preference—down, not up—was going to lead to, she would have kept her mouth shut.

"I never noticed that before." He put his head down for a good look, careful not to block the light. "I'm amazed."

"Why are you amazed?"

"I don't know. It's just interesting, and not something I've seen before."

It was here that she made her second mistake. She said, "I would appreciate it if you would not refer to all the women you have, ah, *fucked* over the years."

That got him. It was so hard to get him, and that did it. For a very short split second, Zoe quailed.

He lifted his head and looked at her, first in surprise and then, just for a second, in distaste. The distaste passed almost instantly into his usual look of benign concern, but she saw it, and it made her jump away from him. Yes, she should have waited three seconds. On the surface, three seconds didn't seem like a very long time, though long enough, she understood from articles on cosmology, for the universe to form itself out of nothing. But she couldn't wait three seconds. She exclaimed, "Fine, that's enough. Do what you want. You always do." She threw herself into an elaborate fuck-me sprawl, and slightly lifted her hips to offer her "eyebrow hairs" for his consideration. He sat up and looked down at her, his fingers in his beard, neither cold nor angry. He knew better than to say anything. Still the three seconds! She pursed her lips shut so that she wouldn't back down. Finally, he said, "It seems to me that you have a pattern of losing your temper when I have sessions with Marcelle Vivier in your presence. Does that seem to be the case to you?"

"Oh, pattern this, pattern that. I don't think in that way. That woman needs to get over it."

"Get over what?"

"Whatever it is that keeps her calling you from France once a week."

"She feels that she is getting something from our work. When she no longer feels that way, I'm sure she'll stop."

"What about you? What are you getting from it?"

"Well, it is my job. And I do think it's interesting. I do think she's interesting. I'm learning from our sessions."

"That's what you always say! Marcelle is interesting! My pubic hair is interesting! George Bush is interesting! What's the difference?"

"Well, there isn't much, really. Probably my feelings about all three of those things are essentially the same."

"Don't you think that's weird? Don't you think that anyone in the world would hear what you just said and think that you were very weird?" Her voice was rising. She knew her voice was rising and she knew he knew her voice was rising, which was yet another point against her, wasn't it? She rolled over in disgust, turning her back on him. In the end, it was always the same with men. Even the enlightened ones took refuge in not saying anything. She closed her eyes, though obviously she was not going to sleep. What she was going to do was lie there all night, churning with indignation, and then she was going to have to get up in the morning and deal with Isabel for one and her mother for another and that woman Elena and her kid for a third, though the kid was good-looking and seemed nice, and he didn't give his mother nearly the hard time Isabel gave her. It was much worse to have a supposedly good kid, who did all the right things, but was angry at you all the time, than it was to have a kid who was sometimes a fuckup but who liked you. What was it Simon had done? Zoe had seen him before dinner, when everyone was cooking, put his arm around Elena and laugh and give her a nice kiss, and not as if he never did that sort of thing and now he was handing it to her on a platter just this once, was she satisfied now, but as if he was used to showing his mom affection. It never occurred to Isabel to suck up. Probably she would rather die than suck up to Zoe. It was a very bad and inflexible attitude, and came straight from Delphine as far as Zoe was concerned.

"Zoe?" said Paul.

"I'm sleeping."

"Are you?"

"No, but I'm thinking about Isabel and my mother."

"What are you thinking?"

"Why do you want to know? Because it's interesting?"

"It is interesting. But, of course, it's interesting to the same degree as anything else is interesting, no more, no less." But he said this as if he were suppressing a laugh.

She sat up and said, "No, it's more interesting." But now she was suppressing a laugh. Because it really wasn't more interesting, it was just the same old mother thing. She thought she could rise to the challenge, though. She cleared her throat. She said, "Okay, it's not interesting, I admit that. But it's no less interesting than Marcelle Vivier's opinions about Iraq, and you spent an hour—"

"Fifty minutes."

"Fifty minutes on those, so—"

"Is this a session?"

"It could be."

"Is it one of your weekly sessions?"

She thought for a moment, then said, "No. May I have an extra session? A half-session?"

"Gratis?"

Now she waited three seconds. She counted them internally. She thought this was a question for him to decide without her urging. After three seconds, he said, "Okay, informal session. Gratis. But only because I'm tired and I'm not sure if I can help you."

She nodded, paused a moment, then began in a more formal tone. "You know, I was terrified of Isabel after she was born. I was sure I was going to make a mistake that would kill her. I even had this dream right before she was born that I went to the grocery store with her, and just happened to put her in the sack before the bagger put the groceries in, and then he put everything in on top of her, and I didn't realize it until I got home, by which time I was really in trouble, you know what I mean? Not to mention that she was in trouble, of course." She cleared her throat. In a session, everything you said, every word you used, was revealing. She glanced at him, but he looked authentically neutral. "The dream didn't even go all the way to unpacking her, just to staring at the bag on the counter, wondering if she was okay. And then, one night when she was only six weeks old, I woke up and saw her in her crib, which was in our room, and the blanket had fallen over her face. I remember thinking, Oh my God, she can't even push a blanket out of her face! I was already wondering what I would say to my mom and Max if she died. She was premature—that was a crisis in itself.

"Whenever she cried or fussed, I knew I was doing a poor job. I used to balance Isabel on her side with blankets rolled against her back and her front so she couldn't fall in either direction, and I would spend ages adjusting those blankets so that if there was throw-up it wouldn't get on the blanket roll in front and be reaspirated or somehow forced back into her mouth, and the one against her back had to be just the right size or she would either roll forward onto her stomach, which I considered to be instantly fatal, or roll onto her back, which would take longer but have the same ultimate result. Every time she cried or fussed, I knew she was blaming me."

"You felt she was blaming you."

"Well, yeah." But after a moment, she recognized the difference between "knew" and "felt."

"My mother was quick. You don't see it so much now; she's pretty stiff. But back then, she was, what, around fifty. She didn't have to think. There was the baby, the baby needed something, my mother was on it before the thought hardly crossed my mind. And Max. Max had his opinions, too. And his mother came out from the East, and Dorothy was always in and out, being helpful. When should you introduce solid food? There was a question. I started solids at two weeks! said Delphine. Two months! said Max's mother. Not until she reaches for it on her own! said Dorothy. Five months! said one book. What seems natural to you? said the doctor. Talk talk talk. Everything about how to treat Isabel was a topic of conversation that had to be exhausted over and over again. I mean, it's not like everyone fought— everyone was very nice—but I was only nineteen, and I'd never even held a baby before Isabel. I don't know." She cleared her throat and fell silent. The silk strap of her chemise had slipped down over her shoulder. She didn't push it up.

Paul gazed at her in a kind of distant way, contemplating, pooching out his lips inside his beard, then pulling his beard idly for a moment. Finally, he said, "Well, it wasn't about the baby."

"What?"

"That whole thing, it wasn't about the baby."

"It sure seemed like it was about the baby. The baby was everything!"

"But of course it was about—" He waited for her to fill in this blank.

"It was about me. I know everything is about me in the end, because I am projecting my entire world and constructing it and creating it, but, you know, I didn't know you then, and I hadn't thought about things in that way, and it sure seemed like we had this baby and there was absolutely no agreement on how to take care of her, and so—"

"And so?"

"And so—" But her mind had stopped working, so she looked at him.

He closed his eyes. This was a sign either that he was receiving something from on high, or abroad, or out there, or within, or that he was making something up. In the quiet, she could hear the hum of the dehumidifier. Outside the sliding glass door, she could see the garden lit up by the moon. He said, "Did you know you were once a god?"

"A what?"

"A god."

Yes, she was startled. She said, "My mother will be interested to hear that."

"Do you know where Oaxaca is?"

"You mean, in Mexico?"

"Yes. It's a very holy site. There's a huge complex called Monte Albán that's only partially been excavated, though when you were the god of thunder it was quite different. Beautiful buildings with wonderful carvings and

luxuries of all sorts, though of course you and your fellow gods and god-
desses were extremely cruel to the human population. Lots of blood sacri-
fices and ritual disembowelments."

"Maybe we didn't know any better."

"Maybe as gods you didn't recognize a problem, and saw the human
population passing from one shape to another, and were just interested or
amused by it, since from an immortal perspective you didn't recognize
death as death."

"Maybe that," said Zoe.

"At any rate, you were the god of thunder, which I take to mean that you
controlled the weather in some way, certainly the rainfall and the extent
and violence of the storms and the length of the rainy season, and therefore
the growth of the crops and the overall prosperity of the community. You
were very powerful. Only the sun god was more powerful, and the goddess
of the earth, who controlled earthquakes, was as powerful as you were, but
somewhat more feared, as you can imagine."

"Oh, sure," said Zoe, "that stands to reason."

"You did a terrible job."

"Oh," said Zoe.

"Some people wanted one thing and some people wanted another, and
they would pray to you and sacrifice to you to get what they wanted. They
were always upping the ante. If one farmer sacrificed his old mother to you,
then the farmer next door would sacrifice his third wife."

"Why didn't they stick with sheep or goats or something like that?"

"No domestic animals to speak of. Excess of human labor, paucity of animal labor. It was a problem throughout the Western Hemisphere, actually.
Of course, they figured you wanted more and more, so they sacrificed
people to you that were more precious and more beautiful and younger.
They began wars just to get sacrificial victims from other tribes, and there
was a premium on getting the very best—not just the king's child, but the
king's best child. This in turn made it very hard for your tribe to get along
with the neighbors, and there was a technological push in the invention of
weapons, which always heightens tensions between warring groups. They
had, for example, been killing each other with axes, but someone invented
two-handed, double-edged axes, and the killings became offensive to some
parts of the society, who considered them excessively brutal and felt that the
breakdown of certain ritualized parameters was a sign of general despera-
tion and breakdown, which obviously it was. The humans came to feel that
nothing worked, that you were always sending the wrong weather."

"Was I?"

"Well, you may have been god of the weather, but you didn't actually control the weather per se. I would say you had some limited effect on upper air patterns and local precipitation, but no more than that and often less. And it may be that this period I am speaking of was a period of general climate change."

"Like now."

"Yes."

"What happened to me?"

"They executed you."

Oddly, Zoe was a bit shocked by this. She exclaimed, "But I was a god!"

"Gods are executed all the time. They went around to all your altars and broke up the statues of you. They defaced and obliterated all representations of you, and stopped saying your name. They made dolls of you and burned you on a pyre. They killed your priests and reassigned your wives to the sun god. They purged you from the records, which wasn't easy, since the records were carved in stone."

"Did I die?"

"I gather that you must have, because you were reincarnated shortly thereafter as a large predatory bird of some kind."

"Did the weather improve?"

"I don't think so. That civilization died out fairly suddenly."

"Well, they were killing each other right and left, it sounds like."

"Usually there is a combination of ecological and sociological factors."

"How is this like Isabel, though?"

"It seems like you are always at the vortex. What you do initiates conflict even when you don't 'want' it to."

"Oh." Zoe was definitely disappointed. She sank down in the bed and pulled the covers up to her chin. She knew it was true. She said, "Even in elementary school I couldn't do the simplest thing without causing a fight of some kind." Then she said, "That's not the same as precipitating the end of a civilization, though."

He didn't say anything for a moment, then he said, "There's nothing wrong with the end of a civilization," and she had this sudden image of some sort of clearing in a jungle, as seen from far away and high up. The figures in the clearing were human, and they were running around at top speed. She knew what they were doing—they were killing one another in battle—but from a distance they looked like they were bumping together, bouncing apart, falling down, jumping up. The scene was alternately light and dark, as the sun rose and set. The figures disappeared, reappeared, disappeared again. The jungle vegetation advanced and receded like a wave on the beach, and the piece of ground was green, then gold, then green again, then gold again. Then she imagined herself looking upward, and in the dark sky, stars began to explode like fireworks. Paul said, "Isabel turned out fine, didn't she?"

"Did she?"

"I was talking to her after dinner about her job and the young man, what's his name?"

"Leo. Wow, I never liked him. He always acted like it was a favor to her that he was dating her, a favor to me if he was eating dinner at my house, and a favor to the world in general if he bothered to smile. And now she says he refuses to move out of their apartment because the marijuana plants that he keeps in the closet under lights are flowering and can't be disturbed."

"So it's good that she's fed up with him, and good that she's ready for another job, and she's healthy and full of energy, so it doesn't matter what happened about the solid food, does it?"

"No. But she's always been such a picky eater. I'm sure that if we—"

"It's not so bad to be a picky eater. Picky eaters tend to have fewer obesity problems. French people, for example, are notoriously picky eaters."

Yes, she did smile, acknowledging that Marcelle Vivier was actually none of her business.

"And it doesn't matter about the end of that Oaxacan civilization, or the end of this one, either, does it?"

"I don't know."

"Well, where is the end of that civilization taking place?"

"In my imagination?"

"Absolutely, so it only matters what you feel about it. What do you feel about it?"

"I don't know. Curious. I mean, it's invigorating more than anything else to think about being a god and then screwing up and being executed by your followers. And it's funny in a way."

"I think so, too." He smiled a big amused smile. She emerged from the covers, which now seemed too warm, and sat up with her legs crossed. She saw him glance down at her breasts, and it was true, she was wearing a peach-colored silk chemise that she had bought on Melrose for just this sort of occasion. It had slender double strands for straps, and the front was cut narrow and loose so that it seemed to be barely clinging to her breasts, which, of course, were something she was known for, the other something being her ass. "Just a minute," she said, and she knelt up onto her hands and knees and reached across the bed for the glass of water she had set on the nightstand before getting into bed. It took her a long time to reach for the glass of water, and when she had reached for it, it took her a long time to drink it, which she did while continuing to present her bare-naked buttocks for his appreciation. While she was drinking, she heard him open the drawer on his side of the bed, and then she heard the slippery, moist sound of his hand anointing what would certainly be his very nice erection with Aqua Lube. A neat and methodical person, he put the Aqua Lube bottle away and closed the drawer before kneeling up himself and introducing his prick. He went in slowly and with some difficulty at first, as if the session and all that talk of conflict had tightened her up. Then, as she felt herself be entered and filled, she also felt his hands on her hips, balancing himself and securing her. He said, "Mmm."

It was interesting, she thought, how this idea of him right behind her, his hairless muscular chest and his beard, his shoulders, arms, and hands, so smoothly and easily succeeded that other image of the stars exploding. Even as he pressed his way into her and she could feel every millimeter of her vagina opening and widening around the pressure of his thrust, she could go in her mind from the thought of him to the thought of the black night and the bursting stars, some close, some far away—that would be some exploding right now and some exploding long ago. She could think how much she liked to be taken without foreplay, because without foreplay she felt it more suddenly and intensely, and right afterward she could remember the waves of green and gold surging and ebbing across the land, and of course there were mountains thrusting upward, too, and, more slowly, crumbling away and thrusting upward again, and once in a while a lake would appear at sunset in the cleft of the mountains like an opal and then vanish, and then her mind would go back to him, so odd that he was named something as dull as Paul. She cried out because he delved too deep, and she pulled away from him, but he pressed against her again, and then again, until she had fallen off the perch of her hands and knees and was collapsed into the bed, and still he was pressing, pulling out, and pressing, and then he pulled out completely and reanointed himself, and then he went in fast and hard and very quickly, and they were both calling and maybe screaming, though he was not howling in her ear as he had done once, because she told him no, under no circumstances, was he to put his mouth near her ear when he was having an orgasm, because he could damage her hearing, and for a singer that was potentially disastrous, but he was leaning back and arching upward and singing out to the rafters while she was crying, "Oh Oh O-H-h-h," and pressing her face into the pillow.

Then she rolled onto her back, and they did it again, and she kept her eyes open and paid attention to his actual physical presence, his beard, his dark eyes, his smallish nose, his thinning hair, the caramel-colored beams behind his head, and the pale stucco on the walls, and she came again, this time a shorter, deeper, and warmer orgasm that was located right between her legs, unlike the outward explosion of the previous one—multiples were always like this, she should ask someone why that was. He did not come again, but he subsided with a smile after she did, and flopped onto the bed beside her, and then he opened his mouth and intoned, "Ommmmmmm-mmMMMMMM," at about G flat below middle C, and she harmonized at D flat above middle C, and then he went down, to about an E, and she went up to an E, so that they sounded quite primitive, like early music, and then they ran out of breath and laughed and she said, "You can make all the noise you want and no one anywhere else in the house can hear you."

Now they got quite comfortable, really more comfortable than Zoe had felt in days, what with the planned trip to the monastery, which she admitted she had been a little nervous about, and not only the roads, but also the monks themselves and the probable accommodations. There was a double room for visiting couples, but only one, which someone else might already be occupying, and if so you had to go uncomplainingly into separate cells. And you were supposed to sit quietly for meditation, which Zoe had trouble with. In fact, in spite of the war and the television, she had been anticipating the monastery with a bit of dread that she had not confided in Paul. She produced a big yawn as Paul settled against her and settled her against him. She shifted her hips slightly back and forth and stretched. She closed her eyes. The last thing she heard was Paul's soothing voice meandering around a bit, telling her a bedtime story, it seemed. He said, "You know, I was thinking about this woman I knew at the monastery in Wisconsin. That was a coed monastery, though of course they called it a 'center.' It wasn't exactly Buddhist, because they talked all the time about Jesus, but he was a very Buddhist Jesus. There was always dancing, especially in the winter, because you had to do something for exercise when there was too much snow to go outside. There was a girl there. Her name was Darling. I mean, her original name was Martha Perkins, but the founder gave everyone new names, and hers was Darling. She was a substantial-looking girl, almost as tall as I am. But she was light as a feather. She seemed to float around the room, and dancing with her was amazing. You felt like your job was to hold her down. One guy was a trained dancer, and he would lift her up above his head and spin her around. He had trained for a long tme, and he could do things like step onto the front of a chair and then the back, and then balance himself while the chair fell over. He said she was miraculously light, lighter than a child. And she never wore a coat, either. She went around in the coldest weather in just a T-shirt. In all my practice and of all the yoga masters I've met, I have to say that Darling was the only one I ever saw firsthand who actually repealed the laws of nature." He pulled Zoe more tightly to him. "No training at all," he said. "No daily practice. Just a name change. I never understood it, really." Now he was mumbling. Zoe didn't ask what happened, but she did imagine the goddess Darling, golden-blonde, yielding her substance smile by smile.

Zoe, reading the morning paper, could see Charlie, across the room, glancing at her. She adjusted the paper slightly so that it shaded her from him, and her eye fell on an awful article, about a man who had been carjacked at Ontario Airport. After the carjacker pushed him out of the car, he got stuck in the shoulder strap of his seat belt and, as far as Zoe could tell, tried to grab hold of the top of the car, but fell under the wheels, and was dragged to the end of the airport drive, where the carjacker got into an accident, and by that time the man was dead. The carjacker, apparently, was upset about lost luggage. This was exactly the sort of article Zoe least liked to read anymore, though at one time she would have read it over more than once in a kind of fascinated amazement at the details. September 11, she thought, had cured her of that sort of fascination, and then Paul came along and told her that she didn't have to reflect upon every gruesome twist of every story, though she could if she wanted—she could choose what to read and think about—and so, rather than letting her gaze drift back to the beginning of this story, she lowered the paper again, which Charlie took as a signal. He came over and sat down. He said, "Hey, Zoe. How are you? I was hoping to talk to you."

Zoe glanced around the kitchen and family room, even though she knew that there was no likelihood of anyone else appearing. She said, "What are you doing up this early, Charlie? It's hardly six." But she smiled.

"Oh, for me it's after nine. I decided when I came out just to stay on New Jersey time. You can get all your business done before anyone else is up. With the Internet, you can keep your eye on the market, no problem. If I'd thought of it before, I'd have spent more time out here for sure." He shook his head.

She offered him the paper.

"Oh, I got one of my own," he said, "I read through it already."

"Well, then. What are your plans for the day? You seem ready to go." She gave him an encouraging smile. He settled more deeply into his chair. He said, "You know, Zoe, you really look great. What has it been, fifteen years since I saw you last?"

"Maybe that."

"Well, if you've changed, you've changed for the better." He stared at her, then went on, "And you looked great then, of course."

She said, "You look good, too, Charlie."

"Do I? I've been working on it. Later I'll show you my stash." He laughed. "You know, I must have run more than a mile and a half yesterday on the beach over there in Santa Monica. I wasn't just jogging, either. I was catching up to lots of the younger guys and passing them. My cholesterol, you know the LDL? It's down to about a hundred twenty-five most of the time. Two years ago, it was over two fifty! I was just waiting for that myocardial infarction, the doctor said, and now it's inside the safe range, and the other indicators are good, too, but, hey, when I pass the forty-year-olds running on the beach and I'm fifty-eight, you know, then that's a good enough indicator for me."

"That's impressive, Charlie," said Zoe.

"That's my story," said Charlie, "and I'm happy with it, but, you know, my story is not important to millions of people around the world! LDL 125 seems like life and death to me, but in the larger scheme of things, who cares?"

"I don't know," said Zoe. "Maybe Max."

Charlie laughed. He said, "That was funny! I was speaking rhetorically, and you thought I was asking a serious question. Well, we'll get back to who cares about Charlie Mannheim later, right?" He laughed again.

"I hope so," said Zoe.

"You know," said Charlie, "this time I'm out here and I realize how much I love Max. I realize how much Max has not changed in fifty years, and it makes me love the guy. I mean, he even looks the same as he did when he was in grammar school."

At a loss for a response to this, Zoe said, "Well, he did shave his beard."

And Charlie laughed again. He said, "Hell, Zoe, I had no idea you were so funny. Your timing is great! They should put you in a comedy! You know, I saw that movie you made a couple of years ago, what was that, let's see, that one where you played the local TV news anchor and you fell for the quarterback on the football team and he got you into drugs of some kind and you overdosed? I mean, it wasn't a big part, but you were great in it. I thought they were going to save you at the end, in the hospital, but they didn't. I guess they had to have a reason for the Eriq La Salle character to feel remorse and turn his life around."

She said, "In the original script, the quarterback killed his friend in a drug-related car accident, and the league hushed it up and paid my character not to investigate the matter, even though she knew all about it. My feeling about the picture they ended up with was that the first half and the second half didn't really make sense together."

"Well, maybe." He waved his hand. "But you could do comedy."

"I'm surprised you saw that movie. No one saw that movie."

"I like sports movies. And they filmed some of it in Trenton. Remember? Not your scenes, but some of the drug stuff, and the quarterback's high-school scenes. I didn't go to see you, but you were the best thing in it. The couple we took to the movie couldn't believe we knew you. I told them about Max, but they'd never heard of Max."

Zoe cleared her throat and then folded and put down the paper, making it as clear as she could that she was going to stand up, but Charlie, his eye caught by the front page of the paper, didn't notice. He said, "What do you think of Elena?"

"She's sweet—"

"I think she's something of a Nazi myself, though I would never say that to Max. Don't tell him I said that."

"A Nazi?"

"Well, a feminazi."

"What's that?" said Zoe.

"You don't listen to Rush?"

"Who's that?" said Zoe.

"Rush Limbaugh. On the radio."

"I don't listen to the radio."

"You drive all over L.A. and don't listen to the radio?"

"I like it to be quiet."

"A feminazi is one of these militant feminists who want to abolish the differences between men and women."

"Like Delphine, you mean?" And Charlie roared with laughter again. Zoe didn't remember his being nearly as good-humored as this when she was married and he and his wife had five kids. He said, "Well, between you and me, your mother is a little scary, but that's just who she is. Elena has a program, though."

"What kind of a program?" Looking over his shoulder, Zoe realized that she could not comfortably evade this conversation, especially as he was opening up the paper and adding to the barrier between her and the rest of the room. What had seemed a secluded corner now seemed like a trap. She said, "You know, I need to—"

"I think she should keep her mouth shut about the war when our troops are in harm's way."

"You do?"

"You can't believe how much Vietnam veterans still hate Jane Fonda. Soldiers don't like to know that they aren't being supported back home. I thought these antiwar protests they've been having were criminal. You didn't go to any, did you?"

Zoe shook her head.

"I didn't think you would. But Elena did, and she took Max. Max doesn't think sometimes."

"Max is a Vietnam vet. He doesn't hate Jane Fonda. We saw her at a party once, and he was quite friendly to her. She complimented him on that movie he made that was a remake of *Topper* set in Hawaii—remember, it was called *Aloha, Topper*? And he told her he liked her in *The Morning After*. He never said a thing to me about hating her, or even disliking her."

"And Max is very strange. I admit that. When we were kids, I considered it my job to look after Max, because it was pretty clear that he couldn't look after himself. And now he's got this feminazi telling him what to do every minute of the day. When we were talking about the war last night at dinner, frankly"—he leaned toward her and lowered his voice—"I was beginning to think she was really, really crazy. I mean, the sort of crazy that ends up in a mental institution."

"She seems to take the war very seriously."

"Well, she's got a thing about the President that's way off the wall, all that stuff about how everything he says is a lie, and he knows it. And what does Enron have to do with Saddam Hussein, I'd like to know. It's crazy leaps like that that let people know you've got a screw loose. And fighting fire with fire is not a war crime. If they come and get us, we have to go get them, that's just the way the world works. Just because you know someone who was at a party at Yale University when the President was going to school there and he came in and swiped your friend's keg under the influence of alcohol—he's the first to admit he was a drunk—does not mean you can call him a sociopath—"

"Why not?"

"Because he wasn't and isn't a sociopath—"

"But she can call him anything, right? I thought the line that you couldn't cross was plotting against him in some way." She let her voice trail off a bit, and she could see that he clearly didn't realize that she was annoyed with him and making fun of him, if only for her own pleasure. She was an actress. She could do whatever she wanted with her voice.

He exclaimed, "Not in a time of war! Calling the President, who is doing his best to keep this country safe, a war criminal is what is a war crime." Charlie was getting a little worked up. "Lots of liberals are for this war! Does she realize that? She is in a very, very small minority here—"

"Well, not here."

"Excuse me?"

"She's not in a small minority in this house, I don't think, judging by the talk at the table last night. And, you know, she didn't say he was a sociopath because he stole the keg. She said he was a sociopath because he punched the owner of the keg in the stomach, even though that guy was supposedly much smaller than he was at the time."

"I thought, 'Christ, Elena, don't you know any boys? That's what boys *do!*'"

"Her boy seems nice."

Charlie rolled his eyes. He said, "Anyway, her house, she gets her way. My take on the conversation last night was that no one wanted to speak up, least of all Max. Her face was all red. Max may not have realized what he was getting into with this one. Steel magnolia and all that."

"I think she grew up in Chicago," said Zoe. This, too, she made sound naïve. In fact, though she worried more about the North Koreans, Zoe did not care for the turn the morning's discussion was now taking. She listened for noises somewhere in the house, heralding the advent of someone who would save her from this man, who was actually breathing hard.

Then he said, all of a sudden, "You know, I love talking to you."

Startled, she cleared her throat. "That's very nice."

"You think so? It's true. I've always loved talking to you. I've always thought you were the kindest, most sympathetic person I knew. I remember that time we visited and Sarah Beth was all bent out of shape about everything, and after she had been a little bitch for four days, you said at the breakfast table, 'I need to go to the Beverly Center for something. Want to come along?' and she went, and you bought her, gosh, boots and a hat of some kind, jeans, a top, and some books and makeup, and it was all very L.A., not the sort of thing Karen would have let her have at all, but cute. A real shopping spree. What was she at that point, fourteen? And at first I admit I didn't approve, and Karen was a little put off for part of the day, but, you know, Sarah Beth was so happy, and I could really see how, when you're fourteen, being taken for a shopping spree by someone you don't have it in for, I mean, being treated as special when you feel ugly and pissed off all the time—I realized that was a great thing you did. We never thought a bad attitude should be rewarded, but what a silver bullet that was! And it wasn't even that you were a movie star, but just getting to do it. So, ever since then, I've felt very close to you, even though, of course, we've hardly had any time to get together."

Zoe smiled. She did remember taking Charlie's daughter to the Beverly Center and buying, buying, buying. What had they spent? Five hundred dollars? Nothing, really. And she didn't do it to be nice. It was just that the girl's expression was so sour, and her skin was so bad, and her bangs were so thick, and her hair was so crimped and curled that at that breakfast Zoe couldn't stand to look at her any longer. At the time it felt more like self-preservation than kindness, but then Sarah Beth turned out to be rather cute when you did her up properly, and then the charitable feeling flowed in and felt good. She said, "Yes, it was fun for me. I guess Sarah Beth has a couple of kids now?"

"Yeah. She married a very big-deal shoe importer from Tennessee. You should see their house. Makes my house look, well, I don't have a house, really, but my old house where Karen's living that we built? All I can say is, we thought it was big at the time." He laughed and shook his head. Then he said, "That's what I'm getting at. My own story is very big to me—the marriage and the kids, and the house we built, and the separation, and now my cholesterol levels and how far I can run on the beach and getting this supplement business going, but coming out here puts it in perspective and makes me know it's just a story. You know, eight million stories in the naked city."

"That's how Paul sees things, too."

"Hmmp," said Charlie, clearly startled by this idea. But he didn't say anything more, and then Simon's bald head appeared, rising out of the stairwell. Charlie glanced in the boy's direction, then picked up the paper. Zoe realized that, over the course of their conversation, his chair had inched toward her, so that the paper was practically touching her. The headline of the article that was right in her face was "State Doubtful FERC Will Grant Refund Request." She leaned forward and said, "Excuse me, Charlie. Mind if I get past you?"

"Oh, not at all," said Charlie, moving his chair. As she slipped through the opening he made, she could not fail to notice how thin his hair was on top. Thin, but not bald. Max looked better than Charlie, she thought, more hawkish and sinewy and Mediterranean. "Hey!" she said to Simon, who had his head in the refrigerator.

"What time is it?" said Simon.

"About seven."

"Why am I up so early?" said Simon, as if he really wanted to know. Zoe laughed and shrugged. He said, "Why are you up so early?"

"We get up early every morning. Paul keeps a strict sched—"

"Oh, the liver and stuff. Did you guys eat that yet?"

"Paul did."

"That's so nasty! My idea of a good breakfast is a liter of Diet Coke and a big bowl of Froot Loops."

"I won't tell your mom."

"She knows, but she doesn't accept." He hiked up the waist of his jeans and said, "All I can find is multigrain bread and four kinds of hummus. And this French butter. That looks okay. But I can see that my stash got thrown away since I left only a week ago."

"Your stash?"

"Well, the aforementioned Froot Loops, plus some nice Milano cookies, the orange-chocolate kind, my Cadbury caramel eggs, the sour-cream-and-onion original Lays potato chips, the Sour Patch Kids, and that Ghirardelli dark chocolate that I use for medicinal purposes. I kept the pork rinds in my room, but I finished those in the middle of the night. I see I am going to have to go out."

She put her hand on his shoulder and whispered in his ear, and he looked at her and said, "Bacon?"

She nodded.

"You buying?"

She nodded again. "Yes!" he exclaimed. He put the excessively nutritious items back in the refrigerator. Zoe said, "You're going right now?"

"I think Gelson's is open."

"Let me get some money."

He followed her out onto the deck and then down the steps. The early-morning sunshine lit up the potted citrus trees, and Simon happily stuck his nose in amongst the fragrant, star-shaped white flowers. "Wow," he said, sniffing excitedly upward, the way you would if you were taking a drug. Zoe laughed. Simon had a frisky way about him and a ready smile. While she powered straight down the forty-eight steps, he seemed to bounce around her, looking at this, glancing at that. It energized her after her interval with Charlie. She took a few deep breaths herself, just to take in his energy.

He said, "I love this garden. Last summer, I worked on the grounds crew at school, and we maintained the horticulture garden. I might do that this summer, but I'm supposed to graduate." She said, "When do you start filming?"

"You mean, when do I start my new career? We have to go over and set up the scene today. They got some sort of big room in West Hollywood, and they even found some old bar from this secondhand restaurant-supply house. We get to have the place for two days, so after breakfast I'm supposed to go over there and help set up the tables and all that stuff. We have to take it down and get everything back to the restaurant-supply house by Friday morning."

"How many actors did they get?"

"Well, five girls and six guys, I guess. Two girls at the tables, two parading around, and one behind the bar. She doesn't wear a fur coat, though. She has a breast costume."

"What does that look like?"

"Well, there was some discussion about that, and I guess they decided that it would be most offensive if the bartender were a black girl and she had about ten pendulous breasts coming out all over her, so I don't know who's making that, but I guess they found some clothing-design and fabric-arts majors. They're using the kind of material they use in wetsuits—what is that?"

"Neoprene?"

"Yeah, black neoprene with bright-pink nipples everywhere! Don't you think that's cool?"

"Sure," she said, "I do. But offensive, of course." And maybe she did. It was easy to agree with someone like Simon.

He took a deep, satisfied breath. "That's the point!"

At the bottom of the steps, the Japanese garden was still in shadow, and at the far end, Zoe could see Paul between the lily pond and the cypress trees. He was in the "standing separate-leg stretch" pose—his feet were wide apart and he was bent double at the hips, with his hands around his heels, his elbows bent, and the top of his head nearly touching the mat he had laid out. Zoe looked at her watch. He would be about half an hour in at this point. She touched Simon on the elbow and turned him toward the door of her room. Simon said, "Look at that! Wow! You know, I bet he can suck his own dick. We should put that in the movie!"

Zoe laughed in spite of herself.

"No! We should! Every college kid in America would like to suck his own dick."

"I don't think Paul puts his yoga practice to that sort of use. Anyway, come back in ten minutes. He does this one where he squats down over the ball of his right foot and puts his left calf up over his right thigh. Then he balances there, with his back perfectly straight and his hands in prayer position in front of his breastbone. You want abs, that position gets you abs. He stays in that position for a pretty long time, too, sometimes left, sometimes right, but he's not quite as strong on the left as the right." Her handbag was right by the door. She handed him a fifty-dollar bill. "Besides bacon," she said, "we are going to be needing those Popsicles that are made with frozen fruit. Paul will eat those. Get the pineapple, the mango, the red grapefruit, or the banana. Paul likes those."

"This is a lot of money for bacon and Popsicles."

"Just spend it all. Cookies. I liked your menu ideas. Think of yourself as a guerrilla insurgent, smuggling contraband sugar into the compound."

As they were running back up the steps, she could see Paul flow into that Eagle Pose. Supposedly there was nothing better for loosening all your joints. Simon ran up the steps ahead of her, distancing her by twenty years every ten steps. Though it was discouraging in a way, he did have that twenty-year-old-boy natural grace that she hadn't dared to appreciate when she herself was twenty. Rarely had she had a relationship with a man less than ten—or was it twelve?—years older than she was. But now that she was forty-three, she could appreciate whatever she wanted to, and she appreciated Simon.

By the time she got to the deck (huffing and puffing a bit, she had to admit), Simon had disappeared inside the house, and she could see through the sliders that others were up, too—Delphine, Elena, Cassie. Charlie was still in his corner—as she opened the slider and entered, he threw her a smile—and Simon was running out the front door, with Elena shouting, "What are you going to get? Get some—"

But the door slammed.

"Some what?" asked Delphine.

"Some soy milk," said Elena.

"We'll shop for that on our way home," said Cassie. "We need to make a list."

Elena glanced at Charlie, who was still reading the paper, then she pursed her lips. Maybe, thought Zoe, things weren't going to be as peaceful as at the monastery after all.

Now Stoney appeared from downstairs, and he was dressed to go to the office. Zoe liked Stoney and was sorry that he was just coasting now. Dorothy was in despair over Stoney, and she and Zoe talked about him once in a while, but neither of them, or any of Dorothy's other friends, could think what to do about him. In Hollywood, thirty-eight was a very dangerous age. Wherever you worked, unless on the technical side (where experience equaled reliability), at thirty-eight you had to prove that you could go on to the next stage. Zoe had proved it well enough by working her ass off that year—three movies, a CD of old punk-rock songs done in a blues style. She'd had a rumored romance with Russell Crowe, who had been her costar in *High Pressure*, but only to boost the picture. Probably her most important career move that year was getting on the cover of *People* magazine in a split picture with Russell. He was wearing a cowboy hat and standing by a horse, and she was wearing a black gown with a low-cut back, going into The Ivy, and the cover headline read, "Off Again." She had also ostentatiously worn a ring, which was ostentatiously missing from her finger when she went to that party at The Ivy with Gabriel Byrne. Jerry Whipple had spent his thirty-eighth year consolidating his control of the agency and packaging Eddie Murphy. But Stoney was spending his thirty-eighth year grieving without even really knowing it, according to Delphine and Cassie. That happened when a death was so big to you that it became the center-piece of your philosophical system.

Now Max came in from the deck. He was carrying a book. He paused in the doorway and looked around the room, then said, "Hey. How about everybody sit down, have another cup of coffee, and I will pitch you a movie. Okay, Stoney?"

Stoney nodded.

Cassie said, "Us, too?"

"Absolutely. I just thought of this, out by the pool, reading the book. Okay? You, too, Chaz. You're the control group. Sit down."

"What does the control group do?"

"The control group keeps saying, 'You've got to be kidding!'"

"I can do that," said Charlie. Zoe saw him glance at her, but when they gathered around the table, pulled out the chairs, and sat down, Zoe sat next to Cassie, around the corner from Elena, across from Max. Stoney sat between Max and Delphine. Charlie sat at the foot of the table. Elena said, "Oh, I wish Simon were here!"

Max opened his book and set it on the table, adjusting his head so he could see the print. He ran his finger down the page for a second, then began to read aloud. "'In the evening, a great change came over the steppe. All its many-hued expanse caught the sun's last flaming reflection, and darkened gradually, so that the dusk could be seen closing over it, painting it dark green. The vapors thickened: every flower, every herb breathed forth its scent, and the whole steppe was redolent. The freshest and most enchanting of breezes barely stirred the surface of the grass, gentle as sea waves, and softly touched the cheek. The music that had filled the day died away and gave place to another—'"

"That would be birds rather than balalaikas," said Cassie.

"Shh!" said Delphine.

Max smiled, then went on: "'The speckled gophers crept out of their holes, sat on their hind legs, and made the steppe resound with their whistle. The chirp of grasshoppers grew louder. A swan's cry was wafted, ringing silvery in the air, from some secluded lake.'"

"Is this some kind of *National Geographic* thing?" said Charlie. "'Asia's Vast Hinterlands' or something like that?"

"It's a movie of this book." Max lifted the book, but Zoe couldn't tell what the book was, because the cover had been concealed in a wrapper, probably by Max, who wouldn't want them to form any preconceptions. "Imagine that steppe that I was just reading about. On it is an encampment, more like a town or a tent village, with a ramshackle, temporary air. Horses, men in beards and boots, wagons, people running around. Lots of weapons—swords and daggers, axes, pikes. No guns. A man, a Cossack, has brought his two sons to the encampment for training as warriors."

Max turned a few pages. "'A messenger comes galloping into the encampment with news from far away, and the news is bad. He says, "Such times are upon us that not even our holy churches are our own!"

"'"How not our own?" shouts someone.

"'"They have been leased to the Jews! If the Jew is not paid in advance, there can be no service . . . and if the damned dog of a Jew does not put his mark on our holy Easter-bread with his unclean hands, it cannot be consecrated!"'"

Isabel said, "They call that the 'blood-libel.'"

Zoe glanced around the table. She was a little surprised that Max would be reading something so anti-Semitic, but Max was mysterious. Way more mysterious than Paul, actually. Max went on, "The next guy says, 'He lies, gentlemen brothers!'"

Isabel smiled a bit, in apparent relief, but then Max read, "'It cannot be that an unclean Jew puts his mark on the holy Easter-bread! Jewesses are already making themselves petticoats out of our priests' vestments. And our chief now lies roasted in a copper pot in Warsaw! The heads and hands of our colonels are being carted from fair to fair for everyone to see!'"

"You've got to be kidding," said Charlie.

"You've got to be kidding that you're interested in this," said Cassie.

"Who are these people again?" said Zoe at last.

"Russians," said Max, "Cossacks. It's a remake of *Taras Bulba*."

"Nineteen sixty-two," said Stoney. "It had Yul Brynner and Tony Curtis. They were huge then."

"I remember it," said Cassie, "but I never saw it. It seems like they put Tony Curtis in everything in those days. What was his name, Bernie

Schwartz, and he looked exactly like what he was, which was a nice Jewish boy, and here you saw him in *Spartacus* and this movie and in some movie about an American Indian. And *The Vikings*! Bernie Schwartz as a Viking! And then he was that Italian guy in that circus movie. I'm surprised they didn't put him in *Camelot*."

There was a period of silence. Then Max said, "Anyway"—he looked back at the book—"Taras is a Cossack. His sons are named Ostap and Andrei. The time is the 1560s. Wars and skirmishes are constant all over the steppe. The Cossacks are stirred up. They go lay siege to a Polish town. Andrei, let's say he's the Brad Pitt character, fights in his first battle, and afterward now, here he is, walking around, looking at the other Cossacks, who are sleeping off their drunken revels." Max lowered his voice to a mellifluous rumble and read, "'He could not sleep and gazed at the sky. The air was pure and limpid, the thicket of the stars forming the Milky Way and girding the heavens was flooded with light. A strange human face seemed to flit before his eyes. Thinking it to be an illusion of sleep, which would at once vanish, he opened his eyes wider and saw that a withered, emaciated face was actually bent over him, its eyes looking into his.'" Max turned a page, skipping down a bit, then he said, "This is an old woman, an envoy from a beautiful princess inside the besieged city—"

"Probably about forty," said Cassie. "Zoe can play her." Everyone laughed.

Max went on, "Her message is, 'Go, tell the knight to come to me if he remembers me, and if he does not, let him give you a piece of bread for my old mother, for I would not see my mother die before my eyes. Beseech him, cling to his knees. He, too, has an old mother. He must give me bread for her sake!' So Andrei, the younger son, remember, steals some bread from the Cossacks' chow wagon and follows the old woman into the town through an underground passageway."

"What attitude are we supposed to be taking toward all of this?" said Elena.

Max shrugged, but he smiled affectionately at her.

"It's a galaxy far, far away," said Cassie. "I think we're supposed to see it like that."

Max cleared his throat. "Everyone is starving. 'Looking about him, Andrei saw two or three people lying motionless on the ground. He strained his eyes to see whether they were asleep or dead.' Then he starts stumbling over corpses. One is a woman. 'By her side lay a child, whose hand clutched convulsively at her lank breast . . .'"

"You should show the breast," said Cassie.

"'. . . and finding no milk there, twisted it with its fingers in vain anger. There was no longer crying or screaming, only the gentle heaving of its stomach showed that it had not yet drawn its last breath.'"

"That's like what people saw when Saddam gassed the Kurds," said Charlie.

Max went on: "The girl lives in a beautiful Italian-style villa. Remember, Andrei is just a nomad from the steppe. He's seen big houses from a distance, but never been inside one. And he sees the girl. 'Her uplifted eyes shone with matured feeling—feeling in all its fullness. The tears were not yet dry in them, and filmed down with a lustrous moisture that struck straight to his soul. Her bosom, neck, and shoulders had reached their full-developed beauty; her hair, which had formerly waved in light curls around her face, had now become a thick, luxurious mass, part of which was braided and pinned to her head, while the rest fell over her bosom in loose and lovely curls and reached to her fingertips.' She eats the bread. He stays with her, abandoning his father, the Cossacks, his religion, for love of her."

"It's very romantic," said Zoe. "I can see it. CinemaScope, as they say."

Everyone sighed.

Cassie said, "Of course, bad things happen in the second act."

"Yes. Because Andrei betrays them, the Cossacks are driven off. When Taras rallies them and they return to the fight, many are killed. In addition to that, since Andrei has betrayed the Cossacks, Taras is required to kill him, which he does. And it's the Jews who tell him all about it. Ostap, the other son, is taken prisoner by the Poles. They lasso him and truss him up and drag him away."

"That's a good visual," said Stoney.

"Is this relevant to modern American society?" said Charlie. "Maybe you could set it in corporate America somehow."

"You could set it in Hollywood, but people hate movies that are set in Hollywood," said Cassie.

"We liked *Sunset Boulevard* and *A Star Is Born*," said Delphine.

"But do people like this kind of thing?" said Elena. "It seems like *The Ten Commandments* to me. Very 1955."

"Nineteen sixty-two," said Stoney, reminding them.

"I always wondered why they made those movies," said Cassie. "Remember *Lawrence of Arabia*? Delphine and I watched it a couple of months ago. It was like watching paint dry, it was so slow. We had to turn it off, because the music was tremendously loud and I just couldn't stand the idea of this blond English guy schlepping through the desert without any sunblock.

Anyway, maybe *Taras Bulba* was a vanity project for Yul Brynner, to repay him for being a spy."

"*Lawrence of Arabia* wore robes," said Delphine. "But it was awfully slow."

"His *face* was exposed," said Cassie. "It was like watching people drive their children around without car seats. Or worse, because you knew they were in the real desert. You know, Yul Brynner spoke not only Russian but also all the major Chinese dialects. After the war and all through the fifties, it was Yul Brynner who told the Pentagon what was really going on in both Russia and China. I can't remember who told me that. I heard it at a party."

"Be that as it may, historically, *Taras Bulba* was a very interesting movie," inserted Max. "It was written by Waldo Salt. It was his first project after he was blacklisted in 1950 because he wouldn't testify before HUAC. He was one of the greatest screenwriters ever."

"But who wants to remake it?" said Zoe.

Max didn't answer. He went back to the book. He read, "Here's how they save Taras. 'His friend took hold of his arms and legs, swaddled him up like a child, replaced all his bandages, wrapped him in an oxhide, bound him up, and, roping him to his saddle, galloped away with him.' I'd like to put that onscreen."

"He's unconscious?" said Delphine.

"He's the sole survivor," said Max. "Here it says, 'Not one remained who had stood up for the just cause.' That would be the cause of sectarian religious fanaticism. Anyway, the Cossack cause is lost. The Poles have won. After he recovers, Taras decides that he has to go look for his older son, he can't help himself. He takes a trip to a town on the Black Sea and looks up a Jew, Yankel, that he once saved from being killed by the Cossacks. He persuades Yankel to take him to find Ostap in Warsaw, which Yankel, being a Jew, I gather, is able to do."

Stoney said, "Being Jewish actually is a conspiracy, you know. That's what my father always said. Not only in Hollywood."

"You're joking, right?" said Isabel.

"I am, but was Jerry?" said Stoney.

"Here's my favorite part," said Max, "'Hear me! Hear me, my Lord,' said Yankel. 'Here is what we will do. Fortresses and castles are now being built everywhere. French engineers have come from abroad and so a great deal of brick and stone is being carried over the roads. Let my lord lie on the bottom of the wagon, and I'll lay bricks over him. My lord looks hale and hearty, and so no harm will come to him, even if it is a little heavy, and I'll make a hole in the bottom to feed my lord through.'

"So they get to Warsaw, and Taras tries to persuade some local Jews to get Ostap out of the city jail. They apparently talk Yiddish, which I think is interesting, and which Taras can't understand. They go out and reconnoiter, but they come back with news that the prisoners are to be executed. Taras, of course, has to see this. So there is a very interesting scene where the Jews dress Taras up in an aristocratic robe and try to smuggle him into the prison, but he gives himself away when one of the guards insults the Russian Orthodox religion, and Taras can't help attacking him. Taras has blown their cover, so they have to bribe their way out of the prison—"

"Or fight," said Zoe. "In an American movie, they would have to fight their way out."

"We'll see," said Max. "But they get to the square where Ostap is to be executed. The square is full of people of all ages and classes, males and females, howling for the executions. They bring Ostap on first, and they strap him to the wheel, because he is supposed to be broken on the wheel before he is beheaded. Taras watches as they torture his son, and the narrator says that you can hear the cracking of his bones all the way to the back of the crowd. Ostap makes no noise, but at the last minute, he cries out, 'Batko! Where are you? Do you hear me?' and the crowd falls silent. In the silence, Taras calls out, 'I hear you!' and then the book says, 'A million people shuddered as one man.'"

Everyone around the table was silent.

Max went on. "Ostap dies smilingly, as they say. Taras goes back to Ukraine and raises a huge army of Cossacks and returns and burns down eighteen towns and forty Catholic churches. He's very angry, and so, it says, 'Lifting the children in the streets on the points of their spears, they threw them into the flames.'"

"I've never seen that on the screen," said Cassie.

"The war continues, until Taras is finally captured. As they are burning him to death, he shouts encouragement to the rest of the Cossacks, who escape by leaping their horses off a high cliff into the Dniester River. The Poles aren't good enough horsemen for this, and they and their horses get crushed and dismembered on the rocks." Max coughed.

Zoe pushed her chair back and rearranged her hair, then glanced at her watch. It was just after eight. Max looked at her. She said, "But what happened to the girl?"

"The implication is that she died in the burning of one of the towns, I guess."

"So," said Elena, "every one of the characters dies—the father, the two sons, the girl?"

"Only the Jews survive," said Cassie.

"And this takes place when, again?" said Elena.

"Well, it was written in the 1830s, but it's supposed to take place in the late 1500s."

"Seems like yesterday," said Charlie.

Max said, "I gather that, in terms of local grudges and historic enmities, it is exactly like yesterday."

"You can see some of those pan shots perfectly. The horses galloping through the tall grass and all. The stars," said Delphine. "The burning towns."

"I just can't see it as mass entertainment," said Zoe. "Everyone dies. The young lovers don't live happily ever after."

Stoney cleared his throat, then glanced at Max, who, Zoe saw, nodded slightly. Stoney said, "Nevertheless, there is a group of investors who want to make this movie, right out of the book, just the way it is, death, torture, horses, costumes, anti-Semitism, and all. Not Americans, but with plenty of money."

"Since all the Jews survive," said Cassie, "it must be some Israelis."

"Or not, depending on your feelings about what the survival of the Jews means," said Zoe. "I think this is very touchy material. Kind of like making a movie of *Uncle Tom's Cabin*. You could do it and it would be a good movie, and, you know, about five years ago, Spielberg sent me the book and asked me if I would like to play the woman Cassy. When they sent it to me, I was amazed at first that they would even think of doing such a project, but I started to read it, and this character of Cassy was so great—the greatest black woman character you would ever want to play—she's smart and brave and beautiful and angry and sexual, and she pulls the wool over the villain's eyes and saves a young girl from a fate worse than death. But the book had so much baggage attached to it that I thought no one could carry it, not even Spielberg, and he was king then. I thought about it long and hard."

"So you didn't make it."

"We didn't. But that wasn't the reason."

"What was the reason?" asked Charlie.

"The Spielberg people found out that someone had already made it for TV about ten years before." Zoe grinned.

Max laughed out loud.

Now the slider opened, and Zoe turned her head. Here came Paul, looking terrifically benign. Zoe said, "Oh, dear one. I wish you'd been here. Max told the bloodiest story. Chock-full of monotheistic religion."

"Oh dear," said Paul.

Delphine said, "Tell me the basic plot again?"

Max answered, "Well, in the first act, Taras decides to make a little war to avenge various crimes and show his sons how life on the steppe is lived. In the second act, Andrei betrays the Cossacks for the sake of a beautiful woman and Taras has to kill him. In the third act, Ostap is captured, and Taras traces him to Warsaw, where he watches his execution, and this is followed by general war."

"I just don't get the theme," said Elena. "What am I, the audience, supposed to learn here? You know what it's like? It's like *The Return of Martin Guerre*, where the guy comes back from the Thirty Years War and says he's this woman's husband, and he moves in and they have a lovely time, and then the *other* redheaded guy comes home, and he's much worse—he's lost one leg and he never was very nice to begin with, and now he's mad as hell, and he manages to prove that he is Martin Guerre, and the wife, who is perfectly beautiful and well meaning, has to watch the fake husband, who is her real beloved, get hanged, and then go home and accept the nasty bastard who is her real husband, and he's even madder now that he knows that she slept with the other guy."

"Talk about a Catch-22," said Charlie.

"Well, it was a wonderful movie, but I was in my twenties when I saw it, and I thought that was just the way life was—unjust, romantic, and sad. I mean, now I think, well, at least she knew true love for a while, and maybe that's worth a high price, but what's the lesson of this one?"

"Does there have to be a lesson?" said Max.

"Think of a Hollywood movie without one," said Delphine. "You can't think of one."

"It's not a Hollywood movie," said Stoney.

"What if it's just like the book?" said Max. "What if it just unfolds, battles, sieges, raids, tortures, conflagrations? Religious hatreds, anti-Semitism, and all? What if the characters are unvarnished and misguided and make the wrong choices and die cruel deaths, the end? I saw *The Return of Martin Guerre*, too. What I liked about it was the hog wallows and the geese in the house and the dark, low-ceilinged rooms and the dully shining pewter on the table and the dirty faces and the strange-looking cattle, and all in color. We could do that, too. Take a camera into the past and show how different it was."

"Like *Rob Roy*," said Cassie. "I remember I saw that movie with some friends, and in the opening credits, you had all these shots of the beautiful Scottish Highlands, and I turned to the other couple and I said, 'These are my people, onscreen at last!' and then they grin and all their teeth are black and rotten."

Everyone smiled.

Charlie said, "So, Max, are you going to make this movie?"

Max shook his head.

Zoe glanced at Stoney, who was looking out the window. Stoney knew, and therefore Zoe understood, that negotiations were not over—they were only just beginning.

Zoe pushed back her chair and got up from the table. One of the things that you noticed over the years in Hollywood was how many of the movies that didn't get made coexisted in your mind with all the movies that did get made. Take that *Uncle Tom's Cabin* movie, for example. She had thought the odds on getting that movie made were a thousand to one. And yet, in her mind, there were scenes from a movie—the slave woman Cassy and the new girl hiding in the attic of Simon Legree's ramshackle house, only coming out at night to haunt Legree as part of Cassy's escape plan. Or Cassy and the girl sneaking through the horrid Louisiana swamps, all the trees draped in Spanish moss, poisonous snakes swimming all around them. And she could perfectly picture scenes without herself at all—Tom on the deck of the paddle-wheeled steamboat, asleep, waking up to the sound of feet running past his head, and then sitting up just in time to watch a girl whose child is going to be sold as she throws herself with the child in her arms over the railing into the river. Or at the beginning, maybe even during the opening credits, the wife of the Kentucky plantation owner breaks the news to the slave girl Eliza, who is otherwise well treated and well dressed, that her child is to be sold to help pay some of the plantation's debts. There would be the great scene where Eliza leaps from ice floe to ice floe as she escapes across the Ohio River. And here's the paddle-wheeler going down the Ohio River, and Morgan Freeman or Sidney Poitier, or someone younger, maybe Danny Glover, standing by the railing on the lower deck, as Tom.

Having a movie in your mind was not like reading a book, where the passing images were loose and a bit vague, and the characters had being but not actual faces. When you were thinking about something for a movie, well, there was Morgan Freeman as Tom, and he was reassuring and wise, and his wife was a grandmotherly type, and the things that were done to Morgan were shocking and unjust the way all attacks on goodness are unjust, and Morgan Freeman's movie was about that. But if Danny were Tom, then he wasn't a grandfather, and his wife, say Oprah, wasn't a grandmother—they were healthy and youthful and good, but also a bit dangerous, without even knowing it, and everything about Danny as Tom while he is going down the hard path he must go down takes more effort and more faith—and that was how she would have played Cassy to Danny's Tom. She, and maybe only she (as Cassy, of course), would have sensed the rebellion that Tom was holding in check, and she would have tried to appeal to it. He would have come to the plantation in a new shipment of slaves, and he would have been imposingly healthy because he would have been treated well in his last place, and he would have been in despair because he had been expecting to be freed, and she, as Cassy, half crazy from working as Legree's concubine and put to work in the fields for insubordination, in spite of her beauty, would have seen this Tom as her only hope. It would have been like a seduction in a way, though not a sexual one. She would have been seducing the side of him that could be tempted to hate and destroy, and the drama and electricity of their conversation would come from the audience's knowledge that such a thing as attacking and killing Legree was still physically possible for Tom because of his size and strength, and also at least remotely tempting for him because he does recognize the injustice of the world he lives in—he not only recognizes it, he also knows that other worlds exist, unlike most of the field slaves on the plantation. It would have been a great scene.

And she would have gotten to escape, to go north, to show Cassy's ability to transform her very being in order to ride trains, walk down streets, to pass, literally, among the enemy, all to save the girl. It was a great, great part.

And then there was the music. The packet of materials Spielberg's company sent with the book included an article by some college professor about how, in the slave period, music was used by the whites for coercive purposes—as long as the slaves were singing, then they couldn't be planning among themselves for escape or rebellion. So the slaves were made to sing, but what they sang about was release and redemption—their release, and the redemption of the world they lived in—and so the music was complex and beautiful. Zoe could hear the soundtrack even without precisely knowing the words to all the songs. Even a song that no one could sing anymore, like "Ole Black Joe," would take on a different meaning altogether, and all the voices would sing out, in chorus and solo. While she was imagining the movie, Zoe had longed to be one of those voices—for that reason alone, she would have participated in the project, just to sing those songs with the full knowledge of what they meant. That Uncle Tom's Cabin project was never to be and existed only in her mind, but so powerfully that she had never bothered to seek out a copy of the TV movie, though the cast was full of actors she liked and respected. The only thing she'd heard about it was that since they filmed in Mississippi there could be no ice floes, so Eliza escaped on a raft of some kind. If Max pursued this movie long enough, thought about it long enough—it would get bigger and fuller, until it seemed like it was actually on film, and only some sort of extraneous factor, like the existence of another version, showed you that it wasn't. Zoe sighed, though not precisely for either Max's project, to which she was mostly indifferent, or Uncle Tom's Cabin. She sighed, she thought, because there were certain thoughts you had that should be realized and communicated, but never would be.

Paul, who had given her a decorous kiss, was standing by the open refrigerator, his nose to the blossom end of a cantaloupe he had found there. The look on his face told her that he found the cantaloupe worthy even though it was out of season. He set it down on the counter and contemplated it, then took out an orange. Then the front door opened and Simon walked in with Isabel. Simon was saying, "And, let's see, chocolate croissants for a healthy start to the day, and a couple of nice Danish for the more adventurous ones like your mom." He smiled. Zoe didn't see how you could resist his smile, but Isabel seemed to. She said, "People don't realize that dairy products are actually bad for you. Small children should not eat dairy products. It screws up their calcium uptake. They should actually be eating kale and broccoli and dandelion greens."

Simon set down his bag on the center island and said, "I *can* eat dandelion greens. I *have* eaten kale and Brussels sprouts. It's just that I *choose* to eat Cap'n Crunch. Right, Mom?"

"Right!" said Elena. "You are incorrigible." She smiled and turned to Isabel. "But he likes tofu, I'll give him that. Who's hungry?"

Max said, "Where's the paper? What day is today?"

"It's Wednesday," said Isabel.

"Day seven of the war," said Elena, "and no one's stopped it yet."

"We're winning," said Charlie, and Elena gave him a tight look.

"It's true," he said. "It's all over the paper. They're moving toward Baghdad as fast as they can. There's hardly any resistance to speak of. Hardly anyone's been killed. I mean, everyone's saying that it's going better than expected."

"Just who is everyone?" said Elena. "The same everyones who concocted the war to begin with, right?" Zoe saw Cassie and Delphine exchange a glance. There had been a few words at the dinner table the night before, but not a real argument.

"Well, the newspeople. Everyone," said Charlie. He looked simultaneously oblivious and aggressive.

"And," said Elena, sharply, "explain to me this 'winning' idea."

Zoe glanced at Isabel and Max. They were glancing at each other and at her. Max had an odd look on his face. He was standing by the toaster, and his toast popped up, and he put his hand out for it, but he didn't pick it up.

"What do you mean?" said Charlie.

"What do *you* mean? What does winning this war mean?"

"Well, obviously, getting rid of the weapons of mass destruction, rousting out the Al Qaeda cells, getting rid of Saddam." He smiled, Zoe thought uncomfortably, but brazenly. It had dawned on him that the person who could be called his hostess was deadly, seriously angry. Zoe, however, had to admit that what he said made perfect sense—obviously you had to do those things. Paul was still cutting up the fruit and setting it in neat wedges on a plate. Charlie went on, "Making sure that they don't attack us, of course."

"Were they planning to attack us?" Elena lifted the knife she was holding, then put it down on the island.

"Yes."

"What's your evidence for that? Are Iraqi troops massing in Mexico and Canada? Are there Iraqi ships sitting just outside American waters, are Iraqi submarines in New York Harbor?"

"Well, they don't have . . ." He laughed at the very thought.

"So—how were they going to attack us?"

"No one knows, that's the problem, they could bring in a dirty bomb or a biological weapon like the plague—"

"Oh, yeah?" she said. Zoe thought Elena's voice was getting a little shrill, though not exactly loud. "You know what I would have done if I were Saddam Hussein? I would have said, 'Yes, I do have nuclear capability, and I did get some uranium, and there is a bomb in a suitcase inside the U.S. that my agents have taken there. It is in an undisclosed location, and as soon as you attack my country, they have instructions to set it off.' Did he say that?"

"That's kind of crazy."

"Why is it crazy? Isn't it more crazy to sit on your weapons of mass destruction while a huge army invades you?"

"Saddam is a tyrant." Now Charlie was getting a little loud. "Are you defending Saddam?"

"What if the Iraqis resist and the Americans have to shoot them?"

"Well, we expect the Republican Guard to resist. Those are his hand-picked—"

"But what if the people resist? What if the Baghdadians shoot Americans from the housetops and blow up American soldiers and do the sort of things that the Palestinians do, and Americans have to shoot them and blow them up, what does winning mean in that context?"

"Honey—" said Max.

Paul finished cutting the fruit. He arranged it on a blue plate. It looked appealing.

"I want him to answer."

But Charlie was silent. Zoe wasn't quite sure why. She wanted him to answer, too, because it was a confusing question.

Paul gathered up the parings and put them in the trash can under the sink. Then and only then did he catch Zoe's eye. She nodded. He walked around Elena, grabbing a couple of paper napkins from a stack on the island, and came toward Zoe, deliberately but not quickly. Elena said, "They always talk about how well it's going to go, and they never talk about what if it goes badly, about what that means."

"But it is going well," said Charlie.

"I don't believe that," said Elena.

"Do you want it to go badly? Do you want Americans to be killed? Do you want the oil fields to be blown up?"

Max cleared his throat.

"Oil!" exclaimed Elena. "Now we get to the bottom—"

Paul opened the slider to the deck. Zoe preceded him into the sunlight. She realized that her heart was pounding. She followed him across the deck to the far corner that overlooked the pool and all the gardens and steps. Across the canyon, the Getty was so bright and distinct in the morning air that she could see tiny dark figures walking there. She said, "We should go to the Getty and look at some art. I haven't been there in a year."

"I would like that," said Paul. He spread a napkin over her lap and handed her a fork.

DAY FOUR · Thursday, March 27, 2003

"Are you awake?"

He had been awake, thought Max. He had been so wide awake that he was contemplating getting up, and then, apparently, he had fallen asleep again, because now he was heavy and thick and it was hard to open his eyes and he no longer had that erection. Hadn't he had an erection? He cleared his throat, rolled over, groaned, and rearranged his balls so they wouldn't get pinched. He said, "I was awake earlier. I had such a big erection that it woke me up."

Elena said, "Oh, Max! Why didn't you just roll me over and stick it in? You know I love that."

"You were sleeping so quietly and soundly, I didn't want to disturb you. It was big, though."

"Describe it."

Max yawned. He felt the yawn roll down through his body, tightening and then loosening every muscle. He stretched his arms above his head, then pulled Elena to him and arranged her head on his shoulder. He said, "Let's see. Well, it must have been that when I rolled over toward you I felt it bang against something, maybe your hip, and that's what woke me up, and then I could sense that it was full and hard, so of course I reached down —"

"Just for technical reasons."

"Yes, of course, just to apply the calipers. You know, I'm always interested in length, circumference, weight, that sort of thing, and it was definitely in the upper quintile of Max, maybe even the top ten percent —"

"Extra Big Classic range —"

"Exactly. So I refined my survey a bit, by feeling it all over, and gave it a little road test, just to see if it could be grown out any—"

"Pushing the envelope, which could be dangerous." She started laughing.

"Theoretically, though"—he tried to sound grave—"I've never heard of any sort of explosion or breakage. You'd think if there had been something like that somewhere, you'd hear about it."

"And so—"

"And so I cultivated it until I felt it had peaked, and—"

"I think I need a better description than that. More detail."

"Let's see." He held up his hand and made a circle. He touched the tip of his middle finger to the tip of his thumb, then spread them a bit. He said, "So maybe it was that big around, but of course you don't really grab it like that. More like this." He changed to a tennis sort of grip. "Anyway, it was a hand-filler. I know what—" Max threw off his covers and got up. His robe was right there. In the kitchen, he saw that Delphine and Cassie were already eating breakfast. "Morning!" he said. They turned and smiled. He grabbed a banana, came back into the room, and tossed the banana on the bed. While Elena was laughing, he took off his robe and threw it over the chair. She was naked, and their covers were on the floor. He picked up the banana and wrapped his hand around it. He said, "About like this." He approximated the stem end of the banana to his groin and arranged his hand as if he were masturbating, but then turned the banana upward. "Actually, more like this." The banana curved upward, and he made the blossom end tap his navel. "Almost exactly like this. Almost exactly the length, circumference, and direction of this banana."

"What a wonderful coincidence!" she exclaimed, but now they were both laughing. He put the banana into her outstretched hand, and got back into the bed. He said, "Don't eat it just right this very minute, okay?"

"I won't. I want to hear more."

"Well, big isn't exactly a dimensional thing. I mean, objectively, it's probably more or less the same size every time, within a few millimeters. What makes it feel big is more about the blood trying to get in, more about a sensation of rigid fullness. That's what I had this morning. Blood just piling up at the gates. And it was right up against my stomach. I could feel that."

"Was it warm?"

"Of course it was warm. It was warm and silky, and my balls were hard, too."

"What color was it?"

They both gazed at it for a moment. He said, "Well, I didn't actually look at it, because it was dark still, but I'm sure it was flushed." He lay back and she knelt over him and kissed him appreciatively and firmly on the lips, then more gently on the tip of his cock. She said, "I'm so glad it isn't pierced." At dinner the night before, Simon had been showing Charlie the tattoo on his leg, and Charlie had asked if tattoos and piercings were still a big deal.

"A big deal to whom?" said Simon. "To parents?"

"To kids," said Charlie.

"Most people have them," said Isabel. "So they're not a big deal."

"So what's the weirdest place to pierce?" said Charlie.

"There's a guy at school who has his ass cheeks pierced and connected by a bar," said Simon. "I saw him at the gym one day."

"How does he sit down?" said Cassie.

"It's up at the top of the cleft."

"Leo and I saw a guy on TV a few months ago," said Isabel, "who did the head of his dick. They called it a 'Prince Albert.'"

"How does that work?" said Zoe.

"Well," said Simon, quite informatively, Max thought, and, you almost might say, enthusiastically, "they gather the skin that's under the head of the penis and pinch it together and pierce it, and then they put a ring or a barbell-type thing through it."

"You're kidding," said Cassie.

"Supposedly," said Isabel, "a 'Prince Albert' is when a ring goes down through the urethra and comes out underneath. Leo couldn't stand to watch long enough for them to explain."

"Maybe it's like a French tickler," said Charlie.

"What's that?" said Simon.

"A condom with a lot of stuff hanging off it," said Stoney. "Sort of like a party hat. Or a Rastafarian wig, with latex Rasta locks."

Everyone had laughed.

"Have you ever used one of those?" said Simon.

Stoney shook his head.

Elena had said, "Do you think they do that piercing for their own pleasure or the pleasure of the partner?"

"I think it's just a sexy thing to do," said Stoney. "I don't think it enhances the pleasure for either one."

"Imagine how much adjusting you'd have to do just to keep it from getting caught in your shorts," said Max.

Then Charlie had said, "When I was in college in the early sixties, there was supposedly a kid in the ag school who could piss over four lanes of interstate highway. He was a farm kid who had been pissing at fenceposts all his life, aiming from farther and farther away. Supposedly, he could shoot it out in a long stream—"

"Say you're a trucker," said Simon, "and you're just rolling down the road, and this arc of pee lands on your windshield—"

"Or you see a tiny, tiny rainbow," said Zoe.

Everyone had laughed.

"Did you," said Simon, "ever see that Web site called 'Clone-a-bone'?"

"What's that?" said Elena.

"It's for making your own personal dildo, or maybe, you know, a monument to your— Well, anyway, they send you this tube and a jar of something you mix up called Buddy Batter, for making the mold, and then some kind of rubber—they have different colors and shades—and when you have it just the way you want it, you fit the tube around it and pour in the Buddy Batter—" But then he had looked at Elena and fallen silent.

The good thing about this dinner-table conversation, as far as Max was concerned, was that there had been no ensuing discussion of the Iraq war. "Or tattooed," he said now. "I'm glad it isn't tattooed. I worked on a paint crew as a summer job, and there was one guy who had tattoos all over his body, mostly cartoon figures. One day we were out behind the school we were painting, taking a leak, and I saw that he had 'FWO' tattooed on the head of his penis. He said it meant For Women Only. That's the only one I've ever seen or heard of."

She snuggled closer, then said, "When we were talking about those things last night, Simon seemed so—"

"Enthusiastic?"

"Well, I was going to say 'knowledgeable.'"

"That, too."

"I feel like he would try anything."

"I think he would try a lot of things, but my guess is that he won't have his penis pierced or tattooed. He's less careful than Isabel, but with boys the question is not 'Will they try it?' but 'Can they handle it?' Just the other day Stoney and I were discussing the dumbest things we did at twenty-one, and obviously Paul took his laps in the risk pool, too. And Charlie did, too, I know for a fact, because I was there, gawking."

"What was the stupidest thing Charlie did?"

"I guess the stupidest was when we were sixteen or so. I came back from some family trip and found out that he and another friend of ours, named Brian Moody, had stolen a stick of dynamite from a construction site, and a blasting cap, too. The day after I got back, we drove around the countryside until they found what they wanted to blow up. It was an old outhouse. The whole time we were driving, they were talking about how you were supposed to do it. I guess everything they knew about dynamite they learned in the movies. One thing they couldn't decide when we found the outhouse was whether to drop the dynamite down the hole or set it on the seat. They finally tossed a coin, and dropped it down the hole. I stood off about a hundred yards. Brian lit the fuse and ran, and then we watched the outhouse shoot up like a rocket. I don't know what the farmer thought. Then, about six months later, we were out in Brian's father's pickup from his work. There were three of us in the cab and three guys in the back, and we were driving down a dirt road between a couple of farm fields that were set lower than the road. Anyway, there was some kind of berm in the road, I don't know what it was, but we were going quite fast, and then Charlie, who was driving, swerved all of a sudden, and the truck went over the edge and rolled into the field. The guys in the back just flew out and landed in the mud. The truck rolled almost all the way over. Man, the tools in the cab were flying everywhere. I was down in the footwell with my arms over my head. Charlie was shouting, 'Whoooooaa! Whoooaaa!' But everyone walked away from it. I guess afterward Charlie and Brian kind of hammered out the fenders and rinsed the truck off, and the father never knew. I mean, it was a work truck, and fairly beat up already."

Elena said, "Oh God, you're making me nervous. Remember that movie *Twins*? With Schwarzenegger and Danny DeVito?"

"I didn't see that one."

"They play two fraternal twins who are the product of a breeding experiment. The DeVito twin has been conveniently disposed of, and ends up a small-time crook on the streets of L.A. Arnie is a genetic superman, so they keep him and raise him with every advantage on a secluded island in the Caribbean. He escapes at about thirty. He's totally innocent and safe and well intentioned and happy. That's what I always wanted for Simon."

"Looks like you didn't get your wish."

"No, I haven't." She sighed. Then she lifted her head and looked at him in what he thought was a peculiar manner, and said, "But you think Isabel plays it safe?" Isabel, Max knew, was an ideal daughter and always had been—happy but serious, straightforward, perfect in every way—but, knowing Elena's concerns about Simon, he didn't want to brag. Instead, he said, "At least she's getting rid of this kid Leo. I never liked him."

"I hear he's a dedicated horticulturalist."

"Yes, I heard that, too. And I'm sure it's an agribusiness with him, not subsistence farming. When he used to come around from time to time, the only thing he ever asked me about was money. He always wanted to know how much things cost. Or else how much you could get for something.

Even when they were in high school, I was doing a movie, what was it, oh, that movie *Imperial* that was the story of Salome but set out in Brawley, that was supposed to be on HBO but they never showed it. Leo couldn't stop asking me about the budget. I almost gave him a copy of the breakdown. I don't know what she saw in him. She doesn't seem to me to care about money, or even things. She buys all her clothes at regular places. That's the way Zoe is, too. If Zoe's ever shopped on Rodeo Drive, I'd be stunned."

"If you look like Zoe, you don't have to shop on Rodeo Drive."

"True enough." Then she looked at him again, and he knew what this look meant—did he care what Zoe looked like? And the answer was, he was so used to what Zoe looked like by now that he hardly noticed, but he doubted whether, if he said that, she would believe him. So he said, "What time is it, anyway? When I ran out there for that banana, I noted that the older generation is already eating breakfast."

"Can we eat the banana yet?"

"Not quite."

"Well, in that case, it's time for a present."

He felt a little charge of pleasure, he had to admit. "A present for me?"

"Yes."

"From you?"

"Oh, yes."

"Is it my birthday?"

"What do you think?"

"No. Is it your birthday?"

"No. My birthday is in September. It's just something I saw, and it might be the wrong thing, but we can return it." She leaned over the side of the bed and reached under the bedskirt.

She pulled out a large-ish box wrapped in blue paper. Inside, Max found a Canon digital video camera, about hand-size. He lifted it out of the box. It was silver. He opened the door on the left side, then closed it again. Just by looking at it, he could tell that it was a nice piece of nonprofessional equipment. He said, "How much was this? I haven't bought a video camera in five years at least."

"About twelve hundred dollars. After we were talking the other day, I was driving down Sunset, and I saw that big video store, and I thought I would just see what they had. Doesn't it seem funny to you that a motion-picture director wouldn't have a video camera?"

He gave her a kiss and said, "Doesn't Mario Andretti usually take the bus?"

Her face fell just for a split second, but then she smiled. "Anyway, I did ask Isabel if you had a video camera, and she said she didn't think so, and

Delphine didn't think so, either, so here it is. Not necessarily the best, though the man in the store said it was the best for the money."

"Do Delphine and Isabel know what I'm going to use it for?"

"I'm sure they think you're going to record family get-togethers, with a long shot of the turkey and before and after shots of the pies."

"I guess they'll be surprised, then."

Elena lay back against the pillows and said, seductively, "I guess they will."

"Are there tapes?"

"Y-e-e-s-s. Look in the box."

"Does it need to be charged?"

"I did that already. I bought it yesterday."

Max took off the lens cap and turned the camera around in his hand. It was compactly appealing. He found the power button and listened while the camera made a few discreet dings and issued a low, whispery hum. He looked through the viewfinder at the door, and then at Elena's face. Both looked good. He said, "I don't know much about digital images, but you look shiny." He panned down the length of her body and then did a close-up of the big toe of her right foot, which she wiggled. He ran the camera up her leg, came to her pubic hair. He did a close-up of her pubic hair. The definition produced by the camera and the light in the room was good enough so that he could see the swelling curves and the subtle color, brick-pink, of her labia. She opened her legs an inch or so. He moved the focus in closer. He said, "Factor-ten close-up is pretty good. Closer than that and I think we wouldn't know what we were seeing."

"Or it would look ugly, like the Brobdingnagians."

"Who are they?"

As he tested how close he could get to the edge of her labia and whether he could make out the hood of the clitoris, she said, "Did you ever read *Gulliver's Travels*? When Gulliver goes to the land of the giants, they are very kind to him, but he can't stand the sight of their pores and moles. Like high-definition TV."

"Well, I can't see your pores. I can see your hairs, but not really well. When they are in focus, they seem quite bright, as if something in the digitization makes them sparkle, and when they're out of focus, they seem quite soft and welcoming." He widened the camera angle, and the rest of her torso came back into the frame. He closed in on her navel, then on her right breast, and then on her right nipple. She said, "Do you like it so far?"

"Yes. Open your mouth."

She opened her mouth. He looked at her whole face, then closed in on her lips and teeth, after that her tongue, which was somewhat pinker and even more sparkly than her labia, because, of course, it was moist. Her teeth glistened, too. She stuck out her tongue. Because the aperture was almost completely shut down, her tongue seemed to balloon at him and then retreat, as she made a point of the tip and then put it away. He said, "Eat the banana now." She moved out of the frame. He didn't watch her with his other eye: he had to keep that eye closed because it was nearsighted. He held the camera steady on the pillow she had been leaning against, and then she appeared again, or, rather, the banana appeared again, peeled and pale, all its little dimples and ridges magnified in the frame. He said, "I never realized what a pleasing color bananas are." Her mouth bit off the top of the banana, and he went for a wider shot, a shot of her whole face as she took the banana down, inch by inch. She said, "You aren't actually filming, right? Because I didn't see you put in a tape."

"No, just experimenting."

"How do I look?"

He took the camera down. He said, "You look great. I love how you look. I want to fuck you."

"Oh, yes, you do. I reciprocate your sentiments." She smiled again.

"Oh, yes, I do want to fuck you. I should have taken advantage of that big one when I had it." He sighed.

Elena sat up. She said, "You're sighing."

"I want to fuck."

"Then stop the war."

He lowered the camera. After a moment, he said, though with a smile, "I'm not sure your analysis is accurate."

"What else could it be? We were fine until Thursday. Even when Colin Powell went before the Security Council and showed all those aluminum tubes and aerial photographs, we were fine. *You* were fine."

In fact, Max thought that this was a rather amusing line of thought, so he went along with it. Whenever she talked about it, it was a relief, better in every way, he thought, that erectile dysfunction not be a personal matter. He especially did not want her wondering about her attractiveness or desirability, and her geopolitical theory was at least better than "I'm just not feeling very sexy lately," an explanation he had relied on in the past. Because, of course, as soon as you said that, you started counting up dates and times and trying to decide when "lately" began and if "lately" might be the dawning of a new era. He was fifty-eight, after all. Fifty-eight had the air of seeming old, and even though when he saw other men his age on TV he was astonished at how old they looked in comparison with himself, when he passed himself in a plate-glass window he sometimes didn't recognize the Max he thought he remembered. She said, "You can be sure that *he* is not suffering any difficulties. I'm sure it's in the DNA. Don't you remember, in the first Gulf War, how the dad really seemed to just get happy as soon as he decided to invade? Here he'd spent two years in the White House, shuffling around, looking depressed, and then he got that coalition together and his whole demeanor changed. You could tell it gave him a boost just to be attacking someone. He was smiling more, standing up straighter. It's only people with consciences that actually suffer when the country goes to war."

Max set the camera inside the box, and removed the box to the floor beside the bed. She was glaring—though, he knew, not at him. After a moment, he said, "Honey. In the last two and a half years, you have done everything you could. You've protested and voted and marched and written letters to the editor. You've subscribed to progressive newsletters and magazines. You've signed petitions and made sure that none of this has been done in your name. You've sent in money and you've made signs. I know you would never take up arms or go outside the system, so you've exploited every single path you have open to you. Maybe you should take solace in the fact that you've done your best, that lots of others agree with you, and that at some point the pendulum will swing back. Maybe you should relax."

"Relax!"

"Well, that's the wrong word. Maybe you should accept that it's out of your hands and that events are going to take their course."

"Maybe I should, but I can't."

"What does that mean?"

"It means that I can't stop feeling offended. Here's what I think. If they hadn't cheated to win the election, I might feel different. First of all, they prevented likely Democratic voters from voting by manipulating the voting lists. They knew they were doing it and intended to do it. Then a cousin of the Bushes on Fox TV called Florida and the election for Bush, even though the election was at least too close to call. Then, when it looked like the recount was going to go our way, they sent in thugs to intimidate the recounters, and after that, the Supreme Court stopped the recount, even though Scalia and Thomas had blatant conflicts of interest. And then they gloated. Cheating and gloating. I mean, people give up power all the time, and it's difficult to do, but in this case the power was stolen because they cheated. Even the Supreme Court justices knew they were cheating, and it's their job not to cheat and to understand cheating and to prevent cheating."

Max shook his head, though discreetly. "It always seemed to me more like what happened was that they gave in to temptation. Yes, they had set up a scam by which Jeb was going to give Florida to his brother, but it was only circumstances that made that one little scam so important. If Gore had won Tennessee, even, the Florida thing would be just one little corrupt wrinkle—"

"But you asked me why I still care. It was the aggressive, open gloating. It was more than a lack of shame. Not only were we supposed to acknowledge that they had the power, we were supposed to admire the idea of cheating as a method of attaining power. They *preened* themselves upon being corrupt and morally bankrupt. If he had gone to his inauguration and said, 'I know I cheated, and I know most of you didn't elect me, and I know I am indifferent to all issues of right and wrong as they apply to me personally, but I'm here and I plan to make the most of it,' I wouldn't be so angry."

Max laughed. The fact was, there was an element of delight that he felt about everything she said. But he tried to speak seriously: "I always think it's funny that the main thing you want is for them to see themselves as you see them, when that's exactly the very thing that they can't do. Honey, you're never going to get that from anyone. It doesn't matter who they are, they get to have that one thing, their own point of view."

"It kills me that the sociopaths have taken over everything. I mean, okay, all through the eighties and nineties we had everyone screaming about how great the free market is, how wonderful it was that everything in the world was going to be defined by self-interest and monetary relations. There were going to be no regulations or sense of obligation, and people were to accept that they were tools of the economy, and the economy was not to have any higher goal than expanding. And the economy was going to *be* the nation. I hate all these theories that you could get something for nothing, that aggregate selfishness somehow turns into a humane society when, quite evidently, it does not. And then the voters did turn away from pure free-market capitalism. They did vote for a guy who cared about global warming, for example. But then the free-marketers stole it anyway, and in the process, they showed that they were as they had appeared all along, that they had no principles. The playing field was not level, there were no rules, and it was just like we always knew the free market really was, not healthy competition, but dog-eat-dog. No, not dogs. Dogs have some sense of propriety. More like crocodile-eat-crocodile."

"But why do you care?" He thought, We're here, in this room. In this room, things are fine.

"Because it's not human."

"It is human."

"Then it's not American."

"It is American. Winning without caring is completely American. Do you know what a 'knock-down, drag-out fight' is?"

"I don't know. A bad fight."

"A knock-down, drag-out fight was a certain type of combat that people in frontier towns used to set up and wager on. Every sort of tactic was legal — including ear-biting, eye-gouging, tongue-biting, testicle-crushing. Men would fight, and other men would watch the mayhem and cheer it on. That was an American form of recreation. Genocide was American. Slavery was American. Witch-burning was American. What conservatives hate about liberals is that liberals repudiate cruelties that are truly American in the name of something larger or somehow alien. Conservatives don't necessarily embrace those cruelties, but they don't mind them, either, because they think they are natural and because they are American. Conservatives figure that, if Americans killed off the native population, then so be it, since Americans did it, it must be okay."

"If Americans invade Iraq, then so be it, it must be okay because Americans are doing it."

"Yes."

"Do you expect me to agree with that logic?"

"No, but I expect you to recognize that it is ineradicable, that it's the price you pay for living here."

"You aren't offended?"

"I am offended, but I'm not surprised. You seem surprised or shocked."

"Well, I don't know that I am. I don't think I'm naïve. But the death and destruction that comes from that sort of logic seems so pointless. If you can foresee the waste, then why suffer it?"

"You know, I'll tell you a story," said Max. "I just thought of it, and I don't quite know how it applies, but it seems to. Maybe, after I tell it, we'll both relax and I'll get an erection." He smiled. "But maybe not. Anyway, when I was in college, there was a kid on my floor who I sometimes talked to, and one night we ran into each other in the coffee room really late, maybe two or three a.m. He had an odd name — Ulli — and I asked him sort of idly where he was from, because he didn't have any sort of accent. He was from Germany. Well, I had never met a German before, not a real German, and it was, what, 1962, so people were very aware of East and West Germany and World War II and everything. And then he told me, without me asking, how his family had gotten through the war. He said that he had an older brother, born in 1933, and another sister, born in 1938. His parents were born in 1910, and they were prominent, wealthy Berliners. On both sides, his family was full of Lutheran ministers and theologians, all the way back to Luther, but his father and grandfather had a dry-goods business, and they were successful and the family was well-to-do. Nevertheless, it was a closely connected extended family, and all the relatives knew each other and spent time at one another's houses. In 1933, when Hitler came to power, Ulli's father, a man named Klaus, and his mother, a woman named Uta, were not convinced that Hitler was a decent man or that the Nazis were good for Germany, and throughout the thirties, Ulli's father continued not only to serve Jews in his shop and to maintain, as far as he could, his Jewish connections, he also went every day to some kind of café that was run by a Jew he knew. Toward the end of the thirties, two SS guards were stationed outside this shop, and every day Klaus greeted them as he walked through the door. They greeted him, and he greeted them, and he always greeted them formally—'*Guten Tag*, Herr Doktor Kommandant Wolfgang Binder,' or whatever. He never in any way showed disrespect, or even irritation, toward the guards, but he always sat down, in the same sort of overtly dignified way, with the café owner, and stayed for half an hour and had a cup of coffee. Eventually, of course, the café owner disappeared, and the café was closed, but Klaus continued to conduct his life with complete integrity, you might say. He never allowed the Nazis, or his relatives, to dictate to him how he was to treat the people he met on the street, and though he never spoke up unasked, he also never kept his opinion to himself when he was asked. Ulli's brother told him that the scariest thing was after the fall of Stalingrad, in 1942, when the Germans, including all the Germans who had been resisting or doubtful, gave up and, at least on the surface, became Nazis because it seemed then as though there was no alternative. Ulli had a picture, which he later showed me, of the street where they lived in Berlin. There was a big parade celebrating the victory at Stalingrad, and flying at every single window was a Nazi flag. Every single window except the three windows belonging to Klaus and Uta, which were closed and not flying any flags. Ulli didn't know who had taken the picture—his father or some informant—but it was a picture he was very proud of, and he kept it in the frame he had of pictures of his parents, between their pictures and the backing. Some of Ulli's relatives never forgave his parents for resisting. I'm sure some other people never forgave them for not doing more, I don't know. He did say that they had become atheists as a result of the fact that all the Lutheran ministers in the family had supported Hitler. But Ulli was proud of them because they had remained more or less themselves in spite of pressure. He didn't call them heroes, and I don't think he thought of them as heroes, but I think he thought that they took into consideration all of the pressures they felt—including the pressures of having to protect and care for two small children—and they acted for the best. The thing that strikes me now, though, is that, even though they might have wished that things had turned out differently, they had no occasion to feel remorse."

"But remorse isn't what I'm trying to avoid. The destruction of the country is what I'm trying to avoid."

"But do countries get destroyed? Germany and Russia aren't destroyed. Hitler lasted twelve years, Stalin lasted about thirty or so, and Communism itself only lasted about seventy years. Milosevic lasted a few years. In Iran, it's been twenty-five years, but I heard that the younger generation doesn't pay much attention to the Islamic revolution anyway. Yes, there may be a political convulsion, but the country and most of the people outlast it."

"But we aren't a country like that. We are a country based on a certain set of ideas about how things are done—how governing is done and how wars are fought, and how the private and the public sectors limit each other's power. If those ideas are destroyed, then there is no country. There is no 'United States,' there's only something else, like non-Canadian North America. 'England' and 'France' are countries. 'The United States' is an abstraction about how to accommodate diversity and unity at the same time. When one faction seizes power and ignores everyone else and just adopts a try-and-stop-me sort of attitude, then the whole system is put at risk. I don't see how they don't understand that."

"They don't understand it because they don't care. Or because they see the country as being based on being special or making it economically, or being victorious, or some sort of social Darwinism. Maybe it's just tribal. For liberals, the question is between right and wrong, but for conservatives, the question is between me-and-mine and not-me-and-not-mine. And anyway, the way the government is supposed to work has often been used as a fig leaf for simply getting what you want. What do you think the motto 'Don't tread on me' was all about? Independence came first, and trying to organize came second. Not being told what to do is the first and foremost American value, not checks and balances. But I see that as our salvation as well as our danger. Are they able to tell you what to do? Are they able to tell me what to do? Are they able to tell anyone at the offices of that magazine you read, *The Nation*, what to do? No, they are not. Don't tread on me. Even if the government ends up being entirely corrupted, millions and millions of people will still adhere to the 'Don't tread on me' principle. Guess what? Waldo Salt was purged by the right wing of his day, and he came back to write, yes, *Taras Bulba*, but then *Midnight Cowboy* and *Serpico* and *Coming Home*. Yes, he was gone for ten years, and for him they were ten years of trouble and hardship, but he was back for almost twenty years, and he regained everything he'd lost and more. Ulli's parents were no doubt terrified and horrified, but they lived to have Ulli, who lived to respect and love them for the hardships they endured."

"A lot of people in Iraq aren't going to live."

"You are absolutely right, and I would not have sacrificed them, either, but opinion is divided in Iraq, too. You can accept that without agreeing with the war, can't you?"

"I can accept that."

"You are not in danger."

"How do you know?"

"What is it you always say, that the statistical likelihood of any given member of the Evangelical Free Church of Sedalia, Missouri, getting blown up in a terrorist attack is infinitesimal, and so why do they vote for the congressman who authorizes the Patriot Act? Well, the statistical likelihood of you, Elena, getting arrested for terrorist connections is infinitesimal, too, as is the statistical likelihood of this house being stormed by an alliance of right-wing Christians, NRA adherents, and Halliburton-employed mercenaries. I won't say it's impossible. I won't say that. But I will say it's unlikely. It's so unlikely that we don't have to prepare for it."

"You're just making my fears sound ridiculous."

"Well, I am trying to get you to laugh."

"Why?"

"Because my take on things is that life is more powerful than death, way more powerful, and if we think about death over and over, look what happens, I can't get it up, and so my sense of being alive is diminished. I would rather be like Klaus. I would rather be an immovable object than an irresistible force. I think you would rather be an irresistible force. But the world is full of people that do harm in the name of doing good. If you are an immovable object, then you are less likely to do harm."

"But you make movies. You depict things. You put stories and images on the big screen and try to have an effect. I think most people would laugh at the idea of a movie director thinking of himself as passive and undynamic."

"Well, I have several ideas about that. In the first place, movies that I make are stories. Even when I try to make it as compelling as possible, I know they are stories and the audience knows they are stories and the actors know they are stories. The thing about a story is that it affects you if you want it to, but you can take it or leave it. It's like Alcoholics Anonymous. Have you ever been to a meeting?"

She shook her head.

He was warming up now, he thought. "What they do at meetings is tell stories. You aren't allowed to give advice or tell people what to do. You're encouraged to tell your own story and leave it at that. The reason they do that is because alcoholics can be volatile and sometimes take offense. Telling stories is the least offensive way to communicate, because it's the least coercive. So that's one of my defenses. Another one is that most movies are bad and most audiences are too sophisticated to buy most movies. I would like to have made a string of movies like *One Flew over the Cuckoo's Nest*, that seem so real while you are watching them that they replace all your own feelings and opinions, but I haven't. Even the guys who made that movie haven't. Michael Douglas went on to make *Wall Street*. *Wall Street* was kind of hokey at the time, and it's more hokey now. *One Flew over the Cuckoo's Nest* was not hokey then, and it's even less hokey now. What happened on the set of *Cuckoo's Nest* was that everything clicked. The script clicked, the set clicked, the actors clicked, Forman, the director, clicked. It was like conducting a sublime performance of the Ninth Symphony. It was not work. Probably it was Nicholson who caused the click. He got along with everyone, and it seems like he's the energy center when you look at him on the screen. But they all clicked, DeVito, Chris Lloyd, Scatman Crothers. Louise Fletcher's performance gets better every time you look at it. When you watch William Redfield, who died after the movie came out, you know that he hates Nicholson's character, and for the moment you can see why, and you hate Nicholson's character, too. When the doctor comes on, who was the real doctor at that hospital, you can't believe what a good job he is doing playing the doctor! That movie is the only thing in the entire world that makes me want to be someone else than myself. I would like to have been Milos Forman just in order to be part of that. But guess what? *One Flew over the Cuckoo's Nest* came and went. It is not life-changing for most people who watch it. It's a story. It may be the most perfect movie ever made, or one of them, but you can still take it or leave it. You can still get up, walk away, and make up your own mind about mental institutions, psychotherapy, electroshock, and even frontal lobotomy, not to mention euthanasia. So I don't see what I do as coercive. In fact, I see it as objective. I offer something for the audience to contemplate, and even though we look like we are being madly active in making our offering, really our offering is as passive as a big stone lion on a pillar. Take it or leave it. And when a movie doesn't jell like that one does, it isn't at all hard to leave it."

She looked at him, didn't say anything and kept looking at him. He could not interpret this look, except that in some sense it was a look of defeat. How long had he known her? A little less than a year. Even before he met her, she'd been in full attack mode for, by her own testimony, at least fifteen months. It suddenly occurred to him, as she looked at him, that perhaps he didn't know her at all. And so he said, "What were you like during the Clinton administration?"

She didn't say anything, only worked her mouth a bit and pushed her hair back, as if maybe he had gone too far. She put her chin in her hand and looked out the window. More than anything, he thought, he would like to pick up that camera and film this set of gestures. Her face was alive with feelings that he couldn't quite read, and, he thought, if he were to look at her through the camera lens, he would be able to read them and figure out what to say next. But he resisted temptation, only taking her hand with the hand he would otherwise have used to pick up the camera. After a moment, she removed her hand from his and picked up the banana skin that had been sitting on the coverlet, and smoothed the edges together, and set it neatly beside the camera box. She said, "I'm trying to encapsulate what I thought about Bill Clinton. I didn't think he was a saint. I mean, Cassie once said he was and is a saint, but I didn't find him attractive or unattractive. I did find him reassuring. I mean, from the very beginning of his administration, when he got in trouble for having his hair cut on the runway at LAX, and then for firing people in the White House travel office, it was apparent that they were out to get him and they weren't going to let him do anything that was even his own business without a fight. That was a shock, but those were the terms of his presidency, and they started right away, and so everyone got used to them. It was like watching a guy walking down a road. The road runs behind a hedge. All you see are his head and shoulders, and he seems like he is having a nice walk. He's happy, he's smiling. Then there's a gap in the hedge, and you realize he's being mauled by a pack of dogs. They've ripped off his pants and they're nipping at his legs and his ass and even his testicles, but he's still progressing, not paying much attention to the dogs, keeping his mind more or less on his destination. It was reassuring. You had the feeling that, even though there was a lot of discord, the country wasn't in danger, because he, Bill Clinton, didn't seem afraid. They weren't going to get him, and that was that, and so you could go about your business, and the economy could expand, and everything would be okay. I think that's what a president does. He takes it, whatever it is, and is undaunted. You know, as soon as Bush got the nod, sometime that December, he said that the economy was going to collapse. Why would he do that? It was like the weapons of mass destruction. He wanted the economy to collapse, in order to instill fear into the citizenry, and so he began talking about it right away. Clinton never did that. So I guess during the Clinton administration I was going about my business, trying to keep Simon moving forward and trying to keep writing. Oh, and I had that call-in radio show for a while on a local public radio station where people called me for household advice, but it didn't really go well, even when we started having authors on, though that was fun. Cookbook authors and house-cleaning authors. My favorite was this woman who knew how to get all the pet stains out of your carpet and upholstery."

"What?" Max relaxed, and then he leaned over and picked up the camera after all. Elena put her hands behind her head.

He turned on the camera again and looked through the viewfinder at her. He focused only on her face, so that it filled the frame. She smiled. Through the camera lens, he could read that smile perfectly. It was amused and nostalgic and friendly. He picked up one of the tapes that were sitting on the bedside table and inserted it. The camera made its dinging noises and came on. He said, "Ready?"

She nodded.

The camera, of course, had autofocus.

"Well, I had this author on the radio, and we weren't getting any calls, so I asked her how she got into the pet-stain cleaning-expertise business. She was British and little and cute, and I'd already realized she was the sort of person who would say anything, so she said, 'Well!' and licked her lips and told me this story." Elena licked her lips. He closed in on them. She went on: "She was out at a bar in Pasadena with some girlfriends, and she got hit on by a guy who was very cute. It turned out he lived in a guesthouse in Arcadia, not far from Santa Anita Race Track. They left the bar and went to his place, and hopped into bed, and made love a couple of times." He backed away from her, then got off the bed and went across the room, until he had all of her in the frame. She stretched a bit, and then pulled up her knees. "When they had stopped wailing in ecstasy the second time—remember, she was saying this on the radio at ten-thirty in the morning—they realized that there was someone else shouting or screaming outside in the dark, and also there was a tremendous squawking, and the guy said, 'Uh, there's something wrong with the chickens.'" She sat up. "So he jumped out of bed, and she did, too, and they got on some clothes and ran outside. Just then, the guy who owned the main house, who bred fighting cocks, ran out of the house with no clothes on and a couple of shotguns under one arm and a big flashlight in the other hand. He sees the two of them, and he hollers that a raccoon has been in the chicken house. This is right in town! So the naked guy runs around the yard, shining the flashlight up in the trees, and, sure enough, there's a raccoon up on one of the the branches, and as soon as the raccoon is discovered, it starts throwing chicken heads at the naked man, and he starts shooting at the raccoon, but of course he can't both hold the flashlight and shoot the gun, not to mention also keep loading the gun, so he gets the girl to hold the flashlight and the guy to load the second gun, while he tries to shoot the raccoon. The raccoon, by the way, escaped once he ran out of chicken heads. So, a week later, the girl got married to this cute guy in Vegas, because, she said on the radio, 'that first night was so utterly brilliant!' And he had seven dogs, 'and, my dear, not all of them were trained!'—not to mention that they brought in dead things and devoured them under the chairs, though never chickens! She got to be an expert at getting organic stains out of clothing, curtains, and carpets. So she wrote the book and got on my show." She put her head back, and he focused on her throat as she said, "Oh, I loved her. Her book had pen-and-ink drawings of dogs peeing and pooping in the house, and dragging in rodent bodies with X's for eyes, with little thought balloons coming out of their heads with comments like 'She said she'd be home at three,' and 'She'll never see it,' and 'She'll think that damned cat did it.' It was so funny."

He turned off the camera and took it down from his eye. He said, "So— do you want to be in pictures?"

"I would put that raccoon in a movie." Then she sighed. "So, anyway, that was the Clinton administration. He wasn't perfect, or even great, but he was undaunted, so you could get on with your life. I didn't feel like we were headed toward the edge of the cliff, so I had more time to relax and enjoy myself, even with all of Simon's misadventures, which of course I took too seriously, too."

"Are you relenting?"

"Well, I did listen to what you said. It doesn't make me relent, but it does make my concerns recede a bit. I'm not so rampantly offended as I was before you made your case, but I'm sure I will be when we get up and read the paper. I could argue, but I guess that I know that I will argue, and so I guess I think I could wait to argue. It's possible to hold my feelings in abeyance for a moment. I mean, this is what I always wonder—do feelings build up like, say, the sewage in a septic tank, until they require some sort of drainage, or do they just come and go, like waves on the beach? If it's the sewage way, then not expressing your feelings is more dangerous, and if it's the wave way, then expressing them is more dangerous. You'd think I would know by now how feelings work, but none of the theories you read about seem to agree. Remember Primal Scream Therapy? That was the septic-tank model. But Parent Effectiveness Training is the waves-on-the-beach model." Now she arranged her pillow again and slid down in the bed. Max lifted the coverlet and got in beside her, only not on his customary side. When he took her in his arms this time, it was his left hand that was free to push the hair out of her face and then press the back of her neck slightly and make a long stroke down her spine all the way to her buttocks, which he fondled, or, rather, he fondled her right buttock, which in the normal course of events was the lower buttock, but now was the upper buttock. In fact, even so minimal a change as this—embracing her mirror image with his unaccustomed left hand—was enlivening and even erotic. She turned her chin toward him, and he began to kiss her, pressing his chest and belly against hers and continuing to stroke her back, waist, and buttocks with long left-handed strokes. She snaked her hand under his arm and around his left buttock and began tickling his testicles from behind, lightly and rhythmically but not idly, rather as if she was systematically enjoying their shape and swell. He had a tiny scar on his scrotum, from his vasectomy, and her three fingertips touched and worried it, but oh so gently. It was exciting. Still they were kissing and kissing. To look at her, you wouldn't think she would have a special talent at kissing. Her lips were not full, but she had a way of meeting his lips firmly, and then a moment later softening and in some way taking his lips into hers. This talent she had, specifically for kissing, did not manifest itself in her appearance at all. You could look at her, and probably many men had looked at her in the course of her adult life, and then you could overlook her, as, by her testimony, most men did. She was small, she was neat, her features were even and pleasing enough. Her clothes were self-effacing. Her hair was well cut, and she did move with grace across the room, but most men, he thought, would look at her and think that they should try for something better. If she were an actress, she would never get cast as the female lead, but always the schoolteacher or the prim older sister, the best friend if she was lucky. Nor would the audience ever know, of course, of the anatomy of her vagina, or her ability, unique in his experience, to squeeze the entire shaft of his cock while he was inside her. All the best parts of Elena were those that were not advertised, that were secret and safely preserved for the one she loved. And the one she loved was him, Max.

Thinking this, he turned her on her back and began kissing her forehead and eyebrows and hairline and earlobes, and he said, "I love you," and she smiled with her eyes partly closed. Her eyelashes were good, too, long and thick, but you only noticed them if you were looking, since they were neutrally colored. This was what Max appreciated about Elena—now that, late in his life, he had enough sense to appreciate her. He had loved three women. Experience showed that most men, given the slightest opportunity, could appreciate Zoe Cunningham. As for Isabel, appreciating her and loving her, for him, and, he feared, for most men, was automatic. Delphine always maintained that the girl had faults, but primarily as a piece of logic—Isabel was human, all humans have faults, therefore Isabel has faults, though what they were in particular often escaped him and Delphine both. Elena, however—well, it seemed as though she was his to appreciate in full, and his alone, and that made her all the more precious to him. After years in Hollywood, he supposed that he was inured to the common, and even general, desire to possess someone because she was desired by everyone else.

Now she was stretched out completely, half smiling, the top of her head pushing into one of the pillows, and the covers on the floor. Sunlight angled across her chest, lighting up her pubic hair with a few morning sparkles. He smoothed his hands around her waist, then lifted her breasts together and kissed each nipple. After that, he took his left hand, his thumb and middle finger, and gently stroked the line of her jaw and the tendons in her neck, which somehow caused her nipples to harden even more, until she giggled suddenly and said, "Oh, I love that." Now he gently parted her knees and spread her legs, then knelt between them, his cock hanging between his legs and her body open before him. While he looked at her, he held her feet in his two hands, feeling the soles with his fingers for a moment, then the toes. As he did this, her back arched and her stomach tightened, as if he were almost tickling her, then he moved his hands and encompassed her heels, giving them little rhythmic simultaneous squeezes. After a few of those, he moved his fingers to her Achilles tendons, and first gently stroked them, and then squeezed the skin between them and her ankle bones until she sighed. Then he ran his hands lightly back up her feet and squeezed her insteps once, before changing his grip and running his hands up the outside of her calves, which were, of course, smooth. He liked that, that she worked in a little oil or cream every day. What was the scent? Lavender or something like that? A fresh, gardeny scent. Thinking of it made it almost there, in the air around him. He stroked her knees, then her inner thighs, which were smooth and silky. He spread her knees wider and wider, just stroking the tender flesh up and out, and there was her cunt, the labia folded together like petals, its shape and color as unique as any face. What a movie that would make, a thousand cunts and a thousand faces, no words, only some music! Her eyes were closed. Her hands were on his thighs, but not doing anything. Some birds were calling outside the window, and then they flew away, and he continued to regard her portal. It was having no effect on his member, but it was having an effect on him, a soothing, pleasing effect. Since he could not do the usual thing with it, looking at it made him feel lighter and more relaxed, as if he had more time than he had ever had, as if he had never been a teenager or a young man, had never wanted anything so much that he overshot the mark and screwed it up. That expression was apt, wasn't it? This thing, these labia, this entry was the goal, but, then, you rarely bothered to look at it, did you?

And, having looked at it, he leaned forward and kissed it. The labia were still dry, but as he kissed them, they swelled slightly—he could feel it with his lips—and she moved against the bed, though she didn't say anything. Anyway, the sound of her hips against the fibers of the bedsheet was arousing enough, the audible signal that his kissing was sending charges through her that were like those he was feeling. He kissed her all over—her thighs, her pubis, the labia again, which he separated gently with his finger, kissing the inner sides and then the outer sides, then the hood over her clitoris, which was beginning to swell. Her hand rested on the top of his head and she cried out. She moved away from him, and he hooked his hands underneath her and anchored her. She cried out again. Now the labia were warm and swollen, not bladelike and nestled, but beginning to open. He felt his cock, but really he didn't have to. His cock didn't care, for whatever reason, except that now when he thought of his cock he did think of Baghdad— how long would it take him to get over that?—and the tanks rolling over the desert even as he was kissing her labia, not the real Iraqi desert but a desert like Death Valley. He kissed her again, and then pulled her labia into his mouth and ran his tongue over them. He could feel her clitoris begin to touch his upper lip. He gripped her tighter, but tried not to press his face too firmly into her. There was a right touch—interested but reserved. You had to keep your wits about you in a way that was not so important when you were fucking. Suddenly she shivered and cried out, and the aroma of her sex mushroomed around him, tangy and rich and erotic. "Ah ah ah ah ooh!" she said, and a moment later pushed his head away. "Oh, it's too much," she said, "I can't stand it," and she laid her fingers over her vagina opening and took a deep breath. He sat up. She often couldn't stand to be touched for the moment or two after she had orgasmed. "Mmmm," she exhaled, then she sighed again. He sighed, too. Then she smiled and opened her eyes. He smiled back at her. Baghdad receded a bit, as if, for example, it were no longer in Death Valley, but somewhere in Nevada or even West Texas. Oh, the camera. What a compact, useful, and attractive object it was. He picked it up again and turned it on. She stretched and eased over, then closed her eyes again.

He put the camera to his eye, took it down again, turned it in his hand. It had a nice weight, enough to seem serious but not inconvenient. He was a little impressed and suddenly curious about what more he could do with it. He said, "Do you think Cassie and Delphine would let me video them having a conversation? I always wonder what they talk about. They've been talking constantly for twenty years. It was Cassie who found this house. She lived next door, and the day she heard it was coming up for sale, she told Delphine, Delphine told Zoe, and Zoe called an agent."

"Ask them," said Elena.

But he didn't think he would. He lifted the camera to his eye again, and focused it just on the curve of her back as it shaped her waist, then swelled into her buttock. When he looked at it with his eyes, it was pleasant but unremarkable. When he looked through the viewfinder, the same curve was bright and erotic, flat in a way, but alluring.

When Max bought his house, it had a two-car garage, fairly standard for the time (at least outside of Bel-Air). There had been a little garden and a boxwood hedge to the right side of the garage. In 1990, he had taken out the hedge, repaved the driveway, and added another bay to the garage, so that it could now hold three cars. These cars were his own Lexus, dark gray, which he had just driven up the hill and parked on the street; the six-year-old Volvo sedan he had gotten new for Isabel when she turned sixteen, white; and Elena's moss-green Subaru wagon, though recently she had ordered a Toyota Prius, dark blue. Personally, he thought the Prius was awfully small, but it was the perfect car for Elena—she could drive it in good conscience almost all the time and know exactly how many miles she was getting every moment of every hour of every day. In fact, the only problem with the Prius was that it didn't seem to offer the Global Positioning option, which would be great for Elena, since knowing just where she was (and what the temperature was, what the time was, and what her average speed was) always relaxed her. "I like to feel well oriented," was what she said. "It's reassuring." He thought the GPS was intriguing himself, except that a friend of his, a lawyer married to another lawyer, had rented a car with that system for a trip to look at autumn color in New England, and his wife and the system had gotten into repeated arguments about the proper route to take. The voice on the GPS would imperturbably announce something like "At Route 128 East, turn south-southwest onto Mars Lane," and the wife would insist that, according to her map, he had to continue to the next right and turn there. There had been no way to turn off either the GPS or the wife. The friend had lamented to Max, "She couldn't help arguing with that voice. She would say, 'Larry, I know it's not a person, but I hate the way she's such a know-it-all!'"

Outside the garage, blocking his ingress, were five cars: Zoe's new Mercedes SL500 convertible, silver with red leather interior, quite a machine, really; Simon's ten-year-old black Jeep that he had bought with money he earned working for a caterer before heading off to college; Cassie's blue Saab; Stoney's vintage dark-red Jaguar, new in 1980, when Jerry and Max had driven it to Las Vegas for a night just to feel it go; and, of course, Charlie's rented lemon-yellow Mustang convertible. Cassie normally didn't park in his driveway, since her own unremodeled two-car garage was right next door, but the trunk was open, meaning they would have been unloading groceries. He looked in the trunk, took out a case of Pellegrino, and then closed it. He set the case of Pellegrino inside the garage door, then resumed his original inspection of the plantings along the driveway. Every year he thought he might redo this area, and in fact, now that the big garden was about as done as it could possibly be without tearing the whole thing up and doing it all over again, it was the perfect time to begin. But the idea of beginning just made him want to go into his bedroom and sit down with a book—it would be a gardening book, maybe a big picture book or maybe something more technical—but it would not be a book that inspired him. It would be a book that soothed him into waiting another day. In the end, this spot was nice enough, and the bougainvillea was thriving, even though it had an outdated air about it. Though the two eucalyptus trees were getting overmature, and they dropped a lot of junk vegetation around the place.

Lately, whenever he contemplated changing the landscaping in this spot, he also wondered, no doubt as a procrastination device, whether he should do some additional remodeling around this end of the house: Still more garage? Bigger and more modern kitchen? Combine a couple of the smaller bedrooms in the lower story? Do something with Isabel's bathroom? Buy a new house altogether, since this one was unconscionably large and rather out of the way—would it be nice to live in another part of L.A., in one of those traditional neighborhoods closer to UCLA, for example? Of course, another deterrent to action was that as soon as you contemplated remodeling you had to wonder if your house wasn't worth more as a teardown. And as soon as he entered upon those sorts of thoughts, the whole thing seemed too much to think about, and so the eucalyptuses stayed put, as did the bougainvillea.

He knew he could move into Elena's little house in the flats, which had only three bedrooms (but Simon was on his way out). If sometimes it seemed to him that his house lay down along the hillside like a big comforter, muffling all things, then her house sat on its corner lot like a tiny power station, transforming big currents into small ones and sending them out into the neighborhood. How many boxes of four-inch, six-inch, and twelve-inch tiles do you order if you want to make sure you have enough for a twelve-by-fourteen-foot bathroom floor? Elena could tell you. What were the eight billing options for electrical power, and what did the surcharges mean? Elena knew. If you were installing a ventilating hood above a gas range, which wire was the ground? Elena knew without even thinking about it.

Should he ask everyone to come outside and rearrange the cars so that he could get into the garage? Or should he give up, leave his car on the street, and go inside, even though he suspected that Charlie and Elena were having it out at last and that everyone else had formed up sides and that dinner would be fraught with tension? In fact, how did it happen that all these people were here in the first place? Every single one of them he liked and enjoyed one on one, even Simon, whom he didn't know very well, even Charlie, whom he knew only too well, and even Paul, whom he considered a fraud. Zoe could come in and out of the house all day. Isabel he was more than happy to see. Delphine he was used to, and Elena it didn't seem he could live without, odd as that was. Stoney and Cassie were Hollywood itself in some way for him—he didn't think he would know where he was in the absence of her stories and his history, and, for now, at least, here was where he loved to be, in this house, looking at the Getty and across the 405 to the delightful but happily remote Elysian Fields of Bel-Air and Beverly Hills. But.

It was all very well, in principle, that his family should foregather at his house as the world, it seemed, was flipping over, taking a new shape, entering a gloomier era. Hadn't he tried to talk Isabel into coming home right after 9/11 and finding a job in L.A.? Or, better even than that, decamping with him and Delphine to his old place on Kauai (even though Zoe had gotten a little hysterical at that, certain as she was that the North Koreans would aim there first)? But Isabel had refused to leave New York, the three of them had not decamped, he had met Elena, and this house had returned to its former identity as his own personal retreat in the Palisades (wasn't that a nice word these days, "Palisades"?), and now here they all were, together, in retreat, carrying in their very selves his entire life all at once. Only Ina, a woman with grandchildren, was missing.

Max did not consider himself an introspective, or retrospective, person. What he liked to do was to make movies, especially contemporary movies. He liked organizing the writer or writers, the actors, and the scenes so that they told a compelling story, and he also liked finding the locations and putting together the costumes and the makeup and the set decorations so that anyone watching the movie even six months later could say to himself or herself, Oh! That picture must have been filmed last March, before the

Starbucks was built on that corner, when kids were still wearing Skechers and dress shirts with ripped sleeves. He was not known for these sorts of movies—only *Southern Pacific*, which he'd made in and around the train station in downtown Los Angeles in 1993, had made any money—but they were his favorites. He was known for being able to organize big productions taking place in distant eras and avoiding the "Ready when you are, C.B." effect. (Cecil B. DeMille is filming thousands of Israelites and thousands of Egyptians on the shores of the Dead Sea. It's a hot day, and it has taken seven hours to set up the shot. There are horses and chariots and elephants and camels and even a few lions for some reason. DeMille is shouting through a megaphone, and the wind is coming up. Action! The scene begins. Ten minutes later, Cut! DeMille turns to the first cameraman, who says, "Gosh, C.B., the camera jammed!" Then he turns to the second cameraman, who says, "Hell, C.B., someone forgot to load the film!" So DeMille puts the megaphone to his lips and shouts to the third camera-man, far in the distance, who is looking intently through his viewfinder. "Jack, Jack!" he shouts. "Jack! Can you hear me?" Jack looks up. He looks happy. He has a big grin on his face. DeMille feels relieved. Then, just flickering on the wind, comes the shout, "Ready when you are, C.B.!") That was a joke Max heard before he ever came to Hollywood—maybe his uncle told him that joke when he was a kid at the dinner table, still planning to fight fires for a living—but he had never forgotten the punch line and often said it—someone said it was time to go, or to start a meeting, or to eat dinner, and he said, "Ready when you are, C.B.," and no one knew what he was talking about. But the joke always reminded him to make sure there was film in the camera, that the camera worked, and that the cameraman had it together. DeMille movies were not his favorites exactly, because they looked like the 1940s and '50s, not 356 B.C. and A.D. 66. Costume movies dated faster than any other kind, probably because of the actresses' hair-styles, but, still, that was what they kept asking him to make. He did not think he was going to make the novel *Taras Bulba* into a movie.

Max knew that around town he was known as "a survivor." It was either the greatest compliment or the smallest compliment. It meant that you had been able to sustain your career, make the best of your talents. That you had been clever and canny and had fit in pretty well. It meant that you had never offended the studios, had a knack for organization, could get along and go along. It was the greatest compliment to people who got up in the morning thinking of the movie business as a field pockmarked with land mines that had to be avoided every day. It was the smallest compliment to people who cared about movies, because it meant that you were not a brilliant or interesting artist, but, rather, a reliable manager. Max cared about movies.

He walked back over to his car, opened the passenger's-side door, and took out the jacket he had laid over the back of the seat. Then he closed the door and pressed the button on his key fob. The doors locked with an expensive heavy click. The Lexus was an okay car, anonymous and Japanese and possessed of sufficient status to not arouse remark. The nicest thing about it was the sound system, which at the touch of a button could mimic the acoustics of any of a number of venues. You could listen to Mozart in a concert hall or a church or your bedroom. You could listen to Neil Young in a club, or in a hundred-thousand-seat stadium. Well, not quite, but the sound system was pleasant to think about, though his hearing was going and he couldn't really tell the difference between the acoustics of the concert hall and the acoustics of the church. Many people in L.A. liked their cars better than they liked their houses. He liked his house better than he liked his car, which showed him to be a certain type of person, not very cool, and probably from the East. So now he opened his front door and walked into the house. It was almost six-thirty.

"Dad!" said Isabel, who was standing in the entryway with a boot in her hand. "What movie did you get?"

"I got the one from the paper this morning, *The Day the Earth Stood Still*."

"I never saw that. I saw *Deep Impact*, though. That was a waste of time. I thought you were going to get the whales one, the *Star Trek* whales one."

He laid his jacket over the back of the bench. "It was out."

She dropped the boot she was holding and put her hand on his shoulder, then kissed him on the cheek. She said, "I'm glad you're home. You should hear the story Cassie's telling. She really does know everyone."

"She does. Who this time?"

"Henry Miller."

"Henry Miller the author?"

"The very one."

He laughed. "I'm impressed. I didn't realize her acquaintanceship extended to literary types."

She put her arm through his, then leaned toward him and whispered, "I don't think they talked about books or art."

Elena and Delphine were cooking dinner. Elena was stuffing vegetable parings down the garbage disposal, flipping the switch off and on as she poked at the onion skins and what looked like celery stalks. When she saw him, she turned off the disposal and came over to give him a kiss. In her book, *Here's How: To Do EVERYTHING Correctly!*, there was a subsection entitled "Meeting and Greeting" in which she pointed out that all mammals have greeting rituals that distinguish between family, friends, and strangers, and therefore an emotionally stable life involves orderly habits of kissing, hugging, patting on the back, making eye contact, and smiling every time your loved ones come and go. He folded her against his chest and it was true, he was reassured.

Cassie was saying, "Well, at that point I was, what, forty? He must have been at least seventy or older. He painted. Our paths crossed. What can I say?"

"Well," said Simon, "what was he like?"

Delphine handed Stoney a knife, a cutting board, and a cucumber. He sat down at the island, and then Isabel sat beside him. He cut a slice off the cucumber, but Isabel stopped him, then took the knife and the cucumber and began to shave off the dark-green skin. Stoney smiled at her.

"He was a talker. I'm not saying he was a big talker, because that would imply that he couldn't back it up, but he did like to talk and talk. And talk dirty, of course. He was quite famous for talking dirty and making dirty talk popular, but mostly he just liked to talk."

"How did you meet him?" said Isabel.

"Oh, I was into art then, too, though I secretly thought all the best work was being done in macramé." She grinned. "He told me a funny story about his life in Paris that I never saw printed in any of his books."

"Oh, do tell," said Zoe.

"Pour me a glass of wine," said Cassie.

She had been idly slicing tomatoes, but now she put down the knife. Stoney reached across the island and took the rest of the tomatoes.

Zoe picked up the bottle, took a glass out of the cabinet, and poured a healthy serving. She gestured to Max, who nodded. It was a Burgundy that he didn't recognize, not from his own cellar, but richly colored and fragrant. Cassie took an appreciative sip and said, "Well, as you can imagine, when Henry Miller first went to Paris, he did not hang out with the best people, but he was good-looking and sexy-looking. He caught the eye of a woman walking down the street—he told me it was 'the exact street that the tumbrels used to go down on their way to the guillotine!' I got the feeling he wouldn't have paid any attention to her if he'd met her in the Louvre. Anyway, this woman invited him to her place one day when her husband was out. Henry thought she might give him something to eat, so he went. It turned out the husband was something like thirty-five years older than the wife. He was a doctor and had all these ideas about sexual energies and sexual hygiene, and so he only slept with his wife every month or so."

Charlie said, "Well, lots of people think—"

"Shhh," said Delphine.

Cassie went on: "Given Henry's predilections and good looks and the wife's frustrations, it took them maybe ten minutes to get to it, and pretty soon, she was mad for him, and she wanted him to come to the house every day. He also liked one of her maids, so Henry was pretty happy. This being France, it was perfectly normal for the wife to pay him for his services, and so she bought him nice clothes. The husband would come and go, but he was a surgeon, so they could always avoid him.

"One day the doctor was in the surgery preparing the anesthetic when he was called to the telephone, and he absentmindedly carried the container of anesthetic with him to the phone—laudanum or something. The phone call was about a huge traffic accident with lots of injuries. The doctor ran out and left the drug by the phone. He told his wife not to expect him for a couple of days, so she called Henry."

Watching Stoney and Isabel slicing tomatoes and cucumbers, Max thought maybe they were flirting a bit.

"Since they had the whole night, they decided to do it in every room. After he tied her up in the bedroom, and she tied him up in the living room, she wanted to do it in the study just to get back at the husband for being so boring; so they went in there, and they were about to do it when the wife decided she needed something to enhance her experience."

"Boots," said Simon, laughing. "A camera!"

"Shh," said Delphine and Elena simultaneously. Max took another sip of his wine. It was pretty clear what was coming. "While she was out, Henry saw the stuff on the desk by the phone. He opened it, took a whiff, and then tried it. He always prided himself on being a transgressor and damn the consequences, and, as he said to me, 'Look at me now. I am unkillable. It didn't matter what I tried. I had to try everything! I knew it even then.' He did pass out on that occasion, though, because the drug was very strong.

"Well, the woman panicked when she came back in the room. Henry was to all appearances dead on the floor. She got the maid. They knew that there would be big trouble for everyone if Henry stayed there. Even though the wife quite liked him, she thought it would be best in the long run to get him out of the house. So the wife and the maid carried him out the back entrance, and down the alley. I guess it was raining, and the wife just couldn't bring herself to leave him there, so they put him inside a big steamer trunk that was sitting under a portico and left the lid slightly ajar on the off chance that he wasn't dead. Of course, he pieced all of this together later.

"Pretty soon, a couple of drunks came walking down the alley, and they saw this trunk. When they went up to it, they happened to bump it so it closed and locked. It was heavy and in this great neighborhood, so they thought it was worth stealing. They picked it up, and they did drop it once as they carried it down the alley, which was good for Henry, because it landed on a rock that broke a hole in the bottom and let in some air, or he might have smothered. He slept on."

Max decided that Stoney and Isabel were definitely flirting. Max took a sip of his wine.

"When the drunks got home, they were tired, so they set the trunk on the back stoop and they went upstairs and passed out. After a while, Henry came to, and he couldn't for the life of him figure out where he was or what had happened to him. He thought he might have been buried alive—it was dark and stuffy and he was very stiff. For a moment he began to panic— though, as he said to me, 'I am not the panicking sort, Cassie. And in those days I was a cool customer—'"

"Did you ever see that famous picture of him in that fedora?" said Stoney. "He was a very cool customer."

"But then," continued Cassie, "he saw the tiny shaft of light coming through the hole that had been knocked in the bottom of the trunk when it was dropped, and he stopped panicking, because really, as he said to me, 'Nothing scared me for long, Cassie, nothing at all, not even German fascism.' He decided to try to turn over, and when he did, the trunk fell off the ledge it was on, and broke in half, and Henry got out. He was still a little groggy, so he looked around for a moment, and then staggered out into the street."

Charlie spoke up. He said, "You've got to be kidding."

Cassie glanced at him, made a small face, and went on. Max gazed at Isabel now, thinking at how serious she was, listening to this story, while Simon was grinning. Then the kid rubbed his hands over his bald head in glee. Max couldn't help smiling, and he couldn't help thinking that Isabel could use some of Simon's lightheartedness even as Simon could use some of Isabel's caution. While he was regarding Isabel and Stoney and Simon and only half listening to Cassie's story, thinking of the kids, not Henry Miller, he had a vivid image of Henry Miller, bald and skull-like, not forty in a fedora but eighty, in pajamas and a robe, staggering in a half-stupor around the streets of Paris, wondering what had happened to him. He said, "Did you ever see the movie they made of *Tropic of Cancer*? It had Rip Torn as Henry."

"I didn't," said Cassie. "But when I knew him, that was a big topic of conversation for him. How it was going to make him a legend. 'Bogart will be nothing to me,' he'd say. They also made *Henry & June*. I never saw that."

"Aren't they all alike?" said Zoe. She shook her head. "Dear one," she said to Paul, who was standing behind her in some funny white pants and a T-shirt, beard, and bare feet, "you're the only man I know who doesn't want to be a Hollywood legend." Paul didn't say anything, but Max wasn't so sure she was right.

"Anyway, here's Henry, all disheveled and groggy, staggering around the Faubourg Saint-Germain with only one shoe on, and the gendarmes pick him up for disorderly conduct, and of course he starts arguing, which gets him in more trouble, because, although he was a very charming man in his way, he did have an authority problem. So they put him in the clink. Everyone he knew from hanging out on the Left Bank is just as happy to leave him in there. But the wife—"

"Named Marcelle, no doubt," offered Zoe, with a glance at Paul, though as far as Max could tell, he made no response.

"—begins to worry. She sends the maid out to look around, and the maid reports that the trunk has been carried off! Now the wife and the maid both go out looking, and they find the broken trunk a few blocks away, lying in another alley, and Henry's left a few things in the trunk—a shoe and a pack of cigarettes—so they know he's still alive. Right about this time, the drunk guys wake up and come down from the *premier étage*—"

"To the *rez-d'-chaussée*," said Isabel.

"—to see what's in the trunk. The woman, who is very well dressed, accuses them of stealing her trunk, and they deny it, but they look guilty, so she knows they did it. But, still, where is Henry?

"The wife and the maid walk up and down the boulevards, and don't see anyone, and the maid discreetly asks at a few cafés if anyone has seen anything of a man with one shoe who maybe looks a little ill."

"*Mal à la tête*," said Isabel.

"Shhh," said Delphine.

"Finally, a waiter at one of the cafés says that the police took him off for vagrancy, and so the maid agrees to dress up nicely and go to the police station. At the police station, they aren't saying anything, but of course this is France, so the maid goes into one of the cells with one of the guards, and the guard is good-looking and the maid is pretty, and she convinces him that Henry is her boyfriend and that it was her fault he drank the opiates, and she can't tell the doctor, and so, in short order, they let Henry out and they give him his shoe and his cigarettes, and they take a cab to the house, and Henry can finally sleep it off in comfort. In the meantime, of course, the doctor comes home, and here is Henry in his bed, but the maid tells him the whole story—how Henry is a great American novelist who has become her lover, and on top of that has come to Paris to learn about life, and he had gotten thirsty and drunk the anesthetic by mistake, and he nearly died, and then the doctor remembers that it was he who left the drug lying about, and so he decides not to press his luck. And after that, Henry kept on with the wife for another few months or so without the husband being any the wiser." Cassie shrugged. "I always thought that was a good story, and I couldn't figure out why Henry didn't include it in one of his books, but he said there was nothing to be learned from it. It didn't fit in with the themes of the rest of his adventures, and anyway, his books were not autobiographical in the strictest sense, but if not, what's the point, I always thought."

"When I was in my English class last year," said Simon, "we acted out a scene from one of his books. My part was to come in one door of the lecture room and shout, 'Ah ah ah!' and then go out again. I had to do that four times."

"What scene?" said Elena from the stove, where she was opening the oven door and bending down to look inside.

"I don't know," said Simon. "I wasn't in the room long enough to make sense of it, but one girl did take her shirt off. I saw that."

"Good heavens," said Elena. She stood up, a fork in her hand.

"Well, she had a bra on. It was fine, Mom."

"'Fine.' I hate that word." But she smiled at Simon, then said, "Anyway, these veggies are done, Delphine."

Max saw Isabel look over at Simon. She did not smile. Stoney was laying the slices of cucumber and tomato on the chopping board in a circle.

"The soup is ready," said Delphine.

"What soup?" said Max.

"Artichoke bisque," said Isabel appreciatively. "My request."

Now the food began to be carried to the table—a big salad, the pot of pale creamy-green soup sprinkled with crispy croutons, a dish of caramelized roasted vegetables (he recognized potatoes, carrots, garlic, onions, fennel, and dark delicious-looking quartered mushrooms), a baguette of whole-wheat bread, another dish of braised asparagus sprinkled with herbs.

Charlie said, "Do you-all ever eat meat?"

"You've got to be kidding," said Isabel.

As they were pulling out their chairs and sitting down at the table, Max was still thinking of Henry Miller. Of course, when he was with Ina, and then right after he came to California, it had been clear to everyone that you couldn't achieve manhood without reading *Tropic of Cancer* and, at least, *Sexus*, if not the whole of *The Rosy Crucifixion*. If you had the time and the money, it was also desirable to go to Greece with a copy of *The Colossus of Maroussi*. If not that, then some time in Big Sur might work almost as well. In college, there were the boys who read *Ulysses* and the boys who read *Tropic of Cancer*, and it was clear that the *Tropic of Cancer* boys were more daring and had more vitality, probably bigger dicks, and a somewhat more brutal sensibility. Max had dutifully done his reading, aspired to be Miller rather than Joyce, and, truth to tell, he couldn't remember a thing about any of the books, but he remembered that feeling he had, that excitement. This book had been banned! All through the life of his father, a person in the U.S. was not allowed to read this book! How precious the book was as a result—so precious you carried it around casually but with the cover carefully obvious, so that everyone in the world—your buddies, your teachers, the mailman, the cop on the corner, your girl— would know that you were friends with *Tropic of Cancer*, on intimate terms, utterly familiar, as unconsciously at ease with *Tropic of Cancer* as you were with your driver's license.

And while he was posing with *Tropic of Cancer*, Max remembered how he would privately ponder Miller's photo. Of course, he saw now, with a professional eye, Miller had a great face, with deep-set eyes and cheekbones and forehead that reminded you subconsciously of a skull, and therefore death, and therefore the fact that he seemed to defy death, and he also had such full, sensuous lips that even if you didn't know the word "sensuous" you could not help responding to those lips as an anomaly for a male, threatening, promising, contradicting the boniness of the rest of the face. And it was even, symmetrical—the other thing about Miller's face was that it was beautifully drawn and got clearer and cleaner as he got older. When you, carrying around your copy of *Tropic of Cancer*, looked at your dad and his friends, with their paunches and droopy jowls, what did they have in comparison with Henry Miller? In fact, they didn't even have Henry Miller! And you did! And so, obviously, you knew something they didn't, since, rather than going to France and engaging with Life in the 1930s, your father and uncles had gone to war, written home faithfully to your mom and your aunts, revenged themselves upon the Germans, taken part in a few celibate, wholesome, and entirely virtuous anti-Nazi adventures, and returned home, still nice American boys, to get married and produce you. Miller had gone to Paris and reveled in what he found, as you would (you thought), whereas your dad and uncles had carried Philadephia with them to Paris and surrounded themselves with it like a force field, not reveling in life but saving lives—a good thing, to be sure, but not an inspiring thing. And, also evidently, it was the only thing your dad was capable of, since now, when you were carrying *Tropic of Cancer* around with you, he was sitting in his La-Z-Boy with his glasses on his forehead and his shoes off, the evening paper in one hand and a beer in the other, tired from a day at his job and ready for dinner at 6 p.m. (pot roast, not boeuf bourguignon). Max smiled. And now he hadn't thought of Henry Miller in fifteen years—who had? He said, "You're reading Henry Miller in school, Simon?"

"We were supposed to."

"We did, too," said Isabel. "In my California-authors class. Let's see, Mark Twain, Helen Hunt Jackson, Jack London, Nathanael West, John Steinbeck, Henry Miller, Wallace Stegner. It was all pretty male. I thought Miller was nicer than the others. More Buddhist. The girls in the class kind of liked him. The boys liked Jack London."

"I heard he was gay," said Stoney.

"Who?" said Zoe.

"Both of them," said Stoney.

"There's nothing wrong with that," said Isabel.

"Henry Miller was not gay," said Cassie decisively, as she helped herself to the roasted vegetables.

"But there would be nothing wrong with it if he were," said Isabel, with a stubborn note in her voice.

It was this very note of mulishness that Max suddenly found provoking. He said, "According to whom?"

Elena looked at him.

"Well, I don't know," said Isabel, a little startled. "According to him, maybe."

"My guess," said Charlie, "is that there would be a lot wrong with it according to him, if he were still alive."

"I just meant that we shouldn't judge him for being gay if he were gay. That's all I meant."

"How about for not being a vegetarian?" said Stoney. "Should we judge him for that?"

Isabel, Max saw, realized that she was being put on the spot, if only playfully. She said, rather stiffly, but aggressively nonetheless, "Meat-eating is a choice, and being gay isn't. You can judge people for choices they make, but not for ways they are that aren't choices."

"Who told you that?" said Charlie.

"I think he was a vegetarian," said Cassie. "From living in Big Sur."

"And following Buddhist precepts," said Paul, gravely.

"It's funny to think of Henry Miller the sex warrior as being a gay Buddhist, don't you think?" said Zoe mildly. "It makes me laugh."

"He lived a long time," said Paul. "You can espouse a lot of ideas in a long life, and most of them will be contradictory."

"That's what I said," said Cassie. "He was a talker. While he was saying any given thing, he tried to sweep you away with it. This whatever it was was the greatest, best thing. Here were all the reasons to convert to whatever belief he was urging upon you. But in the end you couldn't convert to everything he gave you reasons to convert to. Life was too short for that. However, he wasn't gay."

Isabel, Max saw, opened her mouth and then thought better of contributing, and began eating her soup. Simon and Stoney were both looking at her, and the sight of that gave Max a little prickle of alarm, almost a genetic prickle of alarm, a prickle of alarm that as a father he had to feel. After inuring himself to Leo, now he had to watch this? was what the prickle of alarm said, but, really, he had no idea what "this" was. Stoney and Simon were just looking at her, smiling—that was all. Neither of them, necessarily, had designs upon her. He looked at Zoe. Zoe, too, was glancing at Isabel, Stoney, and Simon, but she didn't look alarmed. On the one hand, Max thought, she could be relied upon—she would know through some female sixth sense whether Isabel was in danger—but on the other hand, would she care? Zoe herself, to tell the truth, had been in plenty of danger over the years, the danger, not least, of being a black actress trying to make a career in Hollywood. Maybe her sense of danger was dulled or jaded? Or maybe she didn't realize how her talent and beauty had propelled her through the storm, between the clashing rocks, up the waterfall, over the tops of the trees? Maybe she had inherited, or learned, Delphine's striking way of simply not acknowledging danger of any sort, physical, emotional, social? And so maybe Zoe didn't understand what might happen to a lesser, slightly lesser, or maybe just different, sort of girl, a girl without an evident destiny. A girl that things could happen to, whose life events could deform. Zoe had never seemed like that sort of a girl, even when he first met her singing at a party. No matter what happened to her, she seemed much more like a— what?—a location rather than a person, a phenomenon that was perennial even while things were happening to it. But as Max thought this, he realized he had no idea what he meant.

In fact, having Zoe and Paul around for the last couple of days had been weird for him. He considered his coparenting relationship with Zoe fairly exemplary, and he would not have said that they had lost touch, but there was a little bit of a shock to seeing her in the kitchen first thing in morning, and to hearing her voice waft up from the pool at night, and to seeing her going up and down the stairs as if she still owned the place. What it reminded him of was how much trouble she had been, and how much he had gotten used to not going to that much trouble for a woman. And yet, at the time, he wouldn't have said that. In those days, he thought getting swept up and carried away about a woman was the point. If you didn't think about her all the time, if you didn't, God forbid, sit on the beach and cry at some disappointment or another that she handed you, then how did you know you were in love? The sight of the right woman was supposed to hit you like a blast or a flood, and his first sight of Zoe Cunningham singing, "He's got the urge for going, so I'll have to let him go," and then following that up with "Every breath you take, every move you make . . . I'll be watching you," did exactly that. He had never seen anyone like her. So, of course, in the flush of his own success, he claimed her as his prize, and he was willing to admit, even at the time, that the fact that she was both breathtaking and black gave her still more of that quality of the precious and the rare. Yet, he had never quite thought of Zoe and himself as an interracial couple, because there was nothing so mundane about it as any social or political statements they might be making. She had simply rendered him breathless. He was, what, almost Stoney's age, or thereabouts. Which thought reminded him that when he introduced Zoe to Jerry, Jerry did say, "Represent her, don't marry her. She's a baby." But Max told himself that Jerry's idea of a wife was Dorothy, and he, Max, dismissed that idea as just a version of the Ina idea, which had not worked for him. So he tried the Zoe idea, the blasting, flooding, suffocating idea. And he'd tried it with all the very best intentions, because one look at Delphine indicated that only the best intentions were permitted.

And Zoe had simply overcome him with her energy and her resilience and her everlasting readiness for whatever was next. She was tremendously impulsive, but she didn't see herself that way at all, because acting on impulse never got her in trouble. A perfect example of how Zoe operated was the famous (in the family) story of the BMW. Right after Isabel was born, Max had bought Zoe a compact little white BMW, but she had found the driver's seat uncomfortable, so she had set out one day to take it to the upholsterer and have it customized. As she was driving out to Van Nuys, she passed a Mercedes dealer, and decided to go sit in a Mercedes, to see if that seat was more comfortable. The result was that she traded a brand-new BMW with a thousand miles on it even up for a five-year-old Mercedes with twenty-six thousand miles on it. It was not yet noon when she arrived home in the Mercedes, and Max was still at the studio. As she was taking her groceries out of the back, she noticed that the dealer hadn't cleaned under the passenger's seat very thoroughly, and she pulled out some papers, including some sheets of music, which, of course, she went inside and played through. Songs she had never heard. No name or other identification. So she called the dealer. The previous owner was an elderly man who had died. She mentioned the music. The music! Well, the music turned out to belong to one of the car salesmen, who was moonlighting at the dealership, and by the following Saturday, Zoe had hired him to play backup on her next album, and now he was a sought-after session man and one of Zoe's oldest friends. This sort of thing happpened so frequently with Zoe that she interpreted impulses as her good luck calling out to her. No one was like her. If he'd known himself then as he knew himself now, Max might not have attempted Zoe, but in that case, of course, there would be no Isabel, and he had known for a long time that it was Isabel who was the love of his life, not Zoe.

Even so, or, perhaps, consequently, he didn't often let himself think about what might happen to Isabel. He tried to think of her life as a brick wall she was building that had reached a certain height and was sturdy and aesthetically pleasing so far. She could be relied upon, he usually thought, to keep building in her careful way—to correct this bit here (Leo) and re-inforce that bit there (New York)—in general, even as young as she was, showing herself to be an excellent builder. When he thought of her this way, he did not have to imagine, and then worry about, structural deformi-ties that might topple the building in the future.

So what if Isabel let herself get involved with either Stoney or Simon, one a has-been and one a never-will-be, in Max's private, most brutal, opin-ion? Was it safer for her to pursue her own ambitions and not get involved with anyone at all? To aspire to a nice apartment on the Upper West Side of Manhattan, clean and well furnished and in a secure neighborhoood, no know-it-all lawyer, no overworked doctor, no whining playwright or novel-ist, no shallow business executive, no abusive drug dealer, no alcoholic lyric poet, no tedious do-gooder from a nonprofit organization, no bald-ing, cigar-smoking impresario, no sad-sack high-school teacher, no self-important book publisher? If he had to pick a man for Isabel, would he pick anyone? But did he really want her to wither away with a couple of cats, soli-tary and safe? Of course not. Even so, he was too old now to envision for her what he had envisioned for himself at the same age, all the prospective friends and mates as a gallery of unique and amazing possibilities—Ina! Ruth! Jane! Maureen! Nancy! Mary! If only! if only! a date! or a lunch! or a walk! or a drink! He had been enthusiastic in that teenaged-boy way until Zoe, so focused on the mystery of the girl. If you were lucky enough to get into her space, you would of course inspect all her things, trying to imbibe the wonder of them through your eyes and fingertips. Isabel *should* have that experience. It shouldn't matter if at fifty-eight he saw all the boys as types whose fates were already decided, and not for the best, since all fates, he had discovered, were more or less disappointing or tragic. It was not that the young men were callow or puerile, it was that they were trapped and enclosed by nature, on the one hand, and nurture, on the other, and that what they thought of as surprise twists and happy endings Max knew were just the same old plot points all over again.

He sighed and looked around the table. He was having that moment, even though the soup was good and the roasted vegetables were excellent and the salad was satisfying, that moment when the people around him, the people closest to him, whom he saw every day and cared for and loved, looked benighted and lost and confused and confusing, and of all things the thing he wanted least was to have that thought about Isabel.

Elena's hand fell affectionately on his knee, though, and at her touch he realized that of course he was wrong. He could, for example, privately marvel in a condescending manner at Zoe's choice of Paul here, systematically masticating and experiencing his food, though not, evidently, actually enjoying it. He could see Charlie's life as one doltish, unreflective idiocy after another, many variations on the theme of blowing up an outhouse with a purloined stick of dynamite, or he could take seriously this little burst of pleasure he felt at Elena's touch and presence and leave it at that and try not to worry about the fact that there was no life path he could choose for Isabel that would satisfy him.

"I did an interesting thing today," said Stoney.

"What?" said Isabel.

"Max, do you remember a guy named Howard Greco? Did you ever meet him? He was a friend of Jerry's, but lots older. He's eighty-five now. Anyway, Dorothy wanted me to take something over there that belonged to him, I don't know, it was in a box, I guess Jerry had it for some reason. So I go out there. Howard lives in Pasadena."

"He worked for Disney for years," said Max. "I met him once or twice."

"Remember *Lady and the Tramp*?" said Stoney. "Remember how beautiful certain scenes were? Once, I saw *Lady and the Tramp* as an adult when it came out for a short time on video, and there was that scene where the dogs are chasing the horse-drawn wagon through the rainy streets, under the streetlights, and as the wheels rolled through the mud, the light of the streetlights was reflected in the ruts and puddles. I thought that was the most beautiful scene!"

"Or the opening sequence of *The Lion King*, with the animals galloping over the plain," said Paul.

"I did always think that Disney didn't get enough credit for the detail and beauty of the animation," said Max.

"Well," said Stoney, "Howard Greco was responsible for a lot of that, according to Jerry. Very painstaking and detailed in his work. Studied a lot of art over the years. I mean, he's an expert on not only the Hudson River

School, but also Constable and Turner. Very light-oriented. So I went out there today, and he was glad to see me, and he showed me his hobby."

"What's his hobby?" said Zoe.

"Animated porn," said Stoney.

"I knew you were going to say that," said Cassie.

"He showed me one of his shorts. It was eight minutes long and it took him two years to make, because he doesn't use a computer and does it all in the old-fashioned way, hand-drawing every frame."

"Was it, like, Mickey Mouse does it with Goofy, or, say, a threesome with Minnie?" said Simon.

"No, it was autobiographical," said Stoney. "It was called *Delilah*, and it opened with a shot of Howard's own front entry in his house in Pasadena. You see his hand go to the doorknob, and the door opens, and there's a woman standing there in a pink dress. She looks vaguely like a Disney girl, like Sleeping Beauty or someone like that, but she's clearly forty and has had a hard life, except that she has great skin, kind of luminous. As she turns and says, 'You Howard? You called me?,' it's just like with those puddles in *Lady and the Tramp*—her skin reflects the way the sunlight is falling across the veranda. And then, behind her, he drew in all the flowers in the garden. Pink and white roses and some pampas grass and a lemon tree with lemons hanging on it, and just for a moment you look at these lemons and you see the shadows of the leaves across the fruit. So she comes into the entryway, and her shadow falls across the Saltillo tiles, and she says, 'Put my bag here, that okay?,' and she puts her bag on a table in front of a mirror, and in the mirror you see her back and her ass reflected behind the bag, and behind her, Howard, in his shorts and no shirt, and he really does look about eighty-five. His hair is standing on end, and he's smiling. All around him is the inside of his house, the same house we were in, except drawn in this photo-realist style and suffused with bright colors. I mean, I don't know how it would look on a TV or a small screen, but he'd built himself a screening room just for screening his homemade porn collection, so that he could get the right color values.

"She says, 'You wanna go to the bedroom, right?,' and he says, 'Would you like a drink?,' and she says, 'Not this early in the day, but thanks,' and as they walk toward the bedroom, she keeps looking around at the furniture and the paintings and the mirrors. He even draws her gaze pausing first on the mirror, where she sees herself and makes a little face, and then on a painting, where she makes another face. He draws the painting—it's in a completely different style from the rest of the animation, it's a picture of a waterfall and some mountains in South America, and he animates it so that as they pass it the camera seems to cross it. Can you imagine the work involved in that? I kept sort of marveling, and Howard would say, 'So I'm an old man, what else is there for me to do?'

"He follows her to the bedroom. She starts taking off her clothes, and the animation makes the clothes look filmy and vaporous as she unbuttons them and gets out of them. She is doing a little dance for him. But the best thing about this sequence is his room, which clearly hasn't been redecorated since the 1960s, and has all these curved, shiny surfaces, but nicked and dusty, and it's all in the animation, along with her."

"That junk is coming back into fashion," said Cassie, "I can't believe it myself."

"Well, judging by his film, his is vintage. Anyway, as she takes off her clothes, she moves around the room, and the shadows change. When she turns on a light, the light falls across her body. When he opens a window, the curtain lifts up, and you see the shadow of that. So pretty soon she's naked, and he asks her to go out into the enclosed garden, which she does, and in the midst of her little dance, she begins to smell the flowers, and he shows you that, and also close-ups of the flowers. They're as accurate as botanical drawings. They go back into the bedroom, and she lies down on the bed with her legs spread, offering her breasts in the classic *Playboy* manner, and doing several postures for him, all of which he has carefully drawn. From time to time you catch a glimpse of him in the mirror, and he has stripped down, too. I think the best parts, though, were the animation close-ups of her skin."

"I can't believe this was erotic," said Zoe.

"It wasn't," said Stoney. "I mean, maybe it is to Howard, but the process was so labor-intensive, for one thing, that that would seem to me to diminish the erotic potential of the project even for him. And I thought I would watch him during the screening to see if he was watching it like you would porn, but I was so fascinated by what was happening on the screen that I forgot to look at him."

"So—did they do it?" said Simon.

"Yeah, but it stays completely in Howard's point of view. The sequence of them doing it is all what he sees—the side of her face, the pattern on the pillowcase, the window. At one point, he looks down at her stomach and breasts. They turn over, and he's looking at the ceiling. There isn't any kissing. After a minute, she says, 'So—you done?,' and you see him in the mirror, getting off her, and then he disappears from the mirror and you see part of her body, her leg bending and her buttock. Which looks, even in the mirror, not quite as firm as it once was. Then the bedsprings creak and she sits up, and you see her in the mirror, but she isn't looking at herself. I mean, I have to say that I never saw anything like this. While I was watching it, I thought it was the greatest film I've ever seen. How many frames is eight minutes of animation? And he drew every single one as if it were a painting."

It was here that Max realized that Stoney was telling this story for his benefit, to warn him away from *My Lovemaking with Elena*. Max found this realization amusing, because, of course, there was no similarity between Howard Greco's animated porn and his own live-action depiction of what was to be, essentially, an actual connection, on many levels, between two mature adults. "I'm sure," said Max, "he had some sort of technique for reproducing at least parts of each frame."

"Well, he must have," said Stoney.

"Not much of a story," said Delphine. "How did it end?"

"Well, he shows his hands counting out some money, a hundred bucks, I think, with an extra ten for gas money, and then he offers her a Calistoga water, and she takes the lime flavor, and then he shows her to the door and watches her get into her car, which is a '99 Civic, and then he shuts the door and rolls the credits."

"It doesn't sound very funny," said Simon.

"It wasn't funny at all," said Stoney. "Or erotic. Or even sad. But it was beautiful and interesting. It was like entering the mind of another person, and seeing how he sees his own stuff and his own life. It was eerie. I didn't know what to say afterward. Especially when he offered me a lime Calistoga water."

Everyone laughed.

"Sounds lonely to me," said Elena.

"I guess old age is lonely, you know," said Charlie.

"But it wasn't really lonely," said Stoney, "because it was so painstaking. You realized as you were watching it that if he didn't have all that solitude he wouldn't have been able to make this thing, and the time with Delilah would have just vanished into the past as meaningless."

"It sounds pretty meaningless to me," said Cassie. "I'm not saying that's bad. Every landscape in my gallery is meaningless, when you come to think of it, but where's the proportion? Two years on a sordid little story of the time a certain prostitute came to your house in Pasadena?"

Max laughed.

Stoney said, "But it was so good! I mean, I was so enthusiastic after I watched it that I was ready to get him some kind of film-festival showing, like at Sundance or something. I still might. He has four of them. He said, 'Ah, ya know, Stoney, this one's the photo-realist one. But there's a Pop Art one, too. That's called *Sophie*. I think that's the funniest one. Then I had this girl come, and her name was LaDonna, and she was a black girl, and I thought I should do her like she was out of a da Vinci painting. She had that look.'" Stoney shook his head. "Wouldn't you love to have them?"

"What would you do with them?" said Simon.

Max said, "Run them on a continuous loop, the way they do video installations in museums."

"But then you'd get used to them," said Zoe. "I hate that, when you hear some song you recorded ten years ago over and over again. I think all recordings should self-destruct after five hundred playings."

"What I would do," said Paul, "is watch each one one time, but in a concentrated way, you know, and then give them to someone else."

"What if he dies," said Cassie, "and some relative comes in and throws them out? Without even looking at them? I think you should do something, Stoney." She rolled her eyes, then went on, "I know what I said before, but, actually, the meaning of art is in the technique, after all. Why would these be any more meaningless in the larger scheme of things than *Lady and the Tramp*?"

"Or what if some relative looks at them," said Isabel, "and decides they're nasty and throws them out because of that?"

While this discussion bubbled around the table, Max was thinking of himself that morning, of how Elena's body looked through the digital viewfinder of the video camera. He did feel a surge of reflexive annoyance and, yes, proprietary jealousy at Howard Greco's animated "sex cam" focusing on the pattern of the pillowcase, and then turning over and looking at the ceiling. But, still, only eight minutes! Two years' work and only eight minutes! Whereas his own idea had few commmercial possibilities, Howard Greco's had none at all. Though the film-festival idea was a good one. These days, you could go around to film festivals for most of the year and find yourself quite a big audience. The thought gave him a jolt, and then he remembered what that jolt was. It was anticipation, something he had avoided feeling for a fairly long time now, at least since the bad year 2000, and maybe for longer than that. Under the table, he took Elena's hand between the two of his. The bad year 2000 had opened with his dog, Marco the Barker, half Doberman and half German shepherd, and very lazy (Marco always slept late, and only wandered out of Max's bedroom when he heard people opening the refrigerator door; he then sat down and seemed to survey the shelves at his leisure until the person tossed him something, which he caught and carried to his bed to eat in peace), picking up poison somewhere in the hills and expiring after two weeks of intensive care. His throat swelled up and clenched shut, and he could not be saved. He was seven. Within a few weeks after that, Max himself had gone to have a checkup and ended up in the cardiac unit, having an angioplasty, which was supposed to be an easy-on, easy-off procedure. At one point during the, for lack of a better word, "operation," he had felt a transient pain in his chest, and remarked on it. The surgeon had said, "That's your heart attack. If you ever feel that again, head straight for the emergency room." But six weeks later, he still felt punk, and not as happy as Stoney had thought he should feel at being relieved of that mountain-climbing production. And then, of course, Jerry was diagnosed with his brain tumor ("I don't know what it is, Max, but every time I get on the 405 going north, I feel like I'm spinning"). The bad year 2000 had literally changed his life, hadn't it? But only now, as he felt that single jolt of anticipation with regard to work rather than sex, did he realize how much it had changed his life.

Of course, his movie, by contrast to Howard's, was about a relationship. Who am I? Who is Elena? How do we connect? Howard's idea, of course, was about an exchange. And because it was animated, it was entirely subjective. The camera Max would use would offer the possibility of objectivity, because the camera always sees more than the director intends for it to see, so much more that even when the director and the film editor are staring at the footage, scrutinizing it for continuity problems, they can never catch them all. *My Lovemaking with Elena* would appeal, in part, for precisely the opposite reasons that *Delilah* appealed to Stoney—lack of control in contrast to control. Zoe was right—not much of a story to that *Delilah* thing, nowhere to go except, in eight minutes, to the handing out of greenbacks. But not even Max knew where *My Lovemaking with Elena* would go. Not even Max, the director, knew whether Max, the character, would be able to get it up! Max laughed.

"What?" said Isabel.

"I would like to see that little film, that's all. Or the Pop Art one. Very funny. You should get him a Sundance gig, Stoney. He would be the toast of the festival. And they could seat him on a panel and interview him about the old days at Disney, too. That would be interesting."

"More soup, anyone?" said Elena.

The tureen, Max saw, was almost empty, as was the dish of roast vegetables. A nice dinner, not what he had foreseen as he was standing outside the garage looking at the cars. He said, "We've got *The Day the Earth Stood Still*. Showing in, what, a half an hour? How about that?"

"That's old," said Charlie.

"Nineteen fifty-one," said Max.

"Global warming for the World War II generation," mused Charlie, shaking his head and smiling as he looked around the table. "Someday, you know, they're going to look back at us and say . . ." He was gazing confidentially, even conspiratorially, around the table.

It was amazing to Max how slow on the uptake Charlie was. Surely he had seen the Subaru in the garage. Surely he remembered two nights ago, when Elena was talking about the Prius she had ordered. Surely he had some idea that Isabel had been working for an environmental nonprofit. Isabel, in fact, was now staring at her plate. Elena was staring at Charlie. Her hand went up, and with her index finger she pushed her hair behind her ear.

Zoe said, "Someone sent me a global-warming script a couple of months ago. They've got financing for an all-star production already. A diversified band of patriotic Americans is supposed to outrun tidal waves inundating the Atlantic Seaboard and save their children of many races who are on a school trip to Washington, D.C. As I recall, I was up for the part of the black-studies professor at Columbia. I am a little snippy, and so I am killed when all the tidal waves suddenly turn to ice as the temperature plummets from ninety above zero to ninety below in the course of about an hour, but my child survives and is adopted by my cousin, who is a stay-at-home mom married to a displaced Bengali technician in Quebec City, which I guess is built on a high promontory of some sort, and so is turned into an island. I couldn't make heads or tails of the script."

"It could happen," said Simon.

Everyone laughed, and, next to Max, Elena took a deep breath.

"Good meal," said Max.

"Excellent," said Paul.

"Anyone want some Newman-O's?" said Simon. "They're Oreos by Paul Newman. They had them at Whole Foods when I was there today."

Elena pushed back her chair and stood up with the soup tureen. She said, "What was it you were going to say about global warming, Charlie?"

"Oh, I can't remember," said Charlie.

"Good idea," said Simon.

DAY FIVE · Friday, March 28, 2003

Stoney and Isabel were lying on chaises longues at the farthest edge of the pool, under the shadow of the hillside, in the dark. Isabel suspected that it was way after midnight already. Even the pool light was out, and the water was black and invisible. If she had been making the movie of this conversation, Isabel thought, she would have stippled in some stars in the calm liquid surface of the pool and had them dimly reflect the stars in the sky. She said, "Stoney, do you think that when you are in a hole the way we are here you can see more stars, or is that just an illusion?"

"I have no idea."

It was cool, and she was lying on a blanket, covered with towels. Their edges and corners fluttered just a little bit. It had been an odd day—hot and windy. Now she could feel the wind eddy about; the ridgeline to the west protected them from direct exposure. Even so, she had more of a sense than usual of something dangerous out and about—only the wind, but still—so she had a towel wrapped around her head. It was warm and comforting to be so cocooned.

Stoney said, "I met with those Russians this morning. They told a story. I've been thinking about it all day."

"What was it?"

"Well, they're staying at the Beverly Wilshire, so we were sitting in the restaurant there. Did I tell you before that their names are Mike, Al, and Sergei? Mike is the boss. When he got up to go buy some cigars, Al leaned across the table to Sergei and said, 'You know how Mike got married?' Sergei shakes his head, and Al glances at me, and he says, 'You know Mike is from Kazan, which is almost not Russia. He lives in Moscow now, but he went back to his home district when he was ready to get married, and fell for this girl Adana, but she was determined to finish at the university and have a career, so she turned him down and ran off and hid from him. He tried to set up a deal with her parents, but she still wouldn't have it.

"'One day, Mike is out wandering in the countryside, trying to figure out what to do about Adana—should he forget her, should he try something else, why is she such a cold bitch—and he hears the sound of dogs barking and howling, and he turns around and here comes a naked girl. The dogs are big wolfhound types, and they're chasing her. Behind them is a man on a horse with a gun. The dogs run her down and grab her, and the guy jumps off his horse and goes after her with his gun. Mike has a gun, too, like he always does, so he steps in among the dogs and shoots one and grabs the girl. She's got blood pouring from her belly and her breasts. So Mike holds him off, but thinking that the guy looks familiar, and then the guy says, "Mike! It's not your business!," but Mike won't let him near her. She's crying, one of the dogs is dead, Mike figures it's going to be a shoot-out, which isn't so uncommon in Kazan, but the guy says that he is Mike's uncle Nikolai and that this is Masha, that he is in love with. Now, Mike's uncle is dead, and he figures the guy is lying, so he threatens to shoot the other dog. The uncle says that, yes, he did die, but, unbeknownst to the family, he died by his own hand, out of love for the girl. And after he died, the girl Masha laughed and gloated at his funeral, but then Masha died of a mysterious illness.'"

Stoney sat up, leaned toward her, and whispered, "After her death, the two of them were sent to hell and were cursed, and their curse is this—once a week, just at sunset on Friday, he chases her with the dogs right to this spot, the dogs catch her, and he shoots her."

Isabel said, "Stoney, do you believe everything you hear?"

"And suddenly, as the uncle finishes telling the story, the dead dog leaps up and sinks his teeth into the girl's ass, and she screams. Mike steps back in surprise, the uncle shoots the girl in the head, pulls out a knife, slits her open, pulls out her heart, which is small and hard, and throws it to the dogs, who gobble it down. Then all of them—dogs, horse, uncle, and girl— vanish."

He sat back, out of her gaze, and Isabel looked up at the stars again. She said, "This is a ghost story, right?"

"They said it really happened."

"Ugh," said Isabel. It was true, she thought, that honoring the integrity of other people's cultures was always harder than you thought it was going to be.

"The next week, according to Al, Mike talks Adana and her family into going with him and his family out to this spot. Pretty soon, they're ensconced under some trees, and here comes the horse, the uncle, the girl, and the dogs. She is naked and running and screaming, and as alive and palpable as you or me, and the horse is churning up dust, and the dogs are barking and baying. Right in front of the spectators, they leap on her and bring her down and begin tearing her apart. Nikolai jumps off his horse and wades into the melee, and does the same thing as the week before, shoots her in the head so that her brains spatter all over a nearby tree, and then he rips her open, tears out her little heart, throws it to the dogs, and they all disappear into thin air. Adana's father runs over to the tree and sees that the bark is clean. No blood. No hoofprints. No sign of a bullet. Well, the onlookers are really shook by this—it's 1992, after all, and all the old folks went to Soviet-era schools, and nothing about this sort of thing was ever covered in the curriculum. They do believe in curses, though, so the mother and the father take the daughter aside, and they have a long family conference right there, and Mike starts looking a little better to her. Everyone decides, in the end, that the marriage could be good or bad, but a curse is worse, and so they have a wedding, and Mike brings Adana back to Moscow, and now she works for ITAR-TASS, and they have a couple of kids."

"They told you this with a straight face?"

Stoney nodded.

"This girl is my age?"

"Thirty, actually."

Isabel shivered, looked up at the stars, and listened for the low whoosh of cars on the unseen 405. "They told you this sitting in the restaurant at the Beverly Wilshire?"

"Yeah."

"Did Masha feel the pain?"

"I gather that's what a curse is. You have to feel the pain."

"I guess." Now Isabel could feel the darkness form a second layer of her cocoon. It gathered around her, pressing quietly against her. It was L.A. darkness, reassuring after all, darkness that wafted around places like the Beverly Wilshire and Rodeo Drive and Sunset. Up Beverly Glen to Mulholland, along the PCH, feathered by the whiteness of the breaking surf. Darkness in L.A. wasn't all that dark, in Isabel's experience, and was anyway always broken up and scattered by light. It sounded like darkness in Russia was deeper and more dangerous. Adana and Masha. She shivered. He said, "The way the family interpreted the curse was that the girl returned evil for good—when the guy gave her his love, she not only spurned him, she mocked him."

"So she had no right to her own thoughts and feelings, basically. For her to have her own thoughts and feelings is a danger to the entire town, is that what they were saying?"

"Basically, yeah."

"So what does this have to do with my father?"

Stoney said, "Nothing, except that Mike's the boss and the one with the money. He came back without any cigars and said he didn't like what they had, but I kept wondering if they had set me up with this story to communicate something."

"That sounds very *Godfather*-ish."

"I admit that, but you know what they say about movie critics."

"What?"

"After they've seen three movies a day for a year, they hardly dare to go down the basement steps anymore."

Isabel snuggled down into her cocoon and pulled her turban over her eyes so that she couldn't see anything, but she knew Stoney was looking at her, so she smiled. She heard him go on.

"I mean, it's not like threats and intimidation are unheard of in Hollywood. Bugsy Siegel, Frank Sinatra, William Randolph Hearst, George Raft, and all that. You know who Anthony Pellicano is, right? I mean, it's still happening. If Jerry were alive, he would know how to talk to them."

"What did you say?"

"I said I'd schedule a meeting. Then I came out onto Rodeo Drive, and it was so windy that the trees were cracking. It was kind of apocalyptic."

"Your dad was a tough guy, wasn't he?" Jerry had been a fixture in Isabel's life, but she had never experienced him at all the way Stoney had, no doubt because she was a girl—Jerry treated all females the same way: he complimented their clothes and hair, brought presents, asked them jovially if they had any boyfriends, and then more or less ignored them.

"Well, compared to whom? Compared to De Niro, in *The Godfather, Part II*? Did he do what he had to do when he was a kid? Compared to Pacino in *The Godfather, Part III*? Did he allow the deaths of longtime friends and associates because they had betrayed the code or gotten in the way? I sincerely doubt it. But he was fearless in some ways. He was so intent on the goal that his mind didn't take in threats the way mine does. A threat, for Jerry, was just another factor to be considered while he was deciding his strategy. In the end, people always did what Jerry wanted them to do. Even when he had that brain tumor, he was still like the Terminator. You just couldn't stop him, he was tough like that."

Isabel pushed up her towel and then turned her head and looked at Stoney. Her eyes were so adjusted to the dark now that she could see him perfectly. To all appearances, she thought, he was just talking. With Stoney, just talking inevitably seemed to circle around to Jerry. All the same, she didn't like the idea of her father being vulnerable to these Russian guys, whoever they were, with only Stoney as protection. She said, hopefully, "I guess my dad is a pretty tough negotiator."

"Max isn't a negotiator at all, that's his problem."

"What do you mean?"

"Well, if he really wants to do something, then he will give up anything in order to do it. I mean, when he made *Southern Pacific*—remember that one?"

"With Dennis Quaid. I loved that one."

"Yeah, you and one movie reviewer, I think. Well, Max loved that script, and he wanted to work with that cinematographer, and he had Dennis all fired up, and Jerry had to practically lock him in the closet to keep him from giving everything away. He would have done it for PBS, he would have spent his own money to do it. He thought that his enthusiasm meant something good, but all it meant to the studio was that they could roll right over him. But if they get it cheap, then the project doesn't mean anything to them, that's the way their minds work, and Max should have known that. If you don't play hard to get in this town, then nothing about your project has any value. But if Max is not interested in a project, he just says no, and then he gets pissed when they keep after him."

"'No means no,'" said Isabel. "I can't tell you how many times I heard that over the years."

"Well, in this business, 'No' means 'Call me later and come up with more money.' He should know that by now. Your mom is a great negotiator. She's legendary."

"You're kidding."

"Nope. You know that way she has of reacting to what you say with something that's just a little out of left field? And then you laugh, but you aren't sure she was really making a joke?"

"Yes. It's because she isn't really listening."

"Well, I don't know why it is, but it's always disarming, because all the guys in the room are thinking about one thing, and she isn't thinking about that thing. And then she seems truly not to care about any project more than any other. They think they have to make her care, and of course they think the way to do that is money and perks and points and stuff. But she doesn't really seem to care about that, either, so they offer more. Maybe she's a great actress in those negotiations, but in fact I think she really doesn't care."

"I don't know what she does care about," said Isabel, and saying it felt like a confession. "I don't know who she cares about." There were several things she could add, Isabel thought, but she resisted doing so.

"Are we going to talk about her failures as a mother?"

"We could, but I know what you think."

"And I know what you think. How about you tell me what I think and I'll tell you what you think, and we'll see if we still agree with ourselves."

Isabel sniffed, knowing he was making fun of her, but, yes, she did deserve to be made fun of, at least a little. So she said, "You think she's afraid of me, and just because whenever she calls me or talks to me I act snotty, she gets more afraid of me, and less interested—"

"Less likely."

"Less likely to make an effort."

Stoney said, "You think that she's a selfish narcissist who should take more of an interest in others who are not unsuitable men. That there has actually only been one suitable man, that would be Max, and in the end pleasing him meant fulfilling her obligations to you and Delphine, and that was the deal-killer for her."

Isabel looked at the stars again for a moment, then wiggled around in her cocoon, which suddenly felt too tight. She said, "I guess we understand each other."

"If you say so."

"Our analysis doesn't go very deep."

"I don't think it does, no."

"Well, you know what Delphine told me once?"

"I don't know."

"Oh, I was a senior in high school, I guess, and I was sitting on my bed ranting on about the Legendary Zoe Cunningham, and Delphine was picking up my dirty clothes, and, yes, I am fully aware of what a selfish baby I was being, and anyway she said, 'Your mom is who she is because I bred her.'"

"What does that mean?"

"That's what I said, and so Delphine sat down on the edge of the bed, and she told me about her life. I've never told anyone this story, not even those girls at college who were dying for a comeuppance."

"Okay."

"You know she was born in Jamaica, right?"

"Yes."

"Well, she's never been back there. She said, 'Honey, Jamaica was just one piece of bad luck after another for me, and I turned my back on that place, and I turned my back on that bad luck.' I guess when she was three there was a tremendous flood in Kingston, and it destroyed their house, and her older brother, who was five or so, and her mother and the baby who was just born were all killed. Only Delphine and her father survived, and he lost everything, so that he had to go to work on a sugar plantation out in the country, repairing engines and cars and things like that. She never saw him again for more than a visit. She stayed in Kingston with her mother's cousin, and I guess she was nice enough, but of course—"

"Of course Delphine had lost her entire family."

"Well, yeah, isn't that sad?" They were silent for a few moments, and Isabel suspected that Stoney was thinking of his own mother's death, and, yes, here she was whining about Zoe to someone who had much more to whine about on that score than she did, but who never whined and, indeed, never even mentioned his mother. And so she was embarrassed, but she saw that it would be more awkward and therefore more embarrassing to stop telling her story, so she shifted it a little. "Anyway, she was sent to school. It was an English-type school, where they had to wear uniforms and speak only when spoken to, and basically it was right out of *Jane Eyre*, but for Jamaicans. She was being trained to do something useful, if only to be a high-class servant. 'Here is what I remember about that school, honey, I remember that I was not pretty and that I would never be pretty. I was too tall and too skinny and I had big teeth and my uniform never fit about the waist. In an English school, they always tell you what's wrong with you, and, between you and me, that's not all bad, because then you can make a plan, and you know how the world works, and for Jamaican girls, the world works in one way for pretty girls and another way for plain girls, and that's just the way it is. I don't say they were mean to me. I say they had a job, to make me know myself, and that's what they did.' I mean, really, Stoney, this story is so sad that if I thought about it I wouldn't know how to handle it, but I don't think about it much. I look at her, and she seems healthy and self-reliant, and so I just try to think of it as the adventures of Delphine.

"Anyway, when she got out of school, right after the war, she went to work for a rich woman, as her assistant, and she did that for maybe two years, and then she fell in love with the chauffeur, and they did all the right things—they waited to get married until they had some money, and when they did get married, she was something like twenty-three or twenty-four, and her employer was very fond of her, and they got their own little house on the property, and right away they had a baby girl, and she said, 'I looked at her, and I saw she looked just like me, honey, and my heart sank inside me.' Then the employer got polio, and that whole family took all their money and went back to England, and the new owners of the place fired everyone for political agitation, because Delphine's husband was a leftist.

There wasn't any work, so the husband went off to England looking for a job in the mid-fifties, and Delphine waited to hear from him, because either he was going to come back or she was going to join him, but they didn't hear from him, and then the baby, who was about four by that time, died in a hurricane when the wall of the house they were sheltering in fell on her while she was sleeping. And then a man came from England and told her that her husband had been killed by hooligans on the street almost as soon as he arrived in London. So, she said to me, 'That was enough Jamaica for me. No more floods, no more hurricanes, no more English people. I went around to everyone I knew and asked for some money, and because everyone felt sorry for me, they all gave me a little, and so I got to Miami Beach, where I worked as a maid in the fanciest hotel there,' which I guess was called the Eden something—"

"Eden Roc," said Stoney. "It was very famous." His voice was subdued, and now Isabel was really sorry she had embarked on this story, because, as she told it, it seemed impossibly sad and also so huge that in a way it was happening all over again, perhaps because it was not just a story, but was her own grandmother's experience that could never be expunged. It was so odd that when she had started telling Stoney this, not five minutes before, she had only felt what she had to call the entertainment value, or the shock value, of what she was about to say, but now that she was saying it, she felt the sadness of the child's death, the horror of the husband's death, and also fear for herself, as if these experiences were closing in on her, not because they were Delphine's experiences, but because they were random human experiences that could strike at any time. She sighed and went on. "Anyway, here's what she did in Miami—she seduced a good-looking musician who was playing there. I don't think anyone famous, though she wouldn't tell me who. She said she seduced him during the 1960 presidential campaign, and that he was Irish. She picked him because he was the best-looking man she ever saw, and also flirtatious and also a drinker, which gave her an advantage with him. I was so freaked out when she told me this. I mean, Mom said that her dad died in a plane crash when she was a baby, so I don't know if Delphine's ever told her about this guy. And then she looked at me and said, 'And, honey, when your mom was born, I knew I'd done my job, because she was the prettiest baby I ever saw, from that time to this, including you, and from day one her life was not like mine. Every time she smiled, she made herself a little piece of luck, and since she was a happy baby, she smiled all the time.'"

"You're sure all this is true, right?"

"Well, of course it's true. Why would she lie to me?"

"I'm not saying she lied."

"So you're saying she's crazy?"

"No, of course not. I don't know what I'm saying. I'm saying that I don't know what to say or how to react. She's a very mysterious woman."

"I think so, too. I think the way she looks at it is that she had thirty or so years of bad luck, left Jamaica, changed her name, and then had forty-three years of pretty good luck."

"I've always wondered what she does all day."

"When I was living at home, she took care of me, and, believe me, my pear salad always looked like a face, and my macaroni and cheese was made with aged Cheddar and whole-wheat macaroni. But she reads. She reads lots of books and goes with Cassie every day to the gym. I guess they do aerobics and the stair-climber. She makes lace. That's her needlework hobby. She never watches TV. But I will say that, whenever I would mention a book I was supposed to be reading in high school or college, she would have already read it."

"So, basically, she's a closet intellectual."

"I guess. She read to me for years. But she would never help me with my homework."

"So how did she and Zoe get to Hollywood?"

"How do you think? I mean, it was true. Everyone who saw my mom was struck by her. Some guy in Bruce Springsteen's backup band saw her singing when she was seventeen in a club somewhere in Miami and asked her if she would join their gig, which she did for the few days they were in Miami, and then, three or four months later, when they were finished with their tour and ready to go into the recording studio, someone called her and invited her up to New York to do a few sessions, so, she always says — haven't you heard her? — 'I finished the paper I was writing about *Ethan Frome* and got on the plane to New York.' Delphine went with her, of course, and then her first manager saw her and took her on and got her a party gig in L.A. By that time she was eighteen, and then, while she was doing that gig, my dad saw her and the rest was history. Delphine never let her out of her sight until my dad came along. But I don't know. One time, before she told me this story, I asked her to tell me about some of the fun things they did when my mom was a kid, and she said they didn't have time for fun."

"I think that, as far as Delphine is concerned, you are the fun."

Isabel sighed, suddenly remorseful. She said, "You know, I can't believe I told you that. It was a secret, for one thing, and I was just trying to impress you in some way, for another. But now that I've told it, I can't stand that it happened. Now it seems like it really did happen."

"She said it happened."

"When it was just her telling me, somehow it hadn't happened as much as it has now that I've told you."

"But think of all the things that happen and all the things that people think about and learn, and they get kept as secrets, and then they disappear. What if Delphine's story just disappeared? What if she hadn't told you, and you hadn't told me? It doesn't seem like she's told your mom, and if she's told Cassie, well, it's just another item in Cassie's catalogue of amazing stories. What if every event just disappeared without a trace? I mean, at the very least, there is something important that you wouldn't know about yourself and about Zoe, and now you know it."

Isabel actually rather liked this idea, but she said, "And now you know it. That's the problem."

"I'm not going to tell anyone."

"We do have a history of keeping secrets, don't we?"

"We do." He coughed, then said, "Say, speaking of secrets, you know what Cassie said to me when we were watching the movie?"

"What?"

"Toward the end of the movie, when there's panic in the streets, she turned to me apropos of nothing and everything, of course, the way she does, and said, 'You know when they were looking for Cheney on the afternoon of 9/11?,' and I said, 'He was in a bunker outside of Washington, running the country.' And she said, in that perky tone she has, 'No, he wasn't. He was at a racetrack somewhere, but my friend who saw him and called me on her cell phone was whispering, and so I didn't get what racetrack it was.' So I said, 'What was he doing at a racetrack?,' and she said, 'He was meeting with the Sheikh of Dubai.' Her friend was up in the stands, looking around, and that's what she saw. Here came a big black limo, and before the officials moved her off, it stopped, and out stepped Dick Cheney. And then she went back to watching the movie, and I forgot about it until now."

Isabel said, "Don't tell Elena." She saw Stoney smile in the darkness. Then she said, "These guys who want my dad to make this movie sound really iffy."

"They are iffy. But Ben Avram has been pushing me. And anyway, I'm with Jerry on this. Your dad needs a push. He's sinking into obscurity. And he knows it. He hadn't made a movie in a year when he started doing the pre-production for that mountain-climbing movie, and it's been almost three years since then, so that's four years. Not even any TV. What's he living on?"

Isabel, inside her wrappings, felt suddenly cold. She didn't know the actual answer to this question, but she said, "Oh, something. Investments.

He didn't lose anything when the tech bubble burst. Don't you remember that story?"

"No."

"Oh, it was so weird. A couple of months after the angioplasty, Delphine called me and said that I should know that someone at Max's brokerage had hacked into his account and transferred all his assets to Singapore. I was so shocked! She thought he might have to sell the house, which was why she was telling me this. Anyway, everyone was terrified for about ten days, and then the perpetrator was caught and the assets were returned, but Max changed his brokerage house and his investment plan. He put everything in cash right before tech stocks started to fall, and that's the last I've heard about his net worth." A nice story and a piece of good luck, but, still, she felt cold at the thought that Max had no income, at the thought that Stoney was worried about him, and that even Jerry would have been worried about him. "Of course, he sold the house in Kauai a couple of years ago. I don't know why he did that."

"Well . . ." said Stoney, but he didn't press the point.

Her neck was beginning to stiffen. It was hard to look anywhere but straight up. Her shoulders were getting numb from immobility. The lounge was narrower than a bed, even a twin bed, so it was awkward to turn onto her side, and anyway, her arms were bound by the covers she had wrapped herself in. But even in spite of whatever was happening to Max's career, their privacy and the darkness were pleasurable. It was remotely possible, of course, that there could be an earthquake right now and the rock face could collapse right on her, but she vaguely remembered that she had overheard Max discussing the stability of this formation with someone when she was a kid, and there had been general agreement that it would have to be a very big one, etc. etc. During the Northridge quake, they hadn't even gotten a single crack in any of the walls. Why was she thinking about this when her relatives were ranged around her like sentinels, Delphine high in the guest-house, Cassie overlooking the road down the mountain, Max and Elena in the forward bedroom, surrounded by motion-sensor lights, Paul and her mom in the bowels of the earth, no doubt attuned to some vibrations some-where (she did believe this, though of course Paul was a lunatic). Here she was, safe from bombing, safe from fire (right beside the pool, after all; if a fire raced up the mountain, she could roll right in), safe from biological warfare, at least for now, safe from everything except global warming, and that would take a while. Right now, the interval between herself and global warming seemed almost a treasure.

He said, "Are you cold? I'm getting a little cold."

"Are you going to go home?"

"What time is it?"

"After midnight. It was eleven when we came out here. Can you see the house lights?"

"No."

"Neither can I."

"We could go to your room."

"How would we do that? If we go through the house together, they'll see us, and if I go through the house and you go out and around on the deck, you'll pass my father's windows and set off the motion sensors."

"I would go with you through the house, say good night to everyone, if anyone is up, then go out and get in my car and drive away. When I get down to my house, I'd park the car and walk back."

"You're supposed to be staying here."

"I could say I forgot something. But it seems awfully involved, doesn't it?"

"I have a better idea."

"What?"

Isabel couldn't help lowering her voice. "Kind of make an opening in your towels and unzip your pants."

Stoney laughed. He said, "You are a naughty girl, aren't you?"

"What's naughty? I just want to see your cock. Are you saying your cock is wrong or bad or dirty or, let's see, shameful in some way? You should have been in my human-sexuality class if you think like that. It's just a cock. The world is full of them." She couldn't help giggling.

"You make such a compelling argument." He began wrestling with his wrappings. While he was heaving around on his lounge chair, Isabel thought of his cock, which was, in fact, just one of billions, but somehow compelling to her—almost pointed, not tremendously large, and a little bent, or at least curving. When they had discussed the mechanisms of desire in her human-sexuality class, the professor had introduced the idea of Pavlov's dog. In a good relationship, it was thought, the sight (or smell or touch) of certain markers—the woman's breasts or the man's phallus—that were usually hidden except during explicitly sexual intervals would come to reliably trigger arousal in the partner, but only if such markers were not embedded in confusing experiences. You could ring the bell, then feed the dog, but you could also (and many did) ring the bell and then beat the dog before feeding it, or ridicule the dog while feeding it, or kick the dog just as it began to salivate, or converse with the dog instead of feeding it. Another thing the professor had said was that, contrary to the assertions of mass culture, those breasts didn't have to be perfect melons, and that phallus didn't have to be a log, in order to trigger desire, they just had to be unencumbered, and she had sat in her class thinking of male phalluses she had known (actually, only Stoney's and Leo's and one other, belonging to a best-forgotten freshman from Fresno), and she had thought it would be fun to know more, but the professor seemed to be saying that the phallic Pavlov effect took a while to develop, and if you carelessly encountered too many phalluses (or breasts, for that matter), your experiences could put you off the whole category. In the dark, Stoney's lounge chair creaked and tipped, and he fell off. Isabel sat up. She said, "Are you okay?"

He said, "Believe me, it was a very short drop." Now they were both laughing. He struggled out of the towels. She whispered, "Shh! What if someone comes out here just as you are pulling it out?"

"You still want to see it?"

"More than ever. My human-sexuality professor would say that it's very important that I see it in order to reinforce the positive response that I have toward it."

"Okay, missy." He turned his back on her and set the lounge upright, then arranged the blankets a bit. He said, "Lie down the way you were. We need to get the mood back."

"Okay." She lay back, though a little more tilted toward him, and he stretched himself out on the nest he had made. She saw his hand go to his fly. That made her giggle, too. He said, "Ready?"

"Oh, yes."

She heard the moment of unzipping. He said, "Can you see it?"

"I wish there was a full moon."

"We do need a shaft of light. You could go get a flashlight."

"I like that. That would be funny, to lie out here with me shining a flashlight on your cock."

"Just like summer camp."

"That's what you did at summer camp?"

"Y-e-e-s-s-s-s. In college we graduated to lighting farts, but we weren't allowed to have matches in summer camp, so we contented ourselves with beaming each other's dicks and talking about how to make them bigger."

"And how was that going to happen? Is it out?"

"It's out. We mostly agreed that plenty of hand time was the key, though one kid said that he had seen his dad with weights hanging off it once in the bathroom, and another had heard that if you wrapped it around a broomstick or some other kind of pole or stick and held it that way for a few minutes every day, let's say more than ten but less than twenty, it could double in size."

"I want to see it. Is it hard?"

"No, not yet. Thinking about thirteen-year-old boys at summer camp in the Sierras doesn't make me hard."

"What does?"

"That's a personal question."

"It is, isn't it? Do you have a porn collection?"

"How do you define porn collection?"

"Whatever it is you think of as porn. It might be just photographs of extremely high spike heels without feet in them. I knew a guy in college who had a collection of those."

He said, intriguingly, "That seems to me like an old-man sort of porn collection."

"My human-sexuality professor said that eighty-four percent of American men have some sort of porn collection or other, so probably that would include you."

"For some reason, this conversation isn't helping me get hard."

Isabel turned carefully and hoisted herself on her elbow. There was a faint paleness to the hand he had holding his cock, and in a way that was enough for her—all she had to see was that surface paleness moving and she could sense the rest. She could also see his face. His face, she had to say, had the same Pavlovian effect on her as his phallus. Although he was not handsome in the strictest sense, although by this time of the night his beard was a little heavy, although his hair was thinning and he was getting just a shade jowly, his face was so familiar and so reliably kind and intent upon her, and in fact so revealing of his sadnesses, his self-doubts, and his low aspirations, that she did what she always did when she looked at him, she relaxed and opened toward him and felt the imminence of giving him what he wanted. It had not been that way with Leo. Almost from the beginning, Leo had aroused her urge to resist and to withhold. It had been an invigorating urge, and she had enjoyed it almost to the end, until she realized how exhausting it was. She said, "I was thinking how the very sight of your cock gives me a feeling in my vagina. It's an aroused feeling—I mean, electric in a sense. Obviously, the nerve endings are waking up and making a connection to my, ah, clitoris, which I can also feel swelling a bit, but there's another sensation, too."

He said, "Go on."

"It's kind of an opening up, as if the space had been filled but now the walls are separating in anticipation." She lowered and deepened her voice. "I don't know why that would be. You would think that the walls were swelling and getting juicy and engorged with blood—"

He groaned. She felt herself smile.

"—but it doesn't feel like that. It feels like some kind of expansion. Are you hard yet?"

"Oh, yes."

"Really hard?"

"Mmmm. Pulsing."

"Can I touch it?"

"Please do."

"My fingers are cold."

"I don't mind that. My dick is hot."

She laughed, then reached over toward him. He took her hand in his and guided it toward his member, which was, indeed, quite hard. After a moment, she took her hand away and then grabbed his lounge chair with both her hands and pulled hers toward him. Its metal legs scraped on the concrete. He turned on his back, and she thought she could see his cock pale against the pool in the background, sticking up. She wiped her right hand on one of her towels and then carefully encompassed his erection. He groaned. "Oooh," she said, knowing that it was important to be impressed and to show it. She said, "It is hot."

"And your hand is cold. I like that. It's refreshing."

"May I stroke it?"

"I wish you would."

She held it lightly and moved her hand up and down the shaft. On the upstroke, she closed her hand around it, but on the downstroke, she opened her fingers and made more of a tickle. Up, down. He groaned and his stomach tensed, and then, suddenly, her stomach tensed, too, in response. Her human-sexuality professor had termed this "synchronization"—the effect of hormones, probably oxytocin, he thought, beginning to regulate the two of them simultaneously. This had its origins in the mother-infant bond and the "open loop" connection between the mammal child, who is only partially formed at birth and has to be nurtured in a certain way to achieve the proper brain structure and hormone production, and the mammal mother, who is in turn regulated by the child's behaviors to seek a state of balance and relaxation that can only occur if the child is satisfied. Ideally, of course, the well-regulated infant-mother connection would predispose a mammal entering his or her reproductive years to seek a similar state of regulation in order to promote optimum reproductive outcomes, but of course so much could go wrong. "Aaaaahhh," said Stoney, and Isabel suddenly wanted to fuck him. Here was another pleasant aspect of familiarity. Even as she realized that she wanted to fuck him, she knew that she could—he had been receptive for so long that it was automatic that she would push her chair back and stand up, then shake off her blankets and towels, and take down her jeans and underpants. He had always welcomed her, and now she felt welcomed. She lifted her right leg and sat down slowly, positioning herself and lowering herself carefully so as not to cause him any discomfort.

"Aah," he said again, and she could not help saying the same thing, "Aah," because of synchronization. But then she put her hands over her mouth and his, remembering where they were and the likelihood of their cries' rising, magnified by the shape of the canyon, toward the house. At least her father's windows and Delphine's were on the other side. Her mother, of course, was sequestered in the wine cellar, protected from every sound. Even so, she said, "Shhh! The very walls have ears!" He nodded and lifted his hips, and she felt him come more deeply into her, right into that place that had seemed to be opening up, and now was. She positioned her knees on the lounge chair, which wasn't easy, because it was so narrow. Its metal frame seemed like it had to dig into one of her knees or the other, or else she had to put one knee on the slats, which was more comfortable, and one foot on the ground, which was awkward. "You okay?" said Stoney as she shifted around.

"Do you think the chair might break?"

"No, but maybe we could slither down onto the blankets without actually coming apart."

"Let's try it." Now they were whispering.

It was harder than it seemed it was going to be. He lifted himself by grasping the frame of the chair, then shifted them to his left, her right. She tried to balance using her left foot first, then her right, but it was difficult to decide how much strength to apply—if she stood up too much, they would come apart, and if she didn't stand up enough, he would be unable to lift her. She saw him staring at her as they tried to move carefully, and then, all of a sudden, the chair tilted and slipped out from under them, and they were flopped in the towels. They laughed. He said, "Still together. That's pretty good."

"Are you all right? I'm amazed you're still hard."

"Well, I banged my ass a little, but I love being connected to you—"

And then, when their voices subsided, Isabel heard something. Her foot was caught awkwardly under Stoney's leg, but she ignored it and put a suppressing hand on his chest. She whispered, "What's that?" They both fell silent, and for a moment all she could hear was the liquid sound of the pool, the distant whoosh of the 405, and a bird sound, and then Stoney said, "I believe it's Charlie."

Isabel leaned forward, lowered her whisper even more, right into Stoney's neck, and said, "Oh, shit, where is he?"

In a normal tone of voice, Stoney said, "He's right behind you."

Isabel sat up and turned around, removing her foot from beneath Stoney's leg, but not otherwise changing her position. There he was, staring at them, standing by the pool. He said, "Hey, guys."

"Hey, Charlie."

"Who's that with you, Isabel?"

Stoney said, "Just Stoney."

"You got him pinned, Isabel?"

"Kind of," said Isabel. She could feel that Stoney's erection had subsided entirely. Now it slipped out of her. But she didn't move.

Charlie coughed, then pushed his hair up, what there was of it. He said, "Hey, I was so frustrated. I've got this pillbox—you know, with a little compartment for each day, except they aren't labeled by the day—and I opened up the last compartment, because I was going to fill the whole thing up again for the next week, and the last compartment was already filled, but not with the right stuff. There're supposed to be seven pills in each compartment, and I take all seven at once, but there were only four pills in that compartment, and I couldn't for the life of me remember what happened to the other three or what I'm supposed to do with these four. I thought I took everything this week, and now it turns out that I didn't, so I just got so annoyed with myself that I decided to come out and have a look at the stars—"

"That seems like a good idea," said Stoney in a muffled voice. Isabel was of two minds about whether to lift herself off him—with Charlie behind her, she imagined her ass glinting right in his face—or continue to sit there, but she could feel Stoney shifting uncomfortably against the hard pavement of the pool deck. Finally, she lifted herself up a little, and he pulled out from under her and sat up. He kissed her quickly on the cheek, but they remained between the chairs, sitting on the pile of blankets and towels.

"So, anyway, I heard something over here and thought it might be an animal, like a bobcat, though you guys were making a lot of noise for a bobcat. Bobcats are pretty stealthy. Maybe you didn't realize that. Or I thought maybe it was the wind. The weather report said it was going to switch around to the east overnight. I had no idea you—"

Isabel shifted her position so that she was facing her father's friend. She liked to think that she had been discreet with her ass. She pulled a corner of one of the blankets over her lap. She said, "We were just screwing around."

"I gathered that—"

"I mean screwing around in the more general sense. Having fun."

"Oh." And then his expression changed, and Isabel realized that he knew she was lying, because he had been watching for more than a moment. He cleared his throat, and then Stoney cleared his throat.

Charlie said, "You know, the key to getting these pills off the ground for the general public, which is what I want to do, is figuring out a system that keeps old guys on a schedule. I mean, not only do I have the seven pills I was worried about tonight, but there's fourteen other ones. They're in another box, and that one I loaded up yesterday. This week, I didn't have any problem with that one, but this white box thing they sell you now is for the birds. Yeah, you load them in there, and, yeah, you set your watch so that you'll take them when you're supposed to, but it still doesn't add up. I'm an old guy. I'm forgetful. Other guys say the same. I bet three weeks out of four, or maybe at least two weeks out of five, I've got some left at the end of the week."

Stoney cleared his throat again, and hoisted himself up onto the deck chair, surreptitiously taking a towel with him and covering himself with it. Beneath the towel, Isabel could see him make a few subtle shifts that indicated he was adjusting his clothes. Isabel felt that her main problem was that she didn't have any underwear or pants on and that her underwear and pants were between herself and Charlie, out of arm's reach at this point. She said, "You're taking twenty-one pills every day? What is it you're taking again?"

"Well, of course there's the Lipitor and the aspirin and the Niaspan. And I got this stuff I imported from the Far East that beat the prostate problem I had. I can't remember what that's called. And then there's a bunch of vitamins. E is the main one—"

"You beat prostate cancer with a pill?" said Stoney.

"Well, it was a high PSA, technically. We never— Mind if I sit down?"

"Of course not," said Isabel. This seemed to be the price they were going to pay to keep Charlie on their side. He pulled up another deck chair. As he did so, he kicked her clothes out of the way, apparently without realizing what they were.

"I tell you what, the treatment regimen they have for prostate cancer in this country is no picnic. What happened with me was really pretty fortuitous, though. I was down at the bank right after getting the results of my blood test, and right after the doctor was telling me what they were going to have to do, and, you know, they tell you all this stuff about how careful they're going to be, and this surgeon has a great record and all, so I say to the teller of the bank that I'm a little down because I just got a bad diagnosis about my prostate, and he's shaking his head, and the guy in the line next to me leans over and says, 'You need to go up to the city and go to Chinatown and get some herbs from the Chinese herbologist.' And he writes down an address for me right there in the bank. He said that the Chinese herbologist had cured not only his prostate problem, but also his sister's Bell's palsy, you know what that is? It's when your face gets paralyzed and you can't even blink. She had to close and open her eyelid with her finger! Imagine trying to remember to do that every few minutes. The herbologist cured that in a week, just with some tea, but the prostate thing took longer. So of course I'm skeptical, who wouldn't be, but I decide to just go see the guy. I have to say, my wife thought I was crazy. Karen is by the book all the way, and that's okay for her, but anyway, enough about that. So I went to this address, and there was the herbologist, Ji Yuan his name is, we do lots of business together now. He was about my age, and as soon as I walked in the door we hit it off, and he knew exactly why I had come. One look at me told him all he needed to know. That's what he told me later. The first thing he did was get his cousin in to give me an acupuncture treatment, sort of to set me up for the herbs, and then he gave me the herbs. It wasn't a tea—he had the pills from China, and there were a lot of them, and they were big. But when I was choking them down, I just kept thinking of the surgeon's knife tickling me you-know-where. Oh, Karen was mad that I was putting off the biopsy, but I was right in the end, because the PSA dropped and hasn't gone back up in three years. I went to the doctor after three months and he was floored at my improvement, and then again after six months and all that, the way you do, so Ji Yuan and I have some things going. By the time you kids are my age, medicine is going to be entirely different from the way it is now. That's my considered opinion."

Isabel murmured, "Western medicine is very crude." Charlie's deck chair creaked as he shifted his position, and finally she said, "Do you mind if I put my pants on?"

"Oh. No. Go ahead."

Just out of the corner of her eye, Isabel could see Stoney grin at this, but then he said, "So I guess you have the capital and your friend has the expertise."

"In a sense. I'm looking for investors. We have some interest, but it's slow. Any new thing is slow."

"It is," said Stoney, in a considered way that made Isabel want to laugh.

Then the two men watched her as she stood up with a towel around her, stepped around Charlie, leaned down, picked up her clothes, and crept back to her chair, where she sat down with her clothes in her lap.

Isabel said, "What did you come out to the coast for, anyway, Charlie?"

"Just some sunshine. Weather's been terrible in Jersey this winter. Not even snow, just wind and cold and overcast, day after day. If you're living alone and you're self-employed and you can't just take off and go look for the sunshine, what can you do?"

On the one hand, Isabel yearned for this old man to get up and go away, but on the other, she realized all of a sudden that he was, in addition to being pretty irritating, very lonely.

He had been sitting upright on the deck chair, his forearms on his knees, leaning a little forward, giving her hope that he would get up and go back to his room, but now he turned and stretched out against the back of the chair, arranging his legs comfortably and putting his hands behind his head. She glanced at Stoney, who glanced at her. She sorted her underpants and jeans a bit, as if preparing to slip into them, as her ass was definitely getting cold, but, still, she felt just a little shy about standing up and putting her things on. "So," said Charlie, "what do you think about this Paul guy? Your mom been seeing him for very long?"

"I think since sometime before Christmas," said Isabel. "I guess he had something to do with that kid she was filming the movie with."

"What movie's that?"

"She has a movie coming out with Denzel Washington this summer. It's a thriller."

"Huh," said Charlie, reflectively.

"It's got great buzz," said Stoney. "Kind of *The Sixth Sense* meets *Fort Apache—the Bronx* with a touch of *Kundun*."

"What's that?" said Charlie.

"That was a movie about the Dalai Lama as a boy," said Stoney.

"So—I look at this guy and I can't figure out what your mom sees in him," mused Charlie. "I was watching him do his exercises this morning, and he can corkscrew around in a pretty amazing way, I admit that. But the beard is strange. It gives me the creeps to have it at the dinner table. He might at least trim it. Lots of guys do that."

Isabel didn't quite know how to respond to these remarks. Paul had been friendly to her without seeming to be trying to gain her approval, and he was a vegetarian, apart from the yearly organ-meats thing, and he was always helpful around the kitchen. Besides that, he seemed to be neat, very clean, and so self-contained that Isabel suspected that Zoe found him a little frustrating, which was good. She said, "I like him," by which she knew she meant, and she knew Stoney knew she meant, He suits my purposes with regard to my mother.

"Doesn't look like he has much money. Your mom could have her pick of guys."

"I think she's tried that," said Stoney, and this remark, too, made Isabel a tad uncomfortable. He added, "You know, deep down this is a pretty straight-arrow town. I don't think Zoe ever wanted to be a corporate wife, which would have been the typical thing to happen to her. They don't look like it the way they do in, let's say, Bloomfield Hills, but it's more or less the same lifestyle."

"Maybe you're right," said Charlie.

"He's got his own gig, anyway," said Isabel. "Lots of middle-aged actresses end up with much younger guys who are so clearly on the make. That's so embarrassing. I mean, before Paul met my mom, he was hiking the seven holiest mountains in China."

"Do you believe that?"

"He's got a slide show."

"I'd like to see that," said Charlie.

"Actually," said Stoney, "I would, too."

"Mom saw it. She said it was great." Now that she had begun defending Paul, Isabel could feel herself warm to it. "I guess he was the only person hiking. Every Chinese person he ran across was driving."

"He has very strange-looking feet," said Charlie.

"I hadn't noticed," said Stoney. Isabel had noticed, though, and Paul's feet were strange-looking—horny and flat, with splayed long toes. Just that day, Isabel had watched him dive off the edge of the pool into the deep end, and his feet had seemed to grasp the edge of the pool and then launch him. She said, "I guess if you go barefoot a lot your feet don't look like other people's feet. There's nothing wrong with that."

"Except," said Uncle Charlie, "beard, feet, is this sexy? Frankly, that's what I wonder about. Look at her. She's maybe the sexiest woman in the world. She's sexier in person than she is on the screen, and that's saying something. Just having her around the house gives me a little shock each time I look at her, and it doesn't matter what she's wearing. She could be wearing a pup tent. You kids know what a pup tent is?"

"I can figure it out," said Isabel.

"But he looks to me like a gargoyle."

"You know what?" said Isabel. "I need to put on my clothes. I'm getting cold. I guess we should stop pretending that we weren't doing what we were doing, and that you weren't watching." She stood up and started to pull on her underwear. Charlie, she was glad to note, did look the other way. After she put on her underwear, she pulled on her jeans and sat down again, but only preliminary to saying, "What time is it? I'm about ready for bed."

"I left my watch in my room, but it was way after midnight when I came out," said Charlie. She noticed that he did not say that he wasn't watching. Stoney cleared his throat. He said, "I guess that would mean that I should go home, too."

"I thought your floors were being refinished," said Charlie.

"Well," said Stoney, "I've been going in and out."

Good save, thought Isabel.

Charlie stuck with them all the way up the steps onto the deck, and even into the main part of the house, where, when Isabel followed Stoney to the front door, Charlie went and opened the refrigerator. Everyone else had gone to bed. She followed Stoney out to his car, the old Jaguar that she disapproved of—though, every time she thought her disapproving thought about old emissions standards, she remembered that any new and less polluting car would have to be manufactured of many polluting materials, so that was a trade-off, and a conundrum, global-warming-wise. Stoney was chuckling. She said, "Why are you laughing? This is not good."

"Maybe not, but it is funny." His voice was so familiar. That was its greatest appeal. Its sound in her ear gave her a feeling like she was going to cry, but she didn't cry. Rather, she threw her arms around him and laid her cheek in the crook of his neck. There was a pause, during which he held her tightly. Then he kissed her on the lips, folded himself into his car, and drove down the hill with a wave. She ran up the outside stairs to her aerie. She could feel the press of the wind now, and when she got to her room, she saw that she had left a window open, and papers had blown around the room. She closed the window and stared down the hill. She could see his taillights for one moment before he disappeared around the corner. She got into bed with her clothes on, and pulled the covers over her, but she didn't go to sleep—she sat up and watched and listened to the windows rattling in their frames. It seemed as though she and Stoney were in a different movie now—no longer one in which his presence was familiar and sometimes inconvenient, like a large object that had to be shifted from time to time so that she could work around it, but, rather, one in which he could disappear at any moment, one in which any ignorant word or careless gesture on her part could blow him up. Something, maybe the wind, maybe that thought, made her shiver.

•

It was still windy when Isabel awoke in the bright glare of her room; she was still clothed, too, though she had kicked off the covers, and she had no idea of the time, because she couldn't find her watch and her clock had stopped. She could tell nothing by the light in the room. There was always light in her room. When she got down to the kitchen, she was not happy to discover that Paul and Zoe were forking cantaloupe from the same wedge, Simon was eating some multicolored cereal, her father was buttering toast, Elena was spreading her toast with roasted-garlic hummus, and Delphine was eating an omelet with, it looked like, some bits of ham in it. Charlie had a bagel, split open and smeared with cream cheese. It looked all too busy and convivial to Isabel, who had planned to sleep until everyone was gone, grab a cup of coffee, and sneak out. By the clock on the microwave, she saw that it was only seven forty-one. Elena, Delphine, and Zoe all looked at her, and Zoe said, "You okay, Isabel?"

"Oh, I didn't sleep," she said, and from behind her hair she saw the quickest ghost of a smile cross the lips of Mr. Charlie Mannheim.

Cassie was reading aloud from the paper. She said, "Okay, I'll start over. 'A transgender prostitute who pummeled a 78-year-old retiree during a scuffle in the man's bedroom was found guilty of voluntary manslaughter Thursday after jurors rejected a more serious charge of murder. James Cid, 31, who uses the name Jamie, wept as the verdict was read in Ventura County Superior Court. Prosecutors had sought a first-degree murder and robbery conviction for the slaying of widower Jack Jamar, arguing that Cid deliberately beat Jamar and stole his wallet before fleeing the area. Cid was apprehended in San Diego County after the March 10, 2000, assault, and admitted in a police interview to hitting and kicking Jamar in the man's east Ventura home.'"

"Tell me what 'transgender' means again," said Charlie, biting into his bagel.

Isabel said, "He's had a sex change from woman to man."

"That's what I thought," said Charlie, chewing. "This is such a California story." He picked up his napkin and wiped his lips.

"There are transgendered individuals everywhere," said Isabel. "It's not a California thing."

"Shh," said Delphine.

Cassie went on: "'Outside the courtroom Thursday, three jurors told reporters that prosecutors were unable to prove premeditation or malice, and that the elements for robbery were not proved beyond a reasonable doubt. But jurors also decided the evidence did not support Cid's claims of self-defense based on the testimony of a crime-scene expert who found blood spattered on the bottom of a bedroom dresser, suggesting that Jamar was on the floor during at least part of the altercation. "There was spirited discussion over what was self-defense," juror Denise Barnett said. Barnett said that after seven days of painstaking deliberations, during which the jury asked questions and heard testimony over and over again, the group agreed the evidence pointed to manslaughter.'"

"What does that mean?" said Zoe.

"He didn't intend to kill him," said Max.

"'It also found Cid guilty of petty theft instead of robbery.'"

"Robbery," said Max, "is when you violently steal something, using a weapon or some other sort of intimidation. Theft is just taking possession of something that isn't yours."

"'Barnett and juror Tina Dwyer said they all had different opinions and theories and worked hard just to develop a list of facts they could agree upon. In the end, they said, it was still not clear what actually occurred in Jamar's bedroom. . . .'"

"This makes no sense to me," said Charlie. "Was Jamie the prostitute a male or a female?"

"I think he's a male," said Simon.

"That's funny," said Zoe. "I thought she was a female. I thought she had been James the male but now she was Jamie the female, and that's why the old guy brought her home."

Cassie cleared her throat and continued to read: "'At the trial, West tried to show that Cid beat Jamar, a retired businessman who was known to pick up prostitutes, into a coma and took his wallet after Jamar brought Cid to his Varsity Street house for sex. According to testimony, police officers responding to a possible robbery found a seriously injured Jamar in the bedroom, bleeding from head wounds and wearing only a T-shirt. Jamar's injuries were so severe, West told jurors, that "officers initially thought Jack was shot in the head." Jamar, whose teeth were knocked into his stomach. . . .'"

"Oh my God," said Elena.

"Maybe he just swallowed them," said Max. "'Knocked' is a pretty loaded word."

"'. . . knocked into his stomach during the assault, later died, and prosecutors charged Cid with murder and robbery. But Sheahen told jurors his client, whom he described as a nonviolent individual who suffers from a gender-identity disorder, acted in self-defense after being attacked by Jamar.'"

"See," said Charlie, "the article said 'individual.' My guess is no one knew, or was prepared to say during the trial, whether the perp was a male or a female."

Isabel found this whole discussion irritating. She said, "It seems obvious to me that Jamie had been a female, was now a male, and was taken home by this career john. Boys can call themselves Jamie. The old guy got violent, and Jamie defended himself a little too strongly, and then the old guy fell and hit his head and died. He had probably already given Jamie some money, and that's what they said he had stolen. In the picture he's a man." She found some bread and slid two pieces into the toaster.

"But did he kill the old guy as a man or as a woman? Would a woman really have the strength to do that kind of damage?" said Charlie. "I mean, if she started out as a woman, let's say five eight or so, which is pretty good-sized for a woman but not so big for a guy, would the sex-change operation really endow her as a man with enough strength, not to mention the killer instinct, to beat the guy's head to a pulp and knock his teeth down his throat? But let's say she started as a man; then it makes more sense that there would be residual strength even after the operation for that sort of thing."

"That's what I think," said Zoe. "Don't you agree, dear one? The way I picture it is kind of like that movie *The Crying Game*. The old guy picks up someone he thinks is a regular female prostitute, and when he gets her home, he pays her and she takes her clothes off, but then he doesn't like what he sees, and gets violent—"

Paul opened his mouth as if he meant to say something, but Cassie, looking at the paper, interrupted him: "It says he said the old guy was raping him."

"And what does that mean?" said Simon. "How do you rape a prostitute? Doesn't being a prostitute imply consent? I'm not suggesting anything." Isabel saw him glance at her. "I was just curious."

"Unless," said Paul, "Zoe's right and she was going out as a woman, and she was consenting to vaginal intercourse but not to anal intercourse, and so the one would be consensual and the other would be rape."

"That reminds me of a story I saw on the news once, years ago, back in Chicago," said Elena. "A guy was convicted of rape because the woman he slept with had multiple-personality disorder, and only one of her personalities had consented to having sex. That wasn't a California story."

"I think we should just read what it says and take it at face value," said Isabel, thinking that this discussion was going to drive her crazy.

"It doesn't have a face value," said Max. "The jurors couldn't figure it out, either."

"It would be interesting to know what the defense lawyers knew," said Delphine, who had been reading over Cassie's shoulder. "I mean, they had a choice. Do they send their client into the courtroom as a man or as a woman? Maybe they realized that if the jury couldn't figure it out, then they would have to give the guy the benefit of the doubt. Didn't one of the lawyers say that this proves that the system works?"

"Yes," said Cassie.

"Maybe that's what they meant. I mean, Jamie knows what happened in the bedroom. He's the only one. So he's the only one who knows whether it was murder and robbery or manslaughter and theft, and the only sign of his reaction to the verdict is that he cried. Did he cry as a man or as a woman? Did he beat the old guy as a man or as a woman? How can anyone know?"

Silence descended around the table, and Isabel's toast rose out of the toaster. She reached for the hummus, which was in the middle of the table. Cassie rattled the paper and turned the page.

Zoe picked up one of the inside sections of the paper, and Max picked up the A section, the dangerous section. Isabel didn't have to look closely to notice that there was plenty of Iraq news. She saw that Elena noticed, too, and consciously turned away. Simon got up from his seat, took his plate to the sink, and then rummaged in the cabinet by the sink for a moment and came up with four circular black-and-white cookies. Before Elena said anything, he exclaimed, "Mom, they're Newman-O's. See? Taste one. They're incredibly crisp on the outside and fabulously luscious on the inside." He held one out to her, but she waved his hand away. He said, "I'm sure the frosting is a nutritious mix of tofu and naturally bleached carrot pulp—"

"Yes, Simon," said Elena. "Now, is your filming winding up today?"

"Yeah—"

"Do tell," said Max, folding down the paper, "what scene are you filming today?"

"Well, we might have to do the bartender in the neoprene suit again. The breasts were kind of flat yesterday, and they looked more like flaps than boobs. I think the girls were going to stuff them with something last night. Other than that, there's only one scene left, and that's the men's naked tap-dance. We've been practicing all week, even though it's only about a minute long. All we have to do is step and turn and step and turn, and then tap around in a small circle, and then jump up and land in, what is it, second position, you know, where your legs are apart and your chest is up and your shoulders are back. The director picked the cast for equipment size rather than dancing ability, and I guess I would have to say that a sense of rhythm doesn't seem to correlate with equipment size. And it seems like the more we rehearse the smaller the equipment gets, so he wants to get it on the first take."

"That stands to reason," said Charlie.

"Filming always presents unexpected challenges to the original conception," said Max with a smile. He went back to his paper.

"So you're going back to Davis tonight?" said Elena.

"Well, no," said Simon. "They rented everything for another day, and I don't have to get back till Sunday."

Elena looked at him skeptically.

"If then. Mom, I'm up to date in my classes, I'm refining ideas for my thesis, and there's no problem. I promise. Don't you enjoy having me around? Everyone else is here. I'm helpful and entertaining. I did the dishes last night, right? And I did a good job, didn't I, Cassie?"

"He did a good job," said Cassie.

"Do you enjoy having me around, Cassie?"

"I do."

"Do you enjoy having me around, Delphine?"

"More or less."

"See, Mom, from Delphine, that's very positive—isn't it, Delphine?"

"Very positive."

"Because Delphine has high standards, don't you?"

"Very high." She smiled.

Isabel saw Zoe smile to herself. Isabel felt the tiniest little prick of something at this smile—what was it? She had never had a sibling, of course, and so she was spoiled rotten, of course, and in fact it hadn't occurred to her that Simon could be a rival for her family's affections, and anyway, she was twenty-three years old and beyond caring about that sort of thing, of course, but she cleared her throat and went over to the sink with her plate, and decided that, yes, Simon would be better off back at college Sunday night.

Then Zoe said, "Dear one, we should go see this show at LACMA." She pushed the paper toward Paul. "It's a show of Middle Eastern art. It says, 'But even as art historians and archeologists are warning against the possible destruction and looting of important sites, the L.A. County is preparing a landmark exhibition of historic art and artifacts from the region that includes present-day Iraq.' I'd like to see that."

"I would, too," said Paul, and then Elena said, "Having a war there is like, oh, I don't know—"

"Bombing Dresden?" said Cassie. "Here's a piece about whether analogies between American attacks on Iraq and Allied attacks on Germany during the Second World War are appropriate. It's interesting."

Elena scowled, and Zoe glanced at Paul, evidently sorry she'd brought anything up, but Isabel didn't care whether they talked about the war or not. It was not a subject she thought should be avoided, actually, which is what they all seemed to be doing.

Cassie went on: "'At high noon on March 12, 1945, just eight weeks before the capitulation of Germany to the Allied forces, 1,000 American planes attacked the city of Swinemuende on the Baltic coast of Germany. The city, crammed with refugees from eastern Germany who had been ethnically cleansed and raped by the Red Army, was bombed mercilessly and sprayed by machine gun fire from American dive bombers, which chased people through the city. Of the city's 25,000 civilians, 23,000 were killed that night.'" She cleared her throat.

Cassie glanced down the page. "I think he's objecting to any analogy between the bombing of Iraq and the bombing of Germany at the end of the war. Someone must have made the comparison."

"On TV," said Simon.

"Do you want me to keep reading?" said Cassie.

Elena coughed. No one said anything. Finally, Isabel herself said, "I think it's interesting," and she did.

"I'll skip down. 'Never before in history had a civilian population endured such a military assault. One and a half million bombs were dropped on 161 German cities and 800 villages over five years, leaving half a million civilians dead, including 75,000 children. An additional 78,000 of Hitler's slave workers and prisoners of war were killed. No one was ever punished for these acts. The winners, not surprisingly, didn't indict themselves for war crimes. And, in fact, there was nothing technically illegal about their actions. According to Telford Taylor, the chief U.S. prosecutor of the Nuremberg trials, there was no international agreement limiting aerial bombardment to military targets—so, technically, the bombing was legal. Nevertheless, it was unprecedented and beyond any of the customs of war. The war itself was just, but the means by which it was conducted were unjust and unimaginable.'"

"What about the Blitz?" said Delphine. "And the way they bombed Coventry and Southampton and all those other cities?"

"What about six million Jews?" said Isabel, who only said it because she knew Stoney would have, but as she said it, she thought, Yeah, what about that?

Cassie nodded and went on: "'And worst of all, the bombing was an unmitigated failure. It simply didn't work. . . .'"

"What does that mean?" said Simon. "It destroyed the cities, right?"

"'. . . It weakened Hitler but didn't lead to his overthrow. It didn't destroy morale or incite rebellion; 75,000 children killed and it didn't do anything except, perhaps, strengthen the resolve of the German people against the Allies.'"

"It sounds like he's on your side," Max said to Elena.

"That's what they do, though," said Elena. "They put the reasonable part first. They concede something. That's what he's conceding—that bombing doesn't work. He's going to twist it around by the end. They wouldn't have him on the editorial page if he didn't support the war."

"I think he's just having his say," remarked Paul. "This has been on his mind for years, and now he gets the chance to express it. It doesn't really matter if it fits the circumstances or not."

"You know what I just remembered?" said Max. "Once, my eighth-grade Latin teacher told us about the firebombing of Dresden, which we, of course, had never heard of, and how his mother or his aunt or his grandmother, maybe it was, would huddle in the basement and shake her fist at the Allied bombers as they flew over. I wonder if I went home and asked about it, or if I just filed it away until now. My uncle Walter was a photographer in the belly of one of those bombers. His job was to lie flat and take pictures of the devastation as they flew their missions. I knew all about Uncle Walter, but I never made the connection between the old lady shaking her fist and my uncle in the belly of the plane until now."

"What about my uncle Freddie?' said Charlie. "He was in the Engineer Corps, and it was his company that landed secretly the night before D-Day and made their way up Omaha Beach, disarming land mines in the dark. Not only didn't they want to get blown up, they couldn't reveal that they were there by letting any of the mines explode. By the time the GIs landed, according to Uncle Freddie, he and his men were ten miles inland. But he never talked about it, either. But the war wasn't all bad. Freddie's brother Tom went into the army band as a French-horn player. In the Battle of the Bulge, the German pincer action was so sudden that they had to drop their instruments and run. But they ran east. Pretty soon they came upon the spot where the German band had dropped their instruments, so they picked them up. And they were much better instruments than the ones they had lost. I guess Tom came home with three French horns, and when his own son needed a violin twenty years later, he sold one of them and bought the kid a Stradivarius."

"I had a cousin in the Battle of the Bulge," said Cassie. "His whole unit was wiped out, and the only way he survived was to crawl into the rotting carcass of a horse."

"What happened to him?" said Elena.

"Well, he came home and went into the meat business."

Charlie and Delphine laughed, as did Cassie. Then she said, "But of course he had problems. I don't know that he consciously made the connection between the horse and the meat business."

"What did your dad do?" said Isabel to Max. She was used to Cassie, but did wonder if she knew what she sounded like.

"Well, he always said he wanted to be a flyer, but he was too tall, so he ended up working for the newspaper."

Cassie went on: "'At a press conference last week, Secretary of Defense Donald Rumsfeld noted comparisons had been made between the current campaign and the bombings of Germany. It's a laughable comparison. You cannot compare the mass destruction of incendiary warfare—aimed at killing civilians in extraordinary numbers—with the noisy but relatively precise and targeted attacks on Baghdad. Such comparisons are far too kind to Arthur "Bomber" Harris, the British leader of the Allied campaign. . . .'"

"But you could compare it to the Blitz," said Zoe. "I think."

Isabel saw Elena cast her mother a startled glance, but Zoe had that look she always did—"Who, me? I'm not trying to say anything, I just happen to be talking." As far as Isabel was concerned, the fact that she saw her mother's point, or, maybe, agreed with her, didn't make up for that look, so fake.

"'The difference is this: In Baghdad today, civilian deaths would constitute failure. In World War II Germany, they meant success. The U.S. would be a pariah in world opinion today if it targeted even one Iraqi city the way it attacked German cities relentlessly for five years.'"

"The U.S. *is* a pariah in world opinion today," said Elena.

Charlie stared at her.

Cassie folded the paper and flipped it over. She said, "Last paragraph. 'A better comparison is to Saddam Hussein's weapons of mass destruction. If the Iraqi leader . . .'"

Elena dropped the butter knife and picked it up again.

"'. . . were to use chemical or biological weapons—which strike civilian and military targets indiscriminately over a large territory—that would be comparable. Then Hussein would be the true heir of "Bomber" Harris.'"

"I told you," said Elena. "I told you he was in support of the war."

"Most people are," said Charlie.

"Most Americans may be," said Elena. "That's not the same as most people. Most *people* are not in support of the war, and view Americans as a greater danger to the world than Saddam Hussein. Americans have biological and chemical and nuclear weapons and have used them. Most *people* think they could use them again. A couple of months ago, there was an article in some paper about how the Pentagon was trying to decide on possible nuclear targets in Iraq."

"I can't believe that," said Paul.

"She showed me the article," said Max. "It said that the Pentagon has changed the classification of nuclear weapons so that they are now considered 'conventional' rather than 'special.'"

"It's not like she's making it sound," said Charlie. "There might be targets—"

"Like Nagasaki," said Elena. "There was a good target. Hiroshima, too."

"Now you're bitching about the bombing of Nagasaki and Hiroshima? They were military cities! It's not like they bombed temples or something like that—"

"Well, they firebombed Tokyo and Kobe. Kobe was full of temples. When they firebombed Tokyo, they killed a hundred thousand civilians."

"I saw this anime movie a couple of years ago about that," said Simon. "It was called *The Grave of the Fireflies*. It was a cartoon about these kids who were orphaned in the firebombing of Kobe. The guy I was with couldn't stop crying. We thought it was going to be like *My Neighbor Totoro* or something like that."

"What is wrong with you?" exclaimed Charlie, jumping up from the table. "The Japs attacked first. They attacked Pearl Harbor!"

"They didn't attack Honolulu, did they? They didn't attack, oh, Lihue?"

"But they attacked Nanking! What they did in Nanking makes Rwanda look like a walk in the park! Are you saying that the U.S. should just stand by?" Charlie walked around the table, waving his spoon.

"Well," said Zoe, "the U.S. did stand by and not do anything about Nanking. I don't think the bombing of Tokyo, Kobe, Hiroshima, and Nagasaki had anything to do with Nanking." She glanced at Paul, who was gazing at her—encouragingly, Isabel thought. It was a little irritating.

"I can't believe you said that, Mom," said Isabel.

"Why not?" exclaimed Zoe. "There was a five-year time lag between Nanking and Pearl—"

"No. I mean, I can't believe you know anything about it."

"Well, Mom read that book. Didn't you read that book, Delphine, by that girl?"

"*The Rape of Nanking,* by Iris Chang. I read most of it. It was pretty hard going."

"Well, I read some of it, too," said Zoe. "I picked up the main points. You always treat me as if I were a total ditz."

"Oh," said Isabel. But she thought, Just a ditz, not a total ditz. There's a difference in degree that should be noted.

"That book was on the best-seller list for weeks and weeks," said Delphine.

Charlie opened the front door and went outside. The door slammed behind him. Simon rubbed his hands over his head and said, "Don't come back in." Isabel, and, she assumed, everyone else, could hear Charlie striding around on the deck, and then the door opened again. Simon said, "Whoops. Came back in."

Charlie's face was red. He looked at Max, but he clearly was talking to Elena. He said, evenly and clearly, as if explaining this one more time, but this was going to be the last time, so help him God, "Where *were* you on 9/11? Did you not see what happened? Did you not see those towers fall and those people die? Is that why you propose that we sit around waiting until it happens again?"

"Charlie, they weren't Ira—" said Elena.

"Who do you think the 'great Satan' is?"

"Those were Ira—"

"What's the difference? Nobody has been able to explain to me the difference. This extremist mullah comes from Iran, this extremist mullah comes from Egypt, this extremist mullah lives in Saudi Arabia, this one moved from Pakistan to England twenty years ago. But they are all calling for the end to America. You want to go down without a fight? You want to say, Oh well, you're entitled to your point of view? They want you dead. Why don't you want them dead?"

"Saddam isn't a mullah."

"But he's funneling them money and weapons."

"He says he's not. Lots of people say he's not, because the mullahs hate him and he hates them."

"You believe that? You hate Tom DeLay and Randall Terry on religious grounds, I'm sure, but if it came time for one of them to call out the Air Force and the Coast Guard to defend the country from attack, wouldn't your religious differences fall by the wayside?"

"How can he prove a negative? No one can prove a negative. You've got him in a position where you have made an accusation, and because he has to prove a negative, your accusation automatically becomes a conviction. The inspectors are going around doing their job, but the administration doesn't want them to do their job."

"You're giving Saddam Hussein the benefit of the doubt? After he gassed the Kurds? After he's purged his own population?"

"He used American gas to gas them! Rumsfeld was shaking his hand. He did what they wanted him to do!"

"I don't believe that. I believe that he was like a rogue or a renegade. He did not do what they wanted him to do, and now they have to take him out."

"I think," said Delphine, "that we've gotten away from Nanking and Nagasaki and the Germans."

"What does that mean?" said Zoe.

"The people being bombed aren't Saddam Hussein. He's in a bunker somewhere. They might catch him and they might not—"

"Exactly," said Elena. "We know Al Qaeda people blew up the Twin Towers, but we're punishing Saddam Hussein. That's like I have two kids who are cousins and who hate each other, and I know that one of them blew up the kitchen, so I say to that one, 'Jimmy, you blew up the kitchen, so, just to teach you not to do that anymore, I'm going to give Johnny here, who had nothing to do with it, a whipping.' It makes no sense. Jimmy hates Johnny. Jimmy's glad Johnny gets a whipping. He won! He manipulated me and he got back at the hated cousin."

Simon said, "Go, Mom!"

"That's not what I was getting at," said Delphine. "What I was getting at was the idea of whether there are actually any innocent civilians or not. Are you an innocent civilian, Elena?"

Elena looked at her, a little nonplussed. Then she said, "Well, no. We're all implicated in what the administration is doing. That's what makes me so mad."

"So, if you're implicated, that means, in an extreme case, that firebombing you is justified, because if it turns out that your government is seen by someone else as a rogue government that needs to be stopped at all costs, all costs may include your life."

"Well, I— Yes. I agree with that."

"So what about the Iraqis? Lots of them have left. That means that lots of them had a chance to leave and decided to stay and accommodate Saddam in some way. Most of them have reasons. Let's say one reason is trying to change the regime from within. That's what you've been doing."

Isabel had to admit that she found this line of reasoning a little shocking, but she suspected that Delphine was just making a point.

"Yes," said Elena, nodding.

"So—the Iraqi population, like the German population and the Japanese population and the American population, is not made up of innocent civilians. It's made up of people who saw more or less what was happening and decided for various reasons to take their chances."

"Yes, but—" said Zoe.

"Yes, but what about the children? That's what you're going to say," said Delphine. Isabel did not think Zoe was going to mention the children, but Isabel herself might have. "That's what I was wondering about when I read that piece about Germany. Five hundred thousand casualties and only about fifteen percent of them children. That seems low to me. Where were the children? It must have been like in England during the Blitz. The children got sent away because the parents knew something was going to happen. I don't think that, in terms of guilt and innocence, you can factor the children in or factor them out. They share their parents' conditions even of guilt and innocence until they are, say, fifteen or so. Then they can make their own choices. Anyway, whenever you decide to take your chances, you have to live with chance, and chance might be that you'll get firebombed. So I disagree with the tone of that article, about the poor Germans. Didn't they see *Triumph of the Will*? Couldn't they tell that Adolf Hitler was up to something? Why didn't they stop him? And when the soldiers came home on leave from Nanking, wasn't anyone horrified at what they reported? And if they didn't report anything, wasn't that because they knew they'd committed crimes?"

"Exactly," said Charlie.

Now Delphine turned to him. "I guess you consider yourself an innocent civilian," she said.

"Uh-oh," said Simon. "Run for the hills."

Isabel smiled. She saw that Max was smiling, too. Paul was eating kiwifruit.

"Welllll," said Charlie, recognizing a potential trick, "no one is innocent. But I suppose I consider myself a not-guilty civilian. My guilt has not been proved beyond the shadow of a doubt, and so I am at liberty." He smiled at his own cleverness, and Zoe said, "I see that."

"But you voted for Bush in 2000," said Delphine.

"Of course, but I didn't expect him to start a war. I voted for him for other reasons."

"But are you on board for all of his policies, and in addition to that, do you agree with all or most of them?"

"Yeah, I would say so."

This answer sounded honest to Isabel, like the sort of cocky answer a detainee might unwittingly make to his interrogators early in the questioning process.

"But a lot of his policies are pretty risky. Like this tax-cut thing. Big tax cuts are going to raise the deficit, and if he makes them permanent, some economists think that could put the U.S. in danger of having something happen here like has happened in Argentina and those places, where the economy has collapsed and the middle class has disappeared. What if that happened?"

"Well, I would hope that wouldn't happen. Lots of economists say—"

"But they disagree. It's a risky thing to do, and the gamble could fail, right?"

"Well, I guess. Yeah. For the sake of argument."

"So, if the economy failed, and you were implicated in its failure by voting for and agreeing to administration policies, what would that mean for you?"

"Well, I've got my pension plan and some other investments and—" But he stopped there. "Take the Fifth."

"Money overseas," said Cassie.

Charlie didn't say no. Then he said, "But I'm permitted to save myself."

"Are you?" said Delphine. "Are you permitted to promote risk for others and keep some security for yourself?"

"Well, that's a natural human thing to do—"

"But we're not talking about natural. We're talking about guilty or not guilty. What you're saying is that you are justified in getting away with what you can get away with, right?"

"I guess, right."

"So in that you're in agreement with the administration, too, right?"

"In some sense, right. I admit that."

"So, since a lot of people around the world disagree with the policies you support, you are more or less in the same position as a German civilian or a Japanese civilian before the Second World War. Your ideas could work out, but they might not. Are you ready to pay the price if they don't, and you can't get away with it?"

"Oh, this is a stupid argument—"

"Answer the question," said Zoe. "I think it's a good question, don't you, dear one?"

Everyone looked at Paul, but he looked at Charlie.

Finally, Charlie said, "No. I'm not. First of all, I don't think there is going to be a price to pay, and, second of all, if they want it, they're going to have to come and get it."

"So," Isabel heard herself say, "we've established that Charlie doesn't care that much about guilt or innocence."

Cassie folded the paper and set it neatly beside her plate. "From a certain perspective, though, what's wrong with lots of people dying? Thirty-six million people died in the Second World War, and—boom—they just turned up again, thicker than ever, like cockroaches that get resistant to some pesticide. What was that Greek myth, the Hydra? You cut off a head, and two grow back. Well, you kill a person, and two pop up. The two new ones are a lot more expensive than the original one ever was. The two new cockroaches are bigger, hungrier, and more aggressive than the one you poisoned. It's evolution at work. They talk about technology all the time—technology and human imagination and creative thought are going to save us. I say, what if they actually do? I see those things as a form of mutation, like the mutations in mosquito populations that allow them to carry a virus without succumbing to it. Like humans, they just get more and more lethal."

Max was gazing at Cassie with an amused look on his face. He said, "Easy for you to say."

"Well, of course, so shoot me."

Delphine grinned.

"No, I mean it. Shoot me. I'm seventy-six years old. Personally, I think that birth control hasn't worked. It hasn't slowed or controlled population growth, and it's just changed the composition of the population in a negative way. I think upon retirement you ought to have to apply to continue to exist. You ought to have to show that your life is worth something and that you have something to contribute. If you can't show that, then off you go. Complainers and worriers and crabby old men could be given an ultimatum—mind your manners, get some self-knowledge, or be translated to a higher plane sooner rather than later."

"Present company excluded, right?" said Max.

"No, present company included. Me included, Delphine included, you included, Charlie included. Declare what you have to offer or step aside! What's stopping you? The only thing besides custom and inertia that's stopping you is that it's so hard to do. There's always a mess. When an individual decides to do it, it's a pretty big mess. I think that's actually what stops a lot of people. When there's any kind of mass killing, like a war or an epidemic, it's a huge mess, and everyone who survives is traumatized, but if you had a system where it was understood beforehand that you could live if you accepted certain rules, and one of them was that your life would only be so long—say, sixty-five or seventy years—then you could do your thing, prepare for the end, and go. What could be bad about that? The alternatives are showing themselves to be worse."

"Do you think she's kidding?" said Delphine to Simon.

"I don't know," said Simon.

"She's not kidding," said Delphine.

Cassie shrugged. "Everyone is impressed by hundreds of thousands of deaths, or millions of deaths, or, actually, one death, but what does it do? It doesn't do anything that I can see, except give the survivors a sense that they now uniquely deserve something better than what they had before—"

Elena said, "Yes, well, but now you're playing into the conservatives' hands, because you're discussing all sorts of huge and unrealistic ideas while they go ahead and do something that is illegal and inhumane, which is invade a country and bomb their population and take their assets. It's perfectly fine with Rumsfeld that you debate issues of global life and death, because that occupies you while he deploys his army." She did sound shrill, thought Isabel, although Isabel knew perfectly well that the very word "shrill" was always applied only to women, and only when they were stating strong and usually correct opinions. And so Isabel said, "I agree with that," in a voice that she tried to mold to sound grave, sober, and not shrill.

Isabel saw Zoe look at Elena, then at Max, and then at Paul. Paul had finished his kiwifruit and was now eating grapes. She said, "Dear one, what do you think?"

Paul glanced at her, ate another grape, and then picked up his napkin. He methodically wiped his mustache downward, then smoothed his beard. He set his napkin beside the plate of fruit, which still contained an apple. He said, "Of course, I think it's all an illusion," and in the next second, without any warning, Simon, who was sitting next to him, made a fist, hit him in the jaw, and knocked him off his stool. Everyone gasped—Isabel herself gasped—and then Zoe began to laugh in great merry peals of laughter, her eyes wide in surprise and her mouth open and her golden, legendary laugh filling the room like bubbles. She leaned forward and helped Paul off the floor, then picked up his stool. As he sat himself down and turned his head from right to left and back again, putting his hand to the side of his jaw, Isabel said, "Mom!" and Elena said, "Simon!"

Max said, "Did you rehearse that?"

"No," said Paul, but in an even tone of voice. "We did not rehearse that."

"What in the world were you thinking of, Simon?" said Elena, and Isabel saw that even Cassie and Delphine were shocked. She felt her own shock, which had taken a moment to kick in, begin to swell.

"I was thinking of Bishop Berkeley," said Simon. "He was this guy in the eighteenth century who said that everything was an illusion. So, one day, a couple of other guys were walking down the street. I think one of them was Immanuel Kant. And they started talking about Berkeley and his ideas about the illusory nature of reality, and Kant kicked a stone by the side of the road and said, 'This is what I think of Berkeley.' So that occurred to me when Paul said that word 'illusion,' and I guess I thought I would try a similar sort of thing. It was a sort of philosophical punch. I'm sorry if it was a little hard. I meant it to be more of a slap."

"That is the dopiest excuse I ever heard," said Elena. She went over to Paul and put her hand on his shoulder. She said, "I am so sorry. Would you like some ice? Does it hurt? Oh dear." Isabel thought she really seemed undone by the whole thing.

Max said, "I'm sorry, Paul. I am. But that was the best slapstick routine I ever saw."

"It was. It was!" exclaimed Zoe. "You could not reproduce that timing on film. You couldn't rehearse the look on Simon's face, which was completely relaxed, or how quick it was and how unexpected. I'm so sorry I laughed, dear one! Please forgive me. Would you like to lie down on the couch or anything?" She leaned forward and put her hands on his shoulders and winced sympathetically and then kissed him gently on the uninjured side of his face. When Elena brought the ice, Zoe held it gently to his jaw and said, "Honey, have you ever been cold-cocked before?"

Paul nodded.

Isabel looked at Charlie, who said, "You have? I never have."

"Mmm," said Paul, "that's quite a left hook. Yeah. No, I used to get into fights all the time, and then I became a vegetarian, actually mostly to stop fighting. I was glad to note that I didn't jump up and try to throttle Simon. That's what I would have done thirty years ago, but this time it didn't even occur to me, so that's good." He took a deep breath, then leaned down and picked up the apple that had fallen off the fruit plate and rolled under his stool. Isabel thought he looked a little white around the eye sockets, but, of course, his cheeks were hidden by all that curly hair. Then he said, "What was I saying? Oh." He glanced quickly at Simon. "That all of this is illusory."

"I'm not going to hit you again. I really didn't mean to hit you that hard. I really was just thinking of Kant kicking the rock by the side of the road."

"I don't think it was Kant," said Isabel. "It was someone else." She didn't feel that it was becoming of Simon to try to sound like an intellectual.

"What if," said Paul, "all those people who died in the Blitz and the fire-bombings and the rape of Nanking and the atomic bombing of Hiroshima and Nagasaki and are now dying in Iraq were just playing parts? What if, after the play was over, they got up, took off their costumes, and went on to do something else? What if they had been incarnated to do that, and they were subsequently reincarnated to do something else, and the thing that happened to them in that life, that particular form of suffering, was so momentary that they forgot it immediately?"

Isabel could see that no one had anything to say to this idea, one that she felt was simultaneously tired and irrelevant, but certainly comforting to someone like her mother, who would of course be ever seeking some form of irresponsible belief. She said, "I think that's too easy. It lets everyone off the hook. 'Oh, it's all illusion, everything is fleeting.'" She heard her own mocking voice. "We can just take what we want and do whatever we want, and whatever happens will be fine because it's all illusory anyway. I for one don't think the endangered species are illusory. I don't think plastic bags in the oceans being eaten by seals and birds are illusory. I don't think watching your child die in a bombing is illusory. I mean, look what your generation has come up with. Global warming, environmental degradation, corporate takeover of government, third-world debt impoverishment, failure of the health-care system, the blockbuster movie, and video games. Mercury poisoning."

"They didn't come up with video games," said Simon, seriously. "Or, really, the Internet, either, though —"

"Excuse you," said Isabel.

"Oh, sorry," said Simon.

"If you ask me, I think baby boomers have wrecked the world. But here we are, talking about everything being an illusion! How convenient!"

"Maybe I haven't explained myself very well," said Paul.

"You have! Of course you have. It's not that hard to grasp, you know. I took the History of Religious Thought. When I graduated, the graduation speaker spoke quite eloquently about universal love and Nelson Mandela and seeking a higher form of forgiveness, and why wouldn't he? He lived in Capitola! He bought his house for forty-six thousand dollars and now it's worth about a million! Of course he's conversant with universal love! I would be, too, if I lived in Santa Cruz and had a sailboat."

"You always sound so resentful, Isabel."

"Well, you always sound so shallow, Mom! Maybe you aren't, but blah blah blah! It's embarrassing!"

"You know who really sounded shallow," said Cassie, "was Marilyn Monroe. I met her. But actually she wasn't shallow at all, she—"

"Shh," said Delphine.

"Of course," said Cassie.

Isabel was staring at Zoe, who was staring right back at her. Zoe said, "I don't think the way I am is your real problem with me. I don't think you know how I am or what I'm like—"

"What daughter does?" said Cassie. "I was always glad—"

"Shhh," said Delphine.

"Well, my mother drove me crazy. She was used to good service, because she was quite a beauty and her family was rich, and eventually I was the only one left to serve her. She'd have me drive over there, saying she'd lost her heart medicine, and then her heart medicine would be right there but what she really wanted was for me to find her cigarettes for her in the bedcovers, even though she was forbidden to smoke in bed. I put two smoke alarms above her bed. If I tried to hide her Winstons or keep them from her, she would grab them out of my hand and light up."

"Are you finished?" said Delphine.

"I was just pointing out that it could be a lot worse for Isabel. Did you ever see that movie *Hanging Up*? About Nora Ephron's dad—what was his name?—oh, Henry. He was a charming man from the outside, but he drove those girls crazy, according to the movie. They had Walter Matthau play him. Very dependent, couldn't find a woman of his own age to take care of him, drove the wife away, at least in the movie—"

Isabel could perceive that Cassie was giving her time to back down, as well as giving her a kindly lesson, but she could feel her coming outburst swelling within her anyway, or maybe even because of what Cassie was saying. She could also see everyone else looking at her. Her father looked neutral, as if he had decided not to interfere, which he always did. Elena looked somewhat similar, but with the added knowledge that this was not her business. Simon, of course, looked all too interested, and Paul looked like he had just been punched and didn't really care what happened. She thought that if Stoney were here, the one person that she could rely on, she might have some alternative, but he wasn't, and she didn't, and so she said, in a voice both loud and firm, "No, I am not saying my mom is dependent or hard on me or difficult or even a prima donna, because everyone knows that she isn't. But, Mom! Show me something that you care about! It doesn't have to be the dolphin population or the coral reefs! It doesn't have to be children with AIDS in either Africa or Southeast Asia. You could care about abortion rights or the plight of, of, of anything. You could recognize that there are plights and that you could do something about those plights!"

Zoe continued to stare at her. Isabel was more and more annoyed with herself that she couldn't come up with just the right example that would demonstrate what she meant, but at the same time, she was a little surprised that, of all her grievances against her mother, this was the one she had ended up enunciating. It was as if, after this long time, she had put her quarter in the gumball machine, and now the gumball that rolled down the chute was yellow rather than red, was about her mother's nature rather than about Isabel's nurture. "When Bush was elected, you didn't really care about the Florida vote! You said that you didn't see a dime's worth of difference between them anyway, so you hadn't even voted—"

"Well, I changed my mind later—"

"But then it was too late! But that's just it."

"I'm busy, I—"

"Well, you aren't too busy for Paul, are you?" she said nastily. "Paul comes around and tells you that everything is an illusion, and there we have it. You spend time doing sessions and going to the monastery and refining your practice, but that's shallow, too. If Paul were to go away, all that stuff would be over, just like that, but leaving a residual sense that everything is just okay!" There she was—instead of pointing out that Paul was just another in a long line of her mother's romantic mistakes, she was taking issue with Paul's belief system. But even though she was somehow losing her chance, or so it seemed, her rhetoric had its own momentum.

"People have the right to live their own lives, Isabel," said Charlie, and he did—yes, he did—give her a significant look. So she defied him. She said, "No, they don't. Actually, they do not have that right. They live their own lives because no one stops them."

Paul interrupted her. She had paused to take a breath, so there was a little space for him to intrude, but Isabel knew that they both knew she wasn't finished. That was the first actual beef she had against him. There was nothing overtly wrong with him; guys like him were a dime a dozen in Santa Cruz. Even so, his voice sounded authentically even and steady. He said, "It's not only the bad things that are illusory. It's the good things, too."

She snapped, "What difference does that make?" But of course it did make a difference, and distracted her from what she had been saying, because as soon as he said that she thought again of that moment with Stoney the night before. "Everything is fleeting! I understand that!" Obviously, that's what would make a moment like that moment with Stoney precious.

Paul said, "I didn't say 'fleeting.' I said 'illusory.' What we see around us doesn't have actual being, so the sensations we have about it always betray us, the way they do in a dream. That's all I was saying."

Zoe ignored him. She exclaimed, "What am I supposed to say to you, Isabel? That I'm not shallow, that I have feelings and all of that? I'm not going to do that."

"You can't prove a negative," said Simon. "According to Mom. That's why the justice system is 'guilty or not guilty.' In England it's 'guilty' or 'not proven,' I think. I mean, it's the job of the accuser to make the accusation stick, not of the accused to prove the negative. That's why the Saddam Hussein thing is—"

"Would you shut up, Simon?" said Isabel.

Simon cleared his throat, but he did shut up. Then he began to clean up his place at the counter. He looked at his watch. Isabel turned her gaze back to Zoe, who said, "I don't mind talking to you about this, but I would like to do it in private rather than in front of everyone."

"I don't want to talk about it. It's not like you're going to change my mind. You can't demonstrate to me that you are not who you are. You are who you are. That's fine." But of course it wasn't fine, Isabel saw that everyone could see that. She picked up her own dishes and walked them over to the sink. She put her toast crusts down the disposal and set her plate in the sink. Behind her, Charlie said, "I thought sure we were going to have a big argument about Iraq."

"We still can," said Elena.

"Yes," said Cassie, "there's plenty here. For example, look at this. 'Although a final tab for the U.S.-led war against Iraq remains unknown, the Bush administration does not expect American taxpayers to bear the entire burden for rebuilding the country, Defense Secretary Donald H. Rumsfeld told Congress on Thursday. "When it comes to reconstruction, before we turn to the American taxpayer, we will turn first to the resources of the Iraqi government and the international community," Rumsfeld said.'"

"We invaded you, and you're going to have to pay for it," said Elena.

Simon got up and, as he ran down the stairs to his room, called out, "Okay, I'm going!"

"Yes, yes, yes," said Elena. She turned to Paul. "Did he apologize enough? Is there something else he can do for you?"

"'The administration plans to tap frozen Iraqi assets, revenue from the country's oil fields and contributions from U.S. allies to largely fund the reconstruction effort, said Rumsfeld.'"

"I have a big bridge between San Francisco and Oakland to sell you if you're going to believe that," said Max.

Isabel glanced out of the corner of her eye at her mother, who, she saw, was glancing out of the corner of her eye at her. Then Zoe turned and smiled at Paul, who was feeling his jaw again. Zoe said, "Dear one, that was so strange, wasn't it?"

"I can't tell you how sorry I am," said Elena. "Simon is terribly impulsive. It's been a nightmare for me. His motto since he was a little boy has always seemed to be 'I wonder what would happen if I did such-and-such? If I put this bobby pin into this electrical outlet? If I set this plastic toy on the burner and turned it to high? If I went all the way down this long steep hill on my skateboard but didn't bother to tie my shoes? Could I jump off the skateboard and out of my shoes simultaneously? What if I said "Fuck you" to my math teacher for no reason? What if I tried to jump into my briefs?' That last one, he fell, hit his head on the dresser, and had to be observed for a night in the hospital in case he had a concussion. I used to call it 'the red-button effect.' If his eye caught any sort of red button, like an alarm button, he would just have to press it."

"He doesn't seem hostile," said Zoe.

"Oh, he's never been angry or hostile," said Elena. "Quite the opposite. If I got mad at all of these antics, he would be so surprised, as if trying these things out was just the most natural thing in the world. And it's not like there was peer pressure. He didn't have friends for years. He's such an oddball."

Isabel saw Zoe glance at her, as if she, too, could come up with a word, a mother's sort of word, like "oddball," that would diminish Isabel's most authentic feelings and assign them to a mere kid. Isabel wondered what this word might be—"bitch," probably. But Zoe held her tongue and smiled at Elena. Then she said, "Dear one? May I get you some ibuprofen or something like that?"

Max, in the meantime, had picked up the paper, and now put it down. Cassie said to Delphine, "Are we going?"

"I need my list," said Delphine. "It's supposed to be windy again today."

"Did you see where that fellow got blown out of the basket in one of those cherry pickers?"

"I don't think he got blown out. I think it fell over or something like that." Delphine gave her an absentminded hug.

Isabel continued to stand by the sink. Max got up and came over to her. He took her face in his hands, then he kissed her on the forehead, but he did not say anything about being nice to her mother or being polite or did she want to talk. He smoothed her hair back and kissed her again. One by one, everyone left her there, standing in a shaft of sunlight by the sink. It was nine-fifteen. The Getty, she thought, would open at ten. That would be a good place for her. She could look at some paintings, and then stand on that one west-facing balcony and look for this house from a distance. Sometimes she could see it, and sometimes she couldn't, the roof of her room peeking above every other building on this hillside. Doors slammed. Cars left. She thought that tomorrow morning she would certainly do something smarter—go out for breakfast with a friend, maybe, or take a run on the beach. No, no, no relatives.

DAY SIX · Saturday, March 29, 2003

Paul roused all of a sudden with what he considered to be the most terrifying thought, that he was in time. The way it presented itself to him was deceptively simple—here he was again, waking up again, night and darkness again, days slamming shut ever more quickly behind him with a sound like the sound of machine-gun fire. It was a quick thought, but frightening and stimulating. The shot of adrenaline that accompanied it woke him up thoroughly, and he saw that there was nothing wrong. The room was cool and quiet, Zoe was sleeping, the covers were not disarranged. Only his jaw hurt a little bit. As he gained consciousness, his jaw gained pain. It wasn't agony, but it presented him with an obstacle to going back to sleep. He slid gently upward, so that his head angled higher. He visualized the pain in his jaw draining downward like water, flowing around the back of his neck, and dissipating through the weave of the sheets, the fibers of the mattress, dripping in slow drops from the underside of the box spring onto the carpet, then diffusing into the earth, where it became—what?— bacteria? diamonds? earthworms? Something like pain or something unlike pain? He was adept at visualization, and the pain moved off, locating itself at a distance and staying there obediently.

Everyone had made a big deal about the punch. Even Simon, in his inexperienced way, had manifested true remorse, greater remorse than Isabel had shown for lashing out at Zoe, a more serious symptom in Paul's view. But Paul wasn't at all surprised that he and Zoe would catalyze some sort of violence and conflict. What was surprising, in his view, was that Isabel had suppressed her resentments against Zoe as long as she had, dissipating them with ironic or unkind remarks and avoidance rather than going for the catharsis. In Paul's opinion, this indicated that she was both stronger and more fearful than other girls he had observed. Of course, Zoe would be a worthy and intimidating antagonist for a daughter. One of the things that fascinated Paul about Zoe was what he called her "cloak of visibility"—all the robes and jewels and furs, the public aspect of her beauty and talent and fame, that she always had with her but seemed not to recognize as hers. He could see that Isabel tried not to relate to that part of Zoe, but it was no doubt difficult to avoid. And it was good that Isabel looked like Max and bore his name. She could, as he had heard her say once, "out" Zoe or not, as she pleased. In fact, Isabel's connection to Zoe was a convenient one for a Hollywood child, as close to voluntary as it was possible to get. Isabel, of course, didn't realize this and might never realize it, but Paul thought that, in the fatal compromise that was life in Hollywood, Isabel had gotten away with more of the good things and fewer of the bad things than anyone else Paul had known. No doubt this was owing to Delphine, whose indifference to fame and fortune, at least on the surface, was remarkable and worthy of emulation. Delphine, for Paul, was way more intimidating than Zoe, and if he were a young man and a suitor, he would certainly watch his step with her. Fortunately, he was neither.

He slid a little higher in the bed and arranged his beard a bit. He had taken the ponytail holder out of his hair before going to sleep, so, as surreptitiously as possible, he slipped his hands under the back of his hair and lifted and spread it out. Then he put his hands together over his abdomen, turned his feet directly upward, and performed some floating breaths, maybe ten or twelve of them. He was adept at these, too. He brought the prana first into his mouth, then into his throat, then into his upper chest, then into his diaphragm, then into his abdomen, his genitals, his upper thighs. Then he performed a still finer operation on it—he brought it into his skeleton and muscles, the layers of his dermis and epidermis. By the time it was entering every cell in his body, it was less air than light, but it still worked. With each breath he could sense his layers inflating, not so much a balloon as a sponge. If he really concentrated, he could stand the hairs on his arms right up on end. But that sense of being in time still did not lessen; he remained, as always when this happened, startled and afraid. No doubt the war had something to do with it, as a form of background radiation. It didn't help that he and Zoe had gone to the Middle Eastern antiquities show at LACMA in the afternoon. You couldn't walk through those rooms full of carefully curated artifacts without imagining other, more precious and more mysterious artifacts being blown to atoms at this very minute, by American bombs, under the bright Iraqi sunshine. Paul, of course, had not been to Iraq, but he had been to lots of other archeological sites and ancient temples and holy spots. The closest one to Iraq was in Istanbul, where he had visited both the Blue Mosque and Ayasofya. And

there was Crete, where he had visited the palaces at Knossos and Agia Tri-
ada. And one rainy day in the winter of 1972, he and Sarah Cochran had
walked up the solitary road leading from the train station to the hilltop
fortress of Mycenae, regarded the ruts in the paving stones of the Lion Gate
with considerable awe, entered the beehive tombs, and looked down on the
valley below them, entirely alone with the Bronze Age. Bam Bang Smash.
It was easy to imagine all of those bits of the past that had managed to survive the last three thousand years being pulverized by American bombs.

Zoe turned toward him, but she didn't open her eyes, though she
adjusted her pillow and pushed her hair out of her face. In the dark, he
could hardly see her—he was quite nearsighted, and he didn't want to
admit that he would not be going back to sleep by putting on his glasses or
looking at the clock on her side of the bed. Thus his impression of her was
more imagined than experienced—she was not sleeping next to him in the
blackness as much as she was crisscrossing the room by the light of the bedside lamp, folding her clothes, and setting them inside drawers in the chest
opposite to the bed. The yellow light of the lamp illuminated her hip and
her breast and her chin and the underside of her arms as she lifted her hair,
and then, still talking, she came to the end of the bed and crawled toward
him, smiling. This image of her was not accompanied by sound, though of
course he remembered perfectly what she had been talking about, just as
now he perfectly heard her breath as it went in and out, sometimes catching
behind her lips and emerging as a soft plosive. She had been talking about
Casablanca, which all of them had watched after dinner, or, rather, she had
been talking about a project she'd done with Lauren Bacall in the eighties
sometime. "Remember that movie with Eddie Murphy and Dan Aykroyd?"
she said. "Where Eddie goes to live at Dan's house, and Dan goes to live
with Jamie Lee Curtis, and in the end the three of them engineer some
kind of stock market coup against the old guys who set them up? Well,
Bacall and I were cast in a similar sort of movie, where she played my maid.
She was supposed to be an old Broadway star who had fallen on hard times,
and was working as the cigarette-smoking, hard-drinking secretary to the big
impresario who was going to be played by Woody Allen to begin with, but
he dropped out and we ended up with Carl Reiner. Anyway, Carl discovers
me singing in the restaurant where I have a job washing dishes, but of
course my character knows nothing about anything, so, to avoid the Cinderella thing or the *My Fair Lady* thing but at the same time making use of
both the Cinderella thing and the *My Fair Lady* thing, he installs me in the
Plaza Hotel and has Lauren Bacall tutor me for a couple of weeks or a
month or whatever. And of course we hate each other but then save each
other. One scene we did film was where I am sitting in the living room of

the suite, rolling a joint, and she comes in and sees me and gets all upset, but as soon as I light up, it makes her want a cigarette, so she asks me for a match and pulls out a Lucky Strike. Anyway, it was supposed to be this great Hollywood joke that Lauren Bacall, who looked absolutely gorgeous at the time, had fallen so low as to be picking up after me. There was going to be a scene where my mom, who really is a maid, shows up and they have it out. I wanted them to cast Ella Fitzgerald in that part—I thought it would be fun to see the two of them play that scene. Who's the toughest old girl after all? But they didn't get that far. It was shocking, really. The director was a guy named Sidney Gorman. He got up from lunch and said he was going to lie down in his trailer for a few minutes, and the next thing we knew he was dead. I think we had filmed four or five scenes. The script wasn't in very good shape, so the studio killed the project. I think the main problem was that Sidney and the studio hadn't agreed about who was going to be my love interest." And then she had crawled under the covers and curled next to him, thinking, he knew, that they should make love, but *Casablanca* had not put him in a lovemaking mood and probably had set him up for his dream that he was in time.

During the day he didn't believe in either death or time, but at night he occasionally woke up as he imagined a small animal hidden in the grass might, sensing the shadow of a predatory bird passing over. Even though the rabbit, say, was too young and inexperienced to understand it, it nevertheless reacted with a surge of primeval dread, a dread, Paul was sure, that was worse than actually being picked up and ripped apart and eaten. Pain and death were concrete and specific, and, at least according to victims of near-death events, in some sense not even experienced. But dread was dreadful, and in his own case (lying quietly beside the most beautiful woman in the world, to whom he had made no promises and had no responsibilities other than to keep giving her sessions and to treat her with consistent human kindness) utterly meaningless.

And so he had said little, put his arms around her, which was wonderful to do, and not made love to her. He had just started doing a few breathing exercises, and she had dropped off. He had felt possessed of a wonderful present that he could open at any time—the privilege of touching her and making love to her. Or not.

Paul hadn't seen *Casablanca* in thirty years or more, not since he took Marie Ellis to a showing at a UCLA film-society screening when there were no DVDs or even VCRs and you felt a little special to be eating Lebanese food and then taking in a double bill of *Casablanca* and *Knute Rockne— All-American*. To tell the truth, he hadn't understood *Casablanca* at the time and had never bothered to see it again. Simon and Isabel had stared in disbelief at Bogart crying in his beer, and Simon had said, seriously, "Is this where that expression 'crying in your beer' comes from?" And Max had had to explain to him, in fifty words or less, that there used to be a whole saloon culture where men gathered together without women and got drunk and emoted, either fighting or crying, and that, far from originating the idea of crying into your beer, Bogart had been piggybacking on thousands of years of accepted masculine behavior, and Isabel had said, "You're joking, right?," earnestly seeking to know. "No, I'm not," said Max, and Isabel said, "Hnh," filing this fact away with all the others.

During the flashback to Rick and Ilsa's earlier romance, Isabel had said, "You mean to say that, just because Ingrid Bergman didn't show up at the train, Bogart didn't care at all about the Nazis or the concentration camps or the war? Is that what they're trying to show?"

"Some Americans were more or less disengaged in the early stages of the—" said Max.

"But one wonderful weekend or whatever, and he didn't care at all? Was he, like, a virgin or something like that? Are they saying that, before they met in Paris, Bogart was a virgin?"

"People thought about love differently during the war," said Max.

"I understand that," said Isabel. "But she didn't even tell him her last name or anything about her past. How did they achieve actual intimacy?"

One thing Paul liked about Isabel was the dogged, literal cast of her mind. She was intelligent without being quick, quite different from Zoe. One thing he liked about this visit, even though it was disquieting in comparison with the monastery, was the opportunity it presented of observing the chimps in their natural setting, one of the chimps being himself. Because of course he recognized Max, though Max didn't recognize him. He remembered Max from sixth grade, the year he was a new student at Roosevelt Elementary School, Vineland, New Jersey. Paul, who was now six feet tall and a hundred fifty pounds too, had, at eleven, been about four foot eight and weighed something like sixty-two pounds. Max had been four years older, eight inches taller, and forty pounds heavier. He and two friends had picked up Paul in the hallway of the school, taken him into a classroom, and turned him upside down into one of those tall trash cans they had, then tied the laces of his oxfords together. He had not been hurt, though he got in trouble that evening for breaking his glasses. In the forty-four intervening years, he had come to understand that being bullied was a routine and even essential American school experience. The unique thing was that here he was, and here Max was.

He had not recognized Max right away—even his and Charlie's references to New Jersey hadn't clued him in. But the second night, when they were sitting around the dinner table talking about whether Zoe was too young, at forty-three, to play a grandmother, he had happened to notice a vein in Max's forehead, a small vertical blood vessel, and he had thereupon watched Max's face reorganize itself around that vein. The unfamiliar eyes and the gray hair and the alien cheeks and the beaky nose and the lips and chin visibly reconfigured themselves in relationship to the familiar shape of the vein, and within about a second, he saw Max's face and remembered his name, Nathan Maxwell, and his school locker number, 435. Compared with this, he thought, *Casablanca* was the sheerest realism. His recognition of Max had the effect of collapsing and accelerating time. But though the coincidence was amazing, he could not say that the one incident had even influenced the course of his life. His family had sojourned in New Jersey for one year only, and had then gone back to Michigan, where his father got a better job and they returned to the nest of his mother's family (which he now knew his father had been trying to escape). He had mushroomed in size and taken up football, then come to UCLA, but even that was a mere distraction from his true vocation, which was, of course, given the DNA from his mother's side and the power of the giant X chromosome compared with the fragmentary Y chromosome, God.

The three big boys had come upon him in the hallway, picked him up, and carried him into one of the math teacher's rooms, and they had upended him and tied his shoelaces together, but he remembered what he had been thinking about at the time. He had been thinking about breakfast that morning. He was eating his Wheaties, and his mother was walking back and forth between the stove and the kitchen table. She was scrambling eggs. Paul's sister, Lisa, was saying that she thought she could see the stigmata in the palms of her hands, which were beginning to tingle in a funny way, and also there was a mark on her side. She had pulled up her blouse, and Paul's mother had left the stove, taken off her glasses, and bent down to look at the mark. Then the two of them weighed the pros and cons of what they thought stigmata probably looked like and how stigmata probably began, at which point Paul drank down the milk at the bottom of his cereal bowl, put his bowl in the sink, and ran out of the house. Paul was eleven; Lisa was sixteen. Thank God she went to the high school, because, at the very moment when Max and his friends grabbed him, Paul was praying the stigmata away—dear God, leave her alone; dear God, this is the last thing we need at our house; dear God, I will say ten thousand rosaries if you just give the stigmata to someone besides Lisa. And as it turned out, Lisa did not get the stigmata, and Paul spent several years saying rosaries—he tallied them on a sheet of paper, and got up to 6,014 before losing track of the project.

The brother of one of Paul's ancestors was a saint. Exactly how many generations he and his mother were removed from this saint—Saint Joachim of Neibsheim—he did not know. Saint Joachim's younger brother, Albrecht, was the ancestor. Paul had visited Neibsheim on his own when he was twenty-three and traveling in Europe with Gloria Smithwick. Saint Joachim was considered to be the patron saint of pregnancy and childbirth. If a Neibsheim woman was infertile and she prayed to Saint Joachim, she would get pregnant and have a successful delivery. Gloria Smithwick had found this fact hilarious, given Paul's unceasing desire for sex. After he got home from Germany and broke up with Gloria, he translated the brochure and discovered that Saint Joachim was more interesting than anyone in the family knew.

Saint Joachim had lived a long and sinful life, partly as a small-time lawyer but mostly as a goon for a wealthy merchant. He had traveled all over Europe and was famous for being able to exact payment, with interest, from even the toughest hooligans, such as, apparently, the citizens of Burgundy. He was also famous, according to the brochure, for enthusiastically committing deadly sins. He regaled himself by having sex with anything that moved, whether female or male, human or animal, married or single. He always lied in preference to telling the truth, and he gloried in bearing false witness. He was gluttonous, and regularly ate and drank until he passed out and vomited all over himself. He lived until the age of almost seventy, when he was stricken with what sounded to Paul like either cirrhosis of the liver or kidney failure. He was known to have killed at least four people in anger, not counting those he offed while pursuing his profession. He held money back from his employers out of sheer uncontrollable greed, even after he himself was beaten up by a couple of his goon friends for doing so. As far as Paul could tell, the only sin Joachim did not commit was sloth. As for pride, he paraded his transgressions around town, perhaps as a form of intimidation. Late in his life, his boss, a merchant on a large scale who allowed his customers to buy on credit but then had to get paid, sent Joachim to Burgundy, in France, to collect on some long-outstanding debts. After a day's ride and a heavy meal of some seven courses, Joachim collapsed at the home where he was lodging.

The two brothers who owned the house knew all about Joachim, and they were afraid that if he died in the house, especially without confession or absolution, local thugs would use his death as a pretext for entering the house and having revenge. As the brothers were talking about whether to throw Joachim out in the condition he was in, Joachim called to them, and asked them to get the holiest priest they knew and bring him to his bedside. The brothers were amazed that he would want to confess the kinds of sins he had on his conscience, and they were certain that he could not gain absolution, but they went and got a man famous for his quiet life, Brother André.

Brother André had lived so cloistered a life that he had not heard of Joachim or the two brothers. He asked Joachim if he had recently confessed, and Joachim said that since his illness he had not confessed, the space of about a week, but before that he had been to confession every week for his entire life. Nevertheless, Joachim said, he had terrible sins on his conscience.

The two brothers knelt outside the room, pretending to pray for Joachim's soul, and eavesdropped. They heard him say what his sins were: he had taken two pieces of bread when he meant to take only one, and he had drunk his fill of water one day after a long hot walk (he said nothing about the seven-course meal of goose and carp and venison and doves cooked in wine and onion confit that had done him in, or the twenty goblets of the best red Burgundy). Once he had happened to glance at a girl passing in the street (he said nothing of the three boys he had brought to the house the second night of his visit). He had given only half of his daily allotment of food money to a beggar one day, though he had attempted to make up for that the next day by giving all of it. He said that one time, as a child, he had spoken angrily to his mother. Brother André reacted with enthusiasm—he had never confessed anyone so truly penitent for such minor transgressions! The two brothers were laughing outside the room, but of course making no sound. Shortly after the confession and the last rites, Joachim died.

Joachim had begged Brother André to have his body brought to the monastery, and so it was, and Brother André could not stop exclaiming about Joachim's confession, about what a holy fellow the old guy was, and so humble and punctilious about every little thing! The monks let the body lie in state in the chapel of the monastery for a day or two, and as a result of this public-relations effort, people from the town went to the chapel to see what such a holy man looked like. They began to pray for his intercession with God on their behalf; Brother André said he would jump right to the head of the line and see God almost immediately after death! Within a day, not one but two local townspeople declared themselves healed: one of severe headaches that sounded to Paul like migraines; the other had been inhabited by a devil who caused him to curse and cry out, which sounded to Paul like Tourette's.

The interpretation of these events suggested by the brochure was that, after a sinful life, Saint Joachim made a worthy confession and his soul was cleansed. In the terms of the Parable of the Vineyard, Joachim had managed to get in the gate just before the end of the day—if the grace of God could redeem even this guy, then the grace of God was like the wind inside a tornado, which drove chopsticks through tree trunks and set cars on top of houses. And over the years, Saint Joachim's shrine produced a steady stream of miracles that in the end bore little or no relationship to the life of Saint Joachim himself.

Paul's interpretation was slightly different. As a Buddhist, he did not believe in sin, or virtue, or redemption, or a personal savior, or an individual fate. He saw Joachim's frenzy of activity as pointless and self-defeating, his deadly anger a manifestation of the intensifying unhappiness that always results from the cycle of desires felt and satisfied and then felt again with even greater sting. What interested him about Uncle Joachim was the monumental quality of his appetites—seven courses, three boys, twenty goblets of wine, followed by vomiting and unconsciousness, obviously a form of bulimia.

According to Paul's thinking, Joachim's entrance into heaven was less likely than reincarnation, but there were also two other afterlives. One of these was his afterlife as a saint, and therefore as a concept. Something about Joachim lived in the imaginations of the townspeople of Neibsheim, where his corpse was returned and was entombed some six months after death, richly accompanied by enough stories of miracles in Burgundy to overcome his local reputation. Over the centuries, he became a benign, embracing figure, little Saint Joachim, who was especially interested in babies and children, the patron saint of gestation. His other afterlife was in Paul's family, as the most famous representative of a familial religious impulse, a combination saint and sinner who happened to achieve stardom but who was not much different from certain offspring in every generation. Paul had seen other families like his, all-God-all-the-time families. His was German and Catholic, but he had known one that was English, in which his friend, a Marxist, turned out, unknowingly, to have English Catholic ancestors who lost the family estate in 1605, when they had to flee to Ireland after the failed Guy Fawkes rebellion. What Paul saw in that family was a contrarian, absolutist impulse that was always ready to give up mere real estate in favor of doomed revolution. The other was Ulster Irish, the family of Sarah Cochran. In Paul's own hearing, one of Sarah's aunts, a kindly old lady of the purest orange Evangelical hue, had expressed the opinion that the citizens of Waterford and Wexford did not actually have souls, and that was why they remained committed papists. While his own family members were discussing stigmata and ecstatic flight (had Aunt Eva really risen from the front porch to the crotch of the maple tree in her front yard not through her own will, or was she deluded?), the Cochrans were writing each other letters in which they marshaled pages and pages of doctrinal arguments to demonstrate how and why each of them was right and each of the others was wrong. The goal was to get all the Cochrans into heaven, but God was picky and legalistic, and the rules were complex and hard to understand. Judging by his experience of Sarah, lust was the underlying difficulty, as with many religious families he knew, but actual discussion of lust never got into the letters.

In the meantime, Paul's mother's idea of a vacation was combining a trip to Lourdes, say, with a tour of the Pyrenees and four days in Barcelona—churches, shopping, and beaches. "Have you said your prayers? Have you brushed your teeth? You haven't masturbated, have you? You're serving Mass at six a.m., don't forget."

One girlfriend he'd had, Monica Horner, with whom he had gone to the Grand Canyon and then on to Sedona, in Arizona, and Chaco Canyon, in New Mexico, the home of the Anasazi peoples, and after that made a tour of various medicine wheels around the West, had come from an entirely secular family. They considered religion a topic unmentionable at the table and talked instead about sports, the neighbors, and current events. If heaven existed, they had no doubt that they would be welcomed there as they, a sociable and kindly set, were welcomed everywhere. Before Monica, he had not known that there were such families. Monica truly thought religion was a stage civilization had already passed through. She went on to become a wildlife biologist.

He was stiff. Zoe had turned the other way, and now her shoulder and the back of her neck were pressed against him. Her fragrance was still potent, a combination of the verbena of the soap she used and the lemon-thyme of her shampoo. It made her seem French. His jaw ached again. It was a discrete ache, like a bubble that apppeared, expanded, and popped—possibly it was related to the blood pumping in that area, but it was not repeated or rhythmic. As soon as he thought about it, he also could not help thinking about Stephanie Larsson. Stephanie Larsson was a client he had had who suffered from fibromyalgia and chronic fatigue syndrome. She had worked with him for about three years and also with his friend Barney Chang, who was an acupuncturist. She suffered from constant fatigue and pain. She was unhappy and obsessive. Her history included a car accident that knocked her cervical vertebrae out of whack, and she was allergic to dairy products. She did not have a husband or a boyfriend and was, more or less, isolated. Stephanie Larsson was a stable system, he thought (though Barney did not quite agree with him), and all the elements of Stephanie's stability—her depression, her loneliness, her social awkwardness, her pain, her fatigue, her tendency to bump into things and drop things, her perfectionism, even her desire to find a cause for her condition that could be relieved, as if she could go back in time and relive her life—tended to reinforce one another. He would begin each session with Stephanie with a new idea—to pluck a particular thread out of the tangle of Stephanie's symptoms and understand and then repair that thread. The theory was that getting Stephanie to experience one, and then two positive and pleasurable things would rebalance the whole system, or, rather, unbalance the old system, and move her out of her stable and painful unhappiness, through a mix of unhappiness and happiness, and into a stable system of less pain, more pleasure, and more energy. It became clear as he worked with her that the sort of session she expected, which was to narrate and analyze her particular problem of the day, was not working. She was eloquent, and her own eloquence frightened and in some sense enthralled her. Once she had embodied the problem in words, it was harder to dislodge her sense of its pernicious and unprecedented effects. But if he ever so gently tried to guide her attention away from the current problem and toward something positive, she felt that he wasn't taking her seriously and balked, which was unproductive in its own way. Sometimes, after he directed her toward visualizing beautiful or good things, she might leave his office in a better mood, but when she got home, her own situation, in an unbeautiful neighborhood and surrounded by ugly things, reminded her that she was spending so much money on treatment that she couldn't afford much else. He and Barney agreed that she was a difficult case. On the one hand, she truly believed in her illness; on the other, she was truly ill. They never diagnosed her as stubborn or hypochondriacal. As far as Paul knew, he never showed impatience with her, and Barney certainly did not, but she gave up on the two of them anyway, leaving Paul with the knowledge that the very thing he had put all his faith in up to that point, technique, could turn powerless after all.

He was not so unlike Stephanie in some ways. Or at least in one way—he had an unshakable belief in cause and effect. This belief, he knew, protected him from the dangers of revelation. He had come to think that there were two religious types. One of these was the type who enjoyed being struck by lightning, who gloried in the very unexpectedness of it, because that was what demonstrated the unpredictable power of God. The other type enjoyed shaping the vessel and making it worthy. That was his type. His type followed disciplines and progressed up levels and prepared the spirit and more or less put off the actual transcendent experience as long as possible. Each type had its advantages. The struck-by-lightning type lived in a more exciting way, courting danger and disintegration but also embracing the possibility of overwhelming meaning. If the meanings changed, so be it, the sense that meaning existed was satisfying in itself. His type, by contrast, often received no revelations at all, died, perhaps, in a state of frustration and spiritual emptiness, but created little fuss and no muss. He was temperamentally inclined to prefer nothing to a something that might scatter his atoms completely, and so he ate certain foods prepared in certain ways, he honed his counseling techniques, he systematically excluded negative thoughts, he developed his erotic skills, and he visited ever more far-flung and arduous holy sites. If he thought of himself as a vessel, it was a vessel that was getting cleaner and simpler in design, if, perhaps, smaller. Take the erotic, for example. After much practice, he had arrived, in Zoe, at the apex of most men's erotic ambition. She was not only a talented, beautiful, adept, and famous woman, the best the world had to offer, she was generous and affectionate and more or less suited to his peculiarities. Even her occasional volatility didn't bother him. She was far beyond the erotic fantasies he had had as a young man. But she had arrived in his life at the very time when he not only didn't want to possess her, he didn't want to possess. He didn't want to say she was his, he didn't want to be comforted by her continual presence, he didn't want to have erotic feelings much anymore, and he felt no pride in her attachment to him. Embracing her was like embracing a ghost. In what he felt toward her, he could see that he really and truly had come to believe that all of the material world was illusory. The very palpable and physical sensation he had of her fragrance, and the pressure of her flesh against his, of her beauty and grace and the lovely sound of her voice singing a song, struck him more and more forcefully as not having actual existence.

There were other signs that he was actually achieving enlightenment: He could make light come into his body and make pain go away; he failed to notice things like money and power and influence. He could drive down the road in his little car and make all the lights turn green, intersection after intersection. For about the past year, he had noticed that all he had to do was think of something in order for it to occur. The first notable and specific occasion had been on Valentine's Day the year before. He was walking on the beach with his friend Sophie, whose mistake had been to get a pug puppy. The puppy, named Pepper, had grown into a yapping, undisciplined monster. Because the dog spent the entire day while Sophie was at work barking at the front window of Sophie's apartment, Sophie was about to lose her lease. Paul remembered thinking, "Someone else might like this dog," and before he could add the "but I can't imagine who" clause, a man had come up to them on the beach and said, "Oh, I love your pug! What's his name?" And Sophie had said, "Pepper." And the man had said, "I am such a pug man! How old is he?" And Sophie had said, "He's two. Would you like to have him? He's terribly yappy." And the man had said, "I can deal with that." And she had put the dog and the leash into the arms of the pug man, and she and Paul had walked away without a backward glance or a second thought. But that was only the most dramatic incident. His wishes, if only for the rain to stop or the sun to come out, continued to come true. On his pilgrimage to the seven holiest mountains in China, monks and adepts had greeted him everywhere. If he was standing in a crowd at an overlook or outside a temple door, he would be the one who was chosen to come in and participate in the prayers. If he was hiking up a trail and someone passed him, that man would turn out to be a holy man who would greet him without preliminaries and walk on with him as with a brother. Another thing had not happened to him in China that might have happened to him ten years ago—in each temple, he had looked upon the prayers and rituals with pleasure but felt no sense that maybe there was something in them for him, that maybe those prayers and rituals were more efficacious and worthy than ones he already knew. He had finally truly accepted the fact that you walked up the path because it was the path at your feet. You were not omniscient, omnipresent, or omnipotent. You were specific, and so had to take specific steps up a specific path, but any path was good enough—all the Cochrans would get to heaven in the end, even the ones who were wrong.

Still, on the cusp between a life of desires and a life without desires, Paul found he was awakening with a sense of dread more and more frequently. If not Zoe, what? If not Machu Picchu and Giza, what? Thirty more years of lotus position on the balcony of his apartment in West Hollywood waiting for transcendence to find him? That might have been the question he would have asked some of the monks up north if they had gotten there. But he had known instinctively that Zoe would have carried her cloak of visibility with her even into the monastery and the monks would have been confused. She had that effect, and it took time to wear off. Here, in fact, in this house with these people, might be the only place in the world where Zoe Cunningham left her cloak of visibility by the door. He put on his glasses. Oh, it was 3:19 a.m. He took off his glasses.

Out of the darkness, Zoe's voice said, "Hi."

He said, "Hi. You're awake."

"May I tell you my dream?"

"Of course." He slid down in the bed and turned toward her. She cuddled comfortably against him, and though his body seemed to form itself around hers, his jaw suddenly throbbed. Was there a cause for that? She said, "I was at that restaurant with my old boyfriend Roger Rector, the one at the end of Sunset, right on the beach. It's a seafood place with peanut shells on the floor. I can't remember what it's called, but we were out on the pier. I don't think there really is a pier, but it was like the Santa Monica Pier, and I could see us talking and leaning over our food, and I could also see this huge wave, like a big curl, looming over us, maybe a hundred feet in the air. I wasn't afraid."

"Did it hit you?"

"No, it just loomed. I said, 'Look, Roger,' and he looked up from his breaded shrimp. Then it was over. It wasn't a nightmare."

"Roger Rector?"

"Yes, and his brothers were named Willy and Dick."

"Do you think the parents had any idea of what they were doing when they named those boys?"

"Well, I have no idea about the mother, but Roger always said it was his father's way of blessing them."

Paul laughed, then he said, "I'm sorry if I woke you."

"Did you? I don't know, I thought my dream woke me. You know, one time when I was in my twenties, I was sleeping in my trailer over lunchtime, and I had a dream that I was in my high-school English class. We were all sitting around the table, and the teacher stood up and he said, loud and clear, 'Okay, today I am going to tell you kids the secret of life.' I leaned forward, and we all stopped talking, and he opened his mouth to speak, and right then, right at that exact moment, the PA knocked on my trailer door and woke me up. I mean, how did that happen? Was that just a coincidence?"

Paul rubbed his jaw because it throbbed again, and Zoe glanced at him, but she didn't ask anything. He said, "My immediate response is that there is no secret of life, and so, whenever you think you are going to be given the secret of life just like that, you will back away from it."

She looked at him, then smiled. She said, "I think of you as knowing the secret of life."

"Do you? I think I know a few techniques with which I make adjustments and pass the time."

"But you seem enlightened."

"I seem patient. I am patient."

"Maybe that's the same thing."

"I don't know. Maybe it is."

She inclined her head toward him and pressed against him. She said, "At any rate, it's a rare quality, especially around here."

His jaw throbbed a third time. That was the third time, he thought, in maybe a minute, but even so, as her affection radiated from her body into his, he felt himself relax. And so he slipped downward in the bed, under the covers, and rolled right up against her. It was comfortable. He thought, Was he immune to this, too, to such simple comfort?

Once, he had read an article about the physiology of sleep that said that there was a distinct shift, almost like a switch. You drifted down and drifted down, more and more relaxed but still in a state of being awake, and then your brain performed some function and you were asleep. After reading that article, he had tried to attend to those seconds and moments, until, eventually, he had learned to note the switch, just as he had learned to note the feeling of his brain thinking, of energy, in particular, passing from one side of his brain to the other, through the corpus callosum.

Her affection did comfort him, no doubt a hormonal thing, oxytocin, probably. Nice word, "oxytocin," he thought, as his brain got closer and closer to flipping that switch that he did not know the name of. He felt her take a deep breath and let it out.

He was standing with someone on a narrow parapet. He knew the guy's name but couldn't remember it. He looked like one of the stockers at Whole Foods. He was wearing a uniform, but it wasn't a Whole Foods uniform, it was a military uniform of some kind. He knew that he had to look over the parapet, because the guy kept saying, "Look over the parapet," but he could hardly get his eyes open enough to do so. The guy said, "Look at them. They're getting out."

He asked who was getting out.

"The prisoners!" Finally, he was able to look over the parapet. The yard in front of him was in black and white. It looked like a prison yard in a movie. It was empty. The guy said, "They must have forgotten." Paul remembered that his name was Bit, though part of him, even in the dream, knew that wasn't a name.

"Who?"

"The guards forgot to leave the doors open. They have to be reminded every day."

"To do what?" He was not only sleepy, he thought, he was stupid.

"To leave the doors open! To leave the doors open!"

"Why do they want to leave the doors open? This is a prison."

"Of course it is, but the prisoners have to escape! Didn't you know that?"

Now the prison began to look a bit like the monastery. A beautiful green hillside fell away from the wall, and the sun was shining. Paul, in his dream, felt himself breathe deeply and have a sudden sense of joy. They were going to let the prisoners escape! Things were better than he had thought they would be!

"They have to escape so we can shoot them! We can't afford to try them! We can't afford to feed them! Where is your weapon? Have you lost your weapon? Here they come!"

Bit lifted his weapon and rested the barrel on the parapet. A few people came out into the yard. Paul in his dream didn't recognize them. They looked around and smiled. They thought they were escaping. Bit shot them, one, two, three, four. Then another one came out. It was a man who turned into a dog as soon as it saw the corpses. Bit shot it anyway. He said, "Where's your weapon? We have to shoot them all! They are escaping! They are guilty! It's the best we can do for them. I am cruel only to be kind! Shoot them!"

In the dream, he was stupid, but he did recognize the logic. He also realized he would shoot them. But he cried out and woke himself up. He heard himself say, "We shot them on the film."

"What?" said Zoe.

Paul took a deep breath and twisted his head one way on the pillow and then the other way.

"Were you dreaming of making a movie? You distinctly said, 'We shot the film.'"

"Did I? I thought I said, 'We shot them on the film.'"

"That's not what it sounded like."

"I dreamt I was on a parapet outside a prison in some country like Bosnia or Poland, and I was told that the prisoners were starving, so the prison doors were being left open for them to escape, except that as they escaped we were supposed to shoot them. I dreamt that I thought this was a good idea."

"Don't you remember? Stoney was telling that story after dinner, about one of those guys who want Max to make that movie. He said his grand-father did that with German prisoners in Russian prisons in World War II."

"I don't remember hearing that." He took a deep breath and then another, hoping to accelerate the breakdown of adrenaline in his system that his dream had caused. He closed his eyes. He often thought that if he could really manage his own adrenaline, he could then more perfectly manage his own thoughts.

"Well, you must have. How odd. What a nightmare."

"It was a nightmare."

"Are you okay?"

"I haven't had a nightmare in a long time. I usually don't dream." He stretched and shifted his position against Zoe. He said, "I'm sure this is my nightmare of the Iraq war, my fear that I'll accept its logic, maybe. Or that I already do without knowing it."

"You got an erection."

"What?"

"You got an erection about five minutes ago. I was tickling your testicles and you got an erection, but then it went away before you woke up."

"Why were you tickling my testicles?"

"Because they were there. Because I was awake. Because I had been tickling the insides of your thighs and before that I was stroking your chakras. I thought it might feel good."

Paul turned this over in his mind.

"Do you not want me to tickle you when you're asleep? I was just trying to—"

"Actually," he said, "I think it's good. I think there must have been some blocks in maybe the throat and the base chakra, and your tickling activated those blocks, and I had that dream. You know, for years I could only fall asleep if I was lying on my back with my left hand touching my throat chakra and my right hand touching my base chakra. When I started studying, one of my teachers said that those were my most blocked chakras, and I had to use my hands to open them up and connect them to everything else." He took hold of his head and turned it once to the left and once to the right. He could sense his second and third vertebrae release.

Now he began to feel better. That's what words were for, he had found. Their only virtue, but it was an essential one, was to enter the flow of adrenaline and fragment it by means of interference. The quanta of words tumbled through the energy of feelings and blocked their flow like rocks in a stream, and pretty soon the feelings lost their dynamic and their power. You, whoever you were, were not within the feelings anymore, but beside them or above them, observing them. That was the perennial efficacy of mere words. It was a lovely thing. He said, "No, I like you to tickle me when I'm sleeping. If it arouses a nightmare, so what? I don't mind a nightmare."

"You seem more enlightened than that."

"Oh dear," said Paul. "I don't think enlightenment is about being happy."

"What is it about, then?"

"Well, you know . . ." He could feel himself go into parable mode. "I think about all the archeological sites I've visited. When I go, try as I might to make it otherwise, I just see ruins. But there are others who know more than I do who see what was once there. Right now, that's what I think enlightenment is. It's a sense of all the things that exist having meaning. People's brains are organized to build and perceive patterns, and so the greatest enlightenment is the largest possible construction of meaning, a construction in which every nail and joint and angle and *accident* would have the same amount of meaning as every supporting beam and facing board and brace and *intention*. All the masters say that my construction will eventually be blown up by real enlightenment, and, sure, it will. It has to be. It's like the Tower of Babel. They worked hard on it and built it higher and higher and with greater and greater complexity, and then—boom— God blew it up. Whoops, said the folks on the ground, God is angry. He didn't like our tower. But that's just their perception. It's just as likely that what really happened is that it poufed out or vanished into another dimension, that God saw it was good and it ceased to have material existence. Its disappearance wasn't actually a judgment, but, rather, the explosion was a measure of the difference between God and man. I am operating on the premise that I'm as ignorant at any given moment as I can't help being, but that when I am less ignorant things will have more meaning, until they, and I, cease to be human at all."

She said, "Hmm," as if she had not quite followed this explanation and was now thinking about something else, but Paul rather liked that Tower of Babel idea. He wondered whether he would remember it. "You know," she said, "I should tell you that Simon and I had a little thing today."

He pictured them arguing about something, but what? The punch? (His jawed throbbed.) But Simon seemed genuinely remorseful about that, so, unless there was some irritable, grudge-holding side of Zoe that he didn't know about, he didn't think that was likely. Simon was impulsive but not argumentative or defensive, as far as he could tell. The constant joking seemed truly good-natured. He said, "What about?"

"Well, about the usual."

"You and Simon have a usual source of disagreement already? You've only known each other a few days. Did you get on him about punching me? My feelings about that are—"

"Honey, it wasn't an argument. We fucked. While you were doing yoga and then having that phone session with the girl from Atlanta."

Paul had to admit he was startled, or maybe more than startled, but then it struck him all over again that that was what technique was for. If you are technically adept, then you always know the right thing to say even when you are startled, and so he said, "Does that seem to you to have been appropriate?"

"I don't know. It was fun. He's nice. I realize he punched you, but I'd sort of forgotten about that by the late afternoon."

Nevertheless, his jaw gave another throb.

"He's had lots of experience, as you can imagine, given the way he looks."

Paul cleared his throat in an effort to attain a state of disinterestedness. "Older women?"

"Among others."

"Older men?"

"I gathered that, yes, a few of those."

"Did you use a condom?"

"We didn't have one. It was a spur-of-the-moment thing. It seemed harmless." Her voice was still light, but not quite as light as it had been when she first told him. He said, "I guess, as your counselor, I have to point out that I believe your instincts have led you astray on this one."

"Well, as my counselor, you shouldn't be sleeping with me in the first place, isn't that true?"

He sat up and turned toward her. She looked a tad defiant, which he had to admit was a tad intimidating. He reached around her and turned on the light, reviewing as best he could the agreed-upon unspoken ground rules of their relationship. They seemed to be that she had the right to tell him about things and he had the right to suggest productive and non-self-destructive modes of behavior, and at the same time, he had the right to pursue a sexual relationship with her while she had the right to become attached to him, and additionally that she had the right to spend her money freely on the two of them and he had the right to pursue his various disciplines in the course of the day. He had the right to be honest with her about his opinions, sometimes brutally so, and she had the right to express her feelings, even when they were contradictory and, let's say, unattractive. He took a deep breath. He said, "Yes, some people would say that, but having a relationship seemed to be something we both wanted, and so I didn't feel that there was a mismatch of power that would make either of us unduly vulnerable to the other if I became your counselor."

"Well, I don't think power comes into what I did with Simon at all. We felt like doing it, it seemed like it was going to be fun, and it was. Better than getting it on with Charlie, who's been hitting on me in his way, too."

"But he's slept with men."

"Well, I didn't find out about that until afterward, but he said that he's always been the pitcher, not the catcher."

"Did you douche?"

"Well, I cleaned myself up, of course, but why are you focusing on this part? There are so many parts to focus on, and you've decided that HIV is the important one."

"What do you think is the important one?"

"That he's twenty. That he's my former husband's girlfriend's son. That he's younger than my own daughter, who is in the house. Then, of course, there's the part about him punching you. If this were a movie and you were the villain, then it would be good that I fell for him after that, but if you were the hero, then it would show the true evil of my promiscuous nature."

"How about your continuing discomfort with the sessions I have with women like Marcelle and Anita and Jolene and Diana? That seems to have been part of your motivation today."

She ignored this and said, "But I guess I feel like the punch doesn't really have meaning, apart from what he said about it."

"So you're focusing on the incestuous part."

"Do you really think it's incestuous? I never met him before. We're not related."

She had moved away from him, and now there was about a foot between them, probably a good idea. He said, "I guess I think that there are two ways of looking at that piece of it. Does it feel incestuous?"

"Well, only in the age-difference thing. But I have to admit that, when we were eating dinner and he was sitting across from me, surrounded by the others, I felt a little odd and naughty."

"Zoe—" He was going to exclaim at the irresponsibility of her choice, but he stopped himself, thinking again of the ground rules, and said, "What do you think will happen when the others find out?"

"I don't think they will. Simon says his mother still thinks he's a virgin."

"I truly doubt that."

"Believe me, she can't imagine all the experience he's had. It's like his vocation."

"That," said Paul, "I do understand."

"He said he made up his mind to fuck me the moment I walked into the house. I am the prize."

"He said that? That seems very calculating."

"Well, yes, it does as I repeat it, but it was flattering when he said it. I laughed. I mean, he's got the look of a prize himself, he's so cute."

"So," said Paul, "how was it?"

"Oh, it was fun. Just a fuck. Nothing deep. It's nice to be around a young body."

"I'm sure. But don't you think he's going to brag about this? It would be inhuman not to."

"Yes, but not to his mother. I don't think he's going to brag to his mother."

"But to others?"

"People brag about having slept with me all the time, whether they have or not or whether they've even met me or not, and I don't pay any attention to it. I can't say yes and I can't say no. I just keep smiling and I don't say anything."

"But haven't we had several sessions about whether you should act on impulse in this way?"

"Paul." She sat back on her haunches and looked right at him. "Do you care whether I had a thing—"

"Had sexual intercourse with—"

"—had sexual intercourse with Simon?"

"Do you mean, does it threaten or hurt me in any way?"

"Yes."

"You mean, how do I feel about it as opposed to how do I think about it?"

"Yes."

"You mean, what meaning do I give it?"

"Yes."

"Especially in light of the fact that he socked me first thing in the morning and my jaw still throbs?"

"Does it? I'm sorry about that, honey." She feathered her fingers along his jaw, and he let her. Was this, he thought, the attack he had been dreading, the shadow he had intuited, something as simple, after all, as sexual infidelity? And this bit of information did have an effect—it made his throat ache and his mouth go dry. But he said, "Well, I'll give you my first reaction, my very first thought."

"That should be telling."

"I think it is." He cleared his throat yet again. He said, "The fact is, I'm a little relieved."

"You are?" She looked surprised.

"A little."

"Why is that?"

"Because you are a big responsibility."

"Oh," she said. She looked hurt. He held her gaze. Her expression fixed itself, then shifted and grew a little more remote for a moment. Finally, she looked away, toward the door, then she looked back. She said, "Yes, of course you're right. All you have to do is watch *Sunset Boulevard*, d-a-a-h-h-h-h-ling, to realize that."

He gave her a moment. Then he said, "But you are fun."

She moved across the bed toward him again, almost as if she didn't even realize what she was doing. She snuggled against him. Yes, he thought, it was dishonest. But it was a relief, too. He put his arm around her.

"Look at that," said Cassie. "He dropped the burning cigarette on the wooden floor of the hallway, and stubbed it out with his toe. We used to do that all the time."

"That's true," said Max. "There used to be cigarette butts everywhere. I've been to parties where people actually snuffed their cigarettes out on the wall-to-wall carpet. When they first had nylon carpeting, you put a butt out on that and it would just melt the nylon right down to the matting. Wool, you could get a pair of scissors and cut the carpet out from around the burn, but not, what was it, olefin. And it wasn't just stubbing them out. The burning tips would drop off during parties, and no one would even notice—"

"That's because they would have had so much to drink," said Cassie. "I mean, look at this fellow. Every time he enters a scene, he asks for whisky. That's what acting used to be, smoking and drinking."

Charlie said, "You know, when I first started working, when was that, the early sixties, I worked in this office where we all just threw our cigarette butts into the wastepaper basket, and the secretaries would throw used carbon paper in there, too. No one thought a thing about it until, one day, some of the carbon paper caught fire, and since there wasn't a fire extinguisher, one of the secretaries ran for a glass of water, but the other one stood up and went over and pulled down her panties and pissed the fire out."

"How could she do that?" exclaimed Isabel, skeptically.

"It wasn't actually flaming," said Charlie.

They were watching a movie Paul had never seen before, from England. It was called *The Day the Earth Caught Fire*. Paul recognized only one actor, Leo McKern. It seemed to be a newsroom/romance/apocalypse movie. Paul felt that it was taking a long time to get going. He was sitting on the couch beside Zoe. Simon was sitting on the floor in front of the two of them, in what Paul considered to be a very sonlike position. Isabel was sitting on the other side of Zoe. The others were ranged around the room. The only thing notable about the arrangement was that Elena was as far from Charlie as she could be. The two of them had had a huge argument in the middle of the afternoon, down by the pool, in which he had called her a know-nothing traitor and she had called him a Republican Party robot-apparatchik. The tumult had since died down, but there had been no apologies. Dinner had been strained. It didn't help that the nightly movie seemed to be about climate change.

The movie was heavy on the dialogue, so Paul was with Delphine in this. If they were going to watch it, then everyone should be quiet, but of course everyone was not quiet. The screen was the biggest Paul had ever seen in a private home. Max had told him that the equipment was outdated, but Paul had to admit that he enjoyed the luxury, just as he enjoyed the luxury of the cool and quiet wine-cellar room, and the luxury of the pool, and the luxury of the garden, and the luxury of the location, though all of them, in their way, were outdated.

"I like her," said Zoe of the girl in the movie. "She has a good haircut. Was she ever in anything else?"

Isabel made some noise, rather like a muffled snort, and Zoe reacted immediately, assuming the noise was directed at her. "Well, she does have a good haircut. It shows her independence."

"She was in a few things," said Max. "She died young."

This caused everyone to fall silent.

The movie went on. The premise was that two huge atomic blasts—one at the North Pole, set off by the Russians, and one at the South Pole, set off by the Americans—cause global ramifications. Right now, on the screen, crowds gathered in London for an antinuclear protest happened to notice a solar eclipse. The hero took a picture of it and ran back to his newsroom.

"I think the global-warming stuff is pretty interesting," said Isabel. "You might even call it prescient."

The question about the eclipse was why was it coming ten days early, and why was it tracking across the Northern Hemisphere rather than, as predicted, the Southern Hemisphere? Meanwhile, holiday-makers at Brighton were having a wonderful time. The hero met up with the girl again. She was wearing a skimpy two-piece outfit, and he was wearing a suit, and they were both shining with sweat but smiling. Leo McKern, the science editor, put two and two together for the newsroom and for the audience—the simultaneous atomic explosions had tilted the earth off its axis, changing the location of the equator.

Isabel said, "With actual global warming, Europe will be much colder, not hotter. The weather parts are good, though." So far, the movie had featured torrential rains and blistering heat. As they kept watching, a fog came in, but only a low-level fog, maybe a story or two high. When the characters were at ground level, they could not see a thing. When they went up to their apartments, the brilliant sunlight shone over the white coverlet of the fog and reassured them. Paul said, "It's a good detail that they think it's beautiful in spite of themselves."

"The special effects aren't bad," said Max.

The romance gained speed. The hero knocked on the girl's apartment door just as she was getting out of the tub. She heard the knock and turned toward the camera, and there was the most fleeting view of her breasts, so quick that you almost didn't see it. When she let him in, he asked for a drink, and much was made of the fact that he would have to settle for coffee. Within a few minutes, she was lying on the bed, on her back, and he was leaning over her. Once again, though they didn't complain of the heat, they were shining with perspiration, his face and forehead and her chest.

"Continuity glitch," said Zoe.

"I see that," said Simon. "Her wrap is up under her armpits and across her chest, and then it's down almost showing her nipples, then it's up again, then down again."

"Rage in the cutting room," said Max, and everyone laughed. Zoe ran her hand over Paul's knee in an affectionate manner. In the next scene, the wind came up, dispersing the fog in the night and blowing people, cars, and heavy objects everywhere. "The London Eye would be down in a second with that kind of wind," said Isabel. "Something to look forward to. You know, there were something like twenty-five or -six major flood disasters in the nineties, eighteen in the eighties, eight in the seventies, seven in the sixties, and six in the fifties—"

"Is that what they taught you at the Little Red Schoolhouse?" said Charlie. Paul saw Max give him a kick. Isabel grunted, then said, "There's a Web site not connected with the University of California in any way—"

"Well," said Charlie, "don't you ever pause to wonder—"

"It said on the radio when I was driving here that the winds in L.A. were more than seventy miles per hour today and yesterday. You have to admit that's unusual," said Stoney.

"I don't live in L.A., so I don't—"

"Shhh," said Delphine.

"I don't understand why we're watching a disaster movie in the middle of a war," said Elena. "*The Day the Earth Stood Still* was sort of funny and innocent, but this one actually bothers me."

"I didn't know what it was going to be about," said Max. "I never even heard of it before that article about great disaster-movies in the paper the other day."

On the screen, there were sunny panoramas of London after the storm. Paul knew that the brightness of the cityscape was supposed to seem sinister, but the real effect was to remind him of all those disasters that had struck London over the years and been survived—the Black Death, the Great Fire and the Plague of the 1660s, the Blitz. It seemed a picture of invulnerability rather than vulnerability.

"I might go read in the bedroom," said Elena, but she kept watching.

And just as he was thinking about the Great Fire, it seemed that the filmmakers were, too, because there was suddenly footage of fires—Covent Garden, New Forest (ponies whinnying in the smoke), Epping Forest, then, it appeared, Windsor Castle.

"Do you think that's really England burning?" said Zoe. "The vegetation looks like England, but the fires look like California."

After the fires, the girl, who worked for the ministry of something, leaked to the press (the hero). She met him at an amusement park and, while going around on the Ferris wheel, told him that, yes, the angle of the Earth's axis had been tilted by eleven degrees. They had a disagreement about the government. She said, "Those at the top are cleverer than we are. They know what to do." He then outed her, and she was put in jail.

Simon said, "It was a more innocent time, huh?"

Cassie said, "Look at those smokestacks belching into the sky. You don't see that much anymore."

"But that's prescient, too," said Isabel.

When the hero rushed with the story into the news office, he was in despair at the stupidity of mankind, so much in despair that he didn't even care to write his story. His editor, the Leo KcKern character, looked at him and said, "It's never too late for a good story, well written."

"That would depend on who you are," said Elena, but Paul more or less agreed with the editor. He'd never had a single client who didn't benefit from the telling of a good story.

The weather got hotter—125 in London, 140 in New York—but this information was interspersed with pictures of snowstorms and floods. Finally, the editor got a call from his Moscow correspondent, who told him that the result of the double bomb blast was worse than expected—the orbit of the earth around the sun had been altered as well as the tilt. Leo McKern stepped forward and opined that they had four months until something happened. Paul did not understand whether this something was simply steaming and roasting, à la the orbit of Venus, or whether it was actually the falling of the Earth into the sun.

Stoney said, "This is definitely category-five bad news."

"What's that?" said Simon.

"Well, the end of the world, of course. Category four would be 'incomprehensible, but life goes on.'"

"That's very glib," said Elena.

"Shh," said Delphine.

Leo McKern kept drinking Coke out of old-fashioned small glass bottles, which was what preserved him when the young and handsome errand boy got typhus from contaminated black-market water and died onscreen. Paul saw Zoe's bare foot snake forward and touch Simon on the buttock.

"They thought of a lot of things," said Max. "They really made wonderful use of their budget. A few newsroom sets. Her room. The local pub, some short London street sets. Some other London sets, some artwork, and then some library footage. I'm impressed. They had to depict the end of the world in a very intimate way. No fabulous computer graphics or anything like that. They aren't bombing you out of your seat, but, still—" Max chuckled (with pleasure, Paul knew) and said, "Who's the director again? Oh, Val Guest. Writer, director, producer. Simon, I bet your guys have a bigger budget than he did."

"Well, they have to have a bigger budget, because they had to completely redo the tit suit and reshoot that scene, but it looks a lot better. More like real tits."

Everyone fell silent again. Now there was an announcement from the Prime Minister, in which he acknowledged that mistakes had been made and relayed the information that the authorities were going to try to blast the planet back into a circular rather than a spiral orbit by setting off four simultaneous atomic explosions in the wilds of Siberia. In preparation for this scene, the hero drove into a riot of young people drinking and on drugs, seizing the day, throwing water on one another, playing jazz, and otherwise committing mayhem. The hero saved the girl, who had angered her neighbors by taking a bath. The hero found her fending off the local thugs. Paul didn't quite understand the logic of this scene, but it offered another opportunity to see the girl with no clothes. Danger had the desired effect—she fell for him, he fell for her. The rest of the movie was about the countdown to the big blast. As shots of London, Paris, Rome, the Taj Mahal, and New York filled the screen, different voices said different numbers in different languages. Then, back in the pub, at zero, dust lifted into the air. The ending was ambiguous—one headline read "World Saved"; another read, "World Doomed." When the sound went off, Charlie said, "Must've worked. Here we are."

"But without having learned anything," said Elena.

"People never learn anything from a happy ending," said Delphine.

"I'm sure you're right," said Elena, and Charlie jumped on this immediately. He said, "Am I to assume that you do not want the war in Iraq to succeed?"

"I wonder," said Max, "if people learn anything from an unhappy ending, either."

Paul looked at Zoe's watch. It was early, only about nine-thirty. Her foot, he saw, had returned to her own territory. Just at that moment, Simon shifted position and stretched out on his back, his hands behind his head. In the seventeen hours since Zoe had admitted to her intercourse with Simon, Paul had had the occasion several times to reflect upon the visceral male response he was having to the idea. It was at least partly owing, he thought, to the fact that Simon was youthful and good-looking. Had Charlie, for example, succeeded in bedding Zoe, he would have been far more philosophical. Simon said, "If I am leaving the movie theater in 1962 and I have just seen this movie, what am I supposed to be thinking?"

"I think you're supposed to be scouring the horizon for a mushroom cloud," said Max.

"I would have been doing that, anyway," said Elena. "Cuban Missile Crisis. Better dead than red, you know. My cousin had a friend whose family had a bomb shelter. Whenever he went over to spend the night, the father would explain to him very carefully that if the Russians attacked that very night, they would be happy to take him into the shelter, but no one else in his family, and if they attacked some night when Brian wasn't sleeping over, he better not think that those people would take him in, just because they had a shelter. He explained that to him more than once."

Charlie said, "I remember when we were sitting at the dinner table the night of the Cuban Missile Crisis, and someone asked my father if we were going to try to flee if the bombs dropped, like head into the country or something, and he said, 'No. Life won't be worth living if that happens.' We all nodded and kept eating, then cleared our plates."

Elena said, "I just can't believe that they thought nuclear annihilation was preferable to alternative socioeconomic arrangements. Can you imagine telling your children that it's their fate to sacrifice their lives for the New York Stock Exchange? Or for, let's say, Pan American Airways and the tax privileges of General Electric?"

Charlie, who had stood up and stretched, walked out the back door.

"Yes, Mom," said Simon, "but even so, was I supposed to go out and do anything after watching that movie, or just go home and worry?"

"I didn't think it was scary enough," said Stoney. "I don't think audiences today would be scared by any movie from that period. Like I said, it's comprehensible. It's not real. The governments involved aren't run by madmen—"

"Like North Korea," said Zoe.

"Speaking of the atomic bomb," said Cassie, "you'll never guess who Delphine and I have been working out with all these years without knowing."

"Yes, that was interesting," said Delphine.

"What?" said Isabel.

"Well," said Delphine, "there's a man about my age at the gym, but in much better shape. He's the trainer for the old ladies, really. Tall. High cheekbones. Perfect health."

"Glowing," said Cassie.

"So today he was shaking his head, and he looked upset, so of course we asked him what was wrong, and it turned out that he was retired army, and he was quite worried about the fact that so few people in the army or the State Department speak Arabic, or Iraqi, or whatever, I don't even know what it is, that's how ignorant I am, too. And Cassie said, 'Do you speak a lot of languages?'"

"And he said, 'I speak Russian, German, Czech, some others. You know what I did in the White House? I had an office right next to the President's office, and I was the voice of the red telephone. If he had to call the Soviet Union and speak to the Kremlin, I did the talking.'"

"Wow," said Isabel.

"But here's the amazing part," said Cassie. "He said, 'All those years I worked in the White House, I met every important person who passed through, and I explained to them what my job was, and they were all interested, and they were all pretty nice, too, except I hated one guy. I took an instant dislike to him, and I never changed my mind.'"

Delphine said, "I said, 'Who was that?'"

Cassie said, "And he said, 'John Erlichman.' And I said, 'John Erlichman! I knew John Erlichman!' And he said, 'John Erlichman came into my office the first day, and he sat down and he looked at me, and he said, "So, Colonel, how are you going to feel when you are replaced by a computer?" He was not a nice man.' I thought it was amazing what a small world it is, that he should have such a clear memory of John."

"How did you know John Erlichman?" said Stoney.

"Oh, goodness. When I was the editor of the UCLA *Bruin* in 1946, Erlichman was in charge of circulation and H. R. Haldeman was in charge of advertising. They were the only frat boys we had on the paper. They really didn't fit in, and they weren't nice boys. Of course, they'd already been in the service by then. At least, Haldeman had been in the Marines, because he had that buzz cut. Frank Mankiewicz did sports. He'd been in the army, I think. You know who I mean, Bobby Kennedy's press secretary. And he was McGovern's campaign manager or something like that. Then there was NPR."

"His father made *All About Eve*," said Max, "and his uncle wrote *Citizen Kane* with Welles."

"Yes," said Cassie. "Herman and Joe. Herman died when Frank and I were still friends. Once, I went over there to find Frank for some reason, and Herman let me in, and I said, 'Hi, Herman, how are you? How's Sarah?' and he said, 'Who's Sarah?' and I thought he was senile. I said, 'Your wife, Sarah,' and he said, 'Oh, I didn't know who you meant. Everyone has always referred to her as "poor Sarah."'"

Everyone laughed, and Simon said, "Your editorial board was the center of the universe."

"Well," said Cassie, "not that. But when we graduated, I went to work for Helen Gahagan Douglas, and John and Bob Haldeman went to work for Nixon, and they screwed us, but ultimately they went to jail. We didn't. They're both dead now, of course. They died early, painful deaths." She smiled. "And we didn't. I didn't, and the colonel didn't. The colonel looks like he's going to live forever." Her smile widened. "When I think of the Iraq war, I try to remember what happened to John and Bob."

"There's a happy ending that no one seems to have learned from," said Stoney. "And look at this movie we were watching. The governments make a mistake. They try to fix it. It's reassuring. And then think of stories you've heard that really terrified you. They aren't movies. They aren't art. They can't be comprehended."

"The one that immediately comes to mind for me," said Max, "is that family in Washington, D.C. And this is a true story. My friend Gus Lieberman went to their temple. Do you remember him, Zoe? He lived at the bottom of the street here when we first moved in. He told me about it when we were walking the circuit one day, oh, maybe ten years ago now, but I've never forgotten it. There were a husband, wife, three daughters, and one son. The daughters were in their teens, and the son was maybe twelve. The mother and the son went to New York for a few days to visit some relatives.

In the meantime, they had hired painters to paint the exterior of the house. It was a nice neighborhood. The father was a lawyer or something. Anyway, one of the daughters was home sick from school, and the painter and his assistant raped and murdered her. While they were at it, one of the other daughters came home for lunch, and so they raped and murdered her, too, but she had managed to call the third daughter, who called the father. When the two of them rushed home to save her, the painter and his assistant caught the father and murdered him, then raped and murdered the third daughter. Then they apparently took their equipment and left. The mother and son found everyone when they got home from New York that night."

"Oh my God," said Isabel.

Everyone else was silent for a moment, and Charlie came back in. He said, "What's up?" He seemed, to Paul, as if he was making an effort to be patient. Paul said, "That's a gruesome story, but maybe it would be comprehensible if we knew more about it. If we knew about the trial of the painter and his assistant, for example. If they said what their motive was. Maybe it's not truly incomprehensible, just that there isn't enough data."

"I think the war in Iraq is incomprehensible," said Elena.

"Yes, Mom, we know that," said Simon, but not impatiently. Really, Paul thought, there was something intriguing about Simon's temperament.

"But I spend a lot of time trying to comprehend it. I feel like the fact that I can't comprehend it and others can means that most of the people in the nation are suddenly incomprehensible to me."

"Okay," said Max, putting his arm around her, "but let's not talk about that particular case, at least not yet."

"Wasn't the Rwandan massacre incomprehensible?" said Zoe. "A plane was shot down, and that seems to have been the signal for all the Hutus to drop what they were doing and kill their neighbors with machetes. To me that's way more incomprehensible than Hitler and the Nazis. Hitler spent years cultivating his infrastructure with movies like *Triumph of the Will* and that sort of thing. And then, when he did start massacring the Jews and all the others, he did it secretly, behind walls and in ghettos and outside of Germany. But with the Rwandans, it was like a massive infection, or a poisoning. They weren't doing it, and then they were."

"But how does that make you feel about humans?" said Stoney.

Zoe sniffed thoughtfully, then she said, "It doesn't make me feel one way or another. It's too incomprehensible."

"Well," said Delphine, "my guess is that we don't understand Rwanda because we're ignorant about preexisting conditions there. I heard overpopulation was a problem, and tribal enmities left over from the colonial period. And wasn't there a war there before? Sometime in the sixties? But I must say, that one thing I noticed when I first came to the U.S. was that after the civil-rights movement the whites got more openly fearful, and you could see, during those years when there were riots in Watts and all, that they couldn't help feeling that black people were going to switch over just like that, all at once and in the course of a few days, and start killing as many white people as they could, but in fact black people never thought like that. So it had to be guilt on the part of the whites and a sense of powerlessness on the part of the blacks that prevented it."

"I still find it incomprehensible," said Zoe.

"What about Jeffrey Dahmer?" said Stoney. "Was he comprehensible? If he never said how it felt to be him, if he couldn't explain what was going on inside his head in a way that other people can grasp, then how are we going to be able to comprehend that sort of thing?"

"Why do we want to?" said Simon.

"Because it exists," said Stoney.

"I think it's a fetish," said Paul. "I think there's a brain mechanism and that it's the mechanism of the fetish. Here's a clue. There are people who go to doctors and have healthy limbs amputated. They're called 'apotemno-philiacs.' Most of them, if not all of them, have a specific memory from early childhood of seeing an amputee and becoming preoccupied with that idea or image, then harboring and developing that image as an image of themselves. Pretty much all of them say that they just would feel more right, more truly themselves, if they had an amputation."

"Jeez," said Charlie.

Paul lifted his ponytail off the back of his neck and smoothed down his beard. Zoe was looking at him and smiling, as if she were his presenter, and he smiled back at her. Possibly he had not been especially friendly during the day. He said, "I think it's a kind of conditioning. You know how birds like ducks and geese fix on the first creature they see after they hatch from the egg, and then follow that creature? If it's the mother duck, all well and good, but they might also imprint on a human. All animals do it. They have to, in order to survive. It's a powerful mechanism, and it works by fixing a pattern of response in the brain. That's called a conditioned response. But sometimes the conditioning works idiosyncratically. Like, the kid sees an amputee and he's frightened by the strangeness of that person, and he imprints it. Apotemnophiliacs talk about coming home after seeing the am-putee and trying it out—tying up the leg, or wearing the arm inside the shirt. Pretending to be an amputee. And what that does is confirm the im-printing by repeating the stimulus, and what you might call deepening the groove where the associations the child feels with the amputee exist in the brain. When you have a fetish, you attribute power to that fetish. If you read about fetishes, most of them are sexual, like bound feet or high heels. What the person gets from it is a fixated feeling that results in sexual release of some sort. Let's say a Chinese man of a certain era contemplates the shoe for a bound foot. Obviously, if he's grown up in a foot-binding culture, he is impressed by everything associated with the bound foot—the femininity of the victims, which would include his mother, their evident pain, the difference between them and others, his position in relationship to them. Maybe the way they walk evokes some primal sense of them being alien creatures, and all sorts of strong feelings cluster around that. So, when he looks at the shoe or holds it in his hand, it has a lot of mixed associations that have power for him. He might sexualize those feelings if he is encouraged to do so, or if those feelings are highly sexualized in his society. Same with breasts or red lips or navels in our culture, or ankles in Victorian English culture. Or whips and high boots. All that stuff." He looked around. He could see that they were waiting for him to get to the point. He cleared his throat. "But fetishes are clearly a form of conditioned response that interferes with any actual relationship with another person. You can tell. A man who loves a woman has a certain kind of body language. He looks at her face. His eyes move from place to place. His attention shifts. But if he has a breast fetish, say, his gaze fixes on her breasts. She might be talking, but he doesn't even hear her. He's imprinted on those breasts, and he'll stay imprinted until he has an orgasm. He doesn't love her. There's no actual relationship, with give and take and some version of responsiveness. Instead, he's made her breasts an idol."

"Or her social status. Or her legs. Or her money," said Isabel. "People my age do that all the time. They come into the office and say they're going to marry a tall blonde or a girl from the Upper East Side or someone who was Miss North Carolina last year."

"A lot of things that seem incomprehensible get more comprehensible when you understand the idea of the fetish as a form of imprinting. A fetish is a religious idol. Why did Moses get so angry when he came down from the mountain and the Israelites were worshiping false idols? Because they were ceding power to inanimate objects rather than actually having a relationship with God."

"Remember those stories about John Ashcroft that were in the paper a while ago? He was anointing himself as attorney general. He was pouring oil on his head or something like that," said Elena.

"He was abasing himself," said Paul.

"I thought he was elevating himself," said Elena.

"But that's the point of a fetish," said Paul. "The conscious act of abasement makes you feel a certain way—simultaneously powerless before the idol and powerful in the sense that adrenaline and endorphins begin to pump. My guess is that the adrenaline is related to the imprinting and the earlier fear. It's a modified flight instinct. From what I've seen in my practice, people raised with a lot of fear, in very strict families, get many rewards from abasement, not the least of which is that they avoid the promised beating, and might even be praised for humbling themselves before the power of the parent."

"God is who you thought your parents were when you were a very young child," said Isabel. "One of my English teachers said that one day when we were reading *Paradise Lost.*"

"My clearest memory from being a very young child," said Simon, "is that one day Mom said she was going to tell me about the birds and the bees, but she didn't do it right away. I thought she was going to tell me that Melanie Orton, who lived next door, had something in her panties like a hummingbird, and that if I showed her my pee-pee, her hummingbird would come out and stick its beak down my pee-pee and extract what was in there."

"You're kidding me," said Elena.

"No, I'm not," said Simon, "but that doesn't mean that you failed as a mother. It just means that what you told me wasn't as interesting as what I imagined."

Zoe said, "I want to hear the rest of what Paul is saying."

Paul cleared his throat. "An idol is an idol. Religious feelings and sexual feelings are very closely linked and very powerful. The anthropological evidence for that is universal. If a child grows up in a strongly religious culture and is trained to think that all relationships are extremely hierarchical and power is exciting and fearsome, then, in my view, he will be more attracted to fetishes of all kinds, whether sexual, religious, or whatever."

"Guns," said Isabel. "Guns are an obvious fetish in the U.S."

"And swords are a fetish in Japan. All knives," said Charlie. "You-all are always harping on the U.S., as if this culture is the sickest of all—"

"It isn't the sickest of all," said Paul. "French culture is full of fetishes. So is every other culture. And it's every culture's fetishes that make the least sense to other cultures, especially if we try to impose them. But people can get over their fetishes. They do it by withdrawing the power from them, even finding a way to get bored with them. I had a client who was so addicted to cigarettes that she would light up in the morning before she even put her glasses on and smoke while she was sitting on the toilet. One day, she had to have abdominal surgery, and her mother showed up in her room when she was just coming out of the anesthetic and was feeling quite nauseated. Her mother lit up and blew smoke in her face and talked. By her mother's third cigarette, she never wanted to smoke again, and her relationship with her mother was pretty straightened out, too."

"You're kidding," said Isabel, and everyone else laughed.

"No," said Paul. "No, I'm not kidding. But it was years ago, before widespread smoking bans."

"But how does the idea of the fetish make sense of that Washington, D.C., mass murder?" said Cassie.

"I don't know," said Paul, "because I don't know what was in the minds of the painter and his assistant. But it makes sense of Jeffrey Dahmer."

"I saw a thing on *Nova*," said Max. "It was about a mass murderer who had killed several young women by strangling them. There was nothing evident in his background to show why he'd done that. He was adopted, but he was raised in a loving home, was never beaten or abused, and never suffered any blows to the head. He was intelligent, and he was interested in why he did it, too. So he got together with a neurologist, who interviewed him and tested him. He said that he would just get this urge to strangle these girls and not be able to stop himself, and the neurologist actually listened to him, and he gave him a set of tests. One of them was a fine motor-muscle coordination test, where he had to do this." Max placed both his hands, palm-down, flat on his knees, then made a fist with his left hand and turned it ninety degrees. Then he lifted his hands and alternately made a fist and turned each one and opened and flattened each one. He repeated this gesture a few times. He said, "The guy couldn't do it. Basically, he couldn't rub his head and pat his stomach simultaneously. I don't remember all the tests, but they were fairly simple coordination tests."

"He couldn't play the piano, I'll bet," said Stoney.

"Bet not," said Max. "Anyway, the theory of the neurologist was that fine motor coordination and impulse control are both located in the frontal lobe, and this guy's frontal lobe was poorly developed, so when he had an impulse, which came from somewhere at the base of the brain, the frontal lobe couldn't handle it, and so he was literally telling the truth. And then, when they gave him an MRI, they saw that there was less blood flow in the frontal lobe."

"Strong emotions reduce blood flow in the frontal lobe," said Paul, "so, if something is arousing fear and anger in you, or just adrenaline, even something imprinted rather than present, you're less able to control your impulses and more likely to act. I see that all the time."

"Do we understand Rwanda now?" said Zoe. "Or mutually assured destruction?"

"No," said Delphine, decisively.

"Or the Iraq war?" said Elena.

"Or Genghis Khan?" said Simon.

"Maybe Genghis Khan," said Paul. "In the sense that when society is predicated on hierarchy and fear, people imprint cruel acts as they're growing up, and perform them when they get the chance. Defeating an enemy would unleash an orgy of rape and killing."

"So what?" said Isabel, irritably. "Here we are, we watched that movie, we talked about it. Now we understand. What difference does it make?"

"None that I see," said Charlie.

"And don't agree with me. I find it offensive."

Everyone laughed again, but Isabel scowled.

"I don't feel very welcome here," said Charlie.

Everyone stopped what he or she was doing. Cassie stopped picking up the wineglasses. Delphine stopped straightening pillows. Isabel stopped scowling. Elena stopped stroking the side of Max's head above his ear. Zoe stopped smiling at Simon. Simon took his hand out of his jeans pocket and sat up. Max stopped looking at Elena. Stoney stopped pressing buttons on the DVD player. When the disc drawer buzzed open, he didn't pick up the disc. Paul himself stopped digging his fingers into his beard, without meaning to stop. The evident observation Paul felt hanging in the air was that indeed Charlie wasn't welcome, and that, furthermore, he had invited himself to California for his own reasons. But Elena said, "I'm sorry you think that."

Simon said, "Yeah, it's me who isn't welcome. Mom's been trying to get rid of me all week."

"Yes, I have," said Elena. "But only for your own good."

Charlie said, "You're sorry I don't feel welcome, but that doesn't mean I'm welcome."

"Hey, Chaz . . ." said Max. His tone was cautioning but friendly. It took him a moment to go on. In that moment, Paul decided once again that family life was, in general, something to be avoided, except as an occasion for exercising patience.

Max opened his mouth to continue, but Zoe interrupted him and said, "None of us is welcome, Charlie. Max prefers to be alone. But just because we all imposed ourselves doesn't mean we can't enjoy it." She smiled charmingly. Paul could tell she was making an effort. Or, rather, she was exercising her skills of voice and expression.

"I'm not talking about Max," said Charlie. "I'm referring to general hostility here."

Max smiled and did not try to say anything.

"In my opinion," said Simon, "the hostility is only from Mom. Nobody else really—"

"Simon!" exclaimed Elena.

"Well, you called him, as I remember, a 'soulless, heartless dolt' and a 'blind, deaf, and dumb ignoramus.'"

Paul saw Zoe bite her lips, then straighten her face. She casually pushed back her hair and tossed her head. Truly, every single one of her gestures was graceful and photogenic.

Isabel said, "I don't think Charlie *is* very welcome. I don't think he should be. He doesn't agree with us on anything. I mean, we could just make up our minds not to talk about it, the way most families do, or he could not come visit when there's a war on, but why should we pretend that we accept his ideas when we don't? It's better to be honest." She said this with a low-voiced intensity that Paul found a little surprising.

"You aren't even open to any arguments," said Charlie, but to Elena, not Isabel. "You've all made up your minds ahead of time. The President himself can't get a hearing in this house. You all pat yourselves on the back about how open-minded you are, but you aren't open-minded at all. Yesterday morning I had the TV on for five minutes, and when the President came on to say something, Elena put her hands over her ears and started humming."

"I hate the sound of his voice," said Elena. "That's all."

"Doesn't that seem crazy to you?" said Charlie. He turned suddenly to Stoney. He said, "You strike me as fairly normal. You get out in the world. Doesn't what she did seem crazy to you?"

"It seems extra passionate to me," said Stoney. "And a little funny. But I can see it."

"What has the man done to alienate you? He's president! Max! When we talked about the election in the spring of 2000, and it was Bush, Gore, Bradley, and McCain, you liked McCain! You thought they were all about the same, and would be a relief from Clinton. You didn't hate Bush!"

"Well, I don't think he seemed at the time to be what he turned out to be," said Max in a judicious tone. "Now it turns out that he was talking one way to religious groups and another to the public at large—"

"They all do that! Carter did that! I knew a guy who was an assistant to one of his Cabinet people. He said that, in every meeting, Carter was a first-class hard-ass, not at all like that bleeding heart he looked like on TV. And why shouldn't he be? If he'd shown more of his hard-ass side, he would have been re-elected."

"Personally, I don't hate the President to the degree where I can't stand the sound of his voice. My opinion," said Zoe, "is that he isn't really the President. He's the figurehead for Cheney and Rumsfeld. I saw a thing that said those two have been together for years, ever since Nixon, and they just took him up because they knew that they themselves could never get elected. That's why he takes so many vacation days and goes to bed early and seems to get so much exercise. The country really isn't his business." Then she looked at Isabel and said, briskly, "I read the paper, Isabel."

"I didn't say you don't, Mom."

"You were thinking that."

"You don't know what I was thinking."

"What were you thinking?"

Isabel remained silent. After a moment she said, "I was thinking, 'Oh, right.'" She cleared her throat. "But in fact I don't disagree with you about who actually occupies the seat of power." She said this rather stiffly.

"What do you think, Mom?" said Zoe, turning to Delphine.

"About what?" said Delphine.

"About whether we're acting hostile toward Charlie."

"I think Charlie should be encouraged to speak his piece," said Delphine. She picked up one of the pillows she had plumped, placed it on her lap, and sat down on the couch. She folded her hands over the pillow.

"You mean right now?" said Charlie.

"Why not?" said Delphine.

"It's kind of late."

"It's not even ten o'clock," said Cassie.

"Well, now I feel like I've been put on the spot."

"You have been," said Max, "but you started it."

They all resumed their places. Those whose chairs had been turned more toward the movie screen turned them more toward Charlie. Max pressed a button, and the movie screen itself backed into the wall and shutters closed over it. It was a neat effect. Paul closed his eyes and tucked his feet under himself. He took some quiet floating breaths and then some slower, deeper reviving breaths, and this had the effect of orienting him away from this room and these people, whatever their conflicts. Zoe slipped her hand into his. Her hand was smooth and quiet. The lines in her palm, as he knew, shot across from side to side and top to bottom, deep, straight, and long, making a precise triangle that he had never seen in any other hand, but it probably had no significance. He pictured that triangle in his mind, and also her thumb and fingers folding over it, enclosing and protecting it.

"Okay," said Charlie, "okay. I will say my piece. God knows I've said it every night, lying in bed after one of these evenings of listening to what I consider pretty treasonous, or at least disloyal, chitchat from just about everyone here. Or maybe only disrespectful and irreverent, from some people, but it has made my blood boil a bit." He cleared his throat. "You, for example, Elena—"

"You can't address her," said Delphine. "You have to make your case on its own merits, not in contradiction to what other people are saying. If there's a case to be made, then it has to stand on its own two feet."

"Well, I—"

"I'm just warning you," said Delphine. "You should think about it, because if everything you say starts with how you disagree with someone else, I'll stop you, and then you'll get interrupted a lot, and you'll lose your train of thought. Those are the rules. I just made them up." She smiled a rare smile, and it was pretty, Paul thought, and very like Zoe's smile that was famous all over the world.

"Want a drink?" said Simon. "A beer, maybe? I saw some Negro Modelo in the refrigerator."

Charlie nodded. Simon went to the refrigerator and took out four beers. He kept one for himself, passed one to Max, another to Charlie, and the last to Stoney. They looked good, thought Paul, though he hadn't had a beer in five years. At the sight of them, Zoe got up and went to the refrigerator herself. She brought back two large bottles of Pellegrino and set them, with glasses, on the coffee table.

"So," Charlie said, "I'm making the case for the war—"

"How anyone can—" said Elena, but Delphine looked her square in the face and said, "Shhh!"

Elena put her hands over her lips.

"Okay. I'm going to say even things that everyone knows to be true, just to register them. Then I'm going to say things that some people think are true and others don't, and say how I feel about those things. And then I'm going to give my theory about how all those things fit together. Okay?"

He looked around the room. Paul looked around the room. Everyone nodded.

"Okay. Now, the first thing that everyone knows is that Saddam is a bad man and a tyrant, and Bush Senior should have gone ahead and gotten rid of him at the end of the Gulf War, when we had the advantage and most of the world was on our side. The Iraqi army seemed to be giving up. They backed out of Kuwait, they surrendered, and they threw away their weapons. But there was not a general belief that the coalition would hold if we attacked Saddam and tried to take over Iraq. The Republican Guard was supposed to be different from the regular Iraqi army. The allies hadn't signed on for that, no one knew precisely what it would entail, and, frankly,

Bush Senior wasn't the kind of guy to push his luck. I view the end of the Gulf War as a 'quit-while-you're-ahead' judgment call, and maybe Bush Senior made the wrong call. I think he thought that Saddam had gotten something of a whupping and he would watch his step thereafter. At the time, if they'd asked me, I would have said, 'Go on and finish the job,' but they didn't ask me.

"But Saddam didn't watch his step. In my opinion, he learned the wrong lesson. He learned that we didn't have what it took to go the whole way and take care of him, and he thought that he could pretty much do what he pleased if he kept it secret. And he was set on revenge. That's how those people's minds work, they can't help themselves. They've got to get back at you if you've destroyed their honor and all. And Clinton and the UN did nothing to change his mind about that. He pushed and pushed, and those guys never really pushed back."

Elena squeaked, but said nothing. Charlie glanced at her.

"Now, I'm not saying that 9/11 wouldn't have happened if Al Gore had been elected. It might have or probably would have, but when Bush Junior was elected, that was like a red flag to a bull. Time to get back at the U.S., and specifically at the Bush family, and Saddam was looking for a way. We know he was trying to build nuclear weapons and trying to stockpile biological weapons. We know that. And as far as I'm concerned, the liberals dogged it on that score, because, with something much more iffy, like global warming, they want to take all kinds of precautions, no matter how expensive they are, but with those weapons of mass destruction, they say, 'Well, let's just see what happens.' I mean, we *know* he's got something. The Brits say so, and so do I think it's the Italians. My own opinion is that it's more likely to be germs of some kind, like the plague or anthrax, but whatever. The cautious thing is to take him out. It's a surgical strike. You guys are making an incredibly big deal out of what I consider to be a surgical strike. And almost everyone in this country agrees with me, not with you. Liberals, too. There's lots of reasons to do it, and very few to not do it."

Delphine cleared her throat. She said, "So—it's basically a prudent step to take, that's your thinking."

Charlie nodded emphatically, as if it were obvious that Delphine was agreeing with him, but Paul considered Delphine a tricky one. If he had been in the hot seat, he would have maintained a cooler demeanor. Delphine said, "So—if simple prudence is the important point, why is it such an emotional issue with you, making your blood boil and prompting you to use words like 'treason' and 'traitor' and all of that?"

"Well, anytime the nation goes to war, you have to support it."

"Why? What difference does it make if I don't support it?"

"Well, the war effort is undermined."

"How? I've paid my taxes. The money I might owe is in the kitty. The soldiers are trained, the equipment is paid for. What difference does it make if I agree with it or not?"

"It's important not to aid and comfort the enemy."

"But you said yourself, it's a surgical strike and an essentially prudent policy, completely different from an all-out war. The whole nation doesn't have to gear up for a surgical strike. The whole nation didn't gear up to intervene in Bosnia or Haiti."

Charlie coughed, then exclaimed, "The difference is that we were attacked. I was there! I was in New Jersey that day! People I know saw the planes hit, and other people I know know people who were killed! It was the biggest attack on American soil since Pearl Harbor, and it was important to respond in kind! I am sure the government has information about Saddam's hand in all of this. In fact, I think the war in Iraq is such a big deal that it is prima facie evidence that the administration has good reasons for doing it, reasons in addition to the announced ones, that are possibly too secret to make public. Why do it otherwise? Why take such a big risk? There is certainly more here than meets the eye, and at some point, you just have to trust your government to make the decisions they have to make, rather than second-guessing them all the time." Paul thought Charlie seemed pleased at having stumbled on this line of reasoning. He reiterated it. "Spend billions of dollars and incur the wrath of dozens of countries and tens of millions of people for no good reason? I don't think so. Why would experienced guys like Cheney and Rumsfeld take such a risk? It defies belief. So I don't believe it. I believe that there is a whole fabric of evidence and reasons beyond what they've told the public that simply can't be told at this point, but will emerge sometime later."

He took a deep breath. He seemed almost relaxed now, Paul thought. Elena simply had her head in her hands. Max was patting her on the shoulder. Isabel was biting her lip. The others seemed interested enough. When Zoe opened her mouth to speak, Delphine lifted her forefinger; Zoe didn't say anything.

Charlie went on: "And anyway, everything's a risk. You look at the upside and you look at the downside. I'm sure they saw that the upside to all of this is really positive—allies, real allies in the heart of the Middle East, access to lots of good-quality petroleum fields, acknowledged dictator gotten rid of. Yes, it's a gamble, but if, or when, it pays off, the payoff is enormous." He grinned, having made his point.

"I don't know that it's going that well," Max said mildly.

"For now," said Charlie, "there are some unexpected things. How can that not be true? But, really, what big thing has gone wrong? That's what gets me going around here. Inside this house, it's all doom and gloom and 'I don't want to watch the TV' and 'How could they do such a thing?' But not every newspaper is as anti the war as the L.A. *Times*. If you read the *Journal* and even the *New York Times*, they both acknowledge the necessity of the war. And you can't count on the *New York Times* ever to support a Republican administration, ever. You aren't even going to believe the *New York Times*? Or Tony Blair? Blair was a great friend of Bill Clinton. He's Labour! His leftist credentials are pretty good. Lots of people I would expect to be on your side are not on your side, and you know the reason for that? They accept the results of the 2000 election. They don't hold out this unreasoning hatred and resentment about that. They aren't blinded by what is basically water under the bridge. They are open to the idea that people who were once their opponents, or even enemies, can be right and can do the right and the wise thing. Yes, the election controversy poisoned American politics, but those who got left out don't have to hold a grudge, and lots of people don't, and they are clear-sighted enough to support the war. To see the potential benefits and to put the probable costs in perspective. What did Rumsfeld say in the paper yesterday, that the oil production is going to eventually, and fairly quickly, pay for the whole thing? Sounds like a pretty good deal to me. I guess I am just instinctively for it. My gut says, do it, don't go with the second thoughts and doubts." He took a deep breath and looked around.

Paul could tell he thought he had made a good case. And why not? thought Paul. Why not just accept that case and relax, and forget the whole thing? What was that quote, "full of sound and fury, signifying nothing"? That was the Iraq war for you, especially if you looked at it as Charlie did. Without even trying to, Paul felt himself settle more comfortably into his seat, lean more cozily against Zoe, especially since Simon had gotten up and crossed the room. Paul felt his breaths slow, and he hadn't even realized that they were quick. Elena continued to hold her peace, and even Isabel didn't bother to say anything. That was the sort of authority Delphine had. She was definitely a mysterious woman—maybe, Paul thought, the reincarnation of a long line of matriarchs and high priestesses. She had that businesslike air of someone who had tasks to perform, and whatever they were, even if they were as simple as taking care of Isabel or making mashed potatoes, she performed them with orderly expertise. Zoe never talked about her, except, once, to remark that Delphine never talked about herself. That she was tall, that she was black, that her grammar was perfect, that she had a slight, undefinable accent, that everyone in the family, including Max, treated her with formality, only added to her charisma.

Isabel said, "So, without starting a fight, can I make a few observations about Charlie's case?"

Delphine nodded.

"Well, personally, I like the words 'surgical strike,' and I didn't really care about the Bosnia thing or the Haiti thing, but maybe I was too young at the time to care anyway. And I was twelve during the Gulf War, and I did think that was a big deal. I remember we were in Princeville shopping when we heard about it, and I wondered if there would be Muslims in the grocery store, ready to blow us up right there in revenge. But there weren't."

"I remember that night, too," said Elena. "I was driving toward Mankato, Minnesota, and it was something like twenty below zero and deep snow, and I was looking for Muslim terrorists everywhere."

Isabel went on. "I do think it's very nice the way Charlie makes it seem." She stopped.

"But—" prompted Delphine.

"I don't see any reason to believe that it is the way he makes it seem."

"Right," said Elena.

There was a silence.

"The question is," said Delphine, "why argue about it? He's got his opinions. Other people have theirs. The events are already under way, and we have no way of controlling them or even, I would say, knowing what they truly are. Why talk about it?"

"We don't have to talk about it," Elena acknowledged.

"No," said Delphine, "I'm not saying that we shouldn't talk about it. I'm wondering why we do. What's the source of this drive to talk about it, to think about it, to make up our minds?" She leaned back in her seat and patted the pillow in her lap.

Isabel said, "Well, I—" but just then Charlie jumped out of his chair, the hot seat, the chair by the table that he had dropped into while making his case, and he exclaimed, "Shit! I have had it with this shit!" and he crossed the living room, went through the dark kitchen, and slammed out the door. A moment later, Paul heard the engine of the Mustang start up, and then the sound of the car disappearing down the hill. He saw Elena look at Max, who shrugged a small shrug. Cassie said, "Do you think he's drunk? How much did he have to drink?"

"He hasn't been drinking," said Delphine. "I don't think he can drink really, because he takes all those pills."

"He drank half a beer," offered Simon.

"He said it was something like forty pills," said Stoney.

"I thought it was twenty-one," said Isabel.

"At any rate, he isn't drunk," said Zoe, whose weight next to Paul on the couch suddenly felt heavy and even painful. He tried to shift her without her noticing.

"So what's his problem?" said Simon. "He got to have his say, and Mom didn't even interrupt once."

"Undoubtedly," said Delphine, "he thought his argument was going to make everyone see things from his point of view, and—"

"Well," said Isabel, "it almost did." She looked at Elena, who looked, Paul thought, sour and judgmental. Isabel was intimidated. "I mean, in a way."

Finally, Paul had to move away from Zoe's weight completely, so he stood up. Zoe herself, seeing him looming over her, picked up her feet and pressed herself against the back of the couch. Just then, he had the briefest feeling that it was not he who had been avoiding her all day, but quite the other way.

Isabel droned on: "We talked about this in my Ideology and American Culture class. My professor said that a lot of problems come from the fact that the U.S. has always been, basically, an honor-based culture, and that makes you feel that your opinions are entitled to respect. If you don't get the respect that you need, then you seem to become aggressive, but actually you are becoming fearful because you are losing status in the—"

A certain thing occurred to Paul. It was that he sympathized with Charlie. He thought, "I am wasting my time here." It was as if he had somehow embarked on a cruise, something he had avoided all his life, and suddenly here he was, far out in a sea of languor with a group of people who on land could be avoided, and were therefore fine enough, but here, on this cruise, were insufferable. He sighed. They made him sigh. It was not precisely that they were boring, but more that they caused the expansion of time, so that every second, every moment, swelled to infinity, he himself, in his body and his consciousness, swelled to infinity, and he realized that his long path of exploration, that grand peregrination he had been making for fifty-five years had led to this room, that pointless movie, his old and oblivious antagonist, Max, the view of the eternal Getty Museum dimly white across the hills, the sight of Cassie once again opening her mouth to tell another tale. He groaned and closed his eyes. It was as if he could remember every thought he had ever thought, and every one of them was futile.

Stoney was standing with Simon and Isabel in the corner of the kitchen. Simon had the newspaper in his hand, and was ostentatiously pointing to an article, but actually he was saying, in a smooth but low voice, "Didn't you ever do that, Stoney? I thought everyone did."

Isabel said, "You were in the Gap at the Beverly Center?"

"Well, it happened the first time at Macy's six months ago. This was the third time."

He sounded so relaxed and innocent that Stoney couldn't help smiling, but in fact it had never happened to him. He had never even thought of doing such a thing, which was that Simon, finding himself with a large erection in the jeans department ("peeking out of the waistband of my shorts") and noticing a hot girl not far away, had simply reached up and flipped through some jeans on a high shelf, allowing the girl, if she was so inclined, to notice what was happening to him. Since she was not so inclined, he had simply taken down the stack of jeans, then put his hand in his pocket and rearranged himself.

Isabel wiped the smile off her face and said, with some sternness, "How is that not exposing yourself? I consider exposing yourself an aggressive act."

"Well, I was only about a half-inch exposed. And I didn't force her to notice. I just waited to see if she did notice. I wasn't even offering an invitation, I was just seeing what might happen. My personal impression is that a lot more girls are a lot more interested in a lot more sex than you seem to think. She was pretty well exposed herself, I would have to say. I could see the back of her thong."

"Telling us about it is also a form of exposing yourself."

"Well, in lots of ways, yes—"

Elena, who had been standing by the stove, pouring water into the coffeemaker, said, "I think I'll be going back to my own house today. I think maybe Simon should go with me." Simon fell silent, then glanced at Isabel and at Stoney, and made a nonplussed sort of face, eyes wide, eyebrows high, and mouth drawn down. He said, softly, "The mom sounds a little upset."

Stoney saw Paul glance at Zoe, who said, "We were talking just this morning about clearing out, too. I think Paul should go on up to the monastery, and maybe I'll just go home. Nedra thinks I'm at the monastery, which is why she hasn't called me here all week, but my cell phone is full of messages and text messages. I guess if I want to have a career after the war, I'd better quit hiding out." Nedra, Stoney knew, was Zoe's agent.

It was that phrase "after the war" that made Stoney nervous. "After the war," he would find himself down the hill in his odd and lonely house. After the war, Isabel would go back to New York. After the war, death and injury and horror would be more common than they had been before the war.

Cassie said, "I've hardly been to the gallery in the last week. I even shut it completely for four days because there was so little street traffic, but maybe people are used to the war by now and ready to get out. I should at least open today, and I ought to go clean out my refrigerator. Have I eaten here every night? I think so. Did I miss Wednesday?" She turned to Delphine.

"You didn't miss Wednesday," said Delphine.

Max. Well, Max. Stoney couldn't quite tell. Normally, Max hated visitors, you could see that. But over the course of the last week, he seemed to have gotten used to it, the way you do in a bunker. He had started spending less time in his room and more time in the family room and by the pool. He didn't always have much to say, but sometimes he would erupt with a comment when you hadn't thought he was listening at all. That was a new degree of sociability from Max.

"Are we breaking up, then?" said Simon. "Is Mom getting her way and sending me packing back to Davis even though I've integrated myself so delightfully into the L.A. family? If so, I need forty bucks for gas."

Stoney was tempted to point out to Elena that Davis was a dangerous place, that something could happen to Simon in Davis, just as something could happen to Isabel in New York. Stoney didn't think that, in the midst of a war, they should break up too casually. Any character in a war movie who strolled away, whistling and happy, always got blown to pieces three scenes later.

"I can't believe it's been a week," said Zoe.

Stoney said, "It hasn't. It's not a week until tomorrow." Zoe smiled at him, as if to say that a week was a long time to hide out, but Stoney did not think that a week was at all a long time, if the other choice was leaving the fortress. The siege of Troy lasted ten years, did it not? He said to Isabel, "So where is Charlie? Did he ever come back?"

Isabel shrugged one shoulder. To Stoney, Charlie was a perfect example of how, in wartime, a person could get displaced. He cleared his throat in a nervous way, and Isabel said, "Who cares?"

"I do. You do, too."

She looked at him and said, "Well, yes. In my crabby way, I do care, but no one's said a word about him."

Stoney stepped over to the kitchen window, the one that looked out on the cul-de-sac, and craned his neck to see the cars. He didn't see the yellow Mustang, but, then, he couldn't see his own Jag or Zoe's Mercedes, either. What he could see, or, at least, too easily imagine, was all the cars rolling away, one by one, his own, no doubt, the last. The party over, but not the war. Indeed, not the war. Right there on the kitchen island, on the front page of the Sunday paper, the war was going strong. People were being taken captive. Rocket launchers were launching rockets. People were being caught in cross fire. Baghdad was being considered from a tactical point of view. Stoney took a deep breath and said, "What about this? You know those Russians who want Max to do that remake of *Taras Bulba* —"

"Not them again," said Max.

"Well, they're very persistent. I told them you weren't interested and didn't think your health could stand months on the Ukrainian steppe, winter, summer, all of that, but they want to make one last offer."

"I can't imagine what will —"

"Mike has a house at the top of Bel-Air. I thought it belonged to that friend of Jerry's, Avram Cohen Ben Avram, but apparently it belongs to Mike now. Maybe Ben Avram got him to buy it, because Mike does seem to have all the money in the world. Anyway, they've been remodeling it for the last year, and it's just about finished. I think they still have to bring in more art and do some more on the grounds, but it's otherwise finished, and Mike would like to loan it to you for a few days."

"What for?" said Max. "I have a house."

"There is no one in all of L.A. who has a house like this. I'm not sure there is a house like this outside of Russia. I mean, you know, outside of the Summer Palace of Catherine the Great. Ben Avram told me you can't believe the art. Things that have been gone for centuries are at this place, things by Picasso and van Gogh and even Vermeer. He said that there was a Vermeer. It's big enough to pass as a small resort hotel. If we moved up there, we would definitely not be cramped. It just has a skeleton staff at the moment, but plenty for us. I don't want to miss it myself, but the only way I can get in is if Max agrees to come and stay for a few days." Actually, when Ben Avram told him about the place, he had pictured it as one of those L.A. monstrosities from the thirties, San Simeon on Sunset, but as he talked about it, he got desperately enthusiastic.

"I wouldn't go alone. It sounds lonesome to me," said Max.

"It would be very lonesome for sure if you were alone," said Stoney. Here came his big pitch. "Ben Avram said we can all go with you. And there are no TVs and no newspapers, because they haven't installed the media center yet, and it's a hell of a schlep down to the market, so a certain disputed war could be left behind pretty completely. They have a fabulous screening room and a good collection of movies and videos. Lots of European stuff and Japanese stuff."

Cassie said, "My friend George Lomas went to Saint Petersburg. Or is it just Petersburg now? He went in 1995 with the State Department in some official capacity. He had to take an overnight train from Moscow to Petersburg to meet up with the group. When he and his friend got to the train station in Moscow at about eleven, they found his compartment, and then the friend said, 'Okay, now we have to find the conductor.' And when they found the conductor, George's friend pulled a big pistol out of his pocket and held it to the guy's chin and said, 'If anything happens to my American associate here, I will come back and shoot you.' Then the friend took George to his compartment and had him lock himself in."

"Are we going to be held captive?" said Max.

"No. No, we aren't," said Stoney. He heard the crunch of wheels outside and glanced out the window. Just the corner of the yellow Mustang entered, then backed out of, his line of sight.

A moment later, the kitchen door opened, and Charlie came in. He was unshaven and still wearing his clothes from the night before. He smiled a little bit, then passed between Elena and Zoe and came toward Stoney at the sink. Stoney said, "I don't think we should miss it."

Everyone looked at Max and not at Charlie. Only Max glanced at Charlie. Max groaned good-naturedly and said, "Tell me one more thing about the place."

"Well, Avram said there's supposed to be a jewel-box replica of the Amber Room."

"George saw the Amber Room," said Cassie.

"What is it?" said Isabel.

Charlie said, in an even tone of voice, "I read a book about it. The Amber Room was a whole room in the Summer Palace in Russia. It was paneled in sheets of amber backed with gold leaf. The Nazis stole them at the beginning of the war, and then they disappeared. What your friend saw in Saint Petersburg is a replica." He took a cup out of the cabinet beside the sink and went to the coffeemaker, where he filled the cup. Now he crossed the kitchen and went into the living room and sat down. "But it could all be different by now, of course."

"Given what we know about Mike," Stoney continued, "his Amber Room could be partly the real thing. Maybe it's an amber bathroom or an amber closet. Who knows? Jerry always said that a lot more art from around the world ends up in Los Angeles than the museums have any notion of. Ben Avram has been telling me about it for a year. He was up there Friday and called me. He said it smashes all categories of good taste and bad taste simultaneously." Max still looked skeptical, no doubt merely about crossing the 405.

"I'm sure it's not my type of place," said Elena. "You can go without me and Simon."

"But it is my type of place, Mom. Totally. And yours, too, if you think about it. You can wander around deploring the plunder for three days. You can stand that."

Stoney could see Charlie's feet on one of the ottomans in the living room. Zoe was shaking her head, and Paul, too. Cassie said, "I can't take another day off."

"We've done plenty of cooking already," began Delphine. "I'm . . ."

Everyone had had enough. Only Stoney had not had enough, and Max, he thought, knew that. Stoney thought of Jerry, of something Jerry had done all his life: "Here, here's a hundred-dollar bill, go get yourself some shoes. Here, here's the keys to the Jaguar, go to Ruth's Chris Steak House and have a steak, you look a little peaked. Here, here's two tickets to *Grosse Pointe Blank*. Go get your girlfriend and take her to see it. Tell me how you like it." Stoney knew that Jerry never minded sitting you down in a chair and telling you just what a mess you were making of your life and your career, and using words like "schmuck" and "asshole" and "fucking disappointment to your mother and myself." But the essential Jerry was always slipping you something good and giving you a wink, and maybe it was not the optimal child-rearing system, but he was grateful for it.

Right then, Max put his hands on Elena's shoulders, pulled her toward him, and kissed her on the forehead. "I'll say yes, but only if Elena comes along. And Charlie, too."

"Oh," said Elena. "I—" She was almost but not quite shaking her head. Max whispered in her ear.

"We'll fix him," said Simon. "We'll get him alone and away from all media and fix him good."

"I would like to see it," said Charlie from the living room. "Whatever it

is. I don't quite understand what you're talking about, but I'm game."
Stoney guessed from this that Charlie had had some sort of scary Century
Boulevard adventure during the night—perhaps only as scary as spending
the night in a hotel, but with some of those hotels near LAX, that could be
scary enough.

Max grinned, leading Stoney to believe that Max was fond of Charlie
after all.

Zoe looked at Paul. Paul said, "It does sound interesting."

"Art is always interesting," said Cassie.

Max said, "I think maybe it would be nice to take a complete break from
the war, if only for a day or two," and Stoney saw that Elena heard exactly
what he meant. She said, "Yes, it would be nice," more as if she wished to
mean it than as if she really did, but Stoney respected the attempt. He
glanced at Isabel, across the room. Isabel looked authentically intrigued.
He grinned at her, and she grinned back. He said, "Okay, then, I'll call Ben
Avram and say, what, today? That we'll go up today? The sooner the better,
I think." He tried not to sound excessively relieved.

Cassie said, "Will we need to buy food?"

"I'll ask," said Stoney.

All around him, heads nodded. Max kissed Elena on the forehead, then
he said, "How many cars are we taking?"

"Not mine," said Simon. "I don't want it to feel humiliated. I'll ride with
Zoe and Paul."

"I'll ride with Stoney," said Isabel.

Max said, "I can take four—Elena, Cassie, Delphine, and myself."

"I might not want to stay up there every single minute," said Charlie, "so
I'll take the rental and people can use it if they need to."

And now that he had won them over, now that they were actually talking
about transportation, Stoney's sense of relief shaded toward anxiety. He had
talked them into it, and, yes, it would probably turn out to be a sojourn in
the palace, but, hey, this was Hollywood. It could also turn out to be *The
Haunting*. He pulled out his cell phone and called Ben Avram. Ben Avram
answered at once, as if he had been waiting for the call.

It was always amazing, Stoney thought, what sort of properties could
be found in the hills around L.A. For sure, Mike had more than five acres
here, maybe seven or eight, right in Bel-Air, in fact with a view of the Getty,
though from the opposite side to Max's view—Max viewed the exhibition
hall and the restaurant, whereas Mike viewed the permanent galleries,
though Mike viewed them from somewhat farther away. Today, as Stoney

looked out, the Getty was clearly a building rather than a glacier. The air was so fine that he could see tiny museumgoers strolling here and there on the piazzas. But you only observed the Getty as you were approaching Mike's place along an avenue lined with eucalyptuses that hid almost everything. Then you turned suddenly in front of the house. Apart from the driveway and the view toward the pool, there were so many trees and glades that you had no sense of being high up or exposed—everything was designed for luxury rather than display.

Behind the eucalyptuses, the house was set within an Italian-style garden of alternating pergolas and small lawns punctuated by beds of spring plants that were now, at the end of March, shifting from daffodils (tops tied together) and tulips (heads clipped off) to irises, lilies, and roses (just budding out), as well as more exotic plants that Stoney could not identify. The essential requirement, for southern California, that no burnable brush or trees grow within thirty feet of the dwelling, was elegantly managed by the irrigated lawns. Paths led across the lawns and past the beds. It was tempting to venture onto one of them, and he yielded to temptation, with Isabel, even though he should have been organizing things with the manager, whose name he could not remember. He looked at his watch. It was certainly at least twenty minutes until the arrival of the others. He also thought it would be wise to ascertain from Isabel the precise nature of their show for the other members of the family—his lines, his demeanor, his feelings that were to be made evident.

They wandered down a hill and came upon a tiny circular valley, a mere cleft, but strangely remote from the house, where the grass was thick and bright, amazingly green for California, even at the end of winter. The hillside was dotted with neatly pruned and well-cared-for trees. Some of them were in quite fragrant bloom. Stoney said, "What do you think those are?"

Isabel took a deep breath. "Those are almonds. And there are cherries, plums, olives, avocados, and crab apples, and, of course, you recognize the lemons and the limes and the oranges, because they have the fruit and the flowers at the same time. Oh, I love this. Last summer, I spent so many mornings at the Brooklyn Botanic Garden! That's a bay tree. There's rosemary spilling over the rocks over there. That patch is lavender, but it isn't too fragrant at this time of the year. Smell these. I don't know what they are. This is much wilder than my dad's Japanese garden. I like it."

She crushed a couple of moist leaves between her thumb and forefinger and held them up to Stoney's nose. Their sweetness was light but delicious. She said, "Maybe verbena. I had some soap like that once. It might have been the verbena one." She gazed around. "Isn't this something? You can't even see the house from here. And look. There's a little stream down there."

She trotted down the slope, and Stoney followed her, even though maybe he was hearing another car arrive. The stream, about four feet across and two feet deep, ran clear over what looked like carefully and artistically placed stones of a great variety of shapes and colors set in pure white sand. Stoney had never seen anything like it in California. Isabel said, "It's a made stream. It's a completely idealized, perfect stream, and you only get to see it if you are willing to hike down this hill and back up again. Amazing! I wonder if he pays the sun to shine, too?" She laughed. After a week of strange weather—high, apocalyptic winds and wild clouds—in this spot it was calm. The air was dry and fragrant.

Stoney followed her along the little stream around the hillside to where it entered what appeared to be the swimming-pool area. Avram had said there were three connected pools, and this looked like the bottom pool, at this time of day still partially shaded. It was alluring to be in this private spot with her. He reached for her hand, and she let him take it. The lowest pool was shallow and actually rather warm (he felt the water), certainly heated. Instead of concrete, it was constructed of smooth stones, and a light current eddied from one side to the other, the effect of a small bubbler. "No mosquitoes for Mike," said Isabel. "I love this." They went around the lowest pool and climbed some steps to the second pool, which was much bigger and deeper and in brighter sunlight. This pool seemed to be the main swimming pool; it was entirely constructed of mosaic tiles set in an elaborate floral design, mostly purple and gold. It was hard to make out what the flowers represented on the bottom were meant to be, because of the deep water rippling over them, but maybe wisteria. The sides of the pool were "planted" in alternating white and purple irises, which were depicted as if growing out of thick mosaic grass. Isabel said, "Wow! Did you see this before, Stoney?"

"When Avram had the place, there was a kidney-shaped pool from about 1955 and a rambling adobe. I don't think I've been up here in five years, though. Avram and Jerry and some other guys used to smoke cigars up here."

"Oh, right," said Isabel. "And shoot small animals, I'm sure."

"I'm sure," said Stoney.

They climbed another set of steps alongside the waterfall, which plunged over a third mosaic, this one of some god, probably Bacchus, Stoney thought, with his head back and a bunch of grapes in his hand. The upper pool, which was just below and to the south of the golden house, had a fresco on the bottom of a girl with a unicorn lying in her lap. She, too, had her head back; her eyes were closed. A dress, form-fitting and wet-looking, partially covered her breasts. Her blond hair swept behind her and around the periphery of the pool, which was not terribly large and rather shallow, more for lounging in the water than for swimming. The silvery-white unicorn lay with its legs curled, like a dog, and its head in the girl's arms. She was stroking its cheek with one hand, while the fingers of her other hand were spread over the golden horn that grew from its forehead. Its tail flowed out to the periphery of the pool and entwined with her hair. The unicorn had long eyelashes, and its eyes were closed, too. Stoney said, "Three guesses what that picture is supposed to represent."

Isabel squeezed his hand. "I like the unicorn. I always wanted a unicorn when I was a kid. I thought it would be just like that." She gestured toward the pool. "Me and the ultimate dog/horse combination." Stoney had never heard her express this sentiment before, and it made him smile, it sounded so promising in some way. He said, "Say—" but as they walked along the side of the pool, here came Zoe, Paul, Max, and Elena, who had gone around the other side of the house. Elena caught sight of the pool. She said, "How lovely!"

Stoney looked at his watch.

Isabel said, "Just go down the steps by the waterfall. You won't believe it."

"There's more? You three should go through the greenhouse and aviary we just walked through. It's meant to reproduce some spot in northern Australia, with all these strange rain-forest plants and at least a hundred birds of all varieties. The birdsong in there is deafening. I guess they have three bird people who come in just to take care of them. Parrots, macaws, lorikeets, whipbirds, bellbirds. So many colors! And there's a butterfly house, too. It's like a zoo here, but no big animals, only birds and butterflies."

"I have to find the manager," said Stoney.

Elena smiled. "I don't think we are going to get Delphine out of the bird sanctuary. We saw someone. He was standing on the steps. When we started gawking, he gave us this big wave, as if to say, Go ahead and look."

"We should go back to the house," said Zoe.

"I should, at least," said Stoney. "But how do you get to the front?"

Paul said, "This place sure does kill any ennui you might have been feeling."

Stoney and Isabel now followed a path that wound through the pergolas, around the aviary, and emerged in just the right spot for taking in the façade. Paul and Zoe were behind them. No one was standing on the steps, but the front door was open. They walked across the flagstones toward it. "What style is this building?" said Zoe. It was not modern and it was not California Spanish, but, Stoney thought, it fit with the landscape in a strange way. "Palladian," said Paul, "but not like anything I've seen before. Italian Palladian with, let's say, an overdone, vaguely Russian twist."

"Let's say that," said Zoe, laughing. Stoney laughed, too. The house was built of pale-golden stone. Stoney rubbed one of the columns as they stepped onto the porch. It left bright flecks on the tips of his fingers. The big double doors were wide open, and Cassie stood in the entry hall, talking to a small man in a suit who looked, Stoney thought, like old pictures of Rudolf Nureyev. Stoney half expected him to leap in the air and spin around, but he only smiled, excused himself from Cassie, and glided toward them across the polished floor as a glossy, elegant animal might have, a cheetah, or something smaller, something like a lynx. He reached out his hand to Stoney, and Stoney took it, an apology on his lips. But the manager laughed gaily. He introduced himself as Joe Blow, and waved away Stoney's embarrassment. Cassie laughed, too. He said, "Please, call me Joe. When I came to this country from Russia, for Mike, I found it amusing to take this kind of name, the name that means just any person at all. It was between 'John Doe' and 'Joe Blow' for me, and 'Joe Blow' did not sound so bourgeois, so I chose that one."

"What was your name in Russia, Joe?" said Cassie.

"In Russia, my name is Akaky Akakievich." He grinned again, though Stoney did not quite understand why. But he seemed like a good-natured fellow, and Stoney said, "You must be the manager that Avram told me about."

"Yes, I oversee Mike's property here. We are not quite finished with every room, but we are tremendously happy to have you visit." He nodded to Zoe, and then to Elena, but he addressed his remarks to Max. "Mr. Maxwell. I have seen several of your films and admired them very much, and of course everyone knows Miss Cunningham, and so it is our pleasure and honor to enjoy your company for these few days. Mr. Ben Avram has supplied me with a list of the names of each guest, and so, if you will just inform me who is who, I will be happy."

"But first," said Cassie, "you have to tell them what you were telling me about these tapestries."

"Miss Cassie Marshall, of Marshall Arts Gallery in Pacific Palisades, and I have just been getting acquainted." He stepped back with a smile and turned toward the room. Stoney's gaze followed his gesture, and then he saw the tapestries hanging on the walls. There were eight of them, each some ten or twelve feet high and eight or ten feet wide. They went around three sides of the room and seemed to depict a story.

"These tapestries are a set. They were made in France, at a workshop in the Loire Valley, probably in the beginning to the middle of the fifteenth century. They tell the love story of a couple named Pierre Dieudonné and

Agnès La Belle, but no doubt these were not a real couple. I am certain this couple was intended to symbolize an ideal of true love. Here they are in the first frame."

In the first tapestry, the two lovers seemed to be setting out on their horses. A castle flying banners was depicted in the background, and a dark forest loomed to the left. Agnès was wearing a blue dress with a golden bodice and a tall headdress. Her horse was white, and Pierre was lifting her into the saddle. Pierre's horse, dark brown with a white blaze, whose rein was looped over the branch of a tree, was glancing back toward the castle. Joe said, "You see, they are escaping. He is a prince and she is of low birth, and they have been forbidden to marry—by his father because he wishes his son to make a powerful alliance, and by her father because her father is afraid of his father. And so they have decided to elope."

In the second panel, they were deep in the forest. Her white horse, her headdress, and the white blaze on his horse's face were the only bright spots in the dense, dark mass of limbs and tree trunks. "You see," said Joe, "that here is a fork in the road. If you look up in the right corner of the tapestry, all the way at the top, there is a town with a bit of bright sky above it. That is the town that Pierre wishes to find, where he has some friends. In the upper left corner is a tiny, quite sinister dark castle with a dark sky above it. As you can see, Pierre and Agnès are gazing upon one another as young lovers do, and because they are doing that, Pierre's horse is beginning to take the left fork, and of course Agnès's horse will follow him. That is how they go astray."

The group of them stepped over to the third frame. Joe said, "Now you see that the dark castle is down here in the right corner, and the drawbridge is down. Up here on the left are Pierre and Agnès, and this band of knights gallops toward them. These knights are bandits of the forest, enemies of Pierre and his family. You can see here, Agnès notices them before Pierre does." Stoney could see that—both the girl's face and her horse's head were turned toward the knights; the fear in the horse's expression was more eloquent than that of the girl. Pierre looked as he had in the previous tapestry, all moony with affection and desire.

Joe said, "After this, there seem to be a number of missing panels. In the story, Agnès and her horse run into a very deep and wild part of the forest and are lost. In this next panel that we have, here is a battle between two sets of knights. The original group numbers ten—you can see their helmets all in a row, decked out in black and yellow, the colors of their master. Don't you like the way the weaver has caused them to glint brightly in contrast to the dark branches and leaves of the forest? Coming against them from the right are twelve knights belonging to another faction, and they are dressed in red and green. Gang warfare has not changed much in six hundred years, wouldn't you say? But look, up here in the right corner we have Pierre, and he is wearing only his pants, and his shirt and boots lie upon the ground beside him. Some of the threads have been worn away in this section of the tapestry, unfortunately. In the story, Pierre will have been threatened with torture and hanging by the black-and-yellow group. Now he has escaped, but he has lost his horse."

The next panel was fairly self-explanatory, thought Stoney. Pierre was wandering through the forest, clearly dejected. The tapestry-maker had taken this opportunity to fill the forest with birds and animals, none of which Pierre was noticing, but all of which were noticing Pierre. His path was strewn with flowers, and flowers and fruit seemed to lean toward him from the branches of the trees. The forest was not as wild or hostile as he thought it was, but he didn't notice that. He stumbled along, his sword dangling from his side and dragging on the ground.

They stepped to the following panel. Isabel said, "Why is he in the tree?"

"Well," said Joe, "he has hoisted himself into the tree, and you can see that he has tied himself to the trunk so that he will not fall out while he is sleeping. No doubt, he feels that this is the safest way to spend the night in such a wild forest. And, indeed, here is his horse, being chased across the lower half of the panel by wolves. You see the fear on the horse's face, again. This weaver, whoever he was, was very good with horses. Of course, every tapestry had many weavers, but the expert who has told me about this tapestry maintains that one person might specialize in one theme, such as flowers or birds or, indeed, the facial expressions of horses.

"In our next tapestry, we turn to Agnès, who has found herself refuge in a small house deep in the forest. We see the householder here to the left, in the doorway, and you can just see his wife peeking from behind him. Perhaps he is a woodcutter or a mushroom gatherer. At any rate, his clothes and shoes reveal that he is a humble fellow. The wife's headdress is merely a scarf. Here to the right you see Agnès's white horse, and he is looking around. I think he is surveying the path along which they have come, keeping a wary eye out while Agnès and the couple confer.

"After this panel, there are two missing. In the story, the house is raided in the night by one of the marauding bands, though I do not know whether it is the black-and-yellow band or the red-and-green band, and Agnès takes refuge in a pile of hay, where she narrowly escapes being impaled by a spear belonging to one of the knights. When the knights leave, they steal her horse. Subsequently, Agnès emerges from the hay and persuades the humble couple to accompany her to the nearest castle, where she throws herself upon the mercy of the count who lives there, whose wife turns out to be a friend of Pierre's. I am sure there would have been a panel showing the conversation between the two women, in which the girl tells of the dangers she has passed and the wife compassionates her. We would also be able to see the very elaborate room in which the conversation would have taken place. I am very sorry that this panel has been lost, because no doubt many of the details of dress and furniture would have helped date our tapestry more precisely."

The last panel, thought Stoney, did not seem to fit. It was of many men eating and laughing around a fire, with the sun coming up in the background, and it also included six sheep, five white and one black. He said, "Is this one from a different set?"

"No, indeed," said Joe. "When Pierre wakes up, he discovers a group of shepherds and their sheep not far from his tree, and he goes to them and begs for succor, and here they are giving him food and drink. You can see him a bit in the background. The designer has been far more interested in the fire and the sheep. But here is the bit of blue sky that we saw in panel two, only it is larger. Unfortunately, the last panel is missing, This panel would have shown the reunited lovers, probably taking part in a marriage ceremony which has been brought about by the intercession of the noble lady in the other lost panel I was telling you about." Joe smiled, as if he himself had brought the lovers together.

Max said, "Thank you, Joe. You made it seem like a movie."

Joe inclined his head for a moment, acknowledging both the compliment and the man who was complimenting him.

Cassie said, "Where did you find such a beautiful set?"

"Mike is a great connoisseur of art, and he has agents who are aware of what has become and what is becoming available. Since I have been working for Mike, I have discovered that there is no scarcity of beautiful artworks in the world, just as there is no scarcity of money. The question, as always, is one of distribution." He grinned. "Let me say that some of the rooms of our house here are not ready for your inspection, but many are, and you, of course, may wander around as you please. I trust that in your stay you will have many pleasant discoveries. The rooms that are not ready for you are locked. If you can open a door, you may open the door. Mike is not a secretive man. Our residential staff here includes myself; the two girls, Monique and Marya; and the chef, Raphael. Raphael's cooking skills are quite eclectic. He will be sending in to you a paper every morning, detailing alternative menus for the evening. Whom shall he send this paper to?"

Max gestured toward Delphine, who had come in during the story of the tapestry. "I would like that," said Delphine. "May I meet him?"

"Of course you may. Our staffing arrangements are quite informal at this point, since Mike has not yet been in residence here, pending the completion of the rest of the rooms. Raphael will be quite pleased with your feedback, since you are, in a good way, his guinea pigs." Joe grinned again, and led the way into the library.

The library, which was a circular room with a dome, like a miniature rotunda in some state capitol, was full of books on shelves. A mezzanine ran around the room, with a railing and more books on shelves. A staircase on rollers ran on a track set into the base of the mezzanine, and there were various gates in the railing that the staircase could be rolled to. The floor was carpeted with a custom-made Oriental that was woven and laid to accentuate the circular nature of the room. Other Persian rugs were scattered here and there. The furniture consisted of a large desk and a blond leather couch and chair with a reading lamp. There was also a cushioned window seat inset between two sets of shelves below the mezzanine, and another on the mezzanine. These windows faced east, over the cleft that Stoney and Isabel had just been exploring. Joe said, "Does this library look familiar to you?"

No one said anything except Zoe, who said, "*My Fair Lady.*"

"Yes," said Joe. "That is correct. This library was inspired by the set of Professor Higgins' library in London, in that movie. An amusing thing is that when Mike was a boy that was the first movie he ever saw, and although he did not understand it in any way, because he did not at that time speak English, the luxury of Professor Higgins' library made a great impression upon him, and so he has built this room here in Hollywood. That is his joke, that he is a Russian man from Asia with an English library in Hollywood. He is very globalized. However, there are no media in this library, only books."

"Can you tell us something about Mike?" said Elena.

"Here is a story about Mike. When he got to the university, he did not want to live as we others lived, in a large, drafty dormitory with no privacy. So he found a shower stall that was not working, and he installed himself in there, with a mattress and a lap desk, and he bribed one of the men who worked at the dormitory to remove the shower head and the handles. He did not have a light, but he made sure to do his work by daylight. He was very enterprising even then."

"He lived in a shower stall?" said Simon.

"It did have a door," said Joe. "He lived there for three years. Now perhaps you will be wishing to go to your rooms. If I may ask, will you be needing ten rooms, or not so many?" He smiled. "The rooms are actually small

suites, with a generous bedroom, a sitting area, and, of course, a large bathroom." He paused.

Elena said, "Max and I only need one room."

Zoe glanced at Paul, then said, "Two for us, I believe?" He cocked his
head at her, and she said, "I think so, yes."

At this, Charlie cleared his throat, and then Zoe said, "Paul does need to
be able to receive late-night phone calls from his client in Europe. Also, he
rises at four a.m. now."

"Certainly," said Joe. "I will give you our telephone number for the calls,
and you will have your own extension number, Paul."

"One room for us," said Isabel.

Stoney saw Max's head swivel toward Isabel and heard Max let out a surprised cough. He then glanced at Elena and at Simon, who was standing
next to Isabel. All Simon did was raise the fingers on his right hand about an
inch, but it clearly said, Who me? Not me. Isabel acted nonchalant. "One
room for me and Stoney, I mean." It was then that Stoney remembered that
he had intended to have things out with Isabel somewhere in the garden.
Well, not things, but something. He had forgotten, and now they all looked
at him, and of course he nodded and smiled. He could feel himself smiling.
He nodded again, more emphatically. He said, "That would be good." Joe
must have registered the general surprise, but he made no sign. He said,
"And the others?"

"We come alone," said Simon.

"So—eight rooms. Thank you. Monique and Marya will show you to
your rooms. All of them are on the first floor."

"The *premier étage*," said Isabel. She took Stoney's hand tightly in her
own.

Two smiling girls appeared in the doorway of the library, both blonde.
Simon said, "But maybe we won't leave alone," and Stoney noticed that
Elena gave Simon a look, but then, evidently, it was time for Isabel to
march him out of the library, which she did, and as they came to the center
of the entry hall, where they were surrounded by tapestries depicting true
love, she leaned toward him and kissed him on the cheek in the full sight of
her father. And in front of her mother. And in front of her grandmother.
And Stoney did what he thought appropriate among those tapestries, which
was to pause, turn toward her, and kiss her on the lips, her lips being so
familiar and simultaneously so forbidden that it gave him a zinging sensation not so much in his groin as in his knees. Isabel said, gaily, "Are the
rooms decorated more or less alike?"

"Oh, no," said Joe. "They are all different. I am putting you in what we
call the Amber Room."

Behind them, Zoe laughed aloud. Stoney thought maybe that was a good sign.

After dinner (rack of lamb served with a reduction of red wine and woodland mushrooms, braised bitter greens, and roasted potatoes, plus an artichoke-and-caramelized-fennel frittata for the vegetarians, followed by pistachio biscotti and blood-orange sorbet made with Grand Marnier), Stoney disappeared from the dining room when nobody happened to be looking in his direction—he went out one of the French doors, turned right past the upper pool, and trotted down the steps until he found a seat in the shadows not far from the second pool. The only thing that prevented him from going on down to the lower pool, the one in the grotto, was that he didn't want to seem to be fleeing, even though he was fleeing. When he got to the second pool, he lit a cigarette, his first since Jerry was diagnosed with his brain tumor, which everyone knew came from years and years of smoking and an earlier bout with lung cancer. And he got a buzz from his first drag on that cigarette, no coughing or hacking or adjustment at all, and he felt himself starting back down that very bad tobacco road that led nowhere good and everywhere bad, that he had started down at fourteen and Jerry had started down at eleven, and that he had forsworn, and that Isabel hated, and here was Max.

Max sat down on a concrete bench that was decorated with a mosaic of some sort, maybe six feet from him and a little off to the right. All of L.A., spread over the hills and the mountains in a Milky Way of lights, lay beneath them. The sky above was pale. The moon, as so often in L.A., looked nondescript and tentative. The breeze was cool, almost chilly, and Stoney found himself thinking that, after all, the site of the luxurious house was a little too exposed for his taste.

Max said, "Do you have something to tell me?"

"Would you care for a cigarette?"

"No, thanks."

"I think," said Stoney, after what he gauged to be a thoughtful pause, but was really a blank as far as he was concerned, "that I might like to tell you some things, but unless Isabel and I agree on what there is to tell you, no doubt she would say that we would be entering on an essentially patriarchal discourse that would demean her personhood, so I'm not sure what I have to tell you."

"How is it that I don't seem to have any idea that you and Isabel have a relationship?"

"I think I can divulge that we have made an effort to keep it a secret."

"Can you divulge why?"

Stoney thought about this for a moment, then decided to say the most honest thing he could think of at the time, which was: "My inference from what Isabel has said to me is that she didn't want it to get out, because she didn't want such an unimportant relationship to be formalized by publicity. I think I would have said before this morning that, while she enjoys me, she isn't very interested in me, or at least she wasn't. I'm not sure how she feels now. I was quite surprised when she told Joe Blow that we would be sharing a room."

Max drew in a deep and, to Stoney, threatening breath, and said, "Stoney, are you telling me the truth?"

Stoney sat silent for what he considered to be a long moment, pondering this question. Questions about the truth worried him, because of course he didn't know what the truth was. His own true feelings were always confused, he had no access to any general truths, and if you said you were telling the truth, you laid yourself open to all sorts of contradictions that would ultimately confuse you even further. Whenever "the truth" came up, it was often as a prelude to a lengthy and usually contentious discussion. He reiterated, "I'm really not sure what she feels now, and it was a surprise when she wanted to share a room."

"What do you feel?"

"What do I feel for Isabel, or how do I feel in general, you know, glad, sad, anxious, depressed—"

"What do you feel for Isabel?" Max said this impatiently, and so Stoney's general feeling edged even farther away from more or less happy and toward more or less anxious. He said, "Would a good reply be that I want to do what others—namely, you and Isabel and maybe Zoe and certainly Delphine, but not necessarily my own family—want me to do?"

"That would not be a good reply."

"Can we talk about that?"

"No. Anyway, I didn't ask you what you want to do. I asked you what you feel for Isabel. Is that a question you can answer?"

His impulse now was to tell the apparent truth, and so he did. He said, "No."

"Why not?" Now Max sounded more than impatient, almost belligerent.

He said, "Well, because I have never said how I feel about Isabel, especially to a third party, and so it feels like I am breaking some strict taboo, like saying 'fuck you' to the rabbi, for example, or, let's see, what would be an impossible thing? I guess putting my arm around Dorothy and comforting her, which maybe I should have done when Jerry died, but I simply could not do, because Dorothy doesn't seem to exist in the same universe as that sort of gesture."

And Max chuckled. He said, "No, she doesn't, does she? But anyway, try to tell me how you feel about Isabel." He sounded firm.

"And you're sure that you don't want to just ask her?"

"No. I want to hear it from you."

Stoney cleared his throat. The fact was, he hadn't very often said even to himself how he felt about Isabel, because for many years he had been more or less not allowed to feel anything about her, especially because, until this very day, acting on whatever feelings he had seemed to be foreclosed at every turn. So, once again, he said the most apparently truthful thing he could, which was: "Isabel and I get along perfectly, and we have never had an argument. I always enjoy being with her. Probably, as I think about it, the lack of conflict is because whatever she says goes. I mean, it's not that I am passive, exactly, it's more that she cares about lots of things and I care more about her than I care about anything that she has an opinion about."

"Are you afraid of Isabel?"

"Well, of course. Aren't you?"

Now Max laughed out loud, but then he said, "How old are you now, thirty-eight?"

"Yeah. Almost."

"Do you realize how feckless you sound?"

"Is that the word?"

"What word would you use?"

"Scrupulously truthful."

"Okay," said Max.

The breeze shifted direction, and began to ruffle the smooth sheet of the waterfall and throw up a bit of spray. Instinctively, Stoney pushed his chair back from the pool, even though he was sure the spray would not hit them. Max moved from the bench, which for sure would be hard, Stoney thought, to a chair like his, which he scooted toward him. Stoney said, "You know, Max, I asked her this afternoon what her plan is, and she said, 'Nothing. Acting on impulse. I look around at everyone and listen to the stories they tell, and then I listen to myself, and I seem like the oldest one of all of us. *I am the stick in the mud.* I'm twenty-three. I don't want to be the stick in the mud, and anyway, this is a vacation, right?' That's what she said."

Max said, "Well, Simon does seem to be having more fun than she does. Maybe too much fun, in some ways. I worry constantly about Isabel and not at all about Simon, and Elena worries constantly about Simon and not at all about Isabel."

"Who does Zoe worry about?"

"Herself."

"That was mean, Max."

"Well, she does so in a very charming way. And she has a theory, too. Her theory is that worrying about healthy, normal kids just because they are yours is a form of self-indulgence and lack of faith, whereas worrying about yourself is more likely to be a realistic appraisal of your shortcomings."

Stoney laughed. "That's like something Jerry used to say, actually. Anyway, I worry about myself all the time. But I think it's just a habit at this point. I don't worry about Isabel." Even using this word "worry," though, reminded him that, should the history of his relationship with Isabel come to light, he would indeed have something to worry about. At that very moment, he began to worry. What it felt like was the difference between feeling something and seeing something. What might feel warm and yielding and comforting might look disfigured and ugly. That sort of thing happened all the time when you began to discuss "truth."

Max shifted his weight, and his chair squeaked.

Stoney thought of something, and continued: "Just out of curiosity, Max, you don't worry that Isabel is going to turn out to be a schmuck, do you? Because that's what I always thought Jerry worried about with me."

"No, I don't have the slightest fear that Isabel will turn out to be a schmuck." Stoney saw him smile.

Stoney did not quite dare to go on to ask whether Max worried about whether he, Stoney, would turn out to be a schmuck. He said, "Well, that's something, anyway." He said, "I think we should join the others. If we're the only ones missing, then for sure Isabel will know that we are talking about her."

"Then let's talk about Mike."

Stoney sat up, the way you do when something forgotten but redemptive is suddenly remembered. He said, "Let's do."

"Did you look around?"

"I did."

"Did you see the Vermeer?"

"I saw what they said is a Vermeer. And it looked like a Vermeer to me, or a very good fake. I didn't scrutinize it or peek at the back."

"It's a lovely painting," said Max. "The girl's face is very good-natured. And you could see how such a small Vermeer could get lost in the course of a few centuries, especially if, as they said, the Dutch family that originally commissioned it fell on hard times, and the last heir died intestate, and the house was in a state of disrepair, and a Russian army officer who was in Antwerp bought a bunch of pictures at the auction and boxed them up and sent them home to Moscow and then was killed in a war, and the box went astray, only to be discovered in a government postal lost-and-found by one of the army officer's illegitimate daughters when she herself was fleeing Napoleon's army, so she hid it with friends as a keepsake of her father, whom she had hardly known but remembered fondly, and then one of their sons opened the box twenty years later and saw that insects and mold had destroyed the other three pictures, leaving only this one, and so he hung it in his library, and one day Vladimir Nabokov's grandfather was visiting, and he asked the owner if it was a Vermeer, and they deciphered the signature at the bottom, which has now been worn away, and so they treated it with much more care, so that when the Revolution came one of the daughters took it out of its frame and rolled it up and carried it under her dress to Finland, and then it went in their luggage, sewn into a patchwork coverlet, when they immigrated to the United States, and only a year ago the last son of that family decided to put all his artwork on the market because he wanted to switch all of his investments to gold after the election of the Bush administration, and so it came on the market, and Mike bought it, and feels justified in keeping it, because, even though it was painted by a Dutch painter, it was preserved through the efforts of Russians, and in it he sees all of the ups and downs of Russian history."

"Sounds plausible to me," said Stoney.

"It makes you wonder how any piece of art at all ever survives."

"They put us in the Amber Room, you know. I wonder if it's the real Amber Room."

"They put us in the Flower Room. It has floral wallpaper, a floral pattern in the carpet, paintings of flowers, including what seem to be two Georgia O'Keeffes, and casement windows overlooking one of the gardens. It has its own flowered teacups and teapot, and a collection of flower teas from France. I guess the windows of Delphine's room open out toward the upper part of the aviary, and the decor is a tropical-bird motif. Elena went in to take her something, and Delphine showed her her bedspread and pillows that were hand-embroidered with a scene of parrots and macaws in a forest. And the handles on the faucets in the bathroom were ceramic birds with long tails, blue for cold and red for hot."

"Simon said Charlie's room was all paneled in inlaid tropical woods in elaborate designs, and the flooring is made of bamboo, and Simon's own room is ultra-modern. Lots of glass mosaic tiles and trompe-l'oeil mirrors. He said to me, 'This room is one they could not have put you in, Stoneman. You would have been falling down the steps and walking into the walls, and they must have been afraid of a big liability suit, but to me it's just another challenge. I keep thinking that maid Monique is going to materialize in the middle of the floor and all of her clothes are going to fall right off her.'"

Max laughed. "What did you say?"

"I said, 'Don't call her a maid. You'll have better luck,' and he said, 'Okay, I'll call her a maiden.'" Stoney paused, then said, "But, Max, doesn't the house make you want to do a movie for Mike?"

"No. Frankly, Stoney, I much prefer making movies for a couple of cheap bastards who want to cut corners in every scene, because it's more fun. My guess is that Mike's instinct will be to weight the whole project down with authenticity, so that, for example, every costume will be perfect from the underwear out. So the actresses will all wear some kind of corsets. But twenty-first-century actresses aren't used to corsets, so they'll be distracted by the discomfort of wearing corsets, and they'll look awkward in corsets. So, as a result of that, Mike and I will get into a lengthy discussion of whether the actresses should be made to wear corsets, and the solution will be to try it out, which won't in the end demonstrate anything conclusive. There's thousands of dollars in costume financing wasted and at least a week of filming before we get to the issue of, say, dirt. Is the encampment going to look dirty and authentic, like the sets in *The Return of Martin Guerre*, or is it going to look clean, like the sets in *A Man for All Seasons*? Mike has lots of money, so he's going to think that if we just get all of the details right, then a movie will eventuate, but in fact what will eventuate will be a kind of slow-moving parade of everything we've bought. I like staying here, in other words, but I would never live here."

"Will you meet with Mike?"

"Didn't I say I would?"

"Yes, but I didn't believe you. And it sounds like you can't be persuaded."

"I can't be persuaded by money."

"You need money."

"Do I?"

"That's my impression. You haven't made a movie in four years. You sold the Hawaii house. Stocks are down. My guess is you do need money."

"Well, let me put it this way. If something else were to persuade me, I could thereafter be cajoled into taking lots of money to do the project." He smiled.

"What would persuade you?"

"Something about Mike."

"What?"

"I don't know at this point. Something I don't expect to be there."

"That's so Hollywood," said Stoney. "That's so 'I don't know what I want but I want something and I'll know it when I see it.'"

Max shrugged. Stoney couldn't see Max shrug in the dark, but he knew that he was shrugging. Now they fell silent. The moon had risen and faded even more; the breeze had died. The bubbler that was in one of the pools made a low, intermittent sound, and occasionally there was a call of some sort from the aviary. Suddenly there was a cry from the direction of the glen, too, maybe the sound of a coyote or a bobcat. That was a thought Stoney liked, the thought of some scroungy L.A. County predator expanding his territory to include Mike's property. Come, hawks, he thought. Come, owls and buzzards and crows and Canada geese. Come, feral cats and cougars and deer, gophers and ground squirrels. Partake.

Max said, "Let's go in."

●

Charlie had to admit he was impressed. He kept saying the word "On," and then the other word, "Off," and the lights in the room came on, and then they went off. Clapping didn't do it, coughing didn't do it, bumping one piece of furniture against another didn't do it. Only the word "on" and the word "off," at a normal volume. Shouting the words didn't do it, either. Of course there were switches—one on the lamp beside the bed, and one next to the headboard (a beautiful tall, curved, dark piece out of some tropical wood accented in pale blond). You would expect a backup option, and you could override the general controls by turning various lights on and off individually, and Charlie's private opinion was that this fancy business would prove confusing in the end, and whoever eventually lived in this room would go back to walking around flipping switches, but, yes, he was impressed. He said "Off" in a medium and not-too-self-conscious tone of voice, and the room went dark except for the bathroom and the window lights, which dimmed gradually and then died. He squirmed down under the covers, lay flat on his back, and inventoried his condition.

His condition was better than it had been the night before.

Aches and pains: His left trapezius muscle was hurting from the base of his neck down behind the shoulder blade. His right little finger was throbbing, unknown origin. His right knee hurt at about a three on a scale of ten, not bad, but something to be aware of, possibly from running on the slope of the beach. One thing he'd noticed since taking up fitness and health was that if you hurt yourself running north, say, on an uneven surface, you could not then fix yourself by running south over the same surface, though it seemed like you should be able to.

Digestive system: Mild feeling of bloat, possibly from eating bread and a very little bit of butter at dinner. No actual pain.

Heart and lungs: He put his first and second fingers to his carotid artery. Pulse, about sixty-eight. He took two deep breaths. No discernible congestion. Respiration good. He put his hand over his heart. It was beating. In spite of himself, he felt reassured.

Bowels and urinary tract: He had urinated five times in the course of the day, every time for at least twenty seconds, which he personally thought indicated good hydration. Longest urination of the day, twenty-nine seconds. Onset of urination: good. Two bowel movements, optimal consistency, medium color, no dark spots or streaks or other evidence of blood.

Genitals: No anomalies evident upon palpation. Small pimple just behind his balls, which he would look at in the morning (he resisted the impulse to call out "On" and look right then, because he had found, through experience, that if he gave in to that sort of thing, in the end it was worse). He probably should not have touched his genitals—some guys he knew never touched their genitals when doctors' offices were closed—but he had been lax, and there he was. The pimple would either grow or not before morning; he decided to be philosophical about it.

Skin: Nothing evident, though he suspected he had gotten the merest touch of sunburn on the beach that day. His skin before bed felt a little hot and looked a little red—say, two on a scale of ten. But that could be a bit of niacin flush, too. He would know by morning. His moles didn't worry him—they had been catalogued just before he left Jersey and found harmless.

Looks: Better than many, worse than some. Worse than Max? Hard to tell. Today, when he was running a last time on the beach before coming up here, he paid attention to who seemed to notice him—men, women, young, old. It was fewer in California than it was on the beach in Jersey, but the notice was often friendly rather than hostile, as it could be in Jersey. When you factored in the difference between California and Jersey, that complicated things. Just in terms of looks, people in California got more exercise and probably more sex, but they also got more sun. In his own mind, if Charlie had to choose betwen the eighty-year-old country-club couples in L.A. County, and the eighty-year-old country-club couples in Hunterdon County, he would choose the latter. Old Californians were wrecks, what with sun damage and athletic injuries. Old New Jerseyites, if they lasted that long, looked better. Chances were, at eighty he would look better than Max at eighty. But if he was eighty in Jersey, people might not be as friendly as they would be to Max, an eighty-year-old wreck in California. Just right now, though, it was hard to guess who was going to care what he might look like in twenty-some years.

Charlie cleared his throat and put that thought out of his mind.

He had turned onto his left side without realizing it, bad for the trapezius. He eased onto his back and took a pillow, one of the many that were scattered across the king-size mattress, and stuffed it under the covers, under his knees, which he bent upward. Sometimes a pillow under his knees reminded even his sleeping self not to move from a stable flat-on-his-back position, though five and a half decades and more of sleeping habits made him long to be on his stomach. But his neck couldn't take that anymore, and his lower back needed support, too. Back in New Jersey, he had given up on finding the right mattress. He'd tried a waterbed (two of those, both the old-fashioned kind, made like a giant cushion, and the new kinds, constructed of long plastic water-filled sausages). He'd tried the Swedish foam and thought he'd found the answer, but in the Swedish foam, he never shifted position all night long, and that stiffened him right up. He'd tried the air-mattress thing, and the firm mattress with the softer pillow on top, as well as the softer mattress with the firmer pillow on top. But there was no solving the mattress problem, and his Chinese-medicine crony was no help—he slept on a couch and never complained.

When Charlie had finished rustling around in his bed and rearranged and stilled himself, he noticed again how dark it was, and thought of saying "On," but he didn't want the whole lighting system to wake up. He opened his eyes and closed them. No doubt about it, it was really dark in this room. But cool and yet not cold. Yes, the temperature was quite nice, which he appreciated after Max's place, where climate control was slapdash at best. At Max's, he was always throwing off a blanket or piling one on.

On balance, he was glad he had not acted out his impulse the night before and gone back to New Jersey. Oh, it was easy enough, when you were pissed, to drive the rental to LAX and imagine that you were going to find yourself a flight back to Newark, but the first question you had to answer was, Turn in the rental or not? If you did turn in the rental (and Budget was at least a half-mile from the actual airport), then were you going to walk from terminal to terminal, looking for a reservations desk? And if you didn't turn in the rental, where to park it? And even though there were some red-eye flights to the East Coast, you couldn't just take them at the last minute. And on top of all that, he had to factor in the extra security that came because of the war. So he had found himself a room at the Sheraton, more for the parking lot than for the room, intending to get up and look for a flight in the morning, but then the first three flights on American had been fully booked, and by that time he'd had a chance to look at the Weather Channel, and so he had gone back to Max's, and actually, everyone had been pretty nice to him all day, and then that dinner and this bed, he thought, were some compensation to his pride. Plus the fact that there really was no news of the war up here. It was a relief, though he would never admit that to Elena.

A female voice said, "Hi."

Charlie went rigid among his marvelous linens for a long moment, but then decided that he must have been dreaming. He scratched his head. Yes. It would surely have been an illusion of some—

She said, "Hi, Charlie. Is that what they all call you?"

And Charlie said "On." The room lights came up, revealing the beautiful paneling, the sleek heavy furniture, the large pink Persian rug on the bamboo parquet flooring, the painting of three big dogs taking down a hideously tusked boar, and Monique, standing at the foot of his bed. She smiled.

Charlie felt all of his tissues slam together in shock and only just stifled a holler. Well, a scream. As it was, he did gasp in a very unbrave sort of way, and Monique's smile widened into a grin. At last he said, as indignantly as he could manage, "How did you get in here?"

"There is a door in the paneling of the sitting room. It opens into a little corridor behind the wall, and then into the upstairs gallery. It is a beautifully crafted door. This has been my room, actually, but Joe put me into one of the unfinished ones that we will be using later. It is almost finished, I do not mind, but I"—now her smile turned playful—"I was walking down the gallery, and I just wished to try the secret door. You can lock it from this side, if you want. I'll show you how."

Charlie realized he was in a cold sweat. He had not thought that an actual cold sweat was possible, but his whole body felt clammy and wet under the covers.

She went on, "And anyway, you touched me at dinner, didn't you?"

"Excuse me?"

"When I was passing your corner of the table with the coffeepot, you touched my derriere."

"I did?"

"Didn't you?"

Charlie cleared his throat, then said, "Well, I did. But I didn't realize you'd noticed."

"What would have prevented me from noticing that you patted my ass?"

"Well, it was a little pat, and you didn't react, and your jeans were tight—"

"I did notice."

There was a long pause. She was still standing at the foot of the bed, and she was staring down at him. He had estimated she was about twenty, but as she stared at him, he began to revise his estimate upward. He said, "Are you wanting me to apologize?"

"Don't you think that would be appropriate?"

"Then why do you wear your jeans so tight?"

She frowned and put both her hands on the top edge of the footboard. She was looking older and more resolute every second. He said, "I don't mind apologizing."

"I would like to hear it."

"I shouldn't have fondled your ass. I probably shouldn't even have looked at your ass. I'm sorry I did. I'm not looking at your tits right now, either. I'm looking right at your face, and I'm sorry in advance if my gaze seems to wander. It isn't wandering. My guess is that you are far too young for me to look at, at any rate." He guessed that even Isabel would be satisfied with this apology.

"I'm thirty-three."

Now Charlie sat up in bed, and the covers fell from his chest. He said, "You are? That's amazing. I thought sure you were closer to twenty."

"Twenty?" She came around the footboard and sat down on the end of the bed. "Did you really think I was twenty?"

"Well, twenty-two. Twenty-five at the most. I really did."

"And what are you, about sixty?"

"Fifty-eight, actually. I've looked sixty for years, I suppose, but now I've found a new health regimen. I can tell you about it, but the long and short of it is that sometimes you can't actually turn back the clock but you can stop the clock, in a way, and more or less catch up to it. That's the way I look at it. Are you French?"

"No, I am Russian. We are all Russian here in this house, but I spent some time working in France, at Mike's house there. He has a house in the south, near Menton. I lived there for six years, but I never went out in the hot sun. That is the secret to my youthful appearance. I said before I went there that I was never going to go out in the hot sun, and I never did, and I pursue the same policy here in Los Angeles. Here is my theory; let me know what you think of it. You see that I am pale and blonde. This is what you might call northern coloring. We pale, blonde, blue-eyed types suffer much more from vitamin-D deficiencies than others, but at the same time, we do not have sufficient melanin. We are much more subject to certain types of diseases, such as multiple sclerosis, and certain types of cancer. If we use sunblock, then we don't get sunburned, but we also don't get enough vitamin D, which is a very important vitamin in preventing auto-immune diseases. You may read about this in the British press, not so much in the

American press. Some people even think that cancer itself is inhibited by vitamin D. And if I were to get pregnant with a baby and not get enough vitamin D, my baby could have severe defects. And so this is what I do, I turn the year around. I treat Los Angeles or Menton as if it were Russia. Now we are coming out of winter and going into summer. In the winter I go out without a hat or long sleeves, and in the summer I do not go out, or I go out with sun-repelling clothing on, and so I am preserving my skin and also getting a proper dose of vitamin D. That is my story."

"I see," said Charlie, "that we have a common interest in health."

"Yes, but I am interested in my health, and you are interested in your health. I am not sure I am interested in your health."

Charlie laughed.

Monique made herself a little more comfortable on the end of his bed, leaning back against the footboard and crossing her legs. She was, indeed, a beautiful woman, but now that she had confessed her age, he could see it. He said, "So—are you married?"

"That, too, is an interesting question."

"What do you mean?"

"I was married in Russia, but my husband disappeared, and then I left, and my husband does not seem to have reappeared. He has not contacted my family." She shrugged.

"Don't you care?"

"It has been almost ten years since I saw him. He could well be dead by this time, because he was easily offended—he did not like people telling him what to do. Once everyone in Russia had guns and weapons, the life of someone who was easily offended became very dangerous."

Charlie, who had never been to Russia, didn't know quite what to say about this, so he tried the only thing he could think of. "If you are thirty-three, then you would have been raised a Communist."

Monique gave him a bemused look, then said, "Well, were you raised a capitalist?"

"Of course."

"What does that mean? To be a capitalist, you must have some capital."

"No," said Charlie, with a pleased and rather self-satisfied feeling at what he was about to say, "to be a capitalist, you have to have an idea. Well, a good idea."

"And you had some good ideas when you were a child?"

"I have a good idea now."

"May I ask what it is?"

"Well, in a nutshell, and this is what the best investment-advisers tell you all the time, invest in what you know. I realize that I am just one of a very large group of men who are getting older, and the age cohort behind me is even more vast, and so I am on the cutting edge of an important social phenomenon. Let me show you."

Charlie threw off his covers and walked over to the lowboy, where he opened his case and looked at it fondly. He carried it over to Monique and set it on the bed. He said, "You may not be interested in my health, but plenty of folks are, or should be, because what works for me will work for them."

"You take all of these pills?"

"I do. This, for example, is saw palmetto, which I take for prostate health and repair. This here is Viagra, which is a wonder drug. Here's the aspirin. Did you know that the bark of the willow tree has been used all over the world for all sorts of therapies since—"

Monique was counting. "You have sixteen. No, seventeen types of pills here."

"Yes, I do. It's a complicated regimen, and sometimes I get a little mixed up, but it's doable, and I feel great, better than I have in years. Look at this." He pulled a photo out of a pocket in the lid of the case. He said, "This is what I looked like ten years ago." The photo was of him; he had had Karen take it, and he had been a little surprised that the drugstore was willing to develop it, but not a peep out of them. It was full-front, top to bottom. He said, "It's not just the paunch and the sagging pecs and the loss of muscle mass in the shoulders, or even the jowls. Look at my jowls. They were a lot worse then. You can go to the gym and fix those things, or even—"

"You are showing me a picture of yourself naked."

"Yes." He looked at it again. He had looked at it so many times over the years that in a way he had forgotten that it was at all immodest. "But it's purely informational. See how bad my skin tone was? Loose and pasty and dehydrated. That was ten years ago! I was a fairly young man, but I felt like I was a hundred years old. I was working for Pepsi then, and between you and me—"

She took the photograph out of his hand and slid it back into its sleeve in the lid of his case, then she closed the lid. She said, "Have you taken all your pills today?"

"Well, yes, but I was saying—"

"Then let's talk about something else."

"But we were talking about something else. The regimen of pills I have in here can change the lives of millions of men, and, through them, the lives of their whole families. That's my idea. I have a friend who is an expert in Chinese medicine, and through no fault of his own is stuck in a little shop in Chinatown in New York City. I haven't even told you about the most miraculous—"

All of a sudden, Monique knocked the chest off the bed, and it landed upside down on the carpet.

"Hey!" exclaimed Charlie, thinking he should have known something like this could happen. And then, when he bent down to pick it up and turn it over, she started spanking him with the flat of her hand on his bare ass, which was what reminded him that his ass was bare. Whack, whack. He didn't get away until the middle of the third whack, which went astray and clipped him on the leg. He jumped up, case safely in hand, and turned to confront her. She was grinning. He said, "What the hell are you doing?"

"I'm sorry." But she didn't look sorry.

Charlie set the case down carefully, hoping that he would remember in the morning to sort through the pills, many of which looked similar, but, thank God, not exactly the same. That was another part of his idea—make all the pills look different, color-coded or something, so that old guys—

Her grin faded to something harder. She said, "You have fondled my posterior and shown me a picture of yourself naked and walked around in front of me without any shorts on. It was my feeling that a little discipline would help you learn to mind your manners."

Now Charlie felt his first real burst of anger. He shouted, "What's the matter with you, lady? You showed up in my room at, what is it, eleven-thirty at night, and I am supposed to be welcoming you with a cup of tea and a cookie? Get the fuck out!"

But he was standing there in his nightshirt (a T-shirt, actually, not long enough to cover himself), and he was between the bed and the door, and he was trying not to get any closer to her, so he sensed that his voice lacked a certain measure of authority. For that reason, perhaps, she continued to sit on the bed. He ran his hand over the right cheek of his ass. It stung. Right then, he decided maybe she was crazy. Maybe that talk about vitamin D, though it sounded good, was really some sort of delusion, and this was a Jekyll-and-Hyde sort of transformation. By day she was a perfectly respectable girl working for, admittedly, a set of strange people, but by night she roamed the mansion—

She said, "You didn't think that was even a little fun? Would you like to spank me? I like it myself. Have you ever done it?"

"Get spanked? Or spank?"

"Either one."

"Well, I used to spank my kids. I've never gotten spanked before, at least not since I was maybe four years old."

"Did you enjoy spanking your kids?"

"I don't know. I never thought about it. They needed to be spanked, and they got spanked, and that was the end of it."

She stood up and began to unzip her jeans.

"You know," said Charlie, "I don't think . . ." His anger had given way to just a dot of fear, just a grain of unease. When she had unzipped her jeans, she slid them down maybe six or eight inches, and he saw that she was wearing no underwear, and that, furthermore, she had shaved her pubes in one of those new styles, just a strip, maybe three inches long and, it looked like, dyed. At any rate, it was red. She pushed her ass out of her jeans and turned around, showing it to him. It was a nicely shaped ass. Of course, he had noticed that at the dinner table. He said, "I guess you've decided to take my gesture at the dinner table as an invitation."

Her voice was a little muffled, but it sounded like she said, "I have been mulling that over. I am of two minds about that."

She shifted her weight from one leg to the other, and her ass changed shape. Of course it was tempting. He hadn't actually had anything to do with women since the separation. The few women who made up to him were divorcées or widows more or less his own age, and they didn't appeal to him. And he seemed to be not especially attractive to the women he was interested in. It had not escaped his notice, for example, that Zoe more or less avoided him, though he would have said that he himself was more attractive than Paul. Of course, Paul had no money, but it was clear he had some sort of other capital, however bogus that might be. It sort of got his goat, to tell the truth. Thinking of this, he said, "Did you notice the guy with the beard?"

"Of course."

"What did you think of him?"

"Excuse me?" Her voice was even more muffled.

"Do you find him attractive? On a scale of, say, one to ten, where would you—"

She stood up and turned around and pulled up her jeans. To tell the truth, that was something of a relief to him. She said, "I saw him making yoga postures in the herb garden before dinner. He is very supple and strong. That is appealing in its way."

"But when he gets down to his shorts, you can see there's a lot of sun damage from exercising—"

She sat on the bed again. She held up her finger to him and said, "But, you see, that is what I was saying earlier. He has allowed the sun to naturally envelop him with what you might call a carapace. Yes, he is leathery, but he is evidently very healthy and vital, and what you call sun damage is really a protective layer. It is not so appealing to some, perhaps, but I see the fact that he has done this as a sign of intelligence and experience. I would say that he is appealing in a certain way. He has something to offer. Expertise is sexy."

"Most Americans would just say he is one weird guy. And did you see how Isabel has taken up with the little agent? That surprised me. She must outweigh him by—"

"From the point of view of someone like myself, who has come from Russia and lived in France, most Americans are narrow-minded, ignorant, and provincial."

Charlie was offended at once. He felt his face go red, and he saw that she noticed it. She said, "So now are you ready to spank me? I have insulted your country; Americans hate that sort of thing. Here, I will compound the insult. Once I was at the opera in Saint Petersburg, and there were some Americans sitting near me, a whole group. They were well-dressed adults, and evidently important, because they were sitting in good seats, but they could not sit still in their chairs. They were shifting and talking and squeaking and interfering with the performance. Eventually, several of them dozed off, and then, at the interval, most of them left. It was like watching children. All around them, the Russians were sitting quietly and enjoying the performance."

Charlie didn't quite know how to respond to this, so he said, "Don't Russians hate being insulted?"

Monique threw back her head and laughed. "It is not possible to insult Russians more than Russians insult themselves. For Russians, it is a point of pride to believe that Russians are hopeless. It is like— Have you ever read any books about the Stalinist era? Let's see, there was one by Evgenia Ginsburg. In it, she talks about how, when she was in a retraining camp in Sibir, the soldiers there would drink the antifreeze of their trucks when they had no vodka or other alcohol. And they would live and keep working. This is a point of pride for Russians, that they get so desperate that they would drink antifreeze that would kill anyone else, but that they are so tough that they would live through it. My husband was like that. Once, he was so drunk that he did not see a truck coming toward him, and it hit him and rolled over him, and broke his ankle, but he got up and staggered home anyway, and he only discovered that his ankle was broken the next morning. He was as proud of being stupid as he was of being undaunted. I came to not care for him very much in the end."

"What was his name?"

"His name was Viktor Vassileyevich Storokin. We were from a town inland of Sochi. Have you heard of Sochi?"

"No."

"I am not surprised. But Sochi is a very famous city. It is on the Black Sea, and in Russia, but it has palm trees and tea plantations. It is very tropical and very beautiful. It is the Menton and the Honolulu of Russia. Have you heard of Odessa?"

Charlie thought he had.

"It is rather near to Odessa, though Odessa is now in Ukraine. Sochi is not in Ukraine, but in Russia."

"Is that the sort of place Max would be making his movie?"

"What movie is that?"

"Your boss wants him to make a movie of an old Russian book called *Taras Bulba*."

"Oh. By Gogol. Yes. I have not read that book, but Gogol was Ukrainian from the steppe. He is famous for writing about lots of things, and for offending the Tsar. He wrote a play, and the Tsar got up and left in the first act of the first performance, and so Gogol escaped to Europe that very night, because he was afraid the secret police were going to come get him and throw him in prison. He also wrote a famous book called *Dead Souls*, about a man who buys the property that used to remain in the serfs even after they had died. But at the end of his life, after he had finished it, Gogol thought better of that book, and tried to burn it in his stove. I have read a little of that book, but I don't remember anything except the lonely idea of going around to the impoverished estates in a horse-drawn carriage. I prefer a Russian novel called *Fathers and Sons*. Have you read that?"

Charlie shook his head. He said, "I'm not much of a reader. I like the Discovery Channel, though."

"*Dead Souls* is a very difficult book, but *Fathers and Sons* is about a family. The troubled ones die off, and the family lives on, and there is a baby at the end. It is not very exciting, but it is pleasant, which is a rare quality in Russian books."

Charlie yawned.

Monique looked at her watch. She said, "It isn't yet midnight," as if she was surprised that Charlie was tired. He said, "That seems late to me."

"I, by contrast, am wide awake."

"Maybe you should find your friends Marya or Joe."

"Joe is gay. He's with Raphael. Marya and I spend enough time together. We are friends, but I need a larger group than we have here, and it is too inconvenient to go all the way down to town when I have to be back here early in the morning. And, of course, there is no television or Internet access. When I saw your group, I thought I might find some entertainment among you." She shrugged, as if to say that anyone can be wrong sometimes. "It would be nice to talk to this girl Zoe Cunningham. She is very pretty. I can't quite believe that she is with your group. It seems like a comedown for her after the people she has been with in the movies."

"We're her family. Max is her former husband. Isabel is her daughter, and Delphine is her mother. I'm Max's friend, and Elena is Max's new girl-friend. Simon is Elena's son."

"He is most attractive."

"That's what he thinks."

Monique laughed. She said, "Actually, Marya and I flipped a coin, and she got Simon. I got you."

"I thought you were just walking down the hallway—"

"The gallery."

"—and you came in here on impulse."

"Did I say that?"

"Yes."

"It was more of a game than that."

"Now you're telling the truth, right?"

"Maybe. But what does it matter?"

"I think it's always better to tell the truth. That's how I raised my kids."

"You spanked them until they told the truth?"

"Sometimes I did, I have to say. One of my boys, Jared, he seemed to lie a lot. My wife, Karen, said that it was because he was the second child, and he could see that there were plenty of things that his older brother was doing that we parents had no idea of, so that idea that the older one had, that he would be caught if he did something wrong, the younger one didn't have. He could see the disparities between what was going on and what we knew all too well."

"How many children do you have?"

"Five. They're all married now. I have twelve grandchildren at this point. I bet there's another one on the way, but my wife hasn't told me about it yet. We're separated. We're working on the divorce."

"And so what purpose did it serve for you to leave your home and go off on your own?"

"I get to do what I want. I have to admit that sometimes I don't enjoy what I'm doing and it seems kind of aimless and stupid, but it is what I want to do, and that's better than doing what she wanted to do."

"What was that?"

By now Charlie was sitting on the bed again. He lifted his legs and turned, so that he was leaning against the headboard. His legs looked odd, skinny and sort of droopy, so he flipped the bedspread over them, but the bedspread was so luxurious that now he had in his mind the image of his weird old legs underneath this princely piece of goods. He cleared his throat. "Oh. Are you really interested?"

"Interested enough for now."

That didn't seem like the best beginning to his tale, but it didn't look, from her relaxed gaze up at the ceiling, like she was leaving, so he told it anyway. He said, "I don't guess you've heard of the Catholic Charismatic Movement? That was something that started in the eighties. I don't know much about it, because neither my wife nor I was Catholic. My family was Congregationalist, and her family was Episcopalian. Her name was Cooperman, but the Episcopal church was the 'best' church in her town, so they went there. My wedding took place at a country club where my wife's family belonged. She was half German and half English, all Republican. There were a couple of Jewish relatives, but they just avoided the ham. That was the only way you could tell that any of them were Jews. In those days, we didn't think as much about religion as we do now. Anyway, we had the kids and my career and the house, and she joined various book groups and bridge clubs in addition to our country club, and I think, for a while there in the seventies, she joined a consciousness-raising group, because she got me to buy this white elephant of a big wooden hot tub, I don't even remember how you heated the thing except that it was a pain in the ass, and then she heard about some people in California dying in their hot tub because it was too hot and they were drinking wine and somehow the overheating of their bodies caused them to pass out and die. Literally, that's the main thing I remember from the consciousness-raising period, because I was working at Pepsi fifty hours a week most of the time, and traveling a lot, too, but she met another woman in this group, named Margaret. Margaret had long hair, down to her waist, and she wore it like that for years, just hanging down to her waist, and one time she actually said to me, 'My hair is my glory,' and, I mean, she had nice enough hair, but I ask you. So I guess I could say that I never really got Margaret, but my wife was crazy about her, and they did a lot of things together. Margaret's husband was a proctologist, and he was always working, too, so we hardly ever got together as couples, which seemed to suit everyone just fine. That was all through the eighties. Margaret kept her hair long and, as she said, 'her ideals intact.' She hated Reagan, which in my book was a compliment to him, and the main thing I remember about the eighties was that my kids were teenagers, and once in a while Margaret and I got into screaming political arguments. Anyway, it got to be sort of a joke, like the two relatives at every Thanksgiving dinner who fight about whether FDR was the Joe Stalin of American history.

"In 1993, Margaret joined the Charismatic Catholic Movement, and in pretty short order, my wife was starting to talk about converting. I guess they were going to Mass together, and they got involved with a priest who was giving workshops. The kids were grown up by that time—the youngest, that would be Laurie, was in college or something—and I didn't pay much attention for a while, because of course I had a job and was making a damn good living, but then the pressure built, and Karen was trying to get me to go to Mass with her, so I did, just to keep the peace. The first time I ever went to Mass with her was a shocker, I have to say, because here I was with a woman I had known for thirty years or thereabouts, but I didn't recognize her. And I didn't recognize old Margaret, either. They were kneeling and praying with their eyes closed and this ecstatic look on their faces that made me want to snap my fingers in front of their noses and wake them up. I mean, this very woman I slept up against like two spoons in a drawer the night before, and she was wearing her red-and-white nightgown with the Santa faces on it, and here she seemed to have slid back two centuries. Margaret had her hair up and a thing like a towel covering it, and I have to say that the whole experience freaked me out. I kept very quiet, and as we were leaving the church, I eavesdropped on them talking about rebirthing themselves as handmaidens for Jesus."

"These women sound like lesbians to me."

Charlie paused without saying anything, partly because that thought had crossed his mind more than once, too. Then he went on. "But in sickness and in health, you know, so I kept my mouth shut and tried to cooperate about going to church—or, rather, Mass—when I was asked, and I kept saying to myself that I would draw the line at some point, but I didn't really. After we started going to Mass every Sunday, then she wanted to do another thing on Wednesday, and after that, another thing on Saturday. I was still going to the job and to company functions and working my ass off, and that included when I was playing a little golf at the club, because when you live the corporate life you have to keep up the front twenty-four/seven, as you kids say, but she wasn't going with me. She didn't even realize I was having trouble at the job, and you know, I didn't bother to tell her. After my prostate thing, I just dealt with that on my own, and I'm happy I did. She was spending her whole time at the church, especially when Margaret started being in charge of the altar decorations for the weekends. And then something happened that I knew they had been plotting. You know what an intervention is?"

Monique shook her head.

"An intervention, in the strictest sense, is when you have someone in the family with a bad drug or alcohol problem, and one night you surprise him with the whole family. It's best if the ones from far away, like the West Coast or something, fly in, because he doesn't expect to see them. You also get an expert or two, and you confront him, though it could be a woman—the most famous intervention, at least in our circles, was the Betty Ford intervention. You know who she is?"

Monique shook her head.

"She was the wife of Gerald Ford, who was president for a while. Anyway, you confront the person with his addiction. It's supposed to overwhelm him enough to get him into treatment, and they say it works. You don't hear about it all that much anymore. Be that as it may, one night during the election brouhaha in 2000, I got home from work, and here were all of these people from the church that I didn't give a rat's ass about, and they were going to love me into being converted. They thought I was missing out. It was a kind of conversion intervention, to save my immortal soul. I could tell that it was something Margaret and the priest—Father Donald, his name was—had cooked up, and my wife was more or less going along with, so I pretended to cooperate. It lasted about an hour, and at the end there were hugs and tears all around, and I think Father Donald realized that he hadn't really gotten me—he was no dummy—but my wife was very happy, and that lasted for a while. The proctologist, though, wasn't having any. He and Margaret got a divorce. That just meant that Margaret was around more often, and then she began talking about becoming a lay nun."

"What is that?"

"Well, basically, she's a priest helper, or, in Margaret's case, a priest enforcer, since that's the sort of person she was. Lots of times in the U.S., there aren't enough priests to man all the parishes, so these lay nuns would do lots of the work that the junior priests used to do back in the fifties and sixties, when the seminaries were full. Oh, she was a bossy one, that Margaret. Essentially, she came to have her own parish. I have no idea whether the church condoned this sort of thing officially or not, but, you know, organizations have to deal with their manpower issues somehow, and right around then, they were having the pedophile scandal anyway. But I didn't want to convert, and my wife was pushing me for a yes-or-no answer. Now, I'm telling you all this, but I never told Max any of this, so you can just keep it to yourself, okay?"

Monique nodded. Of course, Charlie thought, her track record as a truthful person was very suspect.

"We were marrying off the kids one by one, and looking like a fairly normal family. I can't say she was neglecting anything, but my impression was that she was offering it up to Jesus rather than being actually interested in our life, and after my job ended, I was working hard on my project, and one day last year I just said to myself, I don't want this to be the only life I am going to have, because, I tell you what, it doesn't seem like it is even my life. It seems like it is her life, and I am only a two-bit player in it. So I told her I was getting an apartment. Now we're working on the next step, though the Catholic church doesn't allow divorce, of course. That's slowing us down."

"How did your job end?"

Charlie cleared his throat. This question always made him a little uncomfortable, especially if it came up suddenly. He said, "Oh, in the usual way. Downsizing, more or less. Every company has to—"

But she interrupted him with some degree of indifference, and said, in a languorous but agreeable tone, "For me, marriage meant Russia and a Russian man. As soon as I went to France, I left marriage behind. In France, marriage is a very particular and, you might say, not-so-important thing. Many people are married, but not many act like they are married or think much about it. In America, I have noticed, being married is a full-time job."

"That's probably true."

"My opinion is that you don't want to have sex because you are not married any longer. You feel there is nothing to be gained by having sex."

"I didn't say that I don't want to have sex. Do you want to have sex?"

"Why else would I come here? I got you, Marya got the boy. We were looking for something to do."

Charlie wondered how he could have read the signs wrong. In the abstract, of course, it would be nice to have sex, but at the moment, it seemed like he was a long way from execution. He felt elderly and unsafe, his Viagra was still in its container, and that stuff took a while to work, anyway. He said, "So do you think they are having sex?"

"Sure."

"What do you think they're doing?"

"Let me find out." She pulled her cell phone out of her pocket and hit one of her speed-dial numbers. After a moment, she said, "How's it going?" Then, "Oh, really? . . . You're kidding." She laughed. She said, "Just a moment." She covered the mouthpiece of the cell phone with her thumb and said to Charlie, "Just when I called, he had been propping her up on pillows so that he could get a good approach from behind."

"So why did she answer the phone?"

"She always answers the phone when she is having sex. If it is someone like me, then she likes to describe it, and if it is someone else—say, a stranger or someone who wants to do business—then it is fun to pretend you are sitting attentively at your desk while you are getting it and being very quiet. Don't most people do that? I thought they did."

"I've never done that."

"See what you have missed? Here, I will put them on speakerphone."

Charlie said, "They're doing it already?" He looked at his watch. From the phone, a hollow-sounding female voice said, "This is our, unh, unh, third time."

"You've done it three times in an hour? Or an hour and fifteen minutes?" said Charlie.

But there was no direct answer to this question, only various noises and cries on the speakerphone, none of which struck Charlie as arousing. It sounded like they were performing in some large, cavernous space—what he envisioned was the waiting room at the Amtrak station in Washington, D.C.—and though he had a good mental image of Simon, his head shadowed with new growth, a gold link in one of his ears, and that perpetual grin on his face, he could not quite remember Marya, except that she had blond, rather short hair and wasn't very tall. Monique seemed to be enjoying it all, though. She was lounging on the bed, one leg bent and her foot on the covers, her head back, and her arm extended, resting on her knee. In her upraised palm sat the open silver phone, and she was staring at the ceiling again, meditative and smiling. Simon's voice said, "How's that? That better?" Marya's voice said, "Oh, that's good, right there," and Simon's voice said, "That's good, that's good, put that up there like that. Oh, yes," and Marya's voice said, "Just move your foot. Yeah." There was a way in which they sounded like they were having sex, it was true, but the image that came to him was that old game people used to play, Twister. Twister in a train station. Do this, do that. Not like in the movies, where the two people always seemed to flow together in tune to some music. Still, it sounded like it was good enough for them. Even though Marya muttered a soft "ouch," within moments there were two not quite synchronous crescendos of cries and respirations, culminating first in a yell from Simon, "Aahhhhh . . . Yes," then a long moan from Marya followed by a laugh. He saw Monique put her free hand into her crotch, first outside her jeans, then, snaking it down without unzipping, inside them, so it must have been good enough for her, too. He said, "Wish you were there rather than here?" but she didn't answer, which was surely just as well. And anyway, he couldn't even lie down comfortably in his bed, because she was sprawled across the foot. Even though it was a good-sized bed. Well, yes, something was aroused in him, and he would have to admit that it was resentment.

He had a good idea. He said "Off." The lights went out, first the room lights, then the one in the bathroom. He hoped she would take the hint. It was late and, really, he liked to maintain his daily regimen. Although he had crept toward California time in the course of the last six days, if he stayed up past midnight, which was three in the East, it could really throw him off. And in the morning, before going for his run, he absolutely had to sort through the pills. That could take as much as an hour right there. He felt her rise from the bed, and immediately slid farther under the covers, until he was a lot more comfortable. He arranged himself on his back, flat, balanced. The pain in his little finger had gone. That was interesting. Nor did he feel bloated any longer. No doubt the moving around had had a positive effect. And here she was, up by his ear. He felt her weight on the bed right beside him, and less than a moment later, she kissed him below the ear, twice. He said, "Are we still on speakerphone?"

"No. I disconnected. They decided to get into the spa in that room. It is big enough for two people."

"I have to say that that was interesting to me as a novelty, but it didn't turn me on."

"It turned me on." She said this in a low voice, clearly implying that the effect on her was his problem.

He said, "Actually, it's getting quite late, and I'm trying not to get completely onto California time. So I think we should call it a day—or a night, if you will—and maybe see what happens tomorrow."

She said, in that same low voice, "I guess I will have to accept that you don't like me," but it didn't sound precisely as though she cared whether he "liked" her or not. He said, "Do you mean 'like' or 'are attracted to'? I can't say yes or no to one or the other. I guess you're not my type. Yeah, I guess that. That seems the simplest answer." And it did. Should he ever have to talk about this incident, he would say, Yeah, this beautiful blonde maybe thirty years younger than me just presented herself to me, in what was probably the most elegant bedroom I've ever seen, and we talked for a while, and she was ready, but, you know, she just wasn't my type. And then he would say, It was as simple as that. "So I guess you should leave now, because I'm ready to go to sleep."

Right next to him, she sighed. Under the covers, he arranged himself again, flat on his back, neck straight, head comfortably supported by the two plump wings of the pillow, knees slightly bent. Hands at his sides. Then he adjusted his genitals, not forgetting the pimple behind his balls, but not

touching it, either, just freeing everything up for a good night's sleep. He set
his hand back down in the sheet, beside his hip, and closed his eyes. She
was still there, of course, but in more ways than one it reminded him of having a kid in the bed. The kid would be squirming around and poking you
and on the alert for the moment when you carried her back to her own bed,
but if you just breathed evenly and relaxed, before you knew it the kid
would be sleeping, and then you would be sleeping, too. He yawned, thinking that if she was still there in the morning, he would report her to Joe
Blow; then he yawned again.

But he didn't go to sleep. The problem was his trapezius. When he kept
his head and neck straight, he could feel a painful little pull going down his
upper back and then throbbing behind his shoulder blade. He had to admit
that that hotel bed had killed him. And of course he had spent the whole
night marshaling his arguments, too, so that tension had made his neck
problem worse. When he turned his head to the right, he almost cried out.
When he turned his head to the left, the pain eased a little, but it also made
him want to roll over on his left side to go to sleep, since that was his habitual way of drifting off. He tried turning his head each way twice, but it
didn't work, and he must have grunted, or cursed, or something, who knew
what, but she said, "Are you all right?"

"No, I have a pain in my back, neck, and shoulder. Are you still here?"

"I was thinking what a comfortable bed this is."

"Oh, Jesus Christ," said Charlie.

"Perhaps you would like me to leave?"

"What gives you that idea?"

"Something about the way you—"

"Of course I would like you to leave. I asked you to leave a couple of
minutes ago."

"Do you mind if I stay just a minute or two longer? I would like to find
something. Of course, I will have to ask the lights to come on."

"Just do it and get it over with."

She said, "On, honey." The bathroom light came up, and then the rest of
the lights turned on. She knelt up, leaned, or, rather, crawled across him,
opened the drawer beside his shoulder, and took out a purple tube readily
recognizable as a dildo, though not terrifically large. She closed the drawer
rather awkwardly and fell back onto her side of the bed, the dildo in her
hand. He said, "That would be your vibrator."

"One of them. I took the other one with me, but I forgot this one. I
wouldn't want you to find it and think ill of me."

He glanced at her, but she wasn't smiling. He suspected she was joking
even so. He said, still resentful, "Let's see you put it to use, then." It was a

dare, he thought, and payback for the spanking, which still annoyed him.
He saw her glance at him out of the corner of her eye and then roll the
vibrator back and forth between her thumb and her palm. Finally, she
turned the black plastic circle at the bottom, and a low buzzing hum
sounded. "What I like to do with this one," she said, "is to touch the tip to
my anus while I masturbate in the normal way with my fingers in front,"
and Charlie felt the first real frisson of arousal that he had felt all night. He
said, "Say that again."

She said, "What I do is, I turn it on about medium, and I pull down my
jeans and lie on my right side. Then I masturbate my clitoris with my fingers while I touch the tip of it to the outside edge of my anus. Right when I
come, I push the tip in a little way, but not far."

"Why?"

"Oh, because it makes the orgasm go really deep, and be a little strange.
More spread around my whole lower area, not so localized."

Charlie coughed. Then he said, "Okay. Let's see it."

She stood up and squirmed out of her jeans, letting them drop right
beside the bed, and then unbuttoned her shirt. She had on a nice bra,
something shiny. The two cups were green, and they grew over her breasts
in satin leaves, or not leaves, but more like the green sepals that flowers
came out of. She said, "If you don't mind, just put your fingers in here, on
my nipple, and squeeze a little, rhythmically, at about, say, a one-two beat.
One-two, one-two. That's good." He sat up to do this, and she jutted her ass
out, then she did what she had said she was going to do: she introduced the
fingers of her lower hand between her legs, which she spread a little bit, and
put the tip of her purple vibrator between the cheeks of her ass. She closed
her eyes. He said, "Tell me what you're thinking about."

"Oh. Let's see. Marya, I guess. When you squeeze my nipple, it reminds
me how much I love to massage her breasts and suck her tits. She has beautiful tits." She said this in a normal, conversational tone of voice. But it was
exciting. "She likes mine, too, but not as much as I like hers. Sometimes we
just stop whatever we are doing in the office, and I suck her tits and think
how if I had a cock I would fuck her."

"You're lesbians, then?"

"Oh, God, no. I can't say we are. I just love her tits. Ahhh. Thinking
about them is turning me on, I must say."

It was turning Charlie on, too. Under the covers, his own cock was
beginning to swell and stir. With his left hand, he was squeezing her nipple,
one-two, one-two. When he put his right hand under the covers to palpate
his stirring and swelling cock (thank goodness he had freed it all up before),
his posture was a little awkward, but, still, it was nice to watch her, and lis-

ten to her, too. No one had ever talked like that in his actual presence, he thought. He said, "What about cocks? Are you thinking about that, too?"

"A little, but not really. I don't have a special cock lately that I can really focus on. And these days I've spent more masturbation time sucking Marya's tits. Just today, while you in the dining room were eating your main course, we went into the pantry while Raphael wasn't looking, and I opened her shirt, which has snaps, you see, and then her bra, which has a front hook, and I sucked her tits like mad and also squatted down and brought myself. That's why we were a little late picking up the plates. I didn't even have time to wash my hands, but I did wash my hands before we brought in the coffee and dessert."

Charlie was so excited by now that he could hardly get out his next observation—"It sounds like you love her."

"Oh, maybe. We're good friends. But sex is more just something we do up here. There isn't much else to do, and we all like lots of sex."

"Does this fellow Mike know that?"

But she didn't answer this question. Instead, she pressed her fingers against her cunt, closed her legs, and also pushed the vibrator, now making a somewhat deeper hum, farther between the cheeks of her ass, then she cried out—Ah, ah—then she went limp. Charlie was hard as a rock now, and threw off the covers. She was so limp that it was easy to turn her on her back, push her legs apart, and go inside her. And it was wonderful in there—from her own orgasm, she was hot and wet. Her knees spread a little farther, then her legs went around him, and he came in a sudden rush, as if his prostate were twenty years old again. As he was coming, it seemed to him that maybe she was coming again—she pushed against him and cried out. Then they both subsided in a heap, and he didn't know what to say. The ideas that came to him—"That was pretty exciting after all," or "Thanks"—seemed lame. So he said "Off." The lights went off, and the bathroom light dimmed exactly in time with his slowing heartbeat.

She said, "Well, I didn't realize you were going to fuck me."

Charlie said, "What does that mean?"

"I think penetration is going a little far."

"You're angry?"

"I don't know. I just don't know. I wasn't foreseeing penetration, and I haven't made up my mind."

Irritated, Charlie said, "There's nothing you can do about it now."

"Your attitude seems quite strange to me. Perhaps it is a result of your advanced age. American men of your generation are often confused about sex, as I understand."

Charlie got up and made his way to the bathroom. When he got there, he turned the light on by means of the switch. The bathroom was unusual in that it had no tile or stone. Like the bedroom, it was brass and wood, with a vaguely oceangoing air. The floor, which he rubbed his toes over, was smooth, though it looked as if it would be rough. It was made of bamboo parquet, like the floor of the room, and was in fact continuous with the floor of his room. The towels were two or three shades of muted green in a jungly leaf print. He took one and sat down on the bidet, facing the wall. His trip to California, which he had thought would somehow ratify his separation and launch him into a more official single life, was turning out to be very strange. He remembered thinking, waiting for two hours in Security at Newark so early last Monday, that he shouldn't bother to go, and maybe he had been right.

On a shelf next to the bidet, six or eight small containers of beauty products were arrayed. He picked them up and peered at them one by one—artemisia, lavender, anise, grapefruit, sandalwood, orange blossom, ylang-ylang. He turned on the water, which was instantly warm, and squeezed a bead of the grapefruit body wash into his palm and began washing and massaging his genitals. The body wash was nice, smooth and slippery. His cock was still plump. In the warm water, his balls hung low and fat. He could still feel the pimple there, but really it didn't feel like much. He washed himself everywhere, front and back, then turned off the water, stood up with his feet still planted to either side of the bidet, and dried himself off with a medium-sized towel. The towel was soft and absorbent. He hung the towel neatly over what looked like a heated drying rack and went out of the bathroom, turning out the light by means of the switch. When he got back to the bed, groping because he refused to call out to the lights, he found that she was no longer in it. Where she was, he had no idea. For all he knew, she was in the anteroom, or stretched out on the floor, but unless he tripped over her, he didn't consider that to be his business. When he came to the bed, he crawled across it to his side and got under the covers. His job was to focus on the main task, which was to go to sleep, get up and sort through his pills, and keep as best he could to his schedule. He stretched himself out flat, then bent his knees, thrusting a pillow underneath him. Fortunately, the exercise had loosened up his trapezius. He turned his head to the right and then to the left. He was pretty comfortable, after all. He closed his eyes.

"I decided," said Cassie, "that they must have put me in the Comedy Room. When I opened the closet to look for the bathrobe, all I found was an overcoat. And then, right in the middle of the room, on a tall pedestal, there is a large plaster nose. And behind my bed is a big painting by a Russian painter I never heard of, depicting four drunk peasants sleeping up against a haystack, and pigs flying through the sky above them. On either side of the door are two Magrittes I've never seen, one of the back of a man's head—he's wearing a bowler hat shaped like a woman's buttocks—and the other one is of the back of a man in a black suit that shades into a horse's tail." She laughed. "But that's nothing compared to the bathroom."

Elena was sitting with Cassie and Delphine under the pergola in the garden next to the aviary. They were on the west side of the house, so they didn't have sun, but the upper reaches of the aviary did, and the birds were awake and singing, calling, whistling, trilling. "That's a whipbird," said Delphine. "I was reading about it in the book in my room. Its call is supposed to sound like the cracking of a whip. Tell her about the bathroom. Elena, I saw this bathroom." Elena looked at Cassie, directing her thoughts away from the fact that she missed the newspaper and had been awake for at least two hours, worrying about the war in a personal way that surprised even her.

"It's upside down," said Cassie. "The ceiling is brilliant green, and detailed to look like grass with the shadows of clouds passing over it, and the floor is blue, like the sky, with the clouds. The sun is off to the side, right where you walk in the door, and the angles are perfect—just where that sun would cast a shadow on the grass from that angle, there's a shadow on the ceiling. But that's not the funny part. It's a pretty big bathroom, and of course it has a sink and a tub and a bidet and a toilet and a cabinet, but right across the room from each fixture is a painting on the wall of that fixture, an exact replica, with a line above it in script, '*Ceci n'est pas un bidet,*' for example, or '*Ceci n'est pas une baignoire.*' Above the painted bath, there are two painted towels and just the word *non.* I was just laughing. Every time I open a drawer or a cabinet, there's something funny in it. I opened one of the drawers in the chest, and there was a sweater glued to the bottom of the drawer, and on the nightstand there's a book glued facedown. It's a copy of a novel called *The Master and Margarita.*"

"I read that in college," said Elena.

"Appearances are deceiving," said Delphine.

"Well, they are in my room," said Cassie.

"I knocked on Simon's door on the way down, because he said his room was quite unusual," said Elena, "but he isn't up yet."

"And there's a gym," said Delphine. "We worked out this morning already. But you know, there's no clock in it. And I forgot my watch. What time do you think it is?"

"I have no idea," said Cassie. "Our friend the colonel would be right in his element here. I wish we'd brought him along."

Elena knew what time it was, as always, but didn't say anything. It was possible that if she didn't acknowledge the exact ticktock of history as it evolved, or devolved, she would succeed in ignoring it. She said, "Max and I thought we'd go for a swim later in the morning, and I think Paul's been in already."

"No doubt," said Delphine. She looked up and then around. "Eight, do you think? Not that late?"

"Delphine doesn't like Paul," said Cassie.

"I didn't say that," said Delphine. "I said I don't see what Zoe sees in him. That's not saying that I don't like him personally."

"He's not very sparkly," said Cassie. "She's more sparkly than he is."

"Don't you think she's more sparkly than just about everyone?" said Elena, picking up a scone and splitting it. Its bottom was hot, savory, perfect. Obviously, Raphael had thoroughly greased the baking sheet with a heavy coat of butter, which had melted in the oven and infused upward. The interior of the scone was scented with lemon peel and dotted with dried cranberries. She broke off a piece and put it in her mouth.

"Well," said Delphine, "it is her profession and vocation to sparkle, when, that is, she is not being asked to smolder—"

"She's really good at that," said Cassie. "Did you see *Wanda Rossini?* People didn't realize it, but it was a very distant remake of *La Bohème,* and she had to sing and smolder for about two hours. I thought she was great in that, but they put Tom Cruise in the lead, and he could not sing, and there was about as much chemistry between them as there is in a green salad."

"I didn't see that," said Elena.

"No one did," said Delphine.

"Fortunately, they blamed him and the director and said that if anything could have saved it, it would have been her. When was that?" said Cassie.

"In '95," said Delphine. "It came out in '95. I think they made it in '93. The Democrats still controlled Congress when they were making it. She sparkles for a living, but at least it's her own sparkle. I wish she would sing more. Did you ever hear her sing 'Just One of Those Things'? Or, for that matter, 'Banks of the Ohio'? That one makes your hair stand on end."

"I never did," said Elena. "Except for the movies, I've only heard her sing one time when I was passing the big bathroom in Max's house. She came out and said what great acoustics it had."

"When we first moved in there, she'd be in that bathroom all morning, doing scales and trying things out. She even made her singing coach go in there with her. He would sit on the stool, and she would prop herself against the sink. I stood outside the door myself a time or two."

"You must be proud of her," said Elena.

Delphine regarded her, and Elena wondered if she had said the wrong thing. Finally, Delphine nodded. "Of course I am. But I don't know that I ever expected anything different. She was the cutest child ever. Once I read an article about it, about the big eyes and the round cheeks and some sort of mathematical relationship between the chin and the width of the forehead. She was made to look at, and when she opened her mouth she was made to listen to. And she wasn't spoiled. I can say that for her, she's never acted spoiled. She has a temper, but that's inborn, as far as I can see. She always had a temper, no matter what I did. Anyway, to make a long story short, I never, ever thought I was going to be her only audience."

"It's just a hair-trigger," said Cassie. "She can't hold a grudge. But the fur flies if the bomb goes off, I'll say that. She's not at all like you, Delphine." Cassie turned to Elena. "If it weren't for the smile, and hands, and skin tone, you would have to wonder whether Delphine had any genetic input at all into the legendary Zoe Cunningham."

Elena felt this was a mildly shocking thing to say, but clearly Delphine had heard it before, because she continued to eat her pineapple with an equable air. "Are you saying that I myself was not destined for stardom?" said Delphine, with a smile.

"Of course you were not," said Cassie. "Fact is, she's a miracle of hybridization." She grinned. A degree disconcerted by this teasing, Elena helped herself to half a grapefruit.

"Ahem," said Cassie. Elena looked up. Zoe was nearly upon them. Delphine didn't flicker. She said, "Morning, Zoe."

"Morning, Mom. Cassie, Elena." She pulled out a chair and sat down. Indeed, she was made to look at. The morning was cool, and she was comfortably dressed. Her long, curly hair was pinned on top of her head. She had on neatly fitting jeans and a yellow shirt nipped at the waist, with an orange collar and turned-up orange cuffs. She wore no jewelry other than a narrow bracelet of lapis-lazuli beads. Both the yellow and the blue were subtly repeated in her brocade flats. She smiled at Elena, then made a wry face at Cassie and Delphine across the table and leaned forward. She said, "I slept for nine straight hours, flat-out, without changing position. I did not get up and go outside and assume the Surya Namaskar Pose to greet the sun, nor did I begin my day by snorting water up my nose and spitting it out through my mouth."

"How did you—" began Cassie.

"I took a long shower with the multi-citrus bath gel and sang a selection of hits by Gary Moore, and I wasn't too bad on those low notes, even if I do say so myself." She cocked her head backward and opened her mouth. "So-o-o long, it was so long ago! But I still got the blues for you!" Above them, the aviary fell silent for a moment, and then roared forth in ever more abundant song. Delphine smiled, and Cassie continued to eat her omelet, but Elena felt herself shoot upward and outward into a state of unexpected visceral pleasure, and even delirium. Just above them, wisteria blooms dangled through the beams of the pergola; before them, the grass was green as it could only be in March in California. "Though the days come and go." In the doorway, the girl Monique was standing with her mouth open at the sound. A peacock on the lawn paused in its foraging, lifted its head, and opened his tail, and Elena thought, I am here. Zoe stopped singing and said, "Paul doesn't actually like me to sing very much. He values silence." She said this idly, while spreading lemon-lime marmalade on her toast, but Elena saw Delphine and Cassie exchange a glance, in which, after a moment, they included her. And she felt her eyebrow lifting without actually wishing to express any opinion at all. "But I'm ready to go on the road again. Do some club dates, at least in New York and London. Just me and Sonny on the piano, and see who shows up to sing along." She bit two chunks out of the toast and swallowed meditatively.

Delphine said, "Last time didn't Sir Paul show up to sing along?"

"Yes. That was fun. We sang 'Brown Sugar' and 'Honky Tonk Woman,' which everyone thought was a daring thing for Sir Paul to do. Once, Dolly Parton showed up to sing along when she and I were both in Atlanta. We sang a duet on 'The Sweet Bye and Bye' and 'Cry Me a River.' She was good. You know who my voice blends with, is that Canadian girl Sarah McLachlan. We've sung together twice—impromptu, of course. We did that old Joni Mitchell song 'Urge for Going,' and 'Highway 61' — 'God said to Abraham, "Kill me a son," Abe says, "Man, you must be puttin' me on"' — great song." She took a sip of her coffee. "There are so many great songs. Lots more great songs than great scripts."

"What's your room like?" said Cassie.

"It's gold," said Zoe.

Elena laughed

"No. I mean, I sat on the bed for maybe fifteen minutes yesterday, trying to talk myself into touching things. Finally, I went over to the wall near one of the windows and actually put my nose right up next to it and peered at the paint, and there were gold flecks in it that Joe Blow says are real. I asked him. And I thought I had seen wretched excess. I gather it's intended to be Mike's own room eventually, but I guess Mike and his family haven't lived here yet."

"You don't like it?" said Cassie.

"I feel I've been misjudged. They thought I was that real-gold-flecks sort of person. I liked your room, Elena."

"Yes, it's overwhelmingly floral. I like it, too."

"Well, I guess I'm the designated Marie-Antoinette. But it's only for a few days. The bed is comfortable."

"What about Paul?"

"Japanese," said Zoe. "Perfect for him, except that there's a pool in the middle of the floor that he could fall into in the dark. I told him he was going to have to come to me rather than me going to him."

"Simon's room has different levels, too," said Elena. "I never think bedrooms or bathrooms should have different levels, especially when there might be guests."

"You know," said Cassie, "years ago, when I was in my forties, I would guess, I went to visit an old friend who had moved into a brownstone in Brooklyn, and she put me in her guest room, which was also the study. The bathroom was just outside the pocket doors, between the bedroom and the kitchen. Anyway, I got up in the middle of the night and opened a door in the dark, and took a step and realized that there was nothing there, so I just grabbed the door frame and arched myself backward. It turned out that what I had thought was a closet was the basement. When I opened that door and looked down in the morning, I saw that falling down those stairs would have killed me, because it was about six steep steps down to a small landing, and then a long flight to the cement."

It gave Elena a chill just to imagine this. She said, "That reminds me of when I was in college in Wisconsin. I lived for a year or so in a farmhouse that was going to be torn down, and toward the end of my lease, the water pump in the basement broke, so there was no water in the house. I didn't have the money to fix it, and the landlord wasn't going to, so I got into the habit of taking containers outside to the well and filling them. I guess I'd been doing that for a couple of weeks. The weather was okay but not warm by any means. One night, toward dusk, I was standing in front of the spigot, and the well cover I was standing on, maybe two and a half feet across and three feet from front to back, just broke away under me. What I had thought was lawn was really just vines that had grown over an old wooden cover. Without even thinking about it, I threw my arms out to the sides and caught myself before I fell in. I remember how I looked down in the kind of dim late-afternoon light and I could see the dark surface of the water about eighteen feet below and the smooth concrete sides. I would have just treaded water until I drowned, I guess, since I was living alone and it was almost night." Thinking about it now made her more nervous than it had then.

The other women were looking at her. "My goodness," said Cassie, sympathetically.

"Oh," said Zoe, "I never know what to think about close calls. One time, I tried to write a screenplay called *Close Calls*, but I couldn't decide whether it was going to be a thriller or a comedy. It was when Isabel was about two and a half, and she was a big, heavy baby, you know, and when I would carry her around, I kept thinking there should be a movie about a woman with two children, a two-and-a-half-year-old and a one-year-old, not mobile children at all, and this woman has to perform all sorts of feats in order to both escape and to foil the villains, but at the same time she has to keep her kids quiet and calm. As she was making her escape, I thought, she would get a lot of dirty looks from people who didn't want her kids to make a noise or a mess. All I had was the title and the first scene. When I pitched it to a studio, they said it was a nice idea but that women with small children don't go to the movies. I was going to star someone much more petite than I am as the woman, I think Sissy Spacek, and put Isabel in as a really big baby."

"She would have been good in that," said Delphine. "She would have kept a straight face the whole picture. I had a close call in a plane once—"

"Someone else's fault," said Zoe.

"—that time I went back to Miami to visit old Mrs. Disantis before she died. We were coming in for a landing, and we were just about to touch down, and suddenly the plane sped up and took off again at a steep angle. I had a window seat up front, so I saw there was a bus on the runway. We missed it, but not by much. That was right after Ronald Reagan busted the Air Traffic Controllers Union."

Elena said to Zoe, "You must have had close calls on movie sets," even though she would have preferred not talking about any more close calls. There was always the chance she could end up telling about her closest call—running off with Simon's father, William McCracken, her adjunct assistant professor of Marxist literary theory and a former Weathermen hanger-on. Simon looked a lot like Bill, only with blue eyes and no hair for the time being. The close-call part was that he had left her while she was pregnant for Miranda Moser, who was taller and better-looking than she was, and he had never contacted her again. No one, least of all Elena, knew what had happened to Bill, but, given his tyrannical predilections, she suspected that he had changed his name and his academic specialty and become a neocon. He had the perfect psychological profile for that sort of thing, but even though she sometimes scrutinized the faces of neocons she saw in the newspapers, she had never seen anyone who looked like Bill McCracken twenty-two years on. Surely he was in a right-wing think tank somewhere. What a relief to know, she had thought lately, that through no fault of her own she had avoided a life with William McCracken.

"On a movie set, the higher your negotiated salary, the fewer close calls you have," said Zoe. "Anyway, Paul would say that close calls are actually moments when the different dimensions of the universe happen to brush against one another. The thing you thought you avoided actually happened in one of those other universes—at least, it happened if you imagined that it might have. If you're truly enlightened, thoughts of bad things don't even occur to you, and you don't even think you had a close call. What time is it?"

"We never figured that out," said Delphine. Now all four of the women looked up toward the top of the aviary, which was shining in the sun. "After eight for sure," said Cassie, "maybe nine."

"It's eight-fifteen," said Elena.

Cassie went on: "I thought I would spend the day looking at the pieces in all the rooms. Joe Blow said we could enter any room that has an unlocked door. I think we should go ahead and be bold about it. I definitely want another look at the so-called Vermeer. And there are lots of Russian artists I never heard of that are quite impressive. Delphine has some pictures of birds in her room that are by a guy named Kamil Bekshev. Beautifully detailed pairs of tropical birds like parrots perched in front of snapshots of objects that are also nicely rendered. One was a '68 red Mustang."

"The bird manager said he would identify all the birds for me," said Delphine. "He said a fellow came here with his clarinet a few weeks ago and got one of the lyrebirds to sing a duet."

"I wonder if the bird knows 'Simple Gifts,'" said Zoe. "I always thought that sounded like a bird's song." She whistled a series of notes that Elena recognized, but no birds answered or joined in. After a moment, she said, "I read that Russian book since we talked about it. *Taras Bulba*," said Zoe. "It's very dramatic."

"Max told me he was going to keep an open mind," said Elena. The others gazed at her. "Or, rather, Stoney asked him to keep an open mind, and he said he would, if that's the same thing." She turned her plate around and rearranged her fork. "I guess he's not too happy with Stoney right now. But he said he's committed himself to talking to the Russians, so he's going to talk to them." It was not clear from their demeanor what Zoe or Delphine thought about the new sleeping arrangement, Isabel-wise, and Elena didn't have the courage to say anything more. Max had been restless all night long. It didn't help that the Amber Room was three doors down from the Flower Room, too close for comfort but too far to stumble toward, feigning sleepwalking, or whatever Max was thinking of doing, which he did not confide in her. And then, after he seemed to forget about it, or else to resign himself to it, he stayed awake, patting her and, it was clear, worrying about this erection thing that had been going on since the first day of the war. Of course, he had pretended not to worry, just to be patting her and from time to time adjusting himself, and, of course, she had presented him with her breasts, her ass, not obviously offering anything, but offering it anyway. She had kissed him and returned the tickling and pretended that she wasn't worrying, either. But of course she had been wondering whether it was time to make that behavioral connection—war–angry woman–impotence—that would show that the failure was her fault, traceable not to geopolitics but to the archetype of the emasculating harridan mother as represented by her, etc., etc. Somehow, this house and the Flower Room intensified what had seemed minor and fleeting in the other house. Although it was also true that she was personally relieved that Simon was safe under the same roof she was under, without his car. She had four things to worry about—the war, the meaning of Max's impotency, Simon, and her feminine failures—and in the course of the night, she had canvassed all of them.

"He's got to do something," said Cassie. "Next thing, he's going to want to make a movie in his own bedroom."

"He already does," said Elena. They laughed. They thought she was joking.

The conversation was very pleasant, and yet was unbelievable to Elena, as if it had been manufactured just for the scene they found themselves in. Its very pleasure seemed to hint at the fact that elsewhere, or everywhere else, the vast and the horrible loomed. These three women seemed happy enough without the papers, but Elena was not. For them, the bad news was intrusive, unwelcome, maybe sometimes even surprising or shocking. For her, the specific items of bad news measured, in their particularity, the even worse things that had not, or not yet, happened. Once, as a child, she had seen a headline in her local paper, "Tornadoes Bypass Town." Right now, on the table in front of her, she would like to see a headline in today's L.A. *Times*: "World Unchanged."

Cassie said, "So the name of your book is *The Idiot's Guide to Doing Everything Correctly?*"

"No," said Elena, "that's a different series. Our series is called *Here's How!* My book is called *Here's How: To Do EVERYTHING Correctly!* We use a lot of caps and exclamation points, but I don't mind that, actually."

"What sorts of things are we talking about?" said Zoe.

"Well, it can be almost anything. The editor wants more rather than less. Obviously, there's what you would consider the usual stuff about how to vacuum and launder your lingerie and clean the fixtures in your bathroom so that they don't have water spots, but there's also a chapter on how to be a congressman. That was actually easier to write than the cleaning chapter, because the issues are more cut and dried. We know instinctively how to get to the end of the day with a good conscience, but we don't know instinctively what good cleaning products are or what their larger ramifications are in the environment. If we discover that infants under a year old have detergents in their bloodstream, then what does that mean about correct cleaning? But if my basic principle for a congressman is 'First, do no harm,' then that cuts out a whole category of potential votes, contacts, conflicts of interest, and all."

Delphine said, "But you've cleaned lots of rooms, so you know the ins and outs of cleaning. You haven't ever been a congressman, so how would you understand their day-to-day dilemmas?"

"That's true, but the chapters about Congress, the presidency, running a multinational corporation, being Pope, and organizing the Pentagon are mostly for comic relief. They're even going to be printed differently, on gray shaded paper. And I doubt that I'll have much of that sort of readership, when all is said and done. I just want the average person who is cleaning her bathroom to have the feeling that her actions have larger consequences and are significant."

"Who do you think is your audience?" said Cassie.

"Oh, definitely people, probably women, who are anxiety-prone. But whose anxiety can be relieved by knowledge, at least temporarily. People like I was twenty years ago, when Simon was a baby, who just don't have a clue, really."

"So what's another chapter?" asked Zoe.

"Transportation is a big chapter. How to buy a bike, how to change the oil in your car. What to do with the oil after you've changed it. Transportation proved to be rather a knotty problem, and I had to wrestle with lots of issues. But I have to say, that's been true of nearly every chapter. When I signed up for the project, I thought that I instinctively knew what to do in almost all situations, because my goal has always been staying out of trouble, and my parents were naturally very systematic and trained me the same way. But it's really been a can of worms. At first the title of the project was *Here's How: To Do EVERYTHING Properly*, but that was a true nightmare, because doing things properly implies either conforming to social codes or achieving excellence. Doing things correctly is more about following instructions. If you're doing things properly, you're wanting to impress someone. If you're doing things correctly, you're just wanting to get them done. It's more inward-looking and task-oriented. I thought that was a more manageable subject."

"But why are you including recipes?"

"Because people have to eat. If they are supposed to learn which knife and fork to use, they should have something good to use them on. It's like the voting chapter. You can't just vote off the cuff anymore, if you ever could. You have to educate and prepare yourself to vote, because lots of Republicans are in the business of making it hard for you to vote and then afterward trying to steal your vote. So, if you are going to have a good conscience at the end of election day, you have to have learned how to correctly request an absentee ballot, or pull the lever on a lever machine, or punch out a chad on a punch card, or whatever. But you also have to have understood your candidates and issues. Correct procedure is one thing, but it makes no difference if there's nothing worth using it on."

"How far along are you at this point?" said Cassie.

"Maybe halfway. But I was just thinking last night that I have to add a chapter at the end called 'How to Correctly Go Down with the Ship.' That would be about if all attempts failed and there you were, stuck in an inescapable disaster not of your own making. I think a lot of that chapter is going to be about how to leave a record so that survivors will know that the whole mess was more complicated than it looked." She knew she sounded as if she were making light of this idea, when in fact it was an idea that she thought about most of the time. "And then, of course, the previous chapter is about how not to go down with the ship. Being prepared for disaster, and all. I mean, did you know that Max had only one working flashlight at that house, and had brush growing right up against the stairs? He had given some thought to using the swimming-pool water to save the house in case of a fire, but I didn't consider him at all prepared for an earthquake."

The other women looked at each other. Zoe said, "Who is? No one I know."

"Well, I'll give you that chapter from my book. It isn't that hard to do, but you have to actually do it."

Simultaneously, they all looked up at the pergola, then at the golden house, then at the aviary, perhaps to see whether anything was shaking, if only slightly. Cassie said, "I slept through the Northridge earthquake, in 1994. I had just flown in from Hawaii, and I was so tired I didn't feel a thing."

"Woke me up," said Delphine.

"I was in New York," said Zoe.

"I felt it," said Elena. "I woke Simon up, and we went out and pitched a tent in our backyard. He thought it was fun."

"That is what you're supposed to do," said Cassie. But then the energy that had been so bright died away, and Elena suspected that, once again, it was she who cast a pall over the conversation with her obsessions, or (she knew it was better to call them) her preoccupations. If someone had the SPF-45 sunblock for sensitive skin ready at hand, it would be her. If someone knew where to get a good bone-scan for incipient osteoporosis, it would be her. If someone's eyes could pick out, in any mass of shrubbery, the varieties of plants most likely to go up like a torch, or to cause contact dermatitis, those eyes were hers. When Simon was a toddler, she could walk into any room and note without thinking the sharp corners, the unshielded electrical outlets, and the proximity of any pointed metal object that a child could pick up and apply to those electrical outlets. Her parents and her family on both sides were the same way. Over the years, they had taken very seriously strontium 90, DDT, PCBs, PBBs, fluoride, the military-industrial complex, racketeering, civic corruption in Chicago, algae levels in Lake Michigan, exactly what lakeside resorts to stay in when they vacationed in Wisconsin. They left nothing to chance. But such care did not make her a desirable companion.

She looked at Zoe, Cassie, and Delphine in their silence for a moment, thinking that, actually, her problem now, here in the Russian house with everything perfectly managed, was that there was nothing at all she could do to offset the momentum of history as it gained downward speed.

Then Cassie said, apropos of nothing except the very thoughts Elena had been keeping to herself, "I wonder if Mike knows anyone on the Council on Foreign Relations."

Delphine rolled her eyes.

Zoe said, "That think tank?"

Cassie cleared her throat and then lowered her voice. "The think tank is just a front organization. They run things. They are the shadow world-government."

Delphine said, "Why would the shadow world-government need a front organization?"

Cassie turned pointedly to Elena. "It was them who had the Kennedy brothers killed."

Zoe said, "I thought that was a combination of the Mafia and some Cubans."

"Maybe at the lower levels. I mean, Jack Ruby had Mafia ties, but, really, there isn't anything that goes on that the Council on Foreign Relations doesn't know about. They are tremendously powerful and in some ways control everything."

"Well," said Delphine, "I can't say they're doing a very good job, all things considered."

Zoe smiled.

Cassie said to Elena, "She and I have had this argument before. I said they are powerful, I didn't say they are omnipotent. And they have their internal battles and struggles about what to do and how to do it, just like everyone else. My view is—"

"Do tell," exclaimed Delphine.

"Okay, I will." Cassie tossed her head. "The Council on Foreign Relations was started by the Rockefellers and the Carnegies and some of their counterparts in Germany and Japan. The Rothschilds. I think it was started in 1900. Anyway, they control so much money, and so many governments, and so much media, that basically the world we all think we live in is really the world they have given us. The money and investments go here, there, and everywhere, and countries rise and fall more or less in line with how these people invest, and politics conforms to their requirements, too. Or most of the time it does. Not lately, I don't think. I think they thought Bush and Cheney were going to go along and do what they were supposed to do, but then the administration slipped the leash, as it were, and now it's a mess. Because, I'll tell you, one thing capitalists at the top don't like is a real mess. Little messes here and there, so there can be some buying low in order to do some selling high, and some war profiteering, but the money has to keep flowing, and the investments have to pan out. When things are a real mess, investments are at risk."

"Why did they kill the Kennedys?"

"Well, according to my source, they killed Robert because he was about to find out that they had killed John. They killed John— Well, I can't quite remember why they killed John. The reason made sense to me at the time, though. The real thing you have to know about the Council on Foreign Relations is that they like there to be a middle class. The Council on Foreign Relations is not in favor of every single place turning into the third world. They know that the middle class always pays for itself. When you don't have a middle class, all sorts of costs are shifted to the state, like right up north, in the Central Valley. In the end, one of the cheapest things you can have is a middle class. A middle class likes schools and roads and hospitals and libraries and parks, and they are willing to pay for them. Rich people hoard their money; the middle class spreads it around. It's that simple. If you don't have a middle class, then you don't have those things, or, rather, you have them, but they are not of good quality and no one takes care of them, and even if they are worthless junk, they cost almost as much as they do when they're good, and the state has to pay for them because there is no middle class to do so."

"So," said Elena, willing to go along, "why has the Council on Foreign Relations allowed what looks to me like the destruction of the middle class over the last twenty years or so?"

"Well, that's a good question. My guess is that the Council on Foreign Relations has its ups and downs and its ideological infights, just like every other organization. You get more nouveau types in there, who maybe only have five hundred million or so, and they feel cramped and oppressed by the demands of labor. They think the pie is finite—"

"The pie is finite," said Elena. "The pie is limited by the capacity of the Earth to supply food, energy, and natural resources for an ever-expanding population of people who want ever more goods."

"Well, the Council on Foreign Relations may be of two minds about innovation and consumption. As I said, they are not omniscient—"

"You said they were not omnipotent," said Delphine.

"But they are omnipresent," said Cassie. "Or at least way more omnipresent than people realize. I see them as a force for good, more or less. And, furthermore, I am sure that the overtures that the Pope has been making toward the Evangelicals is exactly the thing they fear most. We see this all around us—a few branches falling out of the upper canopy that are evidence of the storm that is really going on. I mean, we see how, in the Republican Party, the secular multinational corporations have made an uneasy alliance with the religious multinational corporations run by people like Pat Robertson, because, on the surface, money is money and investment is investment. But, in fact, the religious multinational corporations are infected with a sense of grandiosity that comes from their constant preaching and invocation of God. They begin to believe their own PR, and to treat people like the Rockefellers with a bit of condescension and even disdain. And then you bring in the Pope and and cardinals, with their history of making pronouncements that are supposed to be infallible, and if you are a Rockefeller type, you realize that you really have a problem. When the Pope and the Evangelicals begin pooling their wealth . . ." She shook her head.

"What do they really want?" said Zoe.

"A feeling, an intoxicating feeling. A feeling like you only get when you are in the simultaneous grips of great fear and intense aggression, because that's what extreme religion is all about, fear and aggression. That's why those religions are always talking about the Apocalypse or the Rapture or whatever. The Council on Foreign Relations is not a *moral* organization, it is a *reasonable* organization that would like to avoid the same things that the average person would like to avoid—namely, nuclear war, the destruction of New York, Los Angeles, London, Tokyo, Abu Dhabi, wherever, and the sight of millions or billions of their fellow humans suffering and dying. The extreme religions have that—"

"Fetishistic," said Elena.

"Exactly," said Cassie, giving her a smile, "a *fetishistic* longing for that very thing, the sight of those they fear and those who arouse their aggression suffering and dying on screens that are as big as possible, and they imagine themselves in those scenes like in a movie, of course, just walking along, glorying in being saved, in at last truly having that sensation of *election* that is so elusive in real life."

Elena laughed in spite of herself.

Delphine said, "Frankly, I haven't seen any signs in the last seventy years—since I was, say, six years old—of anyone being in control at all. As far as I see it, no form of control actually works, and all lines of authority break down when they get longer than about two steps. I never saw a single person who realized he was outside of the gaze of the boss who didn't think he knew better than the boss what he should be doing. I never saw that. So—you're telling me that somehow a world government without an evident policing force, without a public presence, without the power to inspire or punish in a practical way, would be more successful at controlling the entire world than a mother is at controlling her children when they are playing by themselves out in the backyard? Yes, there is a Council on Foreign Relations—I know that—and, yes, it may have been started sometime with those goals in mind, and, yes, it may be connected to a secret arm of the CIA that enforces its decisions and policies, and, yes, it might have assassinated the Kennedys, but there is no system that would make it actually work on a day-to-day basis. Whenever we talk about this, I think how nice it would be to have someone at the top who has a reasonable attachment to the idea of the middle class, and to the idea of the quiet, mostly orderly shunting of money around the world, but it ain't human."

Elena, too, thought the Council on Foreign Relations sounded reassuring. There had been a time, of course, when the very idea would have enraged her, but now it was pleasant to hope that someone reasonable was making an effort to discipline the President and the Vice-President and all of the rest of them.

"Well," said Zoe, thoughtfully, running her fork around on her plate and sweeping up stray bits of the mushroom omelet she had been eating, "I guess it's a test case. If they assassinated the Kennedys, then we'll see if they assassinate Bush—"

"It would be a mess and a nightmare if they assassinated him. No shadow government in its right mind would assassinate him and leave Cheney to be president, and if somehow they took out both of them, the country would be in such a turmoil that God only knows what would happen. No," said Delphine, "if the Council on Foreign Relations has a plan at this point, it's a bad plan and doesn't speak well for their competence as a shadow world-government. That's my view."

This last exchange, Elena thought, was so suddenly depressing, after Cassie's earnest but light tone, that she began to contemplate, as she had been during the night, where exactly she could emigrate to. She started on the usual round—Canada, Australia, New Zealand—but then stopped herself. In addition to the fact that Max and Simon had no desire to emigrate and that the thought of her lonely self making a moral pilgrimage to a country that opposed the Iraq war, even if that country were France, seemed like more than she could actually stand doing, there was also this appalling sense of vertigo that entered her every time she thought about it.

Zoe took her handbag from underneath her chair and opened it. She placed her cell phone on the table. As soon as she did so, it beeped, and with her long, graceful fingers, she opened it. She said, "Did you hear the phone ring? I didn't."

"I didn't," said Cassie. Elena had not heard it, either. Zoe pressed some buttons and then listened. After a moment, she said, "It's from Isabel, who says she left in Stoney's car and forgot to get the number of the house, which is why she's calling me. Okay. Let's see. Stoney is here, in the meeting with Max and Mike. Oh, I didn't realize they were already going at it. Did you, Elena?"

Elena shook her head.

"And she has Stoney's cell phone with her. Yes, Isabel, get on with it. Have you noticed how long her messages are? She can never get to the point." Then she grinned and said, "Oh dear. She went into the ladies' room at Starbucks, and as she was standing up from going to the john, the car keys fell out of her pocket into the toilet, and because it was an autoflush toilet, they went down before she realized what was happening, and then, when she called the barista in and they leaned down in front of the toilet, it flushed again." She laughed, and then said, "Well, it is funny! Poor Isabel. Of course, there's also the ultimate humiliation of calling me, which I gather she did because everyone else's phones are turned off." She glanced for just the briefest second at Delphine, a glance that Elena couldn't read, then peered at her own phone. She said, "Well, the signal is very weak up here. I guess that's why we didn't hear a call."

Cassie said, "Stoney's driving that old car of his dad's. I wonder if he even has a second set of keys."

The phone sounded a scale of four or five ascending tones, and Zoe answered it. She said, "Okay. Okay. Oh dear, Isabel. Okay," then looked around the table. "She called Triple A, and they told her it would be at least a two-hour wait and maybe longer, and at that point they would have to tow her to the dealer. It will take even longer to send a locksmith." She spoke into the phone. "I don't know how long that meeting is going to go, Isabel. I think they just started, I don't know. Maybe I'll call Nedra."

"I'll go get her," said Elena. "I don't mind."

"Just a minute," said Zoe into the phone.

And Elena didn't mind at all. As soon as Zoe had said "Starbucks," the first image to enter her mind was the image of newspapers—the L.A. *Times*, the *New York Times*, strewn about on tables, defining just how bad it was in Iraq, and how bad it wasn't. It was all very well to sit here under a lovely pergola between a spectacular house and an amazing aviary with three interesting and friendly women who, moreover, had plenty of insight into Max, about whom she was consumingly curious, and maybe she would not have all that many chances like this, but it was also like floating above the earth inside a large balloon, and knowing that at any time the balloon could pop. She said, "Actually, I'm happy to do it."

"Honey?" said Zoe. "Elena says she'll pick you up. You and Stoney can find another set of keys and go get the car later. Where are you, exactly?" She pulled a slip of paper and a pen out of her bag and wrote down what Isabel was telling her, then hung up the phone. She said, "And why did she leave, anyway? I thought we were in retreat here."

"I guess we'll find out," said Delphine.

As soon as she got into Elena's Subaru, Isabel said, "I knew she wouldn't come pick me up herself."

"I offered to do it," said Elena, and then she rushed to add, "There was something else I thought I would do," but she wasn't yet ready to admit that she was going to buy newspapers.

"Yes, but everyone does her bidding," said Isabel, peevishly, and then she took off her sunglasses and put them back on.

"Well, she is a movie star."

"Don't remind me, please! Anyway, movie stars drive around all the time. I saw Reese Witherspoon just this morning. She was standing on Melrose when I drove past, looking into her handbag."

Elena turned out of the parking lot onto Sunset. She said, "What kind of handbag did she have?"

After a pause lasting a whole stoplight, Isabel said, "Kate Spade."

"You noticed that, just driving past?"

"Well, I did. Actually, I thought, Why does she have *that bag*? I would never have *that bag*. It was pink and turquoise. When I flew out here last week, there was a girl my age sitting next to me on the plane, and she had an eight-hundred-dollar Ferragamo bag. She refused to put it under the seat in front of us. Finally, I said to her, 'If the plane crashes, I don't want to be hit in the head by your bag.'" Elena looked over at her, Isabel looked at Elena, Elena thought how much she looked like Max, and then they laughed. Elena realized that she had never been alone with Isabel before.

But then Isabel frowned and threw herself back in her seat. She said, "Thanks for coming. I can't believe what a mess this is. I really hope Stoney has another set of keys, I really do, but, you know, having another set of keys is not his style."

"What is his style?"

Isabel considered this question. Finally, she said, "Wishing he had bothered to have another set of keys made when he realized that he only had one set."

Elena didn't say anything. One of the first things she always did with a key was duplicate it, mark it, and hang it on the key board in her kitchen closet.

Isabel sighed. "What I really hate is those strings of choices that led to the disaster. For example, I brought two pairs of jeans with me up the hill, only two, because the others were dirty and I hadn't bothered to do any laundry all last week. So, this morning, I looked in my suitcase and I saw the loose ones and the tight ones, and Stoney was coming out of the bathroom and looking at me, and that made me feel very sassy, so I put on the tight ones, but if I'd put on the loose ones, the keys wouldn't have squeezed out of my back pocket as I was standing up, and, you know, I heard the splash, but it just didn't occur to me what was splashing until a moment later, when it flushed, and I realized that the keys had been in my back pocket."

"Why did you go out in the first place?"

"Oh, shit! Where are we? That reminds me! We have to go up to our house, because I went out to get my birth-control pills, because I forgot them. I'm sorry. It's so out of the way."

Elena had to admire the way Isabel slipped that phrase "birth-control pills" into the conversation so naturally. She said, "Better to have them. Maybe we should call and see what other things people forgot." The L.A. *Times*, she knew, could well be lying right there by the front door, and she could pick it up without seeming to be doing anything besides going into the house.

"I guess Dad and Stoney are in the meeting with that guy."

"They were when I left, but none of us saw them."

"He already financed another movie. Did you know that? Stoney and I watched it in our room last night. It was animated. I guess he found a studio in Japan to do it, so it was Japanese with Russian subtitles, but we could make out the story. I enjoyed it."

"What was it called?"

"Something about hawks. I couldn't make that out. Anyway, it begins in 1180, because the date showed on the screen first thing, and the main character is Saladin. At the beginning, you see Saladin and two companions take off their golden robes and put on humbler dress, and then they leave what Stoney thought was Damascus and head west. You know, Saladin was a Kurd. Isn't that interesting? We learned that in my medieval-history class, when we studied the Crusades. The scene changes fairly frequently but smoothly as they travel through Turkey and Greece and Albania, and pretty soon they are in Hungary, and then they go down through the Alps into northern Italy, and I mean this part passes in only a few minutes—it's a beautiful backlit panorama, in anime, of course, of all the landscapes—"

"That George W. Bush could have visited but didn't care to."

"Well, exactly. Anyway, we were fascinated. Somewhere in northern Italy, they're walking along, looking pretty bedraggled by this time, and they encounter two men out hawking. It's almost nightfall. When they've finished talking, the one local man sends the other with the travelers, and as soon as they leave, he gallops home. In the meantime, the second man takes the travelers down the back roads. They arrive at the castle, owned by the first man, and he welcomes them with feasting. You can tell that the man who owns the castle is curious, and that he realizes these guys are important. After everyone is in bed, he sneaks out to where the horses are, and he looks into one of the packs and finds gold coins and silk cloth gleaming in the moonlight. So he sends a messenger into the nearby city to his wife, who is a beautiful young woman in the Japanese anime tradition —"

"Which means?"

"Which means she has long hair hanging over her face, and great big eyes. But she's dressed like a medieval Italian woman. The next day, all the men wake up and they go hawking in the country, and Saladin admires the Italian guy's hawk, and the hawking scenes really are brilliant, the way the hawks fly up toward the sky, then drop on the prey, and everything is reflected in the surface of a lake. When they go into town, the beautiful wife has put on this fabulous feast, and all for these dusty, bedraggled merchants. The next morning, the husband and wife give the travelers five new horses and some new clothes and watch them go off, and from the dialogue even we realized that they think their visitors might have been Jesus and two of his disciples.

"Then it's five years later, and we see Saladin conquering Jerusalem, and there's a lot of typical anime violence, Japanese-style swordplay, and then the next scene is back at the castle in Italy, and the beautiful wife is weeping and saying goodbye to the husband, who is off to the Crusades. There are lots of scenes of sickness, dying, and burial, and then the ones who are left attack Jerusalem and are beaten, and the Islamic army goes through and kills and enslaves whoever is left, which includes our friend. A couple of the Crusaders manage to escape, and the Italian guy gives one of them a message for the wife.

"In the next scene, the Italian guy is dressed in humble robes, wearing a turban, and working in the palace hawkery or whatever it's called, training hawks. The wife back in Italy weeps and grieves at the news of his death, then meets and rejects a suitor. Her brothers come in and threaten to imprison and beat her if she doesn't agree to get married, so she points to a barren tree, from which we gather that when the tree leafs out again she will marry someone, but not before. And then there's a scene of the messenger being waylaid and killed on the way home from Jerusalem. Meanwhile, back in Damascus, Saladin is out hawking. The hawk flies out into the late-afternoon sun in the same way the hawk had done in the earlier scene, and then there's this terrific shot of everything reflecting in the surface of a pool in an oasis, and at that point Saladin looks directly at his captive and realizes that it is that man who had been so hospitable, so, the next scene, you see the Italian as a guest in the palace, eating at a banquet. Then they cut to the tree flowering in the courtyard of the castle, and the wife sitting beneath it, weeping.

"In the next scene, you see her being fitted for her wedding gown. Meanwhile, an Italian shows up at the castle in Damascus, and our Italian visits him, asks the news, and then he runs to Saladin. Cut to the tree, budding out—"

"I love all of this natural stuff," said Elena.

"Well, the story was clearly not a modern story, and more Disney story than anything else. But the backgrounds and settings were mesmerizing and incredibly detailed, the way anime always is. Cut to our Italian, realizing that no ship could get him there fast enough. So—and I love this scene—they take him to a room in a high tower in the palace, and they lay him out on a bed and they give him a potion and he falls asleep, and then Saladin puts many treasures on the bed, and the magician does his thing, and out the bed goes through the window and into the night sky, and it sails over the Mediterranean, and you can see the moon up above and the tiny ships down below, and pretty soon, the bed comes in for a landing, just before dawn, in front of the altar in a church. As the sun comes up, an old sleepy man creeps into the church to light the candles, and—boom— there's this bed with this inert man in it, and the old guy drops his candle and runs, and a few moments later, as our Italian is waking up, the old guy and his boss tiptoe up to the bed, and the two guys recognize each other and hug. The next thing you see is the wedding procession approaching the church, and the bride looks sad, but her brothers are poking her from behind, and when she gets into the church, she sees this strange man in Islamic robes and a beard and a turban, and he keeps catching her eye, so she sends him a goblet of wine, which he drinks, and then he puts a ring in it and sends it back to her. She realizes who it is, and runs to him, and they embrace. The last scene is of them on their horses, out hawking in the light of dawn, and the two hawks fly away together and return, reflected in the surface of the lake."

Elena was passing Mandeville Canyon. She said, "That sounds very nice. Maybe he could, or should, make this Ukrainian movie in anime."

"Well, Stoney suggested that. But Mike told him anime is all very nice for peace, but for war you need real flesh. That's exactly what he said. In English."

"He seems kind of obsessed with the Middle East. I thought he was Russian."

"I guess he's from some part that is more Asian. But look at the place we're staying. He's like the walking manifestation of globalization."

Elena turned up the hill toward Max's house.

Isabel went on, "It was a nice movie. It was reassuring in some way. Here it was made in Japan about Syria and Italy, with Russian subtitles, and no Americans were around, forcing it to be about American needs and wants, or telling it to be a certain way. It was about being friends without any reference to Americans at all."

"If only they could ignore us," said Elena, and Isabel nodded, but then said, "My economics professor always said that soon enough they will be ignoring us, once China is the superpower." Elena groaned. She said, "I find it so hard to get used to being the bad guy."

"Do you?" said Isabel. She pursed her lips and pushed her hair out of her face, then said, "I think that's because you're white. Against all the evidence, white people in America always cling to their own innocence and forgive themselves for whatever they've done, or if they themselves did not do it, whatever was done in their names. We used to talk about that in my job in New York. Is it guilt? I don't think it even rises to that level."

"How about ignorance?"

"Is that all it is? I don't think so. I think of it as a sense of entitlement. I mean, it goes beyond that time we were talking and Charlie couldn't get over the idea that someone might come and try to take his house or his car or something. There are so many histories of the last fifty years that show that Americans haven't been the good guys at all, and that a lot of people in the world are justifiably resentful of American interference in their national life, and I'm not even talking about old genocides against the native peoples and crimes against humanity, like slavery, that it took generations to acknowledge. I'm only talking about assassinated leaders we didn't like, and giving Saddam Hussein weapons of mass destruction that he used on the Kurds. I mean, everyone just goes along thinking that that kind of sensitivity about criticizing white people in this country is justified or normal. So, yeah, you hate thinking of yourself as the bad guy, but why are you only starting to think of yourself as the bad guy right now?" Then she glanced at Elena a bit defiantly.

And, yes, Elena could feel it in herself, even as Isabel described it, that moral resentment—the very things she herself could have and sometimes had asserted with a feeling of self-righteousness irritated her coming from Isabel, tall, good-looking, privileged, twenty-three years old, well educated, and, yes, in the official tradition of race in America, black, but hardly justified in calling herself that. Irritation, the feeling of her pride beginning to engulf her reason and her better nature. But Elena didn't say anything, only continued up the hill, trying to stem that "Who does she think she is?" reaction she was having. She thought of Max, because, of course, here was his house. But Max's image did not stem the vertigo. She thought of Simon. But that was worse. Her greatest attachment was to Simon, and she had cultivated her attachment with love and care, but, truthfully, if she were to admit it, she was a cat who had given birth to a dog. The two of them, mother and son, would not be nesting together ever again. And what would happen to Simon in such a world as this new one?

She pulled up in front of Max's house. Isabel threw open her door and jumped out, but Elena sat there for a moment and reassembled herself. She had to think of her book, her kitchen, her house in the flats of Beverly Hills. She had to think of her clothes and her habits and the cable-knit sweater she was knitting that she hadn't touched in months. She had to think of the orderly manner in which her days had progressed before this war, and to remember that they could progress like that again, task by task, crumb by crumb dropping to the floor of the dark forest, showing the way out again. She had to think of her many convictions and beliefs, and tell herself that they constituted a life, and as she thought of them, she saw Isabel swoop down and pick up the newspapers and carry them into the house, and she knew that she wouldn't have the courage to ask for them.

Meanwhile, back at the manse, Stoney was having several self-defeating thoughts. The first of these was that every man in the room with him, in the *My Fair Lady* study, was both older and bigger than he was. Mike was almost as tall as Max and two sizes larger (forty-six in the chest anyway—though, from the looks of his jacket, his tailor measured him by the millimeter). Stoney himself would have liked to think that he wore a forty; in fact, a forty was a little roomy for him, but, should he admit to the thirty-eight, then that would mean that he wasn't working out as much as he should be and that pretty soon he would weigh less than Isabel, or perhaps not, but last night in the Amber Room, when he took off his shirt, he had tried not to cross directly in front of the mirror. He cleared his throat and tried to project a slightly deeper voice. He said, "Mike, Alex—"

"Al," boomed the third guy, a forty-four for sure.

"Al, and Sergei."

Sergei nodded.

They pulled out chairs and sat around the black-walnut library table. In the middle were two silver pots of coffee, and in front of Mike was a silver pot of tea that looked like a crouching cat. The handle was the tail, curving upward, and the spout was the cat's open lips. Next to the teapot, on a plate, was what appeared to be an antique glass cradled in a silver holder. It didn't seem to be part of the same set as the cat, because the holder was shaped to look like a trellis of leaves bearing a single five-petaled flower. After they all sat down, they all cleared their throats. Stoney cleared his throat.

For most of the night, in the Amber Room, which he considered dark and bizarre but which Isabel liked (at least the bathroom and the dressing room were not paneled in amber, but were mostly white with tigereye accents, like handles and knobs and mirror frames), he had lain awake attempting to imagine Jerry doing this deal. Jerry had perfected a sort of tall-agent method. Loud voice, in-your-face manner, and actual arm-twisting, if he had to go that far. He didn't present it as arm-twisting. He only happened to grab your hand enthusiastically, as if he were about to shake it, but if things didn't go to his satisfaction, as they so often had not when Stoney was in high school and not operating on the most responsible level possible, arm-twisting could ensue before you knew it, either lateral arm-twisting, where he simply turned your hand and wrist until it hurt and you couldn't get out of it, or four-way arm-twisting, where he maintained his grip on your hand no matter what you did and suddenly stepped behind you. Jerry had been tall for a Jew. If you saw him palling around with Sid Caesar and Carl Reiner and some of those old comics he liked, they looked like a set of superannuated wiseguys, and you always stepped aside. Jerry could tell you that he knew best for you, and often, out of sheer fear and even agony, you would agree to what he suggested, and there you were, rich and famous. Or, if you were Stoney, at least not flunking out.

And Jerry had a partner, also successful, also now dead, but very far from tall, named Milt Perera. Milt might have been five feet, and Hispanic-looking, but volatile and Jewish to the core, and his technique was to appear to be about to explode. He would say it—"You don't take this deal, you don't sign on the dotted line here, and you're gonna have to scrape me off the windas and sweep me out the door; I mean it, if you are that stupid so as to not take this deal after I've put it all together for you, who do you think you are, I've got to ask myself, but it's gonna be me that suffers, because I'm not gonna be able to stand it, at the very moment you do not sign this deal, at the very moment you do not say, Milt, this is the best deal I ever saw, at that very moment something will happen to me, I can't say what, but I feel it right here." And then he would make a fist and hit himself on the breast-bone, produce a large burp, and say, "That was nothing. Just don't light any smokes in here."

But imagining Jerry and imagining Milt only reminded him that many many things were riding on this deal, not least the future of Hollywood, if he might be so bold as to think that, and possibly the future of the world, or at least East-West relations and the fate of the Middle East, because he had sat up through the night in the Amber Room with all those candles lit, and he and Isabel had read that book *Taras Bulba* back and forth across the bed to one another for an hour, after that strange anime thing Mike had financed before (best not mention that to Max), and they had seen the whole movie as if it were taking place right on the screen behind the mirror in the wall opposite the bed.

What had struck Stoney about *Taras Bulba* were not the same scenes that, judging by the talk they had had in the kitchen last week, had struck Max—the battle scenes, the scenes inside the besieged Polish city, the romantic scenes with a woman who looked (in Stoney's imagination) like a combination of Zoe and Isabel. What had struck him were the scenes in the Cossack encampment in the middle of a huge plain, under, in some sense within and surrounded by, sky. A wide camera angle could get that feeling of a landscape so large that it curved as the earth did, and men riding across it at the gallop. And then tight shots could capture the tips of the grasses grazing the ears of the horses, the lines of mounted Cossacks parting the flower-decked stems as they galloped through, not over, the grass. Moviemaking technology had arrived at a place where that kind of detail embedded in that kind of panorama was possible—and Max had very much liked *Crouching Tiger, Hidden Dragon* and once had expressed an interest in doing something similar. Of course, he hadn't expressed it lately. But Stoney had imagined how it could be, and Isabel had gotten enthusiastic, too—according to her, you wouldn't have to change the book one bit in order to show the way religious conflict destroyed relationships and families and towns and settlements and the ecosystem. Just one shot of bloated bodies of horses and townspeople and children and Cossacks floating down the river (all done by digital imaging, of course—"No children or animals were harmed in the making of this film") and people would be walking out of the theater as pacifists. Isabel had gotten very enthusiastic.

So here they were, sitting in the *My Fair Lady* study, and Mike, Al, and Sergei looked to be about as far from pacifism as it was possible to be, but who was to say what their true ideals were?

Stoney cleared his throat again and said, "Well, I read through the book again last night, and it really is a wonderful piece of work. Of course, I don't read Russian, so—"

Al said, "Gogol was truly a man from Ukraine. The Russians never understood him, though they were always eager to claim him. The Orthodox, the Soviets, the Tolstoyans. They all said this, that Gogol led directly to them, that he prophesied their coming. My own opinion is that he had stories bursting out of him like rockets. An incident goes in, rolls around, can't help it, must come out, as a great funny story or a great tragic story, and Gogol himself has little control over this. Have you ever driven a Maserati?"

Stoney shook his head.

Al said, "The first time you drive a Maserati, you touch the accelerator and the car is already beyond you, a mile down the highway. Very dangerous. This is what I think it was like being Gogol."

Sergei said, "Al used to be a professor of Russian literature at the university in Tula."

"And now he drives a Maserati," said Stoney. "I appreciate that."

"I appreciate that, too," said Al, straight-faced until everyone laughed.

"This is what is hard for me," said Mike. "I read this book, and I see something that you can only see from reading this book—"

"What would that be?" said Max. He sat behind an empty coffee cup and saucer, and made no move to pour himself a cup. Of course this was a bad sign, as far as Stoney was concerned.

Mike glanced at Max, and paused, then said, "I see beautiful pictures that have never been painted, but have only been thought of. Look at these books here." He waved his arm toward the upper balcony of shelves. "That side is the Russian. That side is the French. The English are right up there. I am a man who likes books. I read something every day. Those French books and those English books, it doesn't matter whether they have been painted or photographed or not. The English books, most of them, you could act out right in this room and not feel that you were missing anything. The dialogue would be witty and the interactions of the actors full of innuendo and tension. The words are the most important things about them. But these Russian books, it is not sufficient for all of them that they are books. Some of them, yes, but not all of them. Merely being books is too private for them. They are asking to appear in front of us and show us something. I thought this one, a great book by a great writer, but one which is not the biggest one, though of course a very magnificent one, should be the first in my project. Then there would be others, of course."

Stoney cast a sidelong glance at Max, who did not react to this, but Al and Sergei suddenly nodded. What business were they in, again? Mining or oil, Stoney thought Ben Avram had said, but it was always the case that everyone wanted to be a movie mogul.

Mike went on, "People in the East hunger for this, to be shown something about themselves that looks better than what they see around them. Here in America, you have forgotten what the effect of movies is, because you are so used to it. You think that it is entertainment, but, really, it is seeing yourself. Seeing yourself so much, all the time, not because you are required to but because you want to, and then you say that that is who you are. Look at these old American actors we think about. Let's take this man Clark Gable, who was not a handsome man, at least to my eyes. He walked and talked a certain way and had a certain easy manner, making jokes and smiling to himself, and being quite tall and yet not being frightening, and people in America said, yes, he is like I am, and so America became great, because Americans used the movies to talk to themselves about who they were."

Stoney looked at Max. Max was nodding at this. That was reassuring.

Mike warmed to his subject. "Henry Fonda and Marlon Brando were cowboys one day, and so those in the audience talked to themselves about that cowboy history. In Russia we did not have this. The movies only talked to us about being a good Soviet citizen. No Russian in his right mind said, Oh, I am a Nikolai Alexandrov type from that movie *I Gave My Life for a Tractor*, and my girlfriend is a Nina Murmanskova type from that movie *Six Fishing Boats Harvest the Northern Sea*. Who would want to be that type? But it is time now, when Russians and Ukrainians, too, wonder about themselves, to give them something to think about."

"Maybe it's too late for that," said Max. "Maybe the newness of movies has passed everywhere, not just in the U.S."

"Maybe, but, you know, in Saint Petersburg many people still go to the ballet and the opera and the theater. People are used to going out and sitting in chairs and watching a show together, and they have not gotten used to something different, the way Americans have gotten used to staying home. Russians are sociable, Ukrainians are sociable, Kyrgyzians are sociable. If there is something on, good or bad, they will see it, even if they complain about it for the next week. Going out to a theater that is decorated in an elaborate way is much preferable to staying home. So—I think it is still possible to impress them with a thing to look at that is magnificent."

"There are Russian directors, both here and in Russia. Why don't you go to one of them? Or a Ukrainian director."

This was the obvious question, so Stoney was a bit surprised that he himself hadn't bothered to ask it.

Mike said, "You are thinking of whom?"

"Well, Konchalovsky, of course. And I saw that movie about the Hermitage, which you must have seen. His name starts with an S. Sukurov."

"And there is Mikhalkov," said Mike. "We have thought of them, and others, too."

Al said, "I talked to Sukurov. He is not out of the question. We are not interested in Konchalovsky, for various reasons. And Mikhalkov is very busy. He never stops filming. For this movie, we need a meticulous planner, which we understand is true of you, Mr. Maxwell, but also someone who seems to be in sympathy with a Russian way of looking at things. I have seen your movie *Grace*, and Mike has seen it twice. To write that movie, you would have to have that sympathy."

"When I was a boy, my grandfather told me those stories, but I'm not that boy any longer, as you can see. I've made lots of other movies since that one—"

"I think," Stoney pushed his way into this remark, "that there is something else going on, if you don't mind my saying so. I think that you do not want this production to be parochial or provincial, am I right? I think that you want it to be world-class, a great Hollywood movie that reeks of Hollywood, that is unapologetically a kind of *Doctor Zhivago* of our day, am I right?" Mike nodded, followed by Al and Sergei. Everyone was saying what they truly thought, but the thing they truly thought that they were not saying, Stoney suspected, was that they were steering away from Russian and Ukrainian directors because those directors would have their own ideas about Gogol and the book, and would be quick to elbow the moneymen aside. As well they should. Max, the best compromise, would be quick to elbow the moneymen aside, too, but as far as Stoney was concerned, he could do that later. He had to make a deal with them first.

"Anyway, as I said," Mike cautioned, "Gogol was not Russian. He wrote in Russian, but he was a man from Ukraine. This is a story about Ukraine that takes place at a time before Russia was Russia and Ukraine was Ukraine. Here are the Cossacks and the Poles and the Turks and the Jews. All of these people have very long memories, as Gogol did. To see this, for them, is to see something that happened the day before yesterday, or a few springs ago. If you go to the steppelands, you see roads and towns, of course, but you also see just what Gogol would have seen and Taras would have seen, and it is not worth seeing only because they would have seen it, but because it is beautiful to see and should be put on film—"

"Before it's changed forever," said Stoney. Then he added, "That's what Isabel thinks. Isabel is Max's daughter. I don't know if you met her."

"Perhaps. But what I was thinking was that a painting of this place is not big enough. Cinerama, or even IMAX would be almost big enough."

"Yes," said Sergei, "I have often thought that *Taras Bulba* in IMAX would be a worthy project."

Max said, "You gentlemen have ideas of your own. You have a vision of your own. This is your movie. Why don't you make it yourselves instead of trying to find someone to make it? I mean, produce it and direct it."

How could this idea be insulting? Stoney thought. And yet there was some way in which it did seem like an insult, as if Max were saying that this was not an interesting enough project for him, that he had better things to do, but also denigrating whatever it was that they did do for a living and implying that he could not be bought. But of course he could be bought, he had been bought many times. Directors in Hollywood of Max's sort rather prided themselves on being bought, because if you could be bought to direct a project that you had not conceived yourself, and you did a good job with it, as Max usually did, then that meant not only that you were technically proficient and a good executive, but also that you could see the look of every subject you were given—in some sense, of every subject in the world.

You could read the material and visualize not only how it would play out but also what there was about it that had a certain sort of meaning. With this actor here and this actor over here and these objects in between them and this wall and ceiling and window in the background and this chair with a certain slipcover on it in the foreground and this shot before and this shot after, you could evoke not only specific feelings and sympathies in the audience, but also specific thoughts and pieces of knowledge. A director who could be bought was above all things intelligent, and not every director was, some were more instinctive. But the sort of director Max was combined a lively curiosity about all sorts of subjects and ideas with strict visual integrity that was similar to, but in some sense more active than, a decided sense of taste. Each shot had to look right, and Max knew instinctively and immediately whether it was right and how to make it right. This was a mere talent, probably a brain function, and yet it brought together all of those other things that Max could do, and it made them all hang together and, always important, look classy. He had made good movies over the years and he had made dogs—*Southern Pacific* was a prime example of a movie of Max's that Stoney considered a stinking dog—but with all of them, the sum of the parts was better than the parts, because of his intelligence and this visual thing he always had.

But Mike did not react as if he had been insulted. He said, thoughtfully, "Mr. Maxwell. Here is the problem with that. It is that I am not a patient man. When I was a boy, it took me a very long time to learn to write. My handwriting was poor for many years, and then I learned to dictate! My mother thought that I would never amount to anything, that I would go out on the street and become a petty criminal, as many of those in my town did indeed do if they were not good students. When I was given a toy to build, a model of something, I could never make the pieces fit together. It was very frustrating. My fingers would not do it. The strategy I developed from this deficiency was to induce my sister to do it for me, and she always did. From this I learned that I didn't have to be patient, or learn how to do something, that there are those who take pleasure in putting the toy together, such as my sister, and those for whom having to put the toy together results in absolute hatred for the toy, such as myself. And so you see my house. It is my job to say to Joe Blow and Mr. D'Amico, the master builder, 'An Amber Room would be nice,' 'A Reformation Room would be nice.' Have you seen the Reformation/Counter-Reformation Suite? It begins with Hieronymus Bosch, who died, of course, the year before Martin Luther actually broke away from Rome. My Bosch is only a drawing for a section of his larger painting entitled *Hell*, but that sets the theme for the suite. It is not a hospitable room because of the drawings of martyrdoms and burnings at the stake, and so we did not put any of your party in there, but the art is unusual, and I go in there sometimes. At any rate, I try to make the most of my impatience by inviting those who are more patient to exercise their talents at my expense. This is one of the few times when I have suggested an idea to someone rather than merely picking and choosing among the items that are available, as I have done in furnishing this house. I am not so new at this now, and what is available doesn't seem so much like an inexhaustible treasure to me now. I see what's missing, and I want to supply it—"

Stoney said, "Thank you so much for that, Mike. It was very illuminating. And, Max, weren't you saying to me just a few weeks ago that Hollywood doesn't make the kinds of movies anymore that they used to, the epic films about history and culture like, say, *The Grapes of Wrath*, or even *Gone with the Wind*? You said it's all some kind of fantasy now, and you were right. This is a way to go back to, or, maybe I should say, to circle around again to, that epic sort of film, to say that, well, the American customer doesn't matter so much anymore, so the adolescent tastes of the American customer don't have to be accommodated every single time anymore, especially if we have a backer with the vision that Mike here has. I see a huge audience for this film, not only Russians and Ukrainians, but all of the audiences that like films about exotic places and exotic times, films that are important enough to win at Sundance and also find their way into the Oscars in the foreign-film category. I mean, didn't you say to my father a couple of years ago that the nominees in the foreign-film category are so much more serious than the nominees in the best-picture category? This is your chance to go there! To become an international director with an international vision—"

"I see that," said Max, "but—"

Now Stoney could feel Jerry's voice coming into him. He sat up slightly and cleared his throat again. Jerry had had a way of looming, and Stoney could feel him looming right there in the *My Fair Lady* study. He exclaimed, "Hell! What else are you doing? You're sitting around your bedroom getting old! You're paying attention to your cholesterol count and the number of trans-fatty acids in your diet! You're listening to Delphine and Cassie every day! You're thinking about gas mileage! You're taking nice little walks and digging in your garden! You're pinching pennies, too. What's the next step with that? Pretty soon you'll be calling your stockbroker every day, and all you'll have for excitement is a little e-trading! Aren't you planning on doing any art? You want to end up like Howard Greco, making animated pornography out in Pasadena about whores coming to the house? What kind of a man are you?"

Stoney noticed that Max was amused at this, and realized that Max thought he was *imitating* Jerry, but he was not imitating Jerry, he was channeling Jerry. He raised his voice a little bit. Mike, Al, and Sergei were staring at him. "You think your reputation is still intact, after that stinking dog *Southern Pacific* and two made-for-TV movies? You're gonna leave it at that, your last finished efforts? You want to be one of those footnotes in Hollywood history, the kind of guy where you turn to the index and it says 'Nathan Maxwell, page 89,' instead of 'Nathan Maxwell, chapter 12'?" Personally, Stoney thought Jerry was going a little far here, but Jerry was Jerry, after all. "First! Husband! Of! The! Legendary! Zoe! Cunningham! Also directed a few movies! Is that how you want it? This guy Mike here, Russian though he is, is offering you a better option—he's offering you redemption after a sorry fading away! He's saying, Get back into the fight, be a man, do what you know how to do! What if he takes the project to some ambitious kid? You know any kid will go for this, no matter what. Any kid with balls, at any rate! A kid says, Ukraine, no problem, are we going on Aeroflot? Are we taking Ukrainian National Airways? Kids are not impressed by far, far away! Kids are not lazy. But can a kid do this project? Can a kid organize things so that Mike doesn't go broke or go crazy? Can a kid *see* this, all these Cossacks and Jews and Russians and Poles? Taras is a father! He has a father's sentiments! Isn't a kid going to focus on the two kids and put the father in the background? Do you want that to happen? You want this movie to be a Ben Affleck–and–Jennifer Lopez vehicle and cut out the father and the older son completely? Because if Mike goes to some kid, that's what's going to happen, and it will be your fault."

Stoney wound up his spiel at the top of his voice, and by this point Max was laughing and laughing, great ha-has, and Mike and Al and Sergei were smiling, though uncertainly, because they had never met Jerry and didn't know what was happening. Stoney sat dead quiet for a moment, breathing heavily with the effort of hosting a guy like Jerry, who was Stoney plus, and then, after Jerry moved off, Stoney himself burst out laughing, and then Max said, "Well, if you're going to put it that way, then how about I put it this way? Why do I have any sympathy at all with Taras? Shouldn't I have sympathy with the Jews who scuttle around here and there, instigating the fights and serving only as go-betweens? What if I do the whole Taras Bulba story, the whole epic history of Ukraine, from the point of view of the Jews in the shtetls and the merchants who have to watch out for their lives and their livelihoods every single minute, because those Cossacks are great unpredictable drunkards who have no self-control and hardly any larger motives other than addiction to drinking, fighting, and killing? What do their lives look like to the old Jewish man who leads Taras to the execution of Ostap? To Taras, it looks like the crucifixion of Christ, but to that man, let's call him Abe, it looks like just another day in the life of the crazy Christians, who pause in their killing of one another only long enough to steal *his* goods and money. That would be where my sympathies lie, if we're talking about sympathies. My idea is not to do an epic. I'm not in the mood for epics anymore—"

Mike eyed Max, and then said, "You see? The material is very rich and complex. Yes, indeed, your sympathies lie with the Jews—whose do not? Are you saying to me that Gogol had the ideas of his time about Jews? Yes, of course he did! And about Cossacks and Poles and Turks. That is part of the pleasure of the material, that small distance we have from the way Gogol looks at it. He brings in this Jew. To him, perhaps, the man is only a Jew doing something that, plausibly, a Jew would do in the middle of the sixteenth century, but to us the man is something different. Why would we make a movie of a book, any book? It is because the book can only exist as it was printed, caught in the time when it was written, but with a movie we can add something. We understand this Jew. He is an old and experienced Jew who has survived doing the one thing he could do in the middle of the sixteenth century, but doing it in a certain way, a way that the actor understands and communicates to me in the audience, something about the tragic nature of the situation. Yes, Taras and this man are watching the execution of Ostap, but the execution is not seen from their point of view. The camera sees it. The camera looks at Taras, then the camera looks at Avram, then the camera looks at Taras and again at Avram. In these shots, we see two men who have different feelings about the execution. One man is somehow astonished, even after a life of violence and killing, that such a thing could have happened to him, and the other man has seen this sort of thing far too often in his life. Where does the tragedy lie? Don't they split the difference between them? Isn't the tragedy that it doesn't matter what you know or where your loyalties are, here, once again, is someone's child being put to death? May we add this to Gogol? If we are making a film, then we must add something. Why not this? Or do you think that the ending of the book promotes violence and war? After Taras vows to avenge Ostap, he puts village after village to fire and sword. Do you think Gogol thought this was good, or do you just think he thought it was inevitable? And was he wrong? There are people here in the U.S. who think that if the people in Iraq give them trouble the American Air Force ought to carpet-bomb the whole country. I have read this and heard it on the radio."

"Yes," said Max, "there are those people. You know the American saying, 'We had to destroy the village in order to save it.'"

"As we make our film, then, we can add the fact that we know this, too. That almost two hundred years of warfare have passed since Gogol and five hundred since Taras, and how we feel about it is different from how Taras and Gogol felt."

Max said, "Of course, you make a good point. But once we humanize all the characters—Cossacks, Poles, Turks, Jews—then we'll be criticized by everyone for softening the story and making it politically correct—"

"Critics never say that if you have enough slaughter," said Stoney. "All the characters can be well meaning, but if there is plenty of gore, then whether they are basically good or basically evil gets kind of lost in the chaos." He looked around the table. He continued, "Jerry always said that. He said the best way to get good reviews was pour on the fake blood, and preferably have it spouting."

"He did say that," said Max with a smile. "But for me that brings up the fact that I don't want to make another bloody movie. I want to make something more intimate."

Stoney began shaking his head, right in Max's direction, warning him off this subject.

"What's that?" said Al.

"Have you ever seen a movie called *My Dinner with Andre?*"

Al shook his head.

"That's a movie where two guys sit in a restaurant for a couple of hours and talk. One of the guys in it wrote a movie you might have seen, or at least be interested in, called *Vanya on 42nd Street.*"

"I have seen that movie," said Sergei. "I did not understand it."

"Anyway, I would like to do a movie like *My Dinner with Andre,* except that, instead of talking in a restaurant for two hours, the two characters make love in their bedroom for two hours."

Mike sat up and looked at Max, then poured himself a fresh glass of tea. He said, "Do they make love in some new way that allows them to keep going for two hours?"

"No, they mostly talk. I've been writing the script. I have about thirty or forty pages. Even though they're naked, I have to say they're having a difficult time getting to the lovemaking. But that's actually more interesting to me than it would be if they were just going at it—"

"What are they talking about?" said Stoney, despairingly.

"Well, in this draft of the script, they are talking a lot about the Iraq war. She's more interested in it, really, than he is, but she gets him worked up at one point. That's the fascinating difference between them. They love each other and they respect each other, but they simply cannot feel the same way about the war. For him, it's just another screwup, but for her, it's the big screwup, the screwup that changes history, and her entire view of human nature—"

"You are promising sex and only giving talk? This also sounds like Chekhov to me," said Al. "Intellectuals will be interested in this movie, but I don't see that it has broad appeal."

"It doesn't have any appeal at all!" exclaimed Stoney.

"I talked to Madonna about it," said Max. "She seemed very interested, interested enough to do it for scale, and she suggested Gabriel Byrne for the lead. He can be very sexy. Or Liam Neeson, but I think Neeson's too tall—"

"Are we talking about the same Madonna who is married to Guy Ritchie and studying the Kabbalah and writing children's books? She wants to be naked with Gabriel Byrne talking for two hours?"

"She said she thought it would be a good intellectual challenge for her, and stretch her acting skills. I wouldn't mind working with her. Her body is iconic. That would be an interesting aspect of the material that I hadn't considered before."

Stoney sensed that Max was joking, but he wasn't sure, so he played along. "There are those who would say that she has no acting skills."

"Well, I didn't commit to her."

"Oh, good," said Stoney. How, he thought, would Jerry stem this tide? He glanced furtively at the three Russian men. He was sure they were thinking that, yes, Max was old. They hadn't realized before how old Max was, but now they did, and right behind this thought was the natural next thought, Why bother with this old man? If there was anything Hollywood had plenty of, it was young men.

But Mike said, "Madonna?" Just like that, just suddenly alert. "I have always seen something of myself in Madonna. She is one woman I would like to meet."

Stoney pondered this.

Max said, "Perhaps I could arrange—"

"For myself," said Al, "I have always wanted to meet Harold Pinter."

"And I," said Sergei, "have often imagined myself having lunch at The Ivy with Vanessa Redgrave."

"Vanessa Redgrave is old enough to be your mother," said Stoney.

"I am content with a fantasy," said Sergei.

Just then, the door of the *My Fair Lady* study opened; Simon put his head inside and said, "Hey, what's going on in here? Mom's car is gone. I think she went on a secret mission to buy newspapers, or at least find an Internet café."

Stoney said, "We've been in here all morning, so—" And then Joe Blow appeared behind Simon, and they stepped into the room together. Joe Blow made what Stoney could only call a very slight bow in the direction of Mike, Al, and Sergei, then said to himself, Stoney, "Mr. Whipple, I have

Mademoiselle Isabel on the line, and she says, do you have a spare set of car keys at your house, and if so, where might she find them?"

"Where are the ones I gave her?"

"They have been flushed, through an unfortunate concatenation of circumstances, down the WC in a Starbucks on Sunset Boulevard. They are beyond retrieval and must be replaced. Mademoiselle Isabel and Madame Elena are at Mr. Maxwell's house in Pacific Palisades, and would like to go to your house and get the spare key."

Stoney said, "But my house key is on the same ring as the car key."

"No shit!" said Simon.

"No shit," said Stoney.

"I can see," said Joe Blow smoothly, "that there are more difficulties here than meet the eye. Please go on with your conference. I will take care of the problem." He walked, seeming to tiptoe, out of the room.

Simon came over to the table, pulled out a chair, and sat down. He looked around with a big smile on his face, and said to Mike, "You must be Mike. This would be your house. I like it. It's really cool. Are you talking about that movie idea, from the old book? I had a thought about that myself the other day. I'm thinking that these characters are not that old. The boys are coming home from some school, so they are, say, sixteen and seventeen, and so Taras himself is in his late thirties, and the wife, who is supposed to be this old crone, she is only thirty-five or less, and the girl the one kid falls for, she is maybe fifteen. Nobody is old in this movie, because in those days nobody had a chance to get old. Fifty was way, way old. I think it would be startling, and it would also look good on the screen, if these were young-looking people but already wrecked, you know, from living such a hard life. That's my idea."

"That's a good idea," said Max.

"Do you have movie experience?" said Mike.

"Very recent," said Simon, with an impish look. "I played a dancing penis in the barroom scene of a student production on the theme of male-female relationships, but they're in the editing stage now, so I'm letting my hair grow in again." He ran his fingers over the shadow of hair he had grown over his head and reached for the coffeepot. He poured himself a cup, then settled into his chair. "It gave me a taste of moviemaking. I liked it. I liked building the set, I liked thinking about the costumes. I even liked the dancing. It turns out I am pretty bilateral on some of those dance steps, good to the left and good to the right. The whole thing was a lot more fun than molecular biology, and pretty much more fun than my photography thesis on the landscape of women's hair."

"What is that?" said Al.

"Oh, it's just what it sounds like. I take extreme black-and-white close-ups of women's heads, and if you manipulate the film in a certain way, it looks like these strange, unidentifiable scenes. One of them looks like a riverscape. Another one looks like a beach. Sometimes I style their hair, or braid it, or mousse it, or put little bits of stuff in it. The point is that when you look at one of the photographs, you are looking at something and thinking it is another thing. One girl had wildlife in her hair, I'm sorry to say, but it made a couple of interesting pictures. I wasn't going to use that set of photos for my thesis, and then I decided I was, but now that I've done this movie, that all seems kind of boring and pretentious to me. I mean, I wish I could say that I have enough photographs for my thesis, because I really feel like I've gone beyond that now artistically, but I need at least ten more."

Stoney said, "Elena is hoping that Simon will return to college tomorrow."

"She is," said Simon, "yes. She is hoping that. But I love this house so much, and I think I've talked Monique and Marya into letting me photograph their hair. On their own time, of course," he said to Mike. "If I get some good ones of them, then maybe I can talk Isabel into something. She has very landscapy hair, especially along the back of her head."

"Did you come in here for a reason?" said Stoney.

"I came in to offer my suggestion," said Simon.

"Oh, right," said Stoney, attempting to insert into his voice the idea that Simon now leave. That Madonna thing had been a gift, and Stoney had thought he could work with that, but now he was experiencing Simon as a stream might experience a rock. The way the men looked at Simon—Who is this kid, what's he doing here?—and Simon looked at the men—This is cool, what can I make of this?—was causing eddies and backflows and a net loss of energy. Stoney cleared his throat. He said, "It's not inconceivable that Madonna would favorably consider the *Taras Bulba* project, if she's in the mood to go back to work."

"She would play the old woman who leads Andrei to the beautiful princess," said Simon. "I can see that."

Max smiled. Then the door opened again, and this time it was Paul. He leaned in, said, "Is Zoe in here? I can't find her. It doesn't help that I still haven't figured out which room is which." But instead of turning around and walking out, he saw the Russians and walked right in, remarking to Al, "You must be Mike—"

Al gestured toward Mike.

"Oh," said Paul, "sorry about that. I don't mean to interrupt, but I just have to tell you how appreciative I am of your house here." He dug his fingers into the giant beard and went on, "I mean, it's very kind of you to let us stay here, but even more than that, I am amazed and thrilled by the degree of thought that's gone into this place. It's unbelievable—"

Simon said, "Paul has been all over the world. Last night he was telling me about climbing the seven holiest mountains in China. He's seen a shitload of stuff—"

"You are a connoisseur, then," said Mike, courteously.

"Of a few things," said Paul. "Of a very few specialized things." He pulled out a chair and sat down at the table, then said, "As a matter of fact, I've made a little study of Russian Orthodox iconography. I am especially interested in representations of God and holiness, and in the theories of the godhead that the various methods imply."

"You are an art historian?" said Sergei.

"Oh, no. I'm a teacher of meditation and yoga techniques, and I also do some counseling. Traveling to holy places is my avocation. Though I would say that I prefer ruins to functioning shrines. Tikal. The Pyramids. I would like to get to the Lascaux Cave this year. That's my plan."

"I didn't know you could go in there," said Al.

Paul smiled.

"Paul goes in everywhere," said Simon. "If he's standing outside, the priests come out and invite him in. It's strange but true. Looking at him, you would never think—"

"I doubt," said Paul "that any Cro-Magnon priests are going to emerge and invite me in."

"Stranger things have happened," said Simon.

"Have they?" put in Stoney. "I think we—"

But Mike leaned forward, looking right at Paul. "What do you think about our movie project?"

"Well, I can't say that I've studied the book at all. Other than Max's synopsis the other day, I've only read it once, and that was years ago. And of course in translation, so I'm sure the subtleties of the whole story escape me. But on the surface, it's very dramatic. The themes, of course, are slightly at odds with the story. I see Taras as a kind of wounded god figure. As I remember, at the end, his presence on the steppe takes on a quality of omnipresence. Notions of good and evil entirely disappear, as if they are too rudimentary to fully encompass the power of Taras' grief. Am I mistaken here? When we weep for Taras, and I do think we are meant to weep for him, the whole notion of men as fallen, and of God as fallen in their fall, is offered as an idea. What do we feel when we think of God weeping for us? Is our own divinity, or potential divinity, enhanced thereby?"

"Gogol was much preoccupied with divinity," said Al. "He made a pilgrimage to Jerusalem, and he did burn much of his work before he died."

"Well," said Sergei, "he destroyed the second half of *Dead Souls* under the direction of his priest."

"I don't think the priest actually told him to destroy it," said Al. "I think it was his own sacrifice."

"When they dug up his grave to rebury him in the Soviet period, he was facedown," said Mike.

There was a moment of silence in the room, then Al said, "It was felt by many that he had been buried alive. In a way, I believe that would have been a fitting end for Gogol, one that even he might have appreciated."

"Ugh," said Simon.

Mike turned to Paul and said, "I like this idea you have about the ending of the book, that Taras is a failed God. It suggests that he exercises his power but is confused about what his power is for. I find that this controversy about God is a constant one. Have you seen—"

"The Reformation and Counter-Reformation Suite?" said Paul. "I went into there about an hour ago. It is a very striking set of rooms." He turned to Max. "One room is full of Northern European art of the sixteenth century, and then there's a bathroom, and then the other room is full of Southern European art of the sixteenth century, Spanish at one end and Italian at the other. But I could not imagine sleeping in there."

"It also has a very elaborate bed from a palazzo in Venice," said Mike, "but it is too short for most modern people. When I have studied religious history, I have found that this idea of God as all-powerful leads to many other ideas that seem very cruel. By comparison to the notion that the destiny of most men is to burn eternally in hell no matter what they do in life, which I believe was a notion of John Calvin, this idea you propose for Gogol that God is so distraught at the mess he has helped create that he exerts his power irresponsibly, or, perhaps I might say, in a state of confusion for a time, this notion seems to imply that God can make errors and then correct them and make amends for the damage he has done. I like this." He turned to Max and said, "I believe it would be a good idea to attach Paul to this project. He has illuminated something for me. I believe he is a man of exceptional insight."

"We don't have a project," said Max. "We're just chatting."

"We don't have a project *yet*," said Stoney.

"That idea, of course, has some interesting theological implications," said Paul. "For one thing, the idea of a wounded God the Father occurs frequently in non–Judeo-Christian myths. The Father has to be saved by the children, as, for example, King Arthur must be saved by the Knights of the Round Table or the land is blighted and sterile. It's an idea that presupposes a nice reciprocity between divinity and humanity. Or think of this—if God makes errors, and then feels remorse and redeems himself, then it is possible for people to do the same thing. And you might also say that if God makes errors and is all-powerful, then he can correct every error even as he is making it. The errors he makes in this universe are not being made in another universe, a universe that is brushing against or bumping into the universe we are experiencing. In the book we have, for example, Taras is so upset by the death of Ostap that he inspires many massacres, but in another book by the same name, written at the same time, Nikolai Gogol rewrites that passage. He decides that Taras has had enough—he does not become a man of peace, that would be implausible for his temperament and his time, but when the moment comes to call for more war, he remains silent, and the warfare diminishes for a time. I see him at his desk—Gogol, that is— with his lamp and his papers and his pen. He is reading over this passage he has written, I think I remember that it is only a few lines, something about the ensuing furious battles all over the region, and he simply draws a line through that and adds in something else, some little thing, about how when the Cossacks regrouped Taras did not add his voice to the clamor for revenge. He doesn't say why not, or that he could not. He simply writes 'did not.'" Paul shrugged. Mike nodded his head slowly and took a meditative sip of tea, as if this made perfect sense to him. Simon nodded, too. He was sitting there in comfort.

Soon enough, it was appropriate for Stoney to go on with what he had been saying in the first place. He cleared his throat again, but not, he thought, in a demanding way, more in a winding-things-up way. "My sense, I don't know about you, is that we've made a lot of progress today, and that many good ideas have come out of our meeting. I've been in other contract negotiations, lots of other ones, where the principals didn't have anything interesting to say. It was only about money and points and perks and stuff, and no thoughts about the project were aired at all, because everyone thought they knew what the others were thinking, even though in fact no one really cared about the project for itself, because it wasn't inherently interesting, just a remake of something else that everyone had seen a hundred times." He turned to Mike. "You may not know this, pardon me if you do, but this is how Hollywood works. You've got the money and I've got the idea, and I come to you and I say, 'I've got a great idea, we'll make a movie about a woman lawyer who's recovering from an alcohol addiction, and Nicole says she wants to do it, so it'll be an updated version of *The Verdict*, but sexier and more upbeat, with a little comic twist, kind of like *Twenty-eight Days*, but with Nicole *Kidman*, but the *early* Nicole Kidman, so there's a hint of *To Die For*, so, really, it has everything, don't you think?' And so they all agree that it does, but actually, they're all only half listening, and going off thinking they're going to make the movie each of them wants to make. The producer is going to add in a little of his favorite movie, which is *Divorce—Italian Style*, and the director is going to add in a little of his favorite movie, which is *Pennies from Heaven*, and Nicole herself is going to add in a little of her favorite movie, which is *Clueless*, and on down the line, and so what I'm saying is that, even though on the surface Max here seems resistant, really he's offering us a golden opportunity to delve into the material. Don't you agree, Max?" But, naturally, Stoney didn't give Max a chance to answer this question. He quickly went on, "And I love that idea that Gogol was found facedown in his grave for some reason." And he did. It was a truly, truly weird idea and perfectly in keeping with how he had felt in the middle of the night, waking up in that abyss they called the Amber Room. He wondered how he could fit someone being found facedown in his grave into a movie of *Taras Bulba*.

Now there was a general loosening of everyone's demeanor, a clear sign that the meeting was over. Max said, "What was that about your car keys?"

"It sounded to me like Isabel flushed my car keys down the toilet somewhere in town, but I don't get it, because I thought Simon said it was Elena who went after newspapers." He looked at Simon. Simon shrugged and said, "I was just asking a question. Actually, I just got up. I was heading for the dining room, and I heard you all in here. I don't know where Mom is or Zoe or anyone."

Everyone pushed back his chair and unbuttoned something. Max unbuttoned the top button of his green polo shirt. Stoney unbuttoned his cuffs. Mike and Al unbuttoned their jackets. Sergei, who had a paunch, unbuttoned, surreptitiously, the button of his slacks. Simon unbuttoned his shirt altogether, revealing the hair on his chest, which curled in a very Adonis-like fashion. Simon was definitely, as Isabel had pointed out to Stoney more than once, suspiciously good-looking. Only Paul didn't have anything to unbutton, since his clothes, made entirely of roughly woven cotton in shades of beige and white, were held together by strings. Though he didn't unbutton or untie anything, Paul did get comfortable. He slipped his feet out of his thongs and then stretched and curled his toes. His toes, Stoney thought, were so long that he could probably manipulate tools with them. He and Mike continued to chat about the divine, which Stoney had an instinctive suspicion of, but if they wanted to introduce some aspect of divinity into this epic, why not?

The task of dealing with those keys, of getting his car from wherever it was parked on Sunset back up the hill, of climbing in one of the windows of his house and finding spare keys in the mess, of being angry or not at Isabel for losing the keys, and angry or not at himself for not having spares ready to hand, these tasks awaited. Better, he thought, to pour a cup of coffee, take a few sips, listen to the ambient conversation, and see if the car situation righted itself on its own.

In fact, the meeting had succeeded in driving from his mind his worries about Isabel. Or was it Isabel and Max? Or was it this new branch his relationship with Max had suddenly sprouted? If someone had told him in the course of the last year not only that he would find a project for Max, who hadn't looked at a project in recent memory, but also that his long-ago relationship with Isabel would revive so suddenly, he would have laughed. He would have scoffed. Or, maybe, he would have prepared himself in some way.

Stoney glanced at his watch. Almost two hours without thinking about it. A relief. It had been all very well, after dinner the night before, to tell Max that he was leaving everything up to Isabel. He didn't mind appearing to be a passive schlemiel. A passive schlemiel was not only more or less what he actually was, it was also good cover for those times when he was not a passive schlemiel but had something more on the ball. Who was it? Some writer whose name he couldn't remember, but a guy who interviewed lots of people and wrote long articles. Even though he couldn't remember the name of the guy, he could perfectly remember his strategy in interviews, which was to play so dumb that the interviewee had to repeat himself over and over, always adding new details, and sometimes even getting angry or impatient with the obtuseness of this writer. But the articles he got out of this method were always better than the articles other people wrote, people who had a desire to appear smart. When had Stoney read about this? In high school or even junior high? It had been a revelation to him, that you could learn more by seeming to be a dork but keeping your eyes and ears open than you could by acting cool.

Even so, in this case, the case of how he and Isabel were going to proceed, appearing to be or actually being a passive schlemiel conferred upon him only limited immunity. Isabel had gloried in their night in the Amber Room, staying up, reading all of the book with him, watching that weird animated movie and making love to him twice while it was going on, eating the fruit and biscotti that were in a bowl, drinking the champagne that someone had left for them, and in general treating the room like her private party. Fucking, pacing, reading, talking, laughing—the whole situation had excited her, and she had been very affectionate, exclaiming over his various parts ("I love the back of your neck, did you know that? I always have"; "Your hands are really beautiful, you know"; "I've always thought that your ass has a certain sassy charm") in a way that made him nervous. Hadn't he counted on Isabel to maintain the positive but skeptical (and, indeed, almost indifferent though friendly) view of him she had always displayed, to more or less anchor him in a world where you didn't fall for anything, and most certainly didn't fall for yourself? And yet, in the Amber Room last night, where he felt mysteriously uncomfortable, as if all the dark corners contained spiderwebs even though he knew they didn't, she had expanded and charged up even while Stoney felt a growing sense of alarm at the way events were accelerating. Something dramatic was shaping up that seemed as though it was certainly going to threaten the colorless life he had been leading in which his dearest hope was that Max would do this movie and get this Russian money, and even that hope wasn't terribly dear. His second-dearest hope was that his floors would be refinished in the next couple of weeks, and his third-dearest hope—well, there hadn't actually been one of those, though now that his car was parked down on Sunset somewhere, he was growing a bit anxious about getting it back. That car was usually not far from where he himself was planted at any given moment, and so it made him anxious, or nervous, or disoriented, or something like that to think that the car was far away and yet not in the custody of the Jaguar dealer.

Max said, "I guess that's that, then."

"In a way," said Stoney, "only in a way," and he looked Max right in the eye—as difficult as that was now that he had ruminated again upon not only the changes in their relationship, but also the fact that Max as yet didn't know what those changes were—but he was rewarded when Max gave him a little smile and a very little nod, as if to say, Okay, okay.

Everyone got up, pushed his chair back, and stretched a bit. There were grunts. Stoney heard Max say he was going for a swim. Paul said he had been for a swim—the water was very refreshing. Al and Sergei conferred about something in Russian. Simon paused and picked up a magazine— Stoney couldn't see which one it was. Max asked Simon if he had taken his car to the Jiffy Lube, but Stoney didn't hear his reply. The group went out the door of the *My Fair Lady* library and spread into the tapestried entry hall. The front door was open, and sunlight fell through it in a bright triangular block that stripped all color from the rug there and said to Stoney, Come out, come out. He muttered to Max, "Are we going to talk?"

Max shrugged and said, "We've talked enough for the time being," but he didn't say it dismissively. They both knew the promise was that Max wasn't saying no just this very minute, that at least for another two or three days, while they were ensconced at Mike's place, the project was alive. Stoney looked up and saw Charlie coming down the elaborate staircase. He looked ill, or exhausted, but he was wearing shorts, a T-shirt, and black-and-white running shoes with small white socks. As Stoney looked up at him, he looked down at the three Russians.

"What time is it?" said Simon.

"Eleven-twenty," said the voice of Joe Blow.

"I think you told me there is a handball court?" said Simon.

"There is," said Mike, and Stoney saw Mike and Simon cock their heads at one another and grin. They turned toward the kitchen.

Max said, "Hey, Chaz, did you miss breakfast?"

Charlie said, "I had some sorting to do. It took a while." Then he glanced at the Russians. Max shrugged. Charlie turned, suddenly perky, and trotted back up the stairs. Max said, "Uh-oh."

Joe Blow said, "We will be serving lunch by the pool at one."

What will I do until one? thought Stoney, languidly, as he glided toward the front door and out into the sunshine. It was Monday. He should call the office, but why go in? Hadn't he done a nice piece of work already? He knew what he should do, of course—he should go get his car and find the keys, and generally take responsibility—but now that Jerry had come into him and then left him again, he felt used up, though in a nice way. There were other movies to watch. Mike had different collections in different rooms all over the house. In addition to that, he couldn't say that he had exhaustively explored the grounds and the aviary, not to mention the garage and what could easily be an interesting car collection—Joe Blow hadn't mentioned that, but this was L.A. Everyone in L.A. who collected paintings also collected cars. He went down the front steps and walked toward the aviary across Mike's pavers, set in an elaborate pattern of interlocking arches. He took note of Mike's Bentley. Next to it was Charlie's bright-yellow rental, and beside that, Zoe's silver Mercedes. She had the back door open, and she was looking under the passenger's seat for something.

Right then, without at first distinguishing it, he heard the rumble of a large engine approaching on the other side of the avenue of eucalyptuses, and then the blue-and-yellow curves of the large front end of some kind of truck appeared. Zoe's head popped up. Stoney noticed that. Then he noticed the words "Sunset Towing," and after that the long bed of the tow truck and on it something red. Oh, yes, he thought for the very smallest moment, and then, as the truck slowed to a halt, he saw a thing he had never imagined in his whole life, Jerry's red Jaguar, windows and headlights smashed, and the finish keyed in long strokes from front to back.

Zoe's voice said, "Oh, Stoney! What happened?" and Max's voice said, "What's going on?," but for the life of him he did not know.

DAY NINE · Tuesday, April 1, 2003

Simon thought that there was still a chance they could get caught by Joe Blow, even though they were back behind one of the sofas in what amounted to the living room but here was called "the salon," which made him think of a beauty parlor, but actually was a hotel-lobby-like space with a bar at one end. If he were to lift his head over the back of the sofa (but of course he was in no position to do so), he would see the stars and the moon through the giant arched true-divided-light window at the other end, and the lawn falling away to the dark trees below. Right above him, where he had just been fellated by Monique, was a huge painting by a Russian artist named Kramskoy. The painting was of a large green-gold field under a blue sky. Near some birches in the corner were a woman, children, and a small dog. It was entitled *Sofya Andreyevna Tolstoy Taking a Walk with Three of Her Children*. Simon, who had no idea how to read Russian, knew this because he had asked Joe Blow about the painting during dinner. Joe Blow had said that it was a great unknown piece of art by a famous artist who had also done a portrait of the woman's husband. Joe Blow suspected that Kramskoy had done this painting while at the Tolstoys' estate, even though there was no record of his doing so. Personally, Joe Blow said he preferred this composition to the famous portrait of the novelist, for the very reason that the figures were so small and seemingly ordinary. "But look," he had said, "how they are having fun. The dog especially is enjoying himself." All of the figures were dappled by the thin shade of the birch leaves. When you looked at them, you wanted to squint your eyes and try to see them more clearly. It was a mysterious and alluring effect. Simon liked the painting very much, but that was not the reason that Monique had been giving him a blow job underneath it, or the reason that he had performed the same operation simultaneously upon Marya. And it had only just turned mid-night; there was no guaranteee that the rest of the household was asleep, or even in their rooms for the night, which was probably the reason the three of them were behind the couch in the salon. Simon's fine appreciation for the pleasurable dangers of possibly getting caught doing sexual things seemed to be shared by Monique and Marya more than by any other girls he knew.

Marya reached over the back of the couch, pulled down a needlework pillow, and placed it under his head. The three of them then settled back, not too uncomfortably, really, on the Oriental carpet. The girls nestled against him. It was kind of cozy. The house was warm, and they were still naked. He bent his knees and put his feet flat on the rug. Marya bent her knees and tucked them under his. That was better.

"He hated sex," said Monique.

"Who?" said Marya.

"Tolstoy," said Monique.

"Who was that?" said Simon.

"Leo Tolstoy," said Marya. "He was a great Russian novelist."

"You mean the husband of that lady in the painting?" said Simon. There was a lot of information that he had passed on acquiring. His mother still told a story about how, when he was six, she had asked him why he thought people celebrated Christmas, and it had turned out after several questions that he didn't know who Jesus was. He said, "I like that painting." He felt he could say this with conviction and authority, because he was a graphic-arts major.

"Kramskoy," said Monique in a clear voice. The lights above the painting came up.

"I know," said Simon. "Joe Blow told me about it."

"I'm not telling you the painter's name," said Monique. "Each of the paintings in the room is programmed to light up individually. Those two over there are both by Ivan Shishkin, so you have to say"—she lowered her voice to a whisper so the paintings wouldn't hear—"'Ivan' for the one by the door and 'Shishkin' for the one by the window."

"Tolstoy hated sex," said Monique. "I read one of his books once. I thought it was going to be about music, but it was about a man who kills his wife because he thinks she is cheating on him. Really, he's already looking for a reason to kill her, because he's ashamed of having sex and thinks that even married people should have as little sex as possible. Of course"—she gestured toward the painting—"he got her pregnant over and over, and they had thirteen children."

"In the book?" said Marya.

"No, in his life," said Monique. "And on their honeymoon, he showed her his diaries about all the whores he'd slept with before he married her."

"Can you imagine?" said Marya.

"She was the one who wrote all his books out longhand. And I'm talking about thousands of pages. I mean, have you ever had one of those boyfriends who, the more you do what they want, the more they actually can't stand you?" said Monique.

"Remember that guy Lukacz?" replied Marya.

"That Hungarian?" said Monique.

Simon felt Marya nod against his chest. "Lukacz, who said he was a gastroenterology medical student? I don't think he really was. I think he worked in a Kinko's on Sunset, because I was walking past there once, and I looked in the window, and there he was behind the counter, and when he saw me looking at him, he bent down and pretended to be putting some things away. I watched him for a minute, but I didn't go in."

"I would have gone in," said Monique.

"He was like that, though," said Marya. "'Put your coat on. Button your blouse. Order the chicken, not the steak. We are going to see *Nightmare on Elm Street.*' I did what he said, and he praised me and told me he loved me, but then he talked to all of his friends in front of me about how women have no ideas of their own and never do anything original, and the whole time he was stroking my thigh under the table. I think he thought he was turning me on, because then he would give me this secret smile, like we shared something."

"Was he?" said Simon. "Was he turning you on, I mean?"

"Simon is still here," said Monique. The two girls cuddled closer to him, and Marya began stroking the hair on his chest.

"Well," said Marya, "I was turned on, but not by that. He was just good-looking. That's enough for a while."

"I do remember that guy," said Monique. "He looked like Colin Farrell."

"That was the first thing I noticed about him when I met him and the last thing I missed when he was gone."

"Do you have boyfriends now?" said Simon.

"Do we?" said Marya.

"I don't think we can say that we do," said Monique.

"The only men around are Joe and Raph and the gardeners," said Marya. "Joe and Raph are gay, and the gardeners are Mexican." She sounded as if these disadvantages were equal and equally self-evident.

"Listen to this," said Monique, and then she began to speak rapidly in what sounded to Simon like Russian. Simon said, "Hey! Be polite." He gave Monique a pinch on the ass, and her ass felt good to the pinch, not hard but full of tensile strength. She laughed and said, "Ouch! I was just telling Marya about our friend Svetlana, who was here before. I'm afraid she's come to a bad end."

Marya giggled.

"I want to know," said Simon.

"Well, Svetlana came with me from France, and the whole time we were on the plane to L.A., she talked about how she was going to be discovered for the movies because she was so beautiful. She thought it would happen the first week. She said she would always remember me and be my friend no matter what happened to her, because she was the sort of person who remembered her humble beginnings—"

"In a town on the Volga, no less!" exclaimed Marya.

"—even though she was so beautiful."

"What did she look like?" asked Simon.

"She looked like Britney Spears," said Marya.

"But there already is one of those!" exclaimed Monique. The two girls laughed. "By the time we'd been here a month, and no stardom, she was beside herself," Monique continued, "and then, one day, she was shopping in Gelson's and a man came up to her and discovered her! He said he was a producer of Christian films, and he wanted her to be in his new movie. But she had to join his church. It was some storefront church somewhere, but this was fine with her, because she thought that she would have stardom and salvation at the same time, and it seemed like she couldn't lose, and so she told Joe Blow that she was going to be in a movie, and she gave notice. She left here, and the man found her an apartment, where supposedly she was an inspiration to him while he worked on the script. She went to his church every Sunday and Wednesday, and that was the last thing we heard of her, but she called me today, Marya, and she said that she had witnessed a miracle, and the miracle was going to be in the movie. She was very excited."

"What was the miracle?" asked Simon.

"I can guess," said Marya.

"This man, I think his name is Roger Something—"

"No doubt," said Simon. "In English, 'Roger' is a slang word for 'fuck.'"

"I never heard that before. So, a few days ago, she was with Roger at the church, and she started nagging him about the movie, and he told her to shut up and gave her a hard time, and she flounced out and was going to try to get Joe to give her her job back. Then, Thursday, Roger came to her apartment and went down on his knees and said that a very strange thing had happened in the night—the angel Gabriel had come to him and reprimanded him and beaten him with a stick! And he had some bruises on his

shoulders and his back, supposedly from this beating. He said that the angel
Gabriel wanted to come to her in the body of a man and pay homage to her
beauty. She was very excited. So, that first day, he said that she could name
the man whose body the angel Gabriel would make use of, and so she said,
'Matthew McConaughey,' and Roger said okay and went away.

"The next day, Roger came back to her apartment and said that the angel
Gabriel had visited him again in the night, and had said that it would be
better for her if he visited Svetlana in the body of Roger. However, he promised that Roger himself would know nothing of the visit. His body would be
there, but his mind would be replaced by that of the angel—"

"Yeah, yeah, yeah," said Simon, laughing.

"That night, Roger shows up at her apartment in a white outfit, and he
parades around telling her about heaven and all the cherubim and sera-
phim, and brings her regards from her grandmothers and also from Tsar
Nicholas—"

Marya laughed at this, and the three of them wriggled into a more comfortable position. Monique interrupted herself and said "Off." The light
above the painting went off, the room turned blue, and she lowered her
voice. She said, "And she said to me, 'And the angel Gabriel came unto me
four times in the one night, and then he slept beside me, but after I fell
asleep, the angel Gabriel vanished.' When Roger showed up later, he acted
completely as though he didn't know what happened, and she believed
him. 'In fact,' she said, 'I tested him, and he had never even heard of Tsar
Nicholas!' They intend to put this miracle in the movie *just the way it
occurred!*" The two girls laughed merrily again.

"That seems like a lot of effort just to have sex with some girl," said
Simon.

"I always said it would take a miracle to get Svetlana into bed," said
Marya, and the two girls laughed again.

Then Monique said to him, "Are you comfortable still?"

"Not especially, but I'm okay." Actually, he had a decided crick in his
neck.

"I want to go to bed," said Monique. "It's after midnight."

Simon knew that her previous night had included Charlie. Marya said to
him, "You can sleep in, but we have to be up by seven." The three of them
sat up and stretched, and Monique began reaching for their clothes, which
were scattered behind the couch. The room was not dark at all. The huge
window was as bright as a movie screen, and the high white ceiling seemed
to gather the light that came from it and reflect it downward, upon the
paintings hanging on the walls and the pieces of antique china and the traditional Russian boxes that sat on the shining tables. Pale areas in several of

the paintings—the sky in the Kramskoy, a campfire in one of the others, the eyes of some forest animals in still another—caught the shimmering light and cast it back. He said, "This is a beautiful room."

"Look at this," said Marya. "This is a silver samovar from the 1840s. Joe says it belonged to the family of General Gorchakov." The moonlight reflected off a tall silver object shaped like a hot-air balloon on legs, with a small protruding tap. The silver was chased and polished, and Simon could make out figures progressing around the perimeter of the widest part— some dogs on a leash, and a man with a gun.

"They are chasing a girl," said Monique. "She isn't wearing much. She's on the back."

The knob on top of the samovar was in the shape of a delicate spiraling shell with a point at the apex. "That shell is called a Neptune," whispered Marya. Exploring the room, both Monique and Marya had become more cautious. When Simon reached for one of the cups, Marya prevented him from touching it. She said, "This is the favorite room. We shouldn't be in here."

Next to the samovar was an antique clock—a horse, rearing up, with jewels for eyes, and on the horse, a man, gold-plated and brightly enameled. Monique said, "When that clock was new, the rider would swing his sword every time it struck the hour, but it doesn't work anymore. The eyes are supposed to be diamonds." She shrugged. The hands had stopped at midnight.

It was much darker in the entry hall—the big double door was closed, of course, and the two windows, one on each side of the door, were tall and narrow. He could not see the tapestries, but he could sense them hanging on the walls, more alive than paintings. Monique gave him a kiss on the cheek, sisterly and kind. Then, very quickly, she stooped down and gave him another kiss, on the fly of his jeans, not sisterly at all. Marya kissed him on the other cheek, and then the two girls whispered, "Night!" They put their arms around one another's waists as they disappeared, yawning, down the corridor that led toward the kitchen wing of the house. Simon went to the bottom of the staircase and looked upward. He actually felt like going to bed. Life here at home was changing his daily routine. At school, he rarely got to bed before 4 a.m., if then.

He put his hand on the carved banister and began to climb the stairs. He suddenly remembered what his mother had said at dinner: "Isn't it strange that here we are and over in Iraq there's a war? And when people look back on this in fifty years, they will think that we voted for that war, when we didn't. We will look to them like those German people in 1939."

And then the men—he had seen it—had all glanced at one another as if his mom had a condition of some sort. Charlie had said, "Luckily, we'll be dead by then, so what they think won't be any of our business."

The fact was, Simon thought the war in Iraq was interesting. He could hear himself say it to his mother: "Interesting! Just interesting, Mom! I didn't say 'attractive' or 'appealing.' I just said 'interesting.'" It was interesting the way a car wreck or a fire or a horror movie was interesting. Once, a couple of years ago, he had been driving late at night somewhere on the flats outside of Davis—he was drunk, and he didn't even know where he was, just sort of on automatic pilot in terms of getting back to his dorm— and he drove past a house burning down in a flat field. The whole house was actually burnt to the ground. The only thing still burning was its outline, a bright flaming set of rectangles in the grass. Even drunk, he had realized that the deserted scene was tremendously mysterious, since if it was a house fire, the firemen hadn't put it all the way out—and that was in California (though in the wet of winter). But if it was arson, then that was mysterious, too. His roommates dismissed the whole thing when he told them about it—just some abandoned building put to the torch by a farmer or his kids—but they hadn't seen it, seen the strange abandoned flaming weirdness of it unexpected in the middle of a dark, overcast night. He hadn't had his camera with him, and had failed to take the best pictures of his life.

So—how could he present to the mom this idea that maybe Iraq was interesting, interesting in a photographic sense, but in another sense, too? The war wasn't supposed to last long, and (he realized completely how selfish this was) he was sorry in a photographic sense to have missed it. What was it Paul had been saying the other day about the smashed archeological sites and old buildings? Iraq was a one-time opportunity, if you looked at it in a certain photographic way. He came to the top of the stairs and gazed down the long corridor of bedrooms. He was thinking about Iraq. He tiptoed past his mom's door, because it seemed like she might easily read his thoughts, open the door, and leap out at him. But she didn't. What if the war were to go on longer? Past the summer, say? What might he do then? He coughed quietly to clear this thought.

Let's see. The room next to his mom and Max was empty—that might be the suite Paul had been talking about at dinner, so that had two doors. On the left side of the corridor was a large closet, and then, he thought, Cassie, and next to her Delphine, surrealism and ornithology. Next to Delphine was Paul; across from Paul, Charlie; next to Paul, his own room; across from him, the Amber Room; past the Amber Room (he paused), the sound of voices. Zoe's room. She had invited him in there sometime in the afternoon, and he had been duly impressed with the grandeur. Zoe professed herself uncomfortable in such a place, and maybe she was, but he had seen her in enough movies—four or five, was it?—that to his eyes the Gold Room was a perfectly fine set for her, as good as any other, and she moved around it gracefully, neither overwhelming it nor failing to balance it. The room remained the immovable object; she remained the irresistible force. But she hadn't asked him to linger, or kissed him, which he had rather expected her to do, given how much they both seemed to enjoy the other day. His visit had soon shaded into awkwardness, and at dinner he had sat on the same side of the table but at the opposite end from her. In the general dinner conversation about her next movie, Max's next project, his own college education, Paul's trip later in the year to France, and Delphine's wish to buy a laptop computer, he and Zoe had exchanged only a few impersonal remarks.

He edged up to the door and leaned toward it. Zoe's was the only voice, intermittent, resonant, and easily understandable. She was not singing, but she might as well have been, since she was projecting from her diaphragm. It was hard to tell whom she was talking to, or, rather, yelling at, since no voice responded when hers fell silent. Was she watching one of her own movies? He glanced at Paul's door, but it revealed nothing. He stilled his body and listened.

In the Amber Room, Isabel had intended to wait up for Stoney, but had drifted off to sleep. The DVD they were watching, of *Harlan County, U.S.A.*, a movie she had always meant to watch, had not turned out to be as compelling as she had wanted it to be, and did not inspire her to become a documentary filmmaker the way she thought it would. It was no longer running; the DVD player was stuck on the introductory table of contents, and had been for at least ten minutes. The room was silent. Isabel was having a dream. The dream was of their old house in Kauai, but it was not on the beach in the southern part of the island, as it had been. While she had been away, her father had had the house moved inland, and now it overlooked that spot—the rainiest spot in the world, at Waipio Canyon—where the trade winds got caught on the summit of the mountain and dropped something like four or five hundred inches of rain every year. In the dream, she was telling her father that he had made a terrible mistake, because, although the view of the waterfall was pretty (and the view from the house in her dream was just like the view she had gotten from helicopter rides), there was nothing to do there now—you couldn't even lie out. Max was shaking his head stubbornly and insisting he had done the right thing because the property was more valuable. In the dream, she kept going up to him and butting her head against his chest, not terribly hard but hard enough to express annoyance, and he kept caving his body so as not to receive the blow, which made her angrier.

The door creaked loudly, and she woke up. When she woke up, she saw that she was in the Amber Room, and that the door had not opened. She was still alone in the Amber Room, propped up on the bed with her head on her chest and a quilt over her legs. Her shoulders hurt from her odd position. The video screen was on. She picked up the remote and turned it off.

She said, "On, left," and more lights came up in the Amber Room. She looked around, and then at her watch. He had only been gone for twenty minutes.

He would be out looking at the car again. She sighed. What had happened to the red Jaguar was not good, but it was not, in the end, mysterious. She had driven to Starbucks, been unable to find a spot in the lot, parked in the thirty-minute spot on the street, and run in. In the chaos of losing the keys, she had forgotten she was in a thirty-minute spot. And when Elena picked her up, they had not called the police or parking control, and sometime after they left, the red Jaguar had been towed to the city impound lot. Joe Blow had found it. But the car that came out of the impound lot was not the same car that went in. The guy who ran the impound lot had not, really, shown a whole lot of either surprise or remorse at the broken windows and lights or the scratched paint. He had shrugged, according to Joe Blow, and said, "You park your car illegally, and you go to the impound lot, and it ain't like going to a private garage, you know? This one fellow sued the city of West Hollywood. Guess how far he got?" And the guy laughed, said Joe Blow. So that was that.

She and Stoney did not see eye to eye on the size and importance of the damage to the car. When she and Elena had gotten back, the car had been parked out in front. She, Isabel, had been shocked and sorry once again that she had dropped the keys in the toilet, but the windows, the headlights, and even the red finish had looked fixable to her. It would be expensive, and the car was unusable for a week or two, but, she thought, it was a car. No lives were lost; no species had gone extinct. They had gone back down the hill and picked up the Volvo.

But it had dumbfounded Stoney. He said, "Did you see it? Did you see it?"

She said, "I did see it. I do see it. I don't know why Joe Blow had it brought here and not taken to the Jaguar dealer. It's the middle of the week. We'll get them to take it right to the Jaguar dealer—"

Stoney could not stop looking at it. She would've had to take him by the shoulders and turn him away and walk him into the house and sit him down and give him some smelling salts or something, right out of a movie, but she hadn't done that. She had gone into the house, exchanged her tight jeans for the loose ones, and then gone into the dining room and had a sandwich. When she went back upstairs for the swimsuit, he was sitting on the bed of the Amber Room with the remote in his hand, but there was nothing on the screen, and it was a perfectly beautiful day out, so she said, "Come swimming with me," and then "I'm so sorry about the car," and then "Oh, come on," and then "What's the matter with you?" and "I think you're overreacting," and then "Oh, for God's sake." In a way, it was his fault that she had kept talking, because he hadn't reacted. It would have been way better if there had been another person with her, someone who had not actually been the cause of the impoundment, because then she could have maintained a remorseful silence while the other person snapped him out of his shock or whatever you would call it. After two more remarks, "I can't believe this" and "What's with you, anyway?," she had flounced off with her suit—yes, she had flounced, unfortunately, and it was only by the time she was out to the pool that she understood the whole thing, the identification of the car with the father, Jerry, and the unresolved trauma of the father's death, and probably his illness, too, and then that opened the door to the earlier trauma with his mother's death, another car-related event that was surely unresolved, because, in addition to the fact that how could anyone deal with that, there was Dorothy, who was a Hollywood rhinoceros if ever there was one, whose favorite remark was "If you show them any weakness in this town, they'll eat you alive!"

But the problem was that, when all of this came to her as she went into the poolhouse and changed into her suit, what she felt was a shiver of apprehension. For the first time in her life, she knew, really knew, that he was way older than she was, and that his complexities were more than set— they were confirmed and habitual. The very thing that she had always responded to in Stoney, that he was reliably himself, had this other side to it that she had never thought about when he was only coming and going (and, of course, she hadn't really seen him in a year); she had never paid much attention to it.

She had dived into the deep end, where the virgin's hair swirled into the tail of the unicorn, and in the middle of her second lap had realized that in fact she was precisely different from the person her father thought she was by the measure of Stoney's influence. It was scientific. Here would be Max's wish, that a young man would come along, someone about her age or a year older, and he and she would be equally idealistic and optimistic, and they would be just self-centered enough so that they would set out confidently to save the world, or some part of it, African felines or babies suffering from malnutrition and dehydration, and they would work out a plan and start a family, not knowing any better, and their life would become a *fait accompli* before they realized how hard it was, and then, after they realized that, they would do as everyone else does, wake up from their idealism and go on to achieve what they could. Typical fuzzy thinking in the older generation, Isabel had always thought.

But, yes, Stoney had ruined her for the raw boys, for their ill-assorted body parts, spotty faces, brash ignorances, lack of money. But he had also, maybe, ruined her for himself, because, as the Jaguar thing was showing her, she wasn't ready for whatever today presaged. The reason, she realized, that Stoney had been reluctant to claim her in front of Max was only in part that he was wrong to have slept with her when she was sixteen, it was also that, to her father, he was a known quantity, a *formed* quantity. Since he had already betrayed his early promise, now his only chance was redemption, and that chance was slim. He knew it and Max knew it. Only she, Isabel, had not known it, but now she did. As she swam her laps, the whole thing unrolled in front of her like a big map, and once she had seen it, she had known she would never see it differently.

And at this very moment, as if scripted, Max had appeared, in his swim trunks, and slipped into the pool. She was swimming laps, and he began to swim laps, and everything about this situation had the marks of a setup of a particular kind—parent needs to have a talk, so he arranges it so that he and daughter will bump into one another in a casual manner. She kept swimming; he kept swimming. Ultimately, though, after thirty-two laps, she had to stop, and he was on her. So she did the child thing, and slithered over to him through the water and, when he stood up, pushed his hair back and kissed him on the cheek, then said, "You can't just paddle around. You have to raise your heartbeat to at least a hundred and forty."

He smiled and said, "Okay."

She stretched out on her back, floating in the water (but with her ears immersed so that she could honestly say that she couldn't hear him). She kept a happy look on her face. Then she had a bright idea and said, "Personally, I think Elena and Simon fit in pretty well. I mean, I'm not asking if you've made any final commitments or anything. But I think it's been pretty comfortable."

"Do you?"

She stood up in the water and showed enthusiasm. "I really do." She gave him a grin.

But he was not to be deflected. He asked it anyway: "So what's going on between you and Stoney? I find this a little surprising."

"What did Stoney say?" But she knew what Stoney had said; they had talked about it the night before. She only asked in order to gain time.

"He said he didn't want to offend your autonomy or your personhood in any way."

"You shouldn't make fun of me, but if he said that, he was right."

"He referred me to you."

She kept quiet, just paddling her hands in the blue surface of the water. Finally, he said, "So. What do you say?"

It came easily, as if she had thought it up and rehearsed it. She said, "We've been friends. A couple of times he was in Santa Cruz and he called me up and took me to lunch, and then, once, he was there overnight, so he took me out to dinner and a movie. I mean, Stoney is such an old friend, I was always glad to see him. And then, since I came back for Jerry's funeral last year, we've been talking on the phone pretty regularly—say, every week or so—and we've had good talks. He's given me a lot of advice about Leo, and actually, I thought he would have mentioned some of those conversations to you, so I guess he didn't?" She glanced at him. Every single word and implication of this was false.

Max shook his head.

"Huh. Well, anyway, I thought we got to be good friends over the last year, and then, suddenly, in the last week, we just got more interested. Don't ask if we're sleeping together!"

"Why not?"

"Because I don't want to talk about that with you." After this, she let there be a moment of complete silence, so that she would seem to be resolute on this score, and, sure enough, he didn't ask. She suspected he decided right then to assume that they weren't having sex, that maybe they were just enjoying the Amber Room together. To reinforce this idea, she said, "It's fun to stay in the Amber Room. It's like going to camp or something."

At this point, Max had ducked under the water, clearly checked, if not yet checkmated, and then he had taken the parental coward's way out—he had said, "This thing with Leo isn't as over as you think it is. Be cautious."

"You know I am." Even though, of course, she wasn't. "Do I act on impulse? Don't you know you can trust me?" She had said that all through high school.

"I worry about you." Parents were supposed to sound apologetic on that one, and he did.

She had finished it off with "I love you, Dad. I love you, Mad Max," her old nickname for him. And he said, fatally to any ongoing discussion, "I love you, too, Isabel. You know how much."

"I do." She hugged and kissed him in the water, and if her fingers hadn't been crossed about her lies behind his back, well, they were crossed in her mind.

Now Stoney had been gone for half an hour, but, really, where would he go? She had the keys to the Volvo in her purse (she checked), and it was important that he feel that he was free to do what he wanted to, wasn't it?

She sat back down on the bed and slipped her feet between the sheets. She picked up the book she had been reading for the last two weeks, *The Botany of Desire*, and turned to where she had been reading about potatoes. It was interesting. Every time she picked it up, it was interesting.

Her justification for bold-faced lying was simple—over and above the fact that women had a perfect right to keep emotional secrets in the context of patriarchy, even benign patriarchy, it was also true that she hadn't the foggiest idea of where the truth, should she begin to tell it, would actually take her. This was exactly the wrong moment for her to be talking herself into anything, and any story she might tell her father would amount to talking herself into something, something with Stoney or without him. As soon as she and Max might agree on even the most trivial point—let's say, that Stoney was tentative and insecure, which he was—then that would be a fact that would have to be contended with.

This conversation had worked well enough—Max didn't pursue the subject afterward. But it also had another effect, which was to alert her to a conversation at dinner that she might otherwise not have noticed.

Cassie had asked Charlie a question. She had said, "Were you talking to Monique? What's she like? She's very interesting-looking. I can't figure out whether she's twenty-five or thirty-five."

"She'll soon be thirty-four," said Charlie.

"You were talking to her."

Charlie lifted his eyebrows with what Isabel saw to be intentional significance, meant to indicate that talking was the least of it. Then he said, "She came to my room. She was interested in my rejuvenation techniques."

The others mostly kept eating, but Isabel said, "Was she nice?"

"She was nice. She is nice," said Charlie. "She's lived in France, too. We had quite a long talk." Then he cleared his throat. Lies, lies, lies, thought Isabel. At that very moment, Monique entered the room carrying two bottles of wine, a red and a white. She had on black jeans and a pink blouse; instead of seeming to wait on them, she seemed to be doing them a favor. Monique set the bottles of wine, which were open, on the table beside Max and walked out of the room again. For Isabel, who hadn't looked very closely at her before, it was a perfect opportunity to give her the eyeball, which she did. Monique was beautiful. She looked like Charlize Theron, but short, maybe five six. After Monique had been gone maybe two minutes, long enough to have gotten back to the kitchen, Isabel said, "Which rejuvenation techniques was she most interested in?"

Now Charlie looked right at her, and she knew that he found her pursuit of this subject suspect. Since that night by the pool at the other house, they

had hardly spoken to one another, and whatever friendliness she had exhib-
ited toward him as a child had completely vanished. But, really, she wasn't
trying to be mean, she was just authentically curious about lying, and also,
what would a girl who looked like Charlize Theron think there would be to
talk about with a guy like Charlie?

He said, "We mostly talked about the Chinese herbs I use. She didn't
know much about Chinese herbs, more about French skin-care products."

"Do you think she wants to break into the movies?" said Cassie.

"No," said Charlie. "She didn't say that she wants to break into the
movies. We talked for quite a long time. She told me about her life in Russia, and her marriage there, and some things about her life here. She asked
me about my life. In some ways, I sensed that she opened up to me. I'm sure
it doesn't mean anything. I think the staff is a little lonely here in a way." He
sniffed. He said, "Anyway." He shrugged and poured himself another glass
of wine. Isabel literally could not believe that anyone would care in the
least about Charlie's rejuvenation techniques. The very thought defied her
entire understanding of human nature. Maybe Monique was paid a premium for conversing pleasantly with the guests? That was the only way
Isabel could account for it. But he was a good liar, and she liked him a little
better for it.

She decided to put her conversation with her father out of her mind.

If she were ever to come back to this house, she would ask to be put in
the Comedy Room. She had spent maybe half an hour in there this afternoon, looking around, and she still hadn't gotten all the jokes. One of them,
though, that she had pointed out to Cassie that Cassie hadn't noticed, was a
small window, maybe twelve inches by twelve inches, in a closet, that
opened onto a simple scene of the driveway. This scene was also painted on
the window, except with one addition, a fly. It was funny in itself, but what
was also funny about it, Isabel and Cassie agreed, was that you had to go
looking for it.

She closed her eyes.

It was a very comfortable bed.

She drew long breaths in an encouraging way, demonstrating to herself
how to stop worrying and go to sleep.

But of course she couldn't. Within moments, she had thrown back the
covers and stood up. Within moments after that, she had crossed to the
door, turned the embossed handle, and opened it. The corridor outside was
dim, but no dimmer, probably, than the Amber Room. She put her head
out and looked right, toward the staircase, for Stoney, then left. She didn't
see him. It was only then that she noticed Simon, who was looking at her, or

at least his head was turned toward her. He was standing across the hall, in front of her mother's door. He was standing, not walking. She said, "Have you seen Stoney? What are you doing?"

He said, "No. I haven't seen him at all. I just came up from downstairs. What are you doing?" And he came across the the corridor toward her and said, in a friendly way, "Hey," and she stepped back and let him in.

Simon had not seen the Amber Room in the daylight, but now, at night, his first thought was that it was a dope-smoker's paradise. Because he was still a little baked from the joint he had shared with the two M's a while ago, he stopped dead in the middle of the floor and stared around. Everything in here glinted or vanished. It was like standing in a forest in the moonlight. He put his hand out and stepped to his right, and his hand met the wall before he had thought it would, or maybe he had thought his hand would enter the wall as if the wall were the surface of water. He said, "Wow." The wall was cool to the touch, not like a painted or a papered wall. Isabel went over to the bed, which was huge and many-pillowed. She flopped down, looking at him, and her feet bounced. She said, "Did you see Stoney anywhere?"

"Was that Stoney in with your mom? She was yelling at someone."

Isabel shrugged and then rolled her eyes. "Were you listening outside her door?"

"Well, I heard her. I was a little surprised. I stopped—"

"Isn't your room at the other end of the corridor?"

Simon considered this question for a moment, then said, "Well, it could have been Stoney in there. But I didn't hear a guy's voice, and I didn't, uh, have a chance to make out what she was saying. I was actually thinking that it might be a DVD playing or something. That's what I was thinking right when you opened the door."

"Maybe he is in there. I hope so, actually, because then I don't have to worry about him wandering around the grounds in a state."

"A state of what?"

"A state of—oh, I don't even know. That's what I was trying to decide when I opened the door. I mean, I was all set to go to sleep, and then I thought about him toppling into the pool with his hands in the pockets of his jeans and sinking to the bottom without even taking his hands out of his pockets. It's like in a movie. His eyes are open and his hands are in his pockets and he just goes down."

"*Harold and Maude*," said Simon. "Or that John Cusack movie—what's it called?—where he tries to commit suicide over and over."

"I didn't see that one."

By this time, Simon had run the palm of his hand along the cool wall, feeling the odd glassy smoothness of its mysterious interface with the air of the room, and he was about to sit down in one of the chairs across from the bed when Isabel said, "Go into the bathroom."

He went into the bathroom and turned on the light. A brilliant gloss of black and ocher stripes seemed to blaze up all around him. It was startling. He recognized it as tigereye immediately, even though he had maybe seen one tigereye necklace in his whole life, when he went to Cabo with two guys his senior year in high school and they looked at some jewelry for some reason. He put out the bathroom light.

"Mom's are malachite. That's green, you know?"

"Huh. You should go down the hall and look at mine. They're inch-thick glass with designs of fish and coral etched on the underside and lit from below."

She gazed at him, and then, after a long moment, she said, almost as if surprised, "Well, maybe I will. I'll do that tomorrow."

"So—why are you always so pissed at your mom?"

Isabel stared at him, and Simon suddenly realized that this question, which he had uttered with mere curiosity, had more than idle importance to Isabel, and he wished he hadn't said anything. He smiled. Usually with girls, his smile was pretty reliable, he had found, but she did not respond to it by smiling, or even softening up. It came to him that if he had had a sister Isabel would have been just the sort of sister he would have wanted, because she was the sort of girl you could prank all day long and she would fall for it every time. This whole thought made him get fond of her right there. Suddenly, instead of waiting for her answer to his question, he said, "Say, why in the world did you get involved with Leo Decker? He's such a stiff. It's like he's never been a kid. One time, I was hanging out with Roman. I mean, we were about eleven, so Leo was maybe thirteen. And we watched him trim a pair of Dr. Scholl's insoles for his loafers with a nail scissors. The whole time, he was explaining to us that he couldn't get them exactly right with a regular scissors." He cleared his throat, and right then she started laughing, ha-ha-ha. Really merry and happy laughter. Simon found himself laughing, too. Then she said, "Oh, God, I've seen Leo do that so many times! Every time he bought a new pair of shoes, at least. Insoles! Nail scissors! That's so funny! He was thirteen?"

"Well, he must have been—"

"What I think now is that I got involved with Leo because I don't have a sense of humor."

"No shit."

"What else would it be? I was with Leo for five years. You know, we went to see *American Pie* and didn't laugh one time. He didn't laugh and I didn't laugh. We went to see *Election* and he kept saying, 'That's funny,' but he didn't actually laugh."

"I've seen you laugh."

"You have?"

"You laughed when we were watching *Casablanca*."

"No, I didn't. I said something, and you laughed. People laugh at me, but I don't have a sense of humor, and I don't laugh."

"Your mom has a sense of humor."

"You've noticed that?"

"Well, sure. I think she says funny things that she knows are funny at the time. But she's good at it. She never goes for the laugh, but a few minutes later, after the conversation has moved on or something, you remember what she said, and you smile." He shrugged. "And you laughed just now."

"Maybe there's hope for me, then." She paused for a long moment, then went on. "Anyway, the very reason I'm here is that Leo has to have time to do some sort of process on his marijuana garden before he can move out, or, rather, before *it* can move out, and I didn't want to live with either him or *it* any longer, so I came out to L.A. But he has to do this whatever it is with a tweezers, and so it is taking quite a long time."

"One thing I learned up at Davis is that agriculture is labor-intensive."

"Do you like it there? I never thought of going there."

"Mom thought I would be safer there. Anyway, when I applied, it was there or Riverside. I didn't get into UCSD or Cal Poly. I was going to major in surfing, but when I didn't get into the surf universities, I ended up majoring in highway driving. I've put a hundred and ten thousand miles on my car in three and a half years."

"That's a lot of emissions." She looked completely serious, and Simon had to admit that, yes, looked at from a certain point of view, that fact only added to the pointlessness of those many pointless hours on the road. She went on, "You should plant some trees."

"What kind of trees?"

"Depends on where you plant them. In some places, you would only want to plant native species, but in other places, you could plant species that had been introduced a long time ago and had adapted appropriately to that particular ecosystem. There are programs that replant the rain forest if you make a certain contribution. A hundred and ten thousand miles would be a thousand dollars or a thousand trees per year."

"You know that right off the top of your head?"

"The math isn't that hard when you start with a hundred thousand. And anyway, I can do that because I don't take time out to make jokes."

"That's a joke."

She stared at him again, then smiled, so he didn't ask her why he should plant trees in Brazil when he was driving in California. Actually, she had a nice smile, wide and sudden. It was the Zoe part of her Max-ish face. But it didn't have the variations and flourishes that Zoe's smile had, and it reminded Simon that he had to continue to think of his adventure with Zoe as precisely that—a one-time adventure—or he would start to think more about it. He looked around, then said, "Don't you think it's kind of dark in here?"

"Well, I was trying to go to sleep. But, yes, this room is more of a daytime room. When the sun is shining in the windows, then everything lights up. It's eye-popping, really, but I have no idea if all the panels are amber, and it seems sort of tasteless and philistine to ask Joe Blow. At night, though, it's a little depressing. Stoney keeps calling this room 'the Abyss.' Maybe he went to sleep on a couch somewhere."

"Do you think it was him your mom was yelling at?"

"That could have been Paul. I sensed at dinner that Paul was due."

"Why was that?"

"Basically, she just doesn't believe in Paul any longer."

"He told me an interesting thing today. He said he knew Max in junior high. Max was in ninth grade and Paul was in sixth grade. In New Jersey. I gather that Max and his friends fucked with Paul in some way. He didn't tell me exactly what they did. But he said that he recognized Max the second day we were at the other house, and he remembered his address, too, because he had to pass your dad's house on the way to school and it always made him nervous."

"Did he tell my dad about it?"

"I don't think so."

"See? That's a perfect example of why Paul can't last. He doesn't have normal instincts. I don't know if his instincts are better than normal or worse than normal, but when you expect him to say something, he doesn't, and when you don't expect him to say something, he does. I think he tries to be enigmatic."

"Well, it's probably just as well, since I don't get the sense that Paul believes in your mother, either."

And now, at this confirmation of her own opinion, her face fell. The two M's were way less trouble than this, he had to admit. At that moment, the door opened inward and, after about a second, revealed Stoney, who looked at him but not exactly in surprise. "Hey," said Simon. Stoney didn't say anything, but when Isabel jumped off the bed and said "Hey!" he kissed her on the cheek and said, "What's up?"

"Where've you been?"

Simon could tell that she was trying to make this question sound casual.

"Oh, I was looking at the car."

"I thought you might be."

"There was a pretty good moon out. Anyway, the driveway is filled with motion-sensor lights. Every time I moved, another light came on, it seemed like." He glanced at Simon, then sat down on the bed and kicked off his shoes. Isabel said, "I caught Simon spying on Mom."

Stoney looked at him, then said, "Got any dope?"

He said, "About half a j."

"Do you mind if I smoke it? Maybe it will put me to sleep."

Simon reached into his pocket and pulled out his wintergreen Altoids tin. He opened it. The joint was longer than he'd remembered. He handed it to Stoney, along with one of the kitchen matches, which Stoney took and struck on the underside of the table beside the bed. The match flared in the Amber Room, and was reflected in the mirror TV screen and, more dimly, in some of the amber panels at the head of the bed. Stoney put the joint to his lips and sucked in a long hit. Then, before he let it out, as dope-smokers were wont to do, he said the most important thing on his mind in a strangled voice that Simon could barely understand: "You know, it's okay about that car. After the shop fixes it up, I'm going to sell it on eBay and buy something else. Another sports car. A little yellow sports car, maybe a Mercedes."

"I would get—" Simon began, but Stoney interrupted him. He said, "I was looking at that car, and I thought and thought about Jerry, and I remembered something he always said that I was forgetting. He always said, 'What are you keeping this for? Life's too short! Didn't you ever hear of John Maynard Keynes?' Then he would explain why you had to keep all your possessions moving. Didn't matter if you liked it or didn't like it, sell it! Donate it! Give it to the homeless person on the corner! I can't tell you the number of times we were walking down the street and he took off his tie and handed it to a homeless guy. Once, he gave a guy his belt; once, he gave a guy his watch; and once, he gave a guy the book he was carrying in his hand, which was a hardback copy of *The Name of the Rose*, and he said to the guy, 'Here. You read it. Maybe you can make head or tail of it. I sure can't.' He would have loved eBay to pieces. He would have had me on eBay every day, selling everything in the house and the office and buying something else. You know how he furnished the Tahoe house? He found out where some cruise line he'd been on refurbished their boats. It was in a town in Alabama. He found a woman in Alabama to keep an eye out for him, and when one of those ships came in to be gutted and redone, he bought chairs and tables and beds and mirrors and a big gas grill and range and a walk-in refrigerator. Dorothy couldn't stand it, she was so embarrassed." He sighed. "But, anyway. So I'll sell the car on eBay. Life's too short, right?"

Isabel said, "Are you asking me for my opinion?"

Stoney nodded.

There was a long moment of silence, then Isabel said, "I have no idea, actually. I mean, about whether life's too short. Or how short life is."

Stoney said, "Well, for the time being, let's say it is."

Without actually planning to speak up, Simon found himself saying, not "How about I go to Iraq," but "I saw my dad last year."

Both heads swiveled in his direction.

He said, "I found him on the Internet. It wasn't hard. He was teaching in Ohio."

"Where?" said Isabel.

"Kenyon College. But he came out to San Francisco, and I met him there."

"Wow," said Isabel.

"I never told Mom, so don't tell her."

Isabel nodded.

Stoney said, "What was it like?"

Isabel said, "What was he like?"

"Well," said Simon, "imagine that you're walking down the street, and you're looking at something in a store window, and you happen to bump into someone because you aren't looking where you're going, and when you look at that guy, there's nothing about him that strikes you. He's just a guy, kind of balding, wearing glasses and a blue shirt, and you both excuse yourselves, and then the voice-over narration says, 'Simon, that is your father.' It was like that. It seemed like I could pick some other guy and have that guy be my father just as easily. That's what it seemed like, but of course he was completely convinced that I was his son, and he had all this verifying information about Mom, so I knew he was the one." Simon shrugged.

Isabel said, "What was his excuse for abandoning you?"

"Mom always said he broke up with her before I was born."

"Oh," said Isabel, her face turning red. "I didn't know that. I was making an assumption."

"There is an ass in assumption," said Stoney. He cleared his throat.

"Yes, there is," said Isabel.

"We can say that he abandoned his zygote. Or maybe his embryo. I'm not sure how far along the pregnancy was. I mean, I haven't quizzed my mom on all the aspects of the fatal interaction." Now there was an uncomfortable silence, which Simon wasn't sure how to break, since he had never had this conversation before, or even expected to have it. He tried to remember more about his encounter with "Bill."

Isabel said, "Does he have other children?"

"Well, he doesn't have a family. He said he was married, but they'd had fertility problems actually, don't tell Mom, but they decided in the end not to adopt. He teaches Milton, non-Shakespearean dramatists of the Elizabethan and Jacobean periods, freshman comp, and American leftist writers of the twentieth century. He's associate chairman of his department and does all the class scheduling and departmental paperwork. Ohio is a nice place, and he and his wife have a large perennial garden and two dogs, a golden retriever—"

"Not a golden retriever!" exclaimed Isabel skeptically.

"—and a mixed breed, part saluki."

"Are you making this up?" challenged Isabel.

"No. I remember lots of the details. I wrote them down. He is writing a novel. He described it to me. Actually, when he was first talking about it, I had this thought that it would be about me, but it was about a guy who starts paddling a canoe on some lake in Wisconsin after going to an Indian pow-wow, and decides to try going out of the lake by means of a little creek he has never explored, and eventually, some six hundred pages later, he finds himself in New Orleans, and in the interim, he has relived all of American literature through a series of dreams. He said the pow-wow and the canoe-ing thing had happened to him, but he had just gone a little way out into the creek, but that the creek actually would lead eventually to the Mississippi, yada yada yada. Anyway, he keeps working on the novel, and has had some interest, but no actual publishing offers yet. He thinks it's maybe a little too complex for today's literary world, especially for the video-game generation."

"Did you like him?" said Stoney.

"Well . . ." Simon had thought a lot about this question. He had not disliked Bill. But he had watched him over lunch. He was the sort of guy who picked up his fork and then his spoon and stared at them, then rubbed them with his thumb to make sure they were clean. He had positioned his water glass just so after every drink, and had kept the foods on his plate neatly separated. Simon said, "You know how Mom always says that when I was little, if there was a red button to push, I would push it?"

Isabel said, "I heard her say that after you socked Paul."

"Well, I didn't not like Bill. But I think I would have been that kid who always had to push the red button, and he would have been the dad who wanted everything to be just so."

"That seems so rational," said Isabel. "I don't see how you can be rational about your dad." Except, of course, she reminded herself, if you had to lie to him.

"I guess if he had been more interesting I would have been less rational. And anyway, our meeting was very short and superficial. A couple of hours, and then he said I could always contact him, and he gave me his card. I think it would be different for Mom, so that's why I never told her about it."

"Just think," said Stoney, "you've avoided the Oedipus complex entirely. You don't even *want* to kill your father and fuck your mother."

"What's an Oedipus complex?" said Simon.

"My point exactly," said Stoney.

"Nobody has those complexes anymore," said Isabel. "You have to have been born into a nineteenth-century German Jewish family to get those. Let's see. Obviously, Simon has a complex of some sort, though. Complexes are just a taxonomy of human idiosyncrasies, is what my psych professor said. And it doesn't have to be Greek, either." She scrutinized Simon for a moment, then smiled. "You know," she finally said, "I think Simon has a Trickster Coyote complex."

"Who's that?" said Simon.

"What in the world have you been taking up there in Davis?" exclaimed Isabel.

"Art. Photography. Geology. I took a couple of horticulture courses."

"Well, we learned about Trickster Coyote in my Non-European Myths and Archetypes class. Just think about a coyote and think about tricks. I mean, not just tricks on other people. One time Trickster Coyote told his ass to keep the fire going all night, and fell asleep, and the fire went out, and so when Trickster Coyote woke up in the cold, he was angry at his ass, and he lit it on fire as a punishment, and burned all his own hair off."

Simon burst out laughing. Isabel smiled. Stoney took another deep toke on the last bit of the joint. Simon said, "Well, that sounds right to me."

·

Afterward, after Elena dozed off, then woke up, then stretched against him, sighed, and opened her eyes, she said, "By the way, I looked for the Yul Brynner version all over the house and asked Joe Blow, but they don't have it. I think we should watch it when we get home tomorrow night. Just you and me."

Max tightened his arms around her and said, "That will be nice." His cock, still not completely detumescent, lay with a certain kind of weight against his leg. He pressed it against her; then she ran her fingertips over it and looked up at him, saying, "You must be getting tired of the crowd."

"I think we could spin off a few, just for a little while. I've held up better than I expected to, I'll say that." They disengaged a bit. He turned on his side and pushed the pillow more tightly against his shoulder. But she was right there. "Charlie is wearing out his welcome."

"Mmm," she said.

"And Paul, lovely man though he is."

"Though not in a physical way." Elena stretched against him again. "Which is not to say that I don't agree with him on many things. It amazes me that I could respect someone's quite unusual choices and yet not feel the slightest spark of interest in him."

"And Zoe and I are divorced, after all. I don't think we've spent this much time together in maybe fifteen years."

"Cassie could spend one night at her own house."

"Delphine could resume her customary distance."

She lengthened against him and put her leg over his. "And Simon could get the hell out and go back to school!"

He kissed her. His own house would be really quiet by now. He said, "I'm sure those floors at Stoney's place are refinished." After his little talk with Isabel, Max thought it probable that mere proximity was the source of their relationship. Proximity was easy enough to fix; time itself would fix it, and if there was something else, well, right this very moment, maybe ten minutes into what you could call his "rebirth" if you wanted to (but might also call "resumption of service," or "reprieve," or "recovery," depending on your model of the original dysfunction), he was gripped by a pleasant feeling of equanimity, especially with regard to love.

Elena said, "I would like to have some time with just Isabel, I think. We have things in common."

"Well, of course." He yawned, not out of fatigue, but out of pure relaxation. "Don't you realize that men my age usually end up with someone like their daughters, not their mothers?"

"What do men do who only have sons?"

"They hang out with the guys. Did you ever see *Goodfellas*? The good fellas are happiest in prison, slicing the garlic with a razor blade, and having no access to firearms."

"I saw that so long ago." Now she yawned. Max laughed.

She snuggled closer. Still she made no reference to the war. Maybe it was over, too, and the Zeitgeist that was no longer pressing against him, apparently, was also no longer pressing against her. "Anyway," she said, "I would like to see *Taras Bulba* by ourselves sometime this week, and then you can talk Mike into filming in Death Valley or over near Bakersfield or somewhere. And everyone can have what they want."

"What do you want?" The question slipped out, a habit from that time, months before, when she might have said, "A cup of mint tea." From the relaxation of her body, he sensed that Elena hadn't thought of the war yet, either.

But she had. She said, "I want to come down from the mountain and discover that Al Gore is president, that 9/11 never happened, which it wouldn't have, because he would have listened to his own administration's warnings rather than dismissing them, that Saddam Hussein died of natural causes, that no elections were stolen and no elderly Jews had found themselves voting for Patrick Buchanan by mistake, that George Bush had been defeated as governor of Texas by Molly Ivins, and that no economic bubbles had burst and no massive tax cuts had been passed. Shall I go on? I want to discover that California has single-payer universal health care and all the labor laws are being enforced, giving every worker, whether a citizen or an illegal, enough bathrooms, enough ventilation, and enough fire exits. I want to find out that my Prius is at the dealer and ready for me to pick it up." As she listed these desires, she was smiling at her game, but suddenly she frowned. After a moment, she said, "I want not to be sliding into a new dark age."

He kissed her between the eyebrows. He said, "That's not a foregone conclusion. We might arrest the slide." But even as he said it, he acknowledged to himself that all the sunshine that seemed to be falling upon them here at the Russian palace was certainly, for him, the effect of their vacation from geopolitics.

She said, "Make a movie." He suspected she meant, Revive your career.

He said, "I'm too lazy to make a movie, didn't you realize that? How about *you* make a movie."

She wriggled out of the coverlet cocoon and glanced at him, startled, but then she put her hands thoughtfully behind her head. After a moment, she said, "Do I have plenty of money?" Her voice was light again, so he said, "All the money in the world."

"Can I go on location?"

"Not outside of southern California. You have to come sleep in my bedroom every night."

She kissed the tip of his nose; the Flower Room became very quiet. It was early, Max could tell by the light, and possibly they were the only ones awake. This room caught the eastern light first thing in the morning, and from the window, a casement opening outward, what you saw when you looked out were the irises depicted in tile under the gleaming surface of the swimming pool. To the right of those, the flowering crab apples and plums alternating with Japanese maples and dogwoods marched down the green hill, frothy white with blossoms, and to the left, purple wisteria hung over the frame of the pergola. The garden had a kind of wildness that he usually didn't care for in comparison with the austerity of his own, but he had enjoyed it after all. She said, "Is it okay to start with the music?"

"For now."

"Do you remember a song Judy Collins sang when I was in high school? It was called 'Farewell to' something. It was about sailing the coast of Greenland, and her accompaniment was the sound of whales singing and waves crashing. Every time I played the album, I cried. I could never get used to it. It seemed like she was saying goodbye to the entire animal kingdom, and they were saying goodbye to her. And it was prescient. We've spent my adult life saying goodbye to the animal kingdom. I would have that song play over my opening titles, because I would want the audience to be crying immediately, without even knowing why."

"And then what? What's your story?"

"Well, the whales aren't in Greenland, they're off the coast of California. The opening scene is a home movie of a girl on a boat with her family, whale-watching. She's six and her brother is seven. They mug for the camera, and then the camera moves and films whales breaching, and then moves back to the children, who are standing still, looking at the whales. And then that dissolves to the same shot of our girl at thirty, on a similar whale-watching ship with her family. She's about to deploy to Iraq with her unit, and this is her last visit home."

"Who is it?"

"The star?"

"Sure."

"Well, of course Nicole Kidman was the first one I thought of, but it should probably be an unknown."

"Never get made."

"Well, J. Lo, then. That's appropriate for California."

Max chuckled at the thought of Jennifer Lopez in this movie, but he went along with her. "Then what?"

"Then the movie just follows her as she goes about her business, leaving her family, and her boyfriend. Doing her job."

"What's her job?"

"Oh, let's see. She went into the reserves years ago with the idea that, since she was bilingual, she would be deployed to natural disasters where the victims spoke either Spanish or English. Now she expects to be some kind of liaison with the Iraqis, though she doesn't know much about the Iraqis. She gets some training in Kuwait. They've been waiting in Kuwait for the last six months. She watches the women there, wearing full chadors and keeping their eyes down. She thinks about that. But she doesn't talk about it. There isn't much dialogue in my movie. Most of what there is, is bullshit—you know, army-speak. Not necessarily anything bad or abusive, just the routine way that people speak by the book in large organizations. Joking. Cursing. Using jargon. Substituting conformist ways of talking for one's own point of view. About thirty minutes into my movie, they start across the desert. That part is very realistic—sometimes boring, sometimes terrifying, sometimes horrible, sometimes exhausting. She sees things that she hadn't imagined, like rockets hitting the convoy in front of her. They try to save the soldiers in the convoy. Civilians by the side of the road, half hidden in the sandstorms, sometimes firing weapons, sometimes being killed. Corpses. Machines. Fires. Darkness. Then they get near Baghdad. It's day thirteen of the war. They are driving along in their Humvee. There are six soldiers in the vehicle. Two women and four men. It's quiet. Everyone is tired, but not too tired to be joking a little bit. Nothing anyone says expresses what J. Lo is thinking, but she doesn't know how to express what she is thinking anyway. She's numb. She thinks of the whales, maybe. And then they drive over a land mine, and the Humvee explodes."

"Is that the end?"

"If only it were. No, we're only fifty minutes into the movie. We have an hour to go. Just as she and her buddies dealt with the rocket attack on the other vehicle earlier, someone else in the convoy shows up and deals with J. Lo and her buddies. Three are dead, blown to pieces. We see that. One is basically okay. Miracles happen. The one who was sitting next to J. Lo, a black guy, let's say Will Smith, is alive, but most of his midsection is blown away."

"An *hommage* to the scene in *Catch-22* where Snowden the gunner dies in Yossarian's plane?"

"Yes, okay. J. Lo herself is a mess. Her face is okay, and her trunk. But the rest of her is a bloody mess. The rest of the movie is about her trip out of Iraq. About the hospital where she goes at first. With scenes of the surgeries. Of what they save and what they can't save. Of the hospital where she goes after that, and the beginnings of rehab. Of the wheelchair. Of how shocked her parents and boyfriend are when they see her for the first time. You can tell by the look on the boyfriend's face that he isn't planning to take care of her for the rest of her life. He doesn't quite know what his excuse is going to be, but he'll come up with something. Her thirty-first birthday in the rehab center. Someone feeding her her birthday cake and holding a glass of 7-Up up to her lips. We see the others who are with her in rehab, some better off, some worse off. We see how she gets back to California. Then, of course, at the end, there would be a reprise of the Judy Collins song, with a lengthier section of the whales singing, and then that tapering off as the credits end. It would be a simple movie. No love interest. No cuts to George Bush or Dick Cheney or peace rallies or her family worrying about her back in Los Angeles. Nothing but J. Lo doing her job, living her life. Almost a documentary, but not quite. That's my movie."

Max didn't know what to say, in part because he could actually see this movie, and it was a sobering movie. As far as he was concerned, it was a movie that could bring the war in Iraq to a dead halt, except that, of course, like all antiwar movies, it would come way too late. If he got up off the bed right now, drove down the hill, and began writing and casting this movie this very day, not to mention trying to find the money, it would still be out of date when it came out. For that matter, J. Lo would be way too old to play the lead. The lessons to be learned from it would be abstract and of mere historical interest, only generally applicable to the circumstances of the time when it would, certainly with some fanfare, have its premiere. Max lamented the utter futility of it.

Elena said, "You would have to star someone big like J. Lo, because you would want the audience to already have a relationship with her. You would want it to be just like seeing someone you know and care about go off and get blown up."

"You show good instincts."

She sat up and stared at him. "Then why am I in the minority about this war? Why, when it seems so obvious to me that there are no weapons of mass destruction and that our supply lines are too long, not to mention the odds of victory and of pacifying the populace? I mean, Saddam is a cruel dictator, but the country is not engaged in a civil war, so we have nothing to offer them *but* civil war—why don't others see this?"

"I don't know," said Max.

Elena burst out of the bed and went into the bathroom. As always, she was naked. As always, she looked lithe and graceful, a neat, un-self-conscious little package, handsome rather than beautiful, and yet evidently the mother of Simon, at whom it was hard to stop looking. They were an interesting pair, Max thought, purely from a casting point of view. You could cast and costume either one of them convincingly as a member of the opposite sex—Simon had the rich grace of a beautiful woman, and Elena had the self-contained, dry skepticism of a young man. And she was right about the violent impact of blowing up J. Lo, and the very thought had evaporated his morning good humor. After all, what were they going to do when they departed this haven in twenty-four hours? It was impossible to tell, and, he thought, impossible to anticipate with any feeling other than dread.

Here he had been so confident that a life in Hollywood had prepared him for any betrayal, any cruelty, any despicable human act, but of course that conceit was as illusory as all the other illusions. It was like when he watched the final cut of A *Very Bad Day*, his one and only blockbuster. Here was Royce Hall at UCLA (in the middle of a student performance of *Medea*, since it was a theater) tilting and tipping into the yawning tar pits, with people fleeing and screaming and dying as the plaza in front of the building caved into a rapidly expanding sea of oily, flaming blackness. After the credits rolled, he and Pete, his cinematographer, and Dom, the producer, and Jerry and the studio execs had all sat quietly for maybe ten seconds, then they had burst out talking and laughing. How great it was! That last scene was fantastic! How did you do that? No one's ever seen anything like that! Wow! Already counting money, and rightly so, since it earned

$103 million when $103 million seemed like a lot. A movie like that did shock you—the tornadoes ripping apart the Beverly Center, and the Hollywood Bowl being crushed by a meteorite did shock you. But how did it prepare you, even if you were the director? The real source of his dread, of course, was that he suspected he was doomed to find out.

Elena emerged from the bathroom again, her face set. She stared at him, then said, "But that is us, you know."

"Who is us?"

"The parents. J.Lo's parents. More or less, now, they've made sure that all our worries for our children will be unceasing, and realistically so."

He knew who she meant by "they." And he knew what she meant by "worries." She pivoted and went back into the bathroom.

•

As she moved about the elegant bathroom, Elena knew she had done it again. The fact was, she said that she couldn't help it—at least, she said that to herself. Every morning, she woke up thinking about Iraq after lying awake at least part of the night thinking about Iraq. She had expected that moving up to this house and avoiding the war would relieve her, especially as the others did now talk about the war less. But she thought about it more last night than the night before, more the night before than Sunday night. It took place in her head no matter what. She was marooned in a mental cul-de-sac compared with Max, compared with Isabel, compared with everyone.

And yet she did not believe in the words "I can't help it." She knew all sorts of techniques that were intended to enable you to put a stop to, or at least to control, intrusive thoughts. For example, she had thought that their conversation was going to come around to Isabel and Stoney, to what was going on between them and what it meant. She had been watching them, and they showed all the signs of a long-term connection. She saw Paul watching them, too, and she could read his mind—Isabel and Stoney were synchronized. The night before, while everyone was watching a movie called *Ghost World* that Simon had found and recommended ("God, Mom! Don't you care about my generation?"—but with a teasing laugh), Isabel and Stoney had gotten into a rhythm. He ate a handful of popcorn, she took a sip of Pellegrino and then offered him one. He took a sip of her Pellegrino, then she picked a few kernels out of the popcorn bowl. Elena had planned, right then and there, what advice she would be giving Max when he noticed this: "Let her bring it up, then tell her exactly what you think. All of what you think. But only one time. She's twenty-three years old. You can make sure she hears you, but you can't make sure she listens to you." But even though he hadn't brought up Isabel, when he invited her to tell her movie she could have told another one, a romantic comedy about a big, loosely knit family, where the beautiful, promising daughter (Nicole Kidman, playing very young) brings home the nerd (Bob Balaban, playing even younger), and some funny and heartwarming things happen, and the father is reconciled. But she could not help herself, and now both of them were depressed.

Her favorite cousin, Lucy, had once retraced a three-hundred-mile drive from Chicago to Des Moines, stopping and checking under every bridge abutment and in every deep ditch and at every rest stop for the injured man she was sure she had hit with her car. It had taken her six hours to make the original trip and two days to retrace her steps; she had slept in her car over the night so that she could begin at first light. Their grandmother, the one she and Lucy shared (Granma Edith), ironed her husband's shorts and undershirts, set the table every night with a freshly laundered and pressed tablecloth. It wasn't until Elena was an adult that she realized that not every grandmother owned a mangle and did her fine laundry in distilled water with homemade soap scented with home-grown lavender. Another cousin, Eloise, known as the careless one, who cooked and cleaned with notoriously hard water, nevertheless weighed her ingredients rather than measure them by volume, as most people did. In fact, Eloise's *Joy of Cooking* (she showed it to Elena) had been entirely notated, in pencil, with conversions in the margins of ingredient measurements, between volumes and weight, but also between English and metric, which Eloise considered finer, and therefore more accurate. Could they help themselves?

And then, when Lucy had been diagnosed with obsessive-compulsive disorder and had informed everyone that you could help these sorts of things with counseling and drugs, everyone in the family had been offended. But, Elena thought as she was carefully drying her hands and laying the damp hand-towel across the warmer rack, Lucy's experience showed that you could help any and all intrusive thoughts, including ones about soldiers getting blown up and ones about politicians having secret agendas and ones about a coming age more violent and fearsome than any she had ever experienced. During her treatment, Lucy had become quite strict—prohibiting her from using the term "obsessed" unless she was, say, measuring the overhang of her bedspread on all three sides with a tape measure to make sure it was even, or holding her junk mail up in front of a bright light before she opened it to make sure it carried no mysterious powdered substances. Elena could not, therefore, describe herself as "obsessed." The term was "preoccupied."

Perhaps a valid difference, according to Lucy's rules, would have been that when Lucy was obsessing it was images she could not get rid of. The image of a man who was holding a traffic sign at the site of some road construction, and whom Lucy had seen, still standing, in her rearview mirror after she passed him. And yet, because of the way the sunlight hit, or the angle of the hood of her car as she passed him, or simply a mistaken thought, she could not dislodge from her mind the sight of him right there, right on the other side of her hood, too close. Perhaps she had brushed him? Perhaps she had hit him, and the view she had of him in her rearview mirror was wishful thinking? Perhaps she was mixed up and she had hit someone else somewhere else, which was why she felt such conviction? When Lucy's friend in Des Moines said to her, "Well, you didn't feel a bump, did you? You would have felt a bump," the idea of a bump lodged in her mind, too. Had she really not felt a bump, *really* not? And so she had driven back to Chicago and then back to Des Moines, looking for the body, and remembering that elderly couple she had heard about, in upstate New York long ago, whose car had slid over an embankment in the snow in the twilight, and not been seen, and the couple had been pinned, and had frozen to death before anyone realized they were in the ravine. And as soon as she thought of that couple, the man she had not hit in the summer became pinned in his car and had to be found before he froze to death. It was after this experience that Lucy had decided she needed treatment.

But it was not images that preoccupied Elena, it was arguments. She thought about this as she flossed her teeth. For example, when she had awakened the night before, she had said to Condoleezza Rice—in her mind, of course, because she didn't want to wake Max—"How are they going to get that mushroom cloud here? By ship? By plane? By car? Are you saying that Iraq has or will soon have the same nuclear and air-force capability that the U.S. had at the end of World War II? That they can build and drop a bomb that will create a mushroom cloud? Or are you saying that it would be like a nuclear test in the New Mexico desert? That they are going to build a framework somewhere, install a nuclear device, and detonate it from afar? If they did get some yellowcake uranium from Niger, are you saying that they are capable of all the steps it takes to transform that uranium into a mushroom cloud, precisely and exactly a mushroom cloud?" She had said all that, and then, the bad sign, she had said it again. "It's remotely plausible that a suitcase full of dirty material could be carried to some American city, be exploded with an improvised explosive, and succeed in contaminating that city, but would that result in a mushroom cloud? Do you, Condoleezza Rice, truly believe that such an act of terrorism would indeed result in a mushroom cloud rising thousands of feet in the air over, let's say, Los Angeles, and if so why?" She had been preoccupied with this argument for more than an hour, between about one and a little after two, before getting back to sleep. Condoleezza, in her mind, had no answer for this argument, but didn't have to, because the image had done its PR work whether Condoleezza believed it or not.

Elena washed her length of floss under the tap and then ran it between her fingertips. It was, she thought, still usable. She wound it up and tucked it inside the cap of the floss package. Normally, she got five or even six flossings out of a single strand, but that was because she flossed at least twice a day, sometimes three times, and her floss never encountered much resistance. She had been weighing whether to put a paragraph about correct flossing in her book or not.

The night before last, she had been preoccupied with the argument about Israel. This argument was with Israelis. It ran: "You know that your supporters in the American right wing are supporting you because they want the final battle to take place in Israel, and then for you to have one last chance to convert, or die and spend the rest of eternity in a burning lake in hell. You know, because they have been open about it, that your destruction is their salvation. They will certainly act if they can, at least unconsciously, to accelerate their salvation and your destruction. And the history of Christianity is of fanatics acting out their fanaticism, so why would you trust and support them? Why would you even take the risk, whatever you think about how deluded they are? Is this some sort of higher-level suicide wish? Is it mere cynicism? Is it blind faith? Isn't what these right-wingers imagine and foresee a version of the Holocaust?" All of these questions ran through her mind as if written out, again and again, not images but words, why why why, sometimes attached to other phrases, like "What in the world is wrong with you that you would think such thoughts or take such risks?," though she tried to maintain, even in her internal preoccupations, a reasonable level of discourse, and not to sink to mere abuse.

The arguments went on simultaneously with everything else she did, everything else she said, which reminded her that when she and Lucy had talked about the history of Lucy's OCD, Elena had been amazed to discover just how long that history was. So many times when she had thought they were just driving down the street looking for an open gas station or shopping for bathing suits, Lucy had been reviewing her day and wondering if, by some inadvertent act, she had injured or killed someone. Somehow, Lucy could say to her sister Lily, "I can't believe you actually wore that outfit out in public," while at that very moment worrying that she had run over a child with her shopping cart without realizing it.

Elena opened the cosmetics closet and took out some French wrinkle cream scented with lavender and began applying it to her temples with the tips of her forefinger and middle finger. It disappeared into her skin instantly, leaving only that floral fragrance in the floral atmosphere of the bathroom. What Elena especially loved about the bathroom was that the green tile floor was edged with elaborately hand-painted tiles of different flowers, almost as detailed as botanical drawings. Right in the center of the floor was a tile bouquet of tiger lilies that you could almost smell, if tiger lilies could be smelled, which they could not.

Perhaps the best argument, though, if not the most logical or even the most moral, but the most effective, was the argument she had made in her movie. The argument of this was: "What happens in war? Is this the price you want to pay? Who is going to pay it? What will you get for it? How close to this high cost are you going to position yourself? Will you pay this price with your own body? With that of your child? (She thought of Simon.) That of your father or mother? That of your daughter? (She thought of Isabel.) How about if the daughter is beautiful? What is the highest price you are willing to pay to secure the abstract benefits of having your way in the Middle East? Amputation? Madness? Blindness? Paraplegia? Quadriplegia? Lifelong institutionalization and helplessness?" (Simon, Isabel, Simon, Isabel, Simon, Simon, Simon.) Obviously, none of the war-makers minded if the Iraqis paid a high price, so she could not make her movie about an Iraqi being maimed. J.Lo might work, though. She capped the bottle of cream and set it back into the cabinet and closed the cabinet door, then she looked around the bathroom. It was clean and neat. The more arguments she made, the cleaner and neater everything around her became. It was a byproduct of the excess energy that the arguments generated. And it was also true that Lucy had always been a demon of activity. Not only was her house perfectly clean, she was a wonderful seamstress, whose every hem and zipper and dart and design was perfect.

She opened the bathroom door and looked at Max, who appeared to have drifted back to sleep. That was good. It seemed to her that he could, as he said, love her for who she was only if who she was was not so potent and concentrated as to irradiate him with the full intensity of her fears.

She opened the closet door and took out a robe. It was an antique silk kimono with a motif of plum blossoms on a black background. The other one in the closet had a chrysanthemum design on a peach-colored background. In her two days in the room, she had paraded around in both of them, and both were flattering. The room was filled with mirrors that reflected all the flowers in the pictures and on the wallpaper back upon themselves, so parading around in the kimonos had been a bit of a forbidden pleasure, if you considered vanity a forbidden pleasure, which normally she did. She went to the window that faced away from the pool. The garden fanned out below as if it had been there for years. A row of palms, each at least twenty feet tall, separated it from the aviary, and the grass grew right up to the base of the palms. What was really beautiful about the garden, though, was that the beds were semicircular, and the blossoms, in their multicolored variety, seemed to twine about one another. From the perspective of her window, the garden made a picture that reminded her of some sort of Arabic or Turkish design, intricate and meditative. She had meant, but kept forgetting, to get Joe Blow to take her up onto the roof so that she could see the garden from an even higher promontory. In the last couple of days, she had stood exactly at this spot any number of times and found it soothing, just as she found it soothing right now. She had conditioned herself to use just this spot to replace other images, as she now used it to replace those images of Simon and Isabel. She took a deep breath, reminding herself that it was profoundly bad (immoral? bad luck?) to think in such a way.

The early-morning light was just brightening, and the sun, still low above the horizon, was picking out some of the yellow and orange flower beds (she recognized the clivia miniata), leaving the purple (Dutch iris) and white (spirea and hawthorn) ones in shadow. Jasmine grew everywhere. The roses had been pruned and were starting to leaf out—Elena expected them to be blossoming in less than a month. She was reminded not so much of Max's garden, more that her own garden required some work. Once, it had been her special small project, an extension of the kitchen and just about as neat, with all of her necessities stashed conveniently in corners—rosemary, thyme, basil, bay, oregano, the grape arbor, the clementine tree, the lemon tree, the freesia, the daisies for the table, the few orchids, etc., but since taking up with Max, she had cut most of it back and hired a gardener to take care of what was still producing. Max's garden was quite intimidating to her, and so the herbs she grew at his house she grew in pots. She had put those citrus trees on the deck and would have liked more—Mike had beautiful flowering trees here, many of which Elena did not recognize. Isabel had said she didn't like this garden very much, because it was not a native-plant garden, but Elena didn't mind that. Her ideal was the tomato, not a plant native to Italy, and yet reaching its zenith right there, where it met up with olive oil, garlic, and basil.

She would say to Tony Blair—

She opened the window in a conscious effort to forestall what she would say to Tony Blair, and as she opened the window, a morning fragrance of dampness, sweetness, and grass entered the room. Max moved and opened his eyes, perhaps at the fragrance. He said, "I dozed off. I was dreaming you were naked." He sounded okay, as if not repelled by her movie.

Instead of telling Max what she would say to Tony Blair, she chose to say, "I am naked inside this silk kimono." She turned, and the silk billowed, outlining her figure, she thought. She lifted her arms and pushed her hair back; the kimono spread wider, and the draft from the window pressed the cool silk against her buttocks and the backs of her thighs and then, "Do you smell the alyssum? I bet that's what it is, though there must be other things, too. Why does Mike get to have a mature garden after only six months, and the rest of us have to wait years?"

"Ah! Mike!" exclaimed Max. "He's very ambitious. Maybe he's the lost great-grandson of Tsar Nicholas. I keep wondering if some ancestor of Mike's and some ancestor of mine met on the streets of Kraków somewhere, or did business, or had a falling-out, or were related in some way. I've always thought that one nice thing about exile, or at least emigration, for Eastern European Jews, is that they don't have to run into the people who beat them and cheated them and sneered at them for all those generations. The people they run into might have beaten and cheated and sneered at other Jews, but not them themselves. So now we have the advent of Mike—"

"You never seem to think of yourself as Jewish," said Elena.

"And then along comes Mike! Is it just the sight of his face that triggers some race memory for me? I don't know."

But he was smiling, so Elena smiled, too. She said, "I have race memories all the time. They are of all those Karstensens and Sigmunds churning butter and making cheese. You know, my grandmother's cholesterol count was almost three hundred, and she lived until she was over eighty. That always made me think that Scandinavians evolved to tolerate high cholesterol. I think it was a body-warming device. If you got lost in the snow, your body would burn the cholesterol until they rescued you." She waited until he smiled, and then smiled herself. Not thinking bad things.

He pulled her down on the bed and kissed her. The kimono floated down over them and she felt it again, smooth across her legs. She lifted her arm and wafted the silk across his face. He closed his eyes. He said, "That smells good." Once again, then, he had induced her to leave that Elena, the shrill, preoccupied, and uncomfortable Elena, behind in the bathroom. She was grateful for that. But she said as if idly, "There are sachets in the closet. But, seriously, you never talk about being Jewish, you never talk about Israel—"

"Jerry used to call me one of the 'half-baked Jews.' He was only partly joking, but we got along, anyway."

"What do you think about Israel, though?" She tried to make this sound casual, as if it were not related to her preoccupation with the Evangelical right wing and other thoughts.

"I don't know what to think about Israel, frankly. You know what my father said about Israel? He only said one thing during my whole childhood that I can remember, and that was 'I don't think it's a good idea to have all the Jews gathered in one place.' And I knew what he meant. In dispersal, safety lies."

This sounded plausible to Elena, but it also brought her argument with the Evangelical Christians to her very lips. She pressed them closed.

He lifted the sleeve of the kimono to his nose again, inhaled, and then said, openly changing the subject, "Do you think Mike thinks of all these details himself?"

When she opened her lips, something normal came out. "I asked Joe Blow about that, and he said some yes and some no. He said to me, 'Madame Elena, Raphael and I together equal one Martha Stewart, and so we are able to put together this one house.' I guess he's a faithful fan of Martha's, and has been since he got to America."

Max laughed, then said, "I hear the Russian troika went back to Russia yesterday to make another billion dollars. I told Ben Avram that Mike needs a sport to occupy his time."

She pressed him just a little bit more. She said, "Didn't you ever have a Jewish girlfriend?"

"As it turned out, no. Though at the time I would have said it wasn't a conscious intention."

Instead of saying, "I hope you never do have a Jewish girlfriend, now," she said, "Tell me about when they made *Grace*. You didn't make it in Russia, did you?"

"Oh, heavens, no. We, but really they, made it partly in Canada, partly in the studio, and partly in Prague, with a second unit shooting a few scenes in Japan. Mostly in the studio, though. The exterior scenes were fewer than you think. There were a lot of scenes in hiding, and if you look at the film very closely, you can see that we used the same set for almost all of them, we just kept redecorating it. The great thing about Lilli Palmer, especially at that point in her career, was that when she was in the scene she was all you looked at. She gave nothing to the kid. Lots of actors hate acting with kids, but she didn't seem to mind, or said she didn't, but when they were in a scene together, it was the kid who just could not stop looking at her. Apted thought that was going to be a problem, but actually, it worked out perfectly, because the kid was the one being saved and Lilli was the one doing the saving, and she made the whole plot very suspenseful."

"I thought it was an English actress in that movie."

"Well, she was married to Rex Harrison for a while, and acted with him in plays. And she took an English name as a young woman, but she was a

Jew from Poland, so she was actually perfect for the part. She wrote a book or two. They weren't bad, either."

Elena kissed him on the nose. She liked it when he talked about his work. Her wish that he would direct this strange movie about war-mad Ukrainians came from sheer ignorance, but every day Stoney said something to her about how Max had to get out of the house, or how Max was letting his talents go to waste, or how Max had turned into an old man since Jerry's death, or how Max was the only person who could plausibly make this movie without having the movie making a fool of everyone involved. She tried asking another question, just a subtle, suggestive question. "Wasn't it quite arduous for her at her age?"

"She was sixty or so if I remember correctly."

"Even going to Canada in the winter and all?"

"She wore furs."

Elena laughed, then said, "Well, sixty is the new fifty." She almost said, "Fifty-eight is the new forty-five," but she stopped herself.

Now he gave her a real kiss, gentle, self-confident, and exploratory, his lips meeting hers in that strange, unreproducible, and almost unrememberable way of kisses that made you wonder about how humans came to be, yes, big brains, yes, opposable thumbs, yes, buttocks as a counterbalancing weight, yes, hairless, but also soft, warm, full, sensitive lips, pressing, retreating, shape-shifting, pressing again, opening, closing. Such lips didn't evolve to kiss babies or suck pomegranates or drink water from a cupped palm, they evolved to precipitate the brain into a hormonal tizzy. She opened her mouth slightly, and touched the tip of his tongue with hers.

Although he was still not quite awake, or maybe because he was still not quite awake, when she turned away from the window and the kimono spread out around her, Max saw the climax to his movie. His movie, not her movie. He had dozed off thinking of her movie, but awakened thinking of his, about her. And now the slanting morning light through the window gilded her hair, the side of her face, and the side of her leg, and the black, red, orange, white, and yellow of the kimono lit up, too. Within its boundaries, there she was, moving, turning, her head tossed back, her neck arched, her breasts lifted, her hip cocked, and her bare leg stepping toward him. It was a perfect last image.

Just a moment later, though, as she was slightly turning her head and repositioning her lips and snaking her arms farther around his shoulders, and he was beginning to forget the movie business entirely (and he could feel a renewed rumble in his crotch that felt reliable and routine rather than miraculous), he closed his eyes and saw the image in a different way. Elena in the kimono was transmuted, for some reason, into Lilli Palmer in a brocade dressing gown—not the Lilli Palmer he had known, an exacting and worldly older lady with an unpredictable sense of humor, but the Lilli Palmer of, say, Berlin in 1935, sleek and mysterious, and the movie she was in was *Taras Bulba*, and the part she was playing was the part of the girl in the besieged Polish city, desperate to save her family, especially her mother, from starvation, and yet also attracted to that dashing Cossack Andrei, a girl whose every preconception has been dissipated and vaporized by the war, and now she is only a bundle of survival instincts, but a beautiful bundle, a bundle that Andrei cannot resist.

As Elena drew the sleeve of her kimono over his face, it was intoxicatingly sensuous and fleeting, compounded of the feel of the silk, some scent he did not recognize, the feeling of being seduced and subdued at the same time. He asked about that scent, and then it was very funny, he thought, that she should start talking about *Grace*, since he had been thinking of Lilli Palmer.

"Wasn't it quite arduous for her at her age?"

"She was sixty or so if I remember correctly."

"Even going to Canada in the winter and all?"

"She wore furs."

Elena laughed, then said, "Well, sixty is the new fifty."

He kissed her then, and had that sensation that he frequently had when he kissed her, that sensation of: Oh! This! How pleasant this is! You could do this all day and never get tired of it! They kissed for a long time, and he felt the immediacy of the kiss—the soft warmth of her lips, the presence of her face and her body, the small cave of her mouth—but the image of Lilli Palmer as a Polish girl never left his mind. Along with it came a lot of images from movies of the thirties, all black and white: Marlene Dietrich in *The Blue Angel*, Mae West in *Go West, Young Man*, Billie Burke in *Dinner at Eight*, Carole Lombard in *Nothing Sacred*, Myrna Loy in *The Thin Man*. Women in those days, of course, had a different body language from the body language of women today. Their self-display had been more subtle but more calculated, less trusting. Even as he had this thought, he realized that in Ukraine those women probably still existed, and there was some girl who could inhabit that part of Taras' movie, and the movie could grow from there; in fact, it could grow outward toward the men by means of the women—the girl's mother (maybe forty, almost dead of starvation), the maid (tough old lady who survives the siege), Taras' wife (arranged marriage when she was thirteen to his thirty, now a crone at thirty-two), and then the men. The men would present themselves, too.

He pulled away from the kiss and rolled over on his back. He said, "I think I'm catching something."

"Oh dear." She felt his head with her small palm. "What?"

"A movie."

"Which movie are you catching?"

"I'm sorry to say, *Taras Bulba*, and it's going to be a major pain in the ass. But we can enjoy the best part right now."

"What's that?"

"Thinking about it."

"What part are we going to think about?"

"Well, you are going to think about what it means, and I am going to think about what it looks like."

"Do I get a credit?"

"Yes, right at the end of the credits it will say, 'Meaning supplied by Elena Sigmund, author of the *Here's How! Guide to Meanings.*'"

"Okay, then."

"Okay, then. I begin with the women. What do you begin with?"

"I begin with the women, too."

"Why is that?"

"Well, why do you begin with the women?"

"Because they're the most difficult to visualize. Is there a woman in America who moves like those women? Whose face has those same habits, whatever they were, geared toward self-preservation? Is there a woman in Russia? In Ukraine? The Soviets set out to eradicate all former ways of thinking and to substitute new ways, more or less European ways, for the old ways, so, if we want to portray the old ways, where are we going to find them? It's a forensic problem. We have this remnant and this remnant and what might be this other remnant over here. How do we put them together so that they look convincing?"

"You said that about the corsets. You told Stoney that the corsets were a deal-killer."

"It goes deeper than the corset thing. But you could send your actresses to Afghanistan or Saudi Arabia and have them observe the body language of those women, and then subtract something, or add something. But you'd have to define what that something is—do you subtract subservience in the princess, or add nomadic toughness in the boys' mother? Even then, you'd only get a rude approximation of the way those sixteenth-century women really were, but if it looked strange enough onscreen, it might work. The actresses could learn and study together, and so at least they could all be rather similar, not the same, but of the same breed." He knew he sounded intrigued. This was the way it always happened—the point of the needle that got under the skin, and pretty soon, ways and means began to occur to you, and to engender more ways and means. First, there you were in a bookstore, and then there you were in the library, and pretty soon you found yourself on a plane scouting locations, the last place on earth that you had imagined yourself before you entered that bookstore. He said, "It's so obviously a man's book that it seems to me that the women are the main problem, and I don't want to solve it in the old Hollywood way, by throwing a big star at it. Elizabeth Taylor as the princess, or even Nicole Kidman as the princess, or even J. Lo as the princess, or even whatsername, Hilary Duff as the princess. Maybe, when we looked at Nicole Kidman as Virginia Woolf last year, she looked okay to us, just the way Janet Leigh looked okay as an eighteenth-century French aristocrat in the 1950s, but now looks like a girl from California in a French-style dress."

Elena said, "The women are the understandable ones. Let's say that the men are just impossibly off-the-wall aggressive and warlike. Every time there are more than two men in any one spot, the first thing they do is fight, two against one, and then more show up, and it's three against two, and on and on. I don't think modern audiences really understand that, even, pardon me for saying so, in Ukraine or Russia or wherever. So the women, who are interested in survival, and family life, and love, even if those things as they know them are distorted and cut short by the endless violence, serve as the emotional guides to the action. Not by talking, since in some ways they can't talk or aren't allowed to talk, but just by reacting. As soon as the boys get home from their school, the mother has to let them go again, and she knows there's a good chance that something bad will happen to at least one of them. That's one thing. Or the princess. She knows how to be seductive, even when the walled city is falling apart around her. In the midst of death, she is seductive. That is so strange and yet right. And even though there aren't many women in the novel, you can have more in the movie. I would have as many women as men, and have the women be a kind of chorus. The men are ignoring them, but the audience isn't."

He said, "I like that. But how do you know any of these women actually care about what we would consider regular, normal sorts of things? Maybe the brutality of their lives has driven that out of them? Maybe they are numb to all human feeling?"

"But the book hints that they aren't. Taras dismisses the wife for being weak because she cries when the boys leave again to go to the encampment. And the author himself says that the girl's concern for her mother is real. Those are our clues. Maybe, in your chorus of women, some of them make remarks that are more brutal. That's how I see the chorus, a kind of ongoing gossip session about events as they transpire. Gossip seems to be perennial and universal. Everyone gossips, so you could use it for your own benefit. Voice-over gossip."

Max could not help loving this idea. "Voice-over gossip" — just fragments of conversations, or groans, or screams, or horses whinnying, or whispers that couldn't be made out precisely. That would be the score, he thought. Normally, the music in a movie didn't leave much room for extra dialogue, but if there was very little music — folk music, mostly, and lots of ambient sound — that could be an interesting experiment. And it was something that you could try and then modify if it didn't work, because you could always put in more music, weaving it into the other sounds. He had never made a movie like that, with that kind of sound, and he really, right at the moment, couldn't think of a movie like that. He sat up higher in the bed. He said, "That gives me a great idea." He described the idea to her, and she nodded.

Her nod made it an even better idea (how many times had that happened, where, as soon as someone agreed with one of his ideas, it got so charged with energy that it became sheer genius?). "You know," he said, "I'm getting a little excited. This room is beginning to seem a little small."

She laughed.

"Mike is beginning to seem a little impoverished."

She laughed again. "Are we launched?"

"Well, we are certainly launched from a supine position under the covers of the bed. I feel a slight urge to go down to the *My Fair Lady* library and look for picture books about the Russian steppe, or even to wander around in the living room. Aren't there a bunch of Russian paintings and artifacts there? Let's take the video camera. I can take some footage of what's in there."

"Will Joe Blow let you?"

"It isn't a museum. Besides, it's Mike's project I'm working on. We could take pictures of every picture of a woman painted by a Russian in this house."

"There was one I saw yesterday—"

"Of course he set this up. Of course this is why he invited us over here, so that the atmosphere would infect us."

"You mean Mike."

"I do." He breathed in the fragrance that now seemed to inhabit the room.

She said, "It's a pretty intoxicating atmosphere."

He said, "This house is a treasury of ideas. Of course, that's no guarantee that we will, or can, make a decent film." He didn't say, though he knew it was true, that the thoughts they were intrigued by now would diminish and be forgotten. This room that seemed somehow to engender them would collapse upon itself into barely an image. He would successively seek out, or endure, or even resist the stages that would take him from here to the movie on the screen—the all-involving research, the all-involving composition of the script, the all-involving beehive activity of actors and technicians, the all-involving logistics of filming in a new place, the all-involving details of finance and money and junk like costumes and houses and cameras and carts and piles of hay and lights and flowers in the grass and armor and weapons and clouds and mounds of turnips and fires and blood, then rehearsals and setup, and the acting out of scenes, the all-involving servicing of the small city that they would be. Cutting, editing, sound, music, and then, of course, promotion and publicity, premieres and festivals, interviews and reflections—one stage after another. Only to have it all fade away in the rearview mirror and become as old, eventually, as *Grace*, or *City Lights*, or

Birth of a Nation. But this catalogue of unavailing efforts, this catalogue of woes to come, well, it perversely energized him, didn't it? He said, "Simon should play Andrei."

"Oh, I don't think so."

"Sure. We'll give him a beard up to his eyes and lots of flowing hair and a little swordplay coaching, a beautiful girl, and let him go. I bet he can do it. Teach him to ride a horse in the Cossack manner."

"I don't think he wants to be an actor."

"But he doesn't have to make a career as an actor. The fact is that a guy who shaves his head in order to play a penis in a student film is a guy who is up for anything. A little trip to Ukraine would be nothing for him. He can go on afterward, across the Silk Road to China, and become a trading representative between Santa Monica and Ulan Bator. Better than having him driving around California with nothing to do."

"Oh well. I'm glad to know you're joking."

"Maybe I am, maybe I'm not." But he was, or, if not joking, then at least giving vent to sudden high spirits. They could all go—Delphine, Cassie, Zoe, Paul, even Charlie. Just to extend this pleasure that he was suddenly aware of, the pleasure of having these particular people around day after day, a pleasure that he had been experiencing without realizing it, or, well, yes, he had realized the pleasure, but he had not admitted it. Now he did. He said, "Delphine and Cassie and Charlie and Zoe and everyone—I'll tell Mike they're my essential creative team, and I'll make them all assistant directors."

"So corrupt and nepotistic! I'm shocked." But she was not shocked; she was amused.

He said, "And Isabel can do the research on authentic ecological details of the period. The steppe is supposed to have been an interesting and unique ecosystem, not just a flat place in the middle of Eurasia, so we can portray that, too. Fulfill our social obligation to record what is probably the end of an era. And as far as that goes, the only things we know about the geopolitical aspects of the sixteenth century are what we read in the novel, but maybe they were more interesting than even Gogol was aware of."

"I'm sure Mike will go for that."

"I'm sure he will. And then he can archive her research, and she can set up a special consulting firm—eco-research for various good causes."

"Yes, but is this a movie or a miniseries?"

"Oh well, you can always get everything into the script until you can't. That's why I prefer to write my own screenplay, because I like to do my own thinking, even if the first draft is three hundred twenty-five pages long. The first draft of *Grace* was more than two hundred pages, and there were basically two characters. One of the problems with *Southern Pacific*, to name only one of the bombs I am responsible for—and I liked that movie, but I am the only one who did—was that, really, it was a seventy-page idea that we tried to pad out with close-ups of the dog."

She laughed again and said, "Let's get up and go downstairs and look around."

He said, "Let's get up and go downstairs and look around." But when she leaned forward, he restrained her, and when she turned toward him, he slipped his hand inside her kimono. She said, "Don't you want to?"

"Of course I do." But he started kissing her again. She resisted for a moment, then yielded completely, and a moment later, they were rolling around in the bed again, less languidly, more like they had something to do but wanted to do this first. She kissed him and kissed him—not only on the lips, but next to the lips, on the nose, on the cheek, under his chin, between his eyebrows. She kissed him until he was laughing, and then she leaned over the edge of the bed and came up with the video camera. She sat up, quickly taking off the lens cap and pressing the power button. She said, "Speaking of archives." And she threw back the covers with one hand, moved the hem of her kimono out of the way, and focused on his erection. He had one. She said, "Think some dirty thoughts," but he didn't have to do that. All he had to do was watch her face as she trained the video camera on his hard-on. She said, "Well, I am impressed," but mostly to herself. He slipped his hand underneath his balls and felt them, then he ran it up the shaft of his cock, so smooth and youthful, that skin, did you ever hear the one about the mohel who ran a luggage shop, and a man comes in and asks to see a wallet? He laughed aloud at this ancient joke, and she laughed, too, just because he was laughing. When his hand closed over the cap, he smoothed it downward again, a little tighter this time, and as he let out an involuntary exclamation, she let out one, too. She leaned closer, and he didn't have to look into the viewfinder to see what she was filming—the head of his cock, emerging from his closed fist, fat around its single dark exit, all the more full because he was squeezing it a bit. She leaned around to the right and got it from the underside, where it stood up out of his pubic hair, and she said, "Is it bigger? It seems bigger."

"You have it on close-up."

She took the camera away from her eye, looked at it, and said with genuine perplexity, "I do?" and then he took the camera out of her hand and put it on the nightstand, not without pushing the power button, and then he stretched her out, opened the kimono, and entered her, and her legs lifted and clasped him around the waist, and her head fell back over the edge of the bed, and it felt like he was entering her up to her throat, that's how big he was, and how big she was, and just as he was thinking this, her entire inner being closed around him, and he also felt that other thing so distinctly, the pulse of her labia against his scrotum. "Mmm," she uttered, and he pressed against her cervix, and it gave way, and he was so glad to be doing this again that he ejaculated almost into a state of unconsciousness.

Well, not really.

But she nearly fell off the bed, and then came a knock at the door, and someone said, "Everything okay in there?" and Elena whispered, "You were screaming," and then she got up and wrapped the kimono around her and went to the door. Max could hear her saying, "Oh, yes, thank you for asking. Nothing at all to worry about. We'll see you at breakfast. You're very kind. Yes, I think the chicken-apple sausage will be delicious. Perfect. Good morning, then."

She closed the door.

DAY TEN · Wednesday, April 2, 2003

Isabel had Zoe cornered in what appeared to Zoe to be a commodious and well-stocked pantry. She was backed up against the double sink, which was next to a window that looked out on the cars. With the corner of her eye, she could see her own little Mercedes. The trunk was open, because she had been putting her suitcase in and realized that she had left her makeup case in the malachite bathroom. Paul's suitcase, such as it was, was not in the trunk. While she was attempting to appear as though she was "actively" listening to Isabel, she was also watching for Paul. She hadn't seen Paul since the night before. He had not said in so many words that he would come to her room in the night, but she'd thought he would. He hadn't. She had left the trunk open, intending to run up and grab her makeup case and come back down. But that was forty-five minutes ago. Isabel had snapped at her as she was entering the dining room thinking of a cup of coffee, in front of Joe Blow and Marya. Zoe had done quite a good job, she thought, of backing out of the room and down the hallway into this more private space, drawing Isabel after her.

Isabel exclaimed, in a low voice that Zoe considered especially mean, "This whole thing is about you, isn't it? Same as always!"

Zoe said, "What whole thing?," but in fact she meant to say, *which* whole thing, the whole argument they were having, or the whole lunch they were about to eat (since Joe Blow had asked Zoe what she would like and Zoe had said that fish would be nice, and so they were going to have a seared salmon, wild rice, and dried-cranberry salad—no salmon for the vegetarians—with a light asparagus bisque and a crisp Riesling that Joe had been holding back, but how did Isabel know that Joe had designed the meal for Zoe?), or the whole experience at the Russian house, during which Joe

Blow and the girls had seemed to be quite deferential, maybe more deferential than they were to the others (how was Zoe to know, how was Isabel to know, unless she had been watching like a hawk?), or some other whole thing that existed in Isabel's mind, as yet to be defined. In fact, Isabel's tone was making her very angry, but Zoe was well aware that (1) her feelings were her own responsibility and she didn't have to express or even feel her anger if she didn't want to, according to Paul, and (2) Isabel sounded much as she herself had sounded two nights ago, when Paul's French client, Marcelle, had mistakenly rung through on Zoe's extension, and Zoe had given her a piece of her mind. As of this morning, Zoe did not know whether Paul knew that that unauthorized interaction had taken place. Had Marcelle called him for her regular appointment the night before and been put through to the right extension?

Isabel whispered, "In fact, it didn't matter whether you came to pick me up at that Starbucks or not! I never thought you would! So you don't have to go up to Stoney and commiserate with him about his poor car when there was nothing you were ever going to do that would have helped in any way, so why bother!"

Zoe said, "I was trying to be polite, Isabel. I didn't want to seem indifferent—"

"Even though you are!"

"Excuse me," said Zoe, and she made just a tiny little effort to push—well, not push, but urge—Isabel to one side so that she could—

"Don't push me!"

"Don't be so predictable. If you don't want me to push you, move out of the way and let me get by."

"I don't feel like it."

"If you are going to have a relationship with Stoney, I would like to be nice to him—"

"My relationships have nothing to do with you!"

"Well, anyway, so what? I already have my own relationship with Stoney." The interesting thing about her conversation with Marcelle was that the Frenchwoman had stayed on the line to listen, rather than hanging up at once, which is what Zoe would have done. She had stayed on the line for seven or eight minutes, and of course you could attribute a few of those—say, two or three—to the pure shock of expecting that you were going to be hearing the soothing but matter-of-fact tones of your therapist, and here you had found a woman's voice saying, "Really, Marcelle, I am only thinking of you. You need to ask yourself what you are getting out of this therapy and why it isn't working for you. It's been, what, seven years? Ten years? You aren't progressing!" Her tone had been fairly light to begin with, and her thinking had been quite Paul-like—the wrong extension was actually a heaven-sent opportunity for Marcelle to hear something that she needed to hear, delivered by someone whom she didn't know, but who had a more objective sense of what was really happening than either Paul or Marcelle. But unfortunately, after a good beginning, she had gotten irritated, because there was something in the Frenchwoman's manner of talking about Paul that struck her. It was too intimate and too possessive. It told Zoe, not in so many words but in so many tones, not only that the two of them had had an affair, but that it was still going on, and it then leapt into her mind that it was Marcelle who kept meeting him on his exotic pilgrimages and climbing those seven holy mountains and going to those Neolithic caves (well, he hadn't done that yet, but this year, and those caves were in France!) and going to the beehive tombs, wherever they were, and why was she calling on the wrong night, anyway? She was his longest-lasting relationship! And here he always presented himself as a solitary seeker after enlightenment, traveling the rock-strewn path ever upward, dallying less and less over the pleasures of the flesh as his being gradually evaporated out of this world. Not bloody likely, Zoe now thought.

Isabel said, "I think you should hear me out for once, Mom!" and she went on.

Zoe had her eyes on Isabel, and she watched her face, which was red. Her forehead was wrinkled and her brows were strangely lifted, as if she wanted to look supercilious but was only faking it. She kept tossing her chin and pushing her hair back, but she was absolutely right, Zoe wasn't actually listening to Isabel having her say. What Paul was really doing was battening on—no, entertaining himself with—one wealthy woman after another, not exactly living off them (though he did charge them all for sessions) but going along for the ride. Why, for example, did his 1982 Honda Civic have fewer than a hundred thousand miles on it? Because he was being driven around in this Mercedes or that BMW or the other Ferrari. And he was driven around. She did all the driving.

And she was not listening because she was cornered. Being cornered, as everyone knew, aroused a primal reaction that felt very much like anger. This competed with her fugitive maternal instinct not to reward bad behavior by paying attention to it. That had been Delphine's main child-rearing principle, expressed as "You will catch more flies with honey than with vinegar. When you can come to me and speak to me in a proper tone of voice, then we can discuss this." And Delphine had been implacable. She never responded to Zoe's anger, ever ever ever. Which meant, obviously, not that Zoe learned how not to be angry, only that she learned that her mother was a strange and mysterious person who could not be understood, at least by her. And Zoe had accepted that—partly, Paul told her, because she had lots of other things to occupy her attention.

Isabel cleared her throat and began again, controlling her tone of voice this time so that it sounded cooler and more rational, all the better to prosecute. Zoe began again, too, making herself think that if she just kept quiet and still and pretended to listen, this could take, at most, ten minutes, and then she could get away from Isabel, from Paul, from Delphine, from Max, from Simon, from Charlie, and the others, who didn't matter except that they chattered away, tossing up interference and keeping the noise level high and irritating. Isabel said, "The thing is, Mom, you don't think I heard what you said, but I did. You said, 'We need to talk about Max's project. Call me.'"

Isabel was right. Zoe had not thought that she had heard that little remark; she had been, in fact, not even sure that Stoney had heard her, and, yes, she had been using her condolences about the car as a way to insert that remark, and, to complicate things further, she didn't even care whether Max made an independent film in his bedroom or not. What she really wanted to do was to get Stoney to talk to her about what was going on between him and Isabel, and she couldn't think of another way, especially in front of Isabel, who had been stuck to Stoney like a second head all morning. Until that moment in the dining room. Now Stoney was nowhere to be seen, and she was trapped by Isabel in the pantry. She glanced up; she couldn't help herself. Stacks of dishes arranged in neat rows by color were arrayed all around them. One of the two girls—maybe Marya?—stopped in the doorway, glanced in, and walked away. Zoe said, "They must want to get in here—"

"I don't care! And if your phone rings, I don't care. Why should Stoney call you about my father's project? What business is it of yours! You are not attached to it!"

"No, I'm not. Fine. Tell Stoney to forget what I said, I don't care."

"But that's not the point. The point is that you said it—"

"I was just taking an interest, Isabel—"

But Isabel said, "That's a lie! You don't just take an interest, in fact you don't take an interest at all, so why pretend that you do? You're pretending that you do because you have some reason to, and I am just telling you to back off, because it's his project, and just because we all happened to spend ten days together for some reason after thirteen years doesn't mean you are part of the family and you can show an interest. If you wanted to show an interest, you should have shown it before this. Now it's too late!" She said the words "show an interest" as if she were spitting out garbage.

Now Zoe had the sense to say, "What are you worried about, Isabel?"

And even though Isabel shook her head and said, "I'm not worried about anything," emphasizing the word "worried," a look crossed her face that indicated that she was worried about something, though whether it had to do with Max or with Stoney, or even with Delphine, Zoe had no idea. Isabel went on, "And if I were worried, you would be the last person I would tell about it, but I'm not. It just drives me crazy that for ten days you've been sitting around, making yourself at home, offering your opinion, parading your new guy around here, just like it's the most natural thing in the world, when it isn't at all! It's not right that we should all act like we're just a happy, normal family when—"

"When in fact we just happened to be thrown into the bunker together, or into the lifeboat, for that matter, or the *Titanic*, or—"

"Go ahead and make fun of me, but there's not going to be this Hollywood ending where we all finally come to respect one another after our harrowing trip together!"

"Fine, Isabel. Please, have it your way. But do step aside, because I want to get out of here."

"That's the very reason I will not step aside."

"Isabel, do you know how crazy you sound?"

"Yes, I do."

"Do you want to sound this crazy?"

"I don't care how I sound to you, as a matter of fact."

Zoe could hear footsteps in the kitchen, maybe the footsteps of two people, and also out the window, in the driveway, tramp, tramp. All at once, she felt all her wishes to be out of here, to be getting into her car, to be somewhere like Paris or Morocco, fall away. Here she was. Here was Isabel. Here was the sink, and here were the dishes and the silverware and the serving platters and the hardwood floor beneath her feet. Yes, excess in here, but plain old excess, not excess with added-on flourishes of excess. No one's imagination had been put to work overtime in here. In here, she did not feel the press of six hundred years of history and culture as she did in the rest of the house. It was actually restful in here, in a way. She took a deep breath and said, "Okay, don't go away. Don't let me out. As long as you've got me here, I'll tell you something about my life." She almost smiled at the brilliance of this trick.

"Oh, God, Mom! All about you again." And Isabel fell for it.

"Well, it's your choice. You can leave, or you can stand there and listen. If you leave, I'll be happy, because I can leave, so if you don't want me to be happy, you can bar my way."

"I'm not listening."

"Fine, don't listen. But I am talking."

Isabel began to hum. It occurred to Zoe to tell her that she was acting like a baby, but instead she began telling her story. She said, "Remember that friend you had for a while, what was her name, Lee Anne, and her mother had been Miss Minnesota back in the 1970s? And she and her sister had a piano in their room, and every child in the family played two instruments and also took ballet? And she wasn't allowed to spend the night because she had to practice the piano first thing in the morning, and to go to bed by eight? You thought they were all so funny."

Isabel stopped humming long enough to toss her head. "Of course I do."

"Well, that was my life with your grandmother, except it was all done in the context of the hotel where she worked in Miami. We got up at five and got dressed. We got to the hotel by six, and she went to work in housekeeping. We didn't have a piano at home, but for an hour before the schoolbus came, I practiced on the piano in the lounge bar. Then I went to school on the bus, and after school, the bus dropped me off at the hotel, and I had lessons. The guy who played the piano at night gave me piano lessons, and his wife, who managed the cabaret dancers, gave me tap and jazz lessons, and after I was eleven, she gave me singing lessons, too. His name was Eddie Farrell and her name was Violet Hartman, and they had done a couple of musicals in Hollywood in the thirties. They had had a school in New York before they gave that up and moved down to Miami. Mom worked overtime to pay for all the lessons. When I wasn't going to school or doing homework, I was having lessons. And I did a lot of shows and recitals. The three of them said that they were grooming me for a stage career at the time, but I think now that, for Mom, it was more about keeping me out of trouble."

"You don't have to tell me—"

"The tale of my tragic childhood? I know that, though I never have really just laid it out for you, Isabel. It was work. It wasn't cooking and cleaning and making beds, but we went about it in the same way. Mom loved all those movies, *Little Miss Marker* and *The Seven Little Foys, Yankee Doodle Dandy,* that sort of thing, where the children are productively employed. She figured if I was making rhythmic noise, either tapping or playing the piano, then I wasn't getting into trouble, and since she was who she was, I went along with it—" She held up her hand to forestall the inevitable protest. "Anyway, it was fine with me, because when I made some money, doing whatever, she would take me shopping, and we always bought clothes for me, and she always said she couldn't find anything for herself that she liked. My reward was that I was the best-dressed kid in school."

Isabel had a skeptical look on her face, but she had stopped humming.

"Of course, she was no dummy, and she knew the difference between

Lena Horne and rock and roll. When some guys at my school asked me to be in a band in Miami, she let me, and she let me wear the Rasta locks and the tank top and everything, but, Isabel"—Zoe made sure that Isabel was looking her in the eye, which she was—"she sat in the audience every night, and when Terry McFadden, who had the van, took me home after a show, he was taking my mom home as well. Every single time. The guys thought it was a joke, but it was okay in a way, too, and, frankly, their own parents liked it, so I put up with it. Our life was not about rebelling, it was about making it. Always had been and always would be. And when we got to California and I met your dad, she orchestrated that, too."

"So you're telling me you were in purdah or something? You were the virgin sacrifice in an arranged marriage? Oh, please, Mom."

Zoe refrained from rolling her eyes, which Paul said was a contemptuous and alienating gesture, *the* contemptuous and alienating gesture, probably even among chimps, and went on. "Why do you think of us as not working-class? Why do you think she didn't put me to work doing what I could do best? The plan was never for me to have a childhood, Isabel, and then rebel and find myself and realize my inner nature—it was always to sing and dance instead of peel potatoes and weed the vegetable patch, and it was also to avoid the occasion of sin, because the big problem with having a baby if you are working-class is that you can't keep working. Didn't any of your economic-theory professors tell you about these things?" That was a good one, thought Zoe.

She leaned forward expressively, and Isabel, perhaps without realizing it, leaned backward. Zoe knew she could probably get out at this point, but she chose not to, as Paul would say. "Max fell in love with me. I knew that. I saw that he liked me and he was good-looking and important, but Mom said, 'Zoe, he is very much taken with you.' Do you think I loved him, or that I knew what love was, or that I was prepared in any way to reciprocate? I was used to doing what I was told, and usually what I was told to do was fun or rewarding. So I thought what I felt for Max was love, and then I got pregnant, and there you were, and I had a movie to be in while I was pregnant, and another movie to be in after you were born, so it seemed perfectly natural that you would be bottle-fed and that Delphine would do most of the baby care. She wanted to do it. It was easier for her to maintain your routine than for the two of us to pass you back and forth, and anyway, the doctor said that the most important thing was a stable routine. And *anyway*, and please pay attention to this, Isabel, for your grandmother, child-rearing was not about Mom and Dad and the baby in their little nest, it was about whoever has the time and the space to do it, does it. That's the way they do it in Jamaica—"

"I've heard this excuse before," said Isabel, in a sullen and dismissive tone of voice. "And I know most of this stuff."

"What's the difference between an excuse and a sequence of events?" said Zoe.

"An excuse lets you off the hook," said Isabel.

"Even so, I think that, for once, you should hear about this 'sequence of events' from my point of view."

Isabel did make a face, but she still didn't move. Zoe stared at her. Her temper was beginning to spark again, even though while she had been relating this information it had soothed her and distracted her from thoughts of Marcelle. For a moment, she paused and did what Paul suggested, imagining dowsing, dripping—the coals and fugitive sparks and occasional explosion being hit by sprays of water. Finally, she said, "Here is what Max said to me. He said, 'I want you no matter what happens.' It was very romantic. I believed him. He was almost twice my age. I thought that all Mom's hard work and mine was paying off at last. I thought it was the American dream."

"Didn't you want to be with me?"

Zoe took a deep breath and decided, after all these years, to be honest, because clearly she had nothing to lose. She said, "I didn't know."

"How could you not know?"

"How could I know? You were a six-and-a-half-pound baby; you scared me because you seemed so fragile, and then, when you were old enough to hold out your arms, you held them out to my mom. When I held you, you cried, and it seemed sort of natural that way. Now, you can go ahead and say that was my fault, and I'm sure it was, but it takes more courage than you think to be a mother, and when someone is always around, giving you an out, and the baby seems to prefer that person, well, you don't really necessarily develop that courage. That's my opinion. Think of it this way, Isabel: when I was your age, you were three and a half years old. You may not remember that you had a point of view, too, but you did, and your point of view was that I was not the preferred person, that I was not really the mom. And that was my point of view, too. Just giving birth didn't actually make me feel like the mom. In my mind, your grandmother simply defined what a mom was, and she seemed to define what a mom was for you, too. I was that young. Now, you tell me, what could I have done about that?"

"You're blaming a baby?"

•

Isabel could not really have said what she thought of this story, because, unfortunately, she was too well educated in sympathizing with working-class women of color not to respond in spite of herself, but though she was accustomed to sympathizing with Delphine, it was novel to be sympathizing, even remotely, with Zoe. It was unfortunate, as well, that Zoe's take on the whole thing was so believable that you could write a paper about it—"Working Girls: The Sociology of Female Stardom in the Hollywood Movie Industry, 1940–1990." Still, she said, "You're blaming a baby?"

Zoe looked exasperated now. She exclaimed, "I'm not blaming you, Isabel. I'm saying that you came into the world with a strong personality and that I was surrounded by strong personalities. Do you think I'm lying?"

Isabel resisted, but then she admitted, "No. But you have a strong personality."

Zoe leaned back and then leaned forward again, which seemed to push Isabel back no matter how much she wanted to hold her ground. Zoe said, "Do I? I have no idea, actually. To me, it seems like I just do as I am told."

In fact, Isabel could not have said exactly how or why she had entered into this conflict at this moment, in this place, on this day. An hour and a half ago, she would have said she was content with things, practically happy. She wanted to go back to her own bright fire-lookout of a room, and she was about to. She wanted to have a really good talk with her dad and actually work out what her next life-step was, and she was about to. Stoney and Simon, in their different ways, had been entertaining, and then— admittedly, stoned—she had slept well. When she woke up this morning, the Iraq war and global warming had actually seemed to be problems she could deal with. But she'd overheard Zoe in the hallway, tossing off that meaningless but intrusive and unwarranted remark, and then she'd been in the dining room and Zoe had come in with that self-satisfied look on her face.

Zoe said, "Anyway, you know she lost a baby when she was in Jamaica."

"I know that."

"So you can imagine that she was obsessed with safety."

"I know that."

"So she kept me absolutely safe."

"I know that, too."

"Well, then, when you came along, and you were premature, though pretty big and healthy, it was automatic for her to decide that my expertise and commitment to safety, at the age of nineteen and having had no real child-care responsibilities in my life, left something to be desired."

"But you didn't have to move out." And now here she was, thought Isabel, saying this utterly obvious and mistaken thing; her line for years had been, Thank God she moved out and took her entourage with her! Just last night, she had remarked to Stoney that it was a shame they couldn't stay here for a day or two without Zoe and Paul and Charlie and, yes, Simon, and even Elena (because, though she liked Elena well enough, Elena was incredibly, though subtly, ubiquitous). Even Cassie could go. Stoney had said, "I'm not sure I'm ready for the unadulterated scrutiny of you and me if we were here with just Max and Delphine," and she hadn't had an answer for that, except, "It's going to happen sooner or later." Her arguments with her mother seemed to have a rhetoric of their own that never, ever truly reflected the complexity of her feelings.

"You and Delphine came to the set with me every day until it was time for you to go to school. You remember that time we filmed in North Carolina? And that time in England? That was part of the contracts. I had those two trailers, and you and your grandmother occupied one and my junk occupied the other, and that went on for five years, and you remember that, right?"

"It was fun." Isabel didn't say that going to the set when Zoe was working was more fun than staying home when she wasn't working, which had seemed utterly dull and isolated by comparison. She didn't say it because it didn't seem to suit her argument, and it did seem as though, with everything she did say, her argument kept dissipating and transforming into something she herself didn't understand.

"Well, you were a cute kid, and everyone always made a big deal of you, and you liked it when the girls would do your hair and put makeup on you and dress you up—"

"And there were horses and other animals sometimes. It was fun." She stressed the "was."

Zoe seemed to ignore the stress. "Well, you were no trouble, except, once, I had to do a scene where I fell in a river and had to drown, and you started screaming and wouldn't stop until I came out and got dried off and dressed and you were sure that I was all right. Delphine actually made the director stop filming for an hour so that you wouldn't have permanent emotional scars. We never let you watch after that, because we weren't sure what you were making of things. But then it was time for you to go to school, and of course that made it different, so you started staying home, and Mom was staying home with you, and it was more like regular people, with me going out to work and coming home at the end of the day."

Then she said, "So the first movie I did that you stayed home from was *Something Good*, that movie with Nick Nolte, did you ever see that? It was something really bad in the end, but we had fun on the set, and that was the first time in my whole life that Delphine wasn't around for some reason." Isabel felt herself go on the alert. She could not have said why, but she wasn't exactly surprised when Zoe continued: "The first time! Isn't that amazing? So of course I fell in love."

Now, as familiar as she was with theories of female sexuality, Isabel moved aside. It was like magic. All her mother had to do was say the most horrifying words, and the key was turned and the door was opened. It would be good, Isabel thought, to leave right now. It would be an exit. She could move gracefully, smoothly. She thought of the girls she had known at school whose mothers, they said, talked to them frankly and openly about sexuality. She was not one of those girls. Nor had she seen any of Zoe's famous sex scenes with Russell Crowe or the notorious almost-nude rooftop scene with Dennis Quaid. (She had seen Zoe shoot plenty of people, though—John Hurt, the old English guy; also Laurence Fishburn; Winona Ryder, on TV; and Faye Dunaway. She had seen her run Gene Hackman down with a car and throw Laura Dern off a bridge, as well as drop suddenly to the floor so that Alan Alda could fall out of a twenty-story window.) The only movie of Zoe's that she actually liked was *Wanda Rossini*, and that was because of the music, of course, but also, she often told people, because at the end of it Zoe had died tragically of a brain tumor.

Zoe went on. There was no stopping her. She said, "The guy who wrote *Something Good* was named Justin Merrill, and he was about a year older than I was, and he was fun. His father was a novelist, and his mother was an artist, and he himself had gone to Amherst, which was better than Harvard, he said, because more exclusive, and I have no idea how he ended up writing that movie, because he never wrote another one, but he was a very naughty, naughty boy, tremendously good-looking, with a drug habit and a car habit and a girl habit." Now Zoe seemed to be positively enjoying herself. "He was every single thing that Delphine hated, and he was so funny that I was falling down laughing every day. I don't know why they had him around on the set—usually the screenwriter is only there if he's rewriting pages—but Justin did whatever he wanted to do. He didn't recognize rules or impossibilities or the desires of others, and he made up his mind to get me to fall in love with him, and I did."

Jason Proctor, Isabel thought, in spite of herself, recalling a guy she had dated for a month between the two halves of Leo, but she tossed her chin in a challenging way and said, "Why are you telling me this?"

"Well, Max never knew and Delphine never knew. Now you know. That was my first taste of having my own life, and after that, everything else was broken. I'm sorry it was, but it was. I didn't want that other life back. I couldn't have it back. Once I knew I could have a secret and keep it, and do what no one else knew I was doing, then that's what I wanted to do. It took a few years for me to act, but . . ."

Isabel recognized that Zoe was being honest with her, and that she had asked for it. Maybe she hadn't meant to ask for it, but she had anyway. She stepped aside. The exit was clear, but Zoe didn't go.

Now they both heaved simultaneous sighs, possibly as a substitute for making eye contact. They did not make eye contact. This was the way Isabel recognized that the long conflict was not over, or even very deeply plumbed, but that, for the moment, they were tired of it. And, of course, in an hour or so they were going their separate ways again. Isabel relented, and said, "I guess they want to get in here."

"I'm sure they do," said Zoe.

Isabel turned and went out of the pantry, and Zoe was right behind her. A short corridor went off to the right, leading to the dining room. Zoe turned there, and Isabel felt it. That she felt the difference was depressing, but that she was no longer in proximity to her mother was a relief, so it evened out. The kitchen—which Isabel admired because it was fitted out to look like one of those ramshackle upscale English kitchens and had one of those stoves that she had never been able to understand—was to the left. Or you could go directly outside, which Isabel did, thinking she would go back in the far door, beside the swimming pool, and then run up to the Amber Room and find Stoney.

But Stoney wasn't as interested as he might have been in her argument with her mother. He said, "I don't mind talking to Zoe about Max's project. She's smart."

"She's smart?"

"She's smart about this business. We've talked about that."

Isabel felt herself make a bitchy and resentful face.

Stoney looked at her for a moment, then said, "Your mother has a certain low cunning that passes for intelligence in the movie business."

She had to chuckle at that.

Stoney knelt down and peered under the bed, put his entire head, in fact, underneath the embossed gold silk bedskirt, and came up with one of her flip-flops. He handed it to her, stood up, and said, "Does Joe Blow look a little subdued to you?"

"I didn't notice."

"It's not exactly that. I don't know what it is."

She unzipped her suitcase and slipped the shoe in. He went around to the other side of the bed, knelt down, and disappeared again. This time, he came up with her book about potatoes. She said, "Simon should read that. There's a whole chapter about the revolution in marijuana growing over the last thirty years. I thought Leo made all that stuff up, but I guess he was reading this book." She took the book and put it in her handbag.

"Did you check the bathroom?"

"I thought I did."

"Then you did." He put his hands on his hips and cocked his head slightly. "And Marya and Monique were whispering about something, too. They were whispering in Russian and so into it that they didn't even see me. It makes me nervous."

"I'm sure they've seen enough to talk about for a month. Zoe Cunningham and her guru, for one thing, but even my dad. Even you. And God knows what they've made of Simon. He seemed on pretty good terms with them when he was talking to us last night."

"He's funny."

"Okay."

"Well, he is."

Isabel admitted that he was. She didn't mind Simon. She was sure she would have minded Simon when she was ten and he was seven or when she was eighteen and he was fifteen, but in fact she didn't mind him now. Stoney went to the window and looked out. It really was amazing, Isabel thought, to stand in the Amber Room on a sunny day and have the walls blaze up like a fire around you, and to stand in the Amber Room in the middle of the night and have the walls vanish in the darkness like forest pools. Last night, her third night, she had been completely disoriented when she woke up and wanted to go to the bathroom. Even after she was wide awake, she could not at first figure out where the bathroom was. Stoney said, "I just have a bad feeling about my deal."

"You don't have a deal, Stoney. He might not do it." She meant, He won't do it.

He turned and looked at her. He said, "You saw them yesterday. They were looking at everything—the pictures, books in the library. They were keeping it quiet, but they were investigating."

"I don't think you should count on—"

"I'm not. Really. But I keep remembering how Jerry used to rant all the time that the business was changing. When he started out, it was great! Every studio had rows and rows of producers, and he took projects to them and they bought them and developed them, and Jerry was rich and powerful and happy. Then he would say, 'These days, I've got to package everything! Why have I got to package everything? I'm not a producer! But now I have to attach the star and I have to attach the writer and I have to attach the director. What are the producers doing all day? Just tell me that one thing.' But I like that part! I think it's fun, and I like this package. Here it is, the book, the director, and the financing! But it makes me superstitious. I'm sure everything's okay. I'm sure I'm just paranoid. Right?"

Isabel picked up her suitcase. She said, "Right."

In the dining room, everyone already had their salads, microgreens from the greenhouse with a champagne vinaigrette. The rolls were Isabel's favorite—nine-grain with poppyseeds on top. And, of course, the French butter. She and Stoney were last to the table, and everyone glanced up at them when they entered the room. The two seats remaining were not next to one another. Stoney took the seat next to Cassie. Isabel had to sit beside Paul (she thought, In the vegetarian ghetto). As soon as she sat down, Marya and Monique began to carry in the soup course. Isabel didn't notice anything different about them. Monique set her dish of asparagus bisque before her. A pink grilled shrimp in its shell, flecked with bits of seasoning, floated in the creamy green of Stoney's soup across the table. Hers had a golden cube of a crouton and two small grilled asparagus tips. Zoe said, "Mom. Tell Isabel about that time when I was a kid and they found the dead body."

Isabel looked up.

Delphine smiled at her, but said to Zoe, "Why do you want to tell that story?"

"I just thought of it. I was telling Isabel about practicing piano before school in the bar there at the hotel, and I thought of that."

Delphine tossed her head. "It was nothing dramatic. No one was shot or anything. One of the patrons had had a heart attack the night before and fallen down in a corner behind a banquette, under some curtains. He was discovered while Zoe was in there playing her pieces before school."

"Who discovered him?" said Isabel.

"I think her name was Hortense," said Delphine. "She would have been the regular cleaner for the lounge."

"And you were sitting there?" Isabel turned to Zoe.

"I was sitting on the piano bench, yes. I always practiced for an hour, so I'd been there a while." She put her hands on the table, picked up her fork, put it down. "It was me. I discovered him. As a rule, I made a beeline from the door to the piano and never went anywhere else in the room. I stayed where I was supposed to be and kept my fingers moving. Before Hortense came in, I saw the foot in its shoe right there by the curtain. It was a brown-and-beige spectator oxford with a capped, pointed toe, and the brown part was either real alligator or fake alligator. I can see it perfectly in my mind's eye." She looked around the table, then right at Isabel. "I knew that because I got up and walked across the room for the first time ever, and I stared down at that shoe, then at his trouser cuff, which was cream-colored, then at his knee, and then I went back to the bench and I played through my piece. I didn't look at his face; the one shoe was enough for me. Then Hortense came in with her vacuum cleaner, and then, a moment later, she screamed."

The asparagus bisque was good, Isabel thought. She finished it, then ate the grilled asparagus.

Delphine said, "Well, I didn't even hear about it until later that day, after Zoe had gone off to school. What grade were you in?"

"I was in fifth grade, so I would have been ten."

Monique took away Isabel's soup bowl and came back a moment later to set down her next course, a mound of wild rice set upon some leaves of Bibb lettuce, with two slices of grilled eggplant beside it, nicely decorated with a grid of black lines.

"That looks good," said Cassie. Those outside the vegetarian ghetto had salmon instead of eggplant.

Isabel saw Stoney nod appreciatively, and then divide the salmon with an expert flick of his fork.

"I've never seen a dead body," said Isabel.

Elena had expected, of course, to think about death at lunch, but not to talk about it. It was appropriate to the times, but also to the room, which was a fantasy of France and specifically of the old market Les Halles. The feathery, soaring metal grillework of that building was neatly painted on the walls, and in the frames created by the faux grillework, the painter had painted long, sunny perspectives of Paris: Eiffel Tower to the west, Luxembourg Gardens to the south, Père Lachaise Cemetery to the east, and Montmartre to the north, all recognizable and in proportion, as if, indeed, you could look out through the nonexistent windows of Les Halles and see what you could not see. There were real windows on three sides, too, with interior shutters. When the shutters were closed, as in the evening, the French scenery encircled the room. When they were open, as now, sunny France and sunny southern California complemented each other nicely and gave the dining experience an air of picnic exuberance. The whole idea had been Joe Blow's—inspired by the chandelier above their heads, Louis XV, that Mike had found in France but had not had a spot for in the Menton house. The trompe-l'oeil artist Joe found had done nice things with the ceiling, too, making the "ironwork" seem, though the ceiling itself was flat, to soar away above the chandelier into misty darkness. Elena thought it was the best dining room she had ever seen. But death was present here—how many protesters against modern chicken-raising methods knew that the poulterers of nineteenth-century Paris had kept chickens in cages in the vaults beneath Les Halles, sending children and servants down to hold candles for the chickens so that they would eat sufficient grain to keep them fat? Since Elena knew this, the decor gave her the vague sense that underneath the dining room there were some sort of mysterious vaults or caves, where animals, vegetables, and wine were imprisoned. Today, too, it was connected in her mind to the Reformation/Counter-Reformation Suite (was that one directly above this one?), where she and Paul had chatted the afternoon before.

"I've never seen a dead body," said Isabel.

Delphine looked at Zoe, and Elena suspected that Delphine was thinking that, therefore, her child-rearing practices were vindicated. And they were, as far as Elena was concerned. Delphine said, "Honey, the best thing to do with a dead body is to sit with it for a while. Till you get used to it. If someone else is around, you should both sit with it, and chat about what that person was like. In my experience, if you can just give yourself time to get used to the way that person is now that he's dead, or she's dead, then all the rest comes easier. Dead bodies are quiet. That's comforting, in a way."

Although Elena expected her to go on, she didn't. Next to Isabel, Paul, who had been very at home in that suite, not impressed at all with the tortures depicted in the paintings, continued to eat in his methodical way. She put her hand under the table, on Max's knee, and felt his hand cover hers momentarily. The main course was good. She had suggested the julienne of fennel to Raphael, and she thought it added a crisp, bright accent that went well with the earthiness of the wild rice. Of course, for her, eating wild rice in April, on the second of April, was somehow an odd thing. She had grown up eating wild rice, but they had always eaten it in the fall, when her father brought home bags from Minnesota and Wisconsin during the deer season. Another thing you could do with wild rice was something Elena would never do, but her mother had often done, which was to make wild-rice–cheese soup (Campbell's Cream of Mushroom and Cream of Potato *both* figured into this recipe). As a child, she had also seen her grandmother pop kernels of wild rice like popcorn, then salt them and use them as a garnish, but she had never tried that herself. She said, "I saw five dead bodies before I was twenty-three. One was my thirty-five-year-old uncle, who was kicked in the head by a horse when I was ten, and another was a boy in our neighborhood who drowned when he was sucked down a storm drain." As she made this remark, she wondered if Simon would take it as his cue to tell her if he had ever seen a dead body, but all he said was "Jeez, Mom!," lifting his eyebrows.

Joe appeared in the doorway and looked at them all. He didn't look as playful and bright as usual. She suspected all four of the staff were happy to see them go. Elena wondered if she would be out of bounds making sure that Isabel, as well as Simon, wrote the Russians a thank-you note within the next three days.

She took a sip of the Riesling. It was too sweet to be one of her favorites, and she didn't think it was quite right with the salmon, but the others seemed to like it well enough. In fact, she dreaded the wine chapter in her book, and had been putting it off for six months, in favor of Congress, the presidency, and auto maintenance. They had chatted in the Reformation/Counter-Reformation Suite for almost an hour. She had been walking down the hall from the Flower Room, and Paul had said, "Have you seen this suite? It's fascinating."

She had said, "I guess I've avoided it."

Paul had said, "This is my fourth time. You shouldn't miss it, really." And so they had gone in, and Paul had shut the door behind them.

She saw Isabel glance sharply at Stoney and then looked at her plate again. Whatever was between Stoney and Isabel seemed to complicate Isabel's attitude, but not Stoney's. Isabel's attitude toward things, truth to tell, was already plenty complicated, Elena felt.

"I want to be buried with my handbag," said Cassie, suddenly.

"What is that about?" said Delphine.

Cassie picked up her handbag, which was next to her chair, and said, "When I was carrying it down the stairs, I realized that. It's not about anything, except at my age these are the sorts of idle thoughts you have."

"Do you know that joke?" said Charlie.

Cassie shook her head. Charlie settled back in his chair and began while everyone else continued to eat. "There's this old guy, and he's incredibly rich, but he's on the outs with everyone in his family except the wife, and she's spent her whole life doing everything he's told her to do. As he gets sicker and sicker, he takes her aside and says, 'Now, Essie, you've got to promise me one thing.' She says, 'What's that one thing?' And he says, 'You promise first, and then I'll tell you. Have I ever treated you badly? Have I ever not had your best interests at heart?' And she agrees that he hasn't. So she promises, and then he says, 'I want you to go to the bank and get all of my money, and put it in my casket in a lead-lined box with me.'

"Well, old Essie is pretty pissed, and she says, 'What about me?' But he says, 'You promised, and, besides that, you've always been a good wife and done what you're told, and Jesus will provide for you because you've done your wifely duty, just the way he always has.' So she calmed down, and pretty soon he died.

"Well, the day of the funeral came around, and, as per instructions, they had it at the church, and no one came, because he'd been such an ornery old cuss. The only people in the pews were Essie and her sister. They were sitting there waiting for the minister, and here comes a man carting a big heavy box, and he sets it into the foot of the coffin and turns and walks away. The sister says, 'Essie, what's that?' And Essie says, 'Well, Ezra made me promise that after he died I would go to the bank and get out all his money and put it in a box and bury it in his coffin with him.' And the sister says, 'Essie, you have always been a sucker since the day you married that man, and you're still a sucker.'

"'Well, he said Jesus would provide, and I did promise, and I never went back on a promise.'

"'How much money is in there?' says the sister.

"'Five million dollars.'

"'And you in this old coat!'

"'Well, Ezra said that Jesus would provide, and I believed that Jesus would provide, and Jesus has provided. It's a miracle.'

"So her sister gets all excited and says, 'What did Jesus do?' And Essie says, 'He told me to write a check.'"

This got a pretty good laugh. Elena herself laughed, though of course she was a little shocked that Charlie would tell a joke that mocked his right-wing political allies, but she had learned her lesson, and she didn't say anything. Charlie himself laughed, pleased at the response. She glanced quickly at Max. He had a good-natured smile on his face.

Cassie regarded Charlie with a straight-man look and said, "I don't care about the money. If I fall over in the street, you can hand it to the nearest homeless person, but I want my handbag, with my wallet and my digital camera and my address book, and my checkbook, and my pen, and, let's see, the car keys—"

"Why the car keys?" said Delphine.

"Because they belong to the handbag. When you sell the car, you can give them the extra set."

"I'm surprised you don't want a Viking burial," said Delphine. "Pushed in the Saab off the end of the Santa Monica Pier."

"I'm not asking to be treated like a king or a queen. I've just never gone anywhere without my handbag, and anyway, I especially like the one I'm using, and I don't want to be separated from it prematurely. You know Ray McGalliard, don't you?" she said to Delphine. "He's eighty-two. He told me he never buys a pair of shoes without wondering if he's going to die before they wear out. And he's perfectly healthy, to all appearances."

Delphine said, "You always talk about your death as if it will be a good joke that you'll be around to enjoy. You don't take it seriously."

"Why should I? It's not my business."

Delphine tossed her head.

In the momentary silence, Zoe said, "Death is actually not first on my list of bad outcomes. What you really don't want is yourself at eighty on *The Tonight Show*, wearing some strange hat and your hands shaking as you light yet another cigarette, to be the last lingering image the public has of you, so that when they go back and look at some movie you made when you were twenty-five, they say, 'She actually was rather pretty when she was first starting out.'"

Joe passed the doorway and looked in again, still not happy. For that matter, Elena got a similar sense from Monique and Marya—that the ten of them had overstayed their welcome. Zoe, too, glanced at Joe, but then she said to Max (with a preliminary glance at Isabel), "Are you going to do an all-naked talking-heads picture in your bedroom with Madonna and Clint?"

Isabel snorted.

Max said, "Actually, Elena and I spent the day in the library yesterday, looking at pictures of Russia. Elena read up a little on Gogol."

"He wore a pageboy," said Elena. "I read some other things he wrote. They were quite funny. Not at all like *Taras Bulba*. That one called 'The Nose' would make a great cartoon."

"Though I think someone did that," said Max.

"Oh," said Elena, and she felt surprisingly crestfallen, as if her incipient Hollywood career, which had begun the day before, had ended already.

Max said, "It could be done again." He looked kind and amused, as if reading her mind. And then, right in that moment, in that room, in front of all his relatives, she was quickened with love for him. Max himself came into sharper focus, and when he then let out the briefest, most delicate sigh, she heard it more clearly. The brightness that suddenly enveloped him, she knew, was the brightness in her own eyes, her own rods and cones, her own optic nerves. The loveliness of his hair and face and shoulders was her own flesh vibrating more intensely at his proximity. But what created this love was a suddenly vast sense of every story he had told her—Max as a boy in knickers (knickers!) walking to school; Max in Vietnam in the latrine, and the latrine suddenly toppling over and sliding down the hill; Max at the dinner table with his girlfriend's mother, eating Chinese takeout with Lee Strasberg; Max and Ina taking photographs of one another in the doorway of some apartment behind LAX, surrounded and overwhelmed by the bougainvillea; Max and Lilli Palmer standing in the snow, her in dark furs; Max on the stage at the Oscars, pushing his hair out of his eyes; Max with a scowling baby Isabel on the beach; Max staring at Zoe, and staring at her again. Max driving his car. Max sitting alertly beside her, watching a movie. Max looking tall and busy, walking down Melrose. Max sleeping on his back in the sunlight in his own bed. Her mind was full of images of Max, and though they were not all complete, they were all immanent—any single one seemed able to manifest at any moment. Some were ones she remembered from times she had spent with him, and others were ones she had imagined from things he had told her, but all were equal in their power to animate her tenderness toward him. Here was Max, fifty-eight years old! So many adventures bundled together and patting her on the knee! Really, she thought, how was it possible to love a young man, a boy, in comparison with loving an old man? She couldn't remember; it was hardly imaginable.

And yet here was Charlie, over on the other side and down. She didn't love him. His adventures left her cool, even put her off. Here was Paul—and she appreciated him more than she had before yesterday, especially the way he sat quietly surrounded by hangings and crucifixions and burnings at the stake, suggesting techniques of mental discipline in an even, deep, steady tone of voice, techniques that part of her found helpful and part of her found simplistic and silly—she would never love him, either. How strange it was, after all.

Cassie leaned around Stoney and stared down the table at Delphine. For once, thought Elena, she seemed a little put out. She said, "Well, then, you tell us how you see your death. You're seventy-six years old, and you've had a long time to think about it."

"Oh," said Delphine. "It doesn't seem that long."

"Long enough," said Cassie, challenging. Elena wondered if there was going to be an argument at last.

Delphine picked up the napkin in her lap, turned it around, laid it in her lap again, and smoothed it with her hands. It was thoughtful but uncanny, like the gesture of a little girl, Elena thought, making sure she was neat and clean before addressing the grown-ups. Finally, she said, "Well, last night I went into the suite, the Reformation/Counter-Reformation Suite. I was looking for a movie to watch, and I'd seen all the ones in my room—"

"What movies are in the Bird Room?" asked Simon.

Delphine looked at him. She said, "*Winged Migration, Green Mansions, The Birds, The Birdman of Alcatraz,* one just called *Birdy.* Let's see, *The Birdcage.*"

"Pretty eclectic," said Stoney.

"Shh," said Isabel, but in fact Elena could see that the interruption had allowed Delphine to regain her customary self-possession.

"Anyway," said Delphine, "I found *The Seventh Seal.* Remember that one?"

Max let out a long hum of appreciation. He said, "I saw that first when I was a freshman in college. I saw it five nights in a row, every night the film society showed it."

"That's about the Black Death, isn't it?" said Isabel.

Max nodded. Elena had never seen the movie, though she had heard of it.

"I need to buy a copy of that," said Max.

"Everyone dies in that movie," said Cassie.

"No, they don't," said Delphine. "Quit interrupting me."

Cassie sat back and made a lip-zipping gesture.

"Who hasn't seen that movie?" said Delphine.

"I haven't," said Charlie. Elena shook her head. Simon said, "Never heard of it."

"I've heard of it," said Isabel.

"That was my mother's favorite movie of all time," said Paul, "except for *Three Coins in the Fountain*."

Max smiled at this, and Paul returned his smile, or seemed to. With the beard, you couldn't really tell.

"It's simple, really," said Delphine. "It's the middle of the fourteenth century, and a knight and his squire are just coming back to Sweden after ten years at the Crusades, and they find out that the plague has preceded them."

"Good immune systems to get that far," said Isabel.

For once, Dephine gave her a look. For once, Isabel was abashed. "They wake up on the beach and start reconnoitering. The squire sees a monk sitting next to a rock and goes over to ask the news, and when the monk doesn't answer, he pulls on his hood, and the camera shows what he sees—the monk's dead face, his eyes picked out by the shorebirds and his skin partially eaten away. Then Death himself appears, a few minutes later. Death and the knight decide to play chess. If the knight wins, he gets something. If Death wins, that's it. It's all black and white, of course."

"I remember it as a scary movie," said Zoe. "Very contrasty, with the faces of the characters a little overexposed and really pale."

"Practically the first thing, the knight and the squire go into a church, and while the squire is talking to a painter—"

"Who says, 'People always prefer a skull to a naked woman'—I remember that clearly," said Max.

"Is that true?" said Elena.

"Only on opening weekend," said Max.

Delphine ignored them. "The knight goes into the confessional and confesses all of his doubts about the existence of God and the meaning of life. Then he brags about his strategy for beating Death at chess. Then the priest, who is Death, turns around—"

"He's fucked," said Simon.

"But not right away," said Delphine. "In the meantime, there's a young couple, Mary and Joseph, and the baby Michael, traveling actors and acrobats. He sees visions and she doesn't.

"The knight and squire come upon a young girl being executed as a witch. The knight wants to find out from her if God exists, but all she can do is cry out."

"You watched this movie voluntarily?" said Charlie. "I gather that I'm in the British Colonial Room, because I watched *The Lives of a Bengal Lancer*. I also watched *A Passage to India* the other night."

Max chuckled.

"Pretty soon, a procession of flagellants comes by, bearing several crosses and whipping themselves and each other, crying out and chanting 'Dies Irae,' which I think means 'Day of Wrath.' The group stops, a priest gives a hellfire-and-brimstone sermon, and everyone falls to their knees, and all of this begins to look dangerous when a smith, whose wife has left him for one of the actors, finds Joseph in the tavern, eating, and goads the patrons of the tavern, with, of course, the assistance of the priest, into tormenting him for no reason other than that he's an actor. But the squire happens to come in, and happens not only to save him, but also to injure the priest, though exactly how I couldn't tell. It looked like he poked his eyes out—"

"Eew," said Isabel.

"—but he seems fine later. In the meantime, the knight has befriended Mary and Michael, and they are chatting together when Joseph and the squire show up. After that, they all decide to take a shortcut through the forest and head for the knight's castle, where his wife has been waiting for him for ten years. On their way through the forest—"

"As I remember," said Max, "the forest scenes were filmed in a backlot in downtown Stockholm, and of course they had to be extra careful with the camera, since modern high-rises were looming all around them."

"The soldiers show up with the witch, planning to burn her at the stake in a clearing. The knight is quite excited by her reappearance, because this time she's lucid, and able to tell him about the Devil. She asks him to look into her eyes, and she says that she sees the Devil everywhere. But in her eyes, he only sees terror, and all around them, he only sees the usual scene. Then the soldiers build the pyre and set it alight, and it's clear that the girl will not be saved. They've broken her hands and tortured her, and she doesn't want to recant, anyway. You have to say to yourself that of course the soldiers must look exactly like devils to her. After watching until they can't stand it anymore, the knight and his friends leave. The girl is lashed to the framework, staring in horror at the bonfire, rigid with fear, and suddenly she relaxes and slumps to the side, and below her you see Death kneeling. It is he who has had mercy upon her, and preserved her from more agony. That's when I realized that *The Seventh Seal* is a comic masterpiece.

"Pretty soon, it's back to the chess game. By this time, the knight knows

Death has him beaten. They play, and chat, and then Joseph notices them, and realizes that the knight's opponent is Death. And the knight sees that the actor knows, so the knight happens to knock the pieces off the board, and while Death is replacing them, Mary and Joseph and the baby escape. Later, in the midst of a storm, the knight, the squire, his girl, the smith, and his wife come to the castle, where the knight's wife has been waiting for them, and in the last scene, while they're sitting at the table, reading from the book of Revelation, Death comes knocking at the door, and they all rise to greet him. Only the knight can't stand it, and he can't understand it, either. He puts his face in his hands and calls out to God, but the others stand quietly, and pretty soon, a shadow comes over them, one by one. In the very last scene, Joseph sees them dancing on the crest of the hill, silhouetted against the sky. And I saw why everyone loves this movie. It's incredibly comforting, because it tells you that if you are in the presence of death long enough, it doesn't matter whether life is meaningless or meaningful."

Delphine looked at Cassie and said, "The knight, I could see, was reared like I was, to always be thinking about God and always be praying for the will to obey and do the right thing, because that's how they disciplined us girls in those days. It was especially important for us little 'Negro' girls to be perfect, because, as far as we could tell from the behavior of the teachers, God was already not well disposed toward us. They said that God was merciful—that even though we were Negro girls, and not English girls, God was willing to take care of us if we did every single thing we were told. If we did every single thing we were told, and things still went wrong, well, we must have missed some little, crucial detail, and surely it was that very detail that God cared about above all others." Her voice was even. "We were told that God had infinite mercy and was infinitely forgiving, but I realized even then that if we were to judge by the way our teachers treated us, that certainly could not be true, because 'strait is the gate and narrow is the way.' So of course the knight was afraid. He was afraid of God, not Death. But the others were smiling, because they didn't have to worry about God."

"It's true," said Paul, "that Jesus has a lot to answer for. My own view is that monotheism has been a pretty toxic idea for humanity. There is a lot of debate right now about whether humans have an inborn, biologically based propensity to belief in the Higher Being, or Beings, and if so, why that would be."

"We talked about that in one of my anthro classes," said Isabel. "I wrote a paper about how it's all nurture. My theory was that since young humans require nurture and authority for such a long time, they can't help constructing an image of authority in their minds that amalgamates all the authority figures that they experience early on, and then culture provides them with a method of naming that image and cultivating it. I tried to devise an experiment that would test if there is an inborn propensity to worship God, but my professor and I couldn't think of a way to remove the presence of authority. I did get an A on the paper, though. She said it was 'carefully thought out.'"

"There's no real evidence that human civilizations do any better under polytheistic systems," Paul went on in his usual careful, or, you might say, pedantic, way. "But it could be that the ritualized displays of human sacrifice that seem to have been ubiquitous in pre–Judeo-Christian-Islamic religions were more about poor technology than anything else. I guess I see the Trade Center victims and the bombing victims in Iraq as types of human sacrifice, the altar being the world stage, and Allah and God being the bloodthirsty deities who require propitiation. Did we talk about fetishes at one point?"

"We did," said Zoe. Elena realized that she no longer called him "dear one."

"Oh, good. Well, that idea seems to me apropos whenever religion comes up as an organized, public institution."

Now everyone was quiet, as well they might be, thought Elena. A sigh came from Max, then from Isabel. Elena herself thought she might sigh, but what sort of sigh? Exhausted? Relieved? Uncertain? Silverware made little clinking sounds as it was placed on dishware. Elena looked at Simon. He had picked up the wine bottle and was perusing the label. He put the wine bottle down and smiled at her. She smiled back at him. Charlie was being quiet. Apparently, Charlie had approached Mike and Al with his investment proposal yesterday afternoon and been turned down not very graciously. Elena didn't know what she felt about that. At any rate, Charlie was being so quiet that Elena was surprised when Cassie said to him, "Whatever you think about the war, do you really want to be all alone for it?"

And Charlie answered, "No."

Max caught her eye.

Stoney said, "What did all you guys say when Jerry died?"

Right then, Cassie, who was sitting beside him, looked at him, then put her arm around him. She said, "Honey, we said, 'Thank God.' We said, 'Thank God he lived, and thank God, given his illness, that he died, and thank God we knew him, because he was one of a kind.'"

Stoney looked at Max. Max said, "I would agree with that."

Now Stoney burst into tears. After a moment, he put his elbows on the table, to either side of his plate, and put his head in his hands. It was sudden. Joe Blow passed the door, and everyone sat very still for a moment.

Elena glanced around Paul at Isabel. Isabel was staring at Stoney, but not in shock or horror—more, Elena thought, in relief.

"Here's a story, Stoney. And actually, it fits right in with this whole discussion," said Max. He arranged his utensils neatly on his plate, then pushed his plate away. "When Jerry was your age, and I think you were about six— when was that? Early seventies sometime?—anyway, we all had bushy side-burns and lots of hair. I think I had a swashbuckler's mustache myself. I didn't know Jerry very well then. He'd picked me out as a hippie type, but a hippie from New York, one he could trust. This particular Saturday morning, he showed up at my apartment. He had on neatly pressed jeans and a nice shirt and polished shoes. I let him in anyway, and he said you had gone to Disneyland for the weekend with your cousins from New York, and since he had two whole days to himself, could we score some LSD? Somehow, he'd decided that I was the LSD type."

Elena glanced at Simon, who was looking at Max with considerable interest. What was she going to say when he asked her directly if she had ever taken LSD? She tried to look unfazed by this aspect of Max's story.

"I wasn't as tuned in as Jerry thought, but I knew a guy in the music business who lived out in Malibu, and so we got into Jerry's car and drove to his place, which was a ramshackle ranch house on a nice private piece of ground. As we drove, Jerry started looking neater and neater, and less and less cool, and I just kept wondering if my friends would think he was a drug agent or not, but it turned out, when I told my friend that Jerry was a *movie* agent, he practically fell to his knees in gratitude that Jerry should come to his humble abode, and so there we were. I remember they had these tiny orange pills, and they called them 'sweet tangerines.' We each took one.

"The house was full of people. Some of the girls were smoking marijuana and baking chocolate-chip cookies, which of course the guys were eating practically off the hot baking pans. Anyway, I kept my eye on Jerry, who was walking around the yard and the gardens, staring at the poppies and the ceanothus and the Indian paintbrush and oohing and aahing the way you did. I would go out the front door, walk around with him for a while, then come in the back door, and every time I came in, one of the girls would be opening the oven and pulling out a fresh pan of cookies. I thought it was a miracle, and what was especially miraculous was that on each pan the cookies were fewer and bigger, until I was amazed to come in one last time and discover that she was opening the oven and pulling out a pan, and on it there was *one big cookie!*"

Paul and Charlie laughed.

"I took this as some sort of sign that we were supposed to leave, so we got into the car."

"Oh dear," Elena could not help remarking.

"Well. We didn't get far. Maybe a mile, because Jerry wanted to stop and wander around a small park. So we did that for a while: we lay down and watched the clouds. For me, they kept turning into pyramids. Jerry kept talking about glaciers, so I think he was seeing something different. He couldn't believe how slowly they moved. Anyway, we were just sitting there, letting the time pass, and I saw a guy come into the park with a couple of dogs. Jerry had taken off his glasses, so he didn't notice them for a bit, and then he did. Jerry liked dogs, so, as soon as he noticed them, he called out to them. They were Dobermans, and they were friendly. When he hailed them, they turned and came running over. I saw that there was something wrong with the one right away, but Jerry was tremendously nearsighted, so it wasn't until the dogs were right next to him that he saw that one of them was sleek and muscular and gorgeous, black and tan, while the other one was a skeleton. You could count every rib and every vertebra. And it came right up to him and licked him on the face. He just sat up and started yelling, 'What's the matter with this dog? What's the matter with this dog?'

"The owner was way behind the dogs, and when he got to us, huffing and puffing, Jerry was about out of his mind, petting the skeletal dog and almost crying, he was so upset. The owner apologized, and said that the dog had been poisoned, and had gotten out of the pet hospital a few days before, and hadn't gained any weight back yet. So Jerry shut up, and the owner walked away with the dogs. He seemed like a nice enough guy. Jerry fell back onto the grass, panting, and when I got around to asking him what was going on, which always took a while when you were doing acid, he said, 'That was Life and Death! I saw Life and Death! I called them to me without knowing which was which, and they both came running! And Death was the friendlier one!' I think I said, 'Death was the female,' and he said, 'Exactly!' But he was really shook. Finally, I said, 'They were dogs. One of them was poisoned.' And he said, 'That doesn't prevent them from meaning something.'"

Stoney had stopped weeping while Max was telling this story. Now he said, "I never heard he did anything but hit the bottle every so often. Well, that and smoke three packs a day."

"I don't think LSD suited him very well. Anyway, he was older than I was, and he had responsibilities. I don't know exactly what that day meant to him as the years passed, but he asked me if I remembered it every so often. That's all I know."

"That doesn't prevent it from meaning something," said Zoe.

Stoney looked at her.

They had finished their main course, and now Monique and Marya came in and began clearing the plates. Elena scrutinized Monique for a moment, then decided for the millionth time in her life to stop being self-conscious. But then, as Monique passed behind Simon, she touched his shoulder. It was just the briefest, most fleeting touch, but it was definitely intended, and it gave Elena an uncanny feeling. She thought right then that Simon probably had seen a dead body, but that he would never tell her about it.

Joe Blow said, "May I bring anyone coffee?"

Elena looked around the table. Delphine was shaking her head. Cassie said, "Not for me." She was reaching under her chair for her handbag. Simon was already getting up from his seat. Isabel and Stoney were gazing at one another. Paul had folded his napkin and placed it on the table. Zoe took a deep breath and then released it, all the while staring out the window. Max leaned forward and kissed her on the cheek, which pushed back his chair. Charlie said, "Well, I . . ." Elena shook her head and gave Joe Blow a cordial, and grateful, smile. She said, "No, thank you, Joe. You-all have been wonderful."

Simon said, "Well, yeah!"

Stoney said, "We really ought to take one last stroll around, given the fact that we might not come back here, and even if we do, it won't be the same, and even if it is, we won't be the same."

"You sound like Paul," said Isabel.

"Well, you know, I was talking to Paul the other day, and he said, 'I don't mind *ça change*, because, in fact, there is also always *la même chose*.'"

Isabel laughed.

Just then, his cell phone rang. He took it out of his pocket, looked at it, put it back. She said, "Who is it?"

"Avram. But he can leave a message. I can hardly hear anything up here anyway, even voice mail. Pleasure before business, I always say." She took his arm, and went with him under the pergola, into the rose garden. The roses themselves weren't blooming, but it was the quickest way to the back lawn.

Most of the others had left right after lunch, though Isabel wasn't sure about Zoe and Paul. Stoney put his arm around her waist, and she put her arm around his waist. He still looked a bit disheveled from lunch. If he had been a girl, he would have gone upstairs to wash his face and comb his hair, but he had only taken a few deep breaths and blown his nose in the table napkin. There was something about this that Isabel found endearing. She squeezed his arm and was about to ask him how he was feeling, but just then he said, "I guess Charlie is driving straight to LAX, even though his plane isn't until six tomorrow morning."

"I'm sure he thinks he had a very weird vacation. Maybe it was weird enough to send him back to his wife. He'd be much better off with her, you know, mowing the lawn and driving the grandchildren to their soccer games, than he is now. You heard what he said."

Stoney nodded. He said, "Some of those old guys who think they're flying at last are really just falling out of the nest. I got this weird feeling looking at him that if she doesn't take him back he's going to be dead pretty
soon, like in a couple of years." He uttered this sentiment just normally, as if
it were a fact of life and no longer the founding principle of his Weltan-
schauung. Then he added, "But he didn't sell us out."

"No, I don't think he did." They continued down the path to the white
stream. She began, "How are you—" but Stoney said, "You know what I call
Cassie's car?"

"What?"

"The 'Enigma-mobile.'"

"What does that mean?"

"Do you understand those two?"

"What's not to understand? They're friends. They get along. I mean,
they're neighborly. I think it's nice. And unusual."

"Well—"

"They're friends." Isabel spoke definitively. And cleared her throat.

After a moment, Stoney said, "Well, yeah."

"You just don't understand female friendships."

"No," he conceded, "I'm sure I don't."

"The interesting thing for me was to watch Mom and my grandmother
for ten days. I mean, I know they haven't spent that kind of time together in
years and years."

"They seemed to get along."

"Yes, I know, but it's like it doesn't occur to Mom not to get along. She's
such a narcissist that she's immune to the swirl of family feelings, good or
bad. I think she's incredibly strange. I thought she was strange before, but
now I think she's even more strange."

"And your grandmother isn't strange?"

"She isn't strange. She's ideal." Isabel said this without any self-
consciousness, just saying at last what she always felt, but Stoney's head
swiveled around and he grinned at her, as if she were joking. She saw that
he saw immediately that she was not.

They came to the white stream and walked along it. Just down from
where they were walking, a small group of colorful agates, broken in pieces,
had been set into the bottom of the stream. The stones were large enough
so that the water split and flowed picturesquely around them. Isabel and
Stoney sat down at this spot. She slipped her feet out of her loafers and
slid them into the cold water, which glistened around her calves. After a
moment, Stoney rolled up his jeans and did the same, saying, "They
brought this sand all the way from Australia. Fraser Island. The sand there is

perfectly white." The weird little stream was so clear that the only way she could tell that it was running was when a fragment of a leaf or a bit of a stick slid telekinetically past. Stoney put his hand through the water and dug his fingers into the streambed. As he pulled his hand from the water, the sand flowed out of his palm and drifted in a silvery ripple around the agates. "And each grain is perfectly spherical. Joe Blow told me about it. That island is in the ocean, but it's full of freshwater creeks that rise near the middle of the island and flow to the sea. Supposedly, they are branches of an underground river that comes to the island below the ocean, from Malaysia. When he was explaining it to me, I didn't quite understand it."

"Do you want to talk about lunch? About that black-dog story?"

"Not right now."

"Do you want to say anything about your feelings?"

"No."

She waited a moment, then said, "I liked this stream the other day, but now it seems odd. I prefer my sand golden. I like the sand on Kauai. This grass is nice, though." She pulled her feet out of the water and shimmied a few feet up the hill, then leaned back and surveyed the hillside. "Look at this grass. Grass like this in California is so luxurious. I'd much rather lie down in a big field of grass than on the beach, I have to say." But what she really wanted to say was, Are you okay? Are you happier? Are you less filled with contradictions and complications? But if she asked those questions and he answered them, then she would have to ask herself questions that she couldn't answer, like "What now?"

He moved up the hill until he was just beside her. She looked at him. He said, "And do you want to say anything about your feelings?"

She knew she should be saying yes, but she said, "No."

Stoney looked up at the sky. He said, "You know why we're sitting here?"

"Are we going to talk about our feelings anyway?"

"You brought it up."

"I brought up your feelings, not mine."

Stoney laughed and lay back. After a moment, he put his arm across his face, to shade his eyes from the sun. She rolled over, and stretched out on top of him so that her head shaded his face. He put his arm around her.

She said, "Why are we lounging here?"

"Because we can't bear to leave."

"I can bear to leave. I think it's strange here. I miss my room."

"Well, that's true. I can bear to leave, though not to get back to my specific chair in front of my specific TV." She kissed him on the nose. "And I think the Amber Room is oppressive and this hillside is bizarre, too. It's like when you go on a movie set at Paramount or somewhere, and the set is, say, a run-down old farmhouse." He pushed her hair back, then ran his index finger across her cheek. "You step up on the screen porch, and not only does it look just like a screen porch somewhere in Illinois—I mean, with the right moldings and the authentic-looking steps—they've also done the boards. If you bend down and look at the floorboards that you're standing on, they have layers of paint beneath the surface coat. They look like they would look if they were sixty years old and had been halfheartedly scraped and repainted two or three times over the years. You think it's amazing!" This time, she kissed him on the lips. After a moment, he went on, "You marvel at the skill and thought of the set decorators and scene painters, but then you think, Who's going to see this? Even the actors aren't going to notice this, and certainly it won't show up on film. But they did it anyway."

"Usually that sort of excessive detail is the result of low labor costs."

"Is it, Miss Smarty Pants?"

She nodded.

Stoney ruffled her hair. He said, "Well, it gives you the willies, and this place gives me the willies in the same way. So it's not that I can't bear to leave, it's that I can't bear to go anywhere."

Isabel heard herself say, "Why is that?"

Now he looked right at her, and he kept looking right at her, only shading his eyes with his hand. He squirmed underneath her, and pulled her more tightly into him. She put her face down against his neck, and the grass brushed her face and gave off its fresh aroma. While they were not talking, Isabel could hear lots of birdsong—calls and trills from the aviary up at the house, but also humbler notes from the trees across the stream. And from the woods there was some sort of little cry, as of a squirrel, and scratching sounds. No traffic. Maybe this was the only place she had ever been in L.A. where no traffic hum intruded. It was true, she admitted, that she knew nothing. Or maybe it was that she knew so many things now, about herself and Stoney and their relationship, that no rational decisions could be made. He was too complex for her. She was too complex for him. And their history was certainly too complex for Max (though, she was willing to admit after today's revelations, possibly not too complex for her mother). Yes, she could tell her father her story, and if she backed it up with a lot of feminist theory, she could talk him into accepting it, just as he always let her do whatever she wanted because she wanted to, but even now, even lying here like this, she wasn't sure what she wanted to do. She suspected that that was what Stoney was saying, too.

She felt his arms release her, then she felt his hands on her shoulders. A moment later, he was looking at her. Soberly. Seriously. He said, "Are you still afraid of being alive?"

She knew perfectly well what he was referring to, but she pretended not to. "What?"

"Remember in the middle of the night that first night, when you asked me whether being suicidal was the same as being afraid of being alive?"

"I was so stoned." She kissed him again, but he made her look at him. She said, "That night was fun. I loved that night."

"Well, are you? You said the baby boomers had wrecked everything and the only thing people your age had to look forward to was everything getting worse and worse."

"Don't you think that's true?"

"I don't know. I leave it to you to distinguish between the personal and political."

"There is no—" But she knew that he knew that she knew that, right at this moment, that was too easy. He was looking at her very earnestly. She said, "Things are likely to get worse and worse." She rolled off him, and then he rolled onto her, pressing her deliciously into the turf. She said, "The probability is that they will get worse and worse, or at least get a lot worse before they get better."

He said, "I think so, too. It makes you think of the Thirty Years' War or the Hundred Years' War, even if you don't know anything about them."

They agreed on this, then. But, really, what was important was that she could not stop staring at him. She had always thought he was handsome, even though no one ever said that about him—quite the contrary. Blair Underwood was handsome. Heath Ledger was handsome. Brad Pitt was handsome. Owen Wilson was handsome. Stoney Whipple was not, by any standard, handsome. And yet. She said, "I know. But I guess, between Mom and Cassie and Simon and everything that they've done to drive me absolutely crazy, I'm not especially focused on that idea right this very minute."

"What idea are you focused on this very minute?"

"I want to ask you a question. Are you handsome?"

"What?"

"Are you a handsome man?"

Stoney's head dropped back, his eyes closed, and he laughed out loud in true merriment. His arms went around her again. He said, "No, Isabel, no, honey, I am not handsome. Jerry was not handsome, and I look just like him. His genetic endowment was too overwhelming for the lovely Diana, at least in my case."

"Then it must be that I love you."

"What?" He lifted his head and looked at her again. She decided again that what she was saying was true, so she repeated herself.

"Then it must be that I love you."

"Oh, Isabel." But his face had softened.

She ran the tip of her forefinger up the bridge of his nose, then brushed her hand across his forehead. His high-and-getting-higher forehead. She whispered, "Because it must be that the love comes first, and then what you love looks beautiful to you. You look beautiful to me, and you always have."

Now he stared at her, so intently that, if she had not known him, she would have thought he was angry, but he wasn't angry. She saw that he was feeling what she said go all through him, and he had to feel every moment of it, she knew that, he had to let it register in every cell, let it become knowledge that his body understood. She saw that she had said something very serious, even though she had never thought of saying such a thing before now. She felt what she had said go through her, too, and install itself. There was a long silent moment, and then, just before he kissed her, he said, "I am yours, Isabel."

·

They, whoever they were, might as well have been dead, Zoe thought when she sat up and looked at her watch. She, at least, had disappeared into nowhere for some period of time, and as she looked around, she could hardly understand where she was. Above a stream? Near some flowering trees? Sitting in the grass beside a mysterious man? Was he the Woodsman? Was he the Wolf? He could not be the Prince, she thought, because he had a wild, long beard. How did she know if she had slept for ten minutes, and not ten days or ten years? How did she know she was not Sleeping Beauty after all? She wiggled her toes. Her shoes had fallen off her feet. She put them on again. She adjusted her shirt and her bra. The Woodsman was still sleeping. Without knowing who she was or who he was, instinctively, as it were, she leaned over him and kissed him full on the lips. He kissed her back. His lips were elastic and responsive, as if she were not in a dream. His eyes opened. Paul, his name was. She knew instantly and without a doubt that they were not going to see one another again after this unless he did something to claim her, something that was entirely outside of "Paul's" personality as she had come to know it. And if he was not going to claim her, what then?

She said, "Paul."

Without opening his eyes, he said, "Zoe."

She said, "My real name is Susan. Susan Brutt. Did I tell you that?"

"No."

"I'll never forget when I turned six, right on my birthday. My mother didn't have any money to give me a present or have a party, so she said, 'I think we should change our names,' and she let me choose the names. I named us. I named her Delphinium, because I knew that was a flower, but she said, no, that was not a woman's name, so she changed it to Delphine. Then we talked about me. I had three ideas. They were 'Dolores,' 'Anne,' and 'Zoe.' She said that 'Dolores' meant 'sad,' and she had had enough of that. So 'Dolores' was out. I wanted 'Anne,' because of Princess Anne, but she said, 'No English princesses.' So we were left with 'Zoe.' That was the only other one I liked. I didn't like 'Laura,' which she thought was pretty, but I thought was common, so she let me have 'Zoe' even though neither of us had ever met another Zoe or knew what Zoe meant at the time." Of course this entire thing with Paul had been a mistake. She knew that.

He said, "'Zoe' means 'life.'"

"Yes, it does. We found that out later. After we did the first names, we chose 'Cunningham' out of the phone book because it was completely safe, we thought. Totally American. There was a whole list of Cunninghams, right between the Cunhas and the Cupps. And there were Cunningham businesses, like 'Cunningham Plumbing Supply' and 'Cunningham's Fine Men's Clothiers.' There was only one 'Brutt'—us. But, really, now that I think about it, I never knew if the goal was to disappear into the crowd or to excel. The other thing about 'Cunningham' was that it was so long we didn't need middle names."

Paul sat up and kissed her again, her face between his hands, a solid, appreciative kiss. She said, "I never told anyone that before. Her name was Ada."

He said, meditatively, "Ada Brutt. Hm."

Now, for just a very short moment, she felt herself close to tears.

He went on. "I called myself 'Deva' for a while. A short while, I admit. And in high school, I was called 'Squirrel' because when I was a junior I got appendicitis, and when my friends came to see me, I went to show them the scar and they saw that my pubic hair had been shaved, so they decided that my genitals looked like a squirrel, for some reason. So I was known as 'Squirrel' for the next year and a half."

That weepy sensation went away. She said, "God knows what Max's real name is. It might be Milstein. I guess his grandfather changed it, or maybe his dad. Nathan Milstein would be his real name. And Jerry Whipple changed his own name, from 'Hillel Goldman.' Stoney was named after his mother's father, so his name really should be Axel Goldman rather than Stoney Whipple. His mother was Diana Carstairs. Did you ever see anything of hers? She made about four movies, but then she was killed on Mulholland Drive. She went right over the edge one night, Max said. I never met her, of course, since I was only about six at that point, and changing my name to Zoe Cunningham. Anyway, her real name was Audrey Putz, daughter of Axel Putz! No kidding! She was from some small town in Iowa that was peopled by Putzes, and even though she died, that still makes me laugh."

She and Paul laughed together.

She went on: "Poor Stoney. So—what I always think is, if there were a biopic of me—which there won't be because I don't intend to live an eventful life, though I wouldn't mind doing a biopic myself, of Josephine Baker—some girl who was born Davina Jefferson but changed her name to, say, Doree Bonard, would play me, Susan Brutt, but as Zoe Cunningham, and it would be directed by Jack Martin, who was originally Aziz Ungatz, and Max Maxwell, originally Nathan Milstein, would be played by some name that is two English nouns, say River Lodge, who was originally Dave Conker." Zoe thought this was a very good joke.

"That's Hollywood," said Paul. This, perhaps, was why they were breaking up, or diverging, or whatever you would call it—his failure to laugh at what she knew were good jokes. He had (she could feel herself growing irritable), you were given to believe, evolved beyond jokes.

"If Isabel and Stoney have a baby, I guess we'll have to call her Ada Susan Audrey Milstein-Putz Goldman, because Isabel is very literal about things like that." She wanted to say, Max may still be wondering what's up between Isabel and Stoney, but for some of us, it's plain as the nose on your face.

No response. He stood up, and then gave her his hand. She stood up. She said, "It's almost four. We won't be back to my place before six, if there's traffic."

"I'll spend the night at my apartment, I think. Then I can be off to the monastery by five."

"That sounds good." She led the way up to the house. She knew that if, as planned, they had gone to the monastery for the last ten days, there would be none of this diverging. Rather, she would have been incorporated into his life, almost without thinking. But it was evident to both of them that he could not be incorporated into her life. The only question, if you could call it a question rather than an impulse, was whether she should respond to this diverging by having a tantrum, as Delphine might say, or giving vent to her honest feelings, as she would say.

They tried the door near the pantry. She thought that she would run up and check her room one last time for anything she might have left behind. She was good at not leaving things behind, because she was always worried about leaving things behind, and she could actually name each of the four things that she had left behind over the years (a not-very-expensive but unique pearl necklace, in which the pearls were encased in individual gold links that were then hooked together; an almost-new flacon of Bulgari Rose

Essentielle; a novel called *Family Pictures* that she had nearly finished; and a silver-framed picture of Isabel at age one and a half, flourishing a spoon).

That door was locked. To get around to the front, they had either to go back down the hillside and all the way around the swimming-pool complex (since the pools were all interconnected, they would have had to enter the water to cross the complex otherwise) or to go through the garden the other way, circumnavigating the bulk of the building and most of the garden beds. It was annoying. Annoyance was swelling.

"Look," said Paul, in his unnaturally cool way, "the drapes are drawn. Aren't those casements the windows of the library? They're closed, with the shades down. And over there, that big arched window at the end of the salon. I didn't even realize that one had blinds. They must have been hidden in the wall somehow."

Zoe backed away from the house, looking up. Every window in the second story was whited out, too. She said, evenly, "I did see that the shutters in the dining room were closed as we were coming up the hill. Well, they haven't lost any time in getting rid of us." But she was beginning to feel something larger than annoyance, something more like fear.

"Or maybe taking the day off. They were pretty attentive for the last four days. I don't know that anyone was getting any time off."

"Well, of course," said Zoe. "But it is a little creepy, don't you think?" She glanced at him. "I mean, I don't mind that everyone is gone"—and as they came around the corner of the house, she saw that her car was the only one left in the driveway—"that's entirely understandable. It's not a hotel, after all." Her voice rose a little. She coughed it back to normal and tried to sound casual. "But everyone looks so completely gone. It's so empty-looking that I almost can't imagine what's in there anymore, or even that we were in there, gawking at not just the paintings and the furniture but the walls and the floors and the amenities." She looked up at the façade. Every window shut and blanked. She said, "But now it hardly looks inhabited. I can't help thinking that somehow Mike died, or the world ended, so no one cares, and it turned back into, what, a bank vault, I guess. Anyway, that's what it looks like now." Yes, she sounded a little upset. "It looks like it might pop."

He said, "There's an interim in the history of every ruin after everyone leaves and before it falls down."

Zoe said, "Ugh. Well, it was a strange place all along. I felt like in every room I was constantly being asked to think about history and the meaning of Europe and things like that. I'm sure Isabel loved it." She went to the driver's side of the silver Mercedes. Paul opened the door to the passenger's side. Her door opened with that quality click she liked so much. The keys were in the ignition, where she had left them. They were swaying ever so slightly, which seemed odd, but, then, it only seemed odd by contrast to the utter stillness of the big golden house, the quiet aviary, the gardens unruffled by any breeze. She shivered, then turned on the engine, put the car in reverse, backed around, put the car in drive. They were pointed toward the row of thick eucalyptuses. She forgot to look back at the house before she was halfway down the avenue, and then it was too late—all she could see were smoky-green leaves and peeling silver trunks. He said, "There's a phrase for what you're feeling," and she was tempted not to respond, but in the end, she was curious, so she said, "What?"

"Existential dread."

"Are you feeling it?"

"No."

But she didn't ask what he was feeling. She was sure she knew. He was feeling relief. Still, they didn't have their first actual disagreement until she turned left rather than right at Mulholland. Paul said, "Why are you turning left? If you turn right, you can just take Mulholland all the way over to Outpost."

"I don't like Mulholland at this time in the afternoon. Or at all, really. This will be quicker."

He said, "For one thing, it's two miles longer by the highway, and for another, I don't think it will be quicker. You're always quicker in L.A. if you go the street way rather than the highway."

"Usually it is quicker to go by the streets, but I don't like Mulholland."

"You don't?"

"I don't."

"I love Mulholland."

"How can you love all those twists and turns? And how can you love any road? You hardly ever drive yourself."

"I just like Mulholland."

This argument got them almost to the 101. As soon as they were on the 101, she saw that maybe the 101 was a little slow after all. She glanced at him. He was looking at the traffic. Or maybe not. He was looking out the front window. He looked serious, or maybe merely enigmatic. What did they have here, seven miles, maybe eight on the 101?

He said, "Or you could have gone out the other way, to North Sepulveda and then left on Sunset and over."

"That takes forever. No one goes that way."

"Well, not on Sunset itself, but—"

She interrupted him. She said, "You know what Bette Davis said when someone asked her how she had managed such a wonderful and productive career in the movies?"

He glanced at her. "No."

"She said, 'I always took Fountain.'"

Paul smiled, and the traffic opened up. Paul said, "I never heard that." At his smile, her feeling of existential dread dissipated a bit. He actually was nice, she thought. Possibly, she didn't really know how nice he was, given his manner. She said, "It's so obvious that Elena is the one for Max, I mean the one who's ready and willing to live in his bedroom with him, and who never thinks of turning him down for sex." Traffic slowed again. "She's just like Ina. I met Ina once. She told me everything I needed to know about Max, French New Wave cinema, nineteenth-century German poetry, puff puff on her Marlboro, Islam, the Reagan administration, her local school-board election, and also me. She looked me up and down and said"—here Zoe went into her Bronx accent—"'When *I* was in Hollywood, Zoe, *I* was too tall and commanding-looking to get parts I liked. I simply did not have the right look for color film. *I* should have been born in time for black and white. You're so much less intimidating than I was, and just the right build. What's your waist, about twenty-five? And your hips, thirty-six? You've had surgery, right? On your tits? Really not?'" Paul smiled again, but kept watching the traffic.

She was willing to admit that she envied Max and Elena. They did get along, and they did have a free and easy affection for one another, and they did evidently have a good sex life, and he was in fact satisfied, and Elena did have no idea how hard it was to satisfy Max. She said, "I think it's nice that Max has finally found himself the perfect female servant."

"Do you?" said Paul.

"Of course I do. And, obviously, she's crazy about him, and both the kids are grown, so that's not a factor, and she seems to accept my mom, so things couldn't be better, it looks like." She turned off onto Cahuenga.

Paul said, "We had a session."

"You and Elena had a session? When was that?"

"Yesterday afternoon, in the Reformation/Counter-Reformation Suite."

Zoe turned onto Woodrow Wilson. "What about?"

"The Iraq war."

"But what did you link it to?"

"The Iraq war."

"Yes, but did it go back to her past life as a Chinese peasant, or anything like that? Or biochemical imbalances in her brain?"

"No. It went back to the Iraq war."

"You let her stay on the surface like that?" Zoe didn't know whether to be insulted or disdainful.

"Well, I acknowledged her tendency to obsessive personality disorder, because she brought that up. But actually, I think it's okay to be disturbed by inhumane and incomprehensible events in the material world. I tried to help her distinguish between productive thought patterns and unproductive ones."

"Is she going to have more sessions?"

Paul cleared his throat. "We talked about closed-loop and open-loop thought patterns. When she's in a closed-loop pattern, she's just thinking the same thoughts over and over again, and can't get out of them, so they get bigger and bigger and she comes to feel more and more helpless. At that point, she needs to divert her thoughts to something else, and keep focused on that until she can relax, then, when she can, as it were, *entertain* thoughts of the war in Iraq, or the Bush administration, and the Christian right, it might be that she would come up with a new idea for effecting change. That's what we talked about."

"Is she going to have more sessions?" Zoe asked again.

"She might. She said she felt less preoccupied after. It could be productive for her. At lunch today, she didn't seem so on edge."

"I thought that, too."

Here was Pacific View. At Outpost, Paul said, "Do you have any more to say about Max and Elena?" Only now did she realize that this was a session. She said, "I guess I'm surprised that he's satisfied with someone who is so ordinary."

"Maybe," said Paul, "he's learned his lesson."

"What lesson would that be?"

"I don't know. It's his lesson." And that was her lesson.

Left onto Senalda, and up the last hill. It wasn't dusk, but it was late afternoon. She stopped the car, opened her window, and pressed the buttons. Her gate opened. By the time Paul switched his things and departed, it would be even later. She said, "You won't be back to your apartment until dark. Would you like to come in?" She drove through the gate, leaving it open. She saw that the gardeners had been there. There was no evidence of wind damage. Her existential dread receded a little more.

He didn't answer her question, but said, as they got out of the car, "Twenty minutes, is all. I go my own way."

"Does it involve Mulholland?"

"No, but I could take Fountain." He smiled.

He was standing there. At some point, there had been no tantrum. It was actually a relief. She went over and put her arms around him under his arms, and laid her head against his chest, just to feel again, for the last time, that rhythm their bodies had together. His arms went around her, and he kissed her on the forehead. She said, "This part is nice." Now her existential dread went away, but she didn't tell him that.

He said, "I think so, too."

"You didn't ask me about Marcelle."

"That was between you and Marcelle. Anyway, she enjoyed you giving her hell. You're famous. It gave her something to talk about for the next five years."

She looked up at him. She saw that she was well and truly forgiven, no caveats or reservations. Him, too, she thought.

Now they kissed on the lips. After that, she pressed the trunk button on her key fob, and when the lid to her trunk popped up, he went over and took out his bag and his beat-up old yoga mat. He opened the passenger's door of his Honda and jammed them in with all the other stuff. His last words were "I'll call you." She knew what that meant. Probably they were not going to do sessions, either. Probably she was going to find herself some other sort of coach—Jungian, Freudian, jazz, piano, Pilates, horseback riding, surfing, more acting. Not yoga. She was, after all, born to take lessons. She watched the beat-up little car turn right out of the driveway and disappear toward Oporto.

When she thought of Marcelle again, it was funny. Paul and Marcelle, at the Lascaux Caves, or at the Pyramids, or at Monte Albán, trudging around in the scorching sunshine or the moist darkness? So what, really? Zoe had been hauled around the world to so many location shoots that no location interested her at all, not the ones she had seen, not the ones she hadn't seen, not Phuket, not Rodeo Drive, not the Champs-Elysées, not the monastery up north. What she really liked, in the end, was a little stage in a little club, with Tony at the piano and good acoustics. Glasses clinking in the background. A laugh from time to time, someone saying "Shh!," plenty of songs to sing, a smattering of applause that she could graciously acknowledge for a moment before singing another song. A glass of white wine on the stool beside her, and a glass of water beside that. All the best locations were evoked in songs, after all—somewhere over the rainbow, the sunny side of the street, down in the valley, up on the roof, under the sun, moon, and stars, easy street, Brigadoon, Oklahoma, Abbey Road. And you didn't have to stay anywhere long, either, just three or four minutes.

Ten days of newspapers and magazines were neatly stacked on the hall table. The only headline she noted before turning away was "Bombing Is

Tool of Choice to Clear a Path to Baghdad." Max was right—they were used to it now, the war, the new world. They had been softened up and obliged to swallow, and it was shocking, except that it was not anymore.

She set down her bag and remembered that she had never put her makeup case actually inside the suitcase, so she went out to get that. The first thing she laid eyes on when she opened her front door was the end of the driveway, where the gate was closed and Paul was no longer poised to make his turn. It occurred to her to sing a song, but the song itself didn't occur to her. Maybe "Just One of Those Things," or "Begin the Beguine," but neither of them was really appropriate. She loved the tune of "Begin the Beguine," though. As she popped the trunk again, she started to hum. Her makeup case had rolled to one side, up against a small, flat, rectangular package wrapped in brown paper. She picked it up and turned it over. On the front, in curly script, was "For Zoe, from Joe Blow." Had she seen it before?

But inside the house, the phone was ringing, so she set the makeup bag and the package beside the door as she closed it (and locked it). After talking to both her agent and her personal assistant, who did seem a little fed up with her, admittedly, long vacation, she went upstairs, then came down and went into her office, then found a bite to eat in the kitchen, then turned on the TV and saw that there was still nothing but the war and *American Idol*, and she considered again whether she wished she had Paula's job on that show, and couldn't decide again if she did or not. Lots of money, she was sure, but they were always giving the poor woman a hard time, too. TV might be fun, if she could play the eccentric best friend rather than the lead, or, better still, someone entirely different from herself, someone male or a nun. (What happened to all those nun movies, like *Two Mules for Sister Sara*—that was Shirley MacLaine with Clint—where they paired you with the toughest guy in Hollywood and you had lots of conversations about daily prayer? That would be a good project for her and Samuel L. Jackson, or, better still, her and Jim Carrey. The thought made her laugh out loud.) So she took a bath and read *Variety* and *The Hollywood Reporter* and *Rolling Stone*, but not the L.A. *Times*.

In the end, it was the fact that it was only nine o'clock and she had nothing to do but unpack that drove her back to the front hall, where she picked up her bag and her makeup case, and saw the package again, and thought to open it.

There was a note in an envelope, handwritten on a half-sheet of paper. She unfolded the paper. It said: "Raphael and I thought you might like this. We want to thank you for your version of 'So in Love.' We not only have the recording, but we heard you singing in your room, once when you had the window open, while you were visiting. We decided this morning that you deserve this more than the tax authorities (or whoever) do." Then there was an explanatory P.S. "We didn't say anything to anyone while you were here, but we believe that Mike and the others have died. Adana believes this. The airplane has disappeared and state officials have already been to her house in Saint Petersburg. She says that they spent two hours going through papers in Mike's office and they have also closed the headquarters of his business. We all agree that this is a very bad sign. We think there might be a story in the *New York Times* tomorrow."

Zoe agreed that it was a bad sign, too. It was shocking, really, though she hadn't actually met Mike and didn't know the names of the other men. She realized she would be calling Max and Stoney very soon, and then there would be days of upset and mystery and revelation, and her memory of every moment of their stay in the Russian house would be utterly transformed, and in ten days, when Paul got back from the monastery, she would have to call him, too. She knew he would say that their discussion of death at lunch had not been a coincidence. But for now, all she planned to do was open the package.

She slipped her hand under the clear tape that held the brown paper closed, then ripped off the paper and set it on the hall table. The object was a painting, upside down. She turned it right-side up. It was the Vermeer.

A girl in a pale-green dress with a white collar, holding a recorder in her hand, had been sitting in her chair, playing music by the light of a partially open stained-glass window. Now she was leaning forward, as if to peruse the music—her finger was resting on the music stand—but she had been surprised at her practicing, and was just turning her head to look at the viewer. The light from the window brightened her cheek and the fold of her white headdress where it touched her on the neck. She wore a plain necklace of amethysts, and a dangling amethyst earring in the visible ear. The recorder was made of ebony with ivory fittings, and it lay in the pale green of her skirt, pressing into the folds. Her face was round and youthful—the face of a thirteen- or fourteen-year-old girl—pretty and pale, not yet smiling, but about to—as if she had only just recognized the intruder, and in a split second she would register her pleasure in seeing him. The intruder, Zoe suspected, was her beloved. It was a beautiful picture, and she stood under her hall chandelier, holding it in her two hands and gazing at it, for a long time, taking in the dress and the collar and the hairdo and the window and the glint of the music stand and the glint of the necklace and the sheen of the black recorder. And the song was in her mind. "Strange, dear, but true, dear . . ." E minor. Or lower, even. D minor. She thought of Joe Blow and Raphael. "So taunt me and hurt me, deceive me . . ." She was humming.

She thought of Mike, and stopped humming. It was shocking. She shook her head to shake away the thought.

She set the picture on the table, propped against the wall. She saw that there was another note, this one in an envelope that had been ripped open. She pulled it out and unfolded it. The paper was thick, on the letterhead of the Getty. It said, "Dear Mr. Blow (ha ha, very funny, Joe), Per your question, it is highly unlikely, in spite of the many legends around this painting, that it is a Vermeer. Practically an impossibility, in my opinion. But I looked around and asked my colleague here, Kirsten (did you ever meet her?), and we wonder if the artist might be a woman of the period named Judith Leyster. It would of course be of exceptional quality for Leyster, but less impossible than this being a Vermeer. Sorry. But hey, Leyster was the only woman artist of her day!! See you soon." Then there was a signature she could not quite make out, and someone, maybe Joe Blow, had drawn an arrow toward the word "woman" and added another exclamation point. Zoe put down the letter and looked at the painting again. She had never thought it was a Vermeer to begin with.

But it was a beautiful picture. What it reminded her of was when you were watching some movie on the DVD and you pressed the pause button, and there were Audrey Hepburn and Cary Grant seated at a table, or Lena Horne, smiling at Bill Robinson, or James Cagney, tap-dancing down the staircase in the White House, and the composition in the frame of the TV screen was striking, original, and evocative. You might leave the TV on, and the DVD player on, and have that picture, that ephemeral moment, on your screen forever, but in fact you always came back from the kitchen with the bottle of Perrier or the bowl of popcorn in your hand, and you always pressed the play button, even if you had seen the movie ten times before. And it never occurred to you that Cary and Audrey and Jimmy and Lena and Bill were dead. You went on with the movie; you could not help yourself. And now she had this still, this stop frame, of the girl in 1663, playing her music one morning in spite of loves lost, in spite of deaths, in spite of the plagues and the fires and the massacres and the genocides and the clashes of armies and civilizations.

She picked it up again. The girl was happy to see someone. It made Zoe smile.

I would like to thank several people who offered information, advice, and aid during the writing of this novel. They are: Miles Berkowitz, Abby Foss, Nick Goldberg, Arianna Huffington, Romi Lisally and her gardening friends, Lynn Pleshette, Mary Pendergast, and, of course, Loren Steck and his lecturers and students at UC Santa Cruz; also Anke Steinecke, who kept us all out of trouble, and David Vladeck. And to every director and commentator on every DVD who bothered to add "Special Features," I couldn't have done it without you.

I would like to thank several people who offered information, advice, and aid during the writing of this novel. They are: Miles Berkowitz, Abby Foss, Nick Goldberg, Arianna Huffington, Romi Lisally and her gardening friends, Lynn Pleshette, Mary Pendergast, and, of course, Loren Steck and his lecturers and students at UC Santa Cruz; also Anke Steinecke, who kept us all out of trouble, and David Vladeck. And to every director and commentator on every DVD who bothered to add "Special Features," I couldn't have done it without you.

Jane Smiley is the author of numerous novels, including *A Thousand Acres*, for which she won the Pulitzer Prize; *Horse Heaven*, which was shortlisted for the Orange Prize; and, most recently, *Good Faith*. She has also written four works of nonfiction, including a critically acclaimed biography of Charles Dickens, and *Thirteen Ways of Looking at the Novel*, a history and anatomy of the novel as a literary form. Smiley was inducted into the American Academy of Arts and Letters in 2001. She received the PEN USA Lifetime Achievement Award for Literature in 2006. Ms. Smiley lives in Northern California.

A Note on the Type

The text of this book was set in Electra, a typeface designed by W. A. Dwiggins (1880–1956). This face cannot be classified as either modern or old style. It is not based on any historical model, nor does it echo any particular period or style. It avoids the extreme contrasts between thick and thin elements that mark most modern faces, and it attempts to give a feeling of fluidity, power, and speed.

Composed by

Stratford Publishing Services, Brattleboro, Vermont

Printed and bound by

Berryville Graphics, Berryville, Virginia

Designed by

Iris Weinstein